TENACITY AND SPIRIT

TENACITY AND SPIRIT

The Story of Rebekah

Terry Overton
&
James K. Stewart

RESOURCE *Publications* · Eugene, Oregon

TENACITY AND SPIRIT
The Story of Rebekah

Resource Publications
An Imprint of Wipf and Stock Publishers
199 W. 8th Ave., Suite 3
Eugene, OR 97401

www.wipfandstock.com

PAPERBACK ISBN: 978-1-6667-9476-2
HARDCOVER ISBN: 978-1-6667-9475-5
EBOOK ISBN: 978-1-6667-9477-9

JANUARY 7, 2022 11:40 AM

This book is dedicated to those who have struggled with self-will and overcome with the help of our Lord.

CHAPTER 1

T HE stories Beth heard about the older woman who lives near the end of Reckoner Street challenged all logic. No one person could have the ability to do the legendary things Rose Maddington was reported to have done. After all, anyone can spin a yarn ten miles long. One full of mystical nonsensical twists and turns designed to capture the imagination of the average listener. According to local gossip, Rose did more than tell tales. She changed lives. Beth didn't understand how the verbal accounts related by this sexagenarian could change the fate of anyone who took the time to hear her tales. The townspeople swore to it; the stories Rose delivered had a life-changing effect on those who listened. Beth Chase didn't believe a word. How did she do it? Was Rose Maddington a counselor? A mentor? A hypnotist? Or simply, an odd woman in a typical little town.

Three months earlier, Beth had been transferred to Sageville. Five years before that, she had begun what was to be an exciting new career in the insurance industry. As it turned out, those five years in Brookville had been the longest she'd ever held a job. Five years was certainly enough time for anyone to settle in, grow roots, and develop friendships. Settling down, growing roots, and especially developing friendships was not something Beth had ever found easy or natural. After three months in Sageville, Beth could tell this place wasn't going to be any different than Brookville. Same small town low-paying jobs, same small-town social climate, but she didn't have a choice. Truth be told, the only distinction between Beth's former town and Sageville was the rumored capabilities of mysterious Rose Maddington.

Walking along Reckoner Street on her way to work, her mother's words stormed through her mind. "Beth Chase, will you ever find what you are looking for; do you even know what it is you're looking for?

Always moving from town-to-town, why can't you settle down? Find someone. You're just as hard-headed as your father."

Never that close, her mother, a very traditional woman, always found it challenging to deal with independent and stubborn people. Beth and her mother were like oil and water. With tension mounting in her neck and shoulders, Beth muttered, "Yes, Mother, I'm still looking." Reflecting on how her headstrong attitude brought her to Sageville, she felt a tiny bit of regret in going over the boss's head with a proposal. This act of disobedience was what he'd been looking for. It was the perfect opportunity to fire an employee whose business sense made him feel inferior. Ironically, Christian compassion and a touch of business acumen caused the Regional Manager to transfer Beth to an office that needed someone who was naturally detailed and meticulous.

Reckoner Street ran directly into the old downtown business district. This peaceful narrow street was adorned with neatly trimmed shrubs and flowers, strategically placed in the front yards of historic, oversized, Victorian homes. Single families lived in most of the old houses, except the one Beth had rented. The owner of this large home had recently converted it into three small apartments, now occupied by one older retired gentleman, a middle-aged widow, and Beth. Each remained in their own space and seldom exchanged words; other than a polite greeting. This arrangement suited Beth just fine.

Balmy spring days helped make the short walk to work refreshing and enjoyable. Lately, on passing Rose Maddington's two-story house, the tales she'd heard at work began causing Beth's anxiety to increase with the temperature. Unable to put her finger on it, there was just something about that picture-perfect house that caused her mind to race. Twice each day, Beth fantasized about this mysterious older woman whom the townspeople rumored was gifted with supernatural skill. The floral wonderland evinced Rose as an avid gardener. Beth knew one had to work hard to maintain those picturesque front yard flower beds. Transferred in the late fall, the wintery walk to work did not provide the opportunity for Beth to get a look at the legendary Rose Maddington. With winter past and spring in the air, Rose finally appeared like a blooming Hosta, albeit not in green. Orange, yellow, mauve, black, vintage Jamaican print dress, with beige work slacks beneath, made it impossible not to notice Rose in her garden of green. This older woman had an air of youth with shoulder-length auburn hair as she moved her gardening implements into the front yard. Unable to take her eyes from this sexagenarian, Beth's pace slowed.

She thought to herself, "She looks normal enough."

Making it past the house without being noticed, or so she thought, Beth, used her break time in the office to research the name Rose Maddington on the internet. Disappointed that multiple searches revealed no record of anything other than the standard information, name, address, and such, Beth searched for the meaning and the history of the name – Maddington. Even that came up empty. Pondering rumors powerful enough to influence an individual's life and hearing the fantastic stories, it just seemed odd that there was nothing written about her? With the daily routine of organizing the files of the agent she'd replaced, Beth felt it was time to increase interaction with her two workmates, Joyce McGilvery and George Engel. Beth had kept to herself for more than three months, but now it would soon be time to start organizing their files and contracts. Everyone knew Joyce and George were salt of the earth people, but not that meticulous in the detail work required in the insurance industry.

Another dull Friday of answering phones and organizing paperwork over, it was time for Beth to walk by the big old white two-story house. There she was, on her knees, digging in the front flower bed. Hopes of not being seen soon faded as Rose Maddington stood up, dusted the dirt from her pants, and looked over the white picket fence to Beth. Turning away, not wanting Rose to catch her eye, her pace quickened, but alas, it was too late.

Rose caught her glancing and called out a warm, "Hello."

Not knowing what to do, Beth feigned a squeaky "Hello," and kept walking.

Again, the sweet voice beckoned, "I was about to have lemonade on the porch. It's quite warm today. Would you like a glass?"

Caught, Beth was stuck. Not being a person who naturally befriended strangers, Beth didn't want to engage in anything, let alone a conversation with Rose. With an empty apartment waiting and laundry the only activity planned for the weekend, Beth was unable to think of a reason to say, "No." Mustering the courage to meet this locally famous woman, Beth reluctantly uttered a quiet, "Okay."

The sweet voice was calming, "Come on up. It will just take me a second."

Timidly opening the garden gate, she entered the yard and took what was to be her first short walk to the porch. Ascending three steps, the fragrance of Jasmine and Gardenia invaded her senses. Scanning the white wicker furniture, Beth chose a chair with a floral-patterned cushion and seated herself. The squeaking screen door announced Rose's return, carrying a tray of lemonade and cookies. Rose placed the tray on the small table between them and sat down with a gracious ladylike genuflect. Knowing the purported powers of Rose Maddington could not possibly hold her spellbound while enjoying a glass of lemonade, she was nevertheless fearful of the words Rose would direct her way.

Rose began, "You know, I've seen you walk by all winter and wanted to have you over. I'm Rose Maddington."

"Nice to meet you; I'm Beth. Beth Chase" came to the bold reply.

"Nice to meet you, Beth. I like to meet all the new people who move to Sageville. It's a small town, and new residents, even visitors, well, they always get my attention." Motioning to the glass, "Here you go. Fresh squeezed."

Taking the tall frosty glass, Beth offered a polite, "Thank you."

"Now, let's just take a moment to enjoy this cold drink. Then you can tell me where you are from, Beth Chase."

Taking a sip of her lemonade, Beth caught a small flash, a twinkle of the eye. Had Rose winked at her?

"Couldn't be," she thought and took another sip.

Placing her glass on the table, Beth tried to dispel her anxiety with, "She seems nice enough."

Beth had always called this type of conversation "The inquisition."

Then it began, "So, tell me, Beth, what brought you to Sageville? Family?"

Always cautious about disclosing personal information, she thought for a moment about how to answer. Not wanting to provide too much information and expose the meaningless life of a single woman, she made it appear as if she were contemplating. Instinctively, she knew where it was going. Beth didn't need, didn't want, help. Figuring things out on her own was an ability she prided herself on, or so she thought. Somehow, her answer needed to convey the fallacy that life was perfect and didn't need any miracle story nor magical remedy.

Realizing she'd been silent for too long, "I moved from Brookville to fill a position with the insurance company here in Sageville," blurted from her lips.

Rose nodded, took another bite of her cookie, and paused to let Beth know that was not near enough detail.

A moment later, "I came here because of the job opening."

Quickly grabbing another cookie, and taking a huge bite, made sure Rose knew she would not be able to talk.

"I see," was the suspicious reaction.

To ease Beth's apparent tension, Rose passed on some personal information of her own. Short and to the point, "I've lived here all of my life. My late husband and I lived in this house for forty-five years."

Thinking the topic of conversation had changed, Beth said to herself, "Thank goodness," and then, feeling at ease, noted, "It's a beautiful house."

"Is your family in Brookville?" directed the questioning right back to Beth. Beginning to feel penned in, she didn't want to tell Rose the real reason for the transfer. Insubordinate was not how Beth wanted to be tagged, but that was the reason used to get her transferred.

"No, I went there for my first insurance company job," was the short answer before quickly filling her mouth with another cookie.

Rose replied with an unsatisfactory, "I see."

Usually brutally truthful, another twinge of anxiety crept into Beth's mind, as trying to be evasive meant not being honest. However, she did not want to be examined or cross-examined. Feeling pressured, all she wanted was to finish her lemonade and head for the safety of her quiet apartment. Then it happened.

"Beth, is there something you want to ask me?" inquired Rose.

Sensing growing anxiety and wanting to escape the intrusion, the reply was sheepish, "No, not really. Why?"

"I've seen you walk by every day, and lately, it seems to me your slow pace indicates there is something on your mind, something you want to ask of me."

Sitting in silent contemplation for an uncomfortable moment, Rose looked Beth straight in the eye and calmly asked, "Perhaps you've heard I'm a storyteller?"

Beth hadn't given Rose any indication that the rumors, the bits, and pieces of the conversation between her workmates, had roused her curiosity. Nonetheless, she decided to provide a truthful but vague answer.

"Yes. I've heard," came the timid response.

"Did anyone suggest that you should ask me for a story?"

Cemented to her seat, all Beth could do was answer with a relaxed and hesitant, "No."

"I see," replied Rose before sitting back.

A curious minute later, "I wonder if anyone might have told you that my stories take several days to tell?"

Now Beth was certain she didn't want to get involved with this older woman and tie up multiple days. A simple answer would have to suffice.

"No, no one said that."

Rose took another sip of her lemonade, looked toward her flowers, and continued with a soft, warm, all-knowing voice, "Stories are like flowers, you know. Each one takes time to fully blossom, but when they do, they are amazing."

"Oh?"

"You see, dear, each story is different, purposely designed for a specific listener."

There it was again, the wink. Beth was sure of it.

Rose continued in a normal voice, "The listener doesn't find a particular story; the story finds the listener. Take yourself. You need a story that will tell you all about being strong-spirited."

"What makes you think I'm strong-spirited," was the snap reply?

"You moved to a new town by yourself, and more than once, it seems. You're a single lonely working girl, right?"

Not able to figure out how on earth this woman could describe her life to a tee in such a short time, Beth searched her mind for the words that would avoid commitment.

"I have just the story for you," continued Rose, "but can only be told if you are willing to listen."

Trapped, but now she was curious to know how some old story could expose her strong-spirited nature.

Hesitant to sit for several days to hear one of these designed stories, Beth began to evaluate, "How on earth could Rose possibly know what I need? We'd only met a few minutes ago." In a feeble effort to escape, her skepticism surfaced, "Rose, we just met. How could you possibly know the perfect story I need to hear after a five-minute conversation?"

Rose went on to explain how Beth was wrong and how her ancient story had relevance for today. For three months, she'd watched Beth walk to and from work. On Saturday mornings, Rose watched Beth do her grocery shopping, oblivious to those around her. Sunday mornings were always the same; Beth, sitting on her balcony drinking coffee, and not even a book in hand. Beth had never noticed Rose walk by on her way to church.

Though their paths had crossed many times, Beth had not noticed Rose. Beth never noticed anyone.

Then came the observation, "In fact, Beth Chase, I'm not convinced you even know yourself."

Unable to process Rose's intuition, Beth reflected on the rumors she'd heard about Rose, especially the fact that Rose claimed to know her. They all defied reason. Maybe it was wishful thinking on Rose's part, but there was no way this odd old woman knew enough about Beth to make a difference in her life. Beth didn't believe that some lame old story could have any effect on her, and that's when she took the bait.

Never having suffered from a lack of courage, Beth's strong spirit challenged Rose, "I don't think you know me as well as you think you do, and to prove my point, I'll hear your story under one condition."

"Just one?"

"Yes. At the end of the story, I get to tell you where you were wrong and why the story wasn't, as you say, designed just for me."

Rose smiled because Beth's response proved her point. She was a strong-willed, independent woman.

Knowing precisely what Beth needed to hear, her challenge was accepted.

"All right then. I'll tell you the story under your condition, but I have one of my own," replied Rose.

"And that is?" came Beth's quick response.

"Afterward, you must tell me truthfully why the story *was* for you."

"Sounds fair."

"We'll begin tomorrow, but you must understand one thing."

Still cautious, Beth asked, "What is that?"

"You must understand that after you hear the story, your life will be different, forever changed."

Beth remembered hearing Joyce say this about Rose, that her stories changed lives. However, she doubted that it would change hers.

"Okay," came the confident, challenging response.

"You come by Monday, right after work. We'll start then."

Once again, Rose's quick wink set Beth's mind spinning.

Beth had not intended to spend the weekend cleaning her apartment, but it was the only way she could get her mind off what Rose had said about changing her life. Finally, sitting to enjoy an afternoon tea, she admitted to herself, "Well, maybe my life could use a little change."

❀ ❀ ❀

Most Mondays at the office, Beth had more than enough to do. There were files to be updated, policies to review, and clients to call regarding conflicting information. Potential clients dropped in from time to time but never to see her. Today, however, was particularly slow. The lack of activity contributed to the dragging of the clock.

Nonetheless, the ticking second hand kept reminding her the dreaded storytime was creeping closer. Beth began to have second thoughts about committing to multiple afternoons listening to a tale that probably had nothing to do with her personal life. Imprisoned in her cubical, Beth began noticing the once quiet clock ticking noisily away. George's cheerful voice speaking with clients dulled the ticking but did nothing for the knots forming in her stomach. In an attempt to snap herself out of the doldrums, she hatched an escape plan.

Tapping her lip, she thought, "There's nothing to say. I have to keep going if I don't like what I hear." Breathing a sigh of relief, she murmured, "I'll just say the story has nothing to do with me and then not go back."

Breaking the trance, Joyce asked, "Did you say something, Beth?"

"No, no, just thinking out loud," was the quick response.

The noise of Joyce and George closing their filing cabinets alerted Beth to the time, five o'clock. No excuses now; Rose would be expecting her. Filing the day's work, Beth cleaned her desk and picked up her purse. With a quick goodbye to coworkers, she was on her way.

With only three more homes to pass before she would open the gate in the white picket fence; anxiety fueling superstition, her feet avoided every crack in the sidewalk until finally, trembling hand on garden gate caused a squeak which signaled Rose to a cheery welcome.

"Hello, Beth Chase."

There she was, in all her colorful glory, waving from the porch. Perched like a southern belle waiting for her caller, it was clear that Rose had stopped gardening early to make preparations for this occasion. Wearing a bright red floral southern short-sleeved summer dress, trimmed in dainty lace around the traditional high scooped neck, she stood to welcome her special guest. A silver tray with finger sandwiches, sweet tea, and cookies, had been prepared in anticipation of Beth's arrival. Feeling honored that someone had taken the time to prepare such a treat, her voice betrayed the surprise.

"Oh my. You've prepared quite the spread."

"I know your time is tight, what with working and all. I thought you might appreciate a light dinner on the days we meet."

"O Rose, I don't want you to go to any trouble."

"Nonsense! We do have to eat, after all. Help yourself; there are small plates and napkins on the table beside you."

Beth carefully lifted a little pimento cheese sandwich onto her floral-patterned crystal plate. The dishes, utensils, and food presentation were just like Rose. Dainty, southern, and charming.

"How was work today?" she asked.

"Slow. I think it's always slow this time of year. You know, people on vacation."

"I hadn't thought about that. I suppose families making traveling plans don't

want to deal with personal insurance. My late husband, Albert, and I used to take a road trip every year."

"Oh? Where was your favorite destination?"

"The Grand Canyon. It was a remarkable trip." Bursting with fond memories, Rose continued. "We listened to old country classics on the car radio all the way there. You know, all the ballads about gunfights, broken hearts, and of course, for the girl left behind in Texas or Mexico." Laughing again. "We had such good times."

"Sounds like fun," replied Beth trying to imagine the scenery.

After finishing her second finger sandwich and lightly dabbing her napkin on her lips so she wouldn't smear her pink lipstick, Rose sat back in her seat and announced.

"Now dear, to the business at hand."

More than satisfied with Rose's delightful sandwiches, Beth sat back in anticipation of how this story was going to change her life.

Rose smoothed her dress over her knees and began, "First, you need to understand something important. There are many parts to the story you are about to hear, and some of those parts are not documented any-where. Having been passed down through the ages by word of mouth, this story was passed on to me long ago. Believe it or not, this story is over four-thousand-years old."

Shocked, Beth inquired, "Wait, Rose. Just a minute. Why would a four-thousand-year-old story be important to me? How could I possibly have anything in common with the people of that time?"

Rose answered matter-of-fact, "I am always surprised myself how events from so long ago have messages relevant for today. What's important to remember is, people today are

the same as they were four-thousand-years ago."

Beth doubted this. There wasn't any way people today are the same as people that long ago. Beth believed people back then had nothing, lived in an uncivilized world.

Making an effort to be polite, Beth challenged, "I don't want to appear rude, but I find that hard to believe. It isn't possible."

"Why?" Rose responded calmly.

"The people four-thousand-years ago were, well, crude and uncivilized."

"You might think so, but they were not."

"But Rose, they had no modern conveniences. No running water, electricity, no motorized transportation. They lived like, who even knows? Savages?"

"The inventions and progress of mankind are not the same as mind and spirit."

Rather than carry this discussion further, Beth decided to let Rose have her way. Allowing enough time to change the trajectory of the argument, she took a bite of one of the cookies and complimented. "Um... so delicious."

Happy Beth had not put up a fight, "Snickerdoodle to you, poodle. Tomorrow, I'll make a special dessert," and then winked again.

Beth savored the taste of the cookie, wondering if she'd return for the second round of storytelling. She couldn't imagine what meaning an ancient story would hold for her, but she had agreed to listen. If the condition were not met, that would be the end. Beth settled in but could not resist asking one more time.

"Rose, are you sure?"

"Sure, about what, dear?"

"That a story that old has anything to do with me?"

"Doubting already?"

Rose refilled their glasses with tea from an intricately decorated glass pitcher. Stacking two small plates on the tray, she stood and paused for a moment.

Watching Beth chewing her cookie, "Tell you what, Beth. We'll start the story tomorrow." Speaking firmly. "You must be ready to listen with a mind free from clutter, or my story will not have any meaning. Now, do you have any more questions for me?"

"Free from clutter?" she asked.

"Yes. You see, for the story to work, there must not be doubting or questioning how people back then were different from people today. You must be open to the fact that what was important then is still important today. Once we get to the end of the story, you will see, and it will all make sense, I promise."

Beth sat quietly, not sure what to think. The story had not yet begun, and already doubt was starting to cloud curiosity.

After taking a moment to consider, "Okay. Tomorrow. I'll come back with an open mind."

"Promise?"

"Yes."

Having prayed that Beth would continue, Rose could not help but smile. After saying their goodbyes, Beth walked home disappointed. She had hoped to at least hear part of the story today. Now, her reluctance meant that Rose wanted her to start in a better state of mind. Reflecting on the first evening, Beth was impressed at how Rose had handled her headstrong stubbornness. The thought was comforting.

CHAPTER 2

B ETH left for work thinking she might change her mind about see-ing Rose, but having agreed, she would not go back on her word. Muddling through the day's work, not sure what to expect, she tried to unclutter her mind. The day over, the moment to leave work and head to the old house on Reckoner Street had come.

Telling herself over and over, "Open your mind, clear your thoughts," passed the time on the short walk.

Opening the white gate, Beth watched Rose waving energetically, obviously happy to have a friend hear her tale. It was becoming apparent that Rose loved color. This day she was dressed in a short sleeve dress, covered with bright orange and yellow flowers.

Her simple greeting of "Hi Beth" was as bright and happy as her dress.

Ascending the three short steps to the porch, Beth could not help but compliment the sumptuous dinner entre, awaiting consumption.

In awe, "This looks lovely, Rose."

"Just good old-fashioned roast beef on a bun."

"Oh, my goodness! What is that we have for dessert?"

"I made homemade ice cream for chocolate fudge sundaes," Rose answered with a touch of pride.

Beth sat looking forward to enjoying this scrumpdillyicious delight.

The sumptuous dinner, the aromatic Jasmine, Rose's generosity, and warmth enabled Beth to relax for once in her life and enjoy a one-on-one women's chat. With the dishes cleared away, Beth snuggled into her wicker chair. Allowing the aroma of Jasmine to invade her senses helped relax her body and unclutter her mind.

Her eyes remained closed as Rose asked gently, "Are you ready, dear?"

"Yes, Rose. I'm clearing my mind."

"Good, let's start."

Beth sat back and inhaled the sweet Jasmine. Rose began,

"The birth of this child is well documented. The childhood years, however, are not to be found anywhere. Those childhood years have many different versions," pausing to laugh, "and I think I've heard them all. What I am about to tell you has come down to me from people I've known and trusted all my life. The undocumented years are from her birth until she was about fifteen; the time many women of that era were given away in marriage."

Beth thought herself, "How will I know what was true and what was a legend."

Unable to hold back, "How will I be able to tell the facts from the myth?"

Rose's calming voice soothed Beth's curiosity, "The truth of the story will find you. As the parts you need to hear come to light, your heart will open."

Not entirely sure of what Rose meant, Beth felt somewhat like the bug tangled in a spider web of mystery.

Noticing the blank expression of her face, Rose added, "Quite simply, you must listen with your heart dear, not your ears."

Beth had heard that saying about love stories, how people needed to listen with their heart, but she doubted Rose would tell her a love story.

"O well," she thought, "if she does, at least it will be entertaining."

"Is this a love story," Beth asked timidly?

Taking her time to construct an answer, Rose knew the importance of accurately relating the truth.

"It's a very different kind of love story. A special love story; so wonderful and miraculous that it continues today, thousands of years later."

Finding it difficult to believe how a love story could continue for such a long time, Beth had to admit it was arousing her curiosity.

"O come on," her cynicism challenged, "no love story continues for thousands of years. Love is a till death do us part thing, and then it's done."

Smoothing her colorful dress over her lap, sitting up straight in her wicker chair, as if she were about to perform a monologue or recite a poem, Rose shook her silver bracelets and looked Beth straight in the eyes. Mesmerized. Beth couldn't look away from Rose even if she wanted. Rose's blue eyes had pierced her very soul. Frozen in place, like a department store manakin, undistracted, with no other desire, Rose's captivating voice transported her back into the ancient world.

"This, my newfound friend, is the story of a most amazing woman. It began more than four thousand years ago. Not long after her birth, Abraham was informed that his brother's son was now the father of an extraordinary girl."

Snapping out of her dreamlike state, Beth asked, "Wait. How could anyone know about her future marriage? She was a baby. Was it their custom to arrange marriages at so young an age?"

Rose paused, then answered, "It was a marriage meant to be. It wasn't so much that it was arranged by men, as God destined it. Now, dear, let's continue with the story. After you hear the entire story, you will know that the marriage was destined to be from the very beginning."

"Beginning of what? This is crazy. Is the story a mystery?" Beth asked.

"The story isn't a mystery. The mystery is in the way God works."

Beth wasn't sure about any of this, but she sat back and prepared to listen.

Allowing Beth a moment, Rose continued, "In ancient times, it was customary for an older woman, known as a midwife, to deliver babies. Usually, three or four women assisted the midwife through the birthing process. It was primitive compared to modern-day medical practice. Nothing sterilized, as we understand sterilization. There were no medical facilities. Only those women who had experience with the birthing process were at the side of the expectant mother. The mother delivered her baby, legs straddled and standing on birthing bricks. Two women assisted the mother by supporting her on each side. A young woman in training knelt behind to keep the mother from falling back. The midwife sat cross-legged in front of the mother and used a ceremonial knife to cut the umbilical cord. Others waited with the necessary clothes to wash and clean the infant. With the infant cleaned and dry, the midwife wrapped the baby in a swaddling cloth and handed the newborn to the mother."

Half conscious, Beth asked, "Was there a place they went to give birth or did this just happen in the open?"

A look of exasperation spread across Rose's face. It was evident Rose wanted Beth to be more into the moment and let her heart feel the story. With Beth still asking questions, it meant she was thinking and not listening with her heart to feel the story.

Reorganizing her thoughts, Rose said, "Tell you what, dear, if you will just relax, I will tell the story in a way that will enable you to picture it in your mind. It will help you understand. So, close your eyes and let me take you back into the red tent. Breathe in the aroma of Jasmine, listen with your heart, and picture in your mind's eye, women in a dull, dreary tent."

"Okay," came the sleepy reply.

"Close your eyes. Relax. Breathe slowly. Inhale the Jasmine. Let your thoughts dissipate. Think of nothing. Feel everything."

Beth relaxed and closed her eyes. The warm breeze wafted the scent of Jasmine over the porch. Inhaling the aroma, Beth heard birds in the distant trees for the first time. Thinking of nothing, she waited for Rose to continue.

"Breathe in deeply, clear your mind, from the top of your head to the tips of your toes," Rose instructed softly.

Beth finally felt her body relaxing, the anxiety ease. Her body, completely relaxed, could feel the warm breeze blowing gently over the porch. The aroma of Jasmine brought her into the red tent as Rose began to speak.

"Your mind is a blank canvas, and we are going to paint a picture."

Somehow, in a slight air of magic or supernatural flow, Rose infused Beth's mind in a way she had never experienced. Beth could see everything just as it was a very long time ago. Rose began.

❊ ❊ ❊

The tent where women gave birth was the most conspicuous one in the village. Pitched at the outer limit, it was a different color but slightly larger than the others. The ancients always made these tents from tanned animal skins, stained red to distinguish it as the women's place. The red tent is where women went to wait out their monthly cycle until men considered them clean. It was also a private place of refuge in which to give birth. A collection of old rugs covered dirt floors. Beds were nothing more than thick blankets, with old pillows to rest the head. Midwives kept supplies of cloths to clean newborn babies and spices to make a poultice in the tent. Village women, the ones considered clean, took turns bringing food twice a day to the confined. Fired clay oil lamps did nothing to brighten the depressing interior.

Life in the ancient world was not easy. Village women worked long and hard every day. While the men tended the herds, sheered the sheep and goats, and hunted for food, the women were responsible for the family life. A typical day for a woman included grinding wheat, kneading dough, tanning hides, training infants, teaching the children, fetching water, washing the garments, and of course, cooking food. Women gathered the clay and made the pottery. Their fingers nimbly spun wool and flax into cloth for robes and fine linen for sashes and traditional garments.

Shiphrah was the finest spinner of linen and always dressed in decorative scarves and sashes, which she also made for the other women in the village. Mysteriousness always surrounded Shiphrah's entire being. She often wore bold hues of red, blue, and green-colored clothing that she had spun into intricate patterns and even trimmed with beads. Her robes and scarves flowed more freely than the clothing of the other women in the village. Perhaps it was because she spun the most delicate linen of anyone. She was the only woman in the settlement who wore multiple bracelets on each arm, except when delivering babies for the women in the region. With her long auburn hair, sometimes adorned with tiny shells, her colorful clothing, silver arm, and ankle bracelets made her unmistakable.

While the men required their women to dress modestly, Shiphrah was always a threat to male authority. She was the only woman in the village men never commanded to do anything. Ancient men feared a mystic. With cleverness paralleling wisdom, she was the most revered individual in the village. With the rate of infant mortality typically high in the ancient world, Shiphrah's knowledge as a skilled midwife was a huge blessing to the village.

When Shiphrah entered a tent, a rich fragrance of Jasmine blossoms always accompanied her. Having refused to share the knowledge of mixing oils or grinding flowers into fragrant perfumes, she freely shared her lovely decorated clay jars of scented oil with women in and around the village. Advancing in years, Shiphrah prophesied that one day a girl would be born among them who would be wise enough to understand the secret process of making the special oils and perfumes women loved. Shiphrah would often say it would be her honor, and her honor alone, to mentor this unique child.

Legend has it that on the day this child was born, Shuah, the wife of Bethuel, straddled the birthing bricks like thousands of women before her. Orna, Talia, two of the older women, supported Shuah on either side.

Yael, a younger girl, a novice, supported Shuah from behind. Another novice, Keila, waited patiently with the ceremonial knife and clean-up cloths. Beside her, the white swaddling cloth. Shiphrah assumed her position at the helm, sitting cross-legged, hands washed and ready for delivery.

Shuah's shawl and outer garment had long since been removed. As the agony of labor increased the pain, large drops of sweat-soaked her shorter linen birthing garment. Yael, reaching around, wiped the perspiration from Shuah's forehead, but it was challenging to do while trying to support her. Concentrating on grasping the depths of her physical being for every once of strength, Shuah focused on nothing but the precious infant struggling to make its way to freedom. Outside the tent, villagers cringed in sympathy as they heard the screams and grunts of Shuah, as well as Shiphrah's coaching.

Instructions to "Push Shuah push!" were issued by Shiphrah, while Talia whispered, "Breathe Shuah, breathe."

One of the younger men fled rapidly from the village to find Bethuel and give him the news.

From the edge of the clearing, he shouted, "Come quickly, Bethuel! Your baby is coming! Your baby is coming."

Excited, Bethuel and his son, Laban, ran through the sheep, up the dirt path, and passed the other tents to the red tent.

On his arrival, Eber, Bethuel's brother-in-law, patted him on the back, saying, "Ah Bethuel! Did you ask the gods to bless you with another son?"

Curious to know if he had a baby brother, Laban, only ten-years-of age, snuck up and peeked inside. Seeing a pair of eyes peering through the curtain, Yael hurried to the opening and pulled the heavy skins aside.

"Not yet. Not yet. Go away!" Yael commanded and then tied the opening.

"Laban!" Bethuel reprimanded, "No men can go in there. Women only."

Understanding of his son's curious nature, Bethuel could only pat him on the back and smile. Truth be known, Laban hoped to have a brother but was not discouraged about the wait. Bethuel, however, was restless and anxious. He wanted another son to help tend the animals, sheer the wool and assist the family. As time passed, he began pacing back and forth.

Finally, after raising his hands in exasperation, he shouted, "She is taking too long Eber."

It didn't help. Bethuel and the villagers watched the sunset. Tempted to look inside the tent himself, he refrained but continually asked Eber, how much longer would it take?

Again and again, Eber reassured, "Bethuel, these things cannot be rushed. The heavens will tell the baby when to come."

Unable to wait any longer, Bethuel started to move toward the red tent.

Eber grabbed his arm and said, "It's not time. Be patient."

As the shadows grew longer, Bethuel's patience grew shorter. Hearing Shiphrah repeatedly shout for Shuah to push was one thing, but hearing his wife scream, was another. He continued to pace and fret.

Inside the tent, Keila frantically arranged the cleaning rags and washbasin several times. As the baby neared entry into the world, Yael found it difficult to keep Shuah from pushing her back. Reaching under the birthing gown, Shiphrah could feel the child's head and encouraged her one last time.

"That's it Shuah. Your baby is close. You can do it. Push!"

One final push. Shuah screamed. The baby landed in Shiphrah's hands. Unable to stand on her own, she collapsed in the arms of Orna and Talia. At that precise moment, lightning cracked. The interior of the tent illuminated as if it were day. Then, rolling thunder, such as had never been heard before, rumbled through the hills. The women froze. Even Shiphrah trembled but had the presence of mind to slap the baby's bottom. *Whaaaa* rang out from the tent.

Outside, the crowd gathered together in fear as the lightning struck so very close to the village. Not far up the hill, a large tree had been knocked over and was still smoldering from the lightning strike.

Laban grabbed his father, saying, "Father, I am afraid."

The villagers looked to the sky in fear, not knowing what this sign from the heavens meant. Inside the tent, a wet, wriggling, slippery tiny baby rested in Shiphrah capable hands. Anxious to cut the umbilical cord, Keila tried to push the knife into Shiphrah's hand.

Refusing the knife. Shiphrah instructed, "Wait, Keila, we must wait for the cord to slow its pulsing."

Moments later, Shiphrah cord cut the cord, and Keila assisted with washing slim from the baby's skin. Orna and Talia, having lowered Shuah from the birthing stones, helped her to a nearby bed. Yael placed another pillow under Shuah's head and wiped her sweat once again. Shuah noticed a different look on Shiphrah's face as she placed the baby in her arms.

Her soft mystical voice announced, "Your child, your child is a girl."

Shiphrah pulled the delicate cloth away from the baby's head, giving a clear view of this exceptional child. The women gathered close to get a better look.

Astonished, Yael whispered, "Her hair. She has red hair."

Shuah stroked the baby's face with her finger as the infant strained to open her eyes. Speaking for the first time to her newborn, Shuah noted, "Tiny one, you have green eyes. You are very special. You have a glow of fire in your sweet eyes." Looking to Shiphrah, I've never seen such beautiful eyes and with such sparkle." Then Shuah gasped. "Shiphrah, what does it mean?"

Shiphrah's demeanor turned to that of an oracle. Staring lovingly at the infant, she raised one hand. Her solemn voice prophesied, "Your child will be wise and strong; she will cause much heartache, and; no man will ever have dominion over her." Turning to Keila, her voice was stern and loud. "No man!"

The women stepped back in disbelief. They knew of no woman not under the dominion of a man. No woman would be so bold. No woman had ever existed in their time that the man of the household did not dominate.

Scrambling to break the tension, Talia asked, "Shall I take the infant to her father so he can name the child?"

Shuah emphatically shouted, "No!" much to the horror of those present, "Her name is to be . . . Rebekah!"

Gasping in disbelief, the women turned their heads to Shuah.

Orna chastened, "But Shuah, it is the father's duty. It is his right to name the child."

"No!" resounded in the tent once again. "You may take the child to Bethuel, but her name is to be Rebekah!"

Talia insisted, "There is no one in your family with such a name. Surely you will name the child after Bethuel's mother. It is tradition."

Outside the tent, following the lightning flash, Bethuel finally heard the slap and first cries of his newborn child. Listening to the women inside the tent arguing, Bethuel waited impatiently for the announcement.

"Why do they argue? What is taking so long? Where is my child?" Bethuel asked.

Grabbing his father, Laban asked, "When will we know Father? When?"

"When we see Shiphrah," came Eber's reply. Eber turned and asked, "Have you decided on a name Bethuel?"

"If it is a boy, he will be named after my uncle, Haran."

"And if it is a girl?"

"A daughter; I will name after—"

"Father! Look! It is Shiphrah!" shouted Laban.

The crowd went silent when Shiphrah appeared in front of the tent holding the infant. Stopping in front of Bethuel, she pulled the swaddling cloth back. All eyes became fixated on the child.

Laban yelled in disbelief, "Father, look, the baby has red hair."

The gathering crowd marveled at the infant's instant beauty and red hair. Observing the baby's face and hair, Eber was stunned momentarily.

Finally, he uttered, "Bethuel, look, your baby has green eyes! Like my grandmother. My grandmother did not have red hair, only green eyes. Your child is extraordinary. The gods have touched her."

Carefully placing Rebekah in Bethuel's hands, Shiphrah said, "Bethuel, you have a strong and healthy daughter."

Pulling the swaddling cloth entirely away from the infant's face allowed Bethuel to examine his daughter closely. A moment later, he held the infant high above his head.

He proclaimed, "May the gods be praised." Beaming with pride, Bethuel turned to the crowd and said, "This day, I have been blessed with an extraordinary child. I shall call her—"

"Rebekah!" boomed loud and clear from the red tent. All eyes focused on the tent curtain as Shuah stepped out and shouted once again, "Rebekah! Her name is to be Rebekah!"

❀ ❀ ❀

Startled by someone touching her arm ad a voice calling her name, Beth's eyes snapped open; she exclaimed, "Oh, my goodness, where, where am I?"

"It's all right. It always happens when I tell a story meant for someone special, and they listen with their heart and feel it in their soul."

"It was like I was right there Rose. I was with those women in the tent helping Shuah. I saw Shiphrah, Rebekah, Bethuel, and little Laban, all of them. Oh dear, it's almost dark. My goodness, how long was I in that tent?"

"Never mind that dear. It's okay."

Taking a moment to compose herself, "You can't stop now. What about Rebekah? Did Bethuel name her Rebekah? I must know."

Rose beamed with pride, knowing it was the perfect story for Beth. In the end, Rose knew she would understand completely.

"We will pick up tomorrow in the same spot."

Knowing this was the end of the day's tale, Beth replied, "Okay then, tomorrow."

"Yes. Now, I need to clean these dishes and tidy the kitchen.

"I'll help you carry them in."

As Beth was leaving, Rose said, "Tomorrow morning, I'll be making a special dessert for our evening's session."

From the bottom of the step, "Thank you, Rose. I'll see you tomorrow afternoon. "Suddenly, there it was again, that magical wink, that twinkle in her eye. Mesmerized, relaxed, intrigued, Beth had to concentrate on how she was walking home.

CHAPTER 3

S LEEP came easier for Beth that night. Asleep faster than any night since moving to Sageville, she slept soundly for a total of eight hours. There was something about the way Rose's relaxing voice calmed her spirit. Waking refreshed, energized, and in a positive frame of mind was another first in a very long time. The reason did not take long to come. Finally, there was something to look forward to after work.

Dressing quickly, a quick bite of toast, and off to work. Cheerfully greeting neighbors on the way out was another first. Practically skipping to the insurance office, the sweet sound of birds chirping had evaded her senses in the past, but not this morning.

George and Joyce seemed uncharacteristically cheerful. Perhaps they had been so in the past, but Beth had never bothered to notice. Today, everything about the office environment seemed extraordinarily pleasant. Clients, upset about policy shortfalls, were spoken to in a kind and understanding manner. No matter how hard Beth tried to suppress the newfound inner happiness, it was to no avail.

Catching Joyce peeking over the divider and trying to hide her smile, Beth said, "Is there something I can help you with Joyce?"

"You seem different today. I don't know, uh, happy?"

"Thank you."

"Anything new going on? "came the obvious question.

From the front of the office, George blurted, "Gotta be a new boyfriend?"

Blushing, she replied, "Heavens no."

Joyce was suspicious. Her mind racing, her eyes darted from George to Beth and back to George again.

No longer able to contain herself, she said very slowly, "Something is going on George . . . What could it be? Wait! Wait! I know."

"What?" George asked, "What."

Joyce gasped after taking a long look at Beth, whose head was down, trying to work nonchalantly. Beth's attitude finally made sense to her.

She exclaimed, "Miracle of miracles! I'll bet you went to see Rose Maddington yesterday, didn't you!"

Unable to contain her joy, "Yes! Yes, I did."

George was surprised by Joyce's intuition. All he could do was affirm, "That explains it. Rose is a miracle herself. Everyone I know has enjoyed their experience with Rose."

Joyce's eyes lit up in excitement. "Are you going back today?"

"Of course. Rose has only just begun."

"Tell her Joyce said 'Hello,' and everything is still good.'" After reflecting on her own time with Rose, "Took me three weeks to hear my story, and I enjoyed every minute of the time I spent with her."

"What was your story about?" came the obvious question.

Shaking her head, "Oh no dear; I can't tell you or anyone. Rose made me promise."

"Rose said that to me as well. I wonder why?" Beth admitted.

George spoke up, "Took me four."

Joyce smiled at Beth and lipped one word, "Men."

Confirming how Rose worked, Joyce said, "Don't worry, you will understand by the time you reach the end."

"But why Joyce? Why does she want people to promise not to tell any of the details?"

"Simple. The story is designed specifically for you and no one else. Always remember, your story is selected for you alone. It will not have the same effect on anyone else. It will not work on others in the same way."

Returning to her desk, Joyce smiled as she remembered Rose saying, "The story always finds the listener."

Returning to her paperwork, Beth could hear a new client enter and ask for George. Taking a moment to ponder how the story was designed for her made sense that no one else needed to know what the story was about; it was personal. Beth was happy that the monotonous job of reorganizing and filing the previous employee's client information was coming to an end. A wistful thought crossed her mind on closing the filing cabinet drawer as she watched George pass the new client a blank form.

She thought, "I wonder when a new client will come in and ask for me?"

Desk cleared, chair squared away, at precisely the same time as the minute-hand reached 5:00 p.m., Beth said her goodbyes and headed out the door.

❀ ❀ ❀

Arriving at Rose's home in no time at all found Rose sitting prim and southern proper on the front porch, with a nice light meal artistically arranged on a tray.

"Tell me," as if she didn't already know, "how was the insurance office today?" as she gestured nonchalantly toward the evening's culinary delight.

"It was good. It went very smoothly as a matter of fact," was the happy response.

Rose smiled. "And did you sleep well last night?"

"I did. Better than the past few months. Thanks for asking."

"It usually happens to the listener once we begin a story."

Beth didn't know how Rose could do so much in just a few hours of storytelling, but it was appreciated. In anticipation of the next episode, about a new baby girl named Rebekah, Beth would have to force herself not to rush through the delicious fare that awaited consumption.

"Now, have your chicken salad, and then, we'll have apple pie with ice cream."

"Rose, you go to so much trouble."

Placing her hand on Beth's, Rose smiled. "This is what I do, my dear. Storytelling brings meaning to my life."

And once again, Rose winked that magical wink. A tiny sparkle twinkled in her eye.

Chatting about the weather and the small-town news helped meal time pass quickly.

Rose cleared the plates and brought out two slices of warm apple pie, topped with a heaping scoop of vanilla ice cream.

"You'll like this old-fashioned vanilla ice cream," Rose said as she curtsied, "Made it this morning."

Rose's many talents amazed Beth. In contrast, Beth knew scant about cooking and felt inadequate in just about all the requisite kitchen skills. Never having made anything from scratch, warming in the microwave, or following simple recipes, was the limit of her creative cooking expertise. Feeling ashamed, she wondered what Rose would think of her habit of eating ice cream right out of the store-bought container. Beth sometimes finished the entire carton in one evening. Eating ice cream on Rose's porch while admiring the prettiest flower beds in town caused her to recall how she struggled to keep even one houseplant alive. Eventually, Beth gave up and bought silk plants to liven her apartment.

"Can I help you with the dishes?" Beth asked.

"Awfully kind of you to ask. I'll just stack the dishes on the kitchen counter and clean up in a bit. We should get started."

Beth stood and said, "Let me help you carry them in."

Rose accepted Beth's offer to help. Stepping into the house for the first time found it to be every bit as dainty and southern as Rose herself. Furnishings were perfectly placed, gentle decor, rooms spotless. Natural light poured in from every window, providing sun for houseplants that cascaded over tables and fern stands. The scent of jasmine wafted through the entire house. Beth began to realize that the fragrance had a relaxing effect on her spirit. On returning to their wicker chairs, it was time to start.

Rose sat, smoothed her floral dress, and began, "Today, we'll continue with the unwritten part of the story. Hopefully, you begin to see why this story is only for you. Now, close your eyes, and I'll continue from where I left off yesterday."

Listening to Rose's relaxing voice, Beth closed her eyes and breathed in the summery jasmine floral aroma. Rose's soft southern voice returned Beth to the middle of the village, four-thousand-years ago. She could see villagers standing frozen, as was Bethuel with baby Rebekah suspended above his head. His eyes fixed on the glare coming from Shuah.

❀ ❀ ❀

The fact that Shuah shouted out her daughter's name before Bethuel had the chance to name the baby angered him. No woman had ever dared to break such an important tradition. It was against everything he knew in his being. Tension rising within, his breathing became deep and heavy. The disrespect was beyond appalling. Women did not behave this way. Yes, women were to be loved but respecting a husband's authority was imperative. Flexibility was never to be tolerated.

Puzzled onlookers in the crowd gasped. Men, women, children all waited to see how Bethuel would react. Women covered their mouths, admitting in whispers how they would never speak out against their husbands. It was the man's place to make all such

designations. Thinking his advice might be required, Eber moved nearer to Bethuel. Studying his face, he saw Bethuel's emotion change from enraged to peaceful bliss. Bethuel's expression relaxed and slowly turned into a beaming smile. After a moment, his face appeared to radiate a glow, as if he had received word from above that his daughter's name was indeed Rebekah. Bethuel looked high to the heavens and raised his daughter once again toward the sky.

Taking a deep breath, he proclaimed, "Rebekah!"

Lowering the infant, he cradled her to his chest. As the crowd moved closer to look upon this red-headed child, lightning struck the earth.

"Father! Your face. It is bright. It is glowing," observed Laban.

"Your face, it is changed. Your face shines," Eber affirmed.

Face aglow, joyful tears filling his eyes, Bethuel announced, "My child, my child is truly a gift from the gods. She is so radiant," Overwhelmed with happiness deep in his soul, "so beautiful."

Filled with pride, Bethuel held her so that the people of the village could walk by, one by one, to view this wonder child. All were amazed by her beauty, striking vivid green eyes, and the wisps of baby-fine hair with the red sheen. She was indeed an extraordinary ethereal infant.

The moons and seasons moved quickly; the years passed. Bethuel and Shuah watched their baby grow into a healthy, energetic child. At five years of age, Rebekah was well known throughout the village for being uniquely different. Unlike any other girl in the settlement, most boys her age had trouble keeping up with her. In addition to her beautiful eyes and hair, she was inquisitive, bold, and wise beyond her years. The villagers often told Bethuel and Shuah how blessed they were to have such a child. At times, this remarkable young girl talked to her parents as if she were an adult. At ten years of age, Laban felt it his place to correct his little sister and call his parents' attention to her actions. No matter how much Laban tried to convince his parents Rebekah needed more discipline, his plea fell on deaf ears. Even when Rebekah was a tiny bit too bold for her age, they simply smiled lovingly at their red-headed wonder child.

One fine sunny day, Laban watched as Rebekah dashed down to the pond to swim with the other village children. He was not worried, as Rebekah was a better swimmer than most children. The older children in the village admired her athletic agility. They liked to goad her antics on, as Rebekah did not let her age stop her. She loved contending and roughhousing with the other children, even those as old as her brother. Always running, never walking, Rebekah raced down the dirt trails, between the boulders, and across the grassy fields. Feeling free as a bird, she loved to explore beyond the village. Always laughing, singing, or screaming passionately, Rebekah enjoyed life and rejoiced in every moment.

Arriving at the clear blue lake, Rebekah watched some younger children swimming near the shore. Older boys were swinging on a rope out over the water. One by one, the boys swung out over the water and did some crazy flying flop into the lake. One boy swung out, let go of the rope, and flapped his arms and legs wildly until he splashed into the water.

"Hey, watch this!" another boy shouted as he climbed to a higher rock and shouted again, "Watch me!"

Grabbing the rope, he swung out courageously, let the rope go, and made a crazy spinning splash into the water.

Rebekah, not to be outmatched, ran to the rope and yelled, "Hey, Amoz! Throw it out, throw it!"

Amoz threw the rope out over the water and watched it swing back. As the rope began its outward swing, Rebekah screamed and launched herself off the edge, grabbing the rope in mid-air with enough force to swing her out over the water. Screaming while swinging, her crazy somersault culminated in a huge cannonball splash.

All the while, the noise of children shouting, "Rebekah! Rebekah! Rebekah!" was heard echoing over the water and back to the village.

Emerging from the cool, clear water, Rebekah heard her friends shouting, "Yeah! Yay! Yeah!"

Anxious to tell her mother about her great flip flop, she swam to the water's edge, scrambled out of the lake, and hustled back up the path to the continued chants of, "Rebekah! Rebekah!"

The children knew Rebekah never refused a dare. They wanted her to return and do the somersault again.

Hearing the distant shouts, Shuah stepped out of her hut smiling with pride knowing her daughter had done something to entertain the crowd of children at the lake.

Frustrated with his sister's behavior, Laban turned to his father and said, "Father, why do you allow Rebekah to do such things?" Chastening his father, "Other girls do not act like her."

Bethuel could only laugh and say, "No one acts like your sister."

"But father, she even talks back to adults. She talks back to you, too."

Placing his hand on Laban's shoulder, Bethuel said, "My son, the gods are with your sister. Look around." Gesturing toward the villagers who had all turned to look toward the lake, he said, "Everyone knows the gods are with her. I do my best, and we must never dampen her spirit." Giving Laban a reassuring hug, he said firmly, "Now, back to work."

Rebekah, proud of the spinning somersault over the water, sprinted up the dirt path to tell her mother. Running as fast as possible, she tripped on a tree root and fell. Rolling in the dirt, she regained her footing without missing a beat and continued running to her mother.

Covered in dust and dirt, she ran by Laban and Bethuel, yelling, "Mommy! Mommy! Mommy!"

Crashing into Shuah's outstretched arms, she was greeted with a jubilant, "Yes, my child?"

"Did you hear? I did the biggest and bestest flip ever! Right into the water!"

Shuah smiled and said, "Yes, my child, yes, and now you can go right back down to the water and do another bestest flip to get that mud off of your clothes."

Rebekah laughed right along with her mother and agreed, "Yes mommy."

Bethuel could not help but feel inner pride at the sight of his beautiful but muddy little girl running wildly, arms thrashing about and yelling.

Passing Laban she exclaimed, "Laban, Laban, look at me! Look!"

Shaking his head, Laban turned toward his father, thinking, "*Surely now father will discipline my sister.*"

Laban's admonition of "Father?" was met with disbelief when his father did not utter a word. Saddened, Laban went back to work, only to hear the continual shouts echoing from the lake, enticing his sister to further challenges.

As the moons and seasons sped by, Bethuel and Shuah watched their little monkey of a girl grow into a smart, adept, and creative child. Unlike girls her age, she was a quick study and permitted to stay in the women's tent to learn the mysterious ways of a midwife. Having taken an early interest in her prodigy, Shiphrah had begun teaching Rebekah the art of herbal medicines needed to treat sickness and injuries. Shiphrah knew that the task of teaching gifted students was a blessing. Having a child keenly interested in learning is a teacher's dream come true. A knowledgeable and talented woman in her own right, Shuah had no idea of the full range of remedies and medical techniques Shiphrah had imparted to her daughter. As a mentor, Shiphrah often spoke of the habits and qualities of various communities, giving Rebekah a greater insight into the nature of all people. In ten short years, Rebekah had gained a lifetime of experience.

Called to assist in the women's tent, Rebekah entered to find Chana, a young woman from the village, lying on blankets, fever-stricken. Realizing death was near, she instinctively knelt behind Chana. She began wiping the perspiration from her forehead and washing her chest with cool water. Orna held Chana's hand at the side. On the opposite side, Shuah checked Chana's pulse and watched her breathing. Chana's struggle to breathe waned. Something needed to be done.

"Mother, her breathing, it is too slow."

Shuah's fearful look over to Talia said it all.

"We must act now Talia. We have no choice. It is time."

Talia retrieved a mortar and pestle from the herbs and spices table. Oils contained in unmarked jars could only be distinguished by those with the knowledge of their shape.

Kneeling beside Orna, Talia opened a small sack of mustard seeds and dropped the contents into the mortar. Orna poured goat's milk over the mustard seed. While grinding the mixture, Talia nodded to Orna to add more milk and a handful of flour to thicken the paste.

Talia looked to Shuah and asked, "Anything else?"

"No—"

"Turmeric, one pinch," was Rebekah's firm instruction.

Talia looked to Shuah, who nodded, "Yes."

Orna added the turmeric from the spice pouch.

"One more," Rebekah said.

Orna looked at Shuah once again, who promptly approved.

Rebekah instructed once again, "Olive oil."

Orna looked at Shuah again and waited for her approval.

"Yes," Shuah replied, "and hurry."

"That is enough. Now mix," Rebekah said.

Orna and Talia found it difficult to comprehend how well mother and daughter worked together. Shuah did not hesitate for a moment or question anything Rebekah had said. With the mixture entirely incorporated, Talia placed a square poultice rag into the mortar bowl and kneaded it into the mix. Rebekah opened Chana's thin linen gown gently and dried the feverish sweat with a cloth. Talia placed the poultice rag on Chana's chest. Shuah softly molded the rag to cover from neck to navel.

Rebekah leaned over Chana and listened closely to her breathing. It was a sight to behold. A ten-year-old girl, whispering in a dying woman's ear, "Breathe . . . breathe deeper Chana, . . . deeper." Rebekah's voice was soft and soothing. Not moving from Chana's side, Shuah's little red-headed daughter continued to nurse her patient.

Rinsing the wiping rag, Rebekah blotted the sweat from Chana's forehead, all the time continually whispering, "Yes, Chana, breathe, breathe."

After repeatedly whispering and applying more mustard to the poultice, Chana's breathing became more distinct. Talia grabbed Orna's hand.

Tears flowed from their eyes as Rebekah's voice encouraged, "That's it, Chana, breathe."

Encouraged, Shuah joined in with her encouragement, "Yes Chana, that's right, breathe . . . come on dear, breathe."

At that moment, Shiphrah entered the tent for the first time that day. Looking at Chana then to Rebekah, a big warm smile brightened her face. The other women watched Shiphrah's magical wink bring a smile to Rebekah's face.

"She looks better. I think she will make it," came the confident observation.

Void of any uncertainty, Rebekah replied, "She'll be fine."

With a tremendous sense of teacher/student pride, Shiphrah's smile lit up the tent.

Helping Rebekah to her feet, Shiphrah complimented, "You are indeed a wise one."

❄ ❄ ❄

As happened the night before, Beth felt someone touching her arm. A voice calling her name awakened her to reality.

"Wait, that's not all? Oh please," cried a disappointed voice.

"No dear, there's much more to the story," Rose answered in assurance.

"Oh Rose, can't you just tell me a little more?"

"Yes dear, tomorrow. Come back tomorrow, and we'll see what happens next."

Beth was hooked. There wasn't anything that could keep her from hearing the rest of the story.

"Can't you give me a hint?" came the plea.

Laughing, Rose said, "I can tell you this much. Tomorrow you will hear what happened in one of the most famous tales passed down through the centuries to my grandmother and now to me. This account has never been recorded but passed on via the ancient Hebrew tradition of the maggid, a storyteller. Once you hear it, you will understand why people always remember it."

Reluctantly, Beth began descending the steps, then stopped.

Turning, she said, "Thank you for the story today, Rose. It certainly was intriguing."

"Thank you dear; you are a good listener."

"I so want to know the whole story."

"You will, dear, you will."

CHAPTER 4

Beth's workday breezed by. Purse in hand, parting salutations made, and she was on her way to Rose's at exactly 5:00 pm. Visions of a little red-headed girl whispering in Chana's ear flashed in her mind. Before she knew it, there was Rose, perched all prim and southern proper in her white wicker deck chair with the ceiling fan whirling its cooling breeze over her bright green and blue summer dress.

As Beth had come to expect, the sincerity of Rose's "Hello dear," warmed her heart. Happy to return the greeting, "Hello Rose," Beth couldn't help but notice a silver tray laden with two large chef salads adorned with slices of hard-boiled egg and freshly baked rolls to the side.

"I hope you like salad and homemade dinner rolls."

"This looks lovely, Rose. You've outdone yourself. I don't know which is better, your stories or your cooking."

Smiling with confidence, Rose said, "When we finish your story, you will know the answer, my dear."

"I guess that's about right."

A touch of sadness crept into Rose's voice as she relayed the sad news about her minister's decision to take another call and leave their church. She was visibly upset but did understand.

Looking down the street to the church steeple, she explained, "He is young and wants a larger church. The younger pastors do that sometimes. But this one, well, in just five short years, he helped us grow our church, create well-attended fellowship events, and gave us stimulating worship services."

Out of curiosity, Beth asked, "What will happen now?" as she had stopped attending church while still in high school. It was the age of enlightenment with her newfound knowledge of evolution. Deciding that believing in such things as God and pastors and churches was a thing of the past, she stopped attending. The reality was, it was to spite her mother's domineering.

"The committee will meet and discuss what to do," continued Rose.

"What are their choices? I mean, what do churches usually do?"

"Either hire an interim, kind of like a substitute teacher, until a decision is made, or start right away by forming a search committee."

"What do you hope will happen?"

"I'm not getting any younger, so I hope we search for a replacement. I don't want to be without a pastor for too long."

"Will you be on the committee?"

"No, not this time. I served on the last three search committees. That's enough. If they need me, they'll call. Now, the apple pie, would you like a slice?"

Beth helped Rose take the dishes into the kitchen. The interior fragrance was initially floral, but the scent of vanilla and freshly baked bread overwhelmed the senses on entering the kitchen. Returning to the porch, Beth's olfactory modality returned to the sweet aroma of jasmine.

Taking their seats, Rose noted, "It warms me so that you've been listening to the story with your heart. Tell me, dear, what thoughts are running through your mind?"

"What do you mean Rose?"

"What do you know so far about Rebekah. What kind of a person is she?"

"Well, let me see; for such a little girl, she was brave, intelligent, and unlike the other women, didn't let tradition dictate her behavior."

Rose had to suppress a smile, knowing that what Beth could see in Rebekah was what she would soon see in herself.

Satisfied with the progress thus far, Rose wanted to begin, saying, "Are you ready to hear what happened that very same afternoon?

"Of course."

Before Rose could tell Beth to close her eyes, she'd already shut them and began to relax.

Rose began by returning Beth to the red tent, saying, "Now, concentrate on the last scene with Rebekah helping Chana. Remember how she was watching Chana beginning to breathe deeper?

"Yes, she was coming out of the fever?"

Beth's mind returned to the exact moment in the women's tent. She could see and feel everything. Rose continued.

❀ ❀ ❀

Rebekah stayed with Chana until she was certain breathing was restored to a steady and normal rate. Watching Chana open her eyes for the first time in two days, Shiphrah smiled at Rebekah and said, "You knew what to do. Very good my child."

Shuah beamed on hearing the words of praise from Shiphrah. Shuah knelt beside Rebekah and listened closely to satisfy herself that Chana's breathing was restored.

Standing, Shuah said, "Come child, let us return to our home."

Rebekah stood beside her mother and smiled at Chana, who returned the smile as best she could. Leaving the women's tent, mother and daughter walked arm in arm toward their hut on the other side of the village.

Looking at Rebekah with pride and adoration, "Shiphrah has taught you well."

"She is a sage, mommy."

Giving Rebekah an extra firm squeeze, "So are you, my dear, so are you, and I am so very proud of you."

They strolled silently, enjoying their time together, then Shuah stopped and looked lovingly at Rebekah.

Dropping to her knees, placing both hands on her daughter's shoulders, she said, "Did you know, from the very first moment Shiphrah looked at you, she said, 'you would be different, that you were a gift from the gods and that you had a specific destiny?'"

"I don't feel any different, mommy, well maybe just red hair different."

As Shuah gave her daughter another hug, two children darted into the center of the village, yelling, "Help! Help! Come quick! The tiger has Uri trapped up the big oak tree!"

Eber shot from his tent holding his spear and shouted, "Get your spears men! Come with me! It's Uri! He is trapped!"

An expression of shock and fear fell over Rebekah's face. Her eyes opened wide.

She screamed, "*No!*" and shot off toward the old oak.

Stunned, Shuah shouted, "Rebekah, come back!"

Protective instinct in full force, Shuah ran after Rebekah but could not catch the fleet-footed redhead as she sped through the village toward the oak tree.

Eber, along with several men, had come to a halt at the edge of the clearing. They halted, unsure of how to proceed. Rebekah burst past them, running full tilt toward the tree. Uri was screaming for help. At the base of the tree, a tiger clawed the bark and roared. It tried jumping to Uri; but it was to no avail. Rebekah stopped when she saw it; a spear had pierced the tiger's hind leg. Inching slowly toward the tree, using the same calming tone to help Chana breathe, she called out, "Malka." This full-grown adult female tiger turned, looked at Rebekah, and growled in pain. Shuah and Bethuel burst into the clearing but came to a screeching halt when they saw their precious little daughter approaching a huge tiger.

With tears in her eyes, Shuah begged, "Rebekah! Rebekah, come back child."

Paying no attention to her mother, Rebekah moved slowly forward. With a voice just above a whisper, she repeated, "Malka, Malka."

Upon hearing the news about Uri and the tiger, others from the settlement gathered in the clearing. With fear in their hearts, the villagers could not believe what they were witnessing. This smart ten-year-old girl was bravely advancing toward a large female tiger. Some of the women in the group held onto each other's arms; others held onto their husbands. At the same time, some of the older children inched closer for a better view. Four of the men, who had begun to circle the tree, spears in hand, stopped forty feet from the most unbelievable sight anyone had ever seen.

Rebekah, now on her hands and knees, cautiously pressed on toward the tiger, all the while calmly calling, "Malka."

Alternating her glances from Uri to Rebekah and back again, Malka allowed Rebekah's hand to stroke her massive shoulder blades.

Kneeling, gently stroking the head of this magnificent animal, Rebekah began whispering, "Down Malka, down," as calmly as possible.

Much to the surprise of all who had gathered in the clearing, Malka lowered herself to the ground. Rubbing the tiger's thigh, Rebekah gradually moved her other hand to the spear.

As calmly as possible, she whispered, "Shh . . . shh . . . rest Malka, rest."

With her left hand on Malka's thigh and her right hand on the shaft of the spear, Rebekah pulled the spear out with one swift yank. This startled Malka. She jumped back, roaring in pain.

In her sweet, calming voice, "Down Malka, down."

Rebekah talked the injured animal into slowly lowering herself to the ground. When Malka's breathing returned to normal, Rebekah removed her shawl and wiped the blood from the tiger's leg. After wrapping the wounded thigh tightly, Rebekah sat with her back against the tree and rested Malka's head on her lap. The villagers watched in utter amazement as Rebekah stroked the tiger's neck. Gradually, the villagers left and returned to the work of the day. Only a few remained to watch Rebekah soothe the tiger until she fell asleep.

When all had quieted, Rebekah began the task of getting Uri down from the tree.

"Uri," Rebekah said quietly.

Louder than he should have been, "Yes?"

"Shh. Quiet . . . Get down and get out of here, quietly!"

Carefully and quietly, Uri climbed down from the tree. Once confident he'd made it far enough to be safe, he ran as fast as he could back to the village. Rebekah remained with Malka until the sun began to set. Walking with Malka, Rebekah stopped, removed her shawl from the tiger's thigh, and sent Malka on her way. On reaching her parents, Shuah scooped her daughter up in her arms, holding tight for a long time. Back in their hut, the family gathered for dinner. No one knew what to say about the incident until finally, Shuah leaned over to hug Rebekah once again.

Sitting back, astonished beyond belief, Shuah said, "Shiphrah was right; you are special, very special."

The family circle became unusually quiet. Still uncertain as to how to broach the subject, Bethuel dipped his bread into the common bowl.

Before taking a bite, Bethuel began, "That was very brave of you today, but very dangerous."

Supporting her husband, Shuah added, "Yes Rebekah, you gave us a terrible fright."

Laban rolled his eyes and glared at his sister, chastising, "Dumb. That's what it was, dumb."

Much to everyone's surprise and in a calm, reassuring voice, "Malka is my friend. She would never harm me."

"Yeah, right, that tiger is your friend," Laban blurted.

Upset at the disbelief, Rebekah replied sharply, "Yes, she is! . . . I've known her all my life."

Placing her hand on Rebekah's shoulder, Shuah confessed, "Oh, my child, sometimes I wish you were like the rest of the children."

"But I'm not mommy. Shiphrah told me she has never had a student like me; ever."

Shocked by this statement, Bethuel's voice became stern, "Shiphrah? What's going on with you and that midwife?" Glaring at Shuah for not speaking to him first about the teaching situation, he tried to continue, "Why didn't anyone—"

"We don't tell men what happens in the women's tent!" Rebekah injected, cutting her father off.

"Rebekah! Hold your tongue. That is your father." Shuah shouted for the first time in a very long time.

Bethuel attempted to regain a sense of calm among the family. He'd always struggled with the problem of how to discipline a gifted child.

Looking directly at Rebekah, he changed his voice and the subject, "Tell me, how did you come to befriend this tiger, this Malka?"

Closing her eyes, Rebekah remembered the exact day it happened.

She began, "A long time ago, I fell asleep against that very same old oak tree. I was dreaming and felt something wet on my cheek. When I opened my eyes, there she was, licking my face." Smiling and looking at her father. "Can you believe it, a tiger licking my face?"

Bethuel and Shuah shook their heads in disbelief. Even Laban was taken aback.

"Rebekah, were you not frightened?" Shuah inquired.

"No, not really. The tiger stopped when I opened my eyes; the tiger just sat there looking at me."

Groaning with disbelief, Laban said, "Yeah, right; the tiger just looked at you."

In a stern tone, Shuah reprimanded, "Laban!" and told Rebekah to continue.

"After a few moments, I started to run my hand over her head and began talking to her."

Laban chuckled, "Ha, ha, ha, and what did the tiger say?"

"Tigers don't talk, silly."

Sitting up a little straighter and looking back at her parents, "She just kept looking into my eyes. She'd move her head from one side and then to the other."

All the family could do was look at each other in utter amazement.

"When I got up to walk home, the tiger walked alongside me. Oh mommy, she was just so majestic that I just had to name her Malka. When we got close to the village, I sent her away."

Astonished, Bethuel remembered, "Shiphrah did say the gods had chosen you."

"And you certainly are special," added Shuah.

Rose touched Beth's arm, but this time, Beth didn't open her eyes, so she tried calling, "Beth. Beth dear."

"Oh, Rose. The story, I was inside the story. Can you believe it?"

"Yes, I can actually, and I know it's one you will remember."

"I'll never forget it, Putting her hand on her chest, "and I'll never forget the size and beauty of Malka.

"As I said, this story has never been documented. It has been handed down through countless generations because nobody forgets such a powerful story as this. And now Beth, it has come to you, and you will never forget it because it's a story you needed to hear."

"I can believe it," answered Beth, as she knew Rebekah's tenacious spirit had begun to resonate within.

"Good," was the all-knowing reply. "Tomorrow, we will begin the next chapter in Rebekah's life. You will see how the tales of old and documented history come together."

"But Rose, can you give me a hint?"

Rose patted Beth's hand and said, "All in good time, my dear. All in good time."

The story had aroused too much emotion for Beth to ask even one more question. At this point, all she wanted to do was go home and fall into bed, and that is what she did.

CHAPTER 5

Beth rose earlier than usual the following day. There was something about spending time with Rose that was beginning to make her feel as if she had, at last, found a home. Rose felt like a favorite grandmother or a great-aunt whom she had known for years. It had only been a few days, but each day felt better than the day before. Not able to articulate her feelings, Beth sensed that she was becoming part of something bigger than herself. What that something was, she did not know?

The heat of the afternoon slowly subsided, giving way to the cool evening breeze. Arriving at Rose's house right on schedule found Rose waiting in her white wicker chair, beaming with happiness.

Beth wondered, "How can she get such happiness out of doing for others?"

On opening the gate, a waving hand and a joyful, "Hello Beth," greeted her entry.

The warm welcome overflowed into Beth's joyful response, whom she happily imitated with, "Hello Rose."

This evening, two dinner plates laden with slender fried chicken strips and homemade potato salad awaited consumption.

Beth cheerfully expressed her concern, "My goodness, Rose. I'm going to gain weight."

"Oh, nonsense! You're as thin as a rail. Shall we eat?" replied Rose as she handed Beth a napkin and a fork before taking her seat. Beth hadn't thought much of it in the past, but every evening before they ate, Rose closed her eyes briefly.

"Is she praying?" Beth wondered.

Allowing Rose time to finish, she quietly took her plate and placed it on her lap.

Rose looked up and asked, as if nothing out of the ordinary had happened, "I thought you might like lemonade rather than tea. We've had tea the last few days."

"Either one is good for me . . . and thank you again for dinner. I'd like to cook for you someday." Beth smiled and laughed, "Once I learn how to cook."

The offer brought a touch of laughter to Rose, who responded, "Now, don't you worry about cooking for me. I enjoy it. Help yourself. Come on; there's plenty."

After dinner, Rose brought out two small plates of cookies, each with three different kinds. Beth couldn't wait to sample each one. While enjoying their sumptuous taste-treat delight, Rose prepared Beth by telling her that the location would change in today's story.

"Oh? Is it still about Rebekah?" Beth inquired.

"Yes, dear, but to understand the story fully, you need to hear about the whole family."

Beth didn't understand where Rose was headed, but she trusted it would be interesting.

"Now, are you ready to begin?" Rose asked.

"Yes, of course."

Rose's soft voice brought Beth back to ancient times, but the scene was not the same as last night. A new village mysteriously appeared in her mind. There were no homes, only tents. Opening her heart, Beth became one of the villagers watching an older man hold up an infant. It was a boy, not a red-headed girl.

❀ ❀ ❀

In the land of Canaan, four thousand years ago, an older man named Abraham lived with his wife, Sarah. After the death of his brother Haran, Abraham's father moved his tribe from Mesopotamia and settled in Padan Aram. God, however, had a more excellent plan for his life and called him to leave his father Terah, his brother Nahor, and journey into the land of Canaan. Sixty years later, following the guidance of the one true living God, Abraham and Sarah settled in this new region. Finally, at ninety years of age, after all those years of barrenness, Sarah's heart was gladdened by the birth of her only child, a son for Abraham.

Holding the newborn infant, Abraham proclaimed, "His name is to be Isaac."

As Abraham named his son, Sarah remembered how she had laughed in disbelief on hearing the angel's prophesy that she would bear a son in her old age.

Sarah said, "I am certainly laughing for joy to at last have such a beautiful baby!"

The one true living God, creator of heaven and earth, had promised Abraham that his seed would be more numerous than the grains of sands of the sea. Furthermore, his descendants would be a blessing to all people on earth. As astonishing as God's promise was, at ninety years of age, it was coming true. Abraham had believed for all those years, and it was accorded to him as righteousness.

Forty years later, after living and prospering in the land, Abraham was nearing death's dark door, and Isaac was not married. He knew it would not be long before joining his wife in the ancestral cave at Machpelah. With large flocks of sheep and goats, more than enough servants to tend the flocks, he was able to enjoy the abundant life. The surrounding tribes considered Abraham richly blessed by his God. However, Abraham lacked one thing; a wife from his father's line for his son Isaac so that his line might continue.

With Sarah at rest with her ancestors and the infirmities of old age making it hard to keep warm, his two servant girls, Bayla and Rina, supplied that warmth once provided by his wife. Sadly, Abraham's material blessings did not ease his troubled mind. He had to find a wife for Isaac before he died. One of the problems faced was the regional practice of idol worship. God abhors the pagan practice of worshiping gods that are nothing but clay images created by men. Abraham knew that if his seed would multiply into a nation, he must find a wife for Isaac from the line God had chosen. One evening, the aged Abraham called for his longtime servant, Chesed.

On entering the tent, Chesed said, "You sent for me, my lord?"

"Yes."

Abraham dismissed his two servant girls saying, "Go! Leave us, but do not go too far. Chesed, come, make yourself comfortable."

Not sure what his master wanted, Chesed sat at Abraham's side, crossed his legs, and readied himself.

"Chesed, you have been my faithful servant for longer than I care to remember."

"Yes, Master. It has been my privilege."

Propping himself up on the pillows, Abraham continued, "I am old, well stricken in years, and have not the strength to travel. So it is, you must undertake this journey in my place."

"Journey Master?"

"Yes, my son Isaac must not marry a daughter of the Canaanite people."

"But Master, all manner of women abounds in this land. Surely there must be one who you would approve?"

"No! There is no one in this land."

"Not one?"

"No!

To ensure Chesed would do as Abraham was about to require, his servant needed to swear an oath. This oath would bind him to find an acceptable wife for Isaac. As was the custom of that day, Abraham instructed him to place his hand under his thigh.

"Come close," Abraham said, "put your hand under my thigh and swear by the God of heaven and earth that you shall not allow Isaac to take a wife from among those tribes with whom we dwell."

"But if not this land, where?" came the bewildered response.

"You shall go to my people, to my kindred, and there you are to choose a wife for my son. My God will send an angel before you as a guide so that you will find a suitable wife for Isaac."

This troubled Chesed, who then asked, "If the woman I find will not follow, am I to bring Isaac back to the land from whence you came?"

"No!" Abraham snapped, then calmed his tone. "Isaac must not return unto the land beyond the flood. He must remain in this land; the land God promised my seed."

Still troubled, Chesed asked, "But what if no woman will follow?"

"If no woman follows, then you are clear from this oath; only take not my son to this land."

Chesed knelt at Abraham's side and placed his hand under the thigh of his master.

Faithfully, he said, "I swear by the God of heaven and earth to do as you have commanded, my lord."

"Good. Now listen."

Chesed sat once again, cross-legged by Abraham's side.

"You will bear many gifts for my nephew's family. Camels for Bethuel, son of my brother Nahor; cloth for his wife Shuah, and jewelry for the daughter you will choose for my son."

"Yes Master, as you have said."

"Good. Now, call Bayla and Rina to return, and Chesed, have them pour us some wine."

Appreciating that Abraham's time was of the essence, Chesed began preparations for the journey that very evening. Enlisting the help of two younger servants, they prepared ten camels. One camel carried two bags of gifts, another, the traveling equipment, while four more camels were fitted with riding saddles. To be presented as gifts, four more camels trailed behind. Provisions in place, Chesed left the following day with two servants to fulfill the oath he'd swore to Abraham.

Leading this procession of camels across the countryside, Chesed traveled past rows of date palms and king palms into an unknown land in search of the Bethuel's settlement, located north of Padan Aram. A caravan of camels, trimmed with magnificent blankets of the finest wool and elaborately decorated riding saddles, followed the old trails. Atop three of the camels, men dressed in fine linen robes with bright linen tunics draped over one shoulder were a sight to behold. Such fine clothing indicated wealth. From a distance, they had the appearance of a spectacular parade of the ancient world. Anyone beholding this caravan knew it was on a mission of great importance.

After long hot days and cool nights under the moon and stars, the caravan arrived on a hillside overlooking Bethuel's village. It was not the small settlement he'd expected. Except for one red tent on the perimeter, all other lodgings were clay brick or large reed mudhifs. With the sun low in the west, it would soon be time for the village's young women to come to the well for the night's water.

Turning to his traveling companions, Chesed said, "We are here. It is as Abraham had said. Look, there is the well."

Dismounting, the men had their camels kneel. It would be an insult to take water without permission. While they waited, Chesed moved to a quiet spot to pray. With both hands covering his mouth and nose, Chesed lowered his head and prayed.

"God of my master Abraham, I pray thee, send me good speed this day. Behold, I stand near the well of Nahor, asking for a sign. Let it come to pass that the damsel to whom I shall say, 'Let down thy water skin, that I may drink,' shall say to me 'Drink, and I will give thy camels drink also,' let the same be she that you have appointed for Isaac, the son of my master."

When Chesed lifted his head, he saw three girls coming to the well carrying empty water skins.

Chesed remarked to his servants, "Look, the one with the red hair, is she not the most beautiful?"

The servants agreed. Chesed admired her striking beauty and gentle face. She was indeed one of a kind. As was the tradition, the three young girls, Rebekah, Keli, and Lora, kept their distance from the men who were strangers. Keeping the well between themselves and the men, the girls filled their water skins one at a time. The male chaperone who had accompanied the young girls for protection stood off to the side.

As in his prayer, Chesed asked of the three girls, "Let down thy water skin, I pray thee, that I may drink."

Without hesitation, the young red-headed girl, no more than fifteen-years-old, stepped boldly forward and said, "Drink, and I will give thy camels drink also."

Handing a ladle of cool water to Chesed, he began to drink but stopped when he saw this beautiful red-headed girl had green eyes.

Accustomed to men taken aback by her beauty, she waved her hand and said, "Drink my lord, drink."

Suddenly, Keli began the barrage of cautionary words, "Rebekah! Do not speak with that stranger."

The others followed, issuing their stern reprimands. Deaf to her companions' rebuke, Rebekah completely ignored Keli and Lora.

She continued, "When your thirst is satisfied, I will draw water for your camels also."

"Rebekah!" Screamed Lora and Keli as they watched Chesed drink from the ladle.

Undaunted, Rebekah walked over and emptied the water into the animal skin watering trough.

With a cheerful voice, she beckoned the other girls to help, "Come on Lora, Keli, give me a hand."

Both girls hurried to assist Rebekah in filling the water trough. Chesed fell to his knees.

Offering a prayer of thanks, he said, "Blessed be God most high. All praise to the God of my master Abraham, who has guided me to the family of the house of Bethuel."

Approaching Rebekah, Chesed asked, "Whose daughter art thou?"

Being overly protective of Rebekah, Lora pulled her away from Chesed and begged, "Please stop speaking to him. It isn't right."

Unafraid and undaunted, she pulled her arm free and proudly proclaimed, "I am Rebekah, daughter of Bethuel, son of Milcah and Nahor. Shuah is my mother, and Laban is my brother."

Chesed's heart filled with joy on hearing this beautiful young girl did indeed belong to his master's family. Making haste to the pack animal, Chesed wondered why the chaperone had remained silent during his encounter with Rebekah. Returning, he removed a nose ring and gold bracelet from a small gift sack. All stood in silent shock as the gifts were of fine gold. The nose ring weighed one half-shekel and the bracelets, ten shekels.

Anxious and invigorated, he handed the gifts to Rebekah and asked, "Tell me please, is there room in thy father's house for us to lodge?"

Lora screamed, "Rebekah! Surely you will not accept gifts from a stranger!

"Yes," came the bold reply.

Again, chastisement rang out, "Rebekah! It is not right for you to offer lodging in your father's house."

Both Lora and Keli protested long and loud at Rebekah's boldness. Then it happened for the first time. Rebekah turned and gave both girls *the look*. Even the chaperone lowered his head.

As her glare returned to a pleasant smile, she looked back at Chesed and said, "We have both straw and fodder, as well as room for you to lodge."

Chesed could not help himself and said aloud, "Praise be to the God of Abraham!"

Lifting the gift sack over his back, he said, "Please take me to your family that I may present these gifts from my Master Abraham, your father's uncle."

Pleased to accept her gifts, she made Chesed wait while adjusting the nose ring and placing the bracelet on her wrists before saying, "Bring your camels. I will go tell my father."

Chesed instructed his servants to take the camels and follow the chaperone. The three young girls took their water skins and hurried after Rebekah. Chesed followed the girls. During the walk back to the village, Lora and Keli continued to scold Rebekah for her bold behavior. Entering the family hut, Rebekah displayed her expensive gifts to her mother, father, Laban, and his wife, Avi. Two servants, Hirsch, an older male servant, and Livia, a female servant, admired the gifts from a distance.

Allowing time for Rebekah to display her gifts, Chesed entered.

Rebekah said, "Look father, this is the man from the well. He said he is the servant of your uncle Abraham."

Surprised by Chesed's sudden appearance, Bethuel reminisced out loud, "Abraham; I haven't seen Abraham in such a long time."

Rebekah continued, "After he gave me these gifts, I invited him to our home to eat and to sleep."

Hirsch spoke out harshly at her audacity, "Bold child, you do not know your place."

Angered by Hirsch's out-of-place comment, she turned and yelled, "*Quiet!*" Stepping face to face, with a glare that could freeze a camel, "It is you who does not know his place."

Hirsch looked at the floor in fear of punishment. Bethuel, however, had learned to live with her boldness. Not only did Rebekah have red hair and green eyes; she was also the student of the mysterious Shiphrah, and no one ever commanded Shiphrah.

Bethuel intervened, "Calm down daughter, calm down. You are too bold for your good."

Turning abruptly to her father, she shouted, "Who is he to tell me my place. Bold! If I were a man, I would whip him!"

Shuah, Avi, and Livia gasped. To break the tension, Bethuel sent Laban to make sure all the camels were corralled properly. Rolling his eyes in disbelief, Laban left. Rebekah hugged her father then hurried eagerly after Laban. Turning to Chesed, who had been standing silently just inside the entrance, Bethuel welcomed him into his home.

After the welcome, he asked, half apologizing, "Is there another child as bold as this one in all the land?"

"No," everyone said without hesitation.

"Hirsch thought to himself, "*Thank the gods for that.*"

Chesed remembered the silent chaperone, "*No wonder the servant said nothing.*"

Not only had Chesed brought five camels for Bethuel, but gits of cloth and jewelry for the women. The gifts were received with grateful enthusiasm. Following the presentation of gifts, Hirsch and Livia finished preparing the evening meal. A hearty lamb stew appeared as a feast to Chesed after his many days of travel. On passing a basket of flatbread to Chesed, Bethuel invited him to eat.

"Come Chesed; you must be famished from your long journey."

Hesitating, out of a need to first state his business, he began, "I will not eat until I have told my errand."

"Pray-tell."

"When I approached your settlement, I prayed to the God of Abraham, asking to be shown a sign so that I would know who the LORD had chosen to be the wife of my Master's son. I prayed that a girl would come to the well, and when I asked for a drink, she would offer me her ladle and water my camels. When I approached your well, it was your daughter who offered me water. Then, as I had prayed, she offered to water my camels. So it is, I believe Abraham's God has led me to you in search for a wife for Isaac."

Rebekah laughed aloud. "They call him, he laughs? Why do they call him, he laughs?"

Laban couldn't help himself. "Because he will laugh when he sees you."

Rebekah stuck her tongue out at Laban and sneered.

"Be still children," commanded Bethuel. "Go on Chesed."

"Abraham made me swear to find a wife for Isaac from among his father's house. He is very old and must know that his Isaac will have an acceptable wife to continue his family line."

Shuah agreed, "Yes, that is our custom."

Chesed added, "I'm forbidden to allow Isaac to find a wife from among the Canaanite tribes."

Shuah emphasized, "And so it should be."

"Bethuel, Shuah . . . your daughter was the answer to my prayer.'

"Oh my!" Rebekah said, blushing for once in her life at the honor.

Chesed continued, "My Master has become very rich and blessed with many sizable flocks, goods of all kinds, and many servants. He has everything, except a wife for his son from the line of Terah." Giving the family a moment to digest the information before continuing, "Now, I must ask, will you give Rebekah as a wife for Isaac?"

Quickly responding, Rebekah snapped, "I'm right here; you may ask me!"

Shuah stomped her foot on the ground and exclaimed, "Rebekah!"

Laban added, "You are too bold, my sister. You must learn to hold your tongue."

Snapping back, "You hold your tongue—"

"Rebekah! Sit!" came the stern command of Bethuel. "I know not what to do with you, child."

Sitting as her father had never before commanded, she anxiously awaited his answer.

Completely aware of his daughter's rebellious nature, he thought for a moment. Bethuel declared, "Rebekah is before you. Take her and let her be the wife of your Master's son Isaac, as your God has spoken."

Rebekah crossed her arms and uttered a sheepish, "Maybe."

❀ ❀ ❀

"Beth. Beth dear. The story is over for today. Beth," Rose said, shaking her pupil.

Beth opened her eyes. "Rose, you can't stop there. Did she go? Did they leave the next day? Did she meet Isaac? Did she like him? You must tell me."

Laughing at her enthusiasm, Rose held Beth's hand and said, "I will tell you this . . . the story does not end there."

"Promise you will tell it all?"

"I promise, dear. Look, it's almost dark?"

"Oh, I'm sorry. I was just thinking. Rebekah was not afraid to challenge authority, was she?"

"No dear, she wasn't."

Concealing her smile, Rose thought, "It won't take long for Beth to make the connection."

Helping Beth to stand, she said, "We'll pick up where we left off on Monday."

"O Rose, I can't wait to hear what happens next."

CHAPTER 6

B ETH was anxious all weekend long. Attempting to kill time, she went grocery shopping; read a romance novel; watched any old movie on television. The fact of the matter was, Beth couldn't get the story of Rebekah out of her mind. No matter what she did, visions of this vivacious young girl, taking a stand against custom and authority, kept running through her mind. Monday morning found Beth scurrying to work.

Thinking to herself, "If I work fast, the day will go by fast."

It didn't work. Filing documents, answering customer inquires did not move the laboriously slow second hand any faster. No matter where she was in the office, her eyes were constantly fixated on the clock. This unusual behavior did not go undetected by her workmates.

From the front of the office, George tried to get the attention of Joyce with, "Psst, psst, Joyce."

The strange-sounding "psst," from the usually boisterous George, roused Joyce's curiosity. It was humorous watching George trying to indiscreetly nod toward Beth, attempting to file a document with her eyes fixed on the clock. Oblivious to the prying eyes of her workmates, Beth's mind strayed back to the vision of Rebekah, sitting with her arms crossed. All of a sudden, she realized Joyce was smirking. At the same time, George, unable to resist any longer, cleared his throat and tried to ask subtly.

"Ahem, say Beth."

Returning to the reality of the office, she answered, "Yes?"

"What do you think of Rose's story so far?"

Joyce peeked over the divider to watch the reaction.

"It's good, and I like it. Why?"

Joyce and George laughed and spoke at the same time, "Because you keep checking the clock."

"Oh," came the sheepish reply.

"She's five days in Joyce." George ventured his guess.

"Don't worry, honey," Joyce added, "George and I were the same. We couldn't wait to hear it all."

"Really?"

"Yes, and the weekends are the hardest. Having to wait until Monday to hear the next part had us climbing the wall at times."

"Yep, and it gets worse," George added.

"What do you mean?" replied a puzzled Beth.

"The more you hear the story, the more you want to know the end," Joyce confirmed. "That's how we were."

"Are you serious?"

"Yes, and the last day," George paused to roll his eyes.

"What happens on the last day?"

"You'll see," was the unison reply.

The bantering was interrupted by the ringing of George's phone. Beth and Joyce returned to their work. Each day thus far, Beth had her desk clean and tidy at precisely five o'clock. Today, however, was different. There she was, desk clean, purse in hand, perched on the edge of her chair, at five minutes to five. After watching the second-hand tick three hundred times, it finally stuck at 5:00 p.m. as Beth bolted for the door. Unbeknownst to her, George and Joyce sat back and laughed at her rapid exit.

"And she's off," announced George as if announcing at the racetrack.

Arriving at Rose's at the same time as always, found Rose waiting with a delectable meal and a very fattening dessert. Beth was beginning to let go of all worries about weight and other obsessions of the past. All she wanted was to hear whatever piece of the tale Rose would weave each day.

A warm smile and friendly "Hello Beth" greeted Beth as she ascended the porch.

"And a warm hello to you, Rose Maddington."

"I made us some deli-style corned beef sandwiches and bread pudding."

Beth wasn't sure what bread pudding was, but she knew if Rose made it, it would be delicious.

While they ate their dinner, Rose told Beth about the church committee meeting held that morning. The chair of the committee called Rose earlier in the day to deliver the news.

Relating the wonderful news, Rose said, "Thank goodness they will begin their search for a new minister soon. I am thrilled they are not going to put it off."

Beth smiled, not understanding why Rose was so concerned about church business. Still, if it were significant to her, she would be supportive.

"Oh, this bread pudding, yum."

"You like it?"

"Yes, never had it before."

"Glad you approve."

"I knew it would be wonderful if you made it."

Rose smiled, stood, and began cleaning before getting to the story. Following the usual routine, Beth quickly closed her eyes and relaxed. Her body tension immediately began to dissipate as the warm summer air transported her back to a time four thousand years ago. Finding herself in Bethuel's home, looking at Rebekah sitting with her arms crossed, Beth could see plain as day, *the smirk*.

The smirk was followed by Rebekah's soft, "Maybe."

❈ ❈ ❈

While her response to the prospect of marrying Isaac still hung in the air, Bethuel snapped, "No maybe! I have spoken, and so it shall be," quieted Rebekah. Folding her arms and sitting back conveyed a sense of false objection to the decision made on her behalf. Rebekah was a woman who wanted to be in control of her fate and would have preferred to have some say in her future. Still, inside, the reality was, she was ready for a new adventure. Desiring to know more about Isaac and where he lived, Rebekah attempted to hide her pleasure. Unfortunately, she could not control her giggle.

Pushing on her shoulder, Laban smirked and said, "Good, now let someone else try and contend with you."

Rebekah smiled, and with her usual bold demeanor, challenged, "Good luck."

Bethuel clapped his hands once and affirmed, "The matter is settled! Now, let us eat."

His errand settled, Chesed could now relax and enjoy the warm hospitality.

The family enjoyed the sumptuous meal prepared by the servants. For the first time in his life, Chesed experienced Qatayef; nuts and cream wrapped in a sweet pancake.

Relaxing afterward, he announced, "Your hospitality is unequaled in all the land, but I need to rest, for our journey back to my Master begins in the morning."

Surprised by the announcement, Bethuel was quick to reply, "Why do you hurry away? Please, stay awhile, let Rebekah stay with us; ten more days."

"Yes, ten days," Shuah added, reaching over to place her hand on Rebekah's. "I fear I shall never see her again."

"That would not be a bad thing, mother," Laban said in his mischievous voice.

"Laban!" Rebekah retorted as he began to laugh.

Chesed, however, was serious, "I beg of you, do not delay my return as my master continues to grow old and longs to meet the wife God has chosen for his son."

Perplexed and hoping his daughter would not want to leave so soon, he begged, "Rebekah. Please dear, you decide."

As if the evening's events had transformed a child into a young woman, Rebekah knelt beside her father and took his hand.

With a voice that could not be denied, "O father, my heart beats so." Looking to Chesed. "I will leave with him in the morning."

Worried that Rebekah might be hesitant to leave her family, Chesed's sigh of relief was louder than it should have been.

Shuah's quivering lips could not hold back her urge to cry aloud, "Oh Rebekah, I will miss you, my child."

Hugging her mother, Rebekah knew she would miss her parents terribly. Still, her future lay elsewhere, and she was not afraid of adventure. Then something strange happened. It was Shuah, not Bethuel, who stood to offer the blessing.

Clasping her hands over her chest, Shuah prophesied, "May you become the mother to thousands of myriads, and may your offspring possess the gates of your enemies."

With tears running from her eyes, Rebekah hugged her mother once again and said, "I will miss you so very much."

Arising at first light, they found Chesed's servants waiting with camels prepared for departure. A camel, with a riding saddle atop brightly colored blankets, had been readied especially for Rebekah. Tent and additional supplies required for the journey through the wilderness were bound behind the saddle.

Taken by the lavish display, she thought, "My husband must be very wealthy." Her mother, tearfully adjusting Rebekah's shawl and touching her new gold bracelets, confessed, "Rebekah dear, I will think of you each day."

Hugging her mother for the last time, "And I will think of you mother, often."

With the two servants waiting, Chesed mounted the lead camel while holding the reigns of the camel awaiting Rebekah.

Much to everyone's surprise, Laban led Chana atop a camel also burdened with a sack of belongings.

Looking to his sister, "You will need someone to remind you of your place." Rebekah smiled and stuck out her tongue.

As so often happened in life, Shuah now issued a new warning, "Rebekah. You are a woman now. None of that!"

Running back to her mother and father for one last hug, she wiped her eyes and allowed Laban to assist in mounting her camel.

With a heartfelt smile, Laban looked at his younger sister and confessed. "I will miss tormenting you, my sister."

"Humph!" came the familiar reply.

After nodding to Chesed, she turned to her family and said, "Goodbye. I love you."

Chesed snapped the reigns, turned the camels toward the desert, and began the long journey home. A few hundred yards into the trip, Rebekah abruptly jumped off the camel and ran toward a nearby ridge. Malka, her childhood friend, and protector had been watching Rebekah ride away.

Horrified, Chesed jumped off his camel and shouted, "Rebekah, come back! Rebekah!" while pulling his 18" sword from the pack. As if finding a red-headed girl with green eyes, bold enough to speak as a man, was not enough, Chesed's wonderment was about to continue. Stopping in his tracks, unable to venture one step further, he watched in amazement as Rebekah knelt to stroke a tiger's head and neck. After giving her friend Malka a parting hug, Rebekah stood up, placed her hand on Malka's head one final time before hurrying back to her camel. All Chesed could do was assist Rebekah into the saddle in silent wonder and return to his camel to continue the journey in silence.

Passing every date palm, every boulder, every cool pond of her childhood, she tried to imagine the landscape of this strange new world to which she journeyed. The only people she knew were Chana, Chesed, and his servants, whom she'd only just met. Her mind raced, wondering if Isaac was strong and handsome? Trying to imagine her new home, would it be bright and cheery? Not knowing anything about the type of foods they ate or clothes women wore, the excitement of the unknown stimulated her imagination. After weeks of uneventful travel, Chesed stopped for the day in a lush green clearing. With the sun beginning its descent into the great sea, it was a suitable place to make camp for the night.

As had happened each evening, the servants watered and fed the camels, then helped Chesed set up makeshift tents for themselves and the women. Rebekah and Chana prepared the fire and the evening meal. With the full moon rising, everyone went to their tents except Chesed and Rebekah. Chesed added more wood to the fire and sat on a log beside Rebekah. Taking in the flickering flames and crackling firewood was relaxing. They sat for a long time without talking. Gazing up at the stars, which looked even more spectacular than back at her village, Rebekah was amazed at how many filled the dark sky.

Finally, in a soft voice, Chesed said, "Rebekah."

"Yes, Chesed?"

"Tomorrow, we shall arrive at my master's encampment."

"He does not live in a village?"

"No, Abraham prefers tents and the freedom to move."

Rebekah, momentarily silent, replied, "Really? My family has never moved, and this is the first time I've ever been away from my home."

"In some ways, you are lucky as it seems that we have traveled the whole world."

"Oh no! The world?" Rebekah gasped.

"Yes, it is true. We have been to many places; followed rivers, crossed mountains, traversed plains, you name it, we've seen it."

"My father said they once lived in tents outside the city of Ur. When scoundrels murdered his brother Haran, they moved far away."

"Yes. That is true. The journey was long and arduous. We traveled for over twelve full moons to a beautiful new land. After Terah died, Abraham's God called him to leave his family and venture into a new land. God promised to establish a new nation from his line; a nation that would eventually be more numerous than the stars in the sky."

"Why was Abraham called to leave his family?"

"Abraham was smart enough to know clay idols are not gods, but just man-made images."

"I feel the same way Chesed. All my life, I have felt an indescribable presence, a feeling in my heart."

"Yes. When I arrived at your well and prayed, I felt that presence."

They sat quietly for a moment before Rebekah asked, "Did Abraham build a city in which to live?"

"O no! Ever since the murder of Haran, Abraham has been suspicious of those who live in clay brick cities. Especially cities such as Damascus. He prefers the openness of the land."

"Yes, it is peaceful here."

"Abraham told me something else. He thinks that when the number of his people grow, the day will come when they too will go back to living in clay brick cities."

Meditating on Chesed's words, "I think he is right."

"I hope it does not happen in my lifetime," Chesed said as he stood, stretched, and continued, "I like the open land, but now, it's time to sleep. We'll continue our journey early, as I hope to arrive at my master's camp tomorrow evening. Goodnight, Rebekah."

"Goodnight, Chesed."

Thinking about all that Chesed had told her, wondering about her family, Rebekah's mind kept spinning. Would she like her new home? Would she even want to live in a tent? Sleeping in a tent while on a trip was one thing, but living in a tent, how would that be? Then, the horror of horrors crossed her mind; what if she did not like her new home, her husband? Would she run back home to mommy? With all the *what-ifs* running through her head, Rebekah found it difficult to fall asleep.

Her curiosity, aroused by the rustling wind, compelled her to step out and call, "Chesed, is that you?"

Suddenly, a bright flame flared up in the fire pit. Growing brighter, it illuminated the silhouette of a man in a white hooded robe sitting cross-legged on the log by the fire. Not certain her eyes were focusing correctly, she was startled when a soft voice called her name.

"Rebekah, . . . come, sit with me."

Unable to comprehend why she did not feel fear, she asked, "Who are you? How do you know my name?"

"I am Elyon, God most high. Abraham's God."

Rebekah fell to her knees, placed her face down on the ground, and said, "My Lord."

While Rebekah knelt, the LORD continued, "I have known you from before the lightning flashed on the night of thy birth. I knew you when you were weaved together in your mother's womb."

Rising to her feet, Rebekah began to speak as if to an old friend, "My mother told me of that mystic night and how the lightning flashed at the very moment of my birth."

"Yes," replied Elyon, "I know . . . I have watched over you from that very moment. I laughed when you opened your eyes to find my friend Malka licking your face."

Rebekah felt her heart sadden as she whispered, "I miss Malka."

Elyon rose and extended an invitation to "Walk with me."

At the water's edge, Elyon said, "Rebekah, look out over the water . . . it was on a night such as this that I stood with Abraham overlooking Lake Assad."

Looking at the silvery moonlight reflecting on the water, "Father told me of that lake and how Terah stood upon the boulder to declare his new home."

"I promised Abraham that his offspring would be as numerous as the stars in the sky. Now, the time has come for you to know that you have been chosen to play a most important role in my promise to him."

"Me? How? I am pledged to marry."

"Yes," Elyon confirmed, "That is exactly how you will play your part. Sadly, Isaac no longer listens. He strays. He takes Hittite women, Canaanite women, into his tent."

"If this is so, am I still to marry him?"

"Yes, my child. I require someone strong enough to carry out my will."

"But Lord, why me? My family does not know you."

"Rebekah, you know me, you have always known me, just as Abraham had always known me before I spoke to him at Lake Assad. Allowing time for Rebekah to reflect, Elyon continued, "Abraham's seed must pass through Isaac, to you Rebekah, to the child I have chosen. Your child."

"Seed? My child?"

"I have chosen you to raise the child in wisdom, strength of heart, and soul."

Sitting upon a rock, hand on forehead, "It is much to comprehend."

"Your father raised you to be strong-willed for a purpose. That is why Shiphrah took you under her wing, became your mentor. It was all to prepare you for this time of life when you will need wisdom and discernment.

"I know not what to say, Lord."

Speaking compassionately, "Not Lord Rebekah, I am the LORD."

Sitting beside Rebekah, the LORD took her hand and said, "Abraham was chosen to be the father of many nations," turning Rebekah's chin to look into her eyes, "so it is, I have chosen you to be the mother."

For the first time in her life, Rebekah felt humbled.

Closing her eyes, she accepted, "Yes LORD, according to thy will."

Visions of Shiphrah returned as she heard the LORD's words, "You must be strong. Do not let Isaac dominate." She smiled as the LORD continued, "Isaac will not be accustomed to women speaking for themselves, so you must conduct yourself wisely."

"Yes LORD," was the response as she thought of Laban always wanting her to be obedient, like the rest of the women."

Then the LORD's promise, "I will be with you always. Pray, and I will answer," brought reassurance to her heart.

When Rebekah opened her eyes, Elyon had vanished.

"Beth. Beth, honey," Rose said, shaking Beth's arm.

Startled, Beth awoke with a string of questions fast on her lips, "Oh, my goodness! Elyon, was Elyon real? And Malka, was Malka real? Was I dreaming?" After a moment to compose herself, "Rose, was I there? Was I actually there?"

"Dear, you will know in your heart when you hear the story in its entirety."

"Rose, it's hard. I want so badly to hear the rest. Does she like Isaac? Does she—"

"Tomorrow dear, tomorrow," Rose said as she patted her hand.

Beth knew what this meant. Tired, curious, excited, mind racing, it was time for her to go. She would just have to wait another day. The problem was, waiting was not one of Beth's attributes.

CHAPTER 7

THERE was no way around it; she needed to learn to be patient. Beth had never realized this was a problem for her until now. Having to wait twenty-four hours to hear the next episode was trying her patience. Not only that, but the thought of another weekend passing before Rose would continue the story did not help. Yes, patience was something she needed to learn. For the first time in her life, Beth sat back in her office chair and began to reflect on her life.

The more Beth thought about her lack of patience, the more she realized it was bigger than waiting for a story. There were other situations in her life where she had reacted impulsively, unable to wait any longer. In her last job, her boss pleaded with her not to submit her proposed company policy change until he had a chance to review the change. Suspecting he wanted some of the credit for the change, she defied him and acted anyway. Labeled insubordinate, she received her notice to leave by the end of the week. Thankfully, the Regional Manager intervened and had her transferred. Then there was the time she left a long-time relationship with the only real friend and love she'd ever known. Too impatient to wait for him to decide about marriage, Beth had given him an ultimatum. Unable to express his feelings for her and unwilling to commit, she broke the engagement.

But perhaps the one thing she questioned the most was her impatience with faith. Having gave up on church many years ago because she didn't have the patience to try and learn more. Attempts to understand her faith, her friends, her life ended in darkness. Remembering how she didn't have the patience to sit in church, the thought of Rose always happy to attend Sunday service played on her mind. Rose had a strong faith. Beth had none.

Thinking, "Maybe if I got to know Rose better, I could figure this faith thing out."

"Beth," Joyce said, interrupting her daydream.

"Oh, sorry."

"Looked like you were, well . . . someplace else."

"No, no, just thinking."

"Okay, well, the Smith file I asked you about, do you have it? I can't find it."

"Yes, I'm sorry, here you are."

George yelled, "Yes!" as he threw his hand up in the air.

"What?" Beth asked.

"It's five o'clock!"

Lost in introspection, Beth gathered her thoughts, cleared her desk, and bolted for the door. Her quick pace up Reckoner Street did not stop the realization that Rose was right; Beth needed to hear this specific story. Happy to see Rose's smiling face, the customary culinary cuisine, and delicious dessert awaiting her arrival, Beth couldn't hold back a hearty greeting.

Flopping happily into the white wicker chair, her enthusiasm was evident. "Hello Rose, I can't wait to hear what happens next."

"You will like it, I think," as she winked her magical wink. With the twinkle of an eye, Rose said, "Now, here you go. I made us egg salad sandwiches and buttermilk pie."

"Oh my! It looks wonderful!" came the delighted response.

Rose talked a bit about her church. She told Beth the committee had placed vacancy notices in all the usual places and was surprised at how quickly the new pastor applications were submitted.

Knowing how important this was for Rose, she said, "I hope it doesn't take too long."

"Tell me, dear, do you have a church?" came the unexpected question.

"No, not here. I had a church when I was growing up, but—"

"I see. Maybe you can come with me sometime."

Beth just smiled and nodded, not objecting to the invitation or to accepting it.

With her mouth filled, she mumbled, "Maybe."

After eating their pie and cleaning up the dishes, Rose and Beth took their seats once again under the whirring of the old ceiling fan on the porch.

"Shall we begin?" Rose asked.

Beth followed the instructions and was immediately transported back to the countryside with Chesed and Rebekah.

❊ ❊ ❊

Chesed led the small caravan through a lush green valley toward Abraham's encampment.

While taking in the new terrain, Chesed said, "Rebekah."

"Yes, Chesed."

"Tell me. Did you hear voices in the night?"

Rebekah bounced gently with the movement of the camel while thinking about his question before answering with, "I heard the wind."

Chesed nodded and smiled. "Yes. It must have been the wind."

Rebekah's mind thought about the night visitor. Feeling the warm valley breeze in her face, she had begun to question their encounter. Had she indeed been paid a visit by Elyon? The experience certainly seemed real enough. Perhaps it was just a vision? A dream maybe? She could not say. All she knew was, the feeling still rested warmly in her heart, and her mind was at peace.

Before leaving home, Shuah bestowed an ancient blessing upon Rebekah to bear many children. For some reason, Shuah could only birth two children for her husband and wanted Rebekah to have many. Shuah's blessing was also for a peaceful life as Rebekah's inability to succumb to blind authority had always brought about contention, especially with men.

Elyon's visit had filled in a blank space. Now with a purpose, something she had begun to feel was missing in life, Rebekah, she felt closer to Abraham's God. The task of raising children, especially a chosen child, in wisdom, heart, and soul, was a worthy challenge but still much to ask. She realized the nurturing of her family and the guidance of Shiphrah had prepared her spirit for the task ahead. The biggest challenge, however, was never to let Isaac dominate while, at the same time, remaining obedient. For many women, this is an impossibility. Resolving herself to this monumental task, she gave her life to Abraham's God and prepared her heart for marriage to an unknown man. Sadly, Rebekah had to prepare her heart to remain barren until the time was right to birth this special child. It was not easy to accept, but it was the way it had to be.

Rebekah was deep in thought when Chesed stopped his camel on the crest of a hill. Moving her camel beside his, she observed a look of calm envelope Chesed's face as he scanned the valley filled with flocks of sheep. It was a beautiful view.

"Rebekah," he said.

"Yes, Chesed?"

"Prepare yourself."

Rebekah inhaled the fresh country air, looked out over the valley, and said, "Why?"

"You are looking over the land of Abraham, your new home."

"Finally. We are here?" Rebekah exclaimed.

Chesed was happy to lead the caravan down the hillside. As he did, Rebekah noticed a man amid the flock examining a lamb. The man stopped what he was doing, looked up, and waved.

"Chesed, who is that man?"

"He is my master's son."

"Isaac," she exclaimed.

Rebekah leaped off the camel, stumbled, and almost fell as she hastened to find her veil and shawl to cover her head and face. It was forbidden for women to reveal their faces to a betrothed until formally introduced by a parent. Abraham, having requested a bride from his brother's family, it was his place to introduce Isaac to his bride.

Chesed assisted Rebekah in mounting her camel as Isaac approached the caravan. Excited to see Chesed, the welcome was warm and enthusiastic. Walking alongside Chesed's camel, he kept looking back at his bride-to-be. After relating how he had prayed to the God of Abraham and how this young woman was the answer to his prayer, Chesed stopped his camel, dismounted, and asked immediately.

"How is your father?"

"He grows weaker, I'm afraid. His servant girls stay with him, trying to ease his pain and keep him warm."

Rebekah listened without speaking; her eyes fixed on Isaac. He was tall, with broad shoulders and handsome.

"He looks strong, not a stranger to working," she thought. Anxious to learn more of her future husband, she thought, "Be patient Rebekah, all in due time."

Without speaking, Isaac accompanied Chesed to Abraham's tent. He remained outside, trying to imagine the beauty of this redheaded girl he was about to marry.

Before stepping into the tent, Chesed distracted Isaac's attention with, "I must tell your father my task is complete."

On entering the tent, Chesed found Abraham sleeping between the two slave women, Bayla and Rina. The women looked at Chesed and smiled.

"Welcome back, Chesed, "Rina whispered.

"Thank you. Now, wake my master."

The women nudged Abraham gently.

Startled, he asked, "What? What is wrong?"

Bayla responded, "Nothing, master."

Looking to the tent opening, and saw Chesed and exclaimed, "Chesed, is that you?"

"Yes, my master. I have someone for you to meet."

Bayla and Rina assisted Abraham to a sitting position. Rina covered Abraham's shoulders with his robe while Bayla arranged the cushions. Ready for the introduction, Chesed motioned for the slave girls to leave.

Outside the tent, Rebekah watched Rina and Bayla exit. The women nodded politely to her as they passed.

Moments later, Chesed, after pulling the tent curtain aside, extended an invitation.

"Come, Rebekah. Meet my master, Abraham."

Rebekah checked her veil and shawl to be sure they were correct before entering.

With Chesed holding the tent curtain open, Rebekah, completely uninhibited, marched straight in and stopped. Abraham could not stop gazing at Rebekah. Even with the veil on her face, he knew right away that her beauty was unmatched in the land. Propped up on pillows, Abraham inspected his daughter-in-law to be, from head to toe. Positioning herself before Abraham, her feet slightly apart, hands posted on her hips, she looked boldly down on Abraham in an attempt to determine if he would approve.

Chesed, standing at her side, noticed the look of shock and disbelief on Abraham's face and became frightened that Abraham would disapprove of his choice.

He intervened immediately, "Master, your daughter-in-law to be, Rebekah; daughter of Bethuel, the granddaughter of Nahor and Milcah."

In a slightly gruff tone, Abraham said, "Come here child; let me look upon you."

The boldness of Rebekah's face softened as she remembered God's words. Knelling beside Abraham, she removed her veil and shawl.

"Red hair! You have red hair!" exclaimed Abraham. Shocked, he uttered, "You are more beautiful than I could have ever imagined."

Amazed by her beauty and never having seen a uniquely beautiful woman, he took her hand and kissed it.

He looked into her eyes and said, "Your eyes! They are green! Chesed, she has green eyes!"

"Yes, master. She has beautiful green eyes."

Stroking Rebekah's face with the back of his hand, he observed, "Shuah, you have Shuah's features. Your cheeks, your face."

"Yes, my father says it is so. I have my mother's features."

Abraham smiled. "God has surely chosen you to fulfill the promise."

"And I have chosen to accept, father Abraham."

Horrified by her boldness, the independence displayed by this beautiful fifteen-year-old girl, Abraham's shock turned into curiosity.

Reasoning within himself about the possibility of his God speaking with a woman, he inquired, "You have spoken with Elyon? You talked with my LORD, the creator of the heaven and earth?"

Without hesitating, Rebekah replied a bold, "Yes."

"Uh-huh. God does work in mysterious ways. Leave us Chesed."

Chesed nodded and departed the tent.

"Make yourself comfortable child. Let us talk."

Rebekah sat beside Abraham, who remained propped up as much as possible.

He began, "Tell me, Rebekah, how is my brother, Nahor? Does he still live?"

"Nahor sleeps with his ancestors."

"Bethuel and Shuah, are they well?"

"Yes, they are well; they prosper, but now they live in mudhif huts and not tents."

Abraham took a deep breath, lowered his head, and shook it from side to side in disbelief. "How soon they forget."

Abraham and Rebekah sat silently for a time before he asked, "The LORD; how did he come to you?"

"In the night."

Abraham nodded, "Yes, go on."

"It was in near a lake. For some reason, I could not sleep."

"Yes, I also."

"I sat up at the sound of rustling wind calling my name."

"It was the same for me. A rustling of the wind."

Rebekah's eyes lit up. It was good to know Elyon had appeared in the same way to Abraham.

"Stepping outside my tent, I observed a man in a long white robe. I was startled but not afraid."

"With a hood?"

"Yes."

"Did the hood cover his face?"

"Except the eyes, there was something about the eyes."

"Ah, yes, I remember the eyes. They looked right through me."

Rebekah nodded in agreement. "I asked, 'Who are you?'"

"And?" inquired Abraham suspiciously.

"I am the LORD thy God," was my answer.

"I mean, were you given a name?"

Abraham was shocked once again by this bold young woman.

Rebekah continued, "No name, just, Hay—"

Panicking, Abraham put his finger to her mouth, saying, "Quiet child, quiet. Melchizedek said we are not even to say that name aloud."

Rebekah boldly whispered in a guttural voice, "Hayah, Hayah."

Abraham wiped a tear from his eye and tried to contain his displeasure at Rebekah's detailed knowledge of his God. Still, he was confident she was the one.

He asked, "Did our God tell you anything?"

"Yes."

"What, pray-tell."

"The LORD told me you would be the father of many nations,"

Abraham nodded.

"and I am to be the mother."

Looking puzzled and upset, he asked, "But why? Why have you been chosen?"

Rebekah was unsure how to respond to this question. She had only been introduced to Abraham and did not yet know Isaac.

Contemplating how best to tell her father-in-law to be, she answered straight on, "Isaac will stop listening."

Abraham could not help but feel sadness, but he knew it to be true.

"Yes, I'm afraid he has not inherited my faith," Abraham admitted sadly.

Rebekah looked Abraham directly in the eye and said, "And like Sarah, I am to be barren for many years."

Abraham lowered his head, remembering the years of pain Sarah had to endure.

Looking up at Rebekah, "Oh Rebekah, I am sad for you. Sarah, my poor Sarah, heartsick for all those years."

"I know not for how long, but I do know my child will be the Chosen One."

Abraham clasped his hands together and said, "Praise the LORD our God."

"Elyon said I am to raise the child in wisdom; strength of heart, mind, and soul."

"Elyon used those exact words?"

"Yes. *Chokmah, labab, nephesh, meh-ode.* Wisdom, heart, soul, strength."

Abraham leaned back and rested on his pillows. He reflected on the words Rebekah had spoken.

Sitting up and taking a deep breath, he proclaimed, "You shall be wed on the first night of the spring full moon."

Rose's touch woke Beth more quickly than usual.

"Oh, Rose. I'm exhausted," exclaimed Beth, "My goodness, poor Rebekah. What a long trip, and then her destiny immediately outlined before her."

"Yes dear, it was."

" Isaac, she'd only just met him. I do hope you will tell me more."

"Of course, dear. Tomorrow, you will see."

"Rose, I think you enjoy keeping me in suspense."

"Patience dear, patience," Rose replied with a slight snicker.

There it was. The light went on. The thing Beth had trouble with the most. Patience.

CHAPTER 8

B ETH's mind traveled down an unusual path for so early in the morning. For some reason, the aroma of coffee returned her mind to the night before. Unable to imagine someone else choosing your husband, the thought of a stranger from a foreign land bartering with parents for the hand of their daughter in marriage to a total stranger was utterly incomprehensible to Beth.

She thought, "How would I feel about not having the ability to make that decision?" Beth asked herself. "How would I feel about being taken to a foreign land with strange customs? How would I feel about marrying a total stranger?"

The answer was simple. "Nope, never going to happen."

Then Beth remembered how Rebekah pretended to object to her father's decision, how the smirk on her face caused Laban to push her shoulder.

"Well, I'll be darned," Beth said, "Rebekah was looking forward to the adventure after all."

Sitting back in her chair, sipping her coffee, Beth realized that she had the same attitude toward life as Rebekah. Beth had never been afraid of change or seeking new adventures.

Looking out her window, north to her mother's house, Beth said aloud, "Okay, mom, you were right, and I'm still seeking."

It was at that moment the realization of why Rose picked this story dawned on her. Beth was more like Rebekah than she first thought. They had similar traits but not the same faith.

"Oh no!" she said after she checked the clock. "I'd better hurry, or I'll be late."

Racing down Reckoner Street to the office, a glance on passing the white picket fence saw Rose busy watering plants at the side of the house.

Entering the office at nine o'clock on the nose, saw. Joyce and George prepared for the day's work.

"There she is," George said as Beth slipped into her chair.

After tucking her purse into the drawer, she returned a hearty, "Good morning."

Joyce replied, "Yes, it is. Another hot one though. My yard is turning brown."

George interjected, "But there is hope."

"Oh?" Beth asked. "Hope for what?"

"Possible chance of thunderstorms this evening."

Joyce agreed, "We do need rain."

Getting right to work, Beth looked at the stack of files on her desk that needed to be processed. She was falling behind, but she hoped a busy day would make five o'clock arrive even faster with so much to do. The wish came true; her workday was over in no time.

The late afternoon sky turned rapidly from light gray to black. She hoped Rose would invite her inside to continue the story. Anxious to hear what happened to Rebekah, Beth ran through the gate and up the steps to find no Rose and no food. The wicker furniture had been pulled up to the wall and covered with a heavy plastic tarp. The thought of not enjoying Rose's company drove Beth's finger to the doorbell. At that very moment, the squeaky screen door opened. Rose was all dressed in another colorful, floral dress, silver bracelets, and a jeweled necklace.

"Come in before the rain starts. I was afraid you might get caught in the storm. The radio report was for high winds."

"Thanks," Beth said as she entered the house. "Nothing so far except wind."

"Yes, it looks like it is going to be a gloomy evening outside. So, I made some soup and a half-sandwich on homemade sourdough bread."

"That sounds heavenly."

"And for dessert, a peach cobbler that I've just taken from the oven. Come on into the kitchen."

Although Rose's house had a large formal dining room, she preferred to eat in the breakfast room off the kitchen.

Rose confessed, "I enjoy looking out of the bay window instead of old furniture and ancient chandelier in the dining room."

The kitchen table was adorned with an arrangement of fresh flowers from Rose's garden.

The sight of hot chicken vegetable soup and dainty sandwiches prompted Beth to compliment, "Another delicious meal, Rose. I can't tell you how much I appreciate all you do."

"Happy to do it," followed by her sparkly wink.

The dishes cleared away, Rose said, "Shall we begin?"

"Of course."

"Now, since the storm is blowing up, I am going to light a couple of these candles just in case we lose power. Once you begin listening to the story, I don't want you to be interrupted. This way, we can just keep right on going."

"Okay, sounds good."

Beth wasn't confident she could concentrate in a bad storm.

"Now dear, close your eyes." Rose began, "You are going back to Abraham's tent, just as Rebekah is leaving."

Beth closed her eyes and relaxed her muscles. With the tension dissipating, her mind traveled back to Abraham's encampment.

❈ ❈ ❈

Escorting Rebekah to her tent Chesed knew she would have much to do before the wedding. He volunteered his services as the spring full moon was only a few days away. Chesed would introduce the servants in the morning and show Rebekah the tent she and Chana would live in until the wedding night.

"Will I be able to spend time with Isaac?" she asked.

"During the day only, and chaperoned, of course."

"Chesed, how can I learn more about Abraham's God?"

"I was a young man when I came into the service of Abraham and have been with him from the day he left his family in Lake Assad until now. I will teach you as much as I know about the God of the earth and the skies."

"Thank you Chesed," she said in appreciation.

Rebekah's tent contained many fine blankets and pillows, a table, and a few items for the wedding preparation. It did not look like a temporary tent except for the smaller size. The interior décor was colorful. Beautiful wool blankets, linen sheets, multi-colored pillows created a longing of the heart for the women's tent back home, especially for her mother and Shiphrah. Remembering her belongings, still packed in the bags and with the camels, she called.

"Chana."

"Yes?"

"Please find my bags. I need some things."

Chana quickly departed and went to the spot where the bags were being offloaded. Inquiring as to the whereabouts of Rebekah's belongings, a servant helped her pick out the bag and carry them back to the tent.

"Ah! Thank you. Help me, Chana. I must sort out my clothes. Shiphrah made me special gowns, shawls, and, most importantly, my wedding dress. We must find it and hang it up." After much digging through the bags, Chana found the items Rebekah needed.

Holding her wedding dress high, she said, "Look! How beautiful! Shiphrah made this for me when I was a little girl. She told me then I would marry someone special and said my family would grow to be very large."

Then Rebekah remembered what Shiphrah said the day she was born. Her mother had told her the exact words.

Whispering, she repeated, *"And no man will ever have dominion over her."*

"What? Did you say something?" Chana asked.

"Oh, nothing."

Rebekah continued unpacking and organizing the items she brought from home. Looking at the various items caused some sadness. Still, she remembered this was an adventure, and her wedding was only a few days away.

The nights spent in the temporary tent were long. Looking at the glow of the approaching full moon through the opening in her tent, she wondered what her new life would be like and how Isaac would be as a husband. Dreaming about the wedding ceremony, she tried to imagine how she would look in her delicate wedding robe and veil. Chesed was true to his promise as Rebekah spent a pleasant afternoon with Isaac, chaperoned by Chesed and two other women.

The days before the wedding were spent preparing her clothing and learning more about Abraham's faith. The one thing she lacked for her wedding day was the wonderful aroma of Shiphrah's perfumes. But she knew how to prepare them.

"Chana, take one of the servants and bring me a basket of wild jasmine blossoms, a little of the finest olive oil, as well as a clay jar, mortar and pestle. I have the other powders in my bag."

Scurrying away on her mission, Chana spent the afternoon correcting the ingredients. Chana returned early that evening, accompanied by two women from the settlement.

Eliana and Sadie had helped collect the supplies and had hoped Rebekah would teach them how to make the much sought-after Jasmine perfume.

Rebekah was gracious but replied, "Yes, but not tomorrow. This one will be special, and I must work quickly."

Sadie and Eliana smiled, nodded, and left the tent.

Rebekah had only two days until the spring full moon. Time passed quickly, and she learned about this new thing Abraham called prayer. Rebekah prayed about her marriage to Isaac and honoring his authority without being dominated. When the night came, she had prepared, mind and body, to spend her life with Isaac, a faithful wife.

With the spring full moon rising in the sky, a silvery blanket of stars lit the heavens the night of her wedding. It was the most beautiful Rebekah had ever seen. The air was warm, the breeze soft, which helped make the night so very special.

Looking to heaven, Rebekah smiled and whispered a heartfelt *"Thank you."*

Returning to her tent, she found Chana waiting to help finish dressing the bride. When the moment arrived, Rebekah held up her arms. Chana slid the pure white dress over Rebekah's head and adjusted it to perfection. The scent of jasmine filled the air, reminding the two women of Shiphrah, Shuah, and the days spent in the red tent. Both women silently wished Shiphrah and Shuah could have attended the wedding. Chana draped the intricately woven linen shawl over her shoulders and positioned the veil so that it only needed to be pulled over Rebekah's face before exiting the tent. Unlike other brides, Rebekah did not wear any jewelry nor beads in her hair. The simplicity made her a picture of perfection; lightly tanned skin; pure white dress; vibrant red hair to the shoulders; green eyes; and missing one final touch. Chana placed a beautiful white jasmine flower in Rebekah's hair and stood back to admire.

The few moments spent waiting for Chesed seemed like an eternity.

Finally, his voice called once, "Rebekah, it is time."

Although Sarah was no longer among the living but resting with her ancestors, the settlement revered Rebekah's place as Isaac's prime wife. Having come to know her, they were happy she would be the new female voice in the village. Everyone in the encampment was delighted about her marriage to Isaac and stood, anxiously awaiting the ceremony to begin.

Chana adjusted the bride's veil, extinguished the oil lamps, pulled the tent curtain back, and stepped out, holding the curtain fully open. From inside the darkened entrance, Rebekah could see Chesed waiting with his arm extended. Dressed in royal splendor, Rebekah wondered for a moment if he was the groom. On stepping into the light, the encampment gasped as they beheld such beauty. On taking Chesed's arm, Rebekah beheld a most beautiful sight. On the outside of every tent in the settlement, oil lamps burned brightly. Flickering flames in the night gave the evening a special glow.

Much to Rebekah's delight, her first step was met with the beat of a *toph* (drum), followed by the pleasant strumming of the *sabbeka* (lute), and finally, the *halil* (flute). All sounds she had not heard in a very long time. At the sound of the *toph*, wedding guests separated, creating a corridor from the tent to the central fire, where Abraham stood, supported by Bayla and Rina. Isaac, wearing a similar long white linen robe, stood awaiting the arrival of his bride. All along the corridor, voices commented on the beauty of Isaac's bride.

"The God of Abraham has blessed Isaac," one man shouted.

"Her hair, have you ever seen such beautiful hair," complimented an older woman.

Stopping just to the left of Isaac, Chesed lifted Rebekah's veil and revealed her radiant beauty to an astounded Isaac. A single white flower adorned her red hair, which fell softly on her shoulders draped with Shiphrah's shawl. Chesed took Rebekah's right hand and placed it in Isaac's left hand. Rebekah looked into Isaac's eyes and smiled. Chesed stepped back, the music stopped, Chesed bowed, then joined the other wedding guests.

Abraham stepped slowly away from Bayla and Rina.

Raising his arms, Abraham began, "My son; my daughter; you stand before the LORD our God as *Ish* and *Ish-shaw*, to become one," and clapped his hands once.

Quiet enveloped the village as Abraham raised his head to the sky and prayed a blessing upon his son's marriage. The wedding homily was not long, but it was profound. Abraham remembered his Sarah to the happy couple, praying that their love would endure forever, as had his love for Sarah. Concluding the homily, Abraham held out his arm, nodded for the *halil* to offer its sweet soft melody. Bayla draped the white scarf of unity over Abraham's outstretched arm.

Much to his delight, Abraham said, "My son, extend your left arm, palm up."

Isaac raised his left arm, and Abraham continued, "My daughter, place your right hand in Isaac's, palm up." Determined not to let any man have dominion over her, Rebekah quickly placed her right hand, palm up, under Isaac's left hand. At the same time, she slapped her left hand, palm down, onto Isaac's hand.

Never having witnessed such boldness by a new bride, the wedding guests gasped.

Abraham, frustrated by the show of disrespect, frowned at Rebekah for a moment. Much to everyone's horror and then surprise, Abraham's facial expression turned from horror to acquiescence. Smiling, he continued with the ceremony.

With the full authority of a tribal chief, he looked directly into Isaac's eyes and commanded, "Isaac, place your right hand on top of Rebekah's," then slowly, "palm down."

Abraham wrapped the wedding scarf around the bride and groom's hands, signifying the marriage was official. Stepping back, proclaiming in a loud voice, "By the taking of hands, two have become one and promise to support each other, in the bond of marriage. May the Lord God bless you with many sons."

The crowd laughed and cheered at the announcement that Rebekah and Isaac were at last husband and wife.

Abraham stepped back and gestured Isaac toward the marriage tent, saying, "My son, your mother's tent awaits." Placing his hand gently on Rebekah's forehead, Abraham looked deep into her eyes. He spoke softly, saying, "Rebekah, may Sarah's great spirit rest upon you always."

Abraham stepped aside. Rebekah placed her hand on Isaac's arm. The horror of the hand incident forgotten in anticipation of his wedding night; Isaac escorted his bride to his mother's tent. Realizing the tent curtain remained tied, Rina hurried to untie and hold back the curtain. The crowd watched in silence as Isaac and Rebekah entered the tent.

Raising both arms toward the tent, Abraham exclaimed, "*Ish; Ish-shaw; Eloheem bawrak*. May God bless this man and woman!"

Once Isaac and Rebekah entered the tent, Rina dropped the tent curtain and tied it. Abraham looked up to the stars and smiled. The wedding guest let up a great cheer as the music began. While a food-laden table was uncovered, servant girls took up large carafes of wine to start serving the honored guests.

As the flickering light of oil lamps were snuffed out, Isaac and Rebekah began their life together as one, *Ish* and *Ish-shaw*.

❉ ❉ ❉

"Beth, wake up, Beth dear," Rose said, touching Beth's arm gently.

Returning to the present and flickering candlelight, Beth uttered, "Oil lamps, full moon, stars, music, merriment . . . O Rose, the wedding was so beautiful, I cried."

Rose laughed. "I thought it might catch you off guard."

"How long ago did your power go out?"

"After the first bolt of lightning, I suppose."

"What bolt?" I heard nothing, except Abraham performing the marriage ceremony."

Rose smiled and said, "But the good news is, the rain has stopped, and the power should be on soon. Now here, I want you to take this flashlight for your walk home. Your power will be off as well."

"The marriage, I need to know how the marriage went. Was it a happy marriage?"

"Now dear, that; is a very long story. We will start it tomorrow."

Reluctantly, Beth stood up and prepared for her walk home. Gratefully taking the flashlight, Beth began the short walk to her dark apartment.

Lighting her way down the steps, Beth said, "Thank you for everything Rose. I will see you tomorrow."

"Yes, dear. Now, be careful walking home."

CHAPTER 9

B ETH woke early that morning, thinking about Rebekah marrying at such a young age. So young, so inexperienced, married when she was only fifteen years old. It made Beth think about her situation. She liked being single. Remembering when she was fifteen, her only cares in the world were learning how to drive a car and hanging out with friends. People were different then, but as Rose said, we are also the same in many ways. Rebekah liked adventure and independence, and so did Beth. Rebekah was impatient at times, and Beth knew she was all the time.

Beth left for work so deep in thought that she completely forgot breakfast. Walking past the old Victorian house, she found Rose working in the front yard picking up branches broken during the storm. Seeing Rose caused a sudden realization: it was Thursday. Calculating that the story would continue at least through next week, the thought of spending another weekend wondering saddened Beth. Rose had said even though Rebekah was married; there was still much more to the story. Now, after befriending Rose, weekends alone had lost their appeal.

Beth knew Rose had a busy life with her church, especially on weekends. If the church ladies weren't cooking for an event, they were planning for the next one. Beth resolved that church was a good place for older women who had nothing but to attend services and plan social events.

Beth laughed while thinking, "I don't have anything to do on the weekends either. Maybe I should consider church? Well, just maybe."

Stepping through the office door, she noticed Joyce flitting around the coffee pot but could not see what she was doing.

Then came the announcement, "George's wife, made coffee cake for us Beth, yum! Come get a slice."

Immediately leaving her desk, Beth confessed, "Great! I didn't have time for breakfast this morning."

"Some night last night with that storm, huh?" George noted.

"It was," Beth agreed.

Joyce took a second slice of coffee cake back to her desk, then asked, "How's Rose?"

"She's doing great. Oh, my goodness, yesterday she made a peach cobbler!"

"She is one of the best cooks in Sageville," George said, "Don't tell my wife, but Rose's desserts are the best I've ever had."

"Your secret is safe with us," Joyce laughed.

The phone rang, and they all snapped into their work mode. Thankfully, the day was hectic and, therefore, over quickly.

The flowers around Rose's front porch were vibrant after the night rain. The storm had brought cooler temperatures, so storytime on the porch would be delightful.

The sound of Rose's warm "Hello Beth" had become routine. As was answering with an equally friendly reply, "Hello Rose," to which Beth added, "that storm certainly helped cool things down."

"Yes, it did. Come, have a seat and a hot bite to eat."

As always, Rose had prepared a nice lite meal. Today's menu included a helping of homemade creamy chicken casserole and a side salad with a peach cobbler for dessert.

"Rose, I don't know how you do it. Maybe someday you can show me some of your recipes and teach me how to cook them."

Rose smiled at the compliment and gave Beth the wink.

Finishing her last bite of cobbler, Rose said, "Shall we begin?"

"Yes! I'm anxious to hear about Rebekah's married life."

"Close your eyes then. You know what to do."

Focusing her mind on Abraham's encampment, Beth was transported back into the red tent.

❊ ❊ ❊

Two weeks after the marriage, it was Rebekah's time to go to the women's tent to wait out her cycle. On entering the red tent for the first time, Rebekah was appalled at the gloom and knew that Shiphrah would not have taken one step further. A dreary atmosphere, worn carpet, old blankets, grungy pillows caused Rebekah to interrupt Sadie's welcome.

She exclaimed, "I'm not putting my head on those filthy things." Looking around disappointed, she said, "Shiphrah would be shocked to see such a tent., and my mother would say, 'There is nothing to celebrate here." Exiting the tent, she yelled, "Chesed!" He was sent to her tent to have Chana bring blankets, sheets, and a big pillow. Stepping back inside, she criticized, "You call this mess a women's tent? Kicking over a pillow, lifting a shawl, "Why do you not have beautiful shawls and big pillows?"

Taken aback, unable to form words of explanation, Sadie stammered, "After Sarah died, no one ever bothered to keep this up. We simply grew accustomed to things and never really noticed how things have faded," Eliana replied.

"That is going to change . . . and it is going to start right now. This tent needs to be bright and cheery. This is our place. It is a place to celebrate being a woman!"

"Is that how it was your village?" Sadie finally inquired.

Sadie and Eliana were afraid to challenge, as they remembered back just a few short weeks to the hand episode at her wedding and the stories circulated by Chesed's servants.

"When Chana arrives, we'll start the makeover."

Sadie offered, "Nayah and Liora will be here in a day or two. They will help."

Eliana was slightly offended, responding with, "But Rebekah, we have what we need, and we take care of each other. What more can we ask?"

"We are the mothers of life, and our gifts need to be celebrated."

"Tell me," challenged Eliana, "how would we celebrate being women couped up in here five days a month?

Ignoring the question, "Who is your best spinner of fine fabric?"

"Eliana makes the best clothing and blankets," replied Sadie. "I used her fabric to make the pillows and shawls for my family."

"It is decided then." Turning to Eliana, "will you make the sashes and shawls to hang about."

"Hang about?" Eliana asked as her tension eased.

"Yes. One over there, and one here and two over there. Special ones for the birthing area. Lamps, we need more lamps. It is like a cave here. We should see each other's faces clearly when we comfort each other and tell stories."

"Your women's tent must have been glorious," Eliana said timidly.

"It was fabulous, and I enjoyed going there very much."

"But what would our men say to—"

"Stop!" Rebekah said, putting her fingers on Iliana's lips, "No men are allowed in the women's tent; ever!"

Sadie and Eliana looked at each other for a moment before the horror on their faces turned to delight.

Half apologizing, Eliana said, "I will be honored to offer my talents."

"Thank you. Women deserve wonderful surroundings in which to pass the time."

After looking around for several moments, "Now, who in the camp can build a table?" Rebekah asked.

As the women grew excited with the conversation, Rebekah asked everything about birthing babies, eating, fellowship, sleeping, and anything else she could think to ask.

Looking at large round stones to the side, Rebekah inquired, "What are these?"

"Stones to stand on while giving birth," answered Sadie.

"Get rid of them. I will ask Omar to bake clay bricks, big bricks, with foot depressions in them. They are easier to stand on while giving birth." A moment later, "Now, give me a hand to sweep this place clean before Chana arrives with my bedding.

"Rebekah," Eliana said softly, "will you teach us how to make perfume?"

Rebekah did not answer but just smiled and said her familiar "Maybe."

The women worked the remainder of the day cleaning. Sadie was strong and helped to adjust the tent poles, making the interior appear larger. This enlargement enabled Rebekah to clean space for herself. When Chana arrived with the clean bedding, two piles of grungy old blankets, shawls, and pillow coverings lay waiting to be burnt.

Looking at a pile of worn blankets and pillows, Chana asked, "What do you want me to do with these?"

"Burn them," came the firm reply.

❀ ❀ ❀

As expected, Liora, Orli, and Nayah arrived the following afternoon. Amazed at the transformation, they stopped just inside the tent curtain.

"The tent looks so much better. What happened?" Nayah exclaimed.

"Rebekah happened," Sadie announced, proud of the transformation.

"It is true," Eliana said, pointing to Rebekah, "she is like Sarah, a take-in-charge woman who gets things done."

Rebekah lifted her head and said, "Isaac told me of Sarah's leadership. He mourns her to this day." Smiling, "Now, my job now is to help him stop mourning."

The women laughed, "Yes. Isaac is better even after a few days of marriage," observed Liora.

As the new arrivals were arranging themselves, Sadie began informing the women of their plans for decorating, lighting, and facilitating birthing. Rebekah remained quiet and started doing something Shiphrah had taught her. Focusing on her new companions' actions and facial expressions helped her determine the individual's temperament. By the time the women had settled in, Rebekah had selected the two women she would teach the time-honored craft of perfumer.

Over the next few days, the women told Rebekah much of their history. When Eliana returned to her husband's tent, she began spinning the decorative materials for pillows and shawls. She took charge of having men bring animal skins to be tanned and colored red. Omar made new poles with hangers for multiple oil lamps. Over the next few months, the women transformed the tent into a comfortable, colorful place, a happy place to relax and enjoy the company of other women. Rebekah also had forbidden the entry of any man from that day forth. What the men never knew was, the red tent now resembled that of a tribal chieftain. With the dramatic transformation, discussions became lively. When Rebekah's time came, her stories made the women laugh, cry and blush.

The red tent became a pleasant place to wait out their cycle or for the birthing of a baby. Perfume for bartering was made away from prying eyes. Herbs were collected, dried and crushed, to facilitate the making of medicines. Rebekah instructed Eliana to make each expectant mother a pure white linen birthing gown and several colorful sashes to hang about the birthing area. Later, Rebekah came up with the idea to have delicate white birthing gowns made for baby girls to honor their purity.

The décor of the women's tent had been a remarkable make-over. Each time Rebekah went there, she remembered so many stories of her childhood and the incredible women she had admired in her village. Sharing her childhood stories inspired the women in the village to speak of Sarah. They would tell of her strong leadership and the pain of her barrenness.

From these women, Rebekah learned of her father-in-law's child by Hagar, Sarah's handmaid. Rebekah understood Sarah's pain of not having a child of Hebrew bloodline and why she asked Abraham to have a child with Hagar. It saddened her to learn that when Ishmael, Hagar's son, was thirteen, mounting tension caused Sarah to send them away. The women believed that Keturah, one of Abraham's concubines, would be sent away as well, along with her children, but that never came to pass as Keturah knew her place.

"But why? Why would Abraham do this?" Rebekah asked.

"To secure the birthright for Isaac," Sadie answered. "Isaac was an infant. Sarah was afraid that thirteen-year-old Ishmael could usurp the tribal leadership. With Abraham getting older, it was not uncommon to murder a brother to gain his birthright. Isaac was her only child, and she was worried."

"What happened to them," Rebekah inquired.

"We don't know," answered Orli, "we heard that a god had come to their rescue, but that is it."

Sadie added, "The many flocks, servants, belongings, and gifts acquired by Abraham must pass through Isaac to his son, your son Rebekah. Abraham's line must forever remain Hebrew. Although she understood, the conversation about Hagar saddened Rebekah's heart. Still, she knew Abraham's God gave Sarah Isaac when the time was right. She believed what Elyon said and that her time would surely come. As it was with Sarah, so too a time of barrenness would be with her. With thoughts of future blessings, she happily resolved to share an exciting life with her husband Isaac in anticipation of that special day to come.

Monthly cycles passed. Full moons turned to seasons, and Rebekah had been married for five years. Although she was only twenty years of age, the barrenness of her womb tugged at her heart, just as it had Sarah's. Over the next few years, Rebekah developed a more suitable birthing area in the women's tent. Shiphrah would have been happy to deliver babies in the brightly colored area set aside for women to give birth. Every new bride longed for the day when she would straddle the birthing bricks and feel new life emerge from her body.

On this day, Mazal, covered with a perspiration-soaked linen gown, straddled the birthing bricks. Breathing labored, tears evincing the pain of childbirth, the groaning grew louder and longer. Sitting cross-legged between the birthing bricks, Rebekah placed one hand on Mazal's right knee while checking the progress with her left.

Looking at Chana, Rebekah reported, "There is no sign; the baby is not near."

Struggling with the horrific pain made it increasingly more difficult to remain standing. From behind, Chana found it necessary to help Orli and Sadie support Mazal on the bricks.

After examining the birth canal once again, Rebekah encouraged, "Push Mazal, push!"

Growing weaker by the moment, her breathing becoming short and erratic, Mazal shouted, "I can't. I can't. The baby will not move."

"Push, you must push!" Chana whispered from behind.

No matter how hard Mazal strained, the baby would not move.

"Errrrr," groaned Mazal.

"Push again encouraged Rebekah.

As Mazal attempted to push again, Rebekah yelled, "stop!"

Leaning forward, Rebekah reached her right hand further to examine the birth canal. A moment later, Rebekah breathed a sigh of relief and said, "There." Looking at Chana, Rebekah smirked said, "It must be a boy; I had to straighten his head."

The women all laughed.

Relieved and confident, Rebekah said, "Mazal, push again. The baby is ready."

Mazal strained, groaned, and with all her strength, quivering from head to toe, pushed as forcefully as possible, then collapsed back into Chana's arms. The needed supplies, clean cloths, a bowl of water, and a knife, had been placed in the proper position and awaited the delivery. With both hands now holding the infant under the birthing gown, Rebekah nodded to Liora to ready the cleaning cloths. Lifting the baby by the ankles, Rebekah slapped the infant's bum, and all heard the thankful sound of a baby's first cry. Orli stood ready with the ritual knife as Rebekah placed the infant on the cleaning cloths. Handing the knife forward, Rebekah shook her head, no.

"Why not Rebekah?" Why do you wait? Orli asked.

"It's best to wait a moment before cutting the cord."

The wait puzzled Liora, who asked, "Why?"

"Shiphrah told me it lessens the shock."

The women looked at each other in amazement.

Mazal, having been washed, her perspiration-soaked gown replaced, now rested on bright, clean blankets, with her head and shoulders supported on large pillows. Each time Rebekah swaddled a newborn and placed the child in a mother's arms, it gave her the same feeling of euphoria it had given Shiphrah. Needless to say, every midwife who successfully delivered a newborn baby felt the same delight.

"You have done well, Mazal," Rebekah congratulated, "He is strong and healthy, like his father."

Mazal's face beamed with pride. Amazed at the instant love she felt for her first son.

"Thank you so much, Rebekah. You are a blessing to our tribe," Mazal replied.

"And now you are the blessed one, Mazal. You have a healthy son. Will you allow Chana to take your child to Peretz? I'm sure he waits anxiously to see his son and to name him, "Rebekah responded.

Mazal passed the baby to Chana.

Outside the red tent, a large fire burnt brightly in the center of concerned villagers awaiting the birth announcement. Peretz, the expectant father, paced back and forth in front of the tent. As the hours passed, the crowd gradually grew with the increasing shouts from within the tent and in anticipation of good news.

"Peretz, don't worry. Mazal is strong," a nearby neighbor comforted, "She will bear you many children in the years to come. This one; it is a boy, I am certain."

"At last!" Peretz shouted as Chana stepped into the light of lanterns hung from the canopy, "My child," shouting louder, "I have a child."

Placing the baby into his father's arms, Chana announced, "You have a healthy baby boy Peretz, a son."

The villagers cheered and came close to see the newest addition to Abraham's tribe.

Allowing plenty of time for the well-wishers to congratulate Peretz, Chana said, "It is time."

Beaming with pride, Peretz said to Chana, "Is he not strong?"

"Yes," Chana agreed, "but Peretz, you must give praise to the God of Abraham for such a healthy boy."

Lifting the infant to the sky, he pronounced, "All glory to the God most high . . . I shall call him Ethan, for he is strong."

"I shall tell Mazal," Chana replied. "Now allow me to return Ethan to his mother."

Rebekah held back her tears as she watched the glow in Mazal's eyes brighten as Ethan began to feed upon the milk of life.

"You will be a wonderful mother," assured Rebekah.

Placing her hand on Rebekah's cheek, Mazal said a grateful, "Thank you."

With everything back in its proper place, Rebekah straightened her robe and left the tent.

Walking to Isaac, she felt an empty sadness in her heart but did not lose faith that, one day, she would be the woman on the birthing bricks.

❀ ❀ ❀

Back on the porch, Rose touched Beth's arm, waking her quickly.

"Oh Rose, Rebekah delivered a baby . . . and she knew what to do when the baby got stuck."

"Yes, and let me tell you, it was one of many," Rose assured and continued, "She was a leader. The women admired her ability to take charge and make things happen."

"She certainly did, but Rose, how much longer before she will have a baby? She will have one, right?"

"Now think for a moment, Beth; was she promised a baby?"

"Yes, she was. Elyon promised."

"And was she also to be barren for many years?" Rose asked.

"O Rose, that must have been hard delivering so many babies for the other women. Can you please tell just a little more?"

"You know the answer, dear."

"I know, tomorrow," Beth quipped.

CHAPTER 10

THE story of Rebekah was steadily taking over Beth's thinking. Her mind was filled with wonder, anticipating what would happen next. "*Surely Rebekah will become a mother in the next episode,*" she thought, "*or, heaven forbid, maybe Rose will tell me of an unforeseen family tragedy.*" Then Beth smiled, "*Or maybe a blessing?*"

Beth had been able to identify certain characteristics displayed by Rebekah that were similar to her own. She completely understood the desire for independence and Rebekah's growing impatience, which she was coming to realize was a test of faith. Still, Beth could not quite make the connection of how this story would change her life. But that is the beauty of a story; it intensifies the listener's curiosity. Beth knew Rebekah would have a baby at some point, it had been promised to her by God. However, that was the part of the story that wasn't similar to Beth's. She was still single. For that matter, she didn't even have a boyfriend or anyone with whom she wanted to date. There must be some other reason besides patience that Rose wanted her to hear this particular story.

"*Patience,*" Beth mumbled, "*I don't even have the patience to wait for five o'clock.*"

"Did you say something?" Joyce asked.

"Oh, sorry, no, just talking to myself."

"Oh, okay, if you say so," Joyce said, followed by a soft chuckle.

George looked at the clock and announced, "Not long now, and I'll be going to my son's first tee-ball game."

"Awe George . . . I didn't know Junior was playing tee-ball. Aren't they so cute in their little uniforms? And those batting helmets they can hardly keep on their little heads!"

"Yeah, Junior sure is a pistol. The two of you should come with me and watch. Oh, wait, Beth is still going to Rose's house. I forgot."

83

Beth smiled, "Yes, in exactly ten minutes."

He laughed. "Yup, she's got you hooked all right."

Beth knew he was right but didn't care. Besides, Rose was her friend. It wasn't just the story that compelled her to anticipate these evenings of food and friendship.

Rose was waiting on the porch dressed as a current-day southern belle. Beth had never seen her wear anything that wasn't perfectly color-coordinated and accessorized with colorful but straightforward jewelry. Truth be known, Beth felt that it was Rose who was the true gem. Even if the story didn't change her life, Beth felt the friendship might.

Grateful she'd decided to step onto Rose's porch a couple of weeks ago, her thoughts were interrupted by the now familiar, "Hello Beth. Come right up and have a seat."

"Hello, Rose."

"I have a good story today, but first, a Cobb salad, crackers, dessert and . . . another buttermilk pie, fresh-made today."

"It certainly looks like you've outdone yourself again."

"Nonsense! Anyway, you say that all the time."

Rose brought Beth up to date on the church news and especially the scheduling of interviews for the applicants.

"We've had some good ones apply."

"I'm happy for you Rose. I know you don't want this to drag on."

"Oh, and, tomorrow," Rose said, "there is a spring bake sale at the church to raise money for the flower fund." Rose knew this was a perfect time, "You should stop by. The ladies offer a large variety of baked goods and, well, you can even buy things by the slice if you wanted to sample a goodie before buying."

"What's the flower fund?"

"We collect money once each year and use it to send flowers to those who are in the hospital and, well, to the families of those who enter the gates of heaven; you understand."

"Yes, in memory of those who have passed away," Beth acknowledged before taking another bite of her delicious buttermilk pie. After taking a sip of her ice tea, Beth continued, "That sounds interesting, but I can't imagine any dessert tasting better than yours."

"There are some good ones and, well, maybe some that are just okay." Rose winked and continued, "It starts at 8:00 am. if you can make it. Now, let's get started."

❀ ❀ ❀

The women in the settlement had collected various items and spun beautiful cloth for the women's tent. It was no longer a place in which the women were sentenced to seclusion during their cycles. The women s tent had become a place for the women to meet and support each other. They shared stories, brought new life into the world, and, the all-time favorite, vented about their husbands or their husband's concubines. However, the most exciting thing that happened in the tent was sharing. Rebekah would share the customs and practices of Bethuel's village, and the women shared similar stories of their traditions. Rebekah knew the most important aspect of sharing was encouraging the women to be strong and yet wise. Women needed to have a say in decisions involving the family.

"How do we do that?" asked Sadie.

"Trickery, of course," Rebekah answered without hesitation.

"Okay, what's the trick?" inquired Orli.

"The trick is," Rebekah answered, "you have to make him think it was his idea."

During the laughter, Orli countered, "That's easier said than done."

"If you want to make a change," answered Rebekah, "suggest something that would make it easier for him, then ask him how he would do it or go about having it done." Using her bewildered feminine voice, Rebekah said, "I am at a loss, Issac; how would you go about it, dear? After the laughter, she said, "Works every time."

Sadie, Eliana, Orli, Mazal, Chana, and the others had to hold their tummies while laughing.

"My husband is good at figuring things out," said Eliana, "so how do I go about leading him?"

"Whatever you would like to have done, or whatever you would like your husband to do, think of all the reasons why it would benefit him. Like I said, pretend to be at a loss, a helpless female." More laughter followed.

Perplexed, Mazal asked, "Tell me, Rebekah, my husband is so tired at night, all he wants to do is drink wine, and I want more children. How can I motivate him and, most importantly, make him think it was his idea?"

Sadie eagerly agreed, "Yes, Rebekah, tell us how."

Rebekah laughed. "This is what I would say with a sad compassionate voice: Oh Yoram, you are always tired, and your work is making you an old man. One day you will be too old to work hard and will need more sons to help. Then stop. Give him a moment to think about what you said. In an encouraging voice, tell him how much you love him, saying, let me give you another son so that you do not have to work so hard and can enjoy your drink at night." Rebekah continued, imitating in a male voice, "Yes, you are right, let us start tonight." The women roared with laugher. Rebekah added, tongue in cheek, "If you like, do not get pregnant too soon. Let him work on it for a while."

Once again, the laughter was heard all through the encampment.

One of the men walking by yelled into the tent, "Are you women alright? Do you need help?"

They quieted their laugher as Rebekah answered, "Oh no. We are fine."

In the days and weeks that followed, the women helped Rebekah collect the plants, herbs, and seeds needed to make several potions and medications. However, she only taught Eliana and Sadie how to mix her mysterious concoctions. Once items were collected, each was kept in a separate jar. Much to the surprise of the other women, there were eleven individually marked jars on the back table. The largest was the one Rebekah kept the ointment used to make their skin soft. Aloe vera was the favorite. It not only hydrated their rough skin but was used on burns as well. Aloe was used to soothe the legs of a young girl who had gotten a rash while in the bush. The women knew anise would break a high fever, but Rebekah knew of usage, much more beneficial.

With her mischievous grin, she said, "There is another use for anise that can help if your husband, well, let us say, makes a noise in the night that smells like camel dung."

At this, the women laughed even harder than before.

"So," Orli asked, "if I use this when making supper, it will stop Amon from stinking up the tent?" A moment later, Orli begged, "Please don't tell Amon what I said."

"May I have a double portion to use in Elam's food?" asked Sadie.

Once again, the women laughed. With their minds off their present woes, Rebekah went on to show the women how to make their skin soft and beautiful.

She told them that, "When the time is right, take your husband's hand and rub it gently over your soft skin. Nature will do the rest."

All the women laughed as Rebekah made a face as she rubbed her skin with the balm.

"Remember," she said, "it's all about making him think it was his idea."

At that, the uproar of laughter was heard once again throughout the encampment.

Rebekah was a natural teacher. She used her organizational skills to prepare for each demonstration, and her natural humor helped the women remember the lesson. It was reassuring to know the women could use these remedies even if Rebekah were not with them. She taught them about using cinnamon for stomach aches and saffron to cheer their husbands' mood or cheer a woman during her cycle. Hyssop was used for sore throats, mint for nausea and headaches, and anise for cramps during their cycle. The women learned much and felt better about themselves.

One day after a lesson, Sadie stayed behind to help Rebekah. While putting the herbs away, she expressed the gratitude of all the women. "Rebekah, you have taught us much, and we are stronger. We feel like we are all sisters."

Rebekah hugged her and said, "We are sisters."

"Tell me, Rebekah, does it trouble you that we have children and you do not?"

"I am pleased for you; really, I am."

Sadie hugged Rebekah and said, "You will have a baby. I just know it."

"Yes, I will Sadie. I will have a child, but it will be in God's time."

A male voice cried out, "Rebekah, you need to come quickly. Rina sent me for you."

Pushing Rebekah out of the tent, Sadie said, "Go, I will finish cleaning the rest of the tent."

Stepping out of the tent, she asked Peretz, "Why is Rina calling for me?"

"Father Abraham, he is not well. She needs you."

After sending Peretz into the hills to inform Isaac, she hurried through the encampment. On entering Abraham's tent, Rebekah found Rina and Bayla at his side. Now one-hundred and seventy-five years of age, Abraham was lying on his bed, completely covered with blankets with his head resting on Rina's lap. Bayla was caressing Abraham's head. Rebekah could see both women were heartsick. Sitting cross-legged for a time, Rebekah monitored his pulse and listened to his breathing.

"Can you not do something Rebekah?" was Rina's plea.

Even though everyone knew Abraham's inevitable destiny was nearing ever so quickly, it did not ease the pain of death. All Rebekah could do was offer assurance that Abraham would soon be with his God. Her voice caused Abraham to open his eyes for one last look at his beautiful daughter-in-law. By his smile, the servants could see that Rebekah's voice pleased him.

Rina tried to hold back the tears as she tried to say lovingly, "We will miss you, father Abraham," but to no avail, her tears flowed.

Abraham uttered a weak, "Yes." Between labored breaths, "I will miss . . . your comforting . . . touch."

Saddened by the realization Abraham was to die without the satisfaction of seeing his grandson, Rebekah looked intently at Abraham as he labored for each breath. Knowing there was nothing she could do, she whispered, "Father Abraham."

"Yes, my child," was the weak reply.

"I am sad that the LORD has not blessed me with a child, a grandchild for you."

Her statement reminded Abraham of Sarah's faith and how she'd struggled to believe for all those years, just as he had.

Barely able to whisper, he said, "All in God's time."

Rebekah sighed. "So many moons, and I'm still barren."

Abraham took a deep breath and said, "Have faith; God's plan will be fulfilled."

Rebekah leaned back, closed her eyes, put her head down, and wept.

His body quivering, Abraham said, "Bayla, Rina, come," gasping, "I am cold."

With Bayla on one side and Rina on the other, Abraham closed his eyes for the last time.

Then, suddenly, Rebekah witnessed something strange. Abraham's eyes snapped open. An uncanny calm fell over him as he looked to heaven and smiled. At that very moment, his breathing stopped.

Aware of the presence of angels, Rebekah said, "Do not be sad; Abraham has gone to be with his God."

Having spent the last few days in the hills inspecting the flocks, Isaac hurried to the encampment when he heard his father lay dying. Entering the tent at that very moment of Abraham's last breath, he cried out, "Father!"

Bidding Rina and Bayla leave with her, Rebekah felt that Isaac might like a few moments alone with his father.

During mourning and preparation for burial, Isaac dispatched Peretz to hasten to Ishmael and inform his half-brother, now settled in the wilderness of Paran, of Abraham's passing. Peretz took the fastest camel as the burial would take place in three days at the cave of Machpelah. Isaac informed Rebekah that the cave at Machpelah was purchased from Ephron the Hittite so that Abraham's line would share the same burial cave. Rebekah took charge to oversee the preparation of Father Abraham's body. Isaac knew his father had purchased the cave, not just for burial, but that his line would always be within the land promised by God so long ago. Isaac also knew that the flocks he had tended for so long were now his. Along with the many servants and treasure always kept in Abraham's tent, Isaac inherited the title of "tribal chieftain."

Peretz was surprised to find Ishmael's encampment so large and prosperous. Ishmael's instruction to servants to saddle his camel and follow with appropriate gifts was even more astonishing. He knew Hagar and Ishmael had been cast out, and this act of reverence took Peretz by surprise. Remarkably, Ishmael did not hesitate. He left with Peretz immediately. A short while later, a small caravan left Paran following the two men.

Isaac and Rebekah traveled with a small caravan to the burial cave. Ishmael and Peretz arrived a short while later, closely followed by his wife Ayesha and a small entourage of servants. Isaac's greeting was polite, and after introductions, the two half-brothers watched as servants lowered Abraham's body from the cart wrapped in white linen. Isaac invited Ishmael to walk with him and lead the procession to the cave.

Stepping aside, the pallbearers entered the cave and lay the body to rest. When the final stones were placed over the cave's mouth, Isaac, Rebekah, Ishmael, and Ayesha took their place before the cave. Bayla, Rina, and Chana stood among the large gathering of villagers and friends.

After a moment of silence, Isaac took a step forward and turned. Acknowledging that Ishmael was also the son of Abraham and therefore his brother, he extended his hand and said, "Join me, brother."

With his brother by his side, Isaacs raised his arms and prayed, "O LORD, God of my father Abraham, creator of heaven and earth, receive your faithful servant Abraham into your bosom. Comfort and bless him as in life he endured much for the sake of your chosen people."

When Isaac stepped back, Ishmael stepped forward and prayed, "Give him rest from his labor and peace from his long and difficult journey through life."

The brothers were silent for a time, allowing mourners time to offer their prayers.

Finally, Isaac turned to Ishmael and said, "Peretz tells me you have done well for yourself."

Ishmael looked at Isaac and responded, "Yes, I have, but now, the responsibilities of a tribal chieftain fall upon you, and I have seen how large Abraham's tribe has grown."

Isaac invited Ishmael back to his encampment to rest and refresh himself before the journey to Padan. The crowd of mourners and friends departed to their settlements.

❀ ❀ ❀

Beth felt Rose shaking her arm and saying, "Beth, Beth dear."

Beth exclaimed, "Rose, she didn't have her baby yet? And Abraham has died?"

Rose smiled and nodded.

Desiring to know, Beth's plea, "Can you tell me more? O please, just a few more minutes."

Beth begged because Monday was two more days away, and the thought of not knowing was still gnawing away at her.

Rose attempted to calm Beth's impatience with, "Now dear, the next part, well, I can't just tell it to you in a minute or two."

"Is it long as well?" replied Beth.

"Yes. Just as long as the other parts."

"Oh, Rose. I must know."

"You will dear; you will … patience."

Beth knew that was the final word as Rose never wavered. Once done for the evening, that was it. Rising from the wicker chair and descending the steps, Beth stopped.

Turning, she said, "You know Rose, I might stop by the bake sale tomorrow. Do you think anyone will have a coffee cake? George and Joyce often bring coffee cake into the office, and I think I'd like to do that as well."

Without hesitation, Rose said, "I know the best coffee cake every year is Myrtle's cinnamon coffee cake. She always makes plenty, but you must get there early."

"That would be great. Will it be inside the church?"

"Heavens no. There are too many tables full of baked goods to fit inside the fellowship hall and have customers milling about tasting things. And, well, you know, people can be messy trying all those samples." Rose laughed. "We have it in the parking lot, outside the sanctuary. To entice people to attend and sample, we offer complimentary coffee and punch with their purchases."

"Okay, where is the church?"

"It's at the end of Hannah Street. Just walk one more block down Reckoner Street and turn right on Hannah Street. It's the large white building with the sign, 'Good Shepherd Christian Church' in front. You will see us there."

"Thank you, Rose."

"See you at the bake sale," Rose said and winked.

Walking to her apartment, Beth realized it was good to have something to do on a Saturday.

CHAPTER 11

Waking early, Beth found herself excited about going to Rose's church for the bake sale. It was the first Saturday since moving to Sageville she hadn't overslept. Springing out of bed, sprinting into the kitchen, pressing start on the coffee machine caused her to pause and reflect on the empty table.

The emptiness caused her to mutter, "Guess I didn't realize how dull my Saturdays have been." Taking her second cup into the bedroom, Beth selected the perfect outfit for a church bake sale. "Yes," she said, "a pair of navy capris . . . um, a lacy white cotton blouse should work nicely and a pair of white pumps." Looking over the church location on her GPS, "Hmm, Good Shepherd Christian Church . . . estimated walking time, ten minutes."

Beth showered, all the time thinking, "*No running water, electricity, or air conditioning. I never appreciated how lucky I am that I do not have to live in a tent.*" Try as she may, Beth could not imagine how hard it must have been not to have a medical center, grocery store, or mall to shop for clothes. Looking at her micro-wave, she thought, "*All I have to do is toss in the frozen package and wallah, supper.*" About to close the closet door after dressing for church, she thought, "*I'd be lost if I had to spin yarn from sheep or goat hair.*" One final check of her well-appointed closet, comfy bed, reading light, and suddenly it dawned on her, "Guess I have it pretty easy. Maybe Rose is right; I have much to learn and much to be thankful for."

For whatever unknown reason, Beth did not hurry to the bake sale. Instead, she began to admire the number of flowering shrubs and trees along the way. Most of the homes along Reckoner Street and Hannah were beautifully landscaped, with an abundance of flower beds snuggled against older but well-kept houses.

She thought to herself, "Why have I never noticed these before?"

The flowers caused her mind to wander back to the homemade perfumes that Rebekah made from flowers, just like these. She longed to turn up the walkways and inhale the wonderful floral aroma but then, walking into a stranger's garden uninvited might not be welcomed. Rounding the corner, she saw the church parking lot. It was, as Rose had said, full of tables filled with baked goods. Parked cars filled the street for this once-a-year bake sale. After all this time in Sageville, Beth had never heard of it until now. Tables filled with pies, cookies, cakes, sweet rolls, and some interesting baked goods she had never seen before lined the lot from one end to the other. Near the end of the line, she spotted Rose and walked to her table.

"Hello, Rose," Beth's cheerful greeting rang out.

"Well, hello to you, Beth Chase. Have you been looking over the tables?"

"I've looked down this row but not the other side."

"Myrtle has a table just over there," winking as she pointed, "now you go get some coffee cake before it all goes. By noon, her table will be empty."

"Good idea," Beth said as she left. "I'll check around as well. I'd like to have some treats for breakfast next week."

Pointing to another table, Rose shouted, "Those cakes on Ida's table freeze well."

"Even better," Beth smiled. "I like a variety."

Purchasing a lemon pound cake from Myrtle for herself and another for the office brought a feeling of joy Beth could not understand. Picking up a bag of assorted cookies from Ida, she continued exploring. Amazed at the creativity and variety, Beth inspected every table before returning to Rose. A father and his large family, were buying treats from Rose. Not intending to eavesdrop, Beth could not but overhear the man thanking Rose for the story she told him years ago. His remark, "You alone turned my life around," caught Beth off guard. Then, there it was again, the wink, as Rose answered, "Now Bert, you and I both know who it was that helped you. Never forget, all things come together for good, according to God's plan."

Bert smiled and laughed, agreeing, "Yes. God is good."

Another family stopped at the table and thanked Rose for her stories. Beth listened as the mother and daughter told Rose how well they were doing compared to the year before. After purchasing two of Rose's pies, they left the table.

"Rose, I got coffee cake, lemon cake, cookies, and muffins," Beth said, showing off her purchases.

"Those look delicious," Rose said and winked.

"Thanks for telling me about the sale, but now, what shall I purchase from you?"

"Oh dear, don't worry about that. In October, we have a fall sale. Not so many baked goods, but more pickled and canned items, as well as holiday decorations."

"That sounds wonderful."

"You might want some holiday decorations for your apartment or to give as gifts."

"Great ideas, thank you."

As another family approached Rose, Beth waved and said, "See you Monday."

Walking away, Beth noticed, *"There was that wink again. There is something mystical about it; I just don't know what?"*

When Monday finally arrived, Beth was up early, had a quick coffee, placed the coffee cake into a tote, and left for the office. Waving to Rose, already busy working in her front yard, she hurried on past. Proudly placing the cake on the coffee counter, she invited Joyce and George to partake.

Her workmates remarked simultaneously, "Myrtle's coffee cake!"

"We just love Myrtle's baking," George said as he placed three small dishes on the counter.

While Beth unwrapped the delectable confection, Joyce retrieved the coffee cream from the refrigerator. Each took a slice and a cup of coffee. Beth took a piece to her desk then dug into this week's files. Mondays had now become the slowest day in the week as storytelling had a three-day interruption. Grateful for the arrival of five o'clock, Beth quickly gathered her belongings and left.

A cheery "Hey Beth" rang out as she opened the white picket gate.

The joyful greetings, the eager wave always made Beth feel so welcome.

"Hello Rose," was Beth's enthusiastic reply.

"I thought we might enjoy a chicken club sandwich today and some of Ethel's apricot cookies from the bake sale."

"Looks lovely Rose."

Without hesitation, Rose happily announced, "The search commit-tee has received five applications to be our new pastor."

"That's exciting."

"Yes, it is. Each one will be interviewed and then invited to preach at least one service." Taking a moment to monitor Beth's reaction, Rose's voice softened, "You could come and help me judge whom you think is the best one."

Taken aback, "O my gosh," replied Beth, "how on earth would I know?"

"Well, for starters, you are the perfect person. The candidate would have to keep your attention for one thing and provide an excellent bibli-cal message that you can relate to your life."

Without realizing she was deep in thought, Beth said, "Sounds in-teresting. Let me know when the interviews begin."

As if returning to reality, Beth thought, "O no, I've gone and done it. I hate commitments, and now I've committed to going to church."

Not surprised in the least, Rose said, "Good. I will let you know."

Uncharacteristically, letting it pass, Beth said, "Rose, speaking of Biblical messages, I can't wait to hear about what happened next to Rebekah."

"Well dear, let's get started. Close your eyes, relax, think of nothing."

Rose took Beth back to the burial cave of Machpelah.

Beth watched the people disperse, Ishmael and Ayesha leave with their servants. After wishing Ishmael a safe journey, Isaac hurried to catch up to Rebekah. Out of the corner of her eye, Rebekah caught Isaac wink-ing at Bayla and Rina, and much to her disgust, Bayla and Rina giggle.

Without turning, Rebekah said in a loud stern voice, "Isaac," then softer, "now that you are the tribal chieftain. Try acting like one."

Isaac did not display the grief Rebekah expected. She feared his spoiled life would be the motivation behind decisions made as tribal chieftain.

Remembering the words of Elyon, that Isaac would not follow in the ways of Abraham, it was apparent he would continue to lie with foreign women.

She thought, "I must remain strong but never dominated."

Isaac would never grow accustomed to Rebekah speaking in oppo-sition to his ideas. Still, her speech would have to be steadfast and wise.

Undeterred by Rebekah's censure, Isaac boasted, "I have waited a long time for this moment. Today, I move into my father's tent. Today, his servants and concubines belong to me; mine; all mine."

Without turning to look at Isaac, she said with much disgust, "Your father's servants may wait on you, but you will not father an heir with them. I will not have you going against the plans God has made for your father's family. That child will be our child! It is God's will."

Isaac winked at Bayla and Rina and then stepped forward to grab Rebekah's arm.

"I will be happy to father an heir to Abraham's line . . . Tonight, you will warm my bed," he said with a slight chuckle, "and every night I call."

The months and years that followed after Abraham's death were hard for Rebekah. Ten years into a childless marriage made her think that twenty-five was too old to bear children. Many women that age had difficult deliveries. Nevertheless, she continued her tedious yet rewarding work with the people of the settlement. Serving as the midwife, medicine woman, and confidant, the villagers began to respect her judgment, not Isaac's.

With Isaac's tribe growing, the steady stream of young women entering the red tent for the first time, the growing number of births each month, and the constant need for medications, kept the older women busy. On top of all that, Rebekah faithfully maintained the affairs of Isaac's household and bartering transactions. Remaining at his beck and call, she could not help but wonder when she would be the one standing on the birthing bricks. Often, Rebekah's struggle with Isaac's desire to dominate drained her energy, but she always remembered that God was with her.

Isaac liked to recline on several pillows under the awning of his father's tent, observing the common folk laboring to complete their routine chores. He was proud that his wife, now twenty-five years of age, remained beautiful. He liked to see her working near the hot clay oven and smell the aroma of freshly baked bread wafting through the settlement. On this particular day, Rebekah sat beside a large flat stone, routinely kneading dough for the day's flatbread. Rebekah would place her kneaded dough onto Chana's bread paddle. Chana then slid the dough into the oven while Rebekah rolled out the next piece of flatbread.

While checking the bread to make sure it was perfect, Chana asked, "Rebekah, how do you remain happy when so many moons have come and gone, and you are still barren?"

"Oh, Chana, I'm not happy all of the time, especially when I see so many wives and concubines continually having children."

She looked at Rebekah and said, "Yet you continue to help bring those children into this life."

Rebekah stopped kneading the dough and said, "Chana, Chesed told me that Sarah bore the same pain for most of her life. She brought hundreds of babies into Abraham's settlement over the years, yet remained barren until her old age."

Chana thought about this for a moment and then asked, "Rebekah, do you think if men knew the pain women bear, they would be more understanding?"

Rebekah had to stop herself from laughing out loud before shaking her head and answering an emphatic, "No!"

In the late afternoon heat, Rebekah and Chana continued to knead and bake their bread. As the sweat rolled down Rebekah's back, Bayla and Rina approached the cooling rack piled high with flatbread. Bayla carried a full wineskin slung over her shoulder. Rina reached out and took a warm flatbread, and placed it into her basket of freshly cooked lamb. Neither one gave Rebekah so much as a glance as they passed by. The women were polite to each other in the red tent. Still, the friction remained because of their wanton service to Isaac, especially after Abraham's passing.

A few steps later, Rina offered a nonchalant, "Thank you," and then giggled. Ignoring Rina's comment, Rebekah watched Rina and Bayla enter Isaac's tent. Isaac rose from his reclined position, stretched, then followed the two females into the tent.

Observing the women's callous behavior, Chana sarcastically remarked, "Those Hittite women certainly enjoy their work."

"Humph! So does Isaac."

"Rebekah," Chana laughed, "You are bad."

"The difference is," Rebekah said as she continued kneading, "we work with our backs. They work on their backs."

Chana could not help laughing before responding with a somber, "And we deliver their babies."

After a moment of reflection, Chana stopped working, looked at Rebekah, and said, "Rebekah, you are strong. Your faith is strong. I believe God will bless you with a child, and soon."

"Chana, the truth is, I must be strong enough for both of us, myself and Isaac. He no longer listens to the God of his father. Elyon had told me this would happen and, on the same night, told me I must remain barren like Sarah but that my time would come."

Chana looked into Rebekah's longing green eyes. "You are a very special woman, and you will be blessed."

❀ ❀ ❀

Having finished the evening's story, Rose shook Beth and said, "Beth, Beth dear."

Snapping to reality, "My goodness Rose, does Rebekah still not have a baby?"

"In time dear, in time."

"You know what is strange about those days?"

"What's that Beth?"

"In that age, people thought twenty-five was old for having a baby. She felt like she was going to be too old to have a baby. Or that it would be hard for her. Oh, Rose, please don't tell me she has a hard time or loses the baby. I would be oh so sad for her."

"Now, dear, we will continue tomorrow afternoon. Now, would you like to take some of Ethel's apricot cookies home with you? I have two dozen."

"I certainly would. Thank you."

Beth took the bag of cookies and left Rose's porch. On the way home, she began to worry about Rebekah. "*Will she ever have a baby?*" she asked herself, hoping tomorrow's episode would find Rebekah finally standing on the birthing bricks.

CHAPTER 12

POURING a cup of freshly brewed Monday morning coffee and treating herself to an apricot cookie, Beth began to see that work isn't the only important thing in life. Recently, Beth had caught herself thinking more about Rebekah, Rose, and even Rose's church, instead of always thinking of work and her career. She had always loved her work and did not have any intentions of doing anything else. Feeling secure and accepted in her new office, the only thing Beth felt impatient about was getting to Rose's house each afternoon.

Joyce's "Good morning" welcome felt warm, as was her invitation to enjoy a slice of Myrtle's coffee cake. Lately, Myrtles' coffee cake was winning out over Beth's desire to remain slim and trim.

"Oh, why not?" was the serene response.

"I've got mine, so the rest is for you two," George announced.

Beth couldn't possibly eat the big piece left on the plate. Cutting it in two and saving half for lunch sounded like a good idea, and fewer calories. Returning to her desk, she began pecking away and the client applications on her desk. She didn't look up or talk with her coworkers for the rest of the day. Working straight through, Beth was determined to complete her review of the documents. Later in the day, Beth was overwhelmed with the sense of change that was beginning to transform her solitary life. Not sure what that change would be or how it would happen, Beth believed it would happen soon. With more certainty than anything she could remember, the feeling was deep in her bones.

Five o'clock roared in thankfully, and waving goodbye to George and Joyce, she left the office and walked rapidly to Rose's house. Knowing that fall was only a few weeks away, the air seemed to be full of change. Beth could feel the season was not the only thing about to undergo a transition.

Sitting prim and southern proper on her porch, Rose offered the customary welcome, "Good afternoon, Beth."

"Good afternoon, Rose, and how are you?"

"I am just fine dear."

"Rose, can you feel the change in the air?"

Rose's smile spread across her entire face. She knew this question; she'd heard it before. Everyone to whom she'd ever told a story asked the same question around this point in their story. She didn't want to spoil it for Beth, so she encouraged her to talk about this feeling of change, just as she had all the others over the years.

"Whatever do you mean?" Rose asked.

"I don't know. I can't explain it, but it is so clear to me. I can feel it. Change is about to happen."

"Well, dear, you know fall is coming soon."

"Yes. I've thought about that, but this is different."

"Tell you what, when you have a better idea of what is changing, let me know. I'm curious to know myself."

Rose knew exactly what was happening, but the transformation was still a long way off. Like all others before her, she had to realize the change herself. Talking nonstop, they enjoyed the soup and salad Rose had prepared and ate apricot cookies for dessert.

When it was time, Rose said, "Now dear, shall we begin?"

Beth nodded in agreement.

❀ ❀ ❀

The weeks rolled by; the usual daily routines continued. The flatbread was basic to almost every meal, and families took turns at the bread oven. While working away, Chesed approached with servants to stock the woodpile. To their surprise, two Hittite soldiers, Selig and Yair, rode slowly into Isaac's camp with the third horse in tow.

Dismounting close to Chesed, Selig asked, "Is this the camp of Isaac the Hebrew?"

"Why do you ask?" Chesed replied.

"We have been sent for the healer woman."

"And why, may I ask, do you seek her?"

"It is Abimelech. He has fallen from his horse. His shoulder is out of place. We seek the healer woman, Rebekah, to attend to him."

Chesed led the men to where Rebekah knelt, kneading dough.

"Rebekah," Chesed said, "These men have come to our camp on behalf of King Abimelech. They are seeking your help for their king."

Rebekah stood, placed her hands on her hips, and said, "How may I help?"

Yair replied, "The king has fallen, and his shoulder is injured. We believe it is out of place."

"Why don't you replace it?"

Selig did not like that kind of a reply by a woman, but still, he asked, "Can you help?"

Biting her tongue to keep from smiling, Rebekah said confidently, "Yes, of course. I will go with you."

Shocked by her independent response, Yair quickly suggested, "Should you not ask your husband's permission to leave camp and go with us?"

In a calm but firm tone, Rebekah replied, "No. I make my own decisions."

The two soldiers were astonished and turned to look at each other. No woman in their settlement would ever think to make such a decision without seeking permission of their husband, master, or father.

While standing fast, staring at the men with confidence in her ability to decide what she would or would not do, Chesed broke the impasse.

He offered a nervous, "I will go with you, Rebekah."

Chesed mounted the third horse and reached down for Rebekah's arm. With a strong pull, he slung her behind him on the horse. The group rode through the valley and over the hills to Abimelech's village. It was a large settlement and had a combination of small huts and larger clay brick homes. Rebekah wondered why there was no women's tent, only houses. Selig and Yair led the group to Abimelech's large, two-story, elaborately decorated, kingly residence. Upon arrival, they heard the moaning of a man in great pain and women's voices coming from the throne room. A well-dressed middle-aged man, Zerach, paced back and forth impatiently as they stepped into the room.

Selig announced, "My king, the healer woman as you commanded."

Two women, female servants, dressed in colorful linen gowns, attempted to comfort Abimelech without success. Yair escorted Rebekah to Abimelech, who was seated on his throne.

Both women looked at Rebekah with pleading eyes that said: "Please help him."

The two young women attempted to support Abimelech as he stood. Placing his left arm against his chest, he cradled his left elbow in his right hand.

Taking a deep painful breath, he said, "Come in. I have heard of your great skill and gift of healing."

"Thank you," Rebekah replied softly.

Yair tried to force Rebekah to her knees, demanding, "Kneel when you speak to the king."

Rebekah glared at Yair and *slapped* his face, replying, "You kneel. He's your king."

All in the room gasped. Rebekah turned to walk out of the door but stopped when Chesed called her name. The servants and others in the room looked at Abimelech and waited for his response. The attitude of defiance and lack of respect was unheard of for a woman. No woman had ever been so bold.

Abimelech looked around. He had no choice, so he said, "I need you to fix my arm."

Without turning, Rebekah said, "I don't kneel."

At this response, the servants in the room whispered amongst themselves.

Abimelech was enraged and said, "I could make you."

"Yes, you still have one good arm."

Chesed shouted the reprimand, "Rebekah!"

Abimelech, wondering what to do in this unheard-of situation, looked at Ahuzzath, who could not answer.

"All right. Can you fix my arm?" Abimelech asked.

Rebekah turned and pointed. "Stand with your good shoulder to the wall."

Aghast, Zerach warned, "You do not tell the king what to do."

"Then you fix his arm," she snapped, turning to leave once again.

Chesed chastened, "Rebekah, just fix his arm so we can leave.

Knowing he was at an impasse, Abimelech said, "Rebekah, please help me. My people do not know what to do. They have tried, and it only hurts all the more."

"Very well. Stand with your right shoulder to the wall."

Abimelech followed her instructions but was careful not to make the injury worse.

"Now, with your right hand on your elbow, lift your left hand to your right shoulder."

Abimelech followed the direction gingerly, cradled his elbow, and waited for his next instruction. Rebekah took a half-inch thick twig from her cloak and placed it in Abimelech's mouth. The entire group of bystanders stood frightened and confused. What would this Hebrew woman have Abimelech do next? Could she heal him? Would he continue to be in pain?

"Now, bite," she said.

Rebekah's vibrant green eyes glared into Abimelech's. The depth of color distracted him momentarily and from what she was about to do next. The king tipped his head as if in a hypnotic trance; the courtiers held their breath. The two female servants held onto each other's arms. While Abimelech focused on her deep green eyes, Rebekah drew her right hand slowly back. Opening her palm, and with all the force she could muster, drove the out-of-place shoulder back into the place. Abimelech's teeth crushed the stick. He screamed and fell to the floor. Female servants rushed to his side. Ahuzzath shouted, "She struck the king!" Guards rushed to Rebekah, pulled her away. Ahuzzath and the servant girls assisted him into his throne as if he were a child with a sprain.

Much to their surprise, Abimelech commanded, "Wine, bring me wine."

A young female servant poured wine into a goblet so quickly; some spilled on the floor. Abimelech gulped the wine rapidly, sat back in his throne, and began to move his arm slowly and gently.

"Well, young lady, that was quite an unexpected shock." Increasing the circular movement of his arm, he said, "It feels better. Tender, but better."

Yanking her arms free from the guards' grasp, Rebekah stepped boldly forward. Touching Abimelech's tender shoulder to satisfy herself that all was well, she said, "Yes, it will be tender for a while. Do not strain it, and it will soon be better."

Ahuzzath stepped over to Chesed and asked, "Wine?"

To settle his nerves, Chesed answered, "Please."

Sitting reclined on his throne, Abimelech invited everyone to partake of his wine. Silver goblets filled, courtiers resumed their idle chatter, but Rebekah did not move. She stood, hands-on-hips, directly in front of the king. Never before had he beheld such a tenacious young woman.

Aware that he would never break her spirit but maintain an air of authority, Abimelech offered a compliment. "Such beautiful red hair."

"Thank you," came the soft reply.

"In all my kingdom, we have never seen anyone with red hair."

"Nor anyone with green eyes," added Zorach.

Having heard these comments all her life, Rebekah casually shrugged her shoulders but remained standing with her hands on her hips. Aware of the king's interest in this young woman, Ahuzzath began walking around Rebekah, slowly inspecting a prospective concubine. Rebekah's glare into his eyes stopped the inspection.

Abimelech remarked, "Isaac tells me you are his sister."

"Oh?"

"Yes," Abimelech continued, "There are many young men in my court that would desire you."

A loud, "*Humph*!" stopped the court chatter.

With his shoulder now healed and to flex his kingly authority, Abimelech decreed, "I could give you to any one of them. Or better still, take you myself."

Rebekah laughed, much to the surprise of those in the court. Tipping her head slightly forward said in a firm challenging voice, "You give me! You take me!" Then turned and walked toward the door.

Before exiting the throne room, with back to the king, Rebekah issued her direction, "You may send your gifts to Isaac's camp."

Rebekah's tenacity stunned everyone. Surely the king would not stand for such an attitude. Standing silently, the courtiers waited for the king's response. To cover the indignity and save face, Abimelech laughed at her boldness.

❊ ❊ ❊

"Beth, Beth," Rose said, shaking her arm gently.

Beth heard Rose's soft voice but did not want to wake up. She wanted the story to go on and on.

Still half asleep, she uttered, "Rose?"

"Are you all right, my dear?"

"Yes. It is just that, well, I wanted the story to go on."

With her all-knowing chuckle, Rose sat back and asked, "What part of the story did you find most interesting?"

Not having been asked anything in a while, Beth thought for a moment, then answered, "Her bravery. She did what no other women had ever considered doing by speaking up to a king."

Rose smiled and asked, "Was that all?"

"No, she was smart about what to say and when."

Rose nodded and answered, "Exactly."

Beth thought for a moment before continuing. "You know, Rose, what I said before . . . about change?"

"Yes, dear."

"I think acting too quickly is not necessarily acting bravely."

"Ah yes, my dear. That is the key, and it makes all the difference."

Beth did not say anything. She just sat there, almost in a trance.

"Now dear, you will hear the next part tomorrow."

Beth rose slowly, head spinning, nodded, and said, "Good night, Rose."

"Good night, dear."

Walking home, memories of the interaction between Rebekah and Abimelech repeated over and over in her mind. Beth was smart enough to have figured it out. The key was to be brave enough to act and smart enough to know what to say. "*When those situations in life arise,*" she thought, "*how will I know when to act and when to question?*"

Beth arrived at her quiet, dark apartment. She began to wonder if living on her own was bravery or a hefty dose of stubbornness. Still unaware of her developing kinship with Rebekah, Beth wondered if her sister from the past would think her brave or just headstrong. Equally unaware of the skill of a good storyteller, Beth still had not realized Rose knew more about planting the seeds of change than she did about gardening. As Beth's eyes closed for the night, her last thought was, "*Am I brave enough to temper my rebellious spirit?*"

CHAPTER 13

S TILL mysteriously haunted by Rose's words, Beth's first thought on waking was, "The key to the whole thing is discernment. The ability to tell the difference between bravery and impetuousness."

Stirring her morning coffee in quiet introspection, Beth realized this was the first time in her life she'd allowed herself to ask difficult but honest questions.

The barrage began, "What is wisdom? What is discernment? What is tenacity?"

Beth knew somehow, even though living blocks away, Rose was working happily in her garden, knowing that the seeds of change were beginning to take root. After all, Rose did know that real change would only come after an individual understood and admitted the personal issues keeping them in a self-contained prison. It was one of the keys to her mysterious storytelling gift.

Answering client inquiries pleasantly was her first notice of a real change. Beth had come to realize the client's questions were more important than her time. Coffee time treats from the church bake sale and conversations with workmates seemed more relaxed and enjoyable. As always, eagerness to hear the next episode quickened her pace to Rose's front porch.

No sooner had she plunked herself down in the cushioned wicker chair than did Rose push through the front door, food tray in hand, and offer a hearty, "Hello Beth Chase."

"Hello, Rose Maddington," came the joyous reply.

"Hope you're hungry. I made ham and cheese with homemade relish," Pausing a moment while she lifted the cloth, "and, for dessert, chocolate peanut butter fudge.

"Looks delicious Rose."

"Sandwiches on my thick sourdough bread are pretty filling, so I only made a few."

"Sounds good to me. I'm famished. I didn't even stop to eat lunch today."

"Hard day, was it?"

"Not really. I wanted to get certain files in order before I left for the day."

"I see. It's nice to know that you love your job."

"Oh yes Rose, I do."

Supper took a little longer this evening as Beth had much to ask. She began, "Rose, I've been doing a lot of thinking lately."

"About what, dear?"

"My life. Listening to Rebekah's story has made me see that she had none of the freedoms women have today. Not only did she have the ability to take control of her life, but knew how to do it wisely."

"Those are good thoughts. No need to be anxious about them."

"When I compare myself to her and all that she did, I realized I've been stuck in the same level position my whole working life, just in different places. I move from one town to the next, just like my mother said, and she was right; I don't know what I am looking for, or where I'm going for that matter. Rebekah, well, she knew where she was going, and at a very young age, had accomplished so much in her life."

"Yes, she was very wise."

"Wisdom. That is something I ponder over. Where does one get it?"

Rose could not help herself. A little giggle snuck out. "I'm sorry dear. I don't mean to laugh at you. But I am very proud of you."

"Proud?"

"Yes. You see, asking yourself honest questions, thinking about how others handle things, that is one of the signs of blossoming wisdom."

"Really? What is the other?"

Rose replied with one shocking word, "God!"

Beth was silent. "God, what does God have to do with the story of Rebekah?" she thought.

Rose could see and feel Beth's dilemma. To comfort her student, she said, "Please do not worry, I have the greatest of confidence you will figure it out by the end of the story."

"Promise?"

"Yes, dear. After all, you have already made the first realization."

"And what is that?"

"You love your job."

Rose let it sink in before saying, "Now, let's finish eating, and then we can begin."

"Okay."

Beth's wisdom was beginning to blossom in that she did not pester Rose for more answers. After clearing the dishes and returning to the front porch, Beth sat and inhaled the aroma of jasmine the whirring ceiling fan was wafting upon her.

"Are you ready?"

Distracted momentarily, she answered, "Oh yes."

Closing her eyes, she listened to Rose's soothing southern voice transport her into that mystical time, four thousand years ago.

❦ ❦ ❦

As the weeks passed, the tale of Rebekah's ability to heal king Abimelech and the boldness displayed in his court had spread far and wide. Each week, visitors from the surrounding tribes appeared in the encampment seeking the healer woman. So well known in the land, some visitors even called her by name. Isaac did not mind as tribesmen always left expensive gifts for *his* beautiful wife. He was proud that people sought the skill and wisdom of *his* wife. He knew that many foreign women, fearing a difficult delivery, were brought to the red tent to ensure a safe birthing. Many women, who had purchased perfume, asked to be taught that craft, but Rebekah always declined. Shiphrah had warned her not to give away her knowledge to greed-driven desire. It was the same with her medications and ointments, except for the mustard seed poultice, which she freely gave, as *the fever* was the most common ailment among tribal women.

Faithful to her newfound God, healing, teaching, and storytelling consumed Rebekah's time and interest. At thirty years of age and married for fifteen years, she continued to complete all the tasks required of women in the home. Dutifully, she came to Isaac each time he called, which was usually at the full moon. After gathering vegetables on another typical day in the life of tribal women, Rebekah and Chana returned to the shade of her tent's canopy.

No longer able to refrain, Chana asked, "Rebekah, do you think God will bless you with a baby soon? It has been fifteen years, and Isaac is now fifty-five."

"I often pray that my blessing comes soon, but still, I wait."

Chana put down her peeling knife and looked beyond two women kneading bread by the clay oven.

A moment later, "Rebekah, look. Your husband's tent."

On the other side of Isaac's tent, two men, neighbors, were struggling with each other. The struggles turned to shouts. Loud, angry voices boomed throughout the encampment. As their voices continually grew louder, Isaac, tying his robe, stepped from his tent to ascertain the cause of the commotion.

"What, is all this shouting?" he bellowed.

Four men rushed to intervene, pulling the neighbors apart. Isaac seated himself under the tent canopy, crossed his legs, and waited. The struggling neighbors were hauled, kicking and shouting, past Isaac's tent. His face, overcome with displeasure, Isaac froze as he watched the four men force the quarreling neighbors to their knees in front of Rebekah and Chana.

Handing her basket of vegetables to Chana, Rebekah calmly asked, "Eiyan, Nissim, what on earth are you fighting about?"

Eiyan blurted first, "His cow! His stupid cow!"

"My cow not stupid! My cow good cow!" refuted Nissim.

"A cow?" Rebekah repeated in disbelief, "This dispute is about a cow?"

Eiyan replied, "His stupid cow broke my fence, ate my vegetables. Stupid cow."

Nissim remarked, "Your fence no good. Broke easy."

Angered, Eiyan responded, "My fence good. It is you! You do not feed cow!"

Nissim replied, "No! You are wrong! I feed my cow! She wants more; always wants more!"

In the distance, Isaac could not listen any longer. He stood and entered his tent.

Eiyan said, "It does not matter; you are responsible for your cow."

Nissim raised his fist at Eiyan and said, "I am—"

"Quiet! That's enough!" Rebekah commanded.

Their argument ceased immediately.

Rebekah continued, "Eiyan, you first. What did the cow damage?"

Sneering at Nissim, Eiyan said, "Cow broke my fence."

Nissim was quick to note, "No good fence—"

"Quiet!" Rebekah demanded.

Eiyan continued, "Ate beans, trampled carrots."

Nissim refuted, "Did not hurt carrots!"

Finger pointed directly into Nissim's face; Rebekah shouted, "I said quiet!"

Both men froze.

A moment of silence followed.

Rebekah began. "Here is my decision. Nissim, you will replace half a bushel of beans.

Quickly looking to Nissim, finger tapping her lips to quell his urge to argue. "You will also give one pitcher of fresh milk to Eiyan." Nissim grumbled as he did not like what he heard but held his tongue. "And, you will help Eiyan repair his fence."

Quick and sarcastic, Eiyan said, "I do not want his help!"

Chana whispered, "Do you think it wise for Nissim to help?"

Rebekah replied for all to hear. "The hungry animal only saw food. Nissim, you did not tie your cow well." Looking to Eiyan, Rebekah's voice was soft but firm, saying, "Eiyan, if you cannot forgive your neighbor, you are no better than that cow."

Rebekah motioned to the four men to allow Eiyan and Nissim to stand. The men rose and stood quietly with their heads to the ground waiting for Rebekah to speak.

"Now Eiyan, can you forgive?"

Eiyan nodded a slow yes.

"And Nissim?"

Imitating his neighbor, he nodded his head slowly.

"Now give your oath; the strife is over."

The two neighbors faced each other, put their right hands on the other's left shoulder, and said in unison, "Neighbor."

Eiyan and Nissim dropped their arms as Rebekah motioned for them to leave.

"Now go mend the fence," Rebekah said in a loving voice, "Oh, and Nissim," the neighbors turned, "Do a better job of tying your cow."

Chana turned to Rebekah and said, "May I ask a question?"

"Of course, Chana, of course."

"How did you gain so much wisdom? You are wiser than any man I have ever known. Even your husband commands no respect for his wisdom. When there is a ruling or decision made, women and men seek your words."

Rebekah knew precisely the source of her wisdom. "Chana, from a very early age, I was tutored by Shiphrah—"

Not intending to interrupt, Chana exclaimed, "What about your mother?"

Rebekah smiled and continued, "and my mother. Both wise women."

"Yes, they were," replied Chana.

"Not long after my third birthday, Shiphrah began, but, at such a young age, I had no idea she was training me. I was so overwhelmed with her wisdom by the age of five that was all I desired. I wanted to be just like her."

Chana thought back to the day she nearly died of *the fever*. It was Rebekah, at ten years of age, who had orchestrated healing.

Allowing Chana a moment to reflect, Rebekah continued. Shiphrah understood people and their motives. Her skill in making medicines and ointments had been passed down by the mystic who trained her. Good judgment comes from the wisdom to think before you speak." "Not like your husband," Chana injected. They both laughed. Continuing, Rebekah said, "It was then I learned to listen to the wind and the tones in a person's voice. So it was, when I heard Elyon's voice, I knew it was a voice to be heard. I learned much about Abraham's relationship with this God from Chesed." Chana interrupted again, "You have learned much." After sitting for a moment to enjoy each other's company, Rebekah finally stood and said, "And now, I must prepare for my husband. He asked me to come to him tonight."

Chana bowed and went to the women's tent to retrieve the perfumes and washcloths to assist Rebekah in preparing for the evening.

❖ ❖ ❖

"Beth, Beth," Rose said.

Beth opened her eyes wide, saying, "Rebekah had such wisdom."

"Yes, she did."

"And just like you said, she desired to learn all she could about the God of Abraham."

"Yes, she did," Rose agreed.

"How would I learn of these things?"

"Beth, do you know who the God of Abraham is? Where to read about him?"

Beth shook her head no, ever so timidly.

"Wait right here," Rose said as she bounded from her chair.

Ducking quietly into her house, she soon emerged, Bible in hand. Holding it out, she said, "This is it."

"A Bible?" Beth said, almost doubtingly.

"All the wisdom in the world is contained in this holy book."

"Really! Come on Rose, all the wisdom?"

Rose nodded and said, "You may have this one. I keep a box of Bibles on hand to give each person who hears one of my stories."

"You do?"

"Yes."

Beth felt the cover of the Bible then looked at Rose. "Where do I start?"

"Prehistory in Genesis, the law, the prophets, are all good beginnings. They are in what we call the Old Testament. I would suggest that a good place to start would be the New Testament. Just open it and explore; there will always be a message. When we finish your story, we will talk more about how to study scripture."

"Okay, I'll look through it and maybe start with the New Testament. Mother always recited verses from the gospels. I think that this weekend would be a good time to start."

Rose nodded. "Now, dear, it is nearly dark."

"Thank you, Rose. I will see you tomorrow."

Chapter 14

Beth left for work right on time, already anticipating today's story. Reflecting on the past few episodes, Beth realized how intelligent Rebekah must have been. Not only did she survive in an ancient, chauvinistic society; she did it on her terms. The saving grace for women like Shiphrah and Rebekah was their mysticism. The ability to heal was rare, and the ability to reason was a gift. Men were superstitious and would not challenge what they feared or did not understand. It took a great deal of craftiness to avoid being dominated by a man. It also took skill to manipulate a man into thinking your idea was his.

Beth did not see Rose working in the garden on her way to the office. She assumed Rose was busy in her house, probably making a new dessert. Beth entered the office at precisely nine o'clock.

"Morning Joyce, morning George," was the cheery greeting.

Intently involved with paperwork, "Good morning" was the only response.

Beth sat down and dug into her workload.

The day went well, and Beth signed two new clients to the insurance agency. Signing two clients on the same day had not happened since Beth moved to Sageville. With the task of organizing office files complete and two new clients signed, Beth related her newfound success to Rose's story of Rebekah. Finally, the first inkling of belief began to take hold. Beth still didn't understand how a four-thousand-year-old story could change a person, but she had to admit, it was making a difference in all aspects of her life.

Beth did not notice Joyce's head peering over the divider until, "Beth."

Oblivious to the time of day, she answered, "Yes?"

"Do you know what time it is?"

Beth's eyes snapped to the clock. It was five minutes past five. "Oh no! I'm late."

Joyce and George began to laugh as frantic Beth tidied her desk, grabbed her purse, and exited in record time.

Walking as quickly as possible, Beth had to catch her breath as she opened the gate to Rose's house. On the porch, next to the display of another lovely tray of delectable delights, Rose sat patiently waiting for Beth to rush up the steps and plunk herself down.

"Hello dear, I was worried."

"I'm sorry Rose, the time just got away from me."

"Busy day?"

"It was."

"Well, now you can relax. I made fresh-squeezed lemonade and two home grilled burgers."

"Burgers? That's a treat!"

During dinner, Rose filled Beth in on the search for a new pastor.

After taking a sip of lemonade, Rose said quietly, "The first candidate will be speaking this Sunday."

Beth knew what this meant, having told Rose she wouldn't mind going to hear one or two of the guest preachers. Strangely, it meant she'd have something over the weekend, even if it meant going to church.

"What time?" she asked without hesitation.

"We could meet in front of the church at 10:45."

"Okay, sounds good."

Rose's face beamed. With a reason to get Beth to come to her church, she said, "Shall we begin?"

"Yes please."

Beth closed her eyes and felt the tension slip away from her body. Returning to the ancient world, Beth found herself in Rebekah's tent.

❊ ❊ ❊

Chana was busy helping Rebekah dress for dinner. Chesed sent word that there would be three Hivite guests attending, and Isaac requested Rebekah make an appearance. Not particularly fond of meeting men from other regions, it was essential to appease her husband, especially in the eyes of other tribal leaders. Now at thirty-five years of age, she wanted to keep Isaac in good spirits hoping that he would soon father a child with her.

"Use this shawl," Chana suggested, "It is lovely."

"I remember when Shiphrah gave it to me. I was only twelve at the time. She said it would be for special occasions. I love how she interwove the colors of teal, jade, and dark blue. Shiphrah certainly knew how to make such exquisite things."

"It is beautiful, and the colors enhance the green in your eyes."

Putting her hand on Chana's, Rebekah said, "Thank you, Chana. Thank you for everything. You are a good friend."

Before Chana could respond, a voice from outside the tent called, "Rebekah, Isaac sent me to escort you to his tent."

"One moment Chesed."

Gathering her long linen robe in her hands, she walked out and took Chesed's arm. Pulling Isaac's tent curtain back, Chesed bowed as Rebekah entered. Rebekah beheld Isaac seated at the head of a long low table, covered with fruit, bread, olive oil, and lamb kebabs. Three Hivite men sat around the table on colorful plush cushions. Bayla and Rina knelt on either side of Isaac. Two spaces remained empty. Six wine goblets awaited the delectable nectar. Rebekah heard the men muttering between themselves but could not understand their conversation. She did, however, have a good idea of what they were saying.

Allowing ample time for the guests to behold his beautiful wife, Isaac finally said, "Come; sit at my table."

After Chesed had aided Rebekah to take her place, he stood behind the first Hivite to make the proper introductions.

Chesed said, "Rebekah, this is Zevlum."

Rebekah nodded.

Moving behind the next guest, he said, "This is Tamir.

Rebekah nodded.

At the next, "This is Oren."

Rebekah nodded a third time.

Full of pride, Isaac boasted, "My friends, this is my wife, Rebekah."

The Hivite men could not take their eyes off such a beautiful woman.

Ignoring their lingering glances, Rebekah motioned for Chesed to sit beside her.

Getting right to the point, she asked politely, "You are Hivites, yes?"

Zebulun was slow to reply, "Yes," while staring into her eyes.

"And may I ask, why have you come?"

Isaac motioned for Bayla and Rina to serve the wine.

Her boldness took the Hivite men by surprise. They were not accustomed to a woman asking such direct questions, especially only moments after the introduction.

Tamir thought to himself, "*She did not ask her husband's permission to speak.*"

Zebulun, still gazing into Rebekah's eyes, replied, "We have come on behalf of our king to ask Isaac to join with us in a war against Husam, the Canaanite."

Oren's voice betrayed the insult as he added, "Husam's shepherds come uninvited and water their sheep at our wells."

Remaining polite, Rebekah said, "You do not need my opinion for such a decision. Isaac is capable."

"Yes, and Isaac has agreed to join us," Oren was quick to respond.

Rebekah wished to end this conversation and return to her tent. She did not want to eat a meal with these particular strangers, so she asked, "Then why am I here?"

Tamir, clearing his throat, said, "Even we Hivites have heard of the fire-haired woman from the other side of the flood. We desire to hear your thoughts."

Zebulun interjected, "Do you agree with your husband?"

Thinking this was a situation that she would like to resolve quickly, she said, "It is not that I agree or disagree with my husband. I disagree with going to war over a well."

Considering what they had just heard, the three men looked at each other to decide what to say next. The shock of a woman not agreeing with her husband had left them speechless.

Rebekah continued undaunted, "You men know full well Husam is only looking for a reason to enlarge his territory."

Tamir nodded, "This is true."

Rebekah took her time to consider how to word her next statement. She thought, "*How can I insult one man without overtly insulting all the men?*" She began in a soft but confident voice. "You are reasonable men, but what you must consider is King Husam's arrogant Canaanite ego, his perverted sense of male pride."

The men looked at one another again. This woman was indeed unlike any they had encountered in the past.

To clarify what he heard, Oren asked, "Pride? How does pride help?"

Rebekah continued, "Have your king send an emissary to Husam. Invite him to use your wells whenever he wishes because you value his friendship."

The three men looked at each other and nodded in agreement.

Zevulun laughed, "Ah, I see. His perverted ego will not allow him to go to war."

"That is correct," Rebekah affirmed.

Isaac smiled, saying, "Thank you, my wife. I knew if there were a way to avoid a war, you would find it.

Rebekah smiled and replied, "You are most welcome. Now, may I leave you to your guests?" Glancing disapprovingly at Bayla and Rina, in their sheer colorful dresses, "I am sure you men have much to discuss?"

"Yes, of course," Isaac replied.

Chesed rose immediately and offered his hand to Rebekah. Still unable to take their eyes from Rebekah, the three men rose and bowed as she left the tent. Returning to her tent, Rebekah and Chana enjoyed a modest supper together. Afterward, Chana brought Rebekah a new clay jar of perfume.

"Let us see what you think," Chana said.

"And who mixed this one?" she asked.

"Sadie. She is trying so hard to perfect the mix."

Wafting the aroma to her nose, Rebekah commented, "I think she might want to add a bit of the quince flower petal and a touch more of the wild olive blossom."

"I will tell her how to mix them the next time we go to the women's tent."

"Yes, and that time is coming soon, Chana spoke sadly."

Taking a deep breath, Rebekah closed her eyes and said, "Oh, I so wish for the day when I do not have to go. I want a child, Chana, child to raise in the knowledge of God. My prayers are frequent, but still, I am barren."

"Oh Rebekah, you must keep the faith. You have the promise of Elyon."

Rebekah combed her red hair and thought about the infant she would bear when God believed the time was right and wondered out loud, "How much longer LORD; how much longer?"

Then, much to her surprise, Chesed's voice beckoned once again, "Rebekah, your husband calls."

Joining Isaac and Chesed at the fire pit, they watched as the three Hivite men rode back to their king with Rebekah's advice.

"Your guests return home?" Rebekah noted.

"Yes. They liked your words Rebekah."

"Thank you."

Chesed added, "You have a rare gift, Rebekah."

"Thank you, Chesed. As do you."

Moving closer to Chesed, Isaac whispered, "I wish to speak with my wife."

"Yes, master," as he moved away immediately.

Leaning to Rebekah, Isaac noted, "Tonight, the moon is full."

Surprised by the romantic tone in his voice, Rebekah readily answered, "Yes?"

"You will come to my tent; tonight!"

Unable to refrain from asking with a touch of sarcasm, she replied, "Will you be alone?"

Isaac did not react to her question, but waited a moment, then said, "You need to bring forth my son."

Rebekah's heart pounded with hope. She joyfully asked, "God has spoken to you?"

"No! Does not matter. I want an heir."

"Perhaps God no longer speaks to you as you no longer listen," slipped from her mouth.

Isaac grumbled but did not respond to her remark. He wanted to have Rebekah this night. He looked back at her and said, "I see God continues to speak with you."

Assuming her now common, hands-on-hips stance, she looked Isaac right in the eye and said, "Yes, and I intend to keep listening."

Isaac turned and walked to his tent. He turned once more and looked at Rebekah. "Tonight!" he commanded before entering his tent.

Floating into her tent, Rebekah's wistful smile said it all.

Chana asked, "Rebekah?"

"Yes, Chana. Tonight is the night. I can feel it. Bring my best perfume, Jasmine. All must be perfect."

❈ ❈ ❈

"Beth," Rose whispered as she touched Beth's arm.

"Oh no! Rose! Don't stop! They were about to go inside his tent! I just know it!"

Rose laughed at how engrossed Beth had become.

"You can't make me wait! O Rose, this could be the night! Rebekah is going to Isaac's tent! I mean, she might become a mother, finally!"

Rose was laughing so hard that tears ran down her cheeks.

"Now dear," still laughing, "We can't rush things."

"But Rose," Beth moaned.

"Just wanted to be sure you would come back tomorrow!" and laughed again.

"Oh! That is mean!"

Putting her hand on Beth's arm, she said, "I haven't laughed this much in a very long time. I had no idea you would be so anxious to get to that particular night."

"You must tell me! Is this going to be the night?"

Laughing again, Rose said, "You will find out tomorrow."

"Rose! She is thirty-five years old! She has waited for twenty years!"

"Yes, she has waited twenty years, and you can wait one more night to find out."

"Rose! This is cruel and unusual punishment!"

Rose laughed again. "You will hear more tomorrow."

Beth didn't know whether to be mad or laugh with Rose. Resolved that this was the end of storytelling for the night, Beth said, "You like teasing me, don't you?"

"I'm sorry dear, but I've never had so much fun teasing anyone as I do you."

Imitating Rebekah, Beth sat back, crossed her arms, and uttered, "Humph."

Standing from her wicker chair, she said, "Oh, all right. Have it your way." Imitating the pout, "I will see you tomorrow."

Thinking she was out of earshot, Beth began laughing. With her excellent hearing, Rose could hear the laughter. Rose had told her stories to many people over the years, but on hearing the laughter, she said to herself, "*I think Beth and I will still be good friends long after the story finishes.*"

Beth couldn't remember the last time she brought laughter into someone's life. She decided to have a cup of tea and look through the Bible Rose had given to her.

Picking the book from the table, Beth said to herself, "Where to start . . . hmm, Rose said anywhere." Beth let the book fall open and read aloud the first line her eyes fell upon, "Come unto me, all ye that labor and are heavy laden, and I will give you rest . . . Wow! Rose was right. I can't believe it."

CHAPTER 15

MESMERIZED at how that passage had spoken directly to her, Beth couldn't get it out of her mind. Rebekah had come up with a simple solution to a complex problem and the wisdom to present her suggestion tactfully. Beth had developed a policy plan to resolve a small business concern but did not use tact. She went over the office manager's head. She presented the proposal directly to the regional manager, and it almost got her fired. Brushing her teeth, putting on her pajamas, climbing into bed, "*Come unto me*," kept running through her mind. Remembered her mother's faith in prayer, she thought, "*Maybe mother was right about this God thing?*" Tired of thinking, Beth fell into a deep sleep.

Sleeping soundly through the night, she awoke earlier than planned. Dressing for work, making coffee, and eating one of Ethel's cookies, the questions came in rapid succession: "*Would Rebekah have a baby? Would the pregnancy be difficult? Would the child be a son, as God had said? Rebekah was the midwife; would deliver the baby?*" Beth knew delivering a baby was much more problematic when a woman was old, but what about then. "*If there were complications? Who would be able to resolve the problem?*" she asked herself.

The barrage of thoughts did not stop. Beth wondered about her plans. Would she meet someone, find a husband, have children? She certainly hadn't met anyone in Sageville. Maybe a bigger city was the answer? No, she didn't like big cities. Never excited about going to places like New York or Chicago, Beth preferred small towns. Her parents thought city life was terrific. They thrived in Atlanta, where Beth grew up, but Beth never felt at home there. What about Sageville? Should she stay, move again, find a new career? How would she know? She wasn't getting any younger. If she remained in Sageville, how and where would she meet someone? Beth poured her coffee and glanced at her breakfast table. She had one cookie left on a saucer sitting next to the Bible Rose had given to her. Without thinking, she placed her thumb almost in the middle and opened the book.

"Hmm… Proverbs? Commit your work unto the Lord, and your plans will be established." Instantly Beth had goosebumps. She repeated the verse to herself out loud. "Commit your work unto the Lord, and your plans will be established. Proverbs 16:3? "Commit your work to the Lord?" She said aloud once again. How would she do it if she was to do this and commit her work to the Lord? She would ask Rose if they had time today. No, she decided she absolutely would ask Rose, and she would do so while they ate dinner.

Beth looked at the clock and knew she had to finish her coffee and hurry to work.

Entering the office to the welcoming words of Joyce's, "Good morning, Beth, I brought a lemon pound cake if you want some with your coffee."

"Thank you. Maybe later." Beth put her purse away and looked at her desk, and mumbled, "Who put these files on my—"

"Did you say something?" George asked.

"Oh, no. Just muttering."

"I put those new files on your desk this morning. Those are clients who left messages asking for you. I contacted a few of them, trying to help you out, but they said they preferred to talk to you personally."

"Okay, thanks, George." "That explains the pile of folders."

"Yup," was the response from good ole' George.

Beth opened the first folder and made the phone call. It was a lovely lady she'd recently signed to a new home policy. They talked for a full thirty minutes, and phone calls set the workload for the remainder of the day. Not remembering most of the people, they were genuinely interested in how Beth was getting on in Sageville. Unbeknown to Beth, when you live in a small town, everyone knows your business. Her weekday evenings on Rose Maddington's front porch had become the talk of the town. By five o'clock, Beth realized she had truly enjoyed the day visiting with her clients.

As usual, she found Rose sitting in her wicker chair, colorfully dressed, with a perfectly matched scarf, next to a tray of gourmet treats.

Walking through the garden gate, with a voice overflowing with enthusiasm, she called out, "Hello Rose."

"Hello Beth, you seem extra happy today."

Scanning the array of crackers, cheeses, fruits, and deviled eggs, Beth answered, "Yup, sure am."

Rose replied, "Well then, I hope you are happy with an assortment of appetizers."

"Wow! They look amazing! You must have spent all day making these treats."

"I had more time in the kitchen today. Not as much gardening to do right now, but it will soon be time to do my fall planting."

"Sounds like a lot of work."

"I do love it though."

Beth took a few of the tasty appetizers and placed them on her small glass plate.

"Speaking of work . . did you have a good day?"

"Yes. I did, as a matter of fact, but I need to ask you a question."

"Oh?"

"It's about a verse in Proverbs."

Rose placed her hand on Beth's. "I'm so glad you are reading your Bible."

"I've only read a little, but this morning I read a verse in Proverbs that said something about committing yourself to work for the LORD so plans will be established."

That is my favorite Proverb Beth, but it says to commit your work unto the LORD, and your plans will be established."

"What does it mean?"

"Are you wondering about committing or establishing?"

"I was thinking more about my work. Why would I commit my work unto the LORD?"

Rose smiled at Beth's naivety. "First of all, in the eyes of the LORD, all work is honorable. So it is that your thoughts and your plans need be honorable as well. When you commit your career, your goals, and your thoughts before God, it demonstrates that you have the faith to trust in God. When you do, God will help establish your plans.

"How?"

"By following what God wants all humanity to do. It includes things like caring for others, and it establishes one's righteousness."

"Others."

"Yes, if your work is honorable, it will not take advantage of others or prosper you at another's expense. God does not want you to live in poverty but does not want you to live the good life at the expense of the poor. When your work is honorable, then it will be established as Godly."

"So, it doesn't mean going to work for the church?"

Rose couldn't contain her chuckle as she said, "Good heavens no."

"But, then what about the planning part?"

Rose sat back in her chair, thinking of the best response. "Have you ever been in a predicament and not able to figure how to get out of it."

"Yes," answered Beth sadly, "and those predicaments have not turned out very well, I'm afraid?"

Rose asked softly, "Did you ever think of asking God for help?"

Beth answered with a puzzled, "No. Why would I do that?"

"I will tell you." Beth sat back to listen. Rose continued. "When I am in a dilemma, not sure what to do, I pray. I turn to God for help, and from out of nowhere, a light goes on, and the answer appears clear as crystal?"

"But Rose, your faith is so strong."

"Beth, all you need is faith the size of a mustard seed, and you will be surprised at how problems seem to resolve themselves. When they do, you will understand the Proverb. It is like a light going on in your mind, and you will know the LORD is with you."

"Really?"

"Yes, dear. Commit the things you do unto the LORD and you will be surprised how a solution will appear. It will set your mind will be at peace.

"To tell you the truth Rose, I've always felt like I've been struggling within, you know, not at peace.

Rose was silent for a moment, trying to keep her emotions from bubbling over in the form of a big smile. Beth was changing, and they both knew it.

Finally, Rose said, "We'll talk about this more, but frankly, I'm surprised you didn't come anxiously anticipating to hear more about Rebekah."

"Oh, my goodness, yes!" exclaimed Beth. "I am anxious to hear if Rebekah will finally have her baby!"

Knowing what was coming, Rose chuckled within and managed to ask calmly, "How about a little strawberry shortcake first?"

Beth enjoyed every morsel of her dessert. After helping Rose with the dishes, she sat back in her wicker chair. Magically transported into Rebekah's tent, she hoped this would be the night.

❀ ❀ ❀

Rebekah could feel tonight was the night, and everything must be perfect. Chana set up the animal skin tub and arranged for pitchers of warm
water. Standing in the tub, Chana washed Rebekah as if she were a princess. Delighted to prepare her mistress, Chana dried, oiled, and jasmine
perfumed Rebekah. Then combed and beaded her hair. There was to be
no doubt in Isaac's mind that his wife was presenting herself just for him.
When all bodily preparations had been made, Chana stepped in front of
Rebekah and held out the most delicate white linen gown she'd ever seen.
The bodice plunged far too low to wear in public, but for tonight, it was
perfect.

"The very one. You know me well."

"I've never seen a nightdress fit so perfectly. You will have to wear
a shawl."

"Yes, it will certainly get his attention when I drop it to the ground."

Both women laughed, that naughty laugh.

"Fits just like the day Shiphrah made it for you."

"Yes. It is so beautiful. Pity Isaac was too interested in other things
to notice on our wedding night."

"Rebekah, I believe tonight he will notice, and you will be blessed."

Rebekah hugged Chana and said, "Yes. I think you are right. I have
committed my plan unto the LORD and trust it will be established."

Chana opened a small box on the table. "Jewelry my lady?"

"I would like the earrings Isaac gave to me for our wedding."

"I've never seen you wear them since that night."

Rebekah sighed. "I did not have much chance. Isaac did not call me
for some time, and when he did, I did not feel he had the right intentions."

Clipping the earrings to Rebekah's lobes, "You look stunning. What
man would not want to give you a child?"

Rebekah smiled. "Chana, I believe God's plan will be established in
me tonight."

Chana laughed, "I know Isaac will have his way."

Patting Chana's hand, she giggled, "You're bad."

Suddenly, Chana said, "Wait, one last thing—"

"What Chana, what?"

"A flower for your hair."

"Oh Chana, would you?"

"Of course," and ran out.

Chana returned with the most fragrant flower anyone had ever seen. Carefully placing the white jasmine flower in Rebekah's hair, she announced, "You are ready princess, I shall call Chesed to escort you."

"Thank you, my loyal friend."

After calling Chesed, Chana placed the shawl over Rebekah's shoulders and held back the tent curtain. Rebekah's long red hair fell over her shoulders and was enhanced by the white jasmine. Standing with her colorful shawl draping over her long white nightdress, Chesed beheld a vision of ethereal beauty. He stood speechless for a moment before offering his arm.

Isaac, for some reason, could not subdue his growing restlessness. He paced the floor, sat on his bed, tried imitating what he thought was the posture of a Pharaoh, but nothing helped. Recalling his wedding night, this was unlike the expectation of pure carnal pleasure. This feeling was like; he didn't know. Thinking to himself, "*For twenty years, all I've ever desired was the pleasure, but now, why do I feel like it is the first night?*" Thinking of his own mother's barrenness, he remembered how his father spoke of the years Sarah waited, barren and heartbroken. He lowered his head and did something he had not done in many years; he prayed, "*God of my father, God of our people, I come to you on behalf of my wife. You alone know when the time will come for her to conceive a child to carry on Abraham's line. O LORD God of thy servant Abraham, hear my plea this night and allow this blessing to come to pass.*"

At that moment, Chesed's voice interrupted Isaac's prayer. "Master Isaac, your wife wishes to enter."

Pulling the tent curtain open, Isaac swept his arm, inviting his wife to enter. "Please," was his only word. Before letting the curtain fall, he said, "Thank you Chesed, that will be all."

Isaac took Rebekah's hand and led her to plush cushions intentionally arranged for this evening. Wanting Isaac to remain in control of the evening, Rebekah was silent. She accepted a silver goblet of wine with a pleasant, "Thank you."

Sitting beside Rebekah, Isaac sipped his wine from a matching goblet. She knew something had come over him when he said, "Even the moon and stars are no match for your beauty." His compliment roused feelings long since forgotten. Time seemed to stop for Rebekah as they enjoyed their wine and nibbling on, what we would call, appetizers. Finally, Isaac stood, offered his hand, and led her to their marital bed. Rebekah allowed him to disrobe and lie down before she stood before him.

Slowly pushing the thin straps from her shoulders, she let the gown drop to the floor. Isaac was speechless as Rebekah nestled next to him, surrendering fully to his every advance. Tonight was the night for which she had prayed. Breathtaking, full of unimaginable love, it was the night of every woman's dream. In all of their twenty years of marriage, Isaac had only taken, never given. Other nights felt rushed, forceful, demanding. This night felt giving. "He is giving me my son," she thought to herself, "and I shall welcome his every advance."

Rebekah felt as if this were her wedding night. It should have been the feeling experienced on her wedding night, but now, that was in the past. Isaac's warm embrace was as it should be. Tender moments of silence interspersed with romantic conversation. Soft flickering lamplight reflected from glowing faces lost in time and space.

Nearing dawn, "Rebekah," Isaac spoke softly, "why did you leave your family and come to be my wife?"

Pausing to give thought to her answer, "It was something, a feeling inside me. I did not know it at the time, but the God of your father had chosen me."

"Does this god speak with you?"

"Yes," . . . but Isaac, it is not, this god, as there is only one God and LORD."

Rebekah could see the concern in Isaac's eyes.

"My son, will I have a son? It has been so very long," he asked softly.

"When you asked me to come to your tent tonight, I could feel tonight was to be the night. It was as if I could hear the voice of God in the wind."

"God approves of our love tonight?"

"Yes, my love."

Rebekah's words took Isaac by surprise. It was the first time in twenty years she had called Isaac "my love."

"Finally, I am to have a—"

Rebekah placed her finger on Isaac's lips and said, "Enough talk for one night. The next time I go to the women's tent, it will be to stand on the birthing bricks."

Isaac embraced his wife once again as she yielded willingly to his amorous advance. This night had been all about warmth and passion. Isaac had not tried to dominate, and Rebekah could feel his desire to share, not take. Not long before the sun broke forth its early morning light, Rebekah fell off into a blissful sleep.

❊ ❊ ❊

"Beth, wake up, dear," Rose called.

Beth opened her eyes, speechless at first.

After a moment, "Oh Rose—"

"It was a wonderful part of the story, don't you think?" injected Rose.

"It was more beautiful than I'd imagined. The fragrance, the flickering light, the whispering between lovers, I could hear it all. After all those years, they finally shared true love."

Rose tried to explain, "It's hard to understand why, for so many years, Rebekah and Isaac were not as loving. I have wondered about that often. It seems like it was a love-hate relationship with both so determined, or maybe, the oldest of all human frailties, hard-headedness?"

All Beth could do was laugh and confess, "I can certainly relate to that."

"Well, if you remember, the God of Abraham said the mother of this special child would have to be determined enough not to be dominated by any man."

"Yes, and she certainly was that and more."

"Yes dear, she was."

"But Rose, love, true love, changed all that, even with Isaac."

"Very good Beth. That is all God has ever asked humanity to do; love, in all its many aspects."

"Wait a minute."

"What dear?"

"I still don't know. Did God finally bless her with a baby?"

Rose looked at Beth and said, "Why was she chosen?"

"Yes, yes, I know, but did she have to wait any longer?"

"Beth, you know what I'm about to say?"

"I know," then sadly, "You'll tell me tomorrow."

Rose laughed, "No dear. Tomorrow is Saturday. You will not hear what happens until Monday."

"Monday!" Beth declared. "Oh Rose, not all weekend, again?"

"Yes, dear, all weekend."

Remembering she would see Rose on Sunday, Beth said, "Rose, I know where the church is, but what kind of church is it? I have never seen a sign, except for the name."

Rose smiled. "It is just like the sign says, Good Shepherd Christian Church. It's not Catholic or Baptist or any other denomination, for that matter. It used to be a Baptist church many years ago. After prayerful deliberation, the congregation decided a church with a specific denominational slant was not what they wanted."

"That's interesting."

"We all agreed that an open church for all who want to come was the kind of church best suited for our community."

"Good, because I want to come."

"I'll see you there?" and there it was, the magical wink.

Stepping off the porch, Beth looked back and waved goodbye. "See ya at church."

CHAPTER 16

B ETH had mixed feelings as she poured her first cup of coffee Saturday morning. Happy for the weekend, but sad for the two days wait. Rebekah's story was creating a burning desire for knowledge. Not just story knowledge, but the awareness of God working in the lives of people, both then and now. Picking up the Bible Rose had given her, sitting in her comfy chair, coffee in hand, she thought, "*Maybe this will alleviate the two-day torture.*" Opening the Bible to the first chapter of Matthew, Beth was impressed that people could pass down such a long genealogy from memory in a world without ledgers and computers. Reflecting, she thought, "*I know who my grandparents were, but that's it. Humm, better start reading.*"

Beth finished reading mid-morning and decided to go shopping for groceries. After spending some time in the baking section, she opted for the frozen dessert section. Walking home with only one bag of groceries, she realized the reason she'd not had to buy much food lately was because of all those delightful dinners at chez Rose.

Her thoughts were broken by a familiar voice shouting, "O Beth, see you at church tomorrow."

There she was, watering her flowers.

"Okay. Yes. See you there," Beth called back.

Returning to her apartment, she put the cold items in the refrigerator and the cans in the cupboard. Lunch consisted of a tasteless pre-made ham and cheese on a bun purchased from the in-store deli. Saturday afternoon found Beth feeding a handful of quarters into the apartment's one washing machine. The frozen turkey dinner was at least tasty, the black and white re-run was funny, and one more chapter of Matthew ended her day.

Sunday morning found Beth still uneasy about going to church but was comforted by the thought Rose would be by her side, just in case. Although, she couldn't think of a *just-in-case* scenario. Beth remembered that her mother always wore a dress and made her wear one as well. As a child, she always amused herself as she dressed, saying, "Must be part of the uniform," and then laughing. She had no doubt Rose would be wearing a typical southern Sunday dress. Probably complete with pearls and maybe even a hat. Her mother never wore a hat. Stirring a large dollop of cream into her coffee, Beth wondered if Rebekah would finally have her baby in the next episode.

Then her self-inflicted barrenness dawned, "Wonder if I'll ever have one?"

This thought did not sadden Beth as she had never really known true love.

Opening her closet and looking at her aging wardrobe, she asked herself, "Whatever will I wear?"

Finding a suitable summer dress, she mumbled, "Needs ironing."

Dusting off the old squeaky ironing board, Beth began ironing clothes she hadn't worn in years. With plenty of time before church, she decided to prepare a corned beef sandwich on rye bread and a salad for her Sunday night dinner, all the while thinking, "*Wish I could cook like Rose.*" Sandwiches were the limit of her culinary expertise,

After her coffee and raisin bread breakfast, Beth showered and got dressed. With still a half hour until she needed leave for church, Beth decided a leisurely Sunday morning stroll to church might be nice. She could surprise Rose by arriving early.

It was to no avail. Rose, in her Sunday go-to-meeting outfit, a teal and blue colored southern skirt, pearls, and a hat, was waiting on the church steps.

"Hello Beth, so glad you could come." Rose said, "Come on up and meet my friend Myrtle." At the top of the steps, "Beth, dear, meet Myrtle."

"Nice to meet you Myrtle."

"Nice to meet you, Beth. Say, didn't I see you at the bake sale?"

"Yes, and your coffee cake, um, so delicious!"

"Why thank you, dear."

Myrtles' portly size evinced the fact she loved food.

As the organ sounded, Rose asked, "Shall we go inside?"

Memories of her mother talking with everyone on the way to her pew surfaced as Rose, in perfect imitation, did the same. Each hymnal contained the day's program. No sooner had Rose seated herself, program in hand, she was reading the pastor's bio. Myrtle did the same. Beth took her time, still taking in her surroundings. When she opened her program, the photo of the pastor, his wife, and baby jumped out at her. "This is an upscale church," she thought, "photos." Once the hymn sing began, Beth fumbled her way through the hymnal to find the right page. Quietly singing along with Rose and Myrtle felt good; she was with friends and felt safe.

The pastor's voice was bold as he delivered a sermon that made people cringe. He seemed upset at how too many people felt the Bible was out of touch with today's world. Giving three examples, he related them to scripture. Beth gave up trying to find the passages.

On the way to the fellowship hall, Rose asked, "Well?"

"He did keep my attention through the whole service, but I have to admit, he frightened me a little," answered Beth.

Beth had thought the bake sale was terrific, but when she saw the array of food spread across multiple tables, she touched Rose's arm and said, "Is this for real? Wow!"

"We have church luncheons about once a month, or when we have important events, such as interviewing a new pastor," was Myrtle's proud reply.

"My goodness, this is a lot of food."

"Yes, it is dear," Myrtle said, pushing Beth quickly into the line.

Rose whispered, "Don't ever try and hold Myrtle back from the food line."

Beth, Rose, and Myrtle sat at a small table where Rose introduced Beth to each person who walked by. *"I'll never remember all those names,"* she thought. However, she'd not soon forget the variety of dishes and desserts. Listening intently, Beth enjoyed hearing Myrtle and Rose chat about their church's history and past preachers who graced their pulpit.

"Want to go to the dessert table?" Rose asked.

"Oh Rose, I am about to pop."

"They will wrap up whatever you want to take with you."

"Now that I can do."

"Okay, dear. Help yourself to the desserts. Myrtle and I want to speak with the committee members, but I will see you tomorrow?"

"Yes, of course, and I hope it's time for the baby."

Rose smiled and said, "See you tomorrow."

After wrapping three large slices of chocolate cake, Beth left the fellowship hall.

Beth arrived at the office early Monday morning and placed two slices of chocolate cake beside the coffee machine.

Returning to her desk, cake and coffee in hand, she overheard George calling to Joyce. "Hey Joyce, come see what Beth brought in."

It was Monday, and that meant she would have more calls to answer. Fridays were generally slow, but on Mondays, people began calling about insurance questions they had been bothered with over the weekend.

"Hey Beth," George asked, "How's your story going?"

"It's getting better and better!"

Joyce laughed and said, "Just wait until the end. She will get you."

"What do you mean? You have both said something unusual happens on the last day of the story. Come on, give me a hint."

George looked at Joyce as she looked back and rolled her eyes. Together they shook their heads and said, "Nope."

"Not gonna happen," George added.

"Let's just say it makes all the time you spent listening to the story worthwhile," Joyce assured.

Beth shook her head and turned back to her work. The phone rang. It was another potential client. After talking with the new client for forty-five minutes, Beth hung up and emailed him the necessary paperwork.

"Beth," Joyce said.

"Yes?"

"Do you realize that is your fifth new client in the last four days and the twentieth new client this month?"

"Oh? I haven't been counting." The truth is, Beth never paid attention to how many new clients anyone in the office signed for policies. She was only concerned about making sure the paperwork was complete and accurate.

As the senior agent, Joyce was the office manager and stayed in constant contact with the regional office. It was the manager of the regional office who brought Beth's performance to Joyce's attention. She hadn't told Beth, but the regional manager had nominated her for "Employee of the Year." Joyce nor George had never been recognized, and Joyce doubted if an agent from the small town of Sageville would ever win the coveted prize. There were no plaques in the small office, except for the gratuitous acknowledgment of the agency's sponsorship of a little league baseball team.

When the regional manager called Joyce on Thursday to ask about Beth, Joyce told him Beth kept her head down and was the workhorse of the office. All of Beth's reviews had been exceptional. Along with the distinction of "Employee of the Year," if selected, Beth would be given a nice bonus and receive a hefty raise. Joyce and George decided not to say anything to Beth until it was official. Then, it would be their job to get Beth to the annual regional recognition dinner in Atlanta. At precisely five o'clock, Beth took her purse and left for Rose's house. She was beyond anxious to hear today's episode.

Rose waved as Beth opened the garden gate. Ascending the porch steps, Beth beheld two heaping plates of chicken salad.

"Looks amazing Rose, as always."

"I was hungry for a mandarin chicken salad and strawberry short-cake dessert."

"Rose, how do you do it? Busy in the garden all day, fix a scrumptious dinner, and still anxious to tell me this wonderful story, and you do it five days in a row."

"You know storytelling and cooking give me a purpose in life," then she winked that magical wink. Changing the subject. "Did you enjoy church yesterday?"

"It was interesting."

What did you think of the candidate?"

"His message made me uncomfortable, but I guess that is what preachers do."

"Not exactly Beth. His message should have been about hope."

"He was like the pastor of my mother's church. I was able to relate but felt uncomfortable."

"That is what Myrtle said this morning on the phone. Now, remember what you thought of him when we consider the next one. Are you ready for dessert?"

"The next one?"

"Why yes, you have to come and compare."

Beth thought to herself, "*What have I gotten myself into . . . stories, now a church. Oh my.*"

Breaking her thought, Rose offered, "Strawberry shortcake?"

"Oh dessert . . . yes please."

After clearing the dishes, Rose asked, "Shall we begin?"

"Yes, please," Beth said and closed her eyes.

Inhaling the aroma of jasmine, Beth found herself in Rebekah's tent. Chana was speaking.

❊ ❊ ❊

When the time came for Rebekah to begin her cycle, she did not have to go to the red tent. It was the same a month later. With her time complete, Chana entered Rebekah's tent and said, "We've missed you, Rebekah. It has been two months. I know as we share the same cycle." Standing directly in front of her mistress, Chana watched a smile form on Rebekah's lips.

"Rebekah," she asked, "are you—"

"Have any of the women said anything?" Rebekah inquired quickly.

"No one has noticed since you go there often to make perfume."

Rebekah took Chana's hands, instructing, "You mustn't say a thing to anyone. Isaac must be the first to know I bear his child. He must be the one to make the announcement."

Still holding hands, Chana let out a soft yelp, jumped up and down, danced around in a circle, saying, "Oh Rebekah! I knew it; I just knew it. When you did not come to the tent the first time, I hoped you had been blessed.

"Shhh! Not so loud dear. And Chana, you are more to me than a servant. You are my true friend."

Hugging Rebekah, she said, "Thank you . . . Oh, Rebekah, your parents would be so proud if they knew."

"Yes. But you must remember not to say anything to anyone."

"When will you tell Isaac?"

"I must ask Chesed to tell Isaac I need to see him."

"Today?"

"Yes, this evening."

"Should we prepare you to go?"

"Yes, please. I do not know if Isaac will want me to stay, but I will prepare."

Chana hugged Rebekah once more. "I will get the best perfume, oh, and your gown; what gown?"

"Perhaps something with a little more room at the top. I am, uh, rather sore."

"Yes. It happens with growth. Soon, you will be showing, and everyone will know. I will hurry. I know the robe you should wear. I will find it when I return with the perfume."

Chana vanished, and Rebekah sat cross-legged on her bed, contemplating. For the first time in her life, she was not sure of what to say what words to use. Finally, after twenty years, she knew the child within would be the one to receive the blessing. Of course it was a son, God had promised. She wondered what advice Shiphrah would offer in this situation? Should she take her time, tease, or maybe erupt straight away and shock Isaac.

Then a barrage of thoughts flashed through her mind; "*O dear, I do not want his heart to stop. How did Sarah tell Abraham?*" No one knew. "*If only I could ask Shiphrah.*"

Bursting into the tent, Chana exclaimed, "I found this one," holding up a clay jar marked *jasmine*, interrupted Rebekah's thoughts.

Inhaling the aroma, Rebekah said, "You know me well. It is my favorite."

"Mine too. Now, you wait here. I will be right back."

Rebekah could not figure out where Chana was going. She only hoped Chana's exuberance would not let the cat out of the bag, so to speak, as Rebekah knew that all women were inherently suspicious of everything. If Isaac did not have the honor of making the announcement, it would be a very great slight to his authority as a chieftain.

Chana returned, holding in outstretched hands one solitary white jasmine blossom.

In a voice soft and loving, "For your hair."

"Thank you, Chana."

"I will return with clean water and cloths, my lady."

Rebekah took the opportunity to look through her wooden trunk for the perfect robe. She did not want the gown with the decorated bodice since it was a tight fit. She needed something elegant and yet comfortable.

"Ah, this one," she said, holding a robe against her body. "This one is perfect."

The robe selected was pale green, with a dark green sash. Noticing the matching shawl Shiphrah had made many years ago, she remembered Shiphrah saying, "The colors enhance your red hair and green eyes."

Entering the tent with warm, clean water, Chana immediately agreed, "Yes, that one, that is the one I would have selected."

Assured of the choice, Chana prepared a dish of nuts and fruits for lunch. Afterward, she helped Rebekah prepare herself. Three gowns were selected, but all were a little too snug. Deciding to go with the dark green gown, Chana placed silver bracelets on Rebekah's arms and silver hoops on her ears. All that remained were a touch of jasmine perfume and the precious white flower in her bright red hair.

Stepping back to admire her friend, Chana placed her hand over her mouth, then said, "O my goodness, I just remembered. Wait one moment," then rushed to the clothing chest. After tying a red sash around Rebekah's waist, Chana placed a light green shawl over her shoulders. "There," she said, "no one will notice a thing." Gently lifting Rebekah's hair over the shawl, Chana said, "One last comb." A moment later, "Perfect."

"Thank you, Chana. Now, you must wait until my return. I will tell you then what Isaac has decided. Can you go and ask Chesed to come into my tent?"

Chesed came immediately, asking, Are you ready?"

"Of course," she said, taking his arm.

Chesed escorted Rebekah to Isaac's tent. Before pulling the tent curtain back, he said, "Master, your wife."

"Good. Please come in," was Isaac's warm response.

On pulling the tent back, Chesed asked, "Shall I wait?"

"I will call when I am ready," Rebekah answered.

"Yes, of course."

On entering the tent, Isaac said, "Rebekah, you look lovely. What is the occasion?"

"A momentous occasion, and you are to be the first to know."

Isaac smiled, put his arms around Rebekah, and looked into her eyes. "You are as beautiful as the day we were married and, of course, that day not so long ago. Now, what is it I must know?"

Looking intently into Isaac's eyes, Rebekah said soft and lovingly, "Our God has blessed us." Placing Isaac's hand on her slightly bulging abdomen, "You are to be a father."

"Is it so?" as his eyes opened wide.

"Yes, my husband. It is so."

Isaac looked deeply into Rebekah's eyes and said, "You must stay with me this night.

Taking Rebekah into his arms, Isaac kissed her and said, "Now, let us relax. I will send Chesed for our evening meal."

The evening meal was delicious. The conversation was delightful as the couple spent time together as it was meant to be, husband and wife.

Rebekah prayed, "Please God, allow this time to last forever."

Isaac and Rebekah enjoyed their romantic supper.

He was surprised when Rebekah declined a goblet of wine and said, "For some reason, wine is not good for a developing baby."

"And you know this how?" was his question.

"I must admit, I do not know how, but Shiphrah told me it was her experience that drink was not good for a woman with child."

In the dim flickering lamplight, Rebekah watched Isaac prepare for bed. Even at his age, his body was firm, his shoulder wide with thick dark hair covering his muscular chest. A newfound joy filled her heart knowing the God of Abraham had brought them together, and she prayed Isaac would change from his wanton ways. She wanted a new beginning, the feeling of a husband's arms holding her tight through the night. When Isaac rubbed his hand over her slightly bulging tummy, Rebekah felt loved and blessed.

❁ ❁ ❁

At that moment, Beth felt Rose rub her arm.

"Rose, Rebekah is going to have a baby."

"Yes, dear, she is."

For some reason, Beth couldn't understand why her eyes were tearing up.

"What is wrong, dear?" Rose asked softly.

"Oh Rose, I don't know. I don't think anything is wrong. I'm not sure why, but the story, the love, the child, they are making me cry."

"Happy tears no doubt?"

"That must be it. I'm so happy; finally, after all those years, a baby. Oh, Rose, you must tell me, is it a boy?"

"Now Beth, you wouldn't want me to spoil the story. You'll just have to wait."

"Rose," was the only response.

"Beth dear. I am only halfway through Rebekah's story."

"Really. Is there that much more to come?"

"Yes. Remember the very first day, when I told you the story would find you, and the parts you need to hear will emerge?"

Beth nodded and wiped her tears with a napkin.

"There are many more parts you need to hear before we get to the end."

"How will I know when it is the end?"

Rose smiled, "You will know."

Beth wiped her eyes again.

"Is there something else upsetting you, dear?"

"It's just the changing. I know something in my life is about to change."

"Uh-huh."

"But I don't know what, how, or why."

"That is the nature of change. You only know after it happens. Now, can I make you a cup of tea? It is Chamomile. It will help you relax."

"Yes, thank you."

Sipping tea made for reflective conversation. Without realizing her developing patience was the source of her calmness, Beth reflected on the words she'd read in Proverbs, "Commit your work unto the Lord, and your plans will be established." Out of nowhere, Beth exclaimed, 'If I commit my plans unto God, will they be established like they were for Rebekah?"

Taking a deep breath of satisfaction, Rose sat back and said, "They've already begun my dear, they have already begun."

Beth felt calmness in her soul as she walked home. The suspense of Rebekah becoming pregnant was over, but the child had not been born. "Oh no," she thought, "I pray all goes well."

Beth had not realized that she had used *pray* instead of the word *hope* for the first time in a long time.

CHAPTER 17

THE day began like any other day in Sageville. Beth took her usual route down Reckoner Street to the office. Arriving at the insurance agency, she would soon find this particular day was anything but typical. On opening the door, Joyce and George threw confetti and yelled, "Surprise!" Surprised all right, and shocked, it wasn't her birthday.

"What? What on earth are you two shouting about?" she asked.

Joyce held up a letter, "You are going to be honored three weeks from Saturday."

"What? What are you talking about?"

Speaking rapidly, "You are one of the finalists for Employee of the Year. You must go, we'll all go. Happy hour, appetizers, free drinks, a scrumptious dinner, and a dance. Oh, Beth, I've always wanted to attend."

Beth took the letter and read it. It was addressed to Joyce as the senior agent. It simply said what Joyce had told her. She was one of several finalists, and her presence was required. Several agents had already been nominated from Georgia, South Carolina, and the northern part of Florida. In the insurance industry, this was the highest honor.

"Oh, my goodness, Joyce, I have been nominated?"

"Yes, you have," George affirmed.

"I don't know what to wear or even if I have something to wear to such a gala?"

Joyce laughed and said, "You and I are going shopping this Saturday and not stopping until we both find the right dress for the occasion."

George pipped in with, "That shouldn't be a problem. Sageville might be small, but we have six ladies' boutiques!"

"Six? I didn't know that," Beth said in surprise.

Joyce laughed. "You have a lot to learn about Sageville. Anyway, we can all ride together. Atlanta is only a four-hour drive. As a finalist, our agency will be booked into rooms where the awards dinner will be hosted."

"I haven't been back to Atlanta since my parents moved to Florida."

"I'd forgotten that you used to live there," George said.

"A long time ago. But, hey, that's a great idea to ride together. It will be fun to get away from Sageville for a night," Beth remarked.

"Yes, it will be. We'll leave Saturday morning and get there in time for lunch. Then, you can show us some of the sights. The reception doesn't begin until five o'clock, so we will have time to relax before the dinner," George suggested.

Joyce added, "This Saturday, we go shopping. We'll meet at Kaitlyn's coffee shop for a hearty breakfast at nine. When the stores open at ten, we'll be raring to go."

"Sounds perfect Joyce."

Beth had trouble getting herself to focus for the rest of the day. She knew the chance of being selected was very slim, but going to Atlanta with her colleagues would be a good getaway. The ringing of her office phone snapped her back to the reality of the job. All the sumptuous suppers at Rose's had started Beth bringing a small lunch from home. On this day, she ate a bagel with herb cream cheese at her desk and worked straight through to five o'clock.

Desk tidy, she waved to George and Joyce, saying, "See you tomorrow," on her way out of the office. Beth hurried down Reckoner Street, anxious to tell Rose the wonderful news.

"Hello Rose." she shouted, passing through the white picket gate.

"Hello Beth." came the curious response.

"What do we have here?" Beth inquired at the beautiful tray of delicious delights.

"Roast beef pie. My grandmother's recipe."

"Looks delicious Rose, and that crust, how do you get it so flaky?"

"I just follow her recipe exactly. It is my favorite way to have roast beef, and it makes a great left-over lunch."

"I can't wait to taste it."

"We are having ice tea tonight."

"Thank you. Oh, and what are these delightful little things?

" Gramma's chocolate chip cookies?"

Beth smiled and said, "Let's eat."

Like always, Rose bowed her head momentarily and then said, "I'm sure you will find this evening's episode very interesting."

"This pie is incredible. Who would think of making a roast beef pie?"

Controlling her urge to burst right out the moment she opened the gate; Beth waited until dessert time to convey the good news of the day.

Munching on a cookie, Beth said, "Rose, I want to tell you the good news. Joyce received a letter today from Atlanta, our regional headquarters."

"Oh?"

"Yes. It seems I'm a finalist for the Employee of the Year award."

"Oh my! Dear, that is wonderful news."

"There are so many other candidates that I know my chances are very slim."

"The nomination is an honor in itself, and you just never know, you could be the very best and get that award. When do you find out?"

"I have to go to Atlanta in three weeks, to the awards' dinner. They will announce it there."

"That is just superb! I am so proud of you and all your hard work. I will pray for you each day until you go."

"Thank you, Rose."

Once they had completed their meal, Rose began the story by taking Beth back into the tent just as Isaac and Rebekah were waking.

❊ ❊ ❊

Isaac began the day by hugging Rebekah and getting a big hug in return.

Having dressed, Rebekah said, "I will return to my tent and prepare for the day."

"What will you be doing?"

Biting her tongue and swallowing her pride for once in her life, Rebekah answered, "Women's work . . . The herbal medicines in the red tent are running low."

Isaac smiled and muttered to himself, "*Women, who knows what they do in that tent*?"

Rebekah could see the skepticism in his eyes, so she added, "Do not worry, one day soon, I shall deliver our son, and I want to be sure all is in order."

"That will be the greatest day in my life."

"I am sad that Father Abraham is not here to see his grandson."

"It will be a day of great celebration."

"Yes, and I will celebrate the fulfillment of God's promise."

Rebekah called for Chesed and returned to her tent.

Waiting for Rebekah to return, Chana had not slept much that night. Greeting Rebekah with a big hug, she asked, "What did he say? Was he pleased?"

"Yes, he was very pleased. He intends to tell the people soon."

"Today?"

"I'm not sure; he didn't say. We must go to the women's tent and replenish all the herbal medicines. I want to have everything ready before I am too big to stand at the medicinal table."

Chana laughed. "Yes, of course."

Rebekah continued with her usual routines knowing Isaac planned to announce Rebekah's pregnancy on the first night of the month *Tish-ei*, two days hence. He felt the beginning of the fall harvest was appropriate. The moon would be full, and the sky filled with stars. Harvest was a time to celebrate God's blessings, and to Isaac, the gift of a son would be the greatest blessing of all. Rebekah was bound and determined to keep her secret out of respect for Isaac and partly out of jealousy. She would never stay in Isaac's tent with Bayla and Rina as she was not just another wife but his prime wife, from which Abraham's line would continue. When Isaac made the announcement, Rebekah would be at his side. The people would know, Rebekah is the prime wife, and she is the one who will bear his heir.

Isaac instructed Chesed to gather the people around the central fire at dusk. He gave Chesed specific instructions to bring Rebekah to him after all the people had formed an arc around him. The scene was set, the moon shone its silver light across the lake, the stars appeared as diamonds, glistening in the night sky. Isaac stood upon the large flat rock used to knead bread. As Chesed walked Rebekah to the large stone, many of the older women put hand to mouth. Not wanting their husbands to hear, they whispered to each other, "*She's pregnant; she is finally pregnant.*"

It was a proud moment for Isaac. Little did he know that Rebekah had instructed Chesed to make certain Bayla and Rina were nowhere to be seen. Oblivious to the absence of his two jealous concubines, Isaac made the long-awaited announcement.

Welcoming Rebekah to his side, Isaac began, "My people, give ear to my words, the God of my father Abraham has blessed me with an heir. We have waited many years, but now, my wife Rebekah is a full two months pregnant, and I pray that we will have a son. Shouts of joy rang out. People cheered and clapped; others began to sing a Sumerian folk song to the happy couple. Well-wishers passed by, some shaking Isaac by the shoulders, others his hand. Many of the women kissed Rebekah's hand and wished her well. It was a night she would never forget. One last well-wisher remained, an older woman, a widow of twenty years. She told Rebekah that that special glow began to radiate from her face from the first day she missed her cycle. Now, Rebekah must get off her feet so that she would not have trouble with her legs in later years.

Isaac whispered, "You will come to my tent tonight?"

"As you have said, so shall it be. I will go prepare for the night."

"Yes."

Rebekah returned to her tent and danced in circles with Chana.

When the dancing stopped, Chana said, "This is wonderful news. I grow tired of avoiding the questions."

"Questions?"

"Yes, in the women's tent when you failed to appear the second time, Ida came to me and asked, but I did not know."

"I thought as much, but for now, I must prepare for this evening. Isaac asked me to come to his tent again tonight."

Chana gave her a big hug and said, "We shall prepare."

As before, Chesed escorted Rebekah to Isaac's tent and then retired for the night. Once again, Rebekah enjoyed the warmth of Isaac's love, remaining in bliss until the sun had risen. When Rebekah said she must go as there was much for her to do, Isaac embraced her.

He said in a soft voice, "Not yet. I need you once more this morning."

Rebekah remained until Isaac was exhausted.

On opening the tent curtain, Isaac said, "Will you return to me tonight?"

"Yes Isaac, as you wish."

Rebekah was escorted by Chesed back to her tent and left. Chana helped Rebekah bathe and then helped with the tasks in the women's tent.

In the women's tent, Rebekah continued working on the medicines and perfumes. As happens in pregnancy, her sense of smell was off. Sadie and Chana had to help her with the aroma of perfume and the mixing of ointment. Two jars of ointment were set aside with strict instructions, "They were for Rebekah only." Several other jars were prepared for the women in the camp and placed at the front of the table.

With the bulk of the work finished, Sadie asked, "My husband needs my help with our tent. He wants to enlarge it as we did with the women's tent. Our children continue to grow and we need more room."

"Go to him," Rebekah replied.

"Are you certain?" Sadie asked.

"Chana said, "Go ahead, I'll finish straightening up."

"Thank you," Sadie said, and then, "Come Rebekah, I'll walk you to your tent."

The full moons waxed and waned. Her tummy grew larger until it seemed unbearable. With the discomfort, Rebekah had stopped going to Isaac months before. Spending more time in her tent because of the increasing discomfort, she began to feel a strange movement within. None of the other women she'd attended had ever expressed such discomfort, at least not until the last few days. This baby would not be still. Movement and kicking were a constant annoyance, sometimes waking her in the night. Not wanting any complications, this worried Rebekah. Having waited for twenty years, she did not want to have any problems.

As the baby continued to struggle within, she whispered, "My Lord, why is this happening to me?"

Then a voice, from where she did not know, said, "Two nations are within your womb, two peoples born of you shall be divided; the one shall be stronger than the other, and the elder shall serve the younger."

Then silence. The LORD had spoken. "*Two within my womb*," she said to herself, then jumped up exclaiming, "I am carrying twins." The shout woke Chana. Rebekah knelt and cried out, "After so many years of longing for a baby, I shall not have one baby, but two," and caressed her abdomen.

"O Rebekah, how can you be so sure . . . does Isaac know?" Chana's questioned.

Rebekah answered, "No, and I'll not tell him. He'll be insulted the LORD has spoken to me and not him." Looking to Chana, "We must keep this to ourselves until I understand what the older will serve the younger means."

Rebekah determined she would love them both and raise them equally. The determination of who was to serve who was up to the LORD. Her time was approaching fast.

❁ ❁ ❁

Rose touched Beth's arm, and she woke up quickly. "Twins? Rebekah will have twins?" she said instantly.

Rose nodded in affirmation, "Yes, she will have twins."

"I can't believe it! After so long without a child, she is having twins!"

Beth was as excited for Rebekah as she would be for a best friend.

"But will the delivery be even more difficult? You know, birthing twins?" Beth asked.

"You will hear about that tomorrow."

"Rose, this gives me a feeling of hope for some reason."

"Why is that dear?"

"It feels like faithfulness and determination paid off for Rebekah."

Grinning from ear to ear, Rose said, "That is a great message, don't you think?"

"Oh, I do, I do. This story is so meaningful, but it sounds like there might be trouble brewing.

"Why?" Rose said with a smile.

"I guess siblings sometimes have problems," was the answer.

Rose nodded, pleased that Beth understood Rebekah was being rewarded for her faithfulness. It is why she picked this particular story for Beth. Rose had sensed from the beginning that Beth had been lost for a very long time.

It was the story Beth needed to hear to enable her to turn a negative life in a positive direction.

Beth popped up and said, "Guess I'd better get going."

"Okay, Beth. See you tomorrow."

CHAPTER 18

ETH'S day began with a review of client files that were up for renewal. Resigning herself to the fact the day would be consumed with phone conversations and emails, the interruptions were still a nice change from organizing and filing. Talking with clients kept her mind off the nomination and Rebekah's baby. What amazed Beth about her contestations was her ability to resolve issues with clients upset with policy changes. After all, keeping clients happy was the key to a successful insurance business; any business. Rarely looking at the clock, time just seemed to fly.

Finishing pricing the policy upgrades for a new client, Beth was about to close the file when George chimed in with, "Almost time Beth."

"What for what George?" Joyce asked.

"Beth's rushing off to Rose's house. Five more minutes."

Alerting Beth's attention to the clock, Beth closed the file, tidied her desk, grabbed her purse from the cabinet, and was ready. It always amazed Joyce how Beth would never take the liberty of leaving the office early. To Beth, it just wasn't right.

"The story still going strong, is it?" George asked.

"Yes, it is, and Rose said we have a way to go yet."

"Must be a long one," Joyce remarked.

Beth nodded and said, "See you tomorrow," as she opened the office door.

Arriving at Rose's front gate found her sitting prime and southern proper in the usual spot.

"Hello dear," resounded her familiar voice.

"Hello Rose," echoed back in imitation.

"Good day at the office, was it?"

"Yes, thank you. I had plenty to keep me busy."

"Those are the best days. You know I can have months go by without having anyone come to hear a story. I do try to stay busy, but it's not the same."

Lowering her voice, Beth asked, "Rose, after you finish Rebekah's story, can I still stop in to see you?" Becoming encouraged, "You are right on my way home." Lowering her voice, "That is unless you have another person needing a story."

"That would be wonderful Beth. After all, I do enjoy your company."

The thought of these times ending had touched Beth deeply. She'd never had a friend to talk with, not like Rose.

"And I yours," Beth said with a touch of heartfelt emotion.

Happy for the friendship, Rose said, "Today, I made us a shrimp cocktail salad."

"I see, and it looks delicious."

"I noticed you took a slice of chocolate cake home after church on Sunday. So, for dessert, I made us a double chocolate layer cake."

"Oh Rose, I love chocolate."

Beth had never before enjoyed the pleasure of talking openly to a good friend. She'd never had one. Following the leisurely supper and the plates cleared away, Rose noticed Beth becoming a little more patient. No longer wanting to rush into the story, Beth took time to relax with a friend. The progress warmed Rose's heart as she straightened her dress and resumed the story.

❀ ❀ ❀

Rebekah was half asleep but felt something was not right. Sitting up on her bed and called, "Chana, wake up."

Spending the last few nights in Rebekah's tent, just in case, Chana's eyes had no sooner snapped open before asking, "Are you okay? Is something happening?"

"My stomach is cramping. The baby is coming."

"I need to get you to the women's red tent?"

"Yes, hurry."

"One moment my lady."

At that, Chana bolted from the tent and returned a short time later. Assisting Rebekah to stand, she placed the birthing gown over her head.

"Where did you go?" Rebekah asked.

"Chesed . . . he will wake the others and then come help us."

Chana was startled when she pulled the tent curtain back as Chesed was at the entrance waiting. Taking Rebekah's other arm, he assisted Chana in getting her mistress to the red tent. Shortly after that, Sadie, Nayah, Liora, Orli, and Mazal arrived. Chesed was told to wait nearby and say nothing. Rebekah did not want the encampment knowing before Isaac. Nayah, Liora spread the animal skin groundsheet; Orli and Nayah covered it with a blanket; Liora placed the birthing bricks. Sadie and Chana made Rebekah as comfortable as possible on another blanket-covered groundsheet. Liora placed a large pillow under Rebekah's head. As Eliana entered with a basin of warm water, Rebekah moaned, her water broke, and the women prepared to birth another child into God's world.

Chana had never been this excited over a birth. Helping Rebekah to stand, she removed the saturated gown from Rebekah's body. At the same time, Sadie and Eliana placed a clean birthing gown over her head. Rebekah's eyes flashed around the tent as she lay down beside the birthing bricks. The scarlet and blue-colored shawls, the red and purple sashes intended to impart a feeling of comfort, meant nothing at this moment. Eliana left and returned shortly with another basin of warm water. Sadie arranged the cleaning cloths, ceremonial knife, and Hebrew swaddling cloth in perfect order.

Stroking Rebekah's forehead, Chana said, "Rest my lady, rest. Your time is at hand."

The one thing Rebekah had never experienced in her thirty-five years was the feeling of a child struggling inside her body, preparing to enter the world. The nervous tension, the joy, the excitement within the tent caused Chana to think, "I wonder if this much fuss was ever made over the birth of a king?"

Rebekah had not wanted to disturb Isaac until the child was born, but it was of no avail. Chesed, unable to sit, was pacing in circles around the red tent. His pacing did not go unnoticed by the women of the encampment as they prepared to start the work of the day. Soon, everyone in the encampment knew, except Isaac. Inside the red tent, Rebekah looked up at Chana and nodded. Jumping to her feet, Chana shouted, "Nayah, Liora, the birthing bricks." Moments later, Rebekah straddled the clay birthing bricks for the first time. Nayah on one side, Liora on the other, and Orli behind for support. Chana sat crossed-legged in front of her mistress, moving as close as possible.

Sitting back, she said, "Eliana, go and inform Isaac that his wife's contractions come frequently."

Covered in a white birthing gown and precariously perched on red birthing bricks, Rebekah's perspiration-covered, pain-ridden face told Chana something was amiss. Chana began to monitor the dilations by placing her left hand on Rebekah's right knee and her right hand between her legs. Eyes closed, head tilted back, Rebekah began breathing slowly and deliberately.

Her face cringed, a panicked *yelp* caused Chana to cry out, "What is it?"

At that moment, a second water sac spilled over Chana's arms and onto the groundsheet.

"Something's not right," Chana exclaimed, "I've never seen water break twice." Grabbing a cloth from Eliana, Chana cleaned her hands and asked, "What is happening? What is wrong Rebekah?"

Rebekah groaned and managed to say, "Twins."

As if she hadn't heard, Chana exclaimed, "You are dilating; push." Rebekah groaned. Chana repeated, "That's it; push; I can feel the child's head." Rebekah closed her eyes and groaned again. Chana said, almost in a panic, "Eliana, raise the gown. The child is here." A moment later, "Good, good, the child comes." As the newborn slid into Chana's hands, she cried out again, "Look; look, a hand holds the heel of the firstborn!"

"What? Another baby?" exclaimed Sadie.

Rebekah could now feel a second baby struggling within. She took a deep breath and pushed. Chana passed the first child to Eliana. Sadie quickly tied a piece of cloth around the baby's ankle, saying, "You are firstborn, little hairy one." Chana commanded, "Push Rebekah! Push, another head comes."

Sadie dropped a cleaning cloth on Chana's lap for the second baby.

"Good girl Rebekah, push," Chana's excited voice shouted.

Rebekah let out a loud gasp and then screamed as she collapsed into the arms of Orli.

It was a scene of bewilderment. Rebekah had not told anyone, not ever Isaac, that the LORD had said she would bear twins.

Chana's voice changed. "Rebekah," she said softly, "look, your second child is not like the first. He is like you, soft brown hair, fair-skinned."

Young Orli asked in all innocence, "Did she have two husbands?"

"No," snapped Chana, "don't be silly."

When the pain of release had subsided, Rebekah opened her eyes and beheld two infants. The first had black hair and a showing of black hair on his arms and legs—the second had a lighter tinge of reddish-brown hair and a fair complexion.

Eliana said, "Rebekah, I have never seen such a thing. Two babies, completely different. What does this mean?"

"That, I do not know," was Rebekah's puzzling answer. She had expected a single child to carry on Abraham's line, but now there were two. Now the foretelling on the LORD, "*The older shall serve the younger*," made sense.

Chana nodded. "It is true; never before has this happened."

After Eliana and Chana finished washing the two babies, Chana forgot that Rebekah always waited a moment said, "Sadie, pass me the knife."

Rebekah reacted quickly, "No; wait!"

The women were puzzled. Chana inquired, "Wait?"

"Yes," came Rebekah's answer, "Shiphrah said it lessens the shock."

Moments later, Rebekah nodded and spoke. "Now, sever the cords."

The women helped Rebekah get comfortable on the bed. Orli propped her up with pillows, and the babies placed in Rebekah's out-stretched arms. Overjoyed with the day's success, the women quickly cleaned the birthing area, put away the birthing bricks, knife, and unused cloths. Nayah washed Rebekah's face while Orli combed her radiant red hair. Liora brought a jar of jasmine perfume to Rebekah. She declined, saying, "The intoxicating effect of perfume is not good for children.

Proud to have been part of the team that birthed the tribal leader's son, Eliana said, "Shall I take the children to Isaac so that he may name them?"

"No," was the flat-out, abrupt reply.

The women froze. Looking at a face of resolve, they all knew something was coming.

"But your husband awaits."

Then, the unexpected happened. Rebekah said, "My mother named me; Sarah inadvertently named Isaac; I shall name my children." Looking into her left arm, Rebekah smiled and said, this one is hairy, like his father. I shall name him Esau. Raising the head of the infant in her right arm, she said, "This one, he is like me, and because he held the heel of his brother, I shall name him Jacob, the one who holds the heel."

Allowing a moment for the unexpected to sink in, Rebekah said, "Now you may take my children to their father." It was too late. Isaac. beyond impatient, burst into the tent. The women screamed for him to get out, as he was not allowed to enter. Ignoring the shouts, Isaac knelt beside his wife and looked upon two children. He looked around, expecting to see another mother. There was none.

"You have two healthy sons," Chana announced.

A smile spread across Isaac's face. He looked closer and said, "Sons! I have two sons? I have been blessed twice?"

Gently removing the swaddling cloth from Esau's head. He laughed with joy, "This one, he is like me; hairy." Removing the swaddling cloth from the head of Jacob, his face grimaced as he said, "This one like you, fair skin." He snapped up straight and demanded, "Which one first? Which my firstborn? Answer me!"

"Esau, the hairy one," Rebekah said as she passed her son to Isaac.

Isaac stood with his firstborn son. Pride overwhelmed his entire being. Then, a moment later, his face turned to rage as he shouted, "You named *my son, my child*? It is not your place to name. It is the father's place to name his sons."

Tenacious and boldly, Rebekah asserted, "He is hairy. His name is Esau!"

"And the other one?"

Rebekah could not hide the smile on her lips as she said, "This one is Jacob."

Gruffly, Isaac screamed, "Heel-holder? Did you name my son heel-holder? Heel snatcher?"

Every woman in the tent was surprised that not a glimpse of fear was evident on Rebekah's face.

Calmly, she replied, "He is my son as well, and I have named him! His name is to be Jacob, *and that is it*," was the loud and final statement.

Isaac began ranting and moving about, still holding Esau and saying, "You! You! Why was I given you? Why did God curse me with you?"

Much to the horror of those present, Rebekah replied, "I have asked the same question."

Beyond angry, Isaac handed Esau to Chana and stormed out of the tent. Chana, placing Esau back in Rebekah's arm, said, "Bad, you are bad."

A glow of satisfaction radiated from Rebekah's smiling face.

❁ ❁ ❁

"Beth," Rose said. "Beth."

Beth kept her eyes closed for one moment longer, hoping Rose would continue, but when Rose did not, Beth said, "And I thought I was bad."

Rose could only laugh.

"Honestly Rose! Isaac and Rebekah are back to their same hard-headedness! I thought their love would not last forever?"

Rose composed herself and said, "Isaac and Rebekah are the personifications of a love/hate relationship. Both have ultra-strong personalities, but they just so happen to be so very different."

"I honestly thought that after the birth, they would remain in love with each other. Why did God cause this to happen?"

Becoming serious, "God did not cause Isaac to do anything. Isaac made his own choices in life," Rose said.

"But was this not God's plan for the nation of Israel to rise out of Abraham's line?"

"The nation to rise out of Abraham's line, yes. The child had to come from Isaac, but God knew Isaac would change, and not for the better, so God needed someone with a strong spirit for those plans to come to pass," Rose explained.

"I don't understand. Why was it meant to be this way? It doesn't seem right."

Rose looked Beth straight in the eyes and said, "God did not create humanity to be puppets. God's advance plan had a woman of faith ready to ensure that the chosen one would receive the blessing.

Beth didn't get it. She could not understand why the story was taking a negative twist. Two very different and independent people had two dynamically different sons to raise. It was apparent to Beth that one would be a daddy's boy and the other, a momma's boy, but she couldn't understand how it could all work out for good.

"Will you tell me the story of the twins?"

"Yes dear, I will tell you all."

"Good. I'll go, even though I want to stay and hear more."

"Beth," Rose called before she got to the gate, "as I told you, the story gets more and more interesting the deeper we get into it."

Beth walked home, almost trance-like, wondering how on earth the story could possibly get any more interesting than it has already been?

CHAPTER 19

Passing Rose's house on the way to the office, Beth thought about all that had happened in Rebekah's life up to this point. Then she thought of Rose's comment, "It will get more interesting the deeper we get into it." Happy it was not going to end any time soon, she still could not imagine the story getting any more interesting. Now, after everything that had happened in her life, two sons had been born in last night's episode, and it didn't take a wizard to figure out there would be sibling rivalry. Opening the office door, Beth said to herself, "Work, focus on work."

Stepping inside the office, Beth went directly to her desk, put her purse away, plunked herself down, and looked at the pile of files George had dropped on her desk.

"Good morning, Beth," Joyce said, diverting her attention.

"Good morning," Beth replied, "Coffee almost ready Hun?"

"Yes, and so is the pudding swirl cake, compliments of George."

"Compliments of my wife Helen," George added.

The files were a result of Beth's initiative a month earlier. Harold Jameson had complained that his premium was too high. Beth had explained that the coverage he required was costly for a small business such as his. Appreciating that Harold had a wife and two young children, she told him that a business policy insuring over fifty employees had a significantly reduced rate per employee. Then she did something that surprised herself.

She said, "If an association of businesses with over fifty applicants was to apply under a blanket policy, she would move the application onto the regional office, with a recommendation. Harold did precisely that. A week later, the Sageville Small Business Association applied for a group policy. With almost sixty members, the association qualified for the lower rate. It pushed Beth over the top with new clients.

Beth could not just put the files into the cabinet. Oh no. They had to be scrutinized, each one. From time to time, she would check with Joyce and George mainly about family information as there was no room for error as far as Beth was concerned. The good part of this scenario was the day would go quickly, and she would be on her way to learn more about those twins.

"Beth, are we still on for Saturday morning breakfast and shopping?"

"I am looking forward to it," she replied.

By the end of the day, Beth was tired and hungry. Having forgotten about lunch, she hurried to what she knew would be a scrumptiously delicious repast with her dear friend Rose.

"Hi Rose," she called from the sidewalk.

"Hello dear. Hope you are hungry."

Looking at plates stacked high with club sandwiches, she said, "You bet, I'm starved."

"And don't forget the potato salad."

"You never disappoint me Rose. I forgot to have lunch today."

"Dear, you are working too hard."

"From the looks of these plates, I'd say you are as well!"

They laughed and visited a host of topics. Then Rose said, "Oh, I wanted to tell you, we have another candidate coming in this week. He confirmed this morning. I am thrilled the interviews are moving quickly."

"What about the pastor from last Sunday?"

"Too much fire and brimstone. It was that kind of preaching which made us decide to become a community church focusing on care and forgiveness."

Beth realized that her mother gravitated to that kind of preaching and why it had seemed normal to her. Her thoughts were broken by Rose handing her a dessert plate.

"Here you go. I made us some pecan brownies with just picked pecans from the trees in my backyard."

"Yum."

The story began as soon as the dishes were out of the way. Rose took Beth back in time to the encampment not long after the twins had been born.

❖ ❖ ❖

Chana handed Esau to Rebekah as Rebekah gave Jacob to Chana.

Rebekah sighed and said, "Nursing twins seems to be a never-ending task, and this one does love to go first. It is a good thing I have two breasts." The women laughed at the comment as Rebekah continued with, "This one is my hairy little bear, just like his father."

"Ah yes," replied Chana, "but Jacob is so sweet." Rubbing Esau's head, she commented, "Even if you came out first, your brother is always first for breakfast!"

From outside of the tent, Isaac called, "Rebekah."

"Yes?"

"I wish to see my sons."

Chana looked at Rebekah and then said, "Enter."

Isaac walked into the tent and looked at Chana. "Ah, I see you are feeding my hairy little son. I will hold the other one, Jacob."

Chana handed him the baby.

"Chana, you may leave us," Isaac said. "I wish to speak with my wife. Wait with Chesed."

"As you wish."

Isaac sat beside Rebekah and watched Esau slurp away, saying, "You have blessed me with an heir."

"It is true my husband."

"And this hairy one," he said, touching Esau's head, "Look how he eats! Is his appetite not ravenous? He loves to eat like me. I shall ask Peretz to help me train him to be the greatest hunter in our village. Peretz knows the habits of wild animals. Esau will hunt, and we will eat the finest game in the land! Rubbing Esau's head once again, he said with a touch of affection, "One day, I will give him my blessing and pass down my birthright."

Ignoring the remark, Rebekah remembered God's word. "*The older will serve the younger,*" once again. Content to let Isaac believe what he wanted, there was no point in causing alarm or starting her sons on the path of never-ending conflict. It was far too early to concern herself with how this would come to pass, but she believed, as God had said, Jacob would be the one to inherit the blessing and the birthright. Like most men, Isaac was oblivious to the thoughts running through the mind of his wife.

Like a concerned husband, he inquired, "Are you well, my wife?"

"Yes I am." came the reply. In the same possessive tone of voice, "Soon, I will be back baking your bread and making stew from the wild game you love so much."

Isaac smiled. "This is good. It has already been one full moon since you bore my sons. Before the next full moon, you will visit my tent and stay the night?"

"As you wish," Rebekah replied, not wishing to cause any conflict.

"The God of Abraham may have blessed me with you, and even though you named my sons, I will be the one to bless Esau and pass on the right of the firstborn."

Rebekah felt her stomach cramping. She did not know if the pain was from her womb shrinking or Isaac's words.

Watching Rebekah's face pale, he asked, "Are you upset?"

"No. It is my stomach."

Isaac touched her hand and said, "I will send Chana in to be with you, and I will look forward to the next full moon."

Exiting the tent, the baby in hand, Isaac passed Jacob to Chana, saying, "Rebekah needs you."

Spending the night with Isaac did not appeal to her. It was all she could do to keep the two nursing sons satisfied.

On entering the tent, Chana said, "You look tired, Rebekah. You need rest."

"Yes, Chana, I do."

Chana placed Jacob in a deerskin cradle swinging from a tripod and then set Esau swinging beside his brother.

With heavy eyes, Rebekah asked, "When the babies are sleeping, please go to the women's tent and bring me fennel and crushed nettle along with the mortar and pestle."

"Why those particular herbs?"

"They will increase the milk flow as my sons demand much milk. As Chana was leaving, Rebekah continued, "And Chana, please bring the black licorice and hot water for my stomach."

"Yes, Rebekah, please rest now. I will have Sadie come and watch over you while I go to the women's tent."

Rebekah nodded and then dozed off.

The days passed, and Rebekah returned to Isaac's tent as he requested. He asked her to come to his tent many nights, and she consented when she was able. Days were spent tending to her sons and completing her daily household chores. When needed, she assisted in the women's tent. In the years to come, Esau and Jacob spent longer times with Isaac. He tutored them in tracking, hunting, fishing, using a bow, and setting a snare. Esau was a natural. At five years of age, he could put the arrow in the bulls-eye every time. At eight years of age, he could set a snare and track a deer. Jacob couldn't care less. He preferred the peace of the field, the bleating sheep. He paid attention to what the sheep liked to eat and how they became spotted when poplar and hyssop branches fell into the drinking water. At eight years of age, Jacob could sheer the wool from the sheep as well as any servant; slower perhaps, but just as well.

While sitting on the hillside overlooking a flock of sheep, Jacob watched Isaac follow Esau into a stand of hardwoods. Jacob knew Isaac would soon enjoy the taste of deer he loved so much.

Returning to his mother's tent, he asked, "Mother, may I enter?"

"Of course, my son, please come in."

Rebekah's eyes sparkled as she watched Jacob sit cross-legged, just like an adult.

"Mother," he said, "tell me, why does father love Esau more? Is it because he is bigger? Or because he looks like him?"

Leaning over to hug Jacob. She answered, "Esau, like Isaac, loves to hunt, and you know how your father loves venison more than lamb."

"Yes mother, I do, but still, I do not feel father's love."

"He loves you, but it's just not the same."

Heartbroken, Rebekah consoled, "You are precious to me. It warms my heart to see you care for our sheep, oversee the servants tending the vegetable gardens, learning the ways of a shepherd."

Jacob responded, "I know mother, but sometimes I wish—"

"You are the one who prospers the village with your lamb and wool." Rebekah's voice was firm and affirming. "You bring me the herbs I use for making medicines and ointments. Esau brings your father venison." Upset, Rebekah blurted, "One day, the older will serve the younger. It is the promise of God."

"Mother, I do not understand. Is this a riddle?"

"It is not for you to understand at this time, but only for you to trust my words."

"Is it good that I don't hunt?"

"It is neither good nor bad, my son. It is the way God created you as an individual. You must follow your God-given nature and not try to be someone you are not. Always remember, I love you just as you are, the way God made you. Mark my words, one day, you will be the one who serves the God of Abraham."

Jacob shrugged his shoulders, still not certain what his mother meant.

"Now, you run to the garden and find me the best lavender flowers. Bring them, as I will need them in the women's tent tomorrow."

"Yes mother, as you wish."

Many moons passed, and the un-identical twins were now ten years of age. While Rebekah worked with other women around the clay oven, Jacob came and watched her remove fresh bread on the bread paddle. He loved the taste of fresh hot bread. While blowing and biting into the delicious treat, Esau walked out of his tent, bow in hand and a quiver full of arrows. Running past Jacob, he purposely bumped him to get his attention. Rebekah looked up and frowned at Esau. Then she looked over to Isaac standing in front of his tent and smiling.

"Watch out!" Jacob said.

"Come on Jacob, I'll teach you to hunt, like a man!"

"I am happy to tend sheep and goats. You go hunt your wild animals."

"Sheep, sheep, stupid sheep! Come and learn something useful. Come and learn to hunt. Anyone can tend stupid old sheep." Esau looked to his father, who smiled and waved. Gesturing Esau to go, Isaac shouted, "Leave him, my son. Leave him to his stupid sheep."

Esau tried to encourage his brother to join him by saying, "Can you not see how happy it would make father if you hunted for the wild meat he loves?"

"I have no desire to hunt. It makes me happy to learn about the crops and tend flocks."

"Awe, come on, momma's boy, hunt with me."

As Esau rand off, Jacob shouted, "I'd rather shear the wool for the clothes you wear."

Disappointed, Esau continued shouting, "Momma's boy! Jacob is a Momma's boy! Jacob is a Momma's boy!"

Jacob turned to his mother, who gave him a reassuring smile and said, "You do what you like. It makes no difference. God honors all work."

Isaac, unable to understand how people could think differently, shook his head and returned to his tent. Sadly for Rebekah, Bayla and Rina were waiting to comfort and warm him.

❖ ❖ ❖

"Beth," Rose said, "It's almost dark."

"Rose, good grief! Rebekah certainly had her hands full!"

Rose laughed. "She did have two sons. Twins. That is a handful!"

"Yes, and it doesn't sound like parenting is going well."

"How do you mean?"

"It's just that, well, Isaac and Rebekah have such different opinions. He favors the wild, and she favors the domestic."

"Parenting can be hard. Parents love all of their children, but all children are different. Esau liked to hunt, and so did his father."

"Do you think it was because Isaac encouraged him to hunt and, since Isaac didn't care much for farming, he just let Jacob kind of find his way?"

"Maybe. As the boys grow older, well, let's just say other differences developed. Not only did they look different, but they also had completely different personalities."

Beth laughed, "Like their parents?"

"Yes. Exactly."

"Rose, do you have a large family? Like brothers and sisters?"

"Yes, as a matter of fact, I do. I have two sisters and two brothers. They all live out of state."

"Really? How did that happen?"

"I am, or rather I suppose I was, kind of like you. I moved away from my family to be on my own."

"Really?"

"Yes, and then I met Albert, and the rest is history. He was in the service when we first married, so we moved about."

"Were you close with your siblings?"

"Sometimes," she laughed. "But those are other stories for another time. How about you? Any brothers or sisters?"

"Yes, two sisters. And, no, we aren't close. They are both several years older and very close to each other. I was raised almost like an only child."

"I see."

Rebekah asked, "Will Jacob and Esau ever become friends, you know, grow to like each other?"

"My dear, that story is for another day."

Beth knew that was Rose's way to sign off for the evening. Rose liked to keep Beth wondering, and right now, Beth was wondering if this story was ever going to end. It seemed like each time the end was in sight; the saga took an unexpected turn. Then again, Beth had to admit that it was one of the reasons she came back each day. Satisfied the sibling rivalry was still friendly, Beth knew it was time to go.

"Well, Rose, I will call it a day."

"All right, dear. I'll look forward to seeing you tomorrow. What about this Saturday? Are you going shopping?"

"Oh yes. Joyce is coming to help me pick out a dress for the awards dinner in Atlanta."

"What about Sunday? Will you still feel like coming to hear our next candidate?"

"Yes, of course. I want to compare this one with the first pastor."

Rose laughed and said, "Me too."

CHAPTER 20

BETH had given up trying to extract advance information. Rose knew the best way to tell a story, and that was that. The only thing Beth could do was focus on work during the day and go to Rose's front porch in the evening. After all, if a job was worth doing, it was worth doing well. It was the same with Rose. She was a person who paid attention to detail in everything she did. Beth knew it was one of the reasons she felt a special kinship with her new friend.

Putting away the last of her work for the week always brought a smile to her face. However, this Friday was different than all the others. For the first time since moving to Sageville, Beth had plans for the whole weekend. Breakfast and shopping on Saturday with Joyce, and church on Sunday with Rose. She felt like life might just be falling into place. For the first time in a long time, Joyce headed for the door before the others. Grabbing her purse on the run, she said, "Can you lock up for me George? I have an appointment?" George looked up and answered, "Sure thing Joyce." Pausing at the door, Joyce called, "Beth, see you at Ida's coffee shop for breakfast?"

"Yes, and I can't wait to explore all the great boutiques with you," Beth replied as the door closed.

Following on the heels of Joyce, Beth was about to exit when George moaned, "You girls have a great Saturday shopping. I'll be sitting in the noon-day sun watching the last girl's tee-ball game of the season. But the good news is, evening baseball starts in four weeks, and Junior is excited about finally being able to play baseball, rather than tee-ball."

"He is growing up fast George! Maybe Joyce and I can come to a game when it isn't so hot," Beth replied before exiting.

"Great, Junior would like that. Enjoy your weekend."

"Don't worry George, I will, bye," Beth said as she let the office door close.

The plates of food waiting for Beth looked inviting, but where was Rose?

Emerging from the screen door, Rose placed a pitcher of lemonade on the table, saying, "Sorry, I was running a bit late today. I talked with Myrtle for over an hour on the phone, poor dear."

"What is wrong with Myrtle?"

"Oh, she is fine really but overwhelmed with all the committee work at church. She asked my advice on how we evaluated the applications last time. On paper, they all look so good, and poor Myrtle was finding it difficult to determine who to invite to speak."

"I can see why Myrtle would be having trouble."

"Yes, and I had to stretch this old brain to remember how our committee handled the selection process. It was well over five years ago Beth."

"You are funny."

"Funny? Me? Why?"

You are telling me a four-thousand-year-old story and can't remember what you did five years ago. That's funny."

"Oh, hush now. Enough of that. Here, help yourself to some stuffed avocados."

"They do look good."

"Avocados, stuffed with crab salad. One of my favorites."

Beth had learned that you do not just eat dinner at the home of Rose Maddington; you savor the flavors. Her food was not to be consumed. It was to be enjoyed. Topping off this culinary delight, Rose brought out banana pudding for dessert.

"Rose, I am so fortunate that you like to cook. Someday I hope you will teach me."

"Of course, dear. That would be fun. I'll look forward to it, but first, you must learn patience. You cannot rush if you want to be a good cook. Now, let's get these dishes squared away so I can tell you more about the twins."

Returning to the porch, Rose took her usual seat and smoothed her dress over her knees while Beth took her seat directly across.

"Are you ready to go back to Isaac's settlement?"

Beth nodded her head, closed her eyes, and said, "On my way."

❀ ❀ ❀

No matter how hard Rebekah tried, Esau and Jacob continued to grow apart as they matured. At twenty years of age, both had evolved into strong, healthy, and handsome young men. When Esau stood beside Isaac, it was apparent he was his father's son. The similarities did not end at looks. Actions, mannerisms were identical. Animals did not often hear them coming. Arrows always found their target. Both cut their meat from spit and ate like starving men. Ironically, Isaac and Esau appreciated Jacob's animal husbandry as the meat and wool were bartered for the best wine in the land, and they did love their wine.

Now one might think this was upsetting to Rebekah, but she had learned it was a common male trait. What upset Rebekah was how easily Isaac's low regard for women had been passed on to Esau. Women, servant or free, Hebrew or other, had one purpose; to serve the desires of men. Isaac's sexist remarks about the attributes of women in front of Esau upset Rebekah. When Isaac bragged of how these women loved to, *uncover his feet* (a Hebrew euphemism), she understood why God did want to have Esau as the progenitor of the chosen people. Isaac was enough.

One particular day, Isaac had not realized Rebekah was near and had to cover up his crude remarks with, "But your mother is the best," as he laughed and winked. Then Isaac carried on uninhibited, "Do you remember the Hittite woman, Zissel?"

"Yes, father. Long hair and big hips."

"Zissel could make your blood sizzle." As father and son laughed, Isaac continued, "Come, let us enjoy some wine."

On her way past Isaac's tent, Rebekah overheard Esau bragging to his father, "Did I tell you about the one I met in the market the other day? Her body was so ripe for the picking.

Jacob, on the other hand, was always interested in knowledge. Wanting to know everything possible, he'd discovered that manure, especially sheep manure, enriched the soil to the point of producing abundant crops. He cut down or fenced off certain trees so the wool would not become spotted. Under the tutelage of Rebekah, Jacob became an excellent negotiator and was unmatched when it came to bartering.

One night, Jacob returned to the settlement late, joined his mother, Chana, and Chesed around the central fire.

After hugging his mother, he asked, "What do the stars tell you tonight?"

"Oh, my son, the stars whisper your name: Ya`aqob, Ya`aqob."

"Is that all they whisper?"

"O no, they tell me you are the wisest man in the camp."

Jacob laughed at his mother's joking and asked, "Why would they say that?"

"Because you are wise enough to stay away from your father and brother when they are drinking and carousing."

"You know I cannot stand the stupid stories they tell and how they humiliate women."

"They are much the same, your father and your brother," Chana said scornfully.

"It is the way of the people in this land, I'm afraid," added Chesed.

Rebekah, watching the sparks rise from the fire, asked, "Do you think it is right for Esau to receive the inheritance? He is unruly, with no understanding of life or knowledge of the God of Abraham?"

Chesed replied, "Life is not fair Rebekah, you know that."

Jacob tried to comfort his mother by saying, "I am glad that you taught me of my grandfather's ways and how he was wise enough to send for you."

"O Jacob, I pray that one day you will come to know Abraham's God and be blessed with a good wife. A wife of our family line and not one of these detestable foreign women." Becoming serious, she warned, "Jacob, if you ever married one of these women, my life would not be worth living."

"Mother, do not say such a thing, do not talk so."

Jacob kissed his mother goodnight, but before he could leave, she said, Jacob, I do not know how it will come to pass, but you must somehow gain Esau's birthright and receive the blessing.

"Mother, you are such a dreamer. Esau will never give me his birthright, and even if he did, his father would not honor it."

As Jacob walked to his tent, Rebekah thought to herself, "I do not know how it will come to pass, but Jacob does not yet know the power of my LORD."

In the morning, refreshed from rest, he left for his flocks in the hills. He wanted to count the females that would be lambing this season. Esau packed a few things and went later that morning to hunt. His hunting trips usually lasted for a day or two as he was a good tracker and an excellent archer. This trip, however, went into the third day and then the fourth. Searching from hilltop to valley floor, without food or water, he began wandering in circles. Even with his water skin empty, his food long gone, Esau's masculine pride would not let him return empty-handed. Not only was he inhibited by pride; his father's approval meant everything to him, and Isaac was expecting venison. Esau had grown accustomed to eating the rich lean meat with his father and drinking the best wine the region had to offer.

Bound and determined, he said to himself, "I will not go home without the game for my father."

Thirsty and starving, he found it difficult to sleep that night. Off he ventured at the crack of dawn, searching for the elusive wild game. Frustration increased the hunger pangs. Barely enough spit to wet his lips, he pressed on. By noon on the fifth day, he crawled over the top of a hill in hopes of finding water. Much to his surprise, he saw a large flock of sheep and smoke from a small fire. Two shepherds were tending the newborn lambs, and Jacob, his brother Jacob, was sitting comfortably on a log stirring the contents of a pot over the side of a fire. Weak from exhaustion, he tried to smile as he crawled toward food and water.

Out of the corner of his eye, Jacob had seen Esau crawl over the hill and knew exactly what had finally happened. "*Well mother*," he said to himself, "*you have always committed your plans unto your LORD, so let us see what happens when I do.*"

Esau continued his quest on hands and knees toward the fire. The aroma of steamy pottage increased the hunger pangs.

He couldn't help but think, "Even pottage smells good when you are starving."

Remaining occupied with stirring his pottage, Jacob did not move until Esau called out, ever so faintly, "Brother."

Reacting as any brother would, Jacob helped Esau to the log and gave him a water skin. The slurping and splashing soaked his tunic, but Esau did not care. Dropping the skin to the side, Esau reached for the ladle in the simmering pot. Jacob grabbed his hand and looked his sweaty, filthy, starving brother in the eye. He reasoned that this would be the opportune time to take advantage of his unwise and undeserving sibling. Esau's dehydrated appearance looked nothing like the robust, loud drinking fool of past nights.

Then words, words' Esau never thought he would hear, especially from his brother, "Your birthright brother, sell me this day your birthright for my pottage."

"What!" exclaimed Esau.

"I will let you have all the pottage you can eat, but first, you must sell me your birthright."

Esau was not altogether foolish; he knew Isaac would never give Jacob his birthright.

So, Esau said, "You know full well father will never give *you* my birthright."

"It is no matter. You and I will know."

Esau thought for a moment and then said, "I am at the point to die: what profit shall this birthright do me?"

"Swear to me this day that the birthright is to be mine."

Esau reasoned, "I am starving. I need food, not a birthright."

Overpowered by hunger, he could fight no longer, so Esau said. "I swear."

Looking at his larger and stronger starving brother begging for food, Jacob smiled, took the ladle, and filled a bowl with his red pottage. After passing the bowl to Esau, he took a flatbread from the sack, broke it, and put it into the bowl, saying, "Enjoy, my brother."

All the while Jacob was thinking, "*I do not know how, but one day, I will enjoy your inheritance.*"

Reasoning within himself if extortion was the right thing to do, especially to his brother, he thought, "Esau is not wise enough to know what to do with father's wealth."

Watching Esau slop the stew into his mouth as fast as he could, Jacob continued to reason. "*He does not care about giving away his birthright, or he thinks father will give the inheritance to him anyway.*"

Jacob lifted a wineskin and poured a goblet full of wine. "Here, my brother, enjoy."

"Umm," Esau grunted, smacked his lips, and drank in large gulps. Wiping his mouth with the back of his hand, he grunted and said, "Would have tasted better with meat, wild meat." He stood and laughed, saying, "Even an old piece of goat would have made this pottage better."

"But my brother, you are no longer starving," Jacob said with a smile.

Esau yelled back at Jacob, "Yes, I live to hunt, and now I will surely find an eight-point buck for father."

By her fifty-sixth year, Rebekah began sitting by the central fire listening to others tell their stories. Chesed and Chana would always sit with her and on these evenings. On this night, Jacob arrived to find only the three.

After greeting everyone, he asked, "Mother, may I speak with you?"

Intuition determined her son desired to speak privately, so she stood and said, "Yes, Jacob, let us go to my tent."

Jacob sat cross-legged on the ground while Rebekah got herself comfortable on the bed.

Looking into her son's eyes, she smiled with pride. His reddish-brown hair and slim muscular body made him very attractive. More importantly, he would make a good husband when the time was right for him to obtain a bride.

"Yes, my son. What troubles you?" she asked.

"Today, Esau found me at the hillside while I watched the sheep."

"Yes?"

"He had been hunting for many days and ran out of food and water. Famished, he came to sneak a bowl of my pottage."

"Did you not give him something to eat?" she asked in surprise.

"Yes, mother, I did, but before I gave him my pottage, I bartered for his birthright."

Trying to hide her smile at her son's cleverness, she asked, "Esau bartered away his birthright?"

"Yes mother, I withheld the pottage until he gave me his birthright."

"Good. You are the one worthy of the birthright, and you are the one who should have it."

"Mother, I need to know one thing."

"Yes, what is it?"

"Will the birthright be honored by my father?"

"Your father will never know unless you tell him, and even then, I doubt if he will honor it. Esau knows full well he will inherit everything when Isaac goes to sleep with his ancestors."

Looking at the ground, Jacob said, "He gave up the birthright easily because he knew father would never honor it." Looking Rebekah directly in the eye, he said, "I will confront him in the morning, and—"

"No! You will do nothing of the kind. When the time comes, the LORD will show us the way. Sleep my son. It is out of your hands."

Before Jacob could leave, Chesed called from outside the tent. "Rebekah."

"Yes, Chesed."

"Isaac calls for you. It is his stomach again."

"Jacob, I must go now but do not worry. All will be well. Now go."

As Jacob left, Rebekah gave instructions to Chana to get a goblet of hot water and some peppermint from the red tent. Chana went immediately, and Chesed escorted Rebekah to Isaac's tent.

❀ ❀ ❀

Rose tapped Beth on the arm, waking her immediately.

"Rose! He took advantage of Esau!"

"Yes, he did, but what happened when Jacob committed his plan unto the LORD?"

"God established his plan."

"Exactly," said Rose with pride.

"So, Jacob was supposed to trick Esau."

"He was supposed to look for an opportunity, and that is exactly what he did."

"I see," said Beth.

"It's hard to judge ethics or morals until one understands the whole story.

"Yes, it is."

Tell me this Beth, of the two sons, who do you think should be the one to carry Abraham's lineage forward?"

"Jacob."

"Why."

"Jacob is better able to make good judgments and for the right reason."

"Good. Now, think about what each son believes is important. What they value."

Beth thought momentarily and responded, "Esau was a little wild He liked to imitate his father. You know, flirting, drinking, and telling jokes about women."

"Exactly."

"What you are saying is that God wanted someone wise, like Jacob."

"Exactly."

"Why didn't God just send a messenger to straighten everything Esau out?"

"You are asking a question that many have asked through the years. In this story, God didn't work that way. God does not think or act like humans. Rebekah was not told when events would occur, only that they would, and she needed to be ready. Throughout her life, she struggled with Isaac. Abraham and Sarah had to struggle with barrenness for ninety years. Part of what makes God's plans come to pass is the faith of people like Abraham and like Rebekah. Beth dear, God does not always remove people from a struggle, but gives strength to endure and the wisdom to guide through the hardship."

"Sounds complicated to me."

"There is a saying I will paraphrase from the Bible: God's ways are higher than our ways, and God's thoughts are higher than our thoughts."

"So, we are not meant to understand it?"

"Beth, I have studied the Bible for twice as many years as you are old. One thing I have learned, and this is a fact to remember, the more you study the Bible, the more you realize it is a mystery that will fill your life with questions. No matter how much you, or anyone, pastor and lay-person alike, study the Bible, you will never know it all.

"Why not?"

"Because God's ways are higher than our ways?"

"But, will Jacob get the inheritance?"

Rose laughed. "You know what I am going to say?"

"I'll hear more when the time comes?"

"Like Monday?"

"No dear. There is much more to hear before you find out about the inheritance."

"Okay, I'll wait. Thank you for everything. You are such a gift to me."

Rose smiled. "Thank you, dear. Now, you get some sleep and good luck tomorrow."

"Oh yes, almost forgot," Beth laughed.

"See you Sunday, 10:45 am."

Rose winked her magical twinkly wink and nodded.

Beth smiled and said, "Goodnight, Rose."

Under her breath, Rose uttered, "She is finally learning to be patient."

CHAPTER 21

F OLLOWING a day of breakfast and shopping with Joyce, Beth returned to her apartment late Saturday afternoon laden with shopping bags. Reflecting on the hours spent looking over dresses, a short lunch break at the Corner Bistro in the town square, and all the *girls' talk*, Beth thought, "*What a wonderful day*." As she viewed her purchases spread out on the bed, she said, "I haven't bought anything new in over five years." Taking a long look.

"Two possible dresses for dinner in Atlanta;

Two dresses suitable for church or an evening out;

Four pairs of slacks and four blouses appropriate for work;

Two pairs of shoes for work, or church, or evening out. That should do it."

Having enjoyed her shopping extravaganza, Joyce had purchased almost as many new clothes and shoes as Beth and was doing the same thing. They had a great time visiting and joking. Beth realized she hadn't taken much time to get to know Joyce in the office, but now she felt they could be good friends.

Looking at her clothing and remembering Joyce's remarks about the dresses, Beth thought, "Evenings out, where did Joyce get the idea that I had evenings out?"

Opening her closet, Beth looked momentarily before saying, "Out with the old, in with the new," and began tossing the clothing no longer wanted into the corner. Everything was in its proper place. Beth turned on the television and sat down to relax for the night. Moments later, she turned off the television and picked up her Bible. Flipping through the New Testament, Beth recognized some of the passages the guest pastor had presented last Sunday. Setting the alarm for eight o'clock to ensure there would be enough time for breakfast before she dressed for church, she fell into bed earlier than usual.

At precisely 10:45 Sunday morning, Beth arrived at church. Rose and Myrtle were waiting for her on the front steps.

"Good morning," Rose said.

"Hi Rose, hi Myrtle," nodding to both women.

"According to his application and his phone interview, this fellow sounds very interesting," Myrtle commented. "Not as old or experienced as the fellow last week, but his letters of recommendation were glowing."

"Sounds like we are in for a good message today," Rose said. "Shall we take our seats?"

The three women sauntered down the aisle, chatting with a few friends, and then sat in the same pew as last week. Rose explained that most churchgoers are habitual; they like to sit in their favorite spot each Sunday. "I'm not sure why. Maybe it's because people feel comfortable when they know what to expect and feel familiar with the surroundings."

"Creatures of habit," Myrtle said, "and speaking of habit, I can't wait to see what food is waiting to for us in the fellowship hall after the service." With a soft giggle, Myrtle continued, "I have a habit of loving to eat."

Rose laughed and leaned toward Beth, "I think this one likes the food more than the message."

Beth laughed. "It was delicious last week."

"I'm glad you liked it. You are planning to stay again?"

"I wouldn't miss it."

The music began, calling everyone in the packed sanctuary to prepare for the usual hymn sing. All eyes turned to the choir director as he introduced the first hymn and invited the congregation to sing along. Beth attempted to sing along with the congregation but was happy when the Associate Pastor stepped to the podium to introduce the guest preacher.

A tall, distinguished-looking man, who appeared to be in his mid-thirties, stepped behind the pulpit. Dark hair with only a strand or two of gray, whose commanding voice carried his warm greeting through the large church, without the use of a microphone, caused Beth's mouth to drop. His deep voice sounded like that of a radio announcer or a documentary narrator. Not able to take her eyes off him, she sat mesmerized for one whole hour. Every word had been perfectly pronounced and the message profound. Pastor Richards asked significant questions about living a purposeful life. Questions that Beth struggled to answer.

"What is your purpose in life?" he asked. "Are you here to simply mark your days, without thinking, without praying, without looking to God? Are you here to find the fastest ways to earn money or purchase a bigger house or fancy car?" Then he paused before slowly and deliberately asking, "Or, are we, each one of us, here to live for God?"

Beth thought this message was similar to the one she'd read in Proverbs that said hard work would result in God making our plans, or something like that. She couldn't remember the exact wording, but now, she understood the meaning.

In between the serious topics and questions, Pastor Richards made a few jokes. He was a genuinely gifted preacher. Not many people had ever been able to keep Beth's attention or interest for that long. Once the service was over, Beth felt a longing to hear more. He was intelligent, witty, and captivating.

Her thought of, "*I could listen to him every day,*" was interrupted by Myrtle energetically asking, "Ready for lunch?" as she headed for the Fellowship Hall.

Following Myrtle up the aisle, Rose asked, "Did you like the service and, of course, the pastor?"

Attempting to cover her breathlessness, she answered a quick, "Yes."

Rose just smiled and continued to the Fellowship Hall.

Once inside, Beth was surprised to see Pastor Richards standing at the entrance shaking hands and greeting each person who walked through the door.

"So nice to meet you," Beth said as she took his hand. "I got a lot out of your message."

"Do you work in Sageville?" he asked.

And then Beth noticed something. That magic twinkle in his eye, just like Rose.

"I'm an insurance agent downtown," Beth said, trying not to sound infatuated.

"Well then, if I am blessed enough to be called to Sageville, I'll have to come down to get a quote on car insurance. I've been thinking about changing for some time."

After gaining her composure and realizing she was still holding his hand, she let go and said, "I'd be happy to help you."

Beth stepped forward and waited for Rose before getting into line at the food table.

Taking their seat across from Myrtle, Rose said, "He's quite charming, isn't he?"

"Very nice," Myrtle agreed and then asked, "can you pass the salt please?"

Unable to contain herself, Beth added, "I thought his sermon was amazing."

"That's good to hear," Myrtle said. I will be meeting with the committee tomorrow and will let them know. I enjoyed it as well. Dynamic and funny on top of delivering a profound message. Now, can you please pass the mustard?"

Lunch was every bit as delicious as last week's, and Beth found enough dessert to take home for later and for the office.

"The committee has a few questions for me Beth. Will I see you after work tomorrow?" Rose asked as they left the church.

"Yes indeed. Bye Rose, bye Myrtle."

The rest of Beth's day was relaxing. She thought about the service and Pastor Richards. Taking the church program out of her purse, she looked at the Bible passages listed. Opening her Bible and re-reading each one, she thought, "It was a great message."

Monday arrived, and Beth was ready to step into the world a new person. Pleased at the way her new dress slimmed her figure and how the comfort of her expensive shoes made the walk to work more enjoyable, she hadn't expected anyone to notice.

No sooner had she stepped into the office when George blurted, "Well, good morning and look at you. Don't you look great!" Beth couldn't remember the last time a man or anyone for that matter had paid her a compliment. "I heard you two had quite the day shopping on Saturday."

"Sorry," Joyce mouthed from the coffee counter.

Beth laughed. Joyce was also wearing a new outfit and shoes.

"Yes, it was a great day," Beth said.

"I don't know who had the most fun, you or me," Joyce laughed.

"I know who spent the most money," Beth laughed.

Beth had been frugal with her earnings for the past five years. In that same amount of time, she had not purchased one new outfit. Feeling good about her new clothes and the ability to mix and match made the purchases worthwhile. Not only that, she had not purchased a single item at full price. Everything was at least twenty-five percent off, and this made her feel even better.

The ringing phone brought everyone's attention back to work, and once engaged, Beth did not look up from her desk until almost five o'clock. At two minutes after five, Beth was already approaching Rose's garden gate.

"Hello Beth." Concerned, Rose said, "You look like you are out of breath."

"Hello, Rose. Not for long. Oh my, look at this." Pointing to the food tray, she itemized, "Baked ham sandwiches, deviled eggs, strawberry pie.'

Rose replied humbly, "I haven't made strawberry icebox pie in years. Hope it's still good."

"I guess it's a good thing I don't have any scales in my apartment."

"Goodness, you don't have any worries. Fact is, you could probably stand a couple more pounds. Take mine," Rose said as she laughed.

Beth smiled and took her plate from the table. As usual, everything was delicious.

The meal went quickly, and Rose prepared Beth to travel back in time to the market in Gerar.

❀ ❀ ❀

Rebekah and Chana strolled through the market, admiring the many booths. Every necessity was before them, food, cookware, and clothing.

Stopping at a vendor selling expensive fabric. "Rebekah, look at these colorful fabrics." Holding up a bolt of cloth, Chana said, "You would look stunning in a robe of jade green."

"Iliana could help me with the sewing," noted Rebekah.

"Yes," added Chana, "Iliana is an expert when it comes to soft linen and fine wool." Taking the fabric in her hand, "It feels so luxurious. I've not seen fabric like this in many years."

"It is settled then." Turning to the merchant, "How much?" Chana asked.

The vendors in the marketplace reminded her of Damascus. Unbeknown to Bethuel, Shiphrah wanted her to experience life in a thriving metropolis when she was twelve years old. It would help her understand why the line of Terah preferred the quiet, safe environment of a village. As a child, she was frightened when a large dreadful-looking man walked toward her. Shiphrah stepped between Rebekah and the man, looked intently into his eyes, and a moment later, he hurried away. To calm Rebekah's nerves, Shiphrah said, "Come with me, my child. I will treat you to the most sumptuous flatbread in the land. Topped with honey, nuts, and sesame seeds, they are irresistible."

At that moment, Isaac put his arms around Rebekah's waist from behind.

Rubbing her stomach, with breath smelling of heqet (beer), he said, "It is time. I want another son. I will make him a great hunter, just like Esau."

"We already have two sons," responded Rebekah, "are they not enough for you?"

Unbeknownst to Isaac, Abimelech stood on his balcony overlooking the city market. He found much pleasure surveying his vast domain. The market was the largest in the region and always bustling with people. Abimelech felt a sense of pride with all his people shopping and merchants selling, all under the umbrella of safety, provided by, Phichol, the captain of his army. Among the crowd of people, a flash of red hair caught his eye. "Ah, Rebekah," he wistfully sighed. Watching Rebekah and Chana with the cloth merchant, he could see Chana place a roll of jade green material in her bag.

Erotic thoughts of what it might be like to take her into his bed caused a smile to form on his lips. The day she slapped his shoulder back in place did not deter his desire to possess this vivacious redhead. A moment later, his attention was drawn to Isaac, approaching his sister from behind. Abimelech's warm smile turned to disdain, then to anger, as he watched Isaac put his arms around Rebekah's waist, caress her bulging stomach. His lips lavish kisses around her neck. Overcome with rage, Abimelech shouted, "Phichol!" Moments later, he stood following the sightline of the king's finger until his eyes lighted upon Isaac squeezing Rebekah's bottom. Ahuzzath responded to the angry shout and stepped onto the balcony in time to see this lewd public display of indecency, generally reserved for late-night raunchiness in the *malown* (inn).

Appalled, Ahuzzath said, "I cannot believe my eyes."

"Look at him stagger," Phichol pointed, "he's been into the heqet."

Abimelech realized, "Rebekah is not his sister."

Aghast, Ahuzzath replied, "My king, our men . . . had it not been for her servant constantly at her side—"

"Our men," shouted Abimelech, "I have wanted to take her into my bed."

Beyond appalled, Abimelech commanded, "Bring the Hebrew to me!"

Phichol turned and marched out without speaking.

Isaac stopped in his tracks when he heard Phichol shout his name. Turning slowly, he answered, "Yes?"

"The king commands your presence; right now!"

Frightened by the abruptness of the command, Isaac, suddenly sober, said, "Of course," and began walking.

Phichol's shout got the attention of many in the marketplace. Among them were Rebekah and Chana and Chesed, who had been bartering with merchants on his own. Chesed rushed to Rebekah's side, uncertain of why the soldiers had come to take Isaac to their king. Chesed could tell Isaac was at a loss as to why but soon recalled Isaac's fondling of Rebekah moments before and remembered Isaac's lie. Suddenly overwhelmed with fear, Chesed said, "Come; we must get back to the encampment and find Esau and Jacob. Hurrying along, he kept silent while being asked what was happening by the frightened women.

Standing on the dais, Abimelech waited, tapping his foot, pacing, tapping his foot. He never liked the judgment seat and refused to sit in judgment for petty crimes, but this was serious, with significant ramifications. He couldn't believe Isaac had lied to him. Pretending Rebekah was his sister had placed the kingdom in moral jeopardy. His people were very liberated, but to take another man's wife was not acceptable.

Abimelech's friend, Ahuzzath, stood with him and watched two soldiers drag a scuffling Isaac into the room. Soldiers and onlookers stood silent with all eyes on the king, waiting to hear what he would say. To their surprise, the king started his inquiry with a soft, unassuming voice. "Isaac, when you came into my land, you told me Rebekah was your sister. Did you not?"

Isaac stood frozen and speechless. His mind flashed back to his squeezing Rebekah's backside and kissing her neck, and he knew trouble was about to rain down upon him. Not knowing what his fate might be, Isaac began to tremble. Abimelech was more than a tribal chieftain; he was a king, and Isaac had lied to a king.

Speaking softly, Abimelech continued, "Now I ask you again; is she your sister," his voice rising a few decibels, "or your wife?"

Isaac remained silent as a horrible fear enveloped his being.

Unable to tolerate Isaac's silence, Abimelech yelled, "Well? I demand you to answer!"

Phichol pushed a sword into Isaac's side.

Hanging his head in shame and regret, "Oh, great king," falling to his knees, he confessed, "she, she is my wife."

A loud gasp rose from the crowd of courtiers.

Abimelech, still shouting, "Did you not know, did you not think of what would happen with that lie? Any one of our men could have taken her. Even I have desired to lie with her."

Ahuzzath shouted from the dais, "Anyone in the kingdom might have lain with her!" Slowly descending the steps, Ahuzzath stopped in front of Isaac and said, "Pick him up." Two soldiers lifted Isaac to his feet. On raising his head, the soldiers pushed it back down. Ahuzzath shouted, "You are not worthy to look upon our king. Have you any idea of the disgrace your lie would have brought upon my king, upon our people?"

Isaac did not respond.

Calming himself, Abimelech stepped from the dais and asked, "Why? Why did you lie? Why could you not tell me the truth?"

Isaac replied in a weak voice, "I lied for fear of my life."

Abimelech shouted, "Your life? I am repulsed." Gathering his thoughts, Abimelech continued. "So, this is what you think of me, that I would murder you to possess your wife."

Returning to the dais, he commanded, "Phichol, tomorrow, before the sun is high, you will see that Isaac and all he has, is driven from our land."

Isaac began softly, "Gracious king—"

"Quiet," Abimelech bellowed.

Continuing his condemnation, "I should have you strung up, wiped, and beheaded, but for the sake of your wife, who was able to fix my shoulder, I will allow you to leave my land."

About to protest, Phichol pushed his sword to Isaac's throat and said, "Silence."

Abimelech raised his arm and commanded, "Guards, remove this despicable Hebrew from my presence."

Those in the court turned their backs as Isaac passed, his plea falling on deaf ears.

❈ ❈ ❈

Rose used her usual method of bringing Beth back to her current reality.

"Rose, what is going to happen now? Where will they go?"

"Dear, that is the next part of the story," and she winked her magical wink.

"Oh Rose, you do make it difficult to practice patience. Sometimes I wish I could just sit listening until you get to the end."

Rose laughed, "I don't think I could go that long without sleep. Much more of the story remains for you to hear."

"Okay, I'll head home. See you tomorrow."

"Goodnight, Beth."

CHAPTER 22

For some reason, nothing was exciting about this day at the office. The best part of the day was, it was finally over.

Again, Joyce was the first one to leave the office. "See you all tomorrow," Joyce shouted as she scurried toward the door.

"What's your hurry?" George asked.

"Big date tonight. It's my anniversary," as the front door closed.

Looking to Beth, "Wow, that's pretty cool," George remarked.

"Okay, George, see you tomorrow," Beth said, following Joyce out the door.

"Hey Joyce," Beth yelled.

"Yes?"

"Wearing that new dress tonight?"

"You betcha! Shoes, too," As Joyce got into her car.

"Have fun," Beth replied.

As usual, Rose was waiting for Beth. The delicious meal of pasta salad, sweet tea, and key lime pie hit the spot, as did the conversation. With dinner over and the plates stacked in the kitchen, they returned to the porch.

Beth asked, "Where did Isaac relocate the tribe when Abimelech kicked him out of the region?"

"Well then, you sit back, relax, and let me transport you back to Abraham's encampment."

❄ ❄ ❄

By the time Isaac returned to the encampment, Chesed had already started everyone packing. Many of the people never knew the reason for their sudden departure. It didn't matter, as it always seemed to them that is what Hebrews did; move. Days later, they found themselves south of

Beersheba. First order of business, dig or find a well. Second-order of business, build a domed bread oven. Not long after opening an old well, Philistine shepherds came and forced them to leave. The harassment continued until Isaac's tribe cleared an old well dug by Abraham and settled in a Valley south of Beersheba. Sadly, the upset, the moving, the harassment by Philistine shepherds was too much for old Chesed to bear; his heart gave out. Isaac did speak well of him at the funeral. Chesed's devotion was acknowledged by how faithfully he had served his father Abraham all his life.

During his last year, Chesed had begun training Hadad to look to the needs of Isaac. In reality, Chesed had spent more time preparing him to care for Rebekah. He confessed to Hadad that there were times when he felt like Rebekah's adopted father. Hadad knew that Rebekah had always been tenacious and high-spirited and that her spirit must never be tempered. Most of all, Hadad was told never to disobey Rebekah. After piling the last stone over Chesed's earthen grave, Hadad waited as Rebekah was the only one to stay behind and pray. Able to see for himself how much Rebekah cared for Chesed, he set his heart to her service.

In Gerar, Ahuzzath began having second thoughts about running Isaac out of the country. He called Abimelech and Phichol to discuss how Isaac's god had prospered him in their land. Ever fearful of what an angry god might do, they gathered a small troop of soldiers and headed south to find Isaac. Reassuring Isaac he would no longer be harassed, they made a small feast and, in the morning, a covenant of peace.

God appeared to Isaac that very night and reaffirmed the covenant of land promised to the children of Abraham. Deciding to remain in the region, Isaac built an altar unto the God of Abraham. Life was good once again, and the people lived there in peace and prospered. Nearing one hundred years of age, Isaac was unable to walk on his own. Standing near the central fire, he was supported by two new servant women, Gila and Tabitha, not yet twenty years old. Wedding flowers adorned a single tent. Oil lamps cast their flickering light upon a few wedding guests. All was quiet. Esau, now forty years of age, stood in a white gown beside his father. The guests waited impatiently for Judith, the daughter of Beeri the Hittite, to be escorted to the groom. People were skeptical of Esau's choices. He had already married Adah, the daughter of Elon the Hittite, and Oholibamah, the daughter of Zibeon the Hivite. Isaac was sad because he knew in his heart, he'd never guided Esau to know that his prime wife must, of necessity, be of Terah's tribal line. It was too late. Esau was his father's son.

Several tents away, Bayla opened the tent curtain and the bride, dressed in white, stepped out to be escorted to Esau. Once the bride was outside the tent, Bayla dropped the curtain. At sixty years of age, Bayla had difficulty hiding the scorn on her face as she walked the fourth of Esau's wives to his side. Unlike a traditional Hebrew bride, Judith, fifteen years of age, did not wear a veil to cover her face or a flower in her hair. Bayla placed Judith on Esau's left side. The happy couple smiled at each other with ogling eyes. Bayla mumbled to herself, "Another heathen bride," then, unable to look at Isaac with his new warming girls, she retreated to her tent and cried. Isaac, assisted by Gila and Tabitha, moved forward and began the wedding ceremony.

Sitting with Rebekah under the awning of her tent, Jacob was saddened to see tears running down the cheeks of his heartsick mother. Disgusted by Esau's choices, her seventy-five years of hard work was beginning to take their toll. She could not hear Isaac, and conversely, he could not hear her. This distance provided the opportunity for Rebekah to voice her disparaging remarks about Esau's latest union.

Turning to Jacob, she said, "Look at those two, smiling like a couple of ninnies."

Jacob shook his head and said, "I don't understand, mother. He has already married Adah and Oholibamah, and now he marries Judith, another Hittite?"

"Your brother believes Isaac will bless him no matter who he marries. He thinks he is the blessed one."

"But that is just the point. Father will bless him. You know he has always allowed Esau to do whatever he wants."

"Esau can do whatever he likes, but Esau will only receive the blessing over my dead body."

Jacob gasped, "Mother, do not talk so of your son, please."

Looking Jacob directly in the eyes, Rebekah said slowly and emphatically, "My son, if you ever married a Canaanite woman, my life would be over. It would be meaningless."

Returning their attention to the wedding ceremony, they watched Isaac wrap the wedding scarf around the hands of Esau and Judith.

Jacob looked at the number of single and eligible young women watching the ceremony, and after a moment of contemplation, asked,

"Mother . . . who will I marry? We are in a foreign land. Both of my uncles live too far away, except, of course, for Ishmael."

"Hush child, not of Ishmael's line, heaven forbid."

"Where then can I go for a bride?"

"I have lived by faith for sixty years, and I know, when the time comes, God will provide? Now, help me up."

Jacob assisted Rebekah to her feet. Nodding toward the wedding tent, they watched the tent curtain fall as Esau and Judith entered.

In a sarcastic tone, Rebekah said, "Well, there it is. In nine moons, Isaac will have another Hittite rug rat to play with."

"Mother!" Jacob said disapprovingly.

"Jacob, I know in my heart you will be the one to receive the blessing, but for now, do not worry about finding a bride. The time will most assuredly come."

From the tent, Jacob heard a weak voice cry out, "Rebekah."

With eyes still red from tears, Rebekah said, "Help me tend to Chana. She will soon rest with her ancestors."

"I am sad for you mother," Jacob said as he opened the tent for his mother, "she has been a good friend."

"I shall miss her."

A few months after Esau's second wedding, Isaac's health suddenly declined. Now blind, lying on his bed waiting to die, he knew his time on earth was coming to an end. Trying to keep him warm, Tabitha and Gila snuggled on either side of Isaac. Chesed had passed away ten years earlier. Before passing, Chesed had trained Hadad to take his place, and now, Isaac needed a servant to assist him more than ever. Waking one morning, Isaac finally realized the end was near.

He called out, "Chesed, come; I need you."

Resting a short distance away, Hadad answered, "Yes Master,"

"Chesed? I called for Chesed. Where is Chesed?"

"It has been ten years, Master."

"Ten years?"

"Yes, ten years since Chesed died."

Isaac shook his head and took another frail breath, "No, no! I called for Chesed. Chesed, bring my son, bring me, Esau."

Hadad knew there was no sense in arguing with Isaac about his name, so he left the tent to find Esau.

Rebekah, at seventy-five, was still helping the women put flatbread into the clay bread oven. Noticing Hadad's quick, she watched him scurry

off. A few moments later, she watched Hadad pulling Esau into Isaac's
tent.

"*This is it,*" Rebekah said to herself. Leaving the bake oven, she
circled a few tents and stopped to adjust her sandals behind Isaac's tent.

Rebekah overheard Hadad ask, "Do you wish me to stay, Master?"

"No Chesed, you may go."

Parting one of the tent seams, Rebekah watched Hadad leave, and
Esau approached his father's bed.

"Gila move, that my son may kneel beside me."

Isaac held his hand out and said, "Your hand, my son, your hand as
I cannot see."

Isaac lovingly ran his hand up and down Esau's forearm, saying,
"Good, it is you Esau. Come near." Isaac dropped Esau's hand and continued. "Behold, my son, I am old, and I know the day comes."

"No, father, please, not yet. The day has not come."

Taking another shallow breath, he said, "You know how I love the
taste of venison."

"Yes father, you know I do."

"I desire that taste, one last time."

Esau tried to assure his father the time had not yet come by saying,
"Father, do not speak in such a way."

"Listen to me. Take your bow and quiver of arrows, go out into the
hills and bring me venison that I may enjoy that savory meat one last
time."

Resolved to reality, Esau said, "Yes, father. I will bring you venison
fit for a king."

"Good, good. Bring me venison that I may eat, and my soul will
bless you before I die."

Esau smiled and thought, "*And Jacob thought he could steal my
blessing.*"

Esau rose and said, "Father, I will hunt into the night and let it hang
until tomorrow afternoon when I shall have Judith make you a savory
dish. It will be like none you have ever had in the past."

"Do not tarry, my son."

In haste, Esau turned and left the tent.

Rebekah watched Esau leave for his tent. Moments after entering, he
rushed out equipped for the hunt. Rebekah ran as fast as she could to the
valley in which Jacob was grazing his sheep. Arriving huffing and puffing,
she bent over to catch her breath.

Oran, one of the shepherds, seeing Jacob was still among the sheep, called out, "Your mother Jacob, your mother."

When Jacob saw his mother huffing and puffing, he ran to her, fearing something dreadful had happened.

"Mother, what is it?" he said on arrival.

Rebekah caught her breath and blurted out, "Your father, your brother."

"Mother, slow down. Come sit."

Rebekah sat down on a log and caught her breath. Jacob sat beside her and took her hand, asking, "What is the matter? Is it father?"

"Yes . . . no. I overheard your father with Esau."

"So, what did he say?"

"The blessing, he plans to give Esau his blessing."

"But I have the birthright mother. Esau sold it to me. The birthright is mine!"

"I know, but without the blessing, it means nothing."

"Nothing?"

"Yes, nothing. It is the blessing that passes on the inheritance."

"He knew it was only a word when he agreed."

Standing, feeling all was hopeless, Jacob said, "We can do nothing. He will not honor his word." Feeling heartsick, Jacob was critical of his mother for the first time in his life and said, "Faith, humph, you said you had faith." Speaking louder. "Where is your faith now?

Silence prevailed while Rebekah thought and prayed. Moments later, she stood, looked at the flock, and said, "Go, fetch two kid goats and bring them to me. I will make a savory meat dish for your father, the kind he loves," Taking Jacob by the shoulders, "and you will bring it to him."

"No Mother. Have you lost your mind?"

"Listen! If you do as I say, we will fool him, and he will bless you. Now go!"

Taking a step away, he stopped. Rubbing his forearm, he cried out, "Mother, Esau is a hairy man, and I am smooth. Father will surely feel my arm and curse me."

"Let your curse be upon me. Now," pushing Jacob toward the flock, "Go, quickly. Fetch two kid goats and bring them to me." As Jacob moved away sheepishly, he heard his mother call out, "And do not worry about your smooth skin."

❈ ❈ ❈

Rose tapped Beth's arm gently and woke her.

"Rose, how can she? How can she possibly fool Isaac? Will she? Will she not get caught?"

Rose smiled. "You will find out."

"Seriously? You're going to make me wait?" Beth asked.

Rose nodded and said, "You must remember that Rebekah had committed her plan unto God."

"All right, all right. I know I'll find out soon enough."

"Yes, Beth, soon enough."

CHAPTER 23

Bᴇᴛʜ greeted Joyce the following day upon arrival with, "How was your anniversary date?"

"It was just wonderful. We drove over to that little country dinner theatre, just off Interstate 75, you know the one?"

"Yes, I've seen it."

"It was a great show, and the dinner was incredible."

"What show did you see?"

"One of my favorites, Saturday Night Fever."

"I saw that on television years ago. Did you enjoy it?"

"Very much so."

"I'll bet the singing and music were terrific."

"Amazing actually, and so romantic."

"How many years now?"

"Fifteen."

"With the same man?"

"Ha, ha. Yes, smarty pants."

"Did your husband like the new dress?"

"Of course, but I didn't tell him the price. He wouldn't have liked it quite as much." They both laughed. Beth's phone rang, and she never got another chance to talk to Joyce or George all day. Happy that Wednesday was behind her, it was time to get to Rose's home for a story that just kept getting more interesting the longer it went.

After another delectable dinner of barbequed chicken and coleslaw, followed by dessert, Rose asked, "Now dear, you remember Rebekah had a scheme to obtain the blessing for Jacob?"

"Oh yes, I thought about it all last night. I wondered how in the world she was ever going to pull it off."

"Okay, close your eyes and relax. We will go back to the time when Jacob brought the goats to Rebekah."

❀ ❀ ❀

With Chana and Chesed having gone to sleep with their ancestors, it seemed like an era had ended. Rebekah, and her new attendant Ariel, watched Jacob string up two goats on tripods, slaughter, bleed, and dress them.

"Jacob," Rebekah instructed, "when you finish skinning the goats, bring me the two meatiest shanks. Oran, you take the soft underbelly to Ariel. She will be waiting to clean and dry the hides."

Puzzled, Jacob went about the task at hand but could not help but wonder what his mother was contriving.

Rebekah knew precisely the way Isaac preferred his wild game. She would use plenty of spices and simmer the meat all afternoon.

Ariel deboned the shanks as Rebekah prepared the pot with the necessary spices.

"Do you think this will work Rebekah," Ariel asked.

"When this meat finishes simmering, even you will not be able to tell the difference between venison and goat. I have prepared this dish many times, and he continues to ask for it, never suspecting the meat isn't venison. You will see."

Turning to Jacob, Rebekah said, "Go to your brother's tent. Find an outer robe that has not been washed and bring it to my tent."

Jacob laughed, saying, "That should be easy."

Everyone went about their specific jobs. Rebekah was a good administrator and before long, the lamb was simmering. Ariel was busy trimming the underbelly skin to the exact specifications.

Jacob searched through the garments strewn about Esau's tent, thinking to himself, *"My brother, how can you live in this mess? You are such a slob."* It was easy to find the right garment. It was in a pile waiting to be washed. Jacob selected the least *aromatic* garment he could find.

Double-checking the repugnant odor, he said, "Perfect." On passing Ariel stirring the simmering pot of goat stew, Jacob breathed a more pleasant aroma and said, Perfect."

After presenting the cloak to his mother, Rebekah shook it and then told Jacob to remove his and put Esau's on.

"Mother, it stinks."

"That's the point. Now, put it on."

A moment later, "Give Ariel your arm."

Puzzled by his mother's request, Jacob timidly extended his arm. Ariel proceeded to slide a perfectly fit underbelly sleeve up Jacob's arm and then secure it behind the elbow.

"Now, the other arm," Rebekah instructed.

After securing the second sleeve, Ariel passed Rebekah a strange piece of the underbelly.

"Bend over," Rebekah said and then placed the piece around the back of Jacob's neck, saying, "There."

"This will never work mother. These skins will not fool Father. I don't want to do this. I'm afraid."

"Quiet! It will work."

Feeling uneasy about his mother's plan, Jacob could not help but worry about the skins moving, or worse, falling off when his father touched him. A twinge of conscience enveloped him as he did care what his father would think of him. He knew what Esau would think, but he had more of a problem with his father's feelings.

Again, he protested, "I am afraid, mother. Father will curse me if I'm discovered, and Esau will kill me if I'm successful."

"Stop your whining. The blessing must come to you. It is the will of the LORD."

"I'm still afraid."

"It must be this way. I will pray for you." Cringing at the aroma of Esau's robe, "Now, let's get the bread and stew your father loves so much."

With the sun dropping low in the sky, Rebekah sent Jacob on his way with a kiss to the forehead and joined Ariel under the tent awning to wait and watch.

Trying his best to imitate Esau's voice, Jacob called out, "Father, I am here with the savory stew you desire."

Poking his head into the tent, he saw Isaac bundled up against Tabitha and Gila. Try as they may, Isaac could not stop shivering.

With his breathing labored, Isaac opened his eyes and struggled to ask, "What? What is it?"

Tabitha replied, "It is—"

"Esau," Jacob said forcefully, cutting off Tabitha and giving both girls *the look*.

"What? So soon? The sun has not yet set."

Isaac struggled to sit against his pillows. Turning to Gila and Tabitha, he said, "Help me. Prop me up."

Gila lifted Isaac from the back while Tabitha built up the cushions. Once propped up, as best possible, Isaac said, "Come."

Jacob stepped into the tent, with bread in one hand and a bowl of stew in the other. Giving Tabitha and Gila *the look* once again, he nodded sharply toward the exit. The two women understood to leave immediately.

On her way out, Tabitha said, "We will leave you with your *son*, master."

Jacob knelt at the side of his father. He wafted the aroma of stew under his father's nose with the back of his hand. The distraction did not work. Isaac was upset that he could not see.

He asked, "Who are you?"

Garbling his voice, Jacob answered, "Esau, your firstborn. I have done all that you asked and have prepared the venison you love so much."

"Venison? So quickly?" Isaac asked as he pushed himself up as much as possible.

"The LORD brought it to me as soon as I entered the clearing."

"Your voice, it is different."

"It is the spice, father," and then he coughed.

"Come near my son."

Jacob shuffled closer so that his knees touched Isaac's side.

Isaac's feeble hand touched the bowl, and then he slid his hand up Jacob's arm and down the other arm, saying, "The voice, it is that of Jacob, but the arms, Esau. Kiss me, my son." Jacob moved forward and kissed Isaac on the forehead. At the same time, Isaac reached up and took Jacob by the back of the neck and drew him near. At the same time as he was rubbing the back of Jacob's neck, Isaac breathed in the aroma of the unwashed robe.

Confused, Isaac said, "Forgive me, for I am old and my hearing is bad. Your voice sounds like Jacob, but your skin is that of Esau. The smell of your robe is that of the field and not stinking sheep," he said gruffly. "Call Tabitha and Gila for me that I may eat.

Jacob did so, and when they entered, he gave them *the look*, once again, and said, "Help my father with his *venison*."

With a nervous hand, Tabitha took the spoon and began feeding Isaac. Jacob moved away from his father but continued to watch the women as they served the stew. As Tabitha fed Isaac the stew, Gila tore pieces of flatbread, dipped them into the sauce to soften.

"Oh, my son, I have waited far too long for the taste of your venison." Smacking his lips. "Your mother tries to feed me that awful goat stew, but I can always tell the difference."

Gila finished wiping out the bowl with pieces of flatbread. Tabitha helped Isaac wash the last piece of bread down with a goblet of wine.

Jacob's silent look was enough for the girls to get up and leave once again.

When alone, Jacob knelt beside Isaac and said, "Thy blessing, father."

His stomach full, Isaac was able to relax and say, "Yes, yes, come close."

Shuffling his knees to Isaac's side, Jacob lifted his father's hand and held it on his forehead.

Isaac's weak voice proclaimed, "May God give thee of the dew of heaven, the fatness of the earth, and an abundance of wheat, wine, and oil. Let people serve thee, and nations bow down to thee, be lord over thy brethren, and let thy mother's sons bow down to thee. Cursed be every one that curses thee and blessed be all that bless thee."

Jacob lowered Isaac's hand, saying, "Rest my father, rest."

Taking one final glance at his father, Jacob exited the tent and motioned the girls to enter. His mother's plan had worked. He had received the blessing but wondered what Esau would do when he learned of the trickery.

Later that evening, Esau opened his father's tent with a bowl of authentic venison stew in hand. He could see his father sleeping between Gila and Tabitha.

Proud of himself for having bagged a deer so soon, he called in a soft voice, "Father, I have brought you the savory meat you desired."

Then his eye caught the goblet and bowl on the ground. Putting his bowl down, Esau lifted the empty bowl to his nose.

Running his fingers inside the bowl and tasting the red sauce, he screamed, "No!" The scream startled Isaac and the two girls as Esau screamed again, "This is goat; stinking goat!"

Isaac struggled to wake and figure out why a familiar voice was screaming.

Dropping to his knees, "Father, what has happened?"

"What? Who are you?"

"I am Esau, your firstborn. I brought you the venison you love."

Isaac trembled. Confused and afraid, he was not able to comprehend what had happened just hours before.

"My blessing father, I have come for my blessing."

"Where is he who brought me venison?" Isaac asked.

"It was a goat!" Esau yelled. "It was not venison. I have the venison."

All went silent. Isaac found the bowl in Esau's hand, dipped his fingers into the sauce, and tasted.

As the reality of the deceit sunk in, Isaac screamed a feeble, "No!" Catching his breath, he cried, "I gave the blessing to your brother!"

As Isaac began to weep, Esau cried, "No! How could you, father?"

Grabbing Gila by the hair, Esau pulled her close and screamed, "How could you let this happen?"

Moving to help her friend, Tabitha said, "We were afraid. Jacob gave us such a horrible look—"

"He made us leave Esau. He made us leave," Gila injected.

Releasing Gila, Esau moaned, "He deceived me again."

A moment later, through his tears and feeling beguiled, Isaac cried, "No! It was not just Jacob. It was Rebekah. My wife has deceived me."

Gila and Tabitha moved away and huddled in the corner of the tent.

Beside himself, angry at himself for selling his birthright many years ago, Esau paced the floor erratically until a calm came over him.

The answer was simple, "It doesn't matter father, bless me," he said, "I am Esau, your firstborn! The blessing goes to the firstborn."

"No, my son, there is only one blessing, and your brother has stolen it."

"He is rightly named Jacob, for he has supplanted me these two times. First, he took my birthright, and now he has stolen my blessing!"

"Oh Esau, my son, my son," Isaac whimpered.

"Father, have you no blessing for me? Have you not reserved one for me? For my birthright?"

"I cannot. I've made your brother lord overall, and all your brethren I have given to him as servants. With wheat, wine, and oil, I have sustained him."

"Oh, father, how can this be?" Overcome with grief, Esau staggered around the tent weeping. Then, cried out one last time, "Has thou not a blessing for me?"

The extreme anguish of the moment caused Isaac to regain temporary control of all his faculties.

Beckoning Esau to his side, he said, "When it comes to pass, that the yoke is broken from your neck, only then will you have dominion over the land."

"What does it mean father?"

"You shall dwell in a land rich with flocks and crops, sustained by dew from heaven. Sadly, you must live by the sword and when the time comes you no longer serve your brother, will you be able to break the yoke from your neck?

Esau stepped outside his father's tent and, at the top of his lungs, yelled, "Jacob! I hate you! After our father dies, so shall you!"

❀ ❀ ❀

The moment Rose paused, Beth woke up. It was the first time she understood the story was finished for the evening without Rose waking her.

"Rose, Jacob stole the blessing?"

Rose nodded and said, "True, Jacob had to act on his behalf, but in reality, it was Rebekah who orchestrated the deceit from start to finish?"

"So, this is why God had chosen Rebekah. She had to be strong-willed and smart enough to come up with a plan at the last minute to deceive her husband for the sake of her son?"

Rose felt a tinge of pride knowing Beth understood how Rebekah, in faith, had committed her plan unto the LORD.

Beth asked slowly, "If God had spoken to Isaac, why was Rebekah necessary?"

"Theologians have struggled with that question forever. All I can say is free will. Everyone must make their own freewill choice to listen, or not to listen."

"Wow! Even though she was barren for twenty years, she remained faithful. Can you imagine?"

"Yes dear, I can. You see, Rebekah had the creativity to work out a plan when the time came. She knew, somehow, Jacob was to receive the blessing. God had selected Rebekah to be Isaac's bride, not only because she was strong-willed but because Isaac would cease to be obedient.

Beth thought about the bigger picture for the first time. "All the years, when Rebekah was growing up, so independent, unconventional and strong; under the tutelage of Shiphrah and her mother were for a purpose, God's purpose.

"Yes Beth, but never forget, Rebekah, like you and I, have to choose to be obedient to God's will."

For the first time, Beth understood that it was her resistance to her mother's faith that brought about emptiness in her life.

Without realizing it, the virtue of patience was blossoming within Beth as she resolved to be content with the day's story.

Rose was not altogether surprised to hear, "I won't ask if Esau finds his brother and kills him. So, I'll just wait until tomorrow."

Rose smiled and said, "That a girl!"

Beth stood and replied, "Okay. Guess I'd better go."

"Goodnight, dear. Sleep well."

CHAPTER 24

THE cooler fall air made the walk to work pleasant. Along the way, Beth noticed how the taller trees were beginning to change color. Relating the change in color to her feelings, Beth knew something was changing inside. Maybe it was the story. After all, Rose had said her life would be forever changed by the end. With the story revolving around so many different characters and conflicts, Beth had not noticed that God was at work in her life. Like Abraham, Isaac, and Rebekah, Beth would have to choose to listen or not. On reaching the office, she thought, "*If there is a plan for life, then there must be a purpose*?" As she fell into a deep sleep the night before, Beth wondered if there was someone different she could talk with about the commit your plan thing?

Opening the office door, she was surprised to hear a familiar voice talking with Joyce.

"Here she is now. Beth, this is Abbott Richards."

When Beth looked up, she had to keep her jaw from dropping. Standing before her was Sunday's guest preacher. "Pastor Richards, my goodness, what are you doing here? It's good to see you."

Surprised, Joyce asked, "You've met?"

"Yes, in church." Motioning to a chair, "Please, pastor, have a seat. I will be right with you."

Beth felt nervous for some unknown reason. Here at her desk was the pastor who delivered a meaningful message just days before. It was a message that she needed to hear. The fact of the matter was, the message felt like it was meant for her alone.

Putting away her purse, she took a seat at her desk and composed herself.

"How are you finding Sageville?"

"I like it a lot. I have wanted to find a church in a town exactly like this one, and I'm praying that I will be called to Sageville and the Good Shepherd Church."

"That would be nice. I'd like to hear you every Sunday," Beth said, almost blushing.

"Thank you. I hope the committee feels the same way," Abbott laughed.

Catching her faux pas, Beth regained her composure and asked, "What can I do to help? You mentioned your car insurance on Sunday?"

"Oh, yes. I wanted to pick up some information about your policies, just in case.

"Just in case," Beth asked.

"Yes, just in case God places me here."

Beth couldn't help but think that Pastor Richards was doing precisely what Proverbs was teaching, "committing his work unto God."

"O yes," he continued, "I'll look over your homeowners' plan as well. Just in case."

Beth reached into her desk file and gathered the information, and said, " I'll put it in a folder for you."

"Thank you."

Handing the file over, she said, "You know, I was thinking about the plan this morning, on the way to work."

"My homeowners' plan?" he laughed.

"No," giggling nervously. "No, not the policies plan." Not wanting to speak too loudly, she lowered her voice and nodded toward the others in the office, and grimaced. Pastor Richards nodded to convey he got the message of wanting to talk elsewhere.

"About God's plan," he asked with a smile.

"Yes, exactly. Would you have time to answer questions about God's planning?"

"That is one of my favorite topics."

"Oh good," replied Beth with a sigh of relief.

Pastor Richards lowered his voice and asked, "Beth, I don't want to impose or seem forward, but maybe you could join me for lunch tomorrow, and I can try and answer your questions?"

"That would be wonderful."

"Well then, since I don't know my way around, could you suggest a place to eat?"

"There is a Bistro on Main Street that has a variety of lunch options and specialty coffees. I could meet you there at 12:30."

"Perfect. The name?"

Laughing, "It is very original, Main Street Bistro."

He laughed, stood, and said, "I will see you then, and thank you for the information."

After Pastor Richards closed the door, Beth saw Joyce out of the corner of her eye, smiling. Not wanting to be grilled by Joyce, or at least not just yet, Beth continued to act as if it was strictly a business conversation.

The Main Street Bistro was crowded, but Beth and Abbott found a table near the back corner. It was quieter in the back section, and Beth thought the quiet might help with the conversation. Once they ordered, Abbott began the discussion. Beth appreciated his expertise since it was a complex subject.

"Now, let's see, you had a question about God's plan?"

"Yes, I do. I probably have too many questions."

"No such thing."

Smiling at his response, she said, "I have only recently begun attending church and reading the Bible. I feel like a little girl back in Sunday School and do not understand anything."

Returning her smile, he said, "Most people feel that way from time to time. The Bible is full of mystery, no matter what age you are. Is there a specific question you have for me?"

Abbott paused as the server placed their lunches on the table. After thanking her, he continued. "I mean, a specific question about the Bible?"

"I have recently come to know Rose. You met her on Sunday."

"Oh yes, and Myrtle," he chuckled. "They are adorable."

"Yes, they are. Rose is a, well, the local storyteller."

"Storyteller?"

"Yes. I have been listening to her story for several weeks now. I go to her house each evening after work, and she continues with a new episode."

"Is this story from the Bible?"

"Mostly, but some of it, well, has been handed down from storytellers over the centuries.

"I see . . . You know, the Jewish people have handed down stories and traditions for centuries. What's amazing is, these stories fill in some of the Biblical voids."

"How interesting, " Beth said, "this story is about Rebekah."

"Rebekah, from the Old Testament. She was an amazing woman."

"But how do we know about God's plan? Rebekah had messages. How do we know if we are doing the right thing when we do not get messages like her?"

"I see why you are puzzled but don't worry, we all are. Even if we know the Bible well, and I think I have a pretty good understanding, we may not know all. It has a lot of unanswered questions for people today." Pastor Richards sat back, took a sip of coffee, and continued, "Let me see, as I understand it, something compelled you to allow Rose to tell you the story of Rebekah; out of curiosity, you were inspired to attend church; my sermon on God's plan and purpose for your life, left unanswered questions; am I right?"

"My goodness, yes."

"Rebekah and Abraham are wonderful stories of faith, but God spoke to each of them, so their obedience was understandable."

"Yes," retorted Beth, "but God also spoke to Isaac, and he did not listen."

"Exactly, each individual must make a freewill choice. God does not force obedience, and all through the Old Testament, Israel only suffered, not from God's doing, but from the results of their refusal to listen and obey."

"You are right. Not once in Rebekah's story did God force her to do anything. In a way, free will is one of the most difficult concepts for Christians to nail down or define."

"Why is that Abbott?" Beth said, feeling more at ease.

"If everything in life, or a particular situation, especially those of health issues, works out for good, it is easy to believe it was God's plan. But what happens when you lose everything, a bad investment, or loved ones die; is that God's plan as well?"

"I don't know."

"Some will say, 'Only the good is God's plan.' but that is poor theology and suggests that God is not in control. So, you can see the complexities of trying to find a single answer that will satisfy every individual."

"What am I to do? What am I to think and believe?"

"First, always go back to the Bible for guidance. Study the life of Jesus, his teaching, his actions. As Jesus said, 'God is the God of the living,' and as such, God wants us to have life in abundance, but, like the Old Testament stories, we have to decide to follow God's will for our lives, or not. Many people will pray, 'God give me this, or God, give me that,' but the fact is, God has already given humanity all they need from birth. All we need do is to trust, develop and use our individual gifts.'"

"Wow."

"Before Jesus ascended into heaven, he left God's Holy Spirit to dwell in our hearts. We simply need to believe and accept. Remember, faith is not about fact. It's about a strong belief."

"But I've always lived by fact."

"The Apostle Paul wrote, 'Faith is the substance of things hoped for, the evidence of things not seen.'"

"Really?"

"Yes, but the fact of the matter is, others see our faith in our actions."

"I remember from Sunday school that the Apostle Paul was an educated Pharisee, and if he did not try and define God's plan, then who on earth can?"

"Exactly."

"That is why it is called the living Word. It is not static. It grows in us with the Holy Spirit."

Both sat in silent contemplation before Beth confessed, "You really haven't answered my question Pastor, but oddly enough, I feel comforted."

"Beth," Abbott said, "I can see why Rose chose Rebekah's story for you."

"Why is that?"

"Rebekah did not know God, but when she heard, she believed and listened."

"Yes, I know that."

"You did not know God, not really, but when Rose spoke, you listened. As Paul said, 'faith comes by hearing.'"

"Thank you, Abbott. I feel much better now." Then Beth's funny side, which hadn't emerged in years, offered, "You do good for someone that doesn't know what he's talking about." At which comment they broke out in a hilarious uproar. With lunchtime over, Beth thanked Abbott and said she would pray he would be called to Sageville.

After work, Beth hurried to Rose's house, anxious to tell her about lunch with Pastor Abbott. She knew Rose would be interested in his interpretation of God's plan.

"Hello dear. Chicken salad and dessert are ready and waiting."

"Thank you, Rose, but first I have to tell you who I ate lunch with today."

"Pastor Abbott," Rose replied immediately.

"Who told you?"

"I think about five different people. You know, small towns. You were spotted at the Bistro." she laughed. "How was it?"

"The food is always—"

"My goodness, not the food . . . the meeting with Pastor Richards?"

"Very nice. We talked about God's plan."

"Oh?"

Beth relayed the conversation, nearly word-for-word. Rose nodded and said his insight was excellent and that his interpretation of the guidance of the Holy Spirit was correct.

"Now, are you ready for this evening's episode?"

"Oh Yes."

Beth found herself in Rebekah's tent as Esau yelled.

❊ ❊ ❊

"Jacob! I hate you! When our father dies, so shall you Jacob! Do you hear me?

Suddenly awakened, a startled Rebekah sat up on her bed to see Jacob and Ariel peeking out the tent curtain, watching Esau rant. Once again, Esau shouted, "Jacob! I hate you! When our father dies, so shall you! Do you hear me, Jacob, do you hear me?"

Frightened, Jacob turned to his mother and said, "See, I told you! I told you Esau will kill me, and father does not have long to live!"

Rebekah replied, "Do not be afraid. Your brother has at least one good quality."

"And what is that?"

"He does not carry a grudge for long."

Ariel added, "And his Hittite women will help him forget."

Ariel's statement triggered a realization for Rebekah, who admonished, "You must not marry Hittite or Canaanite my son. You must flee to my brother Laban and find a wife from among his family."

Ariel protested, "Rebekah, the journey is long. Chesed is no more, and Hadad does not know the way."

"I shall find the way on my own," Jacob said with a newfound sense of confidence.

"Abraham's God will guide and protect him. Jacob will find his way."

"For such a journey, will Isaac not have to bless Jacob on his way?" asked Ariel.

Taking her time to answer, Rebekah said, "I will speak with Isaac in the morning and convince him it is his idea." Ariel added, "As only you know how to do." Turning to Jacob, Rebekah said, "When Esau's wrath is no more, I will send for you."

Entering Isaac's tent unannounced, Rebekah looked down upon Gila and Tabitha and commanded, "Get out!"

The two women knew enough not to have to be told twice and left quickly.

"Who are you to tell my girls to leave?" Isaac tried to command forcefully.

"I'm your wife, remember?"

Gruffly, Isaac asked, "What do you want?"

"I want a proper wife for Jacob. Not one of those despicable, wretched, shameful Hittite women you and Esau are so fond of."

"What's wrong with the Hittite women? At least they obey," he growled.

Instinctively, Rebekah changed tactics, as when she wanted to conceive his child.

Sitting beside Isaac, snuggling close, voice soft and confident, "Isaac, you must remember when we talked of this day? I told you my life would not be worth living if Jacob married one of those Hittite women."

Warming to her voice and rubbing Rebekah's bare arm, he answered, "Ah yes, I remember the good times we had when you would come to my tent. Were those nights not the best?" Rebekah just smiled and ran her fingers over his lips. "You were quite different than all my Hittite women and much better."

"You were always full of passion," answered Rebekah, all the while thinking, "*If only that passion were reserved for me alone, you would have had pleasure beyond imagination.*" Returning to the issue at hand, Rebekah raised her voice and said, "Isaac, stop dreaming. Jacob needs a wife, remember?"

"What can we do? We live so far from our people."

"You do as your father did for you."

"It is too dangerous for a shepherd boy, and Hadad does not know the way."

"It's not too dangerous. The LORD has told me the sun will not smite our son by day nor the moon by night."

Isaac became irritated, growling, "Why does the Lord speak only to you? He does not speak to me as it should be!"

"Isaac," her voice softening again, "the LORD speaks to me because you no longer listen and have not listened for many years."

Isaac closed his eyes and wept.

Rebekah was honestly sad for her husband. He had the potential to do so much more with his life but chose wine and women.

At that moment, Rebekah's heart filled with compassion. She stroked Isaac's head and continued softly, "Soon, you will stand before the God of your father and answer for your disobedience." Isaac could say nothing. "Now do what is right. Bless Jacob and send him on this journey."

His anger began to stir again. Isaac resisted, "He already has my blessing, thanks to you!"

Determined not to let Isaac's tone upset her, Rebekah insisted, "You need to be the one to tell him not to take a wife from the daughters of the Canaanite. He must go to my brother, Laban. It is from his house that the line of Abraham must continue."

"Tell him yourself."

"No! It must be from you. You are the tribal chieftain."

"Oh, you!" Isaac said, making a weak fist, "If only I had the strength, I'd—"

"You'd what?" Rebekah snapped.

"I'd, I'd hit you!"

"You have never had that kind of strength."

"Oh, you, you—"

"I will send Jacob to you, and you *will* bless him on his way."

"Wait; who told you Jacob would be protected, Abraham?"

"No, it wasn't Abraham who spoke to me."

Isaac coughed and began shivering when he finally remembered that it must have been the LORD.

"Don't worry. I will send your two little whores back to keep you warm."

❊ ❊ ❊

Beth was sad about having to open her eyes. "Oh Rose," she said, "Rebekah's life was far from easy, and yet she never lost her faith and desire to serve God."

"That is right Beth."

"And Jacob. I can't imagine having to make such a long and dangerous journey just to find a woman to marry."

"How true. I suppose all you have to do nowadays is join one of those internet dating sites."

Beth laughed, "Not me. I want to meet someone the old-fashioned way."

"Good for you."

"Guess I'd better get home. This part of the story, the conflict between the brothers, the scheming, and the ongoing back and forth rhetoric between Rebekah and Isaac, is mind-boggling!"

"It is, and it is an important part of the story. It will help you understand how God works in your life."

Beth thought back about her desire for independence from her family and her desire for commitment. Maybe someday, she would have the courage to talk with Rose about her decisions. It was a long day, and right now, it was time for bed.

"Goodnight, Rose."

CHAPTER 25

After many days of listening to the story of Rebekah, mornings felt different somehow. Nights became consumed with new thoughts about Rebekah, God, and her purpose in life. No longer feeling content to live without a plan for the future, Beth did something she'd never done before; she began to wonder where she'd be in a year. Sensing the coming change, she hoped it would give her direction. Breakfast over, Beth dressed for work. Today was the day she dreaded the most. It was Friday. Waiting all weekend was difficult. Last Saturday was great, the best Saturday in forever, but tomorrow, same old, same old. Sunday now offered some relief from the boredom, but there was still the long afternoon and evening.

Passing the white picket fence, Beth watched as Rose put down the watering can and motioned for her to come inside the gate. "Good morning, dear. I know you are in a hurry to get to work, I won't keep you."

"That's okay Rose. I'm a little early today. What is it? Is everything all right?"

"Oh yes. I just had to tell you, Myrtle rang and she said the committee offered the position to Pastor Richards yesterday afternoon, and he accepted last night!"

Beth's mouth dropped, her eyes bulged, her heart raced, all the while trying to cover her excitement. "That's exciting for you. He's such a good speaker."

"Yes. Pastor Richards reminds me of the dear pastor we had for twenty years. I hope he will stay at least that long. Our church grew so much by having the same pastor. I believe Pastor Richards will be good for our community. Well, dear, I will see you this evening."

"Yes, thanks for telling me the good news."

Beth felt like skipping to work but just smiled instead. Pleased about Pastor Richards coming to Sageville, she closed her eyes and whispered, "*Maybe*." Not only did she enjoy listening to him preach, but there was something about him that was very special. The way he talked to her at lunch was down to earth yet filled with spirituality and Biblical insight. She wondered if he might teach a Bible study class or even meet one on one to answer the multitude of questions that swirled in her head.

Passing the coffee counter, her thoughts were interrupted by George's friendly, "Good morning, Beth. You look chipper today. Must be glad it's Friday?"

"Yes. I am looking forward to the weekend."

Joyce reminded her, "Week from tomorrow dear, we will all go to Atlanta."

"That's right. It will be fun to revisit Atlanta."

A client stepped inside the office door and asked for George.

"He's at the coffee counter. Please have a seat at his desk. He'll be with you shortly, "Joyce said as she pulled out a chair.

Beth opened her files and got started on her day's caseload. With several clients to call, it kept her mind on her work and off the dragging clock. While nibbling on her homemade sandwich, Beth remembered her luncheon with Abbott. Following her short lunch break, she proceeded to put together the best possible plan. "If I bundle his home, car, and life insurance, he will never find a better price.

The second the minute hand hit five o'clock, George announced, "That's a wrap!" and was out the door on his way to a baseball game.

"Wow, time to go, already? I'd better get to Rose's house."

"I'll lock up," Joyce said, "See you Monday."

Their evening dinner was enjoyable, as usual. Rose thought a change would be nice, so she made a broccoli and cheese quiche with a garden salad, along with carrot cake muffins for dessert. This evening, Beth found herself watching Gila and Tabitha on either side of Isaac, trying to comfort Isaac and stop his shivering.

❀ ❀ ❀

Esau stormed into Isaac's tent unannounced and got right to the point, "Mother told me you blessed Jacob and sent him to Padan Aram to find a wife.

Gasping to catch his breath, he uttered a weak, "Yes."

Getting right to the point, "I take it mother was offended by my choice of wives?"

Although Isaac did not want to insult his favorite son, he replied truthfully, "Yes, my son. It is so."

Esau had not given up on his inheritance. It was the right of the firstborn son. He also understood his mother's approval was not only essential but necessary. Throughout the night, Esau reflected upon the esteem with which the region regarded his mother and how she was the real power behind the throne, so to speak. He was sad over his choices but had contrived a way to regain the blessing, just if Jacob did not return.

He began, "Ishmael is your father's son. It is from this line I will find a wife."

"My son, Ishmael's mother was a slave, not a Hebrew."

Esau shook his head in disagreement. "Father, what does it matter? She only served as the host to Abraham's seed. No different than a grain of wheat planted in mother earth."

Isaac pondered the words from Esau. He was correct that Ishmael was Abraham's son, so what did it matter if Hagar was not Hebrew.

Esau stood and announced, "I shall find a wife from the tribe of Ishmael, and if Jacob does not return, you will have to bless me."

Isaac knew enough to say, "If the God of Abraham is with Jacob, he will return."

Esau quipped, "I'll be waiting. I will be waiting with my new wife to reclaim my inheritance from the supplanter."

After packing water and food, Esau left that day determined to find a wife among Ishmael's daughters.

Earlier that morning, Ariel and Rebekah helped Jacob prepare for his journey. He would have to travel through rugged terrain for many moons and the route would be dangerous. Ariel packed a bag with supplies and placed it on Jacob's back. Rebekah passed him his walking staff as Ariel strapped a knife to his side. Hugging Ariel and his mother, he said his goodbyes and left the tent.

Full of confidence, he said, "When Esau's anger subsides, I shall return with my bride from your brother's family," and marched off.

"His anger will not last long, my son." Rebekah called out, "I will pray the LORD gives you a safe journey across the land."

Ariel and Rebekah found it difficult to turn away, even after Jacob had disappeared over the ridge. Finally turning, they were shocked by the sudden appearance of Esau.

He issued his indictment, "Mother, you have always loved Jacob more, but the birthright is mine, and I intend to regain it."

"It is not so my son. I do love you."

"No matter. I have spoken with father, and I leave for the camp of Ishmael." Marching off in the other direction, he shouted back, "I will find a wife from Abraham's line and will return to claim my birthright."

Rebekah answered, "Esau, whatever happens now, is in the hands of the LORD."

The brothers traveled in different directions, both in search of a bride. One sought Padan Aram and the house of Laban. The other traveled into the wilderness of Suhr and then into the Sinai in search of his half-uncle Ishmael. After many moons of travel, thirst, and near starvation, Esau came upon a long-established encampment resembling his father's. It consisted of many large and lavish tents, a well-used domed bread oven, a central fire, and a large red tent in the distance. From his vantage point, it was easy to distinguish the tent belonging to the tribal chieftain. It was the largest, most colorful, and very elaborate. He hoped it would be the tent of Ishmael.

Mahalath, sixteen, and Bosmath, seventeen, were filling their waterskins at the well. Lips parched from thirst, walking staff in hand, Esau's faint request of, "Please, water, give me water" startled the girls.

Nebajoth, who was nearby, ran to the well. After examining the stranger, he nodded for his sisters to give the man water.

Poured water into the community drinking ladle, made of a simple gourd, Mahalath handed it to Esau. Quickly gulping it down and spilling half onto his tunic, he held the gourd out for a refill. Mahalath obliged and refilled the gourd. After drinking and wiping his face with the back of his hand, he returned the gourd to Mahalath. Other villagers stopped what they were doing when they noticed the stranger.

Nebajoth asked, "Who are you, stranger?"

"I am Esau, son of Isaac."

"Why do you travel alone?"

"I am in search of the man, Ishmael, Isaac's half-brother, both sons of Abraham the Hebrew."

Nebajoth nodded toward the most predominant tent in the village and issued a one-word command, "Bosmath."

Bosmath hurried away immediately. Esau's eyes followed the young girl and observed her entering the large tent unannounced.

Nebajoth uttered a second command, "Follow me!"

Moments later, Esau watched Bosmath step out of the tent and hold the curtain open. A well-dressed man, wearing a black turban, walked out slowly and stopped under the awning.

Esau stopped, bowed slightly, and asked, "Is this the tent of Ishmael?"

"It is as you say. I am he."

"I have traveled far to find you."

"Who are you, and why do you travel?"

"I come in search of a wife from the tribal line of Abraham."

Bosmath and Mahalath began to giggle but stopped when Ishmael cast his eyes their way.

"I will need to hear more." Turning to his son, Ishmael said, "Nebajoth, have the servants prepare a bath for our guest." Nebajoth took Esau by the arm and led him away. "Mahalath, Bosmath, find clean robes and dress our guest for dinner," was his next command.

Esau was impressed with the custom of women bathing him. He thought, "I may begin this custom after I inherit what is rightfully mine." Dressed in elaborate clothing and perfumed, Esau entered Ishmael's large elaborate tent. His eyes were immediately drawn to a low table covered with platters of various fruits, meats, oils, pieces of bread, and goat kabobs. At the head of this feast, Ishmael sat on a cushion, surrounded by four of his sons.

Nebajoth sat to Ishmael's right, then Adbeel. Kedar, was seated to the left of Ishmael and then Mibsam. Esau sat on the cushion between Adbeel and Mibsam, completing the circle. Each man could reach a platter of whatever he desired without having to stretch too far but soon found that was not necessary. Six serving girls, attired with colorful see-through gowns, stood behind the men. The serving girls would ensure wine goblets were replenished as needed. Ishmael clapped his hand, and the servant girls moved about, taking care of the men's needs for food and drink. Uncertain of etiquette, Esau was thankful he waited. All he had to do was to point, and a lovely young servant placed whatever he desired into his mouth.

As the meal progressed, Ishmael inquired, "Esau, you have so many wives. Why do you want another?"

All eyes turned to Esau and waited for his response.

"Jacob, my twin brother."

Puzzled, Ishmael asked, "Twin brother?"

"Yes. You see, many years ago, I had been without food for many days. I came upon Jacob's camp in the valley, where he was watching over his flocks. He took advantage of me and would not give me food and water unless I sold him my birthright." Ishmael and his sons groaned in displeasure when they heard of this impropriety. "I knew father would never give the second-born my inheritance, so I agreed. I was the first-born, and the birthright was mine." Esau paused to sip his wine.

"Go on, please go on," Ishmael required.

"When Isaac lay dying, he called for me and requested his favorite meal of venison. I left immediately with my bow and quiver full of arrows. Entering a nearby clearing, I spotted an eight-point stag grazing in the long grass. One arrow through the lungs and heart, and the deer dropped on the spot."

The men gasped. Nebajoth remarked, "I have never had a shot that clean."

"Neither had I," Esau admitted and then continued. "After bleeding and dressing the animal, I cut off the hind leg and rushed it to Judith, one of my wives. She makes the best venison stew. While she prepared the stew, I returned to butcher the animal for the tribe."

"Ah, yes…venison. I love venison," Ishmael said.

"My father's favorite is a spicy, savory stew. Judith simmered it all afternoon until the meat was so tender, it fell off the bone."

"My mouth waters as you speak," Ishmael said.

Nebajoth asked, "So what was the problem? You did as your father requested and brought him the stew."

Esau gathered himself before speaking again, "My mother has always favored Jacob. Overhearing my father's request for venison and knowing he was about to give me the blessing. Mother rushed to Jacob, had him kill a goat, and cooked a spicy goat stew.

Kedar commented, "Goat is good. I like goat."

"My father is so old, and his taste buds are not what they once were."

"Ah-ha," blurted Mibsam, "your father could no longer tell the difference because of the spices."

"Not only that, my mother made Jacob sleeves of goat underbellies, so my father would feel hairy arms, just like mine?

Ishmael snapped, "If a woman did such a thing in my camp, she would not live."

Nebajoth understood and said, "Your brother brought Isaac the goat stew ahead of you, and that is how he was able to steal your birthright?"

"Exactly, and because father cannot see, my mother was able to or-chestrate the deceit that stole my inheritance . . . Ishmael, I feel rejected by my mother."

The men gasped in disbelief, horrified at Esau's statement.

Ishmael looked at Esau. A tear formed in his eye as he said, "I too have felt the pain of rejection."

"Yes, I know," Esau acknowledged, "Abraham's servant girls told me your story long ago."

Ishmael sat forward and asked, "If Jacob has your birthright, I am puzzled. Why have you come to me?"

"I have Canaanite wives and Hittite wives, but no wife from Abra-ham's line."

Ishmael shook his head and laughed, "Yes, that is their custom." Ishmael's tone changed to critical. "They believe the birthright must pass through a princess and not through a common woman, as if there is any difference."

"Yes, that is our way."

"Now I know why you have come to me."

Esau continued, "At this very moment, Jacob is on his way to Padan Aram to find Laban and a bride from mothers' family line. If Jacob mar-ries one of Laban's daughters and returns, he will have full claim to my inheritance."

Ishmael smiled, "Yes, of course, but if you return first—"

"Yes," Esau yelped, "then you will help me?"

❁ ❁ ❁

"Beth dear."

"Yes, Rose?"

"Are you awake dear?"

"Yes, sorry."

"You were very relaxed."

Beth sat up in the wicker chair and said, "Yes, I was. I was waiting to see if Esau would find a bride. If he does, what about Jacob? Will he return with a bride as well?"

Knowing Beth was into the story hook, line, and sinker, Rose de-cided to tease by asking, "The question is Beth Chase, will you return to hear the rest of the story?"

"O Rose, you know full well the answer to that. Humph!"

Rose knew that Beth was beginning to show all the signs of a developing Christian. Her task was to make sure Beth continued to grow in faith.

Allowing Beth time to pretend to pout, Rose said, "Beth, I want to tell you one of my favorite verses. It is Psalm 37:4. 'Commit thy way unto the LORD; trust also in him, and he shall bring it to pass.'"

Beth sat in silence, considering the verse before she spoke. "Wait a minute . . . isn't that just like Proverbs 16:3, 'Commit your work unto the LORD?'"

"Very good Beth. Committing is the truest form of worship. You can sit in church and sing hymns all your life, but if you do not trust in the LORD, I believe, you do not have faith."

Rose allowed Beth time for this sudden avalanche of information to sink in.

Opening her eyes, Beth began, "Rebekah heard the word of the LORD and waited twenty years to have her children. She waited forty more years to be ready to bring about God's desire for Jacob. For sixty years, Rebekah committed her plans and her work unto the LORD."

"Yes Beth, yes!" Rose exclaimed, unable to hold back her emotions. "I could not have said it any better. When we commit our lives, our work, our plans before the LORD, it is the greatest freewill expression of faith and belief."

"Thank you, Rose," she said as she stood and began to leave, "See you in church."

"Yes dear, goodnight," Rose said with a tear in her eye.

On her way home, Beth thought to herself, "*I've not been very good at committing.*"

CHAPTER 26

Beth decided she was no longer going to be stuck in her apartment on Saturdays. Waking early, hot coffee, soft-boiled egg on a slice of toast, and out the door she went. With new slacks, a blouse, a sweater, and new walking shoes, Beth felt like a new person. Cash and credit card in her purse, it was about time she stepped out to explore Sageville. The change felt good. Life was about living, not surviving. After spending months of solitary confinement in her lonely apartment, the fall air was crisp and fresh, and much to her surprise, the pleasant aroma invigorated her step.

Most of the Main Street shops were just opening their doors. Owners unlocked their doors turned the sign to read "Open." Part-time helpers sweep the sidewalks. For the first time in all the months' Beth had been in Sageville, she noticed the sense of pride folks take in their small town. Not interested in shopping, Beth enjoyed the shops and boutiques on her walk around the town square. Pausing at the statue of a Union soldier on horseback, she took the time to read the plague. A tear came to her eye after reading how Colonel Sage had rescued dozens of slaves from a burning barn. Beth found herself offering a prayer on behalf of people she did not know.

Two blocks past the square, Beth sat in a hexagon gazebo she'd driven past, but never visited. Surrounded by baskets of flowers on all six sides, she viewed a delightful park along a gently flowing river and the sound of water rippling through a large rocky flower bed. "*Delightful*," she thought as joggers ran by. In the warmth of the morning sun, a group of mothers pushed strollers along the river path. Suddenly, a thought occurred, "*Maybe this is paradise? Peaceful. The freedom to walk unmolested with friends. The security in knowing men like Colonel Sage will always be willing to keep us safe from whatever evil threatens our way of life.*"

Beth watched the mothers disappear along the river bend. Spotting a sign that read, "Nature Trail," she decided to follow it past the rippling rapids, over a footbridge, and into the parking lot of a fully restored train station, right out of the 1800s. This was the Sageville Farmers Market Joyce and George talked about so often, but never had enough interest to ask about it. Exploring the tables, she found delightful people offering fresh produce, jars of jams, and preserves. All types of pickles and a wide variety of baked goods prepared by the local Mennonite community were for sale. Knowing Rose appreciated quality; Beth purchased two loaves of homemade artesian bread and a large jar of homemade strawberry jam. For some unknown reason, Beth found it was as easy to chat with vendors she'd never met before as it was with the folks she'd met at church. Speaking from behind her table, one woman said, "I heard Pastor Richards accepted the call to come to our church."

Beth replied, trying to conceal her inner smile, "Yes, I think it's wonderful."

On her way home, Beth found Rose, on her knees, working in the flower bed. The squeaking gate alerted Rose to a visitor. Gesturing to the bag of groceries, Rose said, "You've been busy."

"Yes, I found the Farmer's Market and picked up some artesian bread. Handmade by a delightful Mennonite lady.

"Must have been Ruth. She is always happy?"

"Yes, I think you are right."

"I love that stuff. I'd be happy to take that off your hands and lighten your bag," Rose said with a laugh. "I go to the market almost every week, but today," waving at the flower bed, "I needed to plant my fall bulbs."

"I was just thinking to lighten my load as a matter of fact," Beth replied.

Walking up onto Rose's porch, she placed an individually wrapped loaf of artesian bread on the table and said, "so here ya go."

"Thank you for the bread, dear. I'll see you tomorrow," Rose said as she returned to work and Beth made her way home.

As usual, Rose and Myrtle waited on the church steps for Beth to enter together. This Sunday was not going to be exciting for Beth as an interim minister would be preaching until the induction of Pastor Richards next month. Following the announcement of Pastor Richards' acceptance, the congregation applauded. The statement made Beth happy to know the congregation liked Abbott as much as she did. The music was cheerful, and Beth recognized more hymns from her childhood. The sermon coincided with the fall and harvest season, but it was really about harvesting lost souls. Something at which Rose excelled. Beth had realized that Joyce and George had been brought back to their faith by the type of story Rose had designed for her. Wishing Pastor Richards could move to Sageville sooner, Beth said to herself, "Patience, have patience. It will come to pass." With no luncheon in the Fellowship Hall, the three women went their separate ways. Beth returned to her apartment and began thumbing through her Bible.

Blustering wind, banging branches against her apartment, woke Beth early Monday morning. Checking the weather, she found it would be a touch cooler, and so a light jacket was all she needed for the walk to work. After a pleasant day at the office, Beth arrived at Rose's front porch and took her seat before noticing, the table was empty. No food. At that moment, Rose opened the door and said, "I was afraid we would get blown away out here. Come on inside. We'll eat in the kitchen." As Beth took her seat, Rose said, "I used that delicious artesian bread and made grilled cheese sandwiches to have with our tomato soup."

"Sounds delicious Rose."

"And, we have a choice of desserts, cookies, or apple pie."

"Apple pie for me," was Beth's instant response.

Following a delightful supper, Rose took Beth back into Ishmael's tent.

❀ ❀ ❀

Esau's request for help was met with a warmth he had not expected. Rather than revenge, Ishmael felt acceptance with Esau's acknowledgment that he was indeed an uncle.

"You are not at all like my father, Isaac."

"I too know the pain of rejection and how much hurt it caused my mother Hagar when Abraham told us to leave. I was only thirteen years of age but, by the blessing of God, I survived to acquire all this wealth. As God has been gracious to me, so I will be gracious unto you. Tonight, my daughters will present themselves to you."

Esau was overwhelmed at Ishmael's generosity. He thought he would have to barter or somehow reimburse Ishmael for one of his choice daughters. Neither Mahalath nor Bosmath looked like the Canaanite women, or for that matter, Hebrew women, but they were still beautiful.

Ishmael clapped his hands and announced, "It is settled. Rest and refresh yourself, tonight we will feast, and then, you may select the daughter of your heart's desire."

Esau stood, "Thank you. You are most gracious."

"Take my guest to his tent and bathe him according to our custom. Dress him in the finest of robes, for tonight shall be a night he will never forget."

In the meantime, Esau's twin brother Jacob neared an oasis in the desert, not too far from Laban's settlement. Exploring a lush green pearl in a sea of golden sand before him, Jacob refreshed himself in a small pond. Finding a large flat rock, he sat down to rest. As the sun began to set in the west, Jacob ate a simple meal of bread and cheese. Spreading his blanket, laying his walking staff close to his side, Jacob lay his head on a flat rock and fell into a deep sleep. Late in the night, he envisioned clouds blocking the light of the moon, felt an eerie silence as the palm trees stood motionless, and suddenly, a light appeared in the opening of a cloud. From out of nowhere, a ladder appeared in the opening in a cloud. Angels began ascending and descending, without any regard for his presence. Suddenly, a voice from the top of the ladder called his name, "Ya aqob."

The form of a man materialized, dressed in a long white robe, with a head covering. Eyes from deep inside the hood pierced Jacob's soul. Jacob lay speechless and motionless.

A voice spoke to Jacob's heart. "I am the LORD God of Abraham and Rebekah."

All Jacob could do was nod.

"The land on which you lie, I will give to you and your offspring."

Jacob crossed his hands on his chest and bowed.

"Your offspring shall be like the dust of the earth and shall spread abroad to the west and the east and the north and the south. All the families of the earth shall be blessed in you and your offspring."

Jacob's head moved slowly up and down in obedient acquiescence.

"Know that I am with you and will keep you wherever you go. One day, I will bring you back to this land, for which I promised your forefather Abraham."

In reverse appearance, the LORD, the ladder, and the angels vanished. Jacob awoke, looked into the clear starlight sky. With the full moon illuminating palm branches swaying in the breeze, he said, "Surely the LORD is in this place," and he was afraid. He said, "How awesome is this place! This is none other than the house of God, and this is the gate to heaven."

Rising early in the morning, Jacob stood the sizeable flat stone he'd used for a pillow and poured oil over it, saying, "This place is surely Bethel, the house of God." Just before leaving, Jacob knelt before the stone and offered his vow.

"If God will be with me, and will keep me in this way that I go, and will give me bread to eat, and raiment to put on so that I come again to my father's house in peace; then shall the LORD be my God."

Picking up his staff, he left.

Later that day, he stood atop a ridge and observed three flocks of sheep grazing in the valley below. Six shepherds were resting on the lush grass near an old stone well. Renewed of spirit, and from the night's vision, he hastened toward the shepherds. Upon spotting this stranger hastening toward them, the shepherds rose, took their staffs in hand, and prepared themselves.

Jacob stopped, looked at the Hebrew stripping on the hem of the robes worn by the shepherds. Excited beyond imagination, he said, "My brothers, tell me please, are you from Padan Aram?"

Alub lifted the hem of Jacob's garment and compared it to his, then replied, "Yes, yes we are."

"Laban, son of Nahor, do you know him?"

Alub, still unsure of the visitor, said, "Yes, but how do you know of Laban?"

"I am Jacob, son of Rebekah. Laban is my uncle," he exclaimed.

The shepherds embraced Jacob, gave him a gourd of water, and he drank.

"Have you traveled far, Jacob?" Beor asked.

"Yes, I have traveled two full moons."

Alub asked, "Why have you traveled so far and alone?"

"My mother sent me to find her people so that I may find a bride."

"Are there no wives in your land?" Omni inquired.

"Yes, but, in order for the promise made to Abraham to be fulfilled, the heir must come from among Terah's line?

"You are indeed our brother if you know of Terah," Murash remarked, "and yes, Laban has two fine daughters."

Excited, Beor whispered, "Look, here comes the younger one with her flock. Rachel is a shepherdess, and she is as bold as she is beautiful."

"Quiet," Alub said softly, then added, "Beor is right. She is very bold. Laban says she takes after his sister."

Not realizing there was a stranger among the men, Rachel marched directly to the well in the midst of them and said, "I wish to water my sheep, move."

Beor responded, "It's not the time."

"Move," Rachel demanded.

Jacob stepped to the well and raised the water bag.

Rachel turned face-to-face with Jacob and said, "I do not know you."

Jacob, taken by Rachel's beauty, stood mesmerized for a moment before saying, "I am your father's kinsman, Jacob, son of Rebekah, your father's sister . . . and you . . . you are beautiful."

Jacob took Rachel's face in his hands and looked into her eyes intently, saying, "You have my mother's eyes," and then he kissed her on the forehead.

Frozen momentarily from the shock of Jacob's kiss, Rachel shook herself back to reality, exclaiming, "I must tell father," dropped her staff, and ran to her father's house.

Jacob turned to Alub and said, "I have found my bride as God had promised."

❀ ❀ ❀

Beth's eyes snapped open. Grabbing Rose's hand, she said, "Rose! You cannot stop here. Esau had just arrived to find a wife from the line of Ishmael, and Jacob just kissed the beautiful and brave Rachel! Will he marry her? O please, you must tell me."

"Beth, you will not believe this, but more is to happen before we get to the marriages."

"But they both find wives, right? Oh, Rose, you are leaving me hanging again!"

Rose laughed. " Patience, my dear, patience. I guess you'll just have to come back tomorrow."

"O Rose, you know I will!

CHAPTER 27

Tuesday morning began like all Tuesday mornings, but the end would be different than any other Tuesday Beth had ever experienced. Within minutes of entering the office, taking a cup of coffee to her desk, the phone calls began.

"Morning," George said, hurrying into the office thirty minutes late.

"Where have you been?" Joyce asked.

"Lois wasn't feeling well. Had to take Junior to school."

Careful to keep her mind on work, Beth knew any momentary lapse would find her back in the middle of Jacob's abrupt kiss to Rachel's forehead, and she was just aching to know if they would find romance.

"*Concentrate,*" she thought, turning over another completed file, "*Keep working.*"

Suppressing her thoughts by digging into head office policy changes, the day passed. On her way out, George stepped in front of Beth, saying, "Okay kids, I'll see you tomorrow," and he was out the door at precisely five o'clock.

On entering the garden gate, the customary greetings were exchanged.

Rose, anxious to relay the news, said, "I've got good news!"

"Oh?"

"Yes! Pastor Richards is in town to look over the manse the church provides. He wants to buy some new furniture so he will have it when he moves in."

"Interesting."

"Yes, some of his apartment furniture was not appropriate."

"I did the same when I moved here," added Beth.

"Now, how about some stew? Oh, and you'll never guess what kind?"

Beth's eyes light up as she exclaimed, "Goat."

"Yes," replied Rose, "and I made cream cheese pumpkin muffins for dessert.

"Sounds wonderful."

Rose smiled and passed Beth a basket. "You might want to try some Hebrew flatbread with your stew. It's delicious."

The two enjoyed their meal and chatted about the seasons and the changing weather.

"A cold front is moving in tomorrow, with lows in the forties the rest of the week," Rose said. Taking the bowls and clearing the wicker table, she continued, "I guess we will soon be having more of our meals inside."

"But the cooler weather means the leaves will turn a beautiful color?" Beth said.

"Yes, that's right. It's that time of the year."

Beth thought back about the many weeks that had passed since she first met Rose, and now fall was here, the story continued.

"Rose, tell me, what happened after Jacob kissed Rachel."

"Yes, dear. You sit back and relax. Our story this evening begins in Isaac's tent on Esau's return with his wives.

"What," Beth exclaimed, "two wives!"

"Yes. Esau thought one might not be enough, so he took two."

All Beth could do was laugh.

❈ ❈ ❈

Isaac lay covered with heavy blankets as Tabitha and Gila endeavored to keep him warm. Every breath was a struggle, and like everyone who lives their life in denial, the knowledge of God becomes a frightening reality. Like countless thousands before him, Isaac had taken an audit of his life and actions. Rebekah had seen that fear many times. It was not a fear of death. It was a fear of coming face to face with the creator and accounting for the way they had treated God's children.

Esau entered the tent and held the curtain back for Mahalath and Bosmath to enter. He motioned sharply to Gila to move from his father's side so that he, Mahalath, and Bosmath could kneel beside Isaac.

Shaking his father's shoulder gently, he said, "Father . . . father, wake up."

Eyes closed in total darkness, confused by the new voice, Isaac turned and asked,

"What? Who is this?"

"Father, it is I, Esau, your son. This is Mahalath, and this is Bosmath, daughters of your half-brother, Ishmael."

"Who? What?"

Still confused, Isaac reached out to feel the hairy arm of his son.

"Father," Esau continued, "your brother, Ishmael . . . I married two from Abraham's line." Esau took his father's hand and held it to his forehead, saying, "You can bless me now, father, you can bless me."

Isaac was more confused. "I blessed you already."

"No, father, you blessed Jacob. I need your blessing, father. I have two wives of Abraham's line. Bless me!"

Isaac attempted to raise his hand but was unable. Gila knelt quickly and pressed Isaac's hand to Esau's forehead.

Esau shouted, "Okay father, bless me, bless me now!"

Oblivious to reality, Isaac did his best, "May the LORD bless you, and may you have many children."

Sighing a tear of relief, Esau shouted again, "Thank you, father." To himself, he said, "*When you return my brother, you will find I have stolen back my inheritance.*" Smiling, Esau stood, took the hands of his two new wives, and said, "Come, let me bring you to my tent."

It was not long before the family gathered before the cave at Machpelah to bury Isaac. Two men piled the last remaining stones over the cave opening as the mourners gathered to hear the prayers offered on behalf of their tribal chief. Ariel supported Rebekah, who was now eighty years of age. Mahalath, Judith, Bosmath Adah, Oholibamah, and a dozen children were near Esau.

Esau raised his arms and said, "May the God of Abraham take you in his arms, reunite you with your ancestors and bless you." He lowered his arms and led the people back to their village.

Ariel turned to Rebekah and softly uttered, "He showed more emotion when his dog died."

"Ariel," Rebekah said, "promise me that when they carry me to the cave of my ancestors, you will stay and pray to the LORD God."

Ariel hugged Rebekah, answering, "Yes, Rebekah; I will pray for you, my dear friend."

Five years after the death of Isaac, Ariel abruptly called out to Rebekah. "Are you awake?"

"Yes. What is it?"

"A messenger named Baruch. He is here with a message for you."

"A messenger? From where?"

"Padan Aram; your son, Jacob sent him."

Rebekah sat up, full of excitement, and said, "Come! Show him in."

Baruch entered the tent and was invited to sit near Rebekah.

"You bring me news of my son?" Rebekah said anxiously.

"Your son sent me from the house of your brother Laban."

Ariel knelt beside Rebekah, and they grasped each other's hands.

"Pray-tell is Jacob—"

"Yes," then taking a deep breath, "but he struggles with Laban."

Taken with this news, Rebekah said, "How can this be? Laban was always kind."

"He changed after the death of your father, Bethuel. With the responsibility of two unmarried daughters, the people, and the large flocks, he is now like an old fox."

"No matter. Jacob? Is he married?"

"Please, forgive me, but may I trouble you for a drink?"

Ariel jumped up quickly and poured water into a gourd, and handed it to Baruch.

"Thank you," Baruch gulped the water, then continued. "As soon as Jacob arrived at the house of Laban, he fell in love with Laban's daughter, his younger daughter."

Rebekah placed her hand over her mouth.

"Her name is Rachel. She has your eyes."

"Go on," Rebekah said slowly.

"When Laban saw that Jacob was well skilled as a herdsman, he put Jacob in charge of all of his flocks."

Rebekah nodded, "Yes, he is an expert herdsman."

Within a short time, the flocks were doing so well that Laban asked Jacob how he could repay him.

Jacob said, "You have two daughters, Leah and Rachel. If it pleases you, I will marry Rachel."

"Oh no!" Rebekah uttered.

"Oh yes."

"And Laban agreed?" she exclaimed.

Baruch continued, "Laban smiled and told Jacob, 'if you work for me seven years, you shall have my daughter as a wife.'"

"Oh, I don't believe my brother—"

"Just wait," Baruch continued, "After seven years, the flocks flourished even more. Laban was known throughout the territory for his healthy flocks and excellent wool."

Rebekah shook her head and said, "I still don't believe it. Are you saying Laban arranged the marriage?"

Baruch cleared his throat, took another drink from the gourd, and continued, "As I said, Laban is an old fox. On the wedding night, there was a large celebration. So many people, so much food and wine, so much wine. Poor Jacob, he was so happy, he could not help but celebrate." Baruch tilted his hand up to demonstrate drinking wine. "As is our custom, the bride is escorted to the marital tent to await the arrival of her husband. Laban made sure that Jacob had too much wine before he escorted his son-in-law to the marital tent, saying, 'My son, may you bless me with many children.'" Rebekah and Ariel, hanging on every word, nodded. Baruch continued, "Laban drew the curtain back, Jacob entered—"

"Something's wrong!" Rebekah interrupted, visibly upset.

"Something's wrong indeed. At sunrise, all were awakened by Jacob's screams as he stormed across the camp to Laban's Mudhif."

Her green eyes bulged as she exclaimed, "Oh dear!"

"Jacob kicked Laban's door—"

"Wait, why would he do that?" Ariel asked.

Rebekah snickered, "I know exactly what the old fox had done."

"What?" Ariel asked.

Rebekah answered, "When Jacob awoke, he discovered he had married Leah, the older daughter, as is our tradition."

"It is true. It is our custom, but let me tell you, Jacob was furious."

"I don't blame him," Ariel said.

Rebekah asked, "So, what happened?"

Baruch replied, "Laban was afraid that Jacob would steal away with Rachel, so he made another deal." Rebekah laughed, Baruch continued. "Yes, another deal. Laban said if Jacob performed his wedding duties with Leah for the customary two weeks, he could marry Rachel on the next full moon."

Ariel huffed, "What? On the next full moon, Laban allowed Jacob to marry Rachel?"

Rebekah nodded and said, "Yes."

"But it does not end there. Laban gave him not only Rachel but also Leah's servant Zilpah and Rachel's servant Bilhah."

"Oh come on. In one month, two wives and two concubines?"

After a moment, Rebekah asked, "Did Jacob say when he would return home? My heart longs to see him before I die."

Baruch looked to the floor. "That is why he sent me."

Rebekah asked a hesitant, "Why?"

"Jacob must work another seven years for Rachel."

Tears filled Rebekah's eye as she announced, "I shall never see my son again."

Baruch added, "I am afraid if Jacob wants to inherit his flocks of his own, Laban will make him work even longer."

Rebekah fought as long as she could before she broke down crying.

Baruch said, "You see, Jacob had made Laban a very rich man."

Rebekah quickly regained her composure and asked, "Does Jacob have any children?"

"Yes. Leah has borne him three fine sons, Ruben, Simon, and Levi."

Ariel nodded, "Wonderful."

Baruch continued, "Zilpah has borne him Gad and Bilhah has borne him Dan, all healthy sons."

Rebekah looked into Baruch's eyes, asking, "And Rachel?"

"Sadly, she remains barren."

Rebekah covered her mouth and closed her eyes.

After breathing into her hands, she looked directly into Baruch's eyes and said, "When you return, go to Rachel, " raising her voice, "and only Rachel, and say that a God she will come to know has chosen her to fulfill a destiny."

"A new God?" Baruch asked.

"Yes. New to her. Rachel has a destiny, Baruch. Now, remember Rachel only!"

Looking puzzled, Baruch agreed.

❃ ❃ ❃

This evening, Rose had to shake Beth to wake her.

"Oh, Rose! So much had happened! My goodness! Laban, that scoundrel! How could he? And poor Rachel, no children! You have to tell me, is Rebekah going to be, okay? Will she ever get to see Jacob again? What about Rachel's destiny? Will it be revealed?"

Feeling bombarded, Rose smiled, then laughed. Beth's curiosity and her questions were unstoppable until a knock came at the front door.

"Excuse me," it was a male voice.

On opening the screen door, Rose said, "Pastor Abbott, come in, come in."

"I'm sorry to intrude, but I was out for a walk and, on passing your house, decided to say hello and maybe ask you a few questions about the church."

Beth's mind was racing. No sooner had she heard about Rachel's marriage when suddenly, there was Pastor Richards.

On stepping into the kitchen, Pastor Richards said, "O, hello Beth." Realizing the women were in the middle of a visit, he apologized, "I am sorry to bother you. It looks like you are in the middle of a discussion."

Beth felt a rush of excitement. Something she had not felt in a very long time.

Beth calmed herself and said, "Hello Abbott, good to see you."

Rose smiled, "We were just talking about Jacob and Rachel."

"Oh, I see. That is a fascinating story."

"You're not kidding," Beth said before thinking.

Abbott laughed and then said, "Rose, I understand you are quite a storyteller and well know all over town."

"People have been talking, have they?"

"I have also heard of your ability to restore faith. That is a treasured gift."

Rose graciously nodded.

"You have been a blessing to many," he said.

"Yes, she has," Beth said.

"Well, I will leave you to it. I am staying at the Southern Inn Bed and Breakfast around the corner."

"Yes, of course. Myrtle's daughter and son-in-law own it."

"Yes, nice folks." Turning to Beth, he added, "I am in town to check out the manse and shop for new office furniture. Rose has recommended the furniture store across from your office, and I was wondering if, well, you wouldn't mind helping me select furniture to fit the space, during your lunch break, of course. After all, you do work in an office."

Beth felt her face turning red. No, it was her neck, ears, shoulders, she was downright turning a shade of plum, and she knew it.

"I'd be happy to," she managed to say.

"Perfect. I'll see you tomorrow. Twelve-thirty okay with you?"

"Yes."

"I'll pop by the office."

CHAPTER 28

Beth poured her first cup of coffee, sensing a mysterious feeling of joy welling up inside, knowing her life was changing. No longer isolated or disconnected, coworkers had blossomed into friends; a complete stranger had cracked open a heart hardened by years of self-inflicted loneliness, but most of all, Beth felt a connection to something never before experienced; God's Holy Spirit. Rose had not only become a good friend and a positive influence but the one through whom she'd met Pastor Abbott. Instead of hoping a relationship would develop, Beth prayed for a relationship to bring purpose to her life.

As Beth learned about the people in the community, she began to feel like a true resident of Sageville. Attending church with Rose and Myrtle not only felt good, it felt normal, the way things were meant to be. Moving from one town to the next in the past had always made her feel like a perpetual stranger. Now, people recognized her on the street, greeted her by name in the shops, asked to speak with her in the office, welcomed her into their church, and it made her feel good, just like home.

Selecting a new outfit for the day, Beth was overwhelmed with a feeling of warmth. Abbott would be coming by the office; they would go to lunch; spend time shopping for his home office furniture as he was about to become a resident of Sageville. Abbott's first sermon had a profound influence on her growing faith. Inspiring and knowledgeable, it was almost as if he'd been sent to help Rose re-establish Beth's faith. The words of his sermon felt like they were meant for her. Then she remembered Rose saying, "Faith comes by hearing."

It was becoming evident why Rose said she needed to hear the story of Rebekah. There was a reason Rebekah was the right story for Beth. Rebekah was not only brave and adventurous; she was also stubborn. An attitude with which Beth could relate. Rebekah heard God, believed, and then waited all those years for God's plan to be established. Beth was now doing the same, waiting and praying.

With no sign of Rose working in the garden, Beth figured she was probably enjoying a hot breakfast in her cozy kitchen on a cool morning. Rose was perhaps the best friend she had in her whole life. The thought of a lady in her late sixties who liked her made Beth feel even better. She laughed while thinking, "*Rose knows me and still likes me, wow. Now that is friendship.*"

The jacket selected was too light for a cool morning as Beth entered the office shivering.

"Morning Joyce. Coffee ready?"

"Yes, it is."

"Great. Need it to warm me up."

The slamming front door was followed by George's greeting of, "Brrrrr." Joining Beth at the coffee pot, he observed, "Fall is announcing its presence early this year."

Taking a sip of her coffee, Beth's head nodded in agreement.

"Two more days until we head to Atlanta," Joyce announced.

George's face lit up. " I'm looking forward to it. I've heard the rewards dinner is a lot of fun!"

"Uh-huh," Joyce murmured, "same here."

Beth had not thought about the trip in several days. Somehow, going to the Atlanta rewards dinner didn't seem important, not with other more pressing things on her mind.

Before digging into the files George had placed on her desk, Beth paused for a moment and thought, "*I wonder if Abbott thinks of me as often as I think of him.*" The phone rang, and it was into the day's work. New client referrals, renewals of existing clients, and phone calls consumed her morning. When Beth finally looked up, the office door opened, and Abbott stepped in.

"Hello," Joyce said. "How are you, Abbott?"

"Doing well, thank you."

"How can I help you?"

"Oh, I'm not here about insurance. Beth has graciously agreed to help me shop for office furniture today."

"For the manse," George pipped in.

"Yes. I like doing much of my research at home."

Beth smiled, pushed her office chair under her desk, and walked to the hall tree for her jacket. Abbott's smile warmed as he helped Beth slip it on. George looked to Joyce, who looked back, smiling.

George tried to cover his smile as he said, "See you two in a little while."

Trying to restrain a giggle, Joyce encouraged, "Enjoy your lunch."

A harmonious, "We will," was heard as the door closed.

With so much on her mind, Beth had forgotten that Abbott had suggested lunch before shopping. Lunch suited her just fine. Spending time with Abbott rekindled feelings long since forgotten.

Beth noticed Abbott made a point of walking to the street side, as gentlemen are wont to do when with that special lady. It brought back memories of her father walking with her mother to protect her from any unforeseen danger from the road. It pleased her that Abbott was every bit as much of a gentleman as her father. It was a courtesy her old boyfriend had neglected to extend.

"Would you like to try that quaint café at the corner of Oak and Main?" Abbott asked.

"That would be wonderful."

"I've heard the home cooking is scrumptious," Abbott added.

"Yes, I've heard that as well."

"It will be a first for both of us, then."

"Yes!" as she let her hand brush up against his.

The small café was crowded, but the waitress found a table next to ladies Beth recognized from church.

Mirabel waved and said, "Hello Pastor . . . hello Beth."

"Hello Mirabel," Beth replied with a blushing smile.

Abbott shook Mirabel's hand and went around the table as he was introduced to the other ladies. Beth took her seat, back to the ladies, and waited.

"The people in this town certainly are friendly," Abbott said as he sat.

"Yes, they are." Beth agreed before adding, "It was after Rose invited me to church that I began to get to know the townspeople."

The waitress provided menus and announced the daily specials.

After ordering, Beth continued. "Rose spoke to me first, or rather shouted to me from her porch."

"She is a gem. Any town would be blessed to have someone like Rose. I have heard she brought more people to Jesus and the church than any pastor in town."

"I believe it. Rose is an amazing woman, and oh my, the stories she tells. In fact, she is telling me a wonderful story at present that I am afraid is about to end."

"Remind me."

"Rebekah. Well, mostly Rebekah."

"Ah yes. You do know you can read the whole story for yourself in the Bible?"

"I know, but I don't want to spoil Rose's story! It's magnificent. She knows the facts as well as the myth."

"Oh! Tell me," he asked, "what happened last? In the story, I mean."

"Let's see, Isaac died, Esau and Jacob married, but Jacob got deceived."

"Genesis. You are correct. Rebekah's story is nearing the end, but I won't spoil it for you."

Placing the food order on the table, the waitress inquired, "Anything else, Pastor Abbott?"

"No, thank you. Beth, would you like anything?" he asked.

"Oh, no, thank you, this is great," answered Beth.

As the waitress left, Mirabel's hand fell on Abbott's shoulder as she said, "Enjoy your lunch. We are looking forward to seeing you in church real soon."

After a few bites and comments about the tasty meal, Abbott said, "Beth, there is something I have been wanting to ask you, but I don't want you to feel uneasy. The truth be known, I feel moved to say, I've prayed over this every day since I met you, my first Sunday in Sageville."

Beth's heart was racing. What could he possibly want to ask? What was he going to say? Was it something bad?

Beth found the courage to ask calmly, "Prayed Abbott, I'm curious? Is everything okay?"

He laughed, "Yes, yes. It's better than okay. Somehow, Beth, after I met you the first time and we talked," Abbott tried not to stumble over his words, "I don't know how to explain it . . . you have a very gentle way about you and, well . . . I have to confess; it was you who made me decide to accept the call to Sageville."

Beth's heart almost stopped, "Really?" she blurted, not knowing how to control her emotions.

"Yes. Most certainly. I was offered a charge in a large church in Atlanta, but the one thing that kept drawing me back to Sageville, I don't know how to describe it, was you. The nearest thing I can explain my feelings is when I accepted Christ's call to the ministry. It was that strong. Beth Chase, I want to spend more time with you; get to know you, and I pray you want to get to know me."

Beth felt every ounce of blood rushing to her face. She was certain every customer in the café could see her blushing, and her eyes filling with tears.

"Did I upset you?" he asked anxiously.

It took a moment but, "Oh, no. My goodness no. I have been praying that you would want to get to know me."

Abbott was speechless. All he could do was take Beth's hand and smile.

"I have to tell you," Beth confessed, "for months, I didn't feel I belonged in Sageville, but then I met Rose, she befriended me, began a story that she said would change my life. She invited me to church, I made more friends, and I finally felt like I belonged. Then you walked into my life. In church, if you can believe it. Now, what I want most in life is to spend all my time with you."

"O Beth," Abbott said, "I don't want you to feel rushed, maybe just a dinner, until I am settled."

"Yes, of course, dinner will be very nice."

Beth knew she would be away from the office longer than expected, but she did not care. All she wanted to do was to hold onto Abbott's hand and look into his eyes. After the café emptied and the tables cleared, Abbott paid the bill. It wasn't easy to concentrate on shopping for office furniture. Still, they finally decided on an old-fashioned country roll-top desk with a hidden computer compartment. It would look impressive in his office.

Back at work, Beth's mind would not stop spinning. They had agreed to keep the conversation to themselves and to take things very slowly. The congregation would be told about their dating at a future time. Nonetheless, Beth was finding it almost impossible to contain her joy.

Walking up the familiar steps to Rose's porch, she had a strange sensation realizing the story was about to end. She knew her daily routine of stopping at Rose's house would change, yet, she did not anticipate the ending of something but rather a beginning.

Before she could ring the bell, Rose opened the screened door and greeted her with, "Come in out of the chilly fall air!"

"Oh! You lit a fire. How wonderful. I remember the smell of burning wood."

"It will knock the chill out of the air. Old homes are beautiful, but unfortunately, drafty. Tell me, how was your lunch with Pastor Richards?"

Beth was surprised, but she had learned, there are no secrets in a small town.

"Sorry, I'm too nosey, come on into the kitchen and let's have a bite to eat before beginning our story. We can go sit by the warmth of the fire to enjoy our dessert."

"Rose, you have outdone yourself. This beef stroganoff is incredible."

It was quiet during dinner for a change. Rose, wanting to ask, Beth, dying to tell, but each showing restraint.

Finally, "I made us a peach cobbler and with homemade ice cream to top it off. Go sit by the fire, and I will bring it to you."

As Beth savored each delicious mouthful, she asked Rose if they could depart from their usual routine. "Rose, dear, can we do something different tonight?"

Rose smiled because she knew what was coming. Like every listener before her, Beth could feel the story coming to a close. Rose replied, "Yes dear."

"Tonight, can you tell me the story with my eyes open."

"Of course, dear."

"Good," Beth said and sat back to relax.

"It was a very sunny day when the villagers gathered at the cave of Machpelah. Esau and a small group of mourners watched as men placed the last rocks over the mouth of the cave. Suddenly and mysteriously, the sky began to darken. A strange rumbling was heard in the distance.

Esau lifted his hands and began to offer the burial prayer, "O LORD God of—"

Flash!

Lightning struck the earth above the cave. A small avalanche of rocks and dirt fell over the cave mouth. A *thundercrack* sent fear into the hearts of all gathered. Mourners huddled together; Esau's wives gathered around him; all watched the smoke rise from the hillside. Esau mumbled a few more words and then hurried away, wives and mourners' following.

Unafraid, Ariel walked to the cave, kissed her hand, laid touched the rocks.

With her hand on the rock, she prayed, "LORD God of Abraham, our sister Rebekah has gone to sleep with her ancestors. Please care for her, as in life she was respected and in death regretted. Faithful to your plan, she was obedient to your word. I have been blessed to have known her, even if it was for a short time, and I will miss her terribly. I thank you for her life among your people."

Beth sat silent for some time. Rose knew not to interrupt as she could see tears flowing down Beth's cheeks, and she knew Beth was also offering her prayer on behalf of Rebekah.

Minutes later, "Rose, thank you. Thank you for telling me this story. You were right, this was the perfect story for me, and I have been blessed to hear it. How did you know?"

"You tell me. You know the answer," was not what Beth had expected to hear.

Sitting quietly by the fire, Beth reflected upon her growth and, more importantly, the many changes.

"I am strong, like Rebekah. Too strong at times. I need to temper my tenacity with a spirit of wisdom."

"It is difficult to live in a state of uncertainty, always on the defensive out of fear and uncertainty."

Rose agreed, "It is surprising how faith can conquer fear."

"Yes, and thanks to you, I have only one more fear to conquer."

"And that is?"

"Mother. I will return to my mother and ask her to forgive her head-strong daughter."

"I seem to recall a story in scripture along those lines," Rose said, trying to control her internal laugher. "Now it's time."

"Time for what?"

"Prayer." Beth bowed her head. Rose took her hand and prayed. "Heavenly Father, watch over your prodigal daughter as she experiences the blessing of finding her way. By placing her life in your hands, our sister Beth has come to love the people in this community, as they have come to love her. With a new future awaiting discovery, help her make the right decisions for the right reasons to enjoy life to the fullest. In Jesus' precious name we pray. Amen."

"Thank you, Rose, thank you for everything."

Rose smiled and asked, "Do you have any thoughts or questions?"

"I believe I was lead here for a reason and must confess; I had heard that your stories changed lives."

"I've heard that rumor as well."

"Well, you certainly changed mine."

"Beth! Now think about that a moment."

"I get it. You didn't change my life. God did."

"To be correct, God did because you allowed it to happen."

Sitting in the warmth of the crackling fire, Beth's contentment was overtaken by an air of sadness.

"Rose, I don't want to stop visiting you," she said quietly.

"Don't worry dear, I've been thinking of something you said a while back, and I've been thinking."

"Yes?"

"Something tells me that, well, you might need to learn how to cook for two."

"Why, whatever do you mean?" trying to hide her newfound hope.

"Beth, it's no secret. If it were any more conspicuous, it would be on the front page of the Sageville Times."

Frantic, "What, for heaven's sake, what?"

"The look on your face, and Abbott's, whenever you are with each other. Besides, we could use a few younger women to help out at the bake sale."

With her face as red as a beet, "Rose, I had no idea it was that obvious."

"Oh, it's obvious all right."

The tone of Rose's voice made Beth realize that, for the first time in her life, her heart was beating with the warmth of friendship. It felt comforting. It made her realize that suppressing the true desire of her heart, friendship had eluded her. Now, having laid her plans before the LORD, her dreams were about to be established in ways she could never have imagined. Rose interrupted her thoughts.

"Why don't we start Saturday next? You will be in Atlanta this Saturday."

"I'd like that, Rose."

"It's a deal. Saturday next."

❀ ❀ ❀

After hanging up her jacket, Beth glanced around the living room and kitchen. It had never felt cozy before, but now, it felt warm, warm like home. In all these months, it had only felt like a place to rent with no personal touches. This night, it felt like home, her home. For the first time in her life, Beth sat and looked to the future.

Beth thought, "*It doesn't matter if I win. I've been recognized. I have friends, real friends, and a job I love. Mother will be proud of me when I tell her that I have a church. Finally, there is Abbott, and I will not worry about our relationship as I know God will establish our plans.*"

Sitting back on the sofa, Beth said to her Bible. "It's time you and I became good friends." Looking to heaven, Beth said, "Rose was right. You do work in mysterious ways."

THAT SHINING MOMENT

ERIC LOWANS

TERRAPIN Group Publishing LLC

PROLOGUE AND ACKNOWLEDGEMENTS

My lawyer says that I need to remind the reader that this is a work of fiction. However, some individuals, organizations and events are openly listed here because of their historical significance. This work uses publicly available documents, confirmed by multiple credible sources when using references, comments, writings or other forms of communication and does not attempt to paraphrase any historical figure's publicly expressed ideas or statements.

Private conversations between individuals that are not taken from the official record or press briefings, are hypothetical and purely from the imagination of the author. This is not intended to confuse the reader, but rather to stimulate interest and independent research on all of these topics.

The truth of the matter is that this story was told to me by a long-time friend and mentor named Bob, in a bar in Washington DC about twenty-five years ago, with the caveat that it not be written until after he was gone. Bob left us about ten years ago, and his darling wife, Joni, joined him just before Christmas last year. Thus, the timing seemed right.

Bob was a Marine who served in Vietnam, and then continued to serve his country as a technical specialist with the CIA, before starting his own consulting business near Washington. He and Joni were an awesome couple, filled with curiosity, and occasionally able to provide the back-story to some of the more prominent news items of the time.

But, this book isn't about conspiracies. It is really about heroes. Not the kind that get a plane ticket to the White House for a ceremonial draping of a medal around their neck, because the president likes their music, but rather some heroes that we could not have done without as a society, as a culture and as a nation. Average people.

Don't get me wrong, I enjoy movies and sports, but cringe when I see a sports figure or entertainer receive an award from the President of the United States for "...an especially meritorious contribution to the security or national interests of the United States, world peace, cultural or other significant public or private endeavors...", when their entire contribution was to dribble a basketball or memorize lines of a screenplay. They did it well, and I applaud them, but they already have their own forms of recognition by their peers.

Does the world end if an actor doesn't have a great performance, or a baseball legend strikes out? Sorry, I'm a bit old fashioned and I like my heroes to be larger than life. Real life, not from Hollywood or whatever happens to be popular in the media at the time.

The kind of heroes I'm talking about worked largely behind the scenes, sometimes for many years, and received not a word of thanks for their efforts. And their contributions, if ever revealed, would be seen as a quasar when compared to the entertainers and malcontents who contributed vocally or financially to a particular President's campaign.

Real heroes are the people that got the job done. Maybe it wasn't even a job that they wanted to take on, but they sucked it down, gave it their all, and really made the world a better place. And for the record, I'm not one of them.

Before I go any further, I wanted to recognize four people you've probably never heard of. I can't begin to list the names of the 58,220 US casualties[1] of the Vietnam War, but I think it's important to remember as many of them as we can, because they all came from somewhere. They had families and friends.

Major Dale R. Buis and Master Sergeant Chester M. Ovnand became the first Americans killed in the American phase of the Vietnam War when guerrillas struck a Military Assistance Advisory Group (MAAG) compound in Bien Hoa, 20 miles northeast of Saigon, in 1959. Sixteen years later, the United States would record the names of the last two men who gave all; Charles McMahon and Darwin Lee Judge, killed in a rocket attack one day before the evacuation of Saigon, April 30 1975.

McMahon and Judge were members of the Marine Security Guard (MSG) Battalion at the US Embassy, Saigon and were providing security for the Defense Attaché's Office (DAO) compound. Due to confusion during the evacuation, their bodies were left behind until Senator Edward M. Kennedy of Massachusetts, through diplomatic channels, secured their return the following year.

I wasn't in Vietnam. In April 1975. I was sweating out the last days of the conflict, as a Marine Option Midshipman at a state university in the Midwest, playing Euchre in the wardroom with upper classmen. Thus, the heart-pumping narrative about those last perilous minutes comes not from my imagination, but from people who were there.

If the reader really wants to know what it was like that day, I would urge them to read the article by Bob Drury and Tom Clavin, Air & Space Magazine November 2011, and consider the courage and leadership of Major James H. Kean USMC; Commanding Officer, Company "C", Marine Security Guard Battalion and Ground Support Force Commander United States Embassy Compound, Saigon. What our sons, brothers, husbands, fathers, and Marines, did that day, was heroic.

I won't speculate as to the political motives of governments who see fit to send their fighting men and women into harm's way

---

1   https://www.archives.gov/research/military/vietnam-war/casualty-statistics

for extended periods that transcend presidencies. Vietnam was like a case of herpes. No one wanted it and everyone wished it would go away. But it kept lingering. So, if no one wanted it, why were we there for so long? Maybe because the right people were making money from it?

As a Criminology undergraduate student, I was fascinated by high profile crime, and there was no higher profile crime than the assassination of John F. Kennedy on November 22, 1963. Through the years, I read everything I could on the topic, including nonsensical stories published by the supermarket tabloids. I actually have one of the New York Times' Editions of the Warren Commission Report.

Many of the books and articles I've read through the years are loaded with verifiable eye-opening facts, but then the author takes a wild leap to arrive at some far-out conclusion that one must consider with skepticism. Who knows, maybe they are all right, and everyone wanted to kill Kennedy at the same time for different reasons.

From a purely forensic standpoint, there were problems with the crime scene. There were problems with the autopsy. There were problems with the physical evidence and interviews. A public defender fresh out of law school might have come up with a reason to get Oswald off on a technicality. Nevertheless, I believe that President Kennedy's death occurred as a proximate result of Lee Harvey Oswald opening fire on his motorcade as it passed through Dealey Plaza.

When I've been asked my personal opinions about the assassination, rather than speculate openly, I simply refer people to what I consider two essential primers on the subject; David Lifton's Best Evidence[2] and Bonnar Menninger's Mortal Error[3]. Both books were well-researched and lead the reader through the science of the investigation, allowing them to make up their own minds. These two books aren't so much about motives; just observing what the facts illustrate.

---

2   Macmillan Publishing Company, 1980
3   St. Martins Press, 1992

Regarding the US Government's interest in extraterrestrial visitors, the Air Force alleged that they got out of the UFO business in 1969, when the Condon Committee said that witness reports were not of significant merit to warrant further research. So they subsequently closed Project BLUEBOOK. Of course, the scientific advisor to the project, astronomer and professor J. Allen Hynek, began his tenure as a good scientific skeptic, and then later underwent a conversion when he realized that they could not sweep some of these cases away with hastily prepared, and sometimes laughable explanations.

It wouldn't be until 2017 when the government would officially acknowledge that they had lied to the public and had been running the Advanced Aerospace Threat Identification Program, which (they claim) ran from 2007 until 2012, to investigate the UFO phenomenon. However, some of the US Navy videos and other materials that were released to the media took place between 1969 and 2007. Who was collecting this sensitive evidence during this period?

So, a quick word about classified programs. It is not uncommon for the government to change project names and security clearance classifications throughout the lifecycle of a project. That means when a highly sensitive project goes before congress for funding, and finally gets approved, it is likely that different facets of the project will evolve, including clearance requirements for the subcontracted work, or the name itself, as soon as the money is in the bank.

Important for the reader to remember is that the US Government does not make things. They don't design things, they don't sell things and they don't ship things. They contract with private industry to obtain fresh ideas, develop prototypes and to eventually build something that they alone will use. Often, depending on the nature of the item in question, certain parts of the manufacturing process will be subcontracted to other businesses that are similarly cleared for government work. Companies will build parts to certain specifications, without ever knowing what they will be used for, or how they fit into the final design.

As a humorous anecdote, many years ago I was employed by a defense contractor. I was watching the evening news when a US Senator denied the existence of a particular secret aircraft, the development of which had been leaked to the media. When my wife heard me laughing and asked what I had found so funny, I replied, "I don't know if the airplane exists or not...but I held the XYZ part for it in my hands three weeks ago."

In the Senator's defense, the project name that the reporter had asked him about was no longer valid. It was a name they'd used to obtain funding two years earlier. I have no idea how many times the name was changed before the project was eventually completed (if it even was), but it changed twice in the brief time that I was associated with it. And, in my defense, I am not violating any security protocols for mentioning it because our small piece of the project had not been classified by the Defense Department.

The reason I mention this is because there have been numerous conspiracies passed around since the 1947 crash of something... or somethings, in the desert somewhere between the towns of Corona and Roswell New Mexico. Lieutenant Colonel Philip James Corso, US Army (ret), wrote in his book *The Day After Roswell* (Pocket Books, 1997), that bits of back-engineered alien technology recovered from downed spacecraft had been released to private industry for study and to give us a technological boost. Skeptics have argued that the actual research and patents for most of the inventions mentioned in his book, were due to the hard work of the contractors' innovative employees, and not to an unidentified life form from another galaxy.

However, having worked in the defense industry, I can readily understand how the prime contract holder could sub-out bits and pieces of something to groups of scientists, without them knowing where the technological concept came from originally, giving them just enough information to find it on their own so to speak. I mean, if you handed someone an alien artifact that was inscribed "Made On Alpha Centauri", then we wouldn't be having this discussion (I know. Alpha Centauri is a star system, and the artifact would have had to have been made on one of the orbiting planets in an inhabitable zone.)

Since I never met the author, or any aliens that I know of, I can't assess the credibility of his claims other than to say that his military service record shows him to have been a highly decorated military officer with key assignments in intelligence and the Foreign Technology Division at the right times. He died a year after the book was published.

Similarly, there was the case of Physicist Bob Lazar, who claimed to have been employed at Area 51, back-engineering extraterrestrial craft at a place called S-4. He said publicly on KLAS-TV in 1989, that he had worked on the craft's propulsion system and had identified its fuel as something called "Element 115"; an unknown element that we certainly couldn't synthesize at the time. However, with a bunch of tricky lab work, Moscovium did eventually find its way to the periodic table in 2003, in Dubna, Russia. Lucky guess, maybe?

Even though private employers and academic institutions that were listed on Mr. Lazar's resume claimed that they'd never heard of him, he was able to produce pay stubs from Naval Intelligence, and a telephone directory from one of his employers, with his name and department listed. It appeared that well-connected person(s) unknown were trying to discredit him. They were trying to erase his past.

So, what it comes down to is do you take the Corsos and Lazars of the world at their word, or do you believe your government? A July 2019 study conducted by the Pew Research Center, US Politics and Policy found that "...two-thirds of adults think other Americans have little or no confidence in the federal government."[4] So, if you find yourself leaning towards Corso's and Lazar's respective points of view, by extrapolation, you would be in the majority.

The last twenty years have seen an enormous shift in ownership of government projects into the private sector. In theory, this makes sense, since I earlier commented that the government doesn't really

---

4   https://www.pewresearch.org/politics/2019/07/22/trust-and-distrust-in-america/ Downloaded from the World Wide Web July 14, 2020.

make anything on its own. The problem from a transparency perspective, is that private companies are not required to divulge proprietary information under the Freedom of Information Act (FOIA).

This means that if the government had been collecting information about UFO reports or any type of technology that might have been acquired from crashed vehicles, undocumented Earth immigrants or an alleged technology exchange program, then it would take a stack of carefully worded subpoenas to ever find out about it. It is now proprietary information. Information possessed by the military-industrial complex. The one that President Eisenhower warned us about in his farewell address.

Finally, for those of you who are new to the process of remote viewing (RV), it is the practice of seeking impressions about a distant or unseen target, using extrasensory perception (ESP) or "sensing" with the mind.

There is no way to fully explore the contributions made by the original team at Stanford Research Institute from the 1970s up until the CIA said they closed the program in 1995. Nevertheless, it is real. It has been highly successful, despite claims by anxious bureaucrats that it wasn't. Statistical evidence proves that it works, but mainstream scientists remain skeptical because no one knows *how* it works. It just does.

One CIA official remarked that it had purely been a research project all those years, and that the group had never been operationally tasked by the intelligence community. Since I don't work for the CIA, and I've never been particularly psychic, I would ask the reader to review some of the books by Russell Targ, a laser physicist who began to merge the studies of science with parapsychology in controlled laboratory environments.[5] Or his partner, Hal Puthoff who earned his Ph. D. in Electrical Engineering. Together, they developed protocols, identified some of the variables that make viewing more accurate, and sold the program to the Army, and then to the CIA.

---

5   http://www.remoteviewed.com/remote-viewing-history/ Downloaded from the World Wide Web July 14, 2020

Targ and Puthoff engaged a variety of psychic talent during the early stages of the project as they worked to create controlled laboratory experiments that could be replicated. This was in response to reports coming out of the Soviet Union that psychic research was being taken seriously, and as such was another strategic weapon that our country needed to counter.

There is a vast amount of material out on the internet about Ingo Swann, Hella Hammid, Pat Price, and others, all of whom were from vastly different backgrounds, and who not only possessed tremendous psychic talent themselves, but were able to teach it to others.

The Monroe Institute in Nelson County, Virginia and Courtney Brown's Farsight Institute, offer to teach remote viewing to interested individuals, and have had at one time or another, former government contract psychics on staff. Anyone can learn remote viewing. But, just like learning golf or musical instruments, some will be better at it than others.

Joe McMoneagle, a former US Army Warrant Officer has written several books on the subject that are informative, enlightening, and easy to read. I would encourage readers to take a look at his work and then make up their own minds as to the value and validity of this process.

My point again, is that the volume of evidence indicates that RV has been proven to be a reliable source of intelligence information through the years. And, once again I would ask; should we give more credibility to the heroes who can demonstrate their accomplishments, or to the bureaucrats who claim they didn't get anything out of it?

I'm not a lawyer, but I am a taxpayer. In my previous life as a police officer I learned the difference between the burdens of proof required in criminal cases and civil cases, and bring up that distinction now to help the reader put it into perspective.

In a criminal process, the prosecution must submit to the court *proof beyond a reasonable doubt* against someone, in order to obtain a conviction. But, I've always found that life is more like the civil process, where all it takes to persuade the jury is a *preponderance of the evidence.*

So, if a thousand people at a soccer stadium see unidentifiable lights in the night sky that are not behaving like traditional aircraft, should we agree that they're seeing unidentified flying objects of unknown origin, or should we believe a paid skeptic who argues that they were all hallucinating or watching some sort of migrating spiders? True story.

The late Carl Sagan used to say that "Extraordinary claims require extraordinary evidence."

But as the late nuclear physicist, Stanton Friedman used to remind us, "Absence of evidence is not evidence of absence."

In the end it comes back to a preponderance of the evidence, and even J. Allen Hynek eventually realized that there was more to the story than swamp gas.

1

CHRISTMAS DAY, 1963

D an Reynolds tossed the wet towel on top of the wicker hamper and came out of the steamy bathroom to the familiar smell of a properly basted turkey nearing completion. The new Sylvania contemporary console was blaring in the living room, and he determined that Doris Day was singing *Move Over Darling* a little too loudly for his taste. He slid the wooden door aside and turned the volume knob a little to the left and slid the door back.

It was an extravagance on his salary at the fire department, but he and Millie decided to make it an early Christmas present to each other. Besides, it had everything; AM...FM...phonograph, all in stereo high fidelity. His upcoming promotion to Lieutenant would propel him closer to $5,000 a year, plus his part-time work in construction would bring in a little extra. So, when Mille asked for the huge piece of furniture, he acquiesced, and they had picked it up at the appliance store a week earlier.

"Hey, I like that song!" Dan's wife yelled from the kitchen. "That movie is opening today and I want us to go see it." As Dan entered the kitchen, he saw Millie turn to his brother and, with a wink continued, "And that James Garner is too much man for any one woman! They have a special showing tonight at the Texas Theatre. It's such a beautiful day, we could all walk there and back."

His older brother Dirk was drinking a Coke at the kitchen table, watching the lunch activities, as their wives began locating plates and bowls in the cupboards. "Texas Theater? Isn't that the place they got Oswald?" he asked.

"Yeah," Dan replied, walking over to the refrigerator. "The locals got him about 1:30 and then the FBI came in the next day and confiscated the actual seat he'd been sitting in." Dan opened the near-vintage Crosley refrigerator and found another bottle of Coca Cola. He spotted the bottle opener on the counter and after he popped the cap, he continued, "But, they got the wrong seat because Butch Burroughs had already taken the real seat home as a souvenir."

"Who?" Dirk asked.

"Butch Burroughs...he runs the concessions there." Dan took a swig of Coke, "Of course, he had to give it back." He smiled. "I'm not sure how the FBI wrote that report up later." Both men laughed.

Dirk grinned, "The FBI took the seat he'd been sitting in... seriously?"

Dan nodded, "Uh huh." He opened the cupboard where Millie kept the potato chips.

His brother frowned, "Why the hell would they take a seat?"

"Who knows?" Dan replied. Both brothers had been on enough arson scenes and worked with enough cops to know something about the rules of evidence.

"I mean, if he'd dropped something, they would have found it when they searched the area, wouldn't they? And besides, witnesses said Oswald sat in several different seats while he was in there. He moved around a bunch," Dan said.

Dirk watched his wife, Jeanine bend over to pick up a spoon that had fallen to the floor. Married for a dozen years, she still did things that stimulated him without even thinking about it. The black pedal-pushers might not have been appropriate in Connecticut this time of year, but here in Dallas they made her look fantastic. "It sounds like this case has been handled totally wrong from the start. Nobody thinks that commie acted alone," he said.

Dan had fled the high prices and cold winters of Connecticut eleven years earlier on a whim of becoming an engineer via a football scholarship at Texas A&M. A shoulder injury his sophomore year slowed him down, but a knee injury the following season took him out of the game for good. He was several semesters shy of graduation, and he elected to work in construction for a while to earn some money until he decided what he wanted to do with his life.

Then one day he was at work on a small commercial site that was almost completely framed, when a careless worker mishandled an oxyacetylene torch and lit the entire site on fire. Regrets about seeing his work literally going up in smoke were soon replaced by fascination, as he watched firefighters rush to the scene and attempt to save the building. That day he made the decision to become a firefighter.

Dirk had remained with the extended family in Connecticut. Although the wages at Hartford Fire Department were about the same as they were in Dallas, the cost of living was significantly higher. Dirk was occasionally envious that his brother had been able to afford a nice three bedroom home with a bath and a half, while he was raising two boys in a two bedroom apartment. But, like his brother, Dirk also worked construction projects in his spare time to make extra money.

Dirk's wife Jeanine chimed in, "What would ever possess a man to want to give up his country and move to a place like that...Minsk of all places? Especially a Marine veteran."

Millie shook her head and grimaced, "Sick; he's just got to be sick!"

Millie still retained the athletic form that she had developed in high school. A Dallas native, she was one of the first students to go through the new South Oak Cliff High School when it had opened in 1952. She was proud to have pictures around the house of her days as a Golden Deb, the high kicking cheer team that had been trained by Marianna Brady. Brady had studied dance and traveled to New York City to learn some of the precision secrets from the famous Radio City Rockettes and brought this professionalism back to South Oak Cliff. Her squads, always attired in the trademark golden tuxedos, became well known throughout the country.

Millie carefully placed a stack of plates on the kitchen table and asked the guys, "Why don't y'all go clean up the living room so we can get everyone a place to sit for lunch?"

She looked out the window at the boys playing in the backyard. Only a few patches of snow remained from the large snowfall they had experienced on December 21 and 22. The Greater Southwest Airport recorded a total of more than two inches. But, Emory, about an hour east of them, reported nearly five inches. That dip was rare for Dallas, but not unheard of, with temperatures usually ranging from the high thirties to the low fifties. "Jeanine, can you get the kids in and cleaned up?"

Jeanine wiped her hands on the festive holiday dish towel and went out the back door. A native northeasterner, these temperatures were considered mild, almost tropical for her. She paused to smile at the boys in the backyard galloping around on imaginary horses, having a shootout with the western gun sets that Santa had brought them for Christmas.

She was initially concerned that the movie Millie had gone on and on about might be too mature for them, but the kids had all been excited to see the star of their favorite TV show, Maverick, in living color. Even though she had told them that it wasn't a western, they insisted on going anyway, to see Bret Maverick do something besides deal cards.

Upon hearing Millie's direction, the brothers looked at each other, shrugged and got up from the table. The small living room was a wreck. Discarded wrapping paper was everywhere, hiding obstacles such as Tonka trucks, Lionel train pieces and a track that had been hastily assembled to accommodate the *Goliath Steam Freight* set complete with steam locomotive, tender, caboose and assorted cars. Signaling a change in era, this would be the last year that Lionel produced the 637 steam engines in O-27 gauge. Progress.

Dirk winced as he bent to retrieve some paper and his bare foot found a small plastic soldier. "Damn!" he whispered so that the women wouldn't hear him. "How many of these little buggers are we going to find?"

Dan's boy Mark and Dirk's two sons, Bruce and Elliot, each got a bag of the small soldiers for Christmas. The families had coordinated the gifts this year to ensure that each child received something of similar value and none felt slighted. "I don't know," Dan replied. "I think there were about twenty in each bag." He found a large discarded box from the hair dryer that he'd bought for Millie, "Here, stuff the paper in this."

As they collected paper, bows and ribbon, Dirk lowered his voice, "When are the funerals?"

Dan looked over his shoulder towards the kitchen and then back at his brother, "David's is actually tomorrow and Manny's is Friday."

"Is Millie going with you?" Dirk asked.

"She said she wants to...she was going to ask Jeanine to sit with the kids if that's okay?"

Dirk stuffed some colorful paper into the box and pressed it down, "Pretty bad, huh?"

"The worst." Dan swallowed. "Most of us came over from Central in August when Station 22 opened on Coit Road. We were a pretty tight group. Manny Dominguez had five kids. David Jacobs was a bachelor, but he was the jokester of our group. I can't believe he's gone."

"You said arson, right?" Dirk asked as he bent down to pull some paper and boxes from behind the Christmas tree that was wedged into the corner of the living room. Some of the fake snow Millie had sprayed on the branches came off on his arm and he couldn't tell if the pine scent came from the aerosol can or the actual tree.

"Yeah." Dan retraced the conversation he'd started with his brother during the ride from the airport the day earlier, before being cut off by Millie. He looked again towards the kitchen, "We found several hot spots... and evidence of accelerants on two different floors. They probably started the fire on the second floor and then set another one on the first floor as they were leaving."

"What about the dead guy? Was he an employee or do you think he was involved?" Dirk pressed.

Dan shook his head, "Not sure. He had a military ID in his wallet, but we're pretty sure he was dead already. He was toast on the front, clean on his back...no soot stains around his nose. He...uh..." Dan stopped when he saw Dirk looking towards the kitchen. When he turned, he saw Millie, hands on her hips looking at him.

"Dan, I told you, I don't want to talk about that today! Today is Christmas and I want this family to enjoy the day without thinking about...you know. Our kids just want to enjoy..."

"I know, I know." Dan cut her off as he picked up his pace to get the living room straightened up.

Appropriately scolded, Dirk changed the subject, "We're gonna need another box..."

Once the room had been restored to as nearly an acceptable condition as possible, Dan found the portable card table in the basement and brought it upstairs. He extended the legs and placed it in the middle of the living room. His brother had returned to the kitchen and his near-empty bottle of coke. "Hey Dirk, can you help me bring some chairs up?"

Basements in north Texas were quite rare as a shallow limestone crust usually required costly excavation. However, they had been fortunate to find this home just two days after it went up for sale. Structural engineers claimed that the soil in this area was able to expand more than any other soil in North America. The periodic droughts and wet periods cause it to shrink away from the foundation and alternately squeeze tightly against it. Thus, most basements were considered fragile in the local soil. Their realtor told them that they would need to maintain soil moisture at a nearly constant level to prevent foundation failure over time. Dan, as an engineering student, looked at this as a challenge that he'd gladly accept.

The brothers moved some boxes around and pulled out four chairs that had been folded and stacked against the wall. By the time the card table was ready, so was Christmas dinner.

As Millie fixed a plate for Mark, she told the group, "Aunt Jeanine's gonna take y'all to the Bronco Bowl tomorrow." The famous Bronco Bowl opened the previous year, with Jayne Mansfield headlining the premier event. The venue was well known and in-cluded something for everyone, regardless of age, including slot cars, bowling, pool, dancing and other entertainment.

"Yay!" Mark yelled and told his cousins, "You're gonna love this place!" Mark loved to bowl, even though most of the balls were too heavy for him. He had a certain squat-and-roll technique that he had mastered, and even though strikes were rare, each roll got him seven or eight pins. He considered that success. He didn't care about official scorekeeping.

After dinner, Jeanine and Millie did the dishes and cleaned the kitchen as the boys returned to the back yard to finish their shoot-outs. Dan and Dirk relaxed in the living room with cold beers and tried to find something on TV that could keep them awake.

It was about 5:30 when Millie stuck her head in, "Hey boys, we need to start getting everyone ready if we're going to walk to the theater." The two firefighters shot up in their chairs, realizing that they had each drifted off for over an hour.

Dan's home on North Crawford Street in the Oak Cliff section was less than a mile from the Texas Theater, and a couple of blocks East from Oswald's rooming house. At Jeanine's urging, the couples and the kids donned jackets and walked briskly, so that they would pass the notorious rooming house on North Beckley, where Oswald spent his last days as a free man.

Out of respect for the home's owner, Gladys Johnson, who had owned the place since 1943, the group slowed their pace but did not stop to gawk as so many others had done in the past month.

Jeanine shook her head, "Did his wife live there too?"

Dan spoke softly until they were out of earshot of the residence, "No, she lived up in Irving. Oswald stayed here during the week and then went back there on the weekends."

"Really?" Jeanine asked. "How far is that?"

"Not far," Dan answered. "About ten miles from here."

Dirk looked over his shoulder at the group, "That sounds like a strange relationship. Weren't there any jobs for him in Irving?"

Dan responded, "I don't know; he had only started at the Book

Depository in October. He hadn't been there that long. He'd been going back and forth to New Orleans before that.

"Strange fellow," Dirk grimaced.

"He just had to be a sick man." Millie repeated her earlier appraisal. "So very, very sick."

The Texas Theater opened on San Jacinto Day, April 21, 1931, the anniversary date of Texas' final battle with Mexico, leading to its independence. It was the largest suburban movie theater in Dallas and was the first theater in Dallas to have air conditioning.

Originally part of a chain owned by Howard Hughes, Dan liked it because of its near-fireproof construction of concrete block. It even had special architectural considerations made for the projection booth because back when originally built, movie film was still made from a highly flammable nitrate base. Since nitrates produce oxygen fuel during combustion, a fire in this booth could spread quickly. However, this theater was equipped with metal screens that could slam down, sealing off the fire. In the early days of silent cinema, film projectionists had a mortality rate of 135 per cent compared to the national average. A minor fact that only firemen and insurance actuaries would have cared about.

A safer alternative featuring acetate film was introduced 1909, but the movie studios shied away from its use because the stored film became too brittle. Filmmakers also claimed that it provided inferior image quality. Nevertheless, most home movie film stock of this period was of the safer acetate variety.

The Texas Theater gained its global notoriety on the afternoon of November 22, when Dallas Police responded there on a tip, tracking a suspected cop-killer. Officer J.D. Tippit, an eleven year veteran of the Dallas Police Department had been killed up the street at 10th and Patton Ave. just minutes earlier, and multiple witnesses gave police a description of the suspect and his direction of travel after fleeing the scene. Not long after that, a shoe store manager saw an individual acting suspiciously, who ducked into the theater when police sirens could be heard. Because he went in without buying a ticket, the theater's cashier notified police who surrounded the theater. Oswald was arrested minutes later after a brief scuffle.

Dan and Dirk led the group south on Beckley to West Jefferson Boulevard at a fairly lively pace, covering a little over a mile in less than twenty minutes. The walk was good exercise and easier than trying to pile four adults and three kids into Dan's Pontiac. Besides, he thought, this will burn off some of that sugar the boys had taken in with the selection of pies the ladies had made for Christmas. As they neared the theater, they could see a small line had already formed.

This was eight year old Mark's second trip to the theater, and Bruce and Elliot's first to any theater. Bruce had just turned seven and Elliot was lagging behind at five. They had been to a local play the previous year, but Jeanine and Dirk saw movies as a luxury that they couldn't truly afford yet.

Millie, panting a bit from too many Chesterfields, cleared her throat, "My God Dan, were you in a race or something?"

Dan, a stickler for punctuality replied, "I just wanted to make sure we got here in time." They found their place in line and he continued, "If you get here late, all the good seats will be taken and we'll never get seven together."

Dirk reached for his wallet and waved it at Dan." Tonight is on us! You guys have been so good to have us down here, the least we can do is pick up the tab for a movie."

Jeanine joined in, "And I'd like to pay for the Bronco Bowl to-morrow while you are at, uh, you know." Not wanting to say the word *funeral* on Christmas.

Bruce asked, "Hey, Uncle Dan; can we see where he sat?"

Dan looked at him, eyebrows raised. "Where who sat?"

"Oswald," the seven year old replied.

Millie frowned at Dan as he responded, "Well Bruce, he moved around and sat in several places before the police got him. But the seat where he was actually arrested was about three rows from the rear, five seats from the aisle...and..."

Millie cut him off, "That's enough! We're here to watch a funny movie. Y'all don't have to be so morbid on Christmas Day!"

"Sorry, Babe." Dan said as they neared the cashier window.

Dirk stuck his head near the window and told the young man that there were four adults and three kids, and the cashier mumbled something unintelligible. Dan passed a twenty dollar bill across the surface and the cashier handed him seven tickets and fifteen dollars and ten cents in change.

As they passed through the lobby towards the concession stand, Dirk distributed the tickets.

"Popcorn and cokes only. You guys have had enough sweets today!" Dan said to the kids.

Mark tugged at his dad's arm as Bruce looked on and asked, "Which seat was it?"

His dad looked around to see where Millie was and then answered, "Over there- third row from the back."

Mark looked in the direction and noted the one wooden chair surrounded by all of the other cloth-covered chairs. "That doesn't look right," he said.

"I know. The manager and the FBI took the real one out; that's just a replacement," Dan responded, pulling him along towards the rest of the group.

Once seated, the ladies corralled the kids as Dirk leaned over Elliot and whispered to Dan, "Isn't this the movie that Marilyn Monroe was working on when she died?"

"Yeah, with Dean Martin. She boozed herself out and they had to reshoot it. The studio was worried about the sex so they re-cast with James Garner and Doris Day to soften it up a bit and sell it to more general audiences."

"Marilyn Monroe, really?" he asked, eyebrows raised.

"Yeah. Supposedly, there was a nude scene in the pool that had them worried...but I don't think you could really see anything. They originally called it *Something's Got to Give*.

"Huh, well, I like the song," Dirk added.

Dan laughed, "Yeah. That was actually a Johnny Mercer song

from 1955. It was from that Fred Astaire movie." He loved correcting his brother. More often, he loved the annoyed look his brother would give him when he did so.

The theater lights dimmed and as they showed trailers from coming attractions, Jeanine and Millie made sure the kids had their own popcorn and drinks and were strategically seated where they could appropriately deal with any problems that might occur during the show.

Mark settled into his seat as the movie began. When the credits rolled and the title song began to play, he immediately recognized it as the song that had been playing on the radio all week. In the darkened theater with the amplification of the speakers, it seemed more real.

However, when the music went from the second verse to the bridge, there was something about the harmonics and amplification in the theater that made his back stiffen and caused him to sit upright. He felt a slight tingle over his body, and he felt compelled to look over his left shoulder where he saw a slender young man in the back row, seated next to a woman in her forties or fifties. While the man seemed nervous and his eyes darted from side to side as if looking for someone, the woman sat silent, looking straight ahead.

As the music continued, Mark looked at the screen again for a couple of moments. When he looked back again not more than a minute later, the man and the woman were both gone. But by the time he saw his hero on the big screen in living color, he forgot about them. After all, it was Maverick, and in a suit!

Everyone enjoyed the movie and there were only minor complaints on the long walk back home, centering around who was going to have to take a bath first, and whether or not they could stay up later since there was no school this week.

Later that night as Millie and Jeanine were tucking the kids into beds and sleeping bags, Dan and Dirk sat in lawn chairs on the back porch enjoying a cold beer. A reward for the two mile hike to the theater and back.

After briefly discussing the next day's plans for the funeral of

Dan's co-worker, David Jacobs, they reminisced about their experiences at fire scenes. Dan's most vivid recollection focused on the Texaco fire that had occurred this past August 26. Several fuel tank trucks exploded at the dock where they were being filled, resulting in a huge fire. The trucks were destroyed, but luckily, no casualties were reported.

This, and two more beers, led to a deeper discussion about their departments' respective attitudes and commitments to firefighter safety. Both agreed that it wasn't until the end of World War II that standards began to improve exponentially from where they had been for the previous fifty years. The National Fire Protection Association, founded in 1896, led the various organizations in personal equipment design, and developed firefighting clothing that had become universally accepted as the standard in *bunker* or *turnout* gear, as it was known to some throughout the country.

In addition to helmets designed to allow water to roll off the firefighter's back, they designed a coat with three layers. The outer shell was flame resistant and would withstand temperatures of 500ºF for about five minutes. A middle layer was designed to prevent water from soaking the wearer, and an inner layer that protected against the principal heat transfer methods of convection, conduction, and radiation. Boots and gloves were also designed to be resistant to heat and puncture. For the boots, this meant a steel shank and toe were required for increased protection.

Engineers at Scott Aviation, a company that had made breathing equipment for crews working in airplanes at high altitudes, noticed that the firefighters were still using filter masks and rebreathers that didn't provide adequate breathing air. And thus, the Scott Air-Pack was introduced in 1945.

It was during this discussion that Dan suddenly remembered the film spool that he had shoved into his jacket at the warehouse fire. "Shit!" he exclaimed suddenly.

The interjection caught Dirk mid-swig. "What's the matter?"

"That film canister; I forgot to turn it in. It's still in my turnout coat." Dan paused. "I found it in the mess when we were searching for hot spots the other night. Technically, it's evidence. I can't be-lieve I forgot it!"

Dirk looked at him, "What do you think you'll find on it? That the arsonist recorded his crime and then pocketed the film? And, an accomplice took the camera, since you didn't find one at the scene?"

Dan shook his head, "Naw. I'm not even sure it survived the heat. It might be totally worthless."

Dirk took another pull on his beer, "You know, I have a good friend that works for Kodak back home. I can have him look at it and tell you if it's usable or not. Besides, the investigators would have to send it there anyway because no one in Dallas can develop it if it's damaged." He went on, arousal in his voice, "Look, what if t's just some sleazy porn? You wouldn't want that guy's family to get embarrassed when they collected his personal effects? My thought is, why don't we have a look at it first?"

Dan frowned, "I don't know. I could get in serious trouble if it turns out to be something. Why don't I just turn it in?"

Dirk grinned, imagining what kind of sexually raw material might be on the film, "Oh, come on. All of our lives we've been the curious type, and you know there's something inside you that would like to peek at it before you surrender it. Come on, man! If it's important, you can send it back to the arson team and say you got it mixed up with a home movie. And, if it's raunchy, we'll just, you know, pass it around!" He smiled and winked.

Dan snorted, "That's the lamest excuse I've ever heard!" Both brothers laughed.

"Oh come on." Dirk pressed for a third time, "This guy at Kodak owes me a favor and I'm kinda curious myself. If it's nothing, we'll toss it out and never talk about it again."

Dan thought for a moment, "I think we need another beer to make a rational decision."

Inside the house, Millie went into Mark's room and gave him a brief visual and *olfactory* inspection to ensure that he'd done the right amount of bathing before putting on his pajamas. As Jeanine did the same for her two boys, Millie tucked Mark in and gave him a kiss on the forehead.

Mark smiled, "He was there."

Millie adjusted his blanket, "Who was there, baby?"

"That guy, Oswald. He was in the theater."

"Of course he was there. That's where they arrested him." Millie bent down to pick up a single sock, without a mate in sight.

"No. I saw him, in the back row," Mark continued.

"Baby, Oswald is dead. That Jack Ruby fella shot him at the police station. You probably saw someone who looked like him." Millie hadn't seen anyone sitting behind their group, but since she had concentrated on getting everyone ready for the movie, she hadn't paid that much attention.

"He was sitting next to that lady."

"What lady, baby?" she asked, one eyebrow arching.

"The one in the white blouse and the grey pants...her hair was up."

Millie shrugged, "It was probably his wife. You need to get to sleep honey. Tomorrow is a big day for all of us."

"No, she was older, like fifty. She was pretty. She had black hair."

"Maybe it was his momma, darling. Go to sleep."

Mark wouldn't let it drop. "No. I don't think he knew she was there."

"Well, if they were sitting next to each other, they'd have to know each other was there, wouldn't they?" Since Millie hadn't seen the couple that young Mark had spoken of she wondered if he was still having some delusions or hallucinations that were a result of the scarlet fever episode three years earlier. His fever had hit 105 degrees, but the doctors at Parkland were able to get him stabilized, and he was back to school in a week.

Since that frightening episode, Mark had had some dizzy spells and occasionally reported seeing things that the doctors thought were hallucinations. The experts told her to just ignore it and get him back into his normal cycles of schoolwork and play time. They didn't seem concerned that the spells would continue for long. He seemed to recover nicely and by all accounts, was as healthy as a horse.

Millie followed Jeanine towards the door and as she switched out the light, she said softly, "Get some sleep, cowboy. Tomorrow is a busy day."

2

THURSDAY, DECEMBER 26, 1963

F red Balmain sat at the gray WWII-era Steelcase desk in his office near Main and Griffith Streets. The commercial space had been vacant since early summer, and was now being used as one of the covert command posts for the Dallas FBI agents working the JFK assassination investigation. Agents from other US Government offices were coming and going throughout the day and night, and the Director felt it would be better if they came and went from somewhere other than the Dallas Field Office.

Tall and lanky, Balmain was a bit earthier than the Director usually liked in his agents, but he certainly met the standards. He lived for truth, justice and America and would vocally, or physically oppose anyone who intimated something to the contrary. Barely forty years old, he was a farm-boy-turned-soldier in WWII, who had demonstrated bravery on the battle field and discernment in Headquarters. Even though he had never been to college, he had a depth of knowledge and breadth of experience that made him an intellectual equal of many senior officers. So they promoted him - first to lieutenant and then to captain by the end of the war. He returned home with a Silver Star, Purple Heart, and numerous other commendations.

His uncle, an attorney for the Justice Department, put in a good word for Balmain with an occasional lunch partner by the name of Hoover, and before long he found himself sitting in the Director's office and being asked how he felt about chasing enemies of the nation. In the post-WWII Bureau, J. Edgar Hoover focused on espionage and was looking for agents who had an interest in that field. A bit more opinionated than Hoover usually liked in young agents, they reached an agreement as to conduct and acumen, and before long, Balmain had gained the Director's favor.

Hoover also liked the fact that in addition to Balmain being a thorough investigator, he had a good gut. Hoover recognized that occasionally, with evidence to the contrary, agents had to disregard what the evidence told them, listen to their instincts, and play a hunch. Or, in the vernacular, their *gut*. Balmain's gut was scarily accurate.

After the assassination of JFK in November 1963, President Lyndon B. Johnson ordered the FBI to investigate the murder. However, at that time, the FBI had no statutory authority to investigate presidential assassinations. Jurisdictional conflict between federal, state and local authorities created confusion and organizational one-upmanship in the investigation of the case. But Hoover intended to control the investigation whether it was in his purview or not. He was not about to let the CIA come away from this incident more powerful than before.

Balmain opened one of the thick manila file folders on his desk so that he could familiarize himself with the minute details of the case, before taking his call with the Director. As he flipped through the pages, just like he had done every day for the past month, he looked for something new. He knew there was something in there they were missing. If he found it before anyone else did, then he was on his way to a promotion and a newer desk in Washington.

Planning for the Dallas visit actually began earlier that year at a meeting in which Kennedy, Vice President Lyndon B. Johnson and Texas Governor John Connally were together in El Paso on June 5.

President Kennedy planned the trip with three basic goals in mind. First, to help raise more campaign fund contributions, second, to begin his quest for reelection in November 1964; and more importantly, to help mend political fences among several leading

Texas Democratic party members who appeared to be fighting politically amongst themselves.

The trip to Dallas was first announced to the public in September, 1963. However, the exact motorcade route was not finalized until November 18, and publicly announced a couple of days after that.

Kennedy's motorcade route through Dallas with Vice President Johnson and Governor Connally, was planned to give the president maximum exposure to local crowds before his arrival for a luncheon at the Trade Mart, where he would meet with area civic and business leaders. The White House staff had informed the Secret Service that the President would arrive at Dallas Love Field via a short flight from Carswell Air Force Base in Fort Worth, where he had spoken at a breakfast meeting.

The Dallas Trade Mart had been selected for the luncheon, and Kenneth O'Donnell, President Kennedy's friend and appointments secretary, had chosen it to be the final destination on the motorcade route that day.

Departing from Dallas Love Field, the motorcade had been allotted forty-five minutes to reach the Trade Mart with a planned arrival time of 12:15 p.m. The itinerary was designed to serve as a meandering ten-mile route between the two places, and the motorcade vehicles could be driven slowly, but slightly quicker than parade speed, within the allotted time. The route had been approved and advanced by the US Secret Service.

Driving directly through Downtown Dallas, a route west along Main Street, rather than Elm Street, one block to the north, had been selected. This was the more traditional parade route for Dallas, and provided the optimum building and crowd views. The Main Street section of the route precluded a direct turn onto the Fort Worth Turnpike/Stemmons exit, which was the route to the Trade Mart, as this exit was only accessible from Elm Street. Therefore, the planned motorcade route included a short one-block turn at the end of the downtown segment of Main Street, onto Houston Street for one block northward, before turning again west onto Elm. That way the motorcade could proceed through Dealey Plaza before exiting Elm onto the Stemmons Freeway. The Texas School Book Depository was situated at the northwest corner of the Houston and Elm Street intersection.

After lunch at the Trade Mart, the group had planned to return to Love Field to depart for a fundraising dinner in Austin that evening. For the return trip, the Secret Service selected a more direct route, which was approximately four miles long.

Three vehicles were used for Secret Service and police protection. The first car, an unmarked white Ford, carried Dallas Police Chief Jesse Curry, Secret Service Agent Winston Lawson, Sheriff Bill Decker and the Special Agent in Charge of the Dallas Secret Service Field Office, Forrest Sorrels.

The second car, a 1961 Lincoln Continental convertible, was occupied by driver/Agent William Greer, Special Agent in Charge Roy Kellerman, Governor John Connally, his wife Nellie, President Kennedy, and Jackie Kennedy. The Kennedys were located in the rear, with the Connallys immediately in front of them in jump seats.

The third car, a 1955 Cadillac convertible code-named HALFBACK, contained driver/Agent Sam Kinney, Assistant to the Special Agent In Charge (ATSAIC) Emory Roberts, presidential aides Ken O'Donnell and Dave Powers, Agent George Hickey and Agent Glen Bennett, who were usually assigned to the Protective Research Section but had been temporarily reassigned to the detail due to manpower issues. Secret Service agents Clint Hill, who was Mrs. Kennedy's security agent, Jack Ready, Tim McIntyre and Paul Landis stood on the running boards.

Balmain closed the file and set it aside. His head tilted to the side so that he could read the tabs on the other folders. Finding the one he wanted, he opened it and began to read.

President Kennedy arrived from his stop in San Antonio and spent the night of November 21 at the Texas Hotel in Fort Worth. At a breakfast speech delivered to the Fort Worth Chamber of Commerce, he discussed the emerging Tactical Fighter Experimental (TFX) program. In addition to TFX, Kennedy spoke about military aviation technology and the recent shift in United States foreign policy from isolationism to a conceptual framework that encouraged cooperative international partnerships.

Kennedy boarded Air Force One, which departed at 11:10 a.m., and arrived at Love Field fifteen minutes later. At about 11:40, the presidential motorcade left Love Field for the trip through Dallas, running on a schedule about ten minutes longer than the originally planned forty-five minutes, due to enthusiastic crowds that were estimated to be between 150,000 to 200,000 people. He also made two impromptu stops along the route. By the time the motorcade reached Dealey Plaza, they were five minutes away from the Trade Mart.

The car turned off Main Street in Dealey Plaza around 12:30 p.m. As it was passing the Texas School Book Depository, at least three shots were heard. Bullets struck the president's neck and head, and he slumped over toward Mrs. Kennedy. The governor was shot in his back with the bullet transiting his abdomen and wrist and lodging in his leg. While witness statements were mixed, the majority indicated that the sniper had fired from the fifth or sixth floor of the Texas School Book Depository.

The motorcade immediately headed to Parkland Memorial Hospital, a few minutes away. Secret Service and Dallas police cordoned off the area where the limousine had been parked. At that time, the bubble top components were removed from the trunk and installed on the vehicle. A Catholic priest was summoned to administer the last rites, and at 1:00 p.m. John F. Kennedy was pronounced dead.

The president's body was placed in a casket and taken by ambulance to Love Field where it was carried up the rear port-side stairs aboard Air Force One. At approximately 2:38 p.m., Lyndon B. Johnson took the oath of office, which was administered by US District Court Judge, Sarah T. Hughes.

At 1:30 p.m., Dallas Police arrested Lee Harvey Oswald at the Texas Theater for the murder of Dallas Officer J. D. Tippit. An employee of the Texas School Book Depository, Oswald was soon linked to the assassination. It was his rifle. He was a known subversive.

He had an FBI file and an agent had been assigned to monitor his activities.

Flipping through other witness statements, Balmain saw one from Howard Brennan, who was sitting across the street from the Texas School Book Depository. Brennan told police that he was watching the motorcade go by when he heard a shot that came from above, and he looked up to see a man with a rifle take another shot from a corner window on the sixth floor. He said he had seen the same man looking out the window minutes earlier. Brennan gave a description of the shooter, and Dallas police subsequently broadcast descriptions of the suspect at 12:45 p.m., 12:48 p.m., and 12:55 p.m. Brennan also stated that after the second shot was fired, he recalled that the man he saw in the window was aiming more intently for his last shot, and maybe paused for another second afterwards as if to assure himself that he had hit his mark.

Balmain continued to read to himself, "As Brennan spoke to the police in front of the building, they were joined by Harold Norman and James Jarman, Jr., two employees of the Texas School Book Depository, who had watched the motorcade from windows at the southeast corner of the building's fifth floor. Norman reported that he heard three gunshots come from directly over their heads. Norman also heard the sounds of a bolt-action rifle action being cycled, and cartridges dropping on the floor above them." Dallas police sealed off the exits from the Texas School Book Depository sometime between 12:33 p.m. to 12:50 p.m. to conduct a thorough search.

Balmain looked at the twenty-four hour clock on the wall and waited for the newly modified KY-3 phone system to light up, telling him that Washington DC was calling. Ironically, it was Kennedy that pushed for improved secure communications between the US and the Soviet Union. Under the Defense Communications Agency (DCA), the government identified and implemented a management plan for secure communications at the highest levels. And now, the newly formed White House Communications Agency was the latest iteration of this initiative.

The DCS was essentially a collection of communications systems turned over by the military departments with considerable restrictions. Key among these responsibilities was the establishment of three defense-wide networks that would be known as the Automatic Voice Network (AUTOVON), the Automatic Digital Network (AUTODIN), and the Automatic Secure Voice Communications Network (AUTOVOSECOM).

The technician answered the telephone that rested atop a unit that resembled a hybrid cross between a safe and a small refrigerator. "Yes, sir. He's right here."

Balmain took the handset from the technician and after taking a deep breath, tried to sound as calm as one could when speaking with the Director. "Good morning, sir."

With the new technology built by Bendix Corporation, using wideband radio and telephone channels, and Pulse Code Modulation for speech digitization, Balmain was able to recognize the voice on the other end of the line. This was better than the stuff they'd used in the army, that seemed to garble a person's voice, and then un-garble it just enough to understand some of the actual words.

"Good morning, Fred." The high pitched voice with the mid-Atlantic accent came through the receiver loud and clear. "Where do we stand on the things we discussed before Christmas?"

Balmain drew another breath. "Well, sir, we're still working closely with Dallas PD to identify anyone and everyone that might have had any photographic or other recording equipment in Dealey Plaza. We've gone through the different photos and movie footage to try to identify the exact positions of everyone else with equipment...whether they have come forward yet or not."

He paused and continued, "As you know, sir, most of the high quality, relevant films have already been purchased by the wire services. Where possible, we have confiscated... uh...asked for use of cameras and undeveloped film for laboratory testing. We have had relevant enlargements made so that we can put names to images and try to locate them." He looked up at the large wall opposite his desk and the collage of color and black and white images that had been placed onto a large map of Dealey Plaza that extended from floor to ceiling. A photo was placed in the position from where it was taken, along with the name of the individual who took it or filmed from there.

"And?" the Director inquired.

"And, sir, what we are finding is that some film footage is being reported as missing or damaged during processing, and some negative strips were missing when the owners got their photographs back."

The line was silent for a few seconds. "The President wants to ensure that we are containing this investigation. How do we know what percentage of potential witnesses have actually been interviewed? How do we know what percentage of film and other photographic evidence we have actually seen? And how do we know what percentage of photographic evidence is still available but we haven't seen, because it either hasn't been brought forward or souvenir hunters are hoarding it until they can find a publisher to buy it?"

Balmain frowned. "We've made it clear in newspaper and radio interviews that we need people to bring us anything they might have witnessed in Dealey Plaza, and report any dealings they might have had with Oswald or his known associates in the weeks leading up to the twenty second."

After another pause the Director asked, "Of all the people captured in all the shots, what percentage do you think we have identified, or can identify?"

"Realistically sir?" Balmain hated to give bad news. "Maybe sixty, seventy five percent."

Through the phone, the Director could be heard talking to someone else in the room in Washington, although the conversation was muffled. When he returned, he said, "Look. The Agency is not going to be forthcoming about what they know about him, you know, Oswald. They have informants they identified as LITEMPO and ENVOY that are sharing information about Oswald's time in

Mexico, but as far as the Cuban connection, they claim that HERO went dark in May. They haven't heard anything else from him. They think he's dead."

Balmain knew that LITEMPO was the CIA cryptonym for Mexican intelligence, and that ENVOY was a joint program between the Mexico City CIA station and the Mexican secret police to wiretap the Soviet and Cuban embassies. He had only heard the name HERO associated with intelligence information one time, a year earlier, during the Cuban Missile Crisis.

"Other than the news media and our law enforcement colleagues, is there anyone else expressing an interest in your progress?"

Balmain frowned. "Excuse me, sir?"

The voice on the phone came back, "Was there anything unusual about any of the interviews you conducted?"

Totally confused, Balmain replied, "I'm not sure what you mean, sir. It's a presidential assassination investigation. I'm not sure what constitutes *unusual*."

The Director ignored the comment and asked, "I want you to open a new informant file, under the heading of DL-P1. I will be sending you some information that he is providing. He is new to the Bureau and I have no idea how accurate his information will be. But, he might be able to help us find people who have information, photographs or film footage that we haven't been able to locate."

Balmain grabbed a blank manila folder and wrote the designation on the tab, "DL-P1. Right, sir."

The Director continued, "What can you tell me about the fellow in the railroad tower?"

Balmain dropped the new folder and picked up another. He flipped through a couple of pages before reading. "Lee Bowers, a railroad switchman was sitting in a two-story tower, and advised he had an unobstructed view of the rear of the stockade fence atop the grassy knoll during the shooting. He claimed he saw four men in the area between his tower and Elm Street. These included a middle-aged man and a younger man, standing 10 to 15 feet apart near the triple underpass... uh, who did not seem to know each other, and one or two uniformed parking lot attendants, one of whom he knew. He said that at the time of the shooting, he saw, and I quote, 'something out of the ordinary, a sort of milling around', which he could not identify. Bowers said in his statement that one or both of the men were still there when a Dallas motorcycle officer ran up the grassy knoll to the back of the fence."

Balmain flipped a page and continued, "But, in a later interview, he said that the men he saw weren't behind the stockade fence, but rather between the pergola and the stockade fence."

The voice at the other end of the secure line was quiet for a few moments. "This case is going to have problems. We had no control over the scene at Dealey Plaza. We had virtually no control at Parkland Hospital, and the limousine had already been cleaned up by the time we saw it up here on the night of the twenty-second. The bullet that was recovered was found on a stretcher that we can't positively tie to Kennedy or Connally, and the autopsy report doesn't match the doctors' statements in Dallas relative to the condition of the body and wounds."

The Director took a breath. "In short, if Oswald had lived, any attorney worth his salt would have been able to successfully defend him in court. At least for the assassination. They probably had enough on him for the Tippit killing, maybe, if the defense didn't attack the sloppy handling of the revolver Dallas police claimed to have found on him."

He paused again. "And between our friends in the media and our sister agencies, conspiracy theories are beginning to emerge. As you know, Katzenbach persuaded the President to get Chief Justice Warren to Chair a commission to look into this. They have been meeting since December 5. We are, of course, supporting this commission, but I don't know if they are objectively investigating, or trying to drive a particular result, like the Air Force's BLUEBOOK." He seemed to be thinking out loud more than making a statement.

This discussion was well over Balmain's pay grade. "Any special instructions, sir?" he asked.

"Well, McCone is staying personally involved in this over at CIA, so I intend to remain fully engaged as well. Let's keep a daily call at this time, but if something comes up, I want you to find me immediately. Watch your TELEX."

"Of course, sir," Balmain replied, hearing a click on the other end half way through his response.

Balmain walked across the room to the TELEX machine to ensure that the rectifier and the machine were both on, and that there was blue light coming from the power supply box. Three and a half minutes later, the machine came alive as if someone invisible was typing a letter.

> URGENT   0925 AM EST 12-26-63   1 PAGE
>
> TO   DL33625
>
> FROM   DIRECTOR
>
> FOLLOWUP TO CONV THIS DATE RE DL P1
>
> DL P1 REPORTS RAMEY HAROLD M AF15446860 USAF SSGT. DIED IN FIRE 12-23-63 DALLAS WAREHOUSE
>
> AFOSI MAY HAVE HAD UNDER SURVEILLANCE — MAY BE IN PXXX POSSESSION OF REFERENCED 8MM FOOTAGE. DNC OSI DIRECTLY. REPEAT DNC OSI DIRECTLY.
>
> END AND ACK PLS

Balmain typed *DL33625 ACK* on the keyboard, and carefully tore the message off of the roller. "Do Not Contact?" he read to himself as he walked back to his makeshift office. He realized that this instruction was probably due to what the Director perceived as inter-agency rivalry in the case. But still, how was he expected to interview people about a deceased witness, without someone else finding out about it?

He frowned at the TELEX message as he re-read it, and then turned around and walked out into the bullpen, the open area that had eight desks carefully arranged for the agents to use as their temporary offices. "Hey Scotty," he hailed at the nearest of the two agents who had arrived for work.

"Yeah, boss?" Special Agent Scott Wainwright looked up from his typewriter.

A five-year veteran of the Bureau, Wainwright, like Balmain, had come in from the US Army. Although he had never seen combat like his supervisor, he had been an intelligence officer assigned to post-war West Berlin for the last year of his service. His superior officer evaluation reports and his desire to obtain a law degree was of interest to Hoover. Tall and fit, the bachelor seemed to fit the Director's image of what an FBI agent was supposed to look like.

Balmain approached his desk and asked quietly, "Wasn't there a big warehouse fire across town this past weekend?"

Wainwright thought for a moment and nodded, "Yeah, some textile company. There were three dead, two of them were firemen." He pulled the newspaper out of his briefcase and pointed to a small story on the lower right corner of the page. "The funeral for one of the firemen is today at eleven o'clock. Why?"

Balmain asked, "Can I see that for a minute?" He took the newspaper from his associate and walked back into his office. Sitting with his back to the window he was able to read the article without the desk lamp.

He made some notes on the yellow legal pad and then walked back out to the bullpen. "Here you go."

Scotty took the newspaper and put it back into his briefcase. After all, he wouldn't want his supervisor to think he was reading the paper on company time. "Do you need something?"

Balmain shook his head and replied, "No, thanks." He walked back into his office and stopped short. His senses alert, he looked around briskly and then turned back to Scotty. "Have there been any women up here this morning?"

Scotty smirked and smiled, "Are you kidding? If I'd seen a lady up here, I wouldn't have let her get to you without getting her number first."

Balmain shook his head and sat down behind his desk. For just a split second, he thought he had gotten a whiff of perfume. Nice perfume. But a scent he'd never smelled before. There weren't any women assigned to his team, and their covert location meant they didn't get any non-official visitors. He looked again at the notes he had just made about the fire, got up and moved towards his door, "Scotty!" he said, loud enough to be heard across the room.

"Yeah, Boss?" Scotty replied.

"Get your coat. We're going to a funeral."

3

SUNDAY, DECEMBER 29, 1963

D an Reynolds moved the skillet to another burner so that he could have a few seconds to find the pepper in the cupboard above. Promotable or not, it was his turn to make breakfast for the men on Company A, and with Texas pride, he was determined to make the best Gawdammed breakfast they'd ever had.

He slammed the cupboard door shut with the back of his hand, and sprinkled pepper across the skillet of scrambled eggs like a pro. He'd learned cooking from both his mom and grandma, and realized that no matter where you go in life, you've still got to eat. So, you might as well eat well.

Some of the C Company crew were still finishing up reports and cleaning the apparatus after an early morning trash fire that got them out well before sun-up, when Ed Jeffers, their shift Lieutenant, stuck his head in the kitchen, "Hey, will you have enough for some of my guys?"

Dan nodded without looking up, "Absolutely L-T", using the casual abbreviation of respect for anyone of lieutenant's rank. Dan opened the refrigerator and grabbed the milk and carton of eggs, and started mixing up another bowl of his special concoction to make the additional scrambled product. Scrambled was usually the way to go. People have their preferences when ordering eggs in a restaurant or making them at home, but when there's a dozen hungry firemen waiting for breakfast, scrambled, and plentiful, is the smart bet.

"Thanks!" Jeffers replied. He started to turn and then, "Oh, and also, before I forget, Reno Belcher is coming by later. He wants to talk to you and the guys about the warehouse fire last week."

"Reno?" Dan looked up. "Is he still on the arson squad?"

"Yep." Lt. Jeffers said over his shoulder as he walked away.

In the other skillet, the sausage was already browning, so once Dan gave the flattened mound a flip, he tossed another potato into the boiling water to see if it would heat up sufficiently before he carved it up and fried it in another skillet. A breakfast of fried potatoes, eggs and sausage was a Texas standard, and when you added toast, as long as no one got sick, it was sure to be received with positive grunts.

The position of Cook was not punitive like it had been in the military, but was rather awarded to the fireman who could best meet the needs of the team. Everyone had to take turns cooking meals, pushing brooms, cleaning fire equipment and of course, toilets, but the position of cook was pretty coveted. Once the guys had found their cook, they would volunteer for other more menial jobs just to make sure they got good chow when it was time.

Dirk had the same culinary interests, and the brothers often competed against each other at family events to see who could make the best chili or the most flavorful ribs. Dan pursed his lips and frowned as he used the spatula to dab at the sausage mound, breaking it into smaller pieces. He thought about the conversation with his brother as he dropped him and his family off at Love Field earlier that morning.

"You won't regret it!" Dirk smiled as he took the envelope containing the undeveloped 8MM film spool from Dan.

The corner of Dan's mouth tightened. "I already regret it. That's evidence. Maybe."

After tossing the spool into his suitcase and snapping the latches, Dirk slapped his brother on his shoulder. "It'll be fine Alice. Don't get your panties in a bunch! Five bucks says that it's nothing more than some great porn."

The families had said their good-byes at the house amid hugs, kisses and promises to get together again soon, and then Dan dropped them at the airport on his way into work. Now, two hours later, Dan wondered if he'd made a career blunder by giving his brother the film. As they had agreed, if it was nothing, they'd toss it out and if it turned out to be relevant to the case, it would miraculously show up at the arson investigator's office. Reno Belcher's office.

"Oh shit," Dan muttered quietly to himself. He stared at the pile of scrambled eggs and as he flipped and chopped with one hand, he turned the burner down with the other. His focus was shifting away from breakfast and onto that spool of film that he had handed to his brother a couple hours earlier. A spool that was on its way to Connecticut. "Great timing shit-for-brains!" he said to himself.

An hour later, the dishes done and his team mates fed, Dan flipped through the stories in the newspaper. He looked up when he saw the dark blue Pontiac pull into the driveway and park. He recognized Reno right away, but wasn't certain if he knew the tall lanky fellow in the passenger seat

He neatly folded the newspaper and laid it on the end table as he watched the two men head towards the front door.

As he rounded the corner in the garage bay, he could hear their shift Lieutenant, Bart McDaniel greet the two men. "Hey Reno! Nice looking suit. Sears or Goodwill?"

Reno grinned, "Hey Bart. It's actually my neighbor's, but don't tell him I took it off his clothesline." Dan saw the men shake hands and then look his way. "Hi Dan! It smells like someone just finished breakfast. Anything left?

Dan smiled and shook hands, "Naw, just did the dishes. If I'd known you were hungry, I'd have saved something back for you."

Reno gestured at his guest, and introduced him to the two men, "Lieutenant McDaniel, Dan Reynolds, this is agent Balmain with the FBI."

The men shook hands as Balmain presented his credential book with his left hand. The left handed presentation was a published

FBI procedure; to leave their right hands free in case they had to shoot someone. "Nice to meet you," the Lieutenant said. "What brings you down to our station today?"

Balmain replaced the credentials in the inside breast pocket of his dark gray suit and then bent to retrieve the leather briefcase on the floor beside him. "Sorry to interrupt your Sunday on such short notice, but we thought we'd see if we could catch some of your guys in between runs. Is there a place we can talk for a few minutes?"

Lt. McDaniel pointed back towards the kitchen, "Yeah, we can talk in here. Most of the guys are on clean-up so if you need them, we can call them in."

Dan led them back to the kitchen area where the smell of sausage still hung in the air. They allowed Agent Balmain to seat himself first, and then pulled out chairs nearby as he unzipped his briefcase and extracted a couple of 8X10 manila envelopes and a file folder.

Reno let the FBI agent start the conversation, "First, on behalf of the Director, let me extend our condolences to you and to the families of Manny Dominguez and David Jacobs. It was a horrible tragedy and drives home the level of danger you guys face every day."

Lt. McDaniel nodded solemnly. "Thank you. They're going to be missed around here. We're all family."

Balmain opened one of the manila envelopes and took out a small stack of 8X10 black and white photos. "This may be tough for you, but I want to show you some shots that were taken at the warehouse fire that day."

As he passed the photos to Lt. McDaniel, seated across the table from him, Dan could see that there was handwriting on the back of each photo. Each photo was numbered in the top right corner, but the numbers weren't in sequence, and it appeared that several photos must have been missing. McDaniel examined the first photo and then slid it across the table to Dan. Dan then looked at each one, and in turn passed it back to Balmain, who arranged them on the table between everyone.

"Yeah. That's pretty much as I remember it," Dan said as he looked at Lt. McDaniel for confirmation. The shots were various angles of the inside of the warehouse that showed locations in the center of the first and second floors indicating hot spots - places where the fire may have originated.

Balmain opened the second envelope and pulled out another set of 8 X 10 enlargements, which focused on the civilian decedent. There were no pictures of Dominguez or Jacobs. He slid the first one to the lieutenant. "This one shows the victim, the civilian victim, face down as you found him."

Lt. McDaniel studied it for three or four seconds and then passed it to Dan, as Balmain passed the second photo across the table. "And this one, shows the decedent in a supine, face-up position after you rolled him over."

McDaniel looked at it and nodded, sliding it across the table to Dan. "Yep, that's him. Well, what's left of him."

Dan studied the image for a second and added, "Yeah, he was pretty singed on the backside, but looked kinda, well, peaceful on the front."

Balmain took the other two photos and arranged them to be above the other two rows of enlargements in front of him. "Peaceful. The autopsy said he died of a broken neck, and the absence of any soot around his mouth and nostrils tells us that he was dead before the flames got to him.

Reno joined in, "We didn't find any other shoeprints in the ash, just impressions left by fire boots. So, whoever put him there was out of the warehouse before the shit started coming down around him."

The lieutenant studied the photos again, turning them briefly to get a better look, and then turned them back shaking his head. "I'd agree we have a clear case of arson. But, why is the FBI on this?"

Reno and Balmain looked at each other for an instant, and then Balmain opened the file folder, holding it close like a poker hand that he had just been dealt. "Guys, I need to ask you to treat this information confidentially. Don't discuss this with anyone that we don't interview today. Don't discuss it with your families. Don't discuss it with your parish priests, bartenders or girlfriends."

Dan tensed briefly as he thought about that stupid roll of film that he'd allowed his brother to talk him out of. Now, the FBI was in this for God knows what reason. He felt anxious and queasy.

Balmain flipped a page and read from his report, "Harold M. Ramey, Staff Sergeant, United States Air Force. Does that name mean anything to either of you?"

Dan and Lt. McDaniel looked at each other, frowned, and almost in unison replied, "Never heard of him."

It was McDaniel who pressed, "Who was he?"

"You're sure that neither the face nor the name are familiar to you?" Balmain repeated.

"Not at all," Dan responded, now more curious than anxious at the FBI man's interest.

Balmain turned another page in the file and began, "He was a photographer assigned to Sheppard AFB, the 2054th Communications Squadron. Sheppard is about three hours northwest of here. We're trying to determine how a photographer who didn't file the required paperwork with his superior officer for an off-base leave, ended up in a warehouse fire a hundred and fifty miles from home. Without a car."

Balmain paused and looked at Dan. "Say, do you think I could get a cup of that coffee?"

"Absolutely," Dan said as he got up and went to the percolator on the counter. "How do you take it?"

"Black, thanks," Balmain answered, and then continued, "Well, to be more precise, we found his car, a 1961 Comet two-door, black in color, near his quarters on the base. We checked around and found that he boarded a Greyhound bus at the local station along with four others at 10:30...one woman and three other men. The driver remembers that two of the men were in uniform, and our guy and the man and woman traveling together were in civilian clothes. However, other than the couple, none of the others sat together or seemed to know each other".

"The driver said that the bus made three stops, picked up e even people, but none of them sat with any of the military passengers. The bus arrived at the downtown terminal at approximately four o'clock in the afternoon of the twenty-third." Balmain took a sip of his coffee and toasted Dan, "Thanks! Where was I? Oh yeah. The driver remembered that Ramey was the only passenger on the bus who didn't have any luggage."

McDaniel pursed his lips. "So, he wasn't planning on staying in town overnight?"

Reno answered him, "We don't think so. Since he disappeared at 1600 hours from the terminal downtown, and didn't re-appear until you found him face down six hours later about ten miles away, we're pretty sure he met someone who didn't want him to use his return ticket."

McDaniel thought for a moment, "Drug deal gone bad?"

Balmain shook his head. "We don't think so. Toxicology didn't show any drugs present in his bloodstream. No alcohol either. At the time of his death, he still had his wristwatch and thirty six bucks and some change on him, so we don't think it was any kind of robbery either."

McDaniel looked at Balmain squarely. "Well, your presence here makes me think that there's something you're not telling us, at least completely. What do they do at Sheppard?"

Balmain smiled. "I'm telling you as much as I can. Believe me. As far as Sheppard's mission, it's nothing too secret. Since 1955 it's been the prime training center for the Air Force Department of Guided Missile Training. In particular, the Atlas intercontinental ballistic missile. From 1957 to 1959 Sheppard also became the prime center for the Jupiter and Thor intermediate range ballistic missiles, as well as the Titan intercontinental ballistic missile. It's still a Group Headquarters for The Department of Air Intelligence, but they are looking at moving that back to Lowry AFB in Colorado next year."

Dan's eyes widened. "Nothing too secret?" Everyone laughed.

McDaniel interrupted, "Doesn't the Air Force have an

investigative unit that looks into military casualties. What's it called, the, uh, OSI?"

Balmain winced at the mention of the organization he'd been specifically told not to contact. "Well, the Office of Special Investigations does occasionally look into such matters. But, for national security reasons, we're taking the lead on this." Then, as an afterthought he added, "But, you can be sure that whatever we develop will be shared with our colleagues in that agency."

"National security?" Dan asked with an eye blink that lasted longer than normal. What had he gotten himself into?

Balmain closed the file folder and laid it face down on the table. "I know. Look, I don't want to sound trite here, but a lot of the time, we're only given piecemeal information and asked to investigate and report. So, I'm investigating and reporting. Washington has an interest in this guy for some reason and they've asked me to quietly dig a little deeper into his death."

Balmain reached for one of the photos in front of him as he looked at Reno who suddenly looked down and away. The agent bent down and pulled a magnifying glass out of his briefcase and then passed the magnifier and the photograph across the table to Lt. McDaniel. "Here, use this. Take another look at this photo."

Lt. McDaniel squinted and moved the magnifying glass back and forth until the photograph came into focus for him. "What am I supposed to be looking for?"

"Look at the body," Balmain directed. "In particular, look at the legs of the body."

McDaniel squinted and moved the photo back and forth under the glass. "Corduroys, black socks, loafers... I still don't see what I'm supposed to be seeing."

"Let Mr. Reynolds have a look," Balmain said quietly.

Dan took the magnifying glass and the photo and gave the photo a thorough scan, ending up on the legs of the late Staff Sergeant Ramey. "Yeah, dark corduroys, black socks and penny loafers."

"Look at his socks," Balmain urged.

Dan laid the photo flat on the table and moved it so that the overhead light was able to illuminate it without a shadow. There it was. The lump in the victim's sock. His left sock. The lump that he was certain covered a spool of 8MM film. He swallowed, but tried to keep his composure. "I see, uh, something stuck in his sock."

Balmain started to speak again, but Reno interrupted him. "Yes. It's a spool of movie film. I remembered finding it on him and I was trying to get all of his personal effects into an evidence bag. There was a lot going on, and..." he continued like a child trying to rationalize a failing test score to his parents, "...and at some point, it got, uh, separated. When I bagged everything, it must have fallen out."

Balmain attempted to soften the admission, "It's okay. You'd just lost two of your friends in a horrible fire and I'm sure things were pretty hectic." Balmain reached out his hand and patted Reno's forearm. "It's okay."

Balmain looked at Lt. McDaniel, "But when we went back to check for the film, we couldn't find it. Anywhere."

Dan's heart was racing but he knew he had to control his breathing. He had heard that these FBI guys could spot a liar from across the room. "You looked everywhere?"

Balmain nodded, "Yeah. A couple of Reno's guys and one of mine went back on the 26th to see if we could find it, but, nada."

McDaniel jumped in, "Well, that was three days after the fire; kids could have gotten in there, you know, or scavenger hunters - insurance people."

Balmain began collecting the photos off the table and re-inserting them into their manila envelopes. "Yeah, I know. We really didn't have good control of the scene after the police left on the 24th. And, we have checked with the insurance investigator." He returned the file and the envelopes to his briefcase and zipped it shut. "Lt. McDaniel, would it be okay if I just spoke to the guys who were on the fire scene that night? I don't want to go into too much detail with them. I just want to know if any of them might have seen that spool of film."

"No problem." McDaniel replied and then, turning to Dan, "Can you rustle them up one at a time and bring them in?"

"Right away L-T," Dan said as he got up from his chair and headed to the garage bay.

There were a total of six firemen on station that day who had been at the warehouse fire. One by one, Dan escorted them to the kitchen area so that Balmain, McDaniel and Reno could ask them about the film. He tried to look busy and uninterested, but his heart and breathing were still elevated. What if one of them had seen him pick up the film? However, despite his concerns, none of the interviews lasted more than a couple of minutes and the blue Pontiac headed back down the road twenty minutes later.

When they were gone, Dan Reynolds pulled the lieutenant aside and asked quietly, "What the hell was that all about?"

"Hell if I know," he responded as he started to walk around the pumper truck that had just been cleaned. He paused, took out his handkerchief, and began to polish some of the pressure gauges and the surrounding chrome. "Fingerprints dammit!" He folded the handkerchief and returned it to his pants pocket. "It seems like Reno mucked up and lost something that the feds want."

"I wonder what was on it," Dan speculated ostensibly in an attempt to conceal his guilt.

McDaniel continued his inspection of the other apparatus and didn't bother looking over his shoulder. "Who knows? Who cares? It looks like the Air Force had a photographer who took some pictures of something he shouldn't have, and they want them back. I mean, missiles and shit, really? What gets me is if this is such a sensitive investigation, then why would that FBI agent tell us about it?"

Dan stopped in his tracks. "What?"

McDaniel patted his pants pockets and found a pack of Camel cigarettes. In the other pocket was his cherished Zippo that he had carried with him while serving in the Army in Korea. He snapped the lid open with the distinctive 'tink,' and lit up. Exhaling a plume of smoke through his nostrils, he continued, "If some NCO takes pictures of something classified and then takes a powder with 'em, the OSI and the FBI would work together and get him and the pictures back before he could sell 'em to the Soviets. The public would never even hear about it."

"Hmmm...I guess you're right," Reynolds said, shoving his hands into his pockets. "But what could be worse than missile stuff? I mean, if that's a cover story, then what's the real story?"

McDaniel shook his head, "I don't know; don't really care. My job is to fight fires, not to catch spies. If the FBI thinks this Air Force Sarge was some sort of soviet spy, then they have my blessing to do whatever they need to do to catch 'em. I'll help if I can, and if they want us to go back and search that warehouse again, we'll do it. But they didn't ask."

"Do you want me to take some guys back to have a look for it?" Dan asked, knowing that there was nothing to find.

McDaniel shrugged. "Not really. If it was there, Reno and his team would have found it when they went through. He might not be great at inventorying evidence, but he's pretty damned good at finding it." He took another draw on his Camel. "If you need me, I'll be in my office."

As McDaniel walked away, Dan looked at his watch. Factoring in the time to collect their luggage and the drive time from the airport back to their house, Dirk probably wouldn't be home for another hour. He paced nervously up and down the garage bay as if inspecting the equipment, all the while praying for a fire or some other emergency run to distract him.

Time moved slowly at the station, but seemed to speed up immensely when fighting fires. He never should have given that reel to his brother. Hell, he should have turned it in that night. But why didn't he? Balmain had said it: they'd lost two close friends and no one was thinking rationally.

What would he tell Millie if he got fired? Or worse, what would happen if he got charged for some crime for withholding some sort of national security evidence?

About four miles away, the blue Pontiac turned east on West Commerce street and headed back towards Dealey Plaza. Reno had been driving in silence as Fred Balmain made some notes on his legal pad. As he finished his notes and began to slip the pad back into his briefcase, Reno broke the silence. "What now?"

Balmain drummed his fingers on the arm rest. "How well do you know or trust these guys?"

Reno turned his attention from the street in front of him to look directly at the agent. "With my life. What are you getting at?"

"The photos show the film reel. You picked up a film reel. No film reel got turned in. No one found the film reel when we went back to look again." The drumming intensified. "Either persons unknown gained entry to this warehouse and found it after the police pulled out, or one of your guys picked up the film."

Reno shook his head, "Every one of those guys are solid. If any of them had found that reel, they'd have turned it in."

"Maybe," the drumming stopped. "I'd like to hope so. But, I have to consider all the possible scenarios."

Reno looked back at the road and braked for a car turning left in front of him. "Are you saying they deliberately took evidence from a crime scene? For what reason?"

Balmain's lips tightened almost imperceptibly. "Curiosity, maybe. Or worse."

"Worse?" Reno snapped his head back towards Balmain. "What's worse?"

"Well, you can't overlook the obvious. That fire was set by a pro, and in your business you must know how many firemen get arrested each year for arson?" Balmain kept his voice low and controlled. "Forget personalities and personal relationships. They're your friends. I understand that. But think about the type of people who could successfully set a fire like the one at the warehouse, and get out without leaving anything other than a dead body."

"That's absurd," Reno said, as he slowed for a car attempting to back into a parking space on the street. "These guys are all family men. They're all pros, and they're committed to their work. There's no way any of them would have started that fire."

"I hope not. And, it's highly unlikely," Balmain conceded. "But, we have to consider every possible motive and angle here."

Reno put on his turn signal and slowed to turn into his parking lot at the fire department annex. "So, what's really on that film?"

"I honestly don't know." Balmain admitted. "We were told by an informant that it might have national security information, illegally obtained national security information. I might have some additional background about context, but as you can understand, I can't say any more."

"That's bullshit!" Reno found an empty space and backed the Pontiac in. "I'm willing to help you with anything you need. I want to catch this guy too, but I am certain none of those guys set that fire."

"I accept that, and I appreciate your loyalty." Balmain put his hand on the door handle, "Look, this information came from a relatively new informant. That means that we can't give him any more credibility than any other anonymous tipster. But, we have to check the information out regardless."

"Have you spoken to sergeant Ramey's superiors? His wife?"

Balmain considered the question carefully. "No. We can't just yet."

Reno switched the ignition off and turned in his seat, "What? An informant says this guy pinched some state secrets or something, and you haven't spoken to his boss?"

"Some of the constraints we face in this investigation include the need to avoid approaching Air Force personnel, at least officially. We just don't know who might be involved, and I can't start asking questions until we have an idea of who is on whose team."

Reno's face began to redden, "But you're ready to start accusing my people of arson and murder? Yeah, it's my fault that you don't have your film, so if you're looking for a scapegoat, then I'm your man. But..."

Balmain interrupted, "Reno, no one is accusing anyone of anything. Certainly not your firemen. And, we aren't looking for a scapegoat. I only mentioned it because it's a scenario that people in Washington will eventually get to even if we don't."

"So, who is this informant?"

"Don't know," Balmain answered truthfully.

"When people come to you with information, don't you usually check them out first?"

"He didn't come to me," Balmain admitted. "This came from Washington."

Reno exhaled purposefully. "I'm sorry. I didn't mean to lose my temper. I just can't believe any of our guys would intentionally start a fire, or take a human life in the process." He squeezed the steering wheel until his knuckles whitened. "I don't know how many firemen you know, but we're in this business for a reason. Lord knows, we're not in it for the money or the fame. It takes a special kind of guy to want to race into a burning building when everyone else, and common sense itself tells you to run the other way."

"I hear you, man." Balmain winked and nodded as he started to get out of the car. Then he paused about half way out of the vehicle as something caught his attention. He inhaled deeply and then stuck his head back in the door. "By the way, what kind of perfume does your wife wear?"

"Huh?" Reno asked as he noted the mileage on the department vehicle and wrote it into his logbook. "I'm not married."

"That scent - it's familiar."

"What scent?" Reno grabbed the handle to open his door.

"You don't smell it?"

Reno snorted, "Man, this is a city car. I don't think a woman has ever been in it, and the only scents I smell are stale cigarette smoke and old coffee."

Balmain paused for a second, "Sorry. It's been a busy week, and I'm a bit short on sleep. I probably got a whiff of it down the street. I'll call you later, maybe tomorrow after my morning call with the Director." With that, Reno crossed the parking lot to his office and Fred Balmain walked over to his own car.

Balmain enjoyed the relationships he'd been building with local law enforcement and fire department personnel, and wanted to continue to establish a level of trust, even though most people didn't trust the federal government. Especially in Texas. Nevertheless, he knew that when he made his report to the Director the next morning, the topic of polygraphs might very well come up. And nothing will destroy a professional relationship faster than telling everyone they have to sit for a polygraph exam.

He started his car and sat in silence for a moment. Sniffing his jacket, briefcase and hands, he was perplexed about the source of the fragrance. He smelled the steering wheel and the back of the seats. Nothing.

He turned the ignition switch on and let the car run for a few seconds before backing out of the space and heading towards the entrance to the parking lot. There he sat for more than thirty seconds trying to get that fragrance back into his mind. It was gone now. The first time he'd smelled it in his office, it seemed familiar. But where had he smelled it before? Certainly not on his wife or any of her friends. It smelled exotic, alluring, and expensive.

He turned onto Commerce Street and headed back towards his office. As he stopped for the red light at Commerce and South Ervay, his fingers drummed the steering wheel. In his mind was a Latin beat, something that he and his wife could Cha-Cha to. Maybe a slower rumba, something with the claves clicking out a syncopated rhythm. He looked around the intersection, lost in thought. A woman in her seventies, loaded down with shopping bags crossed the street in front of him causing him to look up. There it was, Neiman-Marcus. If anyone knew about fragrances, certainly someone at their cosmetics counter would know.

He looked at his watch and decided that he had some time before he had to get back to his wife and Sunday dinner, so he did something uncharacteristically whimsical. He looked for a place to park. There was something about that scent that was haunting. It was appealing, and he had to know what it was.

A few minutes later, Fred Balmain looked casually around the sales floor, primarily to see if he recognized anyone, or worse yet, if someone might recognize him. After all, how would he explain being seen shopping in the cosmetic section of Neiman Marcus when his wife's birthday wasn't for another six months? He approached the fragrance counter and stared at the line of perfumes in the glass showcase.

"Good afternoon, sir. May I help you?"

Balmain glanced up to see an attractive woman in her twenties smiling at him from behind the counter. Her blond hair was reminiscent of Brigitte Bardot, with the star's signature bangs, a high ponytail and a cute red bow. Her white skirt and matching jacket made her look wholesome and professional. "I...uh..."

"Something for your wife?" she asked.

He closed his eyes for a moment, "No, uh..." Clearing his throat, he continued, "I, uh, was on the elevator with a woman yesterday and she had the most amazing perfume. I was just trying to figure out what it was."

The lady at the counter smiled, "Oh. Well, was she young or older?"

"What?" he looked up.

"The lady on the elevator, was she young or old? You see some of our fragrances appeal more to women of different ages."

He thought for a moment, "Well, to tell the truth, I really didn't get a good look at her. I didn't notice it really until after she left the car. I was getting in the car as she was..."

"Oh, I understand." The clerk grinned at him. "Why don't I tell you about some of our most popular brands and then you can decide if they smell like the lady on the elevator?" With that, she leaned forward over the counter and presented her neck. "Right now, I'm wearing Shalimar. It was created by the Guerlain perfume house back in 1925, and was the first oriental fragrance supposedly inspired by the Gardens of Shalimar, which the Indian emperor Shah Jahan built for his wife...well, that's what it says on the sales material." She giggled.

Balmain felt more than a little naughty, leaning in to sniff this attractive young woman's neck. As sinfully delightful as it felt, he pulled back a bit and said, "Nice, but that's not it."

"Well you know," she smiled, "...some perfumes smell differently on different women. It has to do with their body chemistry. So, was it close?"

Balmain shook his head, "No, that's just not it. What else do you have?"

"Let me show you what we've got. You can spray them on a piece of paper one at a time and see if any of them remind you of this woman's fragrance." With that, she slid open the glass showcase door and began to place bottles of very nice perfume on the counter in front of him.

"Evening in Paris has been around a long time and is a mix of fruity and floral notes, with a musk and vanilla base." She squirted a dab on the test paper and handed it to Balmain.

He shook his head, "Nope. That's not it either."

One by one, she repeated the same process with Chanel No. 5, which was supposedly Marilyn Monroe's favorite, followed by such brands as White Shoulders, Chantilly, Youth Dew, Arpege and Tabu.

Balmain went back and forth, lightly inhaling each scent with his eyes closed. Nothing. "And these are your top sellers?"

"Oh yes," she explained, "These are the finest fragrances available anywhere. I know they're a bit pricey, but most of our customers don't question the cost."

He glanced at his watch. "Thank you. Money isn't really important. Is there any place else around here that sells exotic perfumes?"

The clerk smiled and shook her head, "No, not really. There are other stores in town that sell some of these brands, but I think we have the biggest selection."

"Thanks," he said as he turned to walk away. "You've been very kind."

He decided he needed to get his head examined. But first, he needed to get prepared for tomorrow morning's meeting with the Director.

4

MONDAY, DECEMBER 30, 1963

D an Reynolds rolled over on his bunk and looked at the clock on the wall. It was just after 3:00 a.m., and he hadn't slept more than 30 minutes the entire night. He couldn't believe that Dirk had managed to drop the film off with his friend at the photo lab quite that quickly, and he rubbed his head as he hazily recalled the conversation.

"What do you mean you don't have it?"

"Mike's place is on the way home from the airport, so I stopped on the way and gave it to him."

"What did you tell him?" Dan asked.

"I didn't tell him anything. I just said that we had found this and we weren't sure what was on it, but wanted it developed privately without drawing any attention."

"Shit!" Dan was disgusted with himself, "How well do you know this guy? How do you know he's not going to say anything to anyone? For Christ sakes, the FBI is on this!"

Dirk was annoyingly calm, "I'm telling you, this guy is cool, really cool!" He paused as he considered his words, "Look, between you and me, I know that he's been seeing Jeanine's cousin, Rachael, okay?"

"Rachael? Isn't she married to a fireman?"

"Yes! That's how I know he's not going to say anything. They've been seeing each other for almost six months. This guy's got two kids and a pregnant wife at home. And, he knows that I know, so his silence is guaranteed."

"How long will it take him to, you know, process it?"

Dirk sounded cavalier, "He said a day or two. Would you relax? Nothing's going to happen!"

"Dirk, the FBI was here with our arson guy. They know that one of the firemen had to have taken it. They're not going to stop looking until they find it!" Dan was exasperated.

After a while Dirk proposed, "Then give them a fucking ro l of film."

"Huh?"

He repeated, "Give them a roll of film. For crying out loud, they already said that they don't even know if it was developed, right? So go buy a roll of Kodak 8MM movie film, take it out to the site and grind it into the rubble. Then, if they are that intent on finding it, they will. Only, the film they find will be fogged, or pictures of someone's pet zebra. How will they know the difference?"

It was like a light went off in Dan's head. Why hadn't he thought of that? "Another roll of film!"

"Yeah!" Dirk told him, "Go to Ft. Worth or someplace away from the city, buy a roll of film; and if you like, run it through a camera; pull the spool off, and then dump it at the warehouse." Then, as an afterthought he added, "Well, and wear gloves while you're loading and unloading the film so that you don't leave fingerprints on t."

That was it! Dan could substitute another roll of similar film and everyone would be happy. All he had to do was pick up the film somewhere, borrow a camera and record something benign. like traffic, the zoo, a party in a backyard somewhere.

Dan had nine hours until his shift was over. Nine hours. He began thinking about all of the photo shops in his area. Whoa, can't use a store in this area in case someone recognized him. Maybe in Garland or Plano? Whom did he know that had an 8MM camera?

Wait. Bob Ritchie had a movie camera and lived in Arlington. That was about ten miles west of him and he knew Bob just well enough from college that he could borrow his camera for a day.

And, Bob would know where to get film. Hell, Bob might even have some film laying around!

Bob was an accountant for some company out there. What was the name of that place? He kept pretty regular hours, which meant that he'd probably be at work by 9:00 a.m. or so. What was the name of that company? But, he certainly wouldn't have his camera with him. The earliest he'd be able to pick it up would be some time after work. That wouldn't matter since he was just going to point it at something and film.

He closed his eyes for just a moment, and it was suddenly 6:15. Today's breakfast menu called for French toast and bacon so he hit the showers with renewed life.

———————————

At exactly 7:59a.m., the KY-3 sprang to life and the technician passed the handset over as agent Fred Balmain closed the file folder and laid it on top of the pile. "Good morning, sir."

"Good morning, Fred. How was your weekend?"

Balmain reached for his notes, "Very good sir, productive. And yours?"

"Fine," was the flat reply, indicating that they had officially concluded the pleasantries. "What do you have for me today?"

The agent picked up the correct file and opened it to his notes. "Well sir, I met with the arson investigator in his office and obtained enlargements of the photos that were taken at the fire scene. Together, he and I met with the firemen at their station and asked them to study the photos. None of the men reported seeing the spool of film. I watched them pretty carefully as they looked at the pictures and I didn't think that anyone was attempting to be deceptive."

Balmain took a quick sip of his coffee to wet his throat. "As you recall from our previous conversation, we checked that warehouse pretty good and couldn't find the film. On the other hand, maybe if we had additional personnel and more time, more light, we might be able to find it. They're going to start clearing it out and re-building next week. I'm afraid if the contractors get in there first with backhoes and shovels, if it's there, it might accidentally get picked up and tossed with the rest of the debris. We'll never see it."

"The fire department already knows of your interest in Ramey and this roll of film, obviously." The Director paused, peeved with the reality that eventually they would have to involve outsiders. "If you think there's a good chance it's still there, then I don't see why you couldn't take another crew back in there and really tear the place apart. But, there may be a problem."

"What's that, sir?"

Pensively, the Director admitted, "Our new informant, Dallas P-1, says the film isn't in Dallas any longer. He says it's been moved north."

"North, sir? What does that mean? Where, specifically is 'north'?"

"We're not a hundred percent sure. Our best guess is somewhere in or around New York. But, we have no idea how credible this informant is, and I'm not sure if I believe in, uh..." he paused for a moment, "So, maybe taking a bigger team back to the warehouse and really going through it with rakes and shovels might be a good way to hedge our bets."

"Just our people, sir? Or can I involve Dallas Fire?" Balmain asked.

"As I said, they already know of our interest, so I don't think it hurts anything to have them supply some manpower for the job. Give them the usual confidentiality reminder and make sure that if they find it, or if they find anything else of interest, that they immediately surrender it to you."

"Can do, sir. I'll get that scheduled right away." Balmain made some notes on his legal pad and propped it up against the telephone on the corner of his desk.

"Any luck on identifying other witnesses in the Plaza on the twenty-second?"

Balmain reached for another folder, "Yes sir. My team has interviewed about everyone who was present outside on the ground, and we went office to office in the Dal-Tex Building, the County Records and Criminal Courts Buildings, the Old Courthouse, and even people that were near the John Neely Bryan House at Commerce and Houston."

He flipped a couple of pages in the folder. "Everyone who was there that day saw or heard something. But no one saw everything. Because of the echo effect, some people thought they heard as many as five shots, and some people report only hearing only two. Some people saw Oswald in a half-dozen different locations when he was supposed to be on the sixth floor of the School Book Depository."

He closed the folder. "Our tipster calls have begun to drop a bit, but we're still hearing from some religious groups that Kennedy was targeted by the Almighty because he was a philanderer, or something to that effect. Some think the Mafia or the Cubans did it. Some suspect LBJ and even the former First Lady. No one has any credible evidence of anything, just conjecture."

The line was silent for a moment, "Are you still getting calls from cranks? Psychics? People with some sort of visions?"

"No, sir." Balmain shrugged. "We had a number of them calling in for a while, but those calls have dropped off as well."

The line crackled for a couple of seconds, "Your fire victim, Ramey; have you turned up anything that would indicate that he might have been assigned to key events or meetings, in particular with former President Eisenhower? Specifically, some meetings he might have had at Edwards or Holloman Air Force Bases several years ago?"

The Director could be heard over the line shuffling some papers, while he spoke. "We were able to quietly check with a source in the office of the Deputy Chief of Staff for Personnel, who oversees the new Air Force Military Personnel Center that opened in April this year. He said that Ramey had been on temporary duty at those two bases in 1953 and 1954, and the dates seem to coincide with official presidential visits. I ask because his involvement in any presidential meetings would certainly increase our concerns, interests, about his demise."

Balmain was taken slightly aback at the question. Where was the Director getting his information? "No sir. But, I haven't been able to dig into his military record yet. I was sure that official questions would alert OSI to our investigation, and you said..."

"Yes, exactly. Let me know if you uncover anything in the search of the warehouse." The Director was off the line before Balmain could respond.

Holloman? Balmain knew that Holloman Air Force Base had operated the White Sands Missile Test range since the late 1940s. He supposed that if a US president decided to pay the site a goodwill visit, then it would be entirely appropriate to have the event recorded by an official photographer, like Ramey. Probably several Rameys; enlisted personnel to follow the official party around and make the event look successful.

Edwards was where Chuck Yeager flew the Bell X-1 out of to break the sound barrier. It was a major Air Force site for testing anything that flew. So, would it also be appropriate for a sitting president to do a courtesy inspection to generate publicity and help fund military programs on the Hill? The visits seemed to make sense. But what, in heaven's name did any of that have to do with the assassination of President Kennedy? And, why would anyone use something like that as a motive for murder?

Besides, Ramey's TDYs to those bases were ten years earlier. He had to have been just starting out in his Air Force career and couldn't have been much higher than an Airman Second Class. At such a low level, he wouldn't have been exposed to anything highly sensitive. His job would have been, very simply, to point his camera and shoot.

Other than a seventy year old who smelled smoke and thought he was having a heart attack, Dan and his team had a relatively un-eventful morning. He busied himself tidying up around the station with the rest of his crew, and tried to keep from looking at the clock. When the men from B Company began showing up just before noon, he went to his locker to change back into his civilian clothes.

He had remembered the name of Bob's company, a chemical manufacturer called Braxall, and found the number in the telephone directory. The conversation was friendly and brief, and Bob agreed to meet him for lunch around 1:30 p.m. in Arlington. Bob said he was happy to loan it to him for as long as he liked, and that he would stop at his home to pick up the camera and a roll of film when he left his office for lunch. He also mentioned that he had several rolls of un-used film that Dan could borrow if needed. Things were looking up.

Dan stopped at home to leave Millie a note. He hated lying to her, but the ruse of having "lunch with friends" wasn't completely untrue. That would give him enough time to expose a roll of film, drop it at the site and get home before she suspected anything un-usual. Today was her hair day so she would be out of the house until at least 3:30 p.m.

Dan walked into the restaurant a little before 1:00 p.m., and found an empty booth. It wasn't long before he saw Bob Ritchie come through the door. The face and the smile were the same, but Bob, just shy of six feet tall, had ballooned to over two hundred, maybe two hundred twenty pounds since he'd seen him on July 4, a year and a half earlier. While Dan's occupation necessitated a high level of fitness, it would seem that a life of accountancy didn't incur the same regimen.

The two men chatted about how they had each been since the party, until the waitress approached them and took their fairly sim-ple order of cheeseburgers, French fries, and cokes. When she left, Bob opened the bag and explained, "Hey pal, I hope this works for you. This is a real cheap camera, a Revere Eight, Model 88. These were made in Chicago in the forties. They were cheaper than the Kodak and Bell & Howell cameras but they work exactly the same."

He showed Dan the controls on the camera, "These are fixed focal length, but you have to manually select the f-stop...the size of the hole that lets light in through the lens. Here." He rotated the lens from left to right. "If you set this on the 2.5 mark, you can use it in lower light conditions, but your depth of field may be shallow."

"My what?" Dan asked.

"Your depth of field. It's the amount of the picture that will be in focus. The more open the aperture, the smaller the depth of field." Bob cranked the lens the other direction, "If you set the f-stop up at 16, you'll have a deeper area in focus, but you'll need more light."

Dan took the heavy camera from him and twisted the lens back and forth. "So if I shoot at f-16 and don't have enough light, like, say, in the fire station, what will happen?"

Bob shrugged. "Then your film will be underexposed; every-thing will be too dark."

Dan nodded, "Got it. So how do I load this?"

Bob took the camera back, and pushed a button on the side, opening the left side of the camera up. "The new roll of film goes on this top peg. You have to thread it so the emulsion side of the film faces the lens like this." He flipped the roll upside down and fed the film through a gate that kept it positioned steadily in front of the lens. "It goes through here, over this guide and then on to the take-up reel. But," he pointed at the label on the empty take-up reel, "once all of the film is run onto this spool, you have to take it off and put it back on the top peg and do this again, because you've only exposed half of your film."

"I don't understand." Dan said, frowning.

Bob elaborated, "This film is actually 16 millimeters wide. But your finished product will only be eight millimeters wide. During processing, they'll cut it down the middle, splice it together, and then you'll get your fifty foot roll of developed film. That's 8 mil-limeters wide. It gives you about four minutes of run time."

Dan smirked. "That sounds complicated, but I think I get it. Two minutes, flip it and two minutes more."

"Here. You try it." Bob removed the roll he'd used for the

demonstration and produced a brand new roll of film from the paper bag and handed it to him. "This was an old spool. I'll give you some fresh stuff that I just bought last month. Let me watch you thread it the first time, and then you can do it yourself if you use more than one roll. Wind it up first." Bob pointed out the lever on the side of the camera that led to an internal spring. "You give it about ten to twelve winds, like an alarm clock."

Dan wound the camera carefully, inserted the roll the way Bob had shown him, and fed the film to the take up reel. "Just like that?"

"Just like that. Now, hit the shutter release for a second or two to make sure that it's feeding right."

Dan complied, and with a soft whirring noise, the camera clicked away and the film began to feed onto the take up reel. He made a mental note that when he'd finished exposing the roll, he'd want to make sure he wiped his fingerprints off of the spool and the film strip.

"There, you're a pro!" Ritchie exclaimed. "What are you going to shoot?"

"Uhmmmm..." Dan busied himself studying the camera as he thought. "Just Millie and the kids in the backyard. Family stuff. I thought if it turns out good, maybe we'll buy one of these."

"Good move," Ritchie commented. "Still photos are great, but catching people in motion will make for some really good memories." He passed the bag across the table and Dan placed the camera and the empty film canister in the bag and rolled the top down.

Dan's anxiety could have been apparent from across the room, since once their meals came, he'd finished his before Ritchie had gotten half way through his burger and a few fries. Ritchie commented, "Wow, you must've been hungry!"

"It's the schedule we keep at the station." Dan shrugged as he finished his last French fry. "With that twenty-four on and forty-eight off routine, your eating habits get a little out of whack." He quietly sipped his Coke and made small talk with his friend until the waitress returned.

"Will there be anything else, boys?" she smiled.

"Ah, no thanks." Dan reached for his billfold and pulled out a ten dollar bill. "Here, this is on me today.

After they shook hands and drove off in different directions, Dan considered the most logical way to shoot his underexposed footage and get the film secreted in the warehouse. He looked down at his jacket lying in a heap on the front seat and an idea struck him. The warehouse was fairly close to being on his way back home. Maybe he should drive by and give it a quick look. No, not yet.

He pulled into a service station and drove over to the tire pump. There was only one car at the gas pumps, and the attendant didn't seem to be paying any attention to him. He took the camera out of the paper bag, shoved it under his jacket, and flipped the shutter release. While the camera whirred beneath his jacket, he began checking the air pressure on his tires. When two minutes passed, he opened the passenger door, took the film out and flipped the reels around as he'd been instructed. Replacing the camera under his jacket, he rewound the spring, and hit the shutter release again before going back to checking his tires.

A couple of minutes later, he got in, checked the camera, and found that the film had been completely exposed. He took his handkerchief out and carefully wiped his fingerprints off of the reel, and the last foot of film, before rolling it up and returning it to the original film canister. He then wiped the prints off of the outside of the canister before sliding it under his jacket.

It should start getting dark around 5:30p.m. What would he tell Millie? She would want to know where he was going. It would take a half hour of travel time and maybe a half hour to find a place to dump the film. What was he thinking? What would be more suspicious than a guy traipsing around a burnt out warehouse at dusk? A voice in the back of his head told him, "Now! You've got to do this now!" The impulsive thought hit him like a refreshing bolt of lightning.

By the time he drove off the lot, his heart was beating rapidly and he could feel his pulse pounding. He looked around for landmarks that would indicate a shortcut to the warehouse, and began checking his rear view mirror every thirty seconds. Mild paranoia was setting in. He adjusted the mirror before thinking that he hadn't done anything wrong, yet. There would, in all reality, be no reason for anyone to have him under surveillance. He saw the building he'd been looking for and made a left turn that would take him down a street parallel to the warehouse.

Looking about as if his head was on a swivel, he circled the block once to make sure that the warehouse was empty and that there were no other cars parked nearby. He found a parking place a half a block away, and using his handkerchief slipped the film canister into his jacket pocket. He locked up his car and donned the jacket as inconspicuously as he could, and walked back towards the warehouse. Satisfied that no one was interested in his activity, he slipped through a hole in the fencing and walked towards the rear of the building.

He knew that the fire department crews had broken through several doors and he didn't think they would be boarded up. He was in luck. A pedestrian door located between two truck bay doors was still partially ajar. Looking again over his shoulders, he quickly slipped in and allowed his eyes to adjust to the darkness. No flashlight. In about a minute, the ambient light coming in through the windows and skylights was enough to allow him to see shoe-printed pathways carved by firemen, inspectors and contractors, and he followed them back to the area where Reno Belcher had staged his evidence the night of the fire.

He found the charred table that Reno had used, and looked around. There, a few feet away, he spotted a metal stool on its side, partially submerged in rubble and ash. He examined the table and the boot prints around it from different angles and then, using his handkerchief, retrieved the film canister from his pocket and set it on the corner of the table. He took a deep breath, and using his middle finger against his thumb, flicked the canister in the direction of the overturned stool.

The sting in his nail bed was quickly forgotten. It was a perfect shot. The canister banked off one of the legs, and embedded in the debris. It looked, for all intents, like it had been inadvertently swept off the table in haste. He looked at it again from different angles. Wouldn't someone have found it there during the previous search? He frowned as he looked at the stool again. Using his handkerchief, he lifted it up and over about two inches, and the canister was covered. Eureka!

He gave the scene a final look, and made sure that the newness of his shoe prints wasn't obvious, and that the scene looked natural. By the time he got back to his car, he was emotionally exhausted. And, by the time he arrived home, about sixteen minutes later, he was drained and was asleep on the sofa in seconds.

He was only vaguely aware of Millie coming through the door at the same time the phone started to ring. Somewhere between consciousness and the haze of the afternoon nap, he could hear her answer.

"Hello?" There was a brief pause. "Hi, Bart. I think he's on the sofa. I'll get him."

A few seconds later, he could feel Millie touching his shoulder, "Hey baby, Bart's on the phone. He says he needs to talk to you right away."

Dan rolled over and rubbed the sleep from his eyes. "Bart? Yeah, okay...be right there."

He sat up on the couch and took a couple of deep breaths through his nose before getting up and walking over to the wall phone in the kitchen. "Hey LT, what's up?"

Bart sounded a bit perturbed. "Sorry to bother you on your time off, but I'm afraid I have to get you back in for some overtime."

Dan was still asleep. "Huh?"

"Reno and that guy from the FBI want us to get a crew together to go back through that warehouse and look for that roll of movie film."

Dan was suddenly awake. He couldn't believe his timing. Thank God he'd listened to that voice in his head telling him to get that film to the warehouse then and there. He looked at his watch; it was a little past three. "What time do they want us there?"

"As soon as you can get there. The FBI is already there, and we're supposed to get as many guys as we can to tear that place apart. Can you be on scene in thirty minutes?"

Dan rubbed his hand through his hair, "Yeah, thirty, maybe forty-five."

"Great!" Lt. McDaniel injected. "I have to round up the rest of the team. They want as many butts as they can get."

Dan stopped briefly at the fire station to grab his turnout gear and then headed on to the warehouse. When he got there, he was stunned by what he saw. There were ten or twelve vehicles and a dozen or so men milling around the entrance. Propped up against a pickup truck were so many rakes and shovels that it resembled the garden section of a local hardware store. After finding a place to park, he got out, opened the trunk and began to put on his gear.

Reno Belcher spotted him, and walked over with a smile. "You weren't thinking that you were about to enjoy a couple of days off, were you?"

Dan continued dressing and answered, "Hah. So, what's going on?"

Reno smirked. "The FBI is convinced that they're going to find that roll of film, one way or the other. They've drawn up search grids for everyone, and we're pretty much going to take this place apart in the next few hours."

Dan, still relieved that he had listened to his inner voice, fastened his bunker jacket. "Yeah, okay. Where do you want me?"

"We're all going to be on the first floor since that's where we...I... last saw the canister." He shook his head, "They've divvied up the floor into work zones, and each man will need to go through every square inch of it like they were cleaning house for their grandmother. Come on, I'll get you an assignment."

Dan followed Reno over to the group of men standing near the entrance where Agent Balmain was pointing at something on his clipboard and gesturing inside the building. He looked up and smiled at Reno's approach, "Good, more talent!"

"Where do you want Dan?" he asked. "I've got two more guys on their way but you can get him started now if you want."

"Thanks for coming, Dan." Balmain showed Dan the drawing of the warehouse and pointed. "I want you and your guys to focus on this far northwest corner. It's not likely that it ended up over there from Reno's staging area, but you never know. Take a flashlight and a rake and when your guys get here, you can split them up as you see fit."

Dan nodded, and was about to reach for a rake when he heard a man yell from inside the building, "Tally Ho!"

Seconds later, two men wearing work boots with their grey flannel suits emerged from the building with huge smiles. The taller of the two yelled, "Fred, we've got it! We need the camera and a collection kit!"

Balmain tossed the clipboard into the bed of the pickup truck, and jogged to the entrance of the building. Reno Belcher followed behind at a brisk pace, as Dan joined in the parade. Some of the other firemen, their curiosity aroused, followed everyone else inside the building.

When they rounded the corner and entered the area where Reno had bagged his evidence, Dan could see that the table had been moved aside, and the metal stool, with which he was familiar, was upside down on top of the table. One of the grey-flannel guys pointed down into the dirt, "We found it right here. We were moving some of this stuff out of the way, and as soon as I lifted the stool, I saw it in the rubble."

Balmain looked at the imprints in the dirt left by the legs of the table, "The table was here? You found the stool right there?" he asked, drawing an imaginary stool with his finger.

"Yeah, right here!" Grey flannel said. "Looks like it got knocked off the table when it was being inventoried. Don't know how they missed it before. I guess they just didn't turn over enough stones." The two suited-ones both laughed.

One of the other agents came inside carrying what looked like a medium sized suitcase. He sat it down and it opened from the top, revealing trays with various evidence collection equipment. He handed a brown paper bag with "EVIDENCE" clearly marked on the front, and a pair of large tweezers to Balmain.

Balmain started to bend to retrieve the canister and then stopped, "Did you guys get shots of this yet?"

"No, sir, not yet," one of the agents replied.

"Oh, for Christ sakes guys, let's not screw this up. Follow procedure!"

The agent with the suitcase reached down inside, and pulled out a Polaroid Land camera. Thanks to Edwin Land, since 1948, people could take a picture of something and have it self-develop in minutes. Now, as of February, Polaroid could also provide color pictures as well as black and white, with their new Polacolor process. He connected the flash attachment, and then snapped several shots of the canister, and then took pictures of the table and chair after laying a measuring tape across the top and the base to give a sense of scale.

Satisfied that they had made an accurate evidentiary record, Balmain knelt down, plucked the canister out of the dirt and soot, and dropped it into the evidence bag. "You're on the next plane to Washington, young man," he said to the nearest grey-flannel guy.

Dan watched the young agent sprint from the room, carrying the bag as if it contained the Hope Diamond, or a fecal sample, and for the first time in days, he felt the weight of the world lifted off his shoulders.

5

THURSDAY, JANUARY 2, 1964

Fred Balmain busied himself in preparation for his Thursday meeting with the Director. He was comfortable enough now that he could handle the KY-3 without the support of his technical assistant, who was needed elsewhere to help create some means of consolidating all of the information they had received on the case into a more useful format. Also, because of the technician's former employment with the CIA, the Director felt it would be better if he wasn't in the room during the calls. It seemed as though no one trusted anyone any more.

He took a moment to look out the window behind his desk at the clear, cool Dallas morning. The flags on the building across the street flapped in the gentle breeze. Hopefully, it would soon be time to dust off his golf clubs and take some time off for himself. When the machine let him know that the Director was on the line, he immediately answered, and they exchanged the customary pleasantries.

This morning, the Director seemed deep in thought, "They processed the film, and I've got the report back from the lab. It seems the entire reel was under-exposed. The question is, whether it was unintentional or deliberately sabotaged?"

Balmain frowned into the handset. "Under-exposed? Ramey was a professional photographer. I don't see how that could happen. How under-exposed is it?"

"Completely," was the reply. "The lab says that it doesn't look fogged, or like it was shot with a lens cover on. It looks like someone either shot in very low light, or covered the camera during exposure. We have no idea how a professional photographer could make a mistake like that. Now the question becomes why he'd deliberately under-expose a reel of film?" The line was silent for a few seconds before Balmain broke it, "And, go to the trouble to hide it in his sock."

"Precisely," the Director replied. "I need you to find a couple of photographs in your files; reference number DL 3151 A and B. They were shot by a pipefitter named Michael Finnegan, who was standing to the right of and below Abraham Zapruder. In the *Exhibit A* shot, Kennedy's limousine has not yet entered Dealey Plaza. Thus, it's immediately before the shooting."

"Finnegan, right. Scott Wainright interviewed him. Nice guy, ex-Army." Balmain scrambled to find the correct file in the cardboard box on the floor, and once he located it, opened the envelope that had the photos. "Got it, sir."

"In the top right corner of that photo, you can see a man on the roof of the US Post Office Building, on the south side of Commerce Street. We blew that section of the photo up, and he appears to be loading film into a movie camera. Moving to the *Exhibit B* photo, which is taken after the ambush begins, it appears that he is filming."

Balmain grabbed the magnifying glass out of his center desk drawer, and examined the photo. The image was grainy, and the figure on the rooftop was several hundred yards away. It was barely distinguishable as a human.

The Director continued, "While he's too far away for a positive ID, his shirt, dark pants and jacket are similar to what SSGT Ramey was wearing when you found him."

"You think that's Ramey, sir?" Balmain continued to study the small section of the photograph.

"Possibly. There's no way to definitively tell, but our lab says the colors match, and they speculate that the figure is a human male, between twenty to fifty years of age. Since we have not identified the individual in the photograph and no one has come forward with stills or movie film from that angle, we can only guess."

The Post Office Building. Damn! This building was also home to various federal agencies including the FBI, CIA and a dozen other organizations. Balmain had not thought to go office-to-office to canvas them. The building was way south of Dealey Plaza, across Commerce. If a government employee had filmed the assassination, then it would have been protocol to turn the film over to him. "Sir, I truly apologize. We didn't do a thorough job of canvassing those offices because, well, because our offices are there."

Balmain continued, "I think we should ask the Dallas SAIC to get his team to immediately determine if there were any employees, or visitors, allowed on the roof on the twenty-second. At the very least, we need to see if the roof entrance is even locked. You know, find out about its accessibility."

"I thought of that already," the Director interjected. "As I mentioned last week during last month's staff call with the SAIC, I raised the issue of potential witnesses, and he indicated that they had already canvassed a number of the personnel located there. He said that many people gathered around windows to watch the motorcade, but that the building manager did not recall anyone going to the roof."

"Well..." Balmain considered a myriad of scenarios, "The photo depicts someone up there, doing something. There's a military recruiting station in there, which means a lot of people going in and out of the building all day. If that was Ramey, there's a possibility that he was familiar with the building, considering his Air Force background. Do we know where he was from?"

"He entered the service in San Antonio, 1951. Basic training at Lackland." The Director could be heard shuffling some papers, "He was promoted to Airman Third Class upon graduation. Several training assignments followed. No derogatory information in his file."

Balmain's mind was racing, "We didn't find a camera. So, whatever he filmed, unless someone stole the camera from him, believing it to contain the film, he didn't film in the time immediately before he was killed. So, we could speculate that..." Balmain had a brief thought, but it momentarily escaped him. There was that haunting fragrance again. Just for a millisecond. It was there and was gone.

"Speculate what?" the Director asked.

The castors squeaking, Balmain rotated the heavy chair so that he could see out his window again. "Let's say that it was Ramey on the roof of the Post Office Building, and he was filming the motorcade during the assassination. Why wouldn't he have just given us, or the OSI, the film? What would have been on the film that would have made him want to sell...or give it away to God knows who?"

Balmain spun his chair around and looked at the photos again, "He couldn't have hoped to get away with profiting from the sale of it. From this angle, it would only be a matter of time before we started piecing together where the footage was shot from and started to narrow down a suspect list. And, if he was at the warehouse that night for some sort of handoff, why would he have shown up with an under-exposed duplicate?"

"Wiped clean of fingerprints," the Director added. "It would seem that Ramey believed the footage to have some sort of value, more so than even the Zapruder film. But, he didn't necessarily trust the parties with whom he was dealing. Maybe he suspected he was being set up, and decided not to take the original with him to the warehouse."

Balmain began tapping his fingers on the desk absent-mindedly. "So, if we assume that the copy we found was just that, a copy, then where is the original? It's too bad we can't work with OSI on this, sir. It would be good to know if Ramey processed it at the Base's photo lab."

The unconscious tapping took on a Latin beat, his fingers striking beats three, six and eight slightly harder. "I mean, if he shot it on the twenty second of November and was killed on December twenty third; that's a whole month. What was he doing for that month? Where was the film during that time?"

The Director cleared his throat, "Well, our informant suggested earlier that the film was on a military installation during that period."

Balmain grimaced, "Our informant? The, uh, P1 guy? Where is he getting his information, sir?"

"I'd rather not say right now, Fred. I don't want to compromise, uh…" The Director rapidly returned to the subject, "I think it's highly likely that Ramey, or one of his confederates processed the film himself. If he considered it that valuable, I don't see why he would trust an outside lab to process it."

"Agreed, sir." Balmain flipped the photos back onto his desk like he was dealing a hand of cards. "So he processes the film, hides it somewhere, and during this period finds a buyer - an outlet for it. Do we have the capability to look at toll calls that might have originated from the photo lab at Sheppard?"

"The Air Force can," the Director admitted. "That would require us to make a formal request. And that also assumes that he might have used government telephone equipment to make his arrangements. If we again consider the value he has placed on his film, then he probably would have used a pay phone off base somewhere."

Balmain pursed his lips. "No prints on the film. He wiped his prints off of a film that wasn't genuine. Why, sir? Was he approaching someone using a pseudonym, and was afraid that they would have the…"

The Director cut in, "The capability to run his prints through an official catalogue."

"Yes sir. Exactly!" Balmain was quietly self-impressed that he was thinking like the Director. "So, which government agency? CIA? Defense Department? Not OSI, his own people?"

"False Flag," the Director said flatly. "He thought he was meeting someone -maybe legitimately - definitely covertly, who was part of government. Perhaps sergeant Ramey had patriotic intentions and sincerely believed he was surrendering evidence of a presidential assassination to the appropriate authority? Maybe he thought he was meeting with us?"

Balmain looked at the boxes and files on his floor and desk, "But, how was the initial contact made? Did he contact someone from OSI, or did someone in government know about the film and make contact with him?"

The Director was deeper in thought. "The chicken and the egg... Aristotle."

"Excuse me, sir?"

"The chicken and the egg question. Did Ramey show up in Dealey Plaza out of curiosity, climb to the roof of a government building without being seen, and record a presidential assassination coincidentally? Or, did someone in his chain of command tell him where to be at 12:30 p.m. on the twenty-second?"

Balmain felt a chill. "Sir, are you suggesting that someone in the government knew that the assassination was going to take place and wanted a record of it?"

"Possibly. "The Director paused for a moment. "But, which government? Despite all of the malarkey about government cover-ups that some of the fringe elements have been proposing, I'm convinced that we did not have Kennedy killed. Maybe Castro was involved, maybe the mob...but not us."

"Chain of command, sir." Balmain reflected. "Ramey was Air Force. His proper chain of command would have been through his squadron's commanding officer and up through the base commander. Unless it was regarding something that occurred off-base, under a temporary set of orders. In which case, for something like this, it would have been to the, uh, OSI."

The Director thought out loud. "But if he had called the OSI to report that he had footage of the assassination, why wouldn't they have just said, *Sit tight, we'll send an agent right over*?"

"I agree, sir. It makes no sense. Why a covert meeting in a Dallas warehouse in the middle of the night. And why set the place on fire?"

The Director continued Balmain's train of thought, "Because they, or whomever, weren't sure that Ramey hadn't secreted the original somewhere in the warehouse. But they didn't search him. He still had the film stashed in his sock."

"Maybe he had *a* film stashed in his sock. Maybe he brought two films: the genuine and a fake and wanted to make up his mind which one to give them after he determined if they were on the level or not." Balmain began drumming his fingers again. "He gave them the real one, and once they decided they had what they needed, they killed him and torched the warehouse."

"Or, maybe *they* got what they wanted, and they slipped a fake into his sock."

Balmain's eyes opened wide. "Of course sir! They would have looked at the first few frames to make sure that they were looking at Dealey Plaza during the assassination."

"That's if Ramey had told his parties that he had already developed the film. What if he had made contact immediately after the event and had been instructed *not* to develop it?" The Director continued at a faster pace, "What if they were expecting an undeveloped spool, and upon inspection realized that Ramey had disobeyed their orders and processed it anyway? Then, they would have to wonder if he had made any additional copies."

"So, in order to ensure that any other copies present in the warehouse were destroyed, they set fire to the place." The Director paused. "How well do you know Sorrels?"

"Forrest Sorrels, the SAIC over here at Secret Service?"

"Yes."

Balmain shrugged, "Everyone kinda' knows him. He's been around as long as, uh, you know, he's been around since the thirties. Why?"

"Do you trust him?"

Balmain was taken aback, "Well, sir, I suppose. I really don't know him that well. I've bumped into him a couple of times at the court house. I think most of his guys like him. Why?"

The Director was pensive. "No reason. There's going to be a lot of finger-pointing up here as this Commission gets further into the facts. I'm hearing back-channel rumors about the way evidence was handled, about liberties that may have been taken with the law. I'm sensing that the facts being presented may not be as accurate as they should be. I'm just trying to understand who is going to be on whose side as all the details go public."

"Where do we go from here, sir?"

After a good thirty-seconds of silence, the Director replied, "Stay away from OSI and the Air Force for now. Also, send me all of the Finnegan photos, all of that 3151 series. Special courier. And, delete them off of your inventory. That goes for his interview report as well."

"Sir?" Balmain asked, stunned.

"I have a bad feeling about this Fred. I don't want those photos, or any reference to them, anywhere but in our safe in Washington until we find out where this leads. Those are classified Top Secret as of now." The Director took a deep breath. "And, you might consider paying Mr. Finnegan a visit to go through his statement again. The events of the twenty second happened so quickly, he wouldn't have remembered seeing anyone on a rooftop that far away, but I am interested in learning how a month has affected his memory."

"Yes, sir," Balmain responded a half-second before the Director hung up.

⸺⸻◉⸻⸺

Dan Reynolds sat nervously in the departure lounge at Love Field, waiting for his flight to New York. Too anxious to sit still, he felt he needed to walk around. The call from Dirk on New Year's Day left him concerned, and downright scared.

"You've got to get up here as soon as possible. I can't talk about this on the phone. This is crazy!"

"What do you mean?"

"I just can't. I don't know who could be listening. Get here as soon as you can!" His brother had rung off before Dan could ask any questions.

So, a day later he paced in Love Field's newest terminal. Actually, it wasn't quite new anymore. It was the third terminal, designed by

Donald S. Nelson, which opened to the airlines on January 20, 1958. Fairly modern, it consisted of three one-story concourses, 26 ramp-level gates and the world's first moving walkway in an airport. Most major airlines served the airport now, including American, Braniff, Central, Continental, Delta, Pan Am and Trans Texas.

He walked past the large bronze statue bearing the inscription, "One Riot, One Ranger," on display, that had been donated in 1961 by Mr. and Mrs. Earle Wyatt. Famed Texas-born sculptress Waldine Tauch created the piece, memorializing an incident in which a single Texas Ranger was supposedly dispatched to quell a riot.

However, during the incident in question, there had never really been an actual riot. It was an expression coined by Captain Bill McDonald in 1896 after having been the sole Ranger sent to stop an illegal prize fight in Dallas, which was to be attended by a large audience that included the legendary Judge Roy Bean. According to the story, when the Mayor met McDonald's train, he asked him where the rest of his Rangers were.

McDonald is alleged to have retorted, "Hell, ain't I enough? There's only one prize-fight!"

This would be Dan's first ride on a DC-8, Douglas Aircraft's answer to Boing's 707, which was now in wide scale production for passenger travel. The long range four-engine jet was introduced in 1958 and offered a slightly larger cargo hold than the 707. For Dan, it was simply the fastest way to get to Hartford. The last airplane he had been on was a Lockheed Electra, a four engine prop job. And today, at more than $150 for a round trip ticket, he realized why he preferred to drive everywhere.

He checked his watch for the fifth time in as many minutes, and realized it would be another ten minutes before boarding. He had been too uneasy to eat breakfast and he was afraid the introduction of food into his system now would result in a vomit situation later at 30,000 feet. He spotted a vending machine along the concourse, and decided that some crackers might be the closest thing to breakfast that he got today.

When he returned to his seat, he found a copy of the *Morning*

News folded up on one of the adjoining seats. After looking around to see if the owner was anywhere close by, he picked it up and returned to his seat. The front page indicated that much was going on in the world.

New York's Idlewild Airport, which was his first destination today, was about to be renamed *Kennedy* as a show of respect for the late president.

A police constable on guard outside the residence of Ghana's president, Kwame Nkrumah, fired five gunshots at him in an assassination attempt. The assailant invaded The Flagstaff House in Accra, and missed with his first shot. Nkrumah's bodyguard shielded the President with his body and was mortally wounded. It marked the sixth attempt on Nkrumah's life since he came to power in 1957. It was murder the old fashioned way.

Also on the front page, USMC Major General Victor H. Krulak, along with a committee of experts who had been asked to provide advice on the Vietnam War, submitted a recommendation to President Johnson for a three-phase series of covert actions against North Vietnam. Phase I, from February to May, called for propaganda dissemination and twenty-odd tactical operations, all intended to result in "substantial destruction, economic loss and harassment," and a second and third phase of increasing magnitude. Dan mused that LBJ was obviously not going to follow JFK's plan to reduce US presence there.

He glanced quickly at several other stories, and when they finally called his flight, he folded the paper back up and returned it to the seat where he'd found it. He joined other passengers in line and when the time came, presented his ticket to the attractive young lady who directed him out the door onto the tarmac. It was only then did he realize that he'd packed his jacket in his suitcase, and that when he disembarked in Hartford he would have to remember to dig it out before leaving the terminal. The temperature in Hartford was expected to hit a high of thirty five degrees.

Sometime after takeoff, the stewardess came around and asked if he'd like breakfast. He declined the offer but gratefully accepted a cup of coffee. He tried to relax, but couldn't drift off with the noise of the engines and the plumes of cigarette smoke being blown over his head causing a distraction. When they finally landed, he felt fatigued and dirty.

Located next to the Grand Central Parkway, the LaGuardia terminal was at full capacity, and he discovered that construction had begun for a 1,300-foot long structure that was to be completed in time for the World's Fair in Flushing. Amid the bustle of the busy terminal, his appetite had returned, and he found a place to grab a hamburger before boarding his connecting flight into Bradley.

It was after 11:00 a.m. when he finally landed in Hartford. He grabbed his suitcase off of the counter and headed for the arrivals area to look for Dirk's car. He walked up and down the sidewalk a few times wondering if he'd forgotten. On that hunch, he strolled over to the bank of pay telephones, dropped a dime in the slot and called Dirk's apartment. Busy.

No worries, Jeanine was probably gabbing away to her friends. He waited ten more minutes and then tried again. Still busy. He was too nervous to wait around any longer, so he hailed a cab and gave the driver Dirk's address on the West End, not too far from the Hartford Seminary. When he arrived, he paid the cabbie, and gave him as much tip as he thought he could afford, before making his way up the stairs to Dirk's second floor apartment.

When he rounded the stairs on the second floor he found Dirk's door open and a medium sized crowd in attendance. Many were firemen. Some were family members that he instantly recognized. A pit formed in his stomach. As he got to the door, his cousin Amy came out, tears in her eyes.

"Oh, Dan, it's just awful," she sobbed. "How did you get here so fast?"

Confused, Dan hugged her, "What's going on? Where's Dirk and Jeanine?"

Amy lifted her head from his shoulder, "Jeanine's in the kitchen." She looked at him quizzically, "You haven't heard?"

Dan dropped his suitcase on the floor, "Heard what?"

She squinted, "Oh, honey, it's just awful! Dirk, uhmmm, Dirk was killed about 5:00 a.m. on a fire!"

Dan couldn't believe what he was hearing. "What?"

Amy repeated the tragic news. "Yes, honey. Dirk was killed this morning over on Mound Street. They were fighting a three-alarm, and the building collapsed."

Dan's heart sank. As gently as he could, he moved Amy out of the way and headed to the kitchen to find Jeanine. He pushed several people out of the way who were attempting to pat his shoulder or offer an embrace. "Jeanine!"

She looked up, eyes swollen from tears, and rushed to him. "Dan! Oh my God, Dan! How did you get here so fast?"

"You didn't know I was coming?" he asked as he took her into his arms.

"Huh uh." She sobbed. "He didn't say anything. He left for his shift while I was at work, so I hadn't had a chance to talk to him since yesterday afternoon. How did you know? How did you get here so fast?"

Dan's mind was in chaos. "What happened? Amy said something about a building collapse?"

It was then that Dennis Becket, a childhood friend and also a firefighter, came in and greeted him. "Hi Dan. I'm really glad you could get here." He shook his head. "I am so very sorry!"

One of Jeanine's friends pushed into the now cramped kitchen and Dan relinquished his grip on her.

"Jesus, Dennis! What's going on? What happened?"

Dennis grabbed Dan by the elbow and steered him through the living room and out into the hall. Shaking his head, he said, "We thought we had this thing knocked down - three story wood and brick structure with six apartments. The people had all gotten out and Dirk and Trevor Forbes went back in to see if we had any more guys left inside. Trevor started back out and then we heard just a ferocious groaning noise and the whole thing caved in."

"Dirk's dead?" Dan asked, not believing it.

"I'm afraid so, man. It took us almost an hour to get to him, and by the time we did, it was too late. Man, I'm sorry. We did everything we could."

Dan sat down on the steps in front of the building and began to weep. Dennis sat next to him and put his arm around his old friend's shoulder. They sat like that for the better part of a half hour before Dan finally rubbed his eyes and stood up. "I guess I need to get back inside and get with Jeanine to make the, uh, you know, arrangements. Do you know if Jeanine's called Millie yet?"

"Yeah, I think she was the first. She's been on the phone all morning."

Dan sniffed. "Where are the boys?"

"They're inside, in their room. They've been sort of quiet all morning. Now that you're here, maybe they'll talk to you." Dennis added, "The Department is going to help you with the arrangements."

"Thanks," was all Dan could muster. He maneuvered back through the crowd to the kids' room and knocked lightly once before opening the door. Both boys were sitting on the bottom bunk elbows on their knees talking quietly. As he pushed the door open, seven-year old Bruce jumped up first, followed by five year old Elliot, and ran towards him.

"Uncle Dan!" both boys exclaimed.

Dan knelt to put his arms around them both at the same time. "Oh my God, guys. Your dad loved you both so much!" It was all he could get out before breaking into tears. Kneeling there, he kicked the bedroom door shut with his foot so that no one would intrude on their private moment.

Over the next hour, he talked about the life of a firefighter and the kind of commitment it takes to want to risk your life to save someone else. He talked about all of the things Dirk had proudly told him about his two sons over the years. He talked about how much Dirk loved the boys and their mom. When he felt the time was right, he told them to try to get some rest because he had to check on their mom.

The afternoon dragged into evening. Consolations, expressions of grief, sadness, and gratefulness for a life well-lived. Stories of Dirk on the job and in his role as father and husband. Dan had called Millie and found that she was already scheduled on the next flight to Hartford, connecting out of LaGuardia. She and Jeanine had spoken earlier. He would pick her up at Bradley a little past 9:00 p.m. It was decided between the two of them to leave Mark with her mom. He would want to be there for his cousins, but he was in school, and the cost of airfare was just too much for them. Millie told him that Mark had been fairly shaken up and would tell him more about it when she saw him that evening.

The Fire Department Chaplain dropped by about 6:30 p.m. and went through some arrangements that his group and Dirk's fire department brothers had put together. Because everyone had left so much food for the family, the chaplain stayed for dinner.

It was to be a formal Fire Department funeral, at no cost to Jeanine. They took as much of the load as they could off of her, to give her and the family time to grieve in their own way. Transportation to and from the funeral home and cemetery would be provided. The services had been outlined, and Jeanine, still in a state of shock, gave her blessing with a subdued, "Thank you."

Around 8:30 p.m., Dan borrowed Dirk's car, which had been dropped off by a couple of the firemen on his shift, and headed to Bradley to pick up Millie. She had relayed her gate information, so by the time she arrived, he was waiting for her in the boarding area, and when he saw her come down the ladder from the aircraft, his heart warmed.

She was everything to him. She tolerated the long shifts, and the occasional parties with the guys. And now, she would be there to help him grieve about the loss of his brother. When she came through the door, he ran to her and hugged her so hard, she thought she would suffocate.

"Oh God, Dan, I don't know what to say!"

Dan released his grip and shook his head, "There isn't anything anyone can say. This is a dangerous business that we get into voluntarily and we all know that bad things can happen."

She ran her index finger along his cheek. "I am so very sorry, baby. So very, very sorry."

Dan fought back the urge to cry. "He was my big brother."

They found Millie's two large suitcases. She had agreed to stay on for a couple of weeks after the funeral to help Jeanine with the boys, and try to help them get back to normal as soon as they could. Dan would return and take care of Mark on his days off and have Millie's mom stay at the house when Dan was at the Fire Department.

Once they were driving out of the airport, Dan asked, "What, uh, how did you tell Mark?"

Millie looked out the passenger side window quietly before answering, "You left before he got up this morning. When I went in, before Jeanine called, he was awake. He was just layin' there, staring at the ceiling. I asked him what was wrong, and he said he hadn't slept well."

She swallowed hard and then continued, "He said...uh...when I asked him if he was okay, he said that there was something wrong with Uncle Dirk."

Dan turned his head to look at her. "What?"

She nodded. "I asked him what he meant, and he told me that there was something wrong with Uncle Dirk, and that I should call Jeanine."

Dan frowned. "What time was that?"

"Just after 6:30 a.m.- right after you left for the airport."

Dan looked at the road and then again at Millie. "That's 7:30 a.m. eastern time. I wasn't in the air yet. They hadn't called Jeanine from the fire department until after five. How did he know?"

Millie continued, "Baby, Mark said he had bad dreams all night long. He said he couldn't sleep because he kept seeing Uncle Dirk under a building."

Dan shook his head. "This can't be those hallucinations from that scarlet fever thing, can it?"

A tear formed in Millie's eye, "I don't know baby, but he said this morning when he woke up, Uncle Dirk was in his room and waved good-bye to him. It wasn't until I called Jeanine that I found out."

Dan came back, "You called her? I thought she called you."

"Huh uh." She wiped at her tears, "After Mark told me that, I felt like I ought to call, just to be on the safe side. And that's when she told me."

"Did he have a fever or anything?" Dan asked excitedly.

"No baby, he sounded just as calm as could be."

Dan drove in silence for a while. There was too much to think about.

6

MONDAY, JANUARY 6, 1964

D an Reynolds ignored the other passengers, and sat in silence for most of the ride back to Dallas. The bump and the chirp of the tires striking the runway brought him out of his reverie and he realized that his first priority would be to spend time with Mark and help him through the loss of his Uncle Dirk. Then, of course, there was the matter of Mark's experiences, his forewarning that Dirk was in trouble. Dan did not understand such things, and in some ways, feared them.

The funeral was well-choreographed by the fire department, poignantly memorable, and served to help friends and family say goodbye to a unique soul. Dirk had been elevated to hero status in the newspapers, and as they wept and grieved, everyone realized that they would have to get on with their lives without him. The chaplain did a great job of combining memories and offering hope, but there would be a hole in their hearts.

So much had happened in the past couple of weeks. Millie and Jeanine began planning their activities as a way to keep structure in their lives and to give the boys some direction. The school acknowledged their loss and allowed them each a three-day absence. But, both Jeanine and the administrators felt that it would be good for them to get back as quickly as possible. Regardless, structure was important.

Not wanting to tip his hand, Dan had asked Becket to allow him to go through Dirk's locker for personal effects. He went through all of his bunker gear, toilet kit and every other place he could think to look without arousing suspicion. No film.

As time permitted when Jeanine and Millie were out of the apartment, he looked through Dan's things; pockets, drawers, tool kit and anywhere that someone could hide a reel of film. No luck.

He even took the car apart in the hopes that the film might have been secreted under the spare tire or even wedged between the seats. Nada. The film was nowhere to be found.

Now, as he returned to Dallas by himself, he felt empty and foolish. No film. No brother. He rubbed his eyes as he stared out the window at the terminal building and reflected on the chances that they took every day; fighting fires, trying to save others. Truly a noble profession, but not one without risks. Certainly it was stimulating and emotionally rewarding, but quite dangerous as well.

The aircraft rolled to a stop in front of the gent holding the orange sticks, crossed over his head in an X, and it wasn't long before the hatch opened and the passengers were allowed to disembark. The fresh air smelled clean and warm compared to Hartford. And, for no apparent reason, Dan felt a minor jolt of energy pulse through his body as his feet touched the tarmac. Something told him that life was moving on.

———◦«◯»◦———

Fred Balmain parked the Bureau's four-door Oldsmobile Dynamic 88 in a space near the entrance of the Cheyenne Oil & Gas Supply building, and asked Scott Wainwright if he wanted to lead the conversation. Since Wainwright had interviewed Finnegan earlier, and seemed to have a good rapport with him, the two agents decided it would make for a more relaxed exchange. This wasn't so much an interrogation, but rather an opportunity to find out anything else he might have known and whom he might have told.

Balmain locked his door and pocketed the keys, "What do you feel like for lunch today?"

Scotty shrugged, "You know me, boss, steak and fries always hits the spot!"

Balmain reached the lobby door first and held it open for Wainright to pass through. Like any good FBI agent, they quickly scanned the area and noted that the reception area was sparse and industrial-looking, befitting the nature of the business, and the reception desk was empty. Balmain looked around for a bell or buzzer to ring but found none. "I guess we wait?"

Scotty looked at the door marked *Employees Only* and gestured, "Maybe not. Let's see what's behind this door." He turned the knob and gently pulled it open, revealing a small hallway with offices on either side, leading into a larger manufacturing space.

He yelled "Hello!" as both men walked cautiously down the hall past the empty offices into the manufacturing area. Near the end of the hall, Scotty held up his hand, stopping their advance.

Balmain came up behind him and looked around the corner at the group of men and women who stood in a circle, their heads bowed in prayer. When one of them said, "Amen," and the group started to disperse, Balmain and Wainright approached quietly.

"Good morning," Balmain addressed the group above the noise of the machinery. "Are one of you the manager?"

A sturdy woman in her late forties stepped away from the group and replied, "I'm Cheyenne. I'm the owner. Can I help you?"

Wainright stepped up and smiled as he presented his credentials. "Good morning Ma'am. We're agents Balmain and Wainwright, with the FBI. We wondered if we could speak with Mike Finnegan. It'll just take a minute."

Cheyenne looked at him and then at the ground. "You just missed him."

"He left for lunch?" Wainright asked.

She looked back up at the agent, "No. His sister just called. She said he died a little while ago at the hospital. He was doing some welding Saturday and fell off of a scaffold. I guess he wasn't wearing any kind of harness. They took him to Parkland, but he didn't make it."

The agents looked at each other straight-faced. "Where did this happen?" Balmain asked.

"Over there." Cheyenne pointed to the east side of the manufacturing area where several scaffolds had been erected to support teams working up near the ceiling. "I guess he was focused on his welding and not his footing, and he slipped and went over."

Balmain and Wainright approached the indicated area where Finnegan's body hit the concrete. As both men looked at the scaffold from top to bottom, Balmain asked, "Did anyone write a report on this?"

"I did," she replied. "Our company attorney came by Saturday afternoon to find out, you know, how it happened. He said even though it was an accident, we should have something in the file. Do you want to see it?"

"Yes, Ma'am!" Balmain replied.

Cheyenne nodded, and disappeared back towards the main entrance to the facility.

"What do you think?" Wainright asked after Cheyenne was out of earshot.

"Strange timing." Balmain rubbed his beard stubble as he looked up and down at the offending scaffold and then at the adjacent structures. "I don't know, Scotty. It could've been an accident." He moved to the back of the scaffold and then to the side to get a perspective from all angles. "Why would anyone want to help him over the side? How could anyone help him over the side? Witnesses?"

"Man, he turned his stuff over to us a month ago. He'd already made his statement." Scotty began looking at the floor and the area surrounding the scaffolding. "Unless he owed somebody money, boss, my vote would be for *accident*."

Balmain shook his head, "Why do I have a bad feeling about this? This was to be a quick follow up interview. A closing memo of sorts. No one knew we were coming here today." He subconsciously clicked his molars. "There's absolutely no reason to think that he had any other information of value, or that he was even aware of what his photo captured in the background."

Cheyenne's boot heels hit the concrete with a lively series of thuds as she crossed the floor to meet them. "Here you are, boys."

Balmain read the neat, hand-printed report as Wainright looked over his shoulder to follow along:

"On January 4,1964 Michael Finnegan, a 36-year-old male with Cheyenne Oil & Gas, was performing welding activities inside on the East side of the facility, on a scaffold, about 22 ft. above a concrete floor, marking and rigging pipe routes. Finnegan was not wearing a body harness; the scaffolding did not have guardrails or netting installed. Witness Martin Stansfield remembers marking the rafters, and then he stated that he 'heard someone falling, as he was descending an adjacent scaffold.' Finnegan was transported to the emergency room at Parkland Hospital by Donner Ambulance (operated by Donner Funeral Home). He suffered multiple broken bones including a skull fracture, bruises to his back and laceration to his forehead. He was admitted for treatment. He succumbed to his injuries approximately 0100 January 6, 1964.

Investigation Findings:

1. *Finnegan was working on scaffolding when he fell about 22 ft. onto a concrete floor.*

2. *Finnegan erected the scaffolding himself.*

3. *The scaffolding was rented from McKinley Builder Supply in Ft. Worth.*

4. *Finnegan was not wearing a body harness or seat, and the scaffolding did not have guardrails or safety nets installed.*

5. *The witness did not see the fall, but heard noise that*

captured his attention in time to see Finnegan on the ground.

6. *Although Finnegan was a Journeyman Pipe Fitter, he did not have any recent fall protection and scaffolding training.*

7. *The job site facility was a single-story manufacturing site approximately 750,000 square feet.*

8. *Finnegan had 10 years of experience with the employer and the weather conditions outdoors were sunny with clear skies at the time of the accident."*

When he and Scotty had each read the report, Balmain glanced up at Cheyenne, "I don't suppose you have a..."

"Xerox 914?" she answered, as if reading his mind. "Yeah. Give me a minute and I'll make you a copy."

Wainright added, "Also could you let us speak with this Martin Stansfield, the fellow that witnessed the accident?"

Cheyenne shook her head, "I can't today. He was still pretty shook up, so he took the day off."

Balmain asked, "Do you have his home address and phone number?"

"I think so," she said as the agents followed her back to the offices. "We should have a pretty current application for him. He just started a couple weeks back."

The agents looked at each other. "He was new?" Wainright asked.

"Yeah." She placed the report upside down on the glass of the large copier, covered it with the rubber door, turned the machine on, and then hit the "Print" button. "The union sent him over. We had a guy leave - got married pretty fast, and moved to Tulsa. I needed a man, and they sent Marty."

"Good employee?" Wainright asked as the Xerox 914 whirred.

She shrugged. "He's okay. It seems like he knows his stuff, but he isn't a real go-getter if you know what I mean." The machine spit out the copy of the report and she handed it to Wainright.

In the other corner of the room was a row of filing cabinets. She squatted down to find the drawer containing files beginning with *S* and backed up as she slid the drawer out. One by one, she paged through the applications in that file, replaced it in the drawer and pulled the files labeled *R* and *T*. After flipping through all of the files in those folders, she frowned. "Sorry boys. I can't seem to find it right now."

She scratched her head. "I know it's got to be here somewhere. It must've been misfiled. Let me look around for it and I'll give you a call when I find it."

"Please do." Wainright said. "Thank you for your time."

When the agents were seated in their car, Wainright looked at Balmain. "Well?"

After backing out of the parking space, Balmain shifted the transmission into drive and headed for the street. "I've got a bad feeling about this."

<hr />

Millie called Dan a little past three to make sure he'd arrived safely, and to check on Mark.

"Mark is okay. We're talking. He understands what happened," Dan said pensively.

At Millie's request, he put Mark on the phone for a brief minute to talk to his mom. When they had finished, Mark handed the phone back to his Dad.

Dan scratched Mark lightly on the head. "Give me a minute and then I'll make us some dinner."

Dan, still a little choked up, said, "We haven't really talked about his dreams yet. I thought I'd kinda bring it up and see if he feels like, you know, talking about it."

"Yeah baby. I love you. Sorry to rush, but if this call goes more than three minutes, we'll get extra charges." She paused, "By the way, did you pick the mail up over at Martha and Jack's?"

"Oh shit," he replied, somewhat embarrassed that he'd forgotten. "Naw. I'll head over and get it in a bit. I've just been too preoccupied."

"I know baby. I'm so sorry. I'll call you tomorrow." She kissed the phone on the other end and rang off.

Dinner was easy. Mark loved hamburgers done on the grill, and after they each downed two of them, Dan watched Mark do his school homework while he did the dishes. After he put the last plate in the strainer, he dried his hands. "How's it coming?"

"Good, dad. Almost done."

Dan hung the towel on the oven rail to dry, "I'm going to run over to Jack and Martha's to get the mail. You okay for a couple minutes?"

"Yeah, Dad." He grinned.

When Dan returned a couple of minutes later, Mark had cleared the kitchen table and had gone to his room. Dan dumped the paper shopping bag that Martha had given him onto the table. He shook his head. The heaviest part of the week's mail was Millie's magazines; *McCall's, Ladies Home Journal, Good Housekeeping*. He pushed them aside and stacked them on the corner of the table before sorting through the various bills and cards.

He turned over a thicker dark manila envelope and froze as he recognized the handwriting. It was from Dirk. Judging from the thickness, he had a good idea what was in it, and he furtively looked over his shoulder towards Mark's room to make sure that his son wouldn't see him tear it open. Inside was the developed version of the spool of film that he'd handed his brother at the airport, just days before. Taped to the container was a brief note from Dirk, "Sorry - I didn't want to hang onto this. Too crazy!"

He stared in amazement at the film and the note. His brother's final words to him. He quickly sorted the rest of the mail and set it aside. Carefully, he opened the container and gently pulled the reel out. He unwound the first few inches and held it up to the light. The color images were small, but clear enough for him to realize that he was looking at Dealey Plaza.

"Oh my God!" he said out loud as he unwound more of the film and held it closer to the light. The first few frames showed the police lead vehicle before Kennedy's limousine came into view. "Christ! This is the assassination!" He quickly rewound the film on the spool and ran to the telephone.

"Martha?" he said breathlessly when his neighbor answered. "It's me again. Does Jack still have that movie projector?"

"Why sure he does," she replied.

"I need to borrow it for a couple of minutes. I'll be right over." He replaced the handset in the cradle before Martha finished speaking.

Ten minutes later, he was back home with their projector, and his nerves were on fire. He felt like he'd had a gallon of coffee. He got Mark cleaned up and put to bed and he took the projector and the film to the basement.

He went to the corner of the room and began to pop the legs out on the portable card table. The last time he'd done this, Dirk and he were getting ready to sit down to Christmas dinner. He sighed unevenly, a momentary wave of grief subsiding. After locating an extension cord, he got the projector plugged in and pointed at a space of white wall.

He carefully fed the film through the various sprockets and tracks, took a deep breath and turned it on.

From the view, it looked like the photographer was south of Dealey Plaza - maybe on a roof, shooting north. The images were remarkably steady, like they'd been shot for the evening news.

Five motorcycles came into view from Main Street and headed north on Houston towards the Texas School Book Depository. Behind them, a white Ford, or Mercury four-door sedan. And then, there was the Presidential Limousine, Kennedy waving proudly at the crowds. The First Lady's pink outfit stood out smartly in the noonday sun.

Looking above and in front of the limousine, he could see

Oswald, well, whomever everyone assumed was Oswald, looking out the sixth floor window. Kennedy disappeared briefly as the limo rounded the corner from Houston onto Elm. When he reappeared, the rifle barrel was visible in the window as Oswald took aim. In the film, Oswald could be seen firing, working the bolt, firing, working the bolt, and firing again before withdrawing inside the window.

The limousine, after slowing briefly to allow a Secret Service agent to climb on back, sped off under the triple-underpass, presumably enroute to the hospital. Dan shook his head. There was history, right in front of him. He stopped the film and reversed it, watching the cars back up through Dealey Plaza. It was an interesting piece of film, to be sure. But, certainly not anything as earth-shattering as Dirk had made it sound. He pulled the projector back a couple of feet to make the image bigger on the wall, and then re-focused the lens.

He switched the projector back on. There were the motorcycles, the lead car, JFK's limo and the large Cadillac convertible carrying extra agents. With the larger image, Dan was able to get a clearer view of the action. Oswald fired. As people began to look for the sound of the shots, some looked confused. A Secret Service agent sitting on the back of the Cadillac follow-up car reaches down and grabs a rifle off the seat and appears to chamber a round. Oswald seems to fire a third time, and the President's head explodes. Another Secret Service agent runs forward, jumps spread-eagle on the limousine and forces the First Lady down inside the vehicle. The cars go under the triple-underpass.

Dan shook his head slowly. He wondered what would make this film so controversial. As the vehicles entered the Stemmons Freeway and disappeared from view, there was a break in the film. Dan started to reach for the projector to rewind it again, but then checked himself. The photographer was now running, the jerky view of concrete moving past, indicating that he was running quickly, his right arm swinging the camera as he moved.

When the camera began to return to horizon level, he wasn't looking at Dealey Plaza anymore. Instead, it was a clear day at an airport. Dan initially surmised that the same photographer had journeyed to Love Field to catch Air Force One leaving with JFK's body. However, having just returned from there, Dan soon realized that he wasn't looking at Love Field, but rather, a US military base somewhere, the water tower painted in the red and white checkerboard pattern visible in the distance.

In the first two or three seconds, Dan saw a group of eight senior military officials: colonels and generals judging by all the braid on their service hats. The mix of Air Force and Army officials seemed to be impressed with something, smiling and pointing and patting each other on their backs. Then, the view of the lens moved up to something in the sky.

There were two of them. At first, Dan thought the camera was being jerked side to side, but then recognized that one of the objects remained perfectly still in hover, while the other flitted back and forth, up and down, like a hummingbird. They looked like stainless steel disks with upside down coffee cups on top. He had no idea how large they were because he couldn't tell how far from the camera they were. His heart and breathing quickened as he attempted to interpret what he was actually seeing on the film.

Then one landed. On the flight line. In front of the generals. On a US military flight line. The officers approached it cautiously and the photographer followed at a distance. When it seemed like officers were within ten feet of it, Dan surmised that the craft was probably about twenty feet in diameter. It was two to three feet off the ground, but there were no visible landing gear. What the hell was it resting on?

The generals became motionless, with one pointing at the craft. The crackle of the end of the film moving through the sprockets signaled the end of the show. The space on the wall where the images had been projected now turned white, bright enough to light the basement.

Dan swallowed hard. He sat down in one of the folding chairs and tried to mentally process what he had just seen. His thoughts raced. Sometime in the hours or days after the President of the

United States was gunned down, flying saucers landed at a US military base? Was this a joke? Was this someone in Hollywood creating a science fiction movie set? That's what had gotten Dirk so excited! Not the assassination, but rather the flying saucer footage!

He removed the full spool and moved it up to the other arm of the projector so that he could rewind the film back to its original reel. Once he'd done that, he re-fed the film onto the sprockets so that he could watch the entire movie one more time. He pulled the projector back as far as he could, almost to the other wall, to make the image as large as he could. He turned out the basement lights to improve the contrast of the images on the wall.

He shook his head vigorously and said aloud, "This is nuts!" before heading to the stairs. He went into the kitchen and found the bottle of Four Roses whiskey that he'd been given a little over a year earlier at Christmas by Jeanine and Dirk. He grabbed the aluminum ice cube tray out of the freezer and yanked the lever to break up the cubes. He put four large cubes in his glass along with a double shot of whiskey before returning to the basement.

Dan switched the projector on one more time. After refocusing for the new distance, he took his drink up to the wall so that he could watch from as close as possible. When he saw his shadow blocking the lower right portion of the image, he moved aside a bit. His mind now on weird spacecraft, he all but ignored the motorcade once again moving through Dealey Plaza. The whiskey tasted good and felt therapeutic. Oswald shoots. Agents respond. Motorcade heads to the hospital.

He was ready for the break in scenes and focused intently on the senior officers and their objects of interest. Three seconds on the generals, and on to ... there they were! While one seemed to hover motionless, the other would dart around the sky with impossible speed and angulation of turns. Then, while that one hovered, the other would seemingly move so quickly that it disappeared from one spot and instantaneously reappeared in a new spot. They were putting on quite a show. Some of the generals applauded.

Nevertheless, try as he might, Dan couldn't get any more

footage out of the film. The photographer had filmed as much as he could, right up to the end. Over the course of the evening, he ran the tail end footage of the strange craft a half dozen more times, and filled his glass with whiskey at least three times, maybe four.

As drunk as he was, his curiosity eventually turned to anxiety as he pondered the notion that the poor chap in the warehouse fire on December 23 could have been killed over this. What could Dan do with the film now? Dirk had been right, this was some crazy stuff. He couldn't give it to the police or the FBI without them prosecuting him because he stole evidence from a crime scene. The film had to have been classified; those generals wouldn't have wanted their faces on the next *Life* or *Look Magazine* covers, standing next to a flying saucer. Dan's emotions ran wild, figuring that if someone was willing to kill Ramey over this, then they'd be willing to kill him as well.

Yet, something told him not to destroy it. He needed time to think. As he began to put the projector back in its case and fold up the chairs and table, he looked in the corner of the basement where a 2X4 board had become loose from atop the concrete block that made up the lower six feet of the basement wall. He wrapped the film canister in a sock, and gently wedged it into one of the cores of the block, and then secured the 2X4 back over the top. He took a couple of steps back, almost stumbling in his stupor, and determined that it was as safe a hiding place as he could imagine. He grabbed the projector and his whisky glass, and flipped the basement lights off as he returned to the kitchen.

He dropped the projector by the front door and staggered to the kitchen and the now well-used bottle of Four Roses. He poured another shot of the brown liquid remedy over the partially melted ice remaining in his glass, and sat at the table with his head in his hands. Someone had killed a guy over this film. Maybe this footage was so sensitive that someone would kill anyone who...he sat up and stared straight ahead at the refrigerator. Someone would kill anyone. Dirk?

Dirk's friends and fire department brothers had been with him the night of the collapse. It was bad luck. That's all it was, bad luck. It was inconceivable to think that someone could have staged a building collapse so precisely that it only killed one person. One specific person. No way – that's just crazy! There were dozens of witnesses.

And what were those flying saucers, really? Were they some new government secret weapon? He'd read in so many trash tabloids about the potential for intelligent life - beings from other star systems, visiting our planet. Maybe even crashing here. Total garbage! He was a good Baptist. Well, most of the time. Since the church frowned on alcohol, he wouldn't be viewed favorably by the pastor right this second. Nevertheless, he'd been told through the years that God made the earth, and then rested. The heavens and the earth.

He'd also been told by many of the same people, that psychic phenomenon was evil. But, Mark was certainly nothing of the sort. His son was good and kind and pure. Yet, his own son knew something was going to happen to Dirk. His own son said that he saw Dirk in his room on the morning that he died. This was just too much!

He looked at the drink in front of him, and frowned. Tomorrow was a new day. He had to get back to normal, and that meant that Mark had to get back to normal too. He picked up the glass with the Four Roses sedative in it and dumped it in the sink.

7

TUESDAY, JANUARY 7, 1964

B almain stared at the phone book in front of him and then looked at his notes before speaking again, "You mean to say that there is no pipefitter named Martin Stansfield in your union? You didn't send him to Cheyenne?

"Nope," was the flat reply. "I've been here for more than fifteen years, and I think I know every member. I've never met a Martin Stansfield. Never heard of him. And we haven't sent anyone to Cheyenne in a few months."

Balmain thanked the rep from the Pipefitters Union, and hung up. His concern about the credibility of the sole witness to Finnegan's death was increasing. He looked at the TELEX he had received from his contact at the Texas Department of Public Safety, which lay wrinkled on the desk in front of him. Apparently, they had never heard of him either. No driver's license, no union membership and no listing in the telephone white pages from Dallas, Ft. Worth or any of the surrounding towns.

The Director had pushed their daily call to 10:00 a.m. Central time today, due to a schedule conflict with the Attorney General. So, he decided to make the most of this extra time by running down information on Stansfield. Now, the missing employment application was looking less like sloppy filing, and more like a criminal act intending to cover someone's tracks. But, why? Why kill Finnegan?

Balmain looked at Wainright's original interview report.

Finnegan had joined the Army at age 18, but by the time he had completed Basic Training, the war was over. Like many infantry troops, he was reassigned into a non-combat role. His choice had been with a civil engineering unit. It was there that he learned his trade and gathered the skills and experience that made him successful in his civilian life following his Honorable Discharge, four years later.

His record was spotless. No trouble while in the Army, and no problems with the law since getting out. Married to the same woman for the past eight years, but no children. Balmain shook his head, there was nothing sinister there. He plumbed and piped; nothing subversive about that!

When the KY-3 sprang to life, he tossed the folder on the top of the pile accumulating on his desk.

"Good morning, sir."

"Good morning, Fred. What do you have regarding Finnegan?"

Balmain encapsulated the previous day's activity. "Not good, sir. Wainright and I ran over to his business yesterday to find that he'd fallen from a scaffold this past Saturday and died Sunday night at the hospital. We looked at the scene, but nothing seemed contrived or suspicious about it. However..." He paused for a moment, "The only witness, if you can call him that, was a guy named Stansfield, who, well, sir, he's a ghost."

"I beg your pardon?" the Director interrupted.

"We asked the owner if we could speak with him and learned that he'd taken the day off. When she tried to pull his personnel file, it was missing. I followed up with Texas DPS and the pipefitters union, and they have no record of a Martin Stansfield either. No listing in directory assistance."

The Director sounded concerned, "When you say witness, what exactly did he say happened, and with whom did he speak?"

"According to Cheyenne Wells, the owner, he was first on the scene. He told her he was climbing down one scaffold when he heard something that made him look around. That's when he saw Finnegan on the floor unconscious. He finished out what was left of his shift. But as you can imagine, with an accident of that nature, not a whole lot of work got done the rest of the day. Yesterday, he called off sick and told her that he just couldn't make it in."

"He...heard a sound? What kind of sound?"

Balmain replied, "Mrs. Wells said he wasn't specific, so we don't know."

After a moment, the Director summarized his morning meeting with the Attorney General, "As you know, the AG and I met this morning, along with Mr. Dulles. Their belief is that the Warren Commission is proceeding along the correct path of inquiry at a responsible pace. All other investigations being run that are not ancillary to theirs, are to cease immediately."

"Cease, sir?" Balmain asked baffled. "But, we're nowhere near done with this. There are still..."

The Director cut him off, "Take it down, Fred. Close it up. Your agents will all be re-assigned by the end of the day, and their service on this special task force should not be discussed with anyone, ever. Please remind them individually about their need to honor their oaths and maintain absolute secrecy. You've done well, but the Warren Commission is going forward with their own objective. Regardless of any evidence, no matter how minute, Oswald did it, he acted alone and the case will be closed. Each agent will receive a commendation in his file, but this task force never existed."

"What about the files?" Balmain asked.

"Box them up and ship them to me. As a matter of fact, have an agent escort them up here. And Fred, after everything is shipped. Clean the office."

"Clean it?" Balmain wanted to be sure he understood the connotation of the Director's statement.

"Top to bottom." The Director paused, "I think your wife will enjoy Washington. You've earned it!" And he was gone.

———— ((●)) ————

It was almost noon, and Dan Reynolds still felt a throbbing in his head. "Come on buddy, I promised your teacher I'd get you there by 12:30." It had been a long time since he had consumed as much alcohol in any one setting and today, his body was paying the price for the indulgence.

"I know Dad, I'm hurrying," Mark replied lacing up one of his shoes.

Dan sat down on the bed next to his son. "So…how are you doing? I mean really, how are you doing?"

Mark shrugged as he laced up the other sneaker. "I'm okay Dad. I miss Uncle Dirk, and I know you do too. We just have to get along with each other I guess. Well, and mom!" He smiled. "Do you think Aunt Jeanine and Bruce and Elliot will want to come back and stay with us for a while?"

Dan put his arm around Mark and pulled him close for a hug. "You bet slugger. But, it probably won't be until school is out."

Mark grabbed his note pad and school books off of his dresser, and followed his dad out to the car. He wasn't used to going to school half way through the day, and was entertained by all of the activity on the street. By the time they pulled up in front of the school, he was humming a song from one of the movies he'd seen. "Thanks, Dad!" he said reaching for the door handle. "See you tonight!"

Dan rubbed Mark's head briskly. "Count on it! It's spaghetti night!" He watched his son run up the drive to the school entrance and go inside.

For no apparent reason, Dan pointed the car towards Dealey Plaza. The radio was on softly and the local station was airing the news in the background, a story about something called the Typhon missile. After spending more than 230 million dollars to develop the thing, the U.S. Navy was abandoning further work on the project.

General Dynamics had contracted with the Navy to design a shipboard surface-to-air missile that could launch missiles simultaneously against a number of aircraft, but the system was too large for use on most of the ships in the American naval fleet.

"Wouldn't they have thought of that before building it?" he said to himself, turning the radio off.

He slowed as he drove past the Post Office building. Judging from the angle of the movie footage he had seen the previous evening, the photographer would have had to shoot from somewhere high up here. Probably the roof. Without thinking, he pulled up, and parallel parked into a space on Houston that had just been vacated by another car zipping away.

When traffic opened up, he crossed the street to take a closer look at the new building under construction just east of the Post Office building. The steel girders comprising the framework rose to at least eight stories and it looked like there would be even more by the time it was completed. High rise buildings brought their own challenges for firefighters. The higher the fire, the tougher it was to fight it.

He watched a man welding about five stories up and remembered his own days in construction. He remembered the welding accident that caused him to rethink his career path. Was he better off now? He enjoyed being able to point to something and tell people "I built that." The fire department offered its own rewards but it wasn't quite the same. Not worse, not better. Just not the same. There were plenty of buildings in Dallas that he could point to and say, "I kept that from being destroyed."

He moved on north and waited to cross Commerce Street with a dozen other men and women, most of whom appeared to be tourists with their cameras and street maps. By the time he came abreast of the Old Court House, he could see that Dealey Plaza was alive with activity. There were dozens of people, walking, pointing, and snapping pictures. He could see that across Elm, on the north side of the street, people had built a makeshift shrine out of f oral bouquets and crosses to mark the spot where Kennedy's fatal head shot occurred. There was a city traffic crew working on the signal light that hung out over Elm, just east of Houston. They seemed to be focusing their attention on the metal arch that suspended the traffic light over the street. In front of the Texas School Book

Depository, there were three men in suits and sunglasses making notes on a clipboard.

Things had been busy in Dealey Plaza about every day since the assassination. On November 27, the Secret Service had shut down the area to conduct a day of reenactments, which included running a substitute limousine along the same route over and over again so that it could be photographed and recorded from a dozen different angles.

Agents assumed different roles and took up positions in cars and in buildings, so that a photographic record could illustrate how Oswald killed the President. What were they trying to prove? They had Oswald. They had the rifle. Oswald had lived in Russia and there were reports saying that he'd traveled to Mexico and Cuba as a spy. He had a Russian wife, who spoke very little English.

Along with other visitors, Dan stood near the entrance to the School Book Depository, and craned his neck looking up at the window on the sixth floor. People spoke in subdued tones as if at a funeral. One of the group of men with the clipboards spoke into a walkie-talkie, the obnoxious static seemingly irreverent for this setting.

He turned and looked at the Post Office Building that was south of him, at least three hundred yards away. That seemed to be about the same distance he'd estimated the night before, watching the movie on his basement wall. He looked up at the roof. The angle seemed about right as well. He grunted and thought, *someone had to get all the way up there to take pictures of something right here.*

He maneuvered around the three men in suits, and as he passed by one of them, noted the five-pointed star logo of the US Secret Service on the top page of his clipboard. The gentleman's walkie-talkie crackled, and he pulled it out of the leather holster on his belt. Dan recognized it as a Motorola HT-200, similar to what he had used at the fire department. Commonly known as, *the brick,* the radio was a true workhorse but was built like, and similar in weight to a brick.

As Dan walked further west along Elm, he overheard the agent begin a conversation with someone, which was basically unintelligible. But, as he progressed towards the grassy knoll and the makeshift shrine, he passed by the traffic crew that was servicing the stoplight, and slowed as he heard their walkie-talkies squawking the same conversation as the men who were presumably Secret Service.

Why would the Dallas Traffic Operations Maintenance Department be on the same radio frequency as the United States Secret Service? He stopped and turned. It looked like they were replacing the traffic light that hung out over Elm Street. They were in a City truck. They had tools. Dan shrugged and moved on down to the area where dozens of people had left flowers in remembrance of President Kennedy.

"Excuse me, Mister?" Dan looked up at the middle aged man and his wife, who was offering him their camera. Hanging from the man's neck by a strained leather strap was a camera with a lens that looked like it could be a foot long. "Would you mind taking a picture of my wife and I here - maybe get the Book Depository in the background?"

"Holy cow!" Dan exclaimed as the man handed him the bulky rig. "What is this thing?"

As the man's wife rolled her eyes, the man proudly explained, "This is a Nikon F. It's one of the new single-lens reflex cameras. You just look through the viewfinder and everything you see in there will be in your photo."

Dan inspected the heavy contraption, the large lens throwing the center of gravity well off. "What about your lens?"

His wife crossed her arms over her chest. "Please don't get him going on this."

The man waved her off with a smile. "I'm a retired engineer, and I'm afraid photography has become my latest hobby."

"An obsession," she added.

"This lens is the coolest thing you've ever seen. It will zoom from 85MM, which is just slightly closer than a normal shot - all the way out to 250MM, which really brings in the background!" He moved the ring up and down the cylinder of the lens, exposing the different markings that showed precisely which magnification was in use. "This kit has everything:100% viewfinder frame coverage, interchangeable focusing screens, interchangeable viewfinders, large bayonet mounts, mirror-up devices, and..."

The woman dove in, "For crying out loud, George, let the man take the picture and be on his way!"

"Sorry," he went on. "You basically frame your shot through the viewfinder, and then you focus by twisting this ring, and if you want to move in or back up, you slide this back and forth until you get the picture you want."

"You make it sound simple," Dan said has he hoisted the camera to eye level and took aim through the view finder. "Whoa...I think we're too close."

The retired engineer responded, "That's okay, I left the other lens in the car. We were just walking the plaza, trying to get some close-up detail of the buildings. And, well, the uhm, Grassy Knoll. If you step back a few feet and move the ring back to the 85MM line, you'll be fine."

Dan backed up a few feet and began to sight through the lens. The engineer and his wife stood together in front of the floral shrine, his arm around her. Dan moved the ring until they were in the frame and in focus and then depressed the shutter release button. "Now what?"

George motioned with his thumb and index finger, "That lever on the right there; that's the frame advance uh, the winder. Pull it out and let it spring back, and that'll advance the film."

Dan complied, and as he raised the camera back to his eye, the engineer continued, "Why don't you turn the camera a quarter turn to your left. That'll make the image come out vertically and you can get some of the depository in the background."

Dan rotated the camera as instructed, and as he adjusted the focus ring again, he froze. He increased the telephoto to its maximum power and looked at the man in the suit who joined the group of agents in front of the book depository. It was that FBI agent who had interviewed him at the fire station. Balmain.

He watched as Balmain shook hands with one of the men, and handed him a dark 8" X 10" envelope. The other two men ignored him as if he wasn't there. The Secret Service agent looked at the envelope, and then slipped it up under the other documents on his clipboard. They spoke softly for a minute during which Balmain glanced at the progress of the supposed traffic crew, and then they shook hands once more. He looked up at the sixth floor window of the Book Depository, shook his head solemnly and then calmly turned and walked away south on Houston Street.

Dan followed him through the powerful lens of the camera. At this level of magnification, it was difficult to hold it steady, so he cupped the lens in his left hand, and drew his elbow into his torso to help stabilize it as if taking a rifle shot. He tracked Balmain until he turned east on Main Street and out of view.

"Hey!" The engineer asked, "Is anything wrong?"

Dan shook his head, "Oh, no. I was just looking at how well this lens brings everything in up close. Really impressive!" He depressed the shutter release, advanced the film while taking a step to the side, and then took two more shots to give the couple a variety of poses.

He handed the camera back to George. "Here you go. I hope they come out okay." The men shook hands and Dan paused to look at the flower arrangements left by people from all over the country. His hands in his pockets, he followed a group of people up the hill to the pergola where Abraham Zapruder had stood while shooting his famous coverage of the attack.

What the hell was Balmain doing in Dealey Plaza? What was in the envelope? He'd seen an envelope just like that at the fire station. It was the type of envelope from which Balmain had produced photographs of the fire scene and the late sergeant Ramey. His intuition told him that Balmain must have pieced together, or been told, that sergeant Ramey's film had something to do with the assassination. What had Balmain really known about the film when he'd come to the station with Reno? His mind scampered but the throbbing in his head returned.

"No more drinking," he said as he crossed Elm Street to walk the plaza. He wandered and people-watched for a while. They were all different, but they were all here for a common purpose. It was doubtful that any of them had ever even met President Kennedy. He was just that well-liked. They felt a loss as Dan did, grieving his brother.

Dan looked at his watch and headed back to his car. If they were going to have spaghetti tonight, he'd need fresh hamburger from the grocery.

By the time he had returned home, it was almost three, and just not enough time remained to allow him to grab a nap. He did some cleaning and straightening-up to pass the time and before long decided he needed to head out to pick up his son from school.

Dan rolled up to the drive, leaned across the seat, and released the door handle, giving the door a push to open it. Mark opened it the rest of the way, and threw his books on the floor, beaming.

"How was school, slugger?"

"Oh Dad, it was great!" He started, "At first, I didn't feel right because the kids kept coming up and saying they were sorry about Uncle Dirk. I don't like it when people you know, talk to me like that. I don't like people to, ya' know, feel sorry for me."

Dan shifted into drive, and after looking over his shoulder, moved the car back into the street on their way home. "Well, they were doing what we call, *paying condolences*. It means letting someone know that they are sorry for a certain loss and want to show their friendship." He got to the stop sign and put on his turn signal, "So, everything's okay?"

"Yeah, Dad!" Mark was excited. "That lady was there. We were playing ball out on the playground, and she was standing there. She was so, you know, nice. She told me that everything was going to be alright, and that I was going to be fine."

"What lady? One of your teachers?" Dan asked, making the left turn.

"No, Dad - the lady from the other night. At the theater."

Dan was still thinking about the events of the day and wasn't sure he understood what was just said. "What theater? What are you talking about?"

"It's like I told mom. Christmas night, when we went to see that movie at the Texas Theater. There was a lady that sat behind us with Oswald, the guy that looked like Oswald."

Dan tilted his head to look at his son. "Huh? I still don't know what or who you mean."

"Geez, Dad." Mark smiled in mock frustration. "I told Mom about it. At the movie there was a really nice lady who sat behind us. Her hair was up and she had on a white blouse and gray pants. She was watching the movie with a guy that looked like Oswald. They weren't talking. She just sat there."

He now recalled Millie mentioning it, but he had done his best to make light of it in the hopes that his son had been mistaken. Or confused. "She showed up at your school today? On the playground?"

"Yeah! I knew it was her. She was wearing the same clothes she wore at the theater on Christmas."

"But, she's not a teacher?"

"No. I've only seen her that one night at the theater. I don't know who she is. But, she made me feel better. It's like, I don't know. It's like she really knew that I was going to be okay. I just felt it!"

"What else did you two talk about?" Dan tried to sound as casual as he could.

"Well nothing..." Mark paused in thought..." Now that you mention it, it's like we really didn't actually, uh, talk. I mean I felt her talking to me. But, now that you say it -I don't think we talked about much at all. She just wanted me to know I'd be okay. She said to be myself and trust my feelings."

Dan thought for a moment, "Were there any other kids around when you were with her?"

"Huh uh; it was just the two of us. I saw her on the side of the field smiling, and I felt like she was watching me, so I just walked over to say hi. No big deal."

Dan allowed his thoughts to catch up with him, "You said you saw her sitting with someone at the theater? If she was just sitting in the dark how'd you know she was wearing gray slacks that night?"

Mark wouldn't allow anything to dampen his high spirits. "I don't know. I just know she was. Are we still having spaghetti tonight?"

Dan nodded with a small grin, "Of course!"

Dan drove on in silence for a couple of blocks before deciding to lighten the conversation. "Well, did she say anything about me?"

"Nah..." He grinned, "We just talked about me."

Dan smiled and nodded. "It figures."

<hr />

Fred Balmain shook his head as he looked at his watch. It was half past five and he was going to be late for dinner, again. She'd understand. She was an FBI wife. Pursuant to the Director's instructions, he'd called the movers and the special janitorial company, and then called his staff in one by one to give them the news. He thanked each for their service, reminded them of the need to maintain total security and then gave them their new assignments, which had been sent via TELEX after his conversation with Washington. Scotty was the last of the group.

"Well, shit," he began unceremoniously, "For what it's worth, I really enjoyed working with you, and hope that you can adjust to Miami."

His conversation with Scotty was to be less formal than the ones he'd had with the rest of his unit. Scotty was almost a friend. If you could have friends in this business.

"Miami?" Scotty replied, grinning. "Are you kidding? Do you know how many single women are running around down there looking for someone to marry?" His eyes darted to the window and then back to Balmain. "So what's the real story, boss?"

"I'm not sure I could tell you, even if I knew." He looked at the younger agent, "I thought we had some good leads to follow, but our plug has been pulled. Maybe one day we'll figure out how we fit into the grand scheme, but for now, enjoy your leave." Every agent had been given thirty days of transit leave to close out their affairs in Dallas and get to their new duty station. They'd also been allotted $700.00 for travel and moving expenses.

"See you around, boss, one of these days!" They shook hands and Scotty turned to leave.

As a parting toast, Balmain hoisted an imaginary glass at him, "One of these days!"

When everyone was gone and the movers had loaded the desks, empty file cabinets and telephone equipment, Balmain walked around the hollow space, kicking the phone cables and their Amphenol connectors out of the way to avoid tripping. With his hands on his hips, he stood in the center of the large room that had housed covert FBI activity for the past couple of months.

"What a waste," he said to himself.

He wondered if he'd made a mistake, or worse, violated his loyalty oath, by giving Barnes the duplicate photos of sergeant Ramey, along with the typewritten, but unsigned summary of what they knew about him. Barnes was Secret Service. They'd lost a president. They had every right to know what the FBI knew about the assassination. He recalled the brief conversation at the foot of the Depository earlier that day.

"Here," Balmain had said, passing Barnes the package.

"Thank you. Believe me Fred, you're doing the right thing," he said as he slipped the envelope under the sketches they'd been making of Dealey Plaza. "You and I, we work for the same boss, and I assure you, no one will ever know where this came from."

"I hope not," Balmain said pensively. "I don't know what's going on, but someone is going to great lengths to keep aspects of this investigation quiet. People are dying and disappearing." The two men shook hands again and Balmain admonished, "Take care of yourself."

The janitors would be in at midnight and by 8:00 a.m. tomorrow, the office would be sterile. Like they were never there. He took one last look around and began shutting off the lights. As he headed to the door, he detected the all-too-familiar fragrance in the air. He didn't stop this time, but as he closed the door behind him, he paused and said in a loud whisper, "Fuck you lady! I hope you got what you wanted."

8

WEDNESDAY, APRIL 30, 1975

Once called "The Pearl of the Orient", Saigon was a bustling metropolis with a strong French influence. During this period of unrest, it was considered a wide-open city with crowded streets and a unique and heterogeneous population of more than two and a half million people. Both fascinating and complex, it had become a dangerous city for westerners and their collaborators, with Viet Cong agents and sympathizers surreptitiously causing damage and unrest. When least expected, huge rockets would land and explode in different parts of the city.

Saigon had every problem of most over-crowded cities, and by this time, most of its citizens had little faith in their government. For police, it was a living nightmare. To complicate matters even further it was in a combat zone. Among the Saigon population, were thousands of Americans living and working there, on leave, or passing through. These included: military personnel from various countries, diplomats, civilian workers, and members of the media. To the Americans working there, no spot on earth provided a greater challenge. Diplomatic and security work there had been sensitive, demanding, complex, and now unpredictable.

Mark had done his best to get used to his first posting. Other than boot camp in San Diego, this was the longest he had ever been away from home, and certainly the farthest. Nevertheless, he liked being immersed in the drama of it all, and he wanted to understand the issues that had caused such a drawn out war.

As the North Vietnamese forces continued their advance south, the Saigon population who had supported or worked for the Americans or other western interests for the past decade, saw the end coming quickly. They were looking for a way out. Many had been promised sanctuary in the United States, and were flocking to the embassy and other US diplomatic offices to arrange their exit.

Now, on this Wednesday morning, Lance Corporal Mark Reynolds did the best he could to control his fear as he stared through the gates at the thousands of people on the other side. At nineteen, he was one of the youngest members of the Marine Security Guard Detachment at the US Embassy Saigon. He was worried. He was worried both for himself and for his Marine brothers who wondered how long Saigon would last now that Da Nang had fallen to the North Vietnamese.

Da Nang had been one of the world's busiest aircraft hubs during the Viet Nam War with an average of almost 3,000 aircraft traffic operations every day. That was more than any other airport in the world at that time. Even though U.S. ground combat operations had actually ceased in August 1972, the 3rd Battalion, 21st Infantry Regiment had been the last unit to officially complete their patrols. This remaining force had been known as "Operation Gimlet." After the official withdrawal from the conflict, in the final stage of the conquest of South Vietnam by North Vietnam, Da Nang fell to the communist forces on March 30, 1975.

Mark stared blankly through the steel gates at the mob on the other side, being crushed against the gates by row upon row of people trying to bribe or cajole their way inside the compound. As the choppers began making their lifts that morning, the anxious horde realized that freedom, and a ride to the United States, was only a few feet away. The people left behind would be beaten, killed or sent away for undetermined periods to so-called re-education camps. The Marine Security Guard Detachment was part of the dwindling diplomatic presence remaining in South Viet Nam. Their

role was security, not combat, and Mark had accepted the assignment with great pride. He was now a part of a battalion-sized organization of the United States Marine Corps, whose detachments
provided security at American embassies, consulates and other official United States Government missions such as the NATO headquarters in Belgium.

The USMC had a long history of cooperation with the U.S. State
Department in this provision of security, going back to the early days
of the country. The permanent use of Marines as security guards
had begun with the Foreign Service Act of 1946, which authorized
the Secretary of Navy to assign Marines to serve as support personnel under the supervision of the senior State Department diplomatic officer at an official post.

Mark's primary mission as a Marine Security Guard (MSG) was
to provide security, particularly the protection of classified information and equipment that was important to the national security of
the United States at America. And, in this role, he worked closely
with personnel from the Diplomatic Security Service, especially
Regional Security Officers (RSO's), who were the senior U.S. law enforcement representatives and security attachés at U.S. diplomatic
posts around the world.

He had occasionally been asked to provide security for visiting
American dignitaries and to assist the RSOs in supervising the local
security forces that provided additional security for the exterior of
the embassy. The MSGs fell under operational control of the local
RSO but were still administratively controlled by the Marine Corps
Embassy Security Group.

The secondary mission of his unit was to provide protection
for U.S. citizens and U.S. Government property located within his
designated area during exigent circumstances, which could require
immediate action, such as the mob of Vietnamese people now
pushing up against the embassy gate with crushing force. There had
initially been hundreds. Now, thousands.

It had been chaotic in Saigon since Mark's arrival in September
the previous year. As a part of his acclimatization and orientation

to his new post, he had been assigned to do security inspections of the Embassy compound with more senior enlisted Marines and one of the RSOs. Mark was intensely serious about his new job taking detailed notes, and making highly accurate sketches of everything that the experienced men pointed out during their inspections. They seemed to know their stuff.

The United States Embassy in Saigon was first established in June 1952, and moved into a new building in 1967 in response to a bombing attack that had occurred two years earlier. Due to security concerns, military and diplomatic leaders determined that a new embassy with greater protection should be constructed. They chose a 3.18-acre site known as the Norodom Compound at No 4 Thong Nhut Boulevard at the corner of Thong Nhut and Mac Dinh Chi Street. The American embassy was next to the French embassy, opposite the British embassy, and located near the Presidential Palace.

Although originally designed in early 1965 by the firm Curtis and Davis, their plan had only called for three stories. Due to the increased U.S. commitment in Vietnam, a larger building was immediately needed. As such, in November 1965 the firm Adrian Wilson and Associates were selected to redesign the building, but with six floors.

The construction project employed a workforce of 500 Vietnamese, primarily using materials from the U.S., due to the scarcity of commodities in South Vietnam at the time. Despite that, the sand and gravel used in the concrete mix, along with the walkway tiles, and the bricks used in all the interior walls were sourced from Vietnam. The embassy was opened on September 29, 1967, after more than two years of construction and cost a total of 2.6 million US dollars.

The embassy consisted of two separate compounds: a consular compound sealed off by a separate wall and steel gate, and the embassy compound containing the Embassy Chancery building. Behind the Chancery was a parking lot, and a two-story villa used as a residence by the Mission Coordinator, who served as a civilian assistant to the Ambassador. There were two entry gates: a pedestrian entrance on Thong Nhut Boulevard and a vehicle entrance on Mac Dinh Chi Street that were included in the security assessments.

The new Chancery was a distinctive six-story white concrete building, with a concrete lattice facade that served to both cool the building and deflect rockets and other projectiles. Due to both aesthetics and security, the Chancery was set back from the street, and was enclosed in the walled compound that measured 437 feet by 318 feet, which brought its area to just over three acres. The structure was located 60 feet inside the compound, protected from both streets by an 8 feet wall with a 6 inches-thick mixture of cement and marble chips. The lattice facade extended from the first story to the roof, covering the entire building in a protective white terrazzo sunscreen. It was separated from the concrete walls and the shatterproof Plexiglas windows of the chancery by five feet of space.

The chancery was designed to accommodate a staff of 200, with nearly 50,000 square feet of office space for 140 offices. There were also executive offices on the third floor for the Ambassador's office and other high-ranking members of the Mission. Thankfully, it was air conditioned, had its own water filtration system, and at the rear of the compound, had a power plant consisting of four 350 kilowatt generators. The chancery also had small helipad on the roof. A concrete awning extended from the Chancery out over the pedestrian entrance on Thong Nhut Boulevard.

The old embassy on Hàm Nghi Boulevard remained in use as an embassy annex. During his orientation, Mark asked good questions, and the senior Marines were impressed with his maturity and basic understanding of security principles.

But now, facing the throng pressing against the gates, he tried not to look into their eyes. He did not want to feel their desperation. Neither did he want them to see the fear in his. He wished he was back inside on Post One.

At the embassy, Post 1 was the official designation of the primary interior security post. And, traditionally, it was in the lobby or main entrance of the building housing the Chief of Mission. This post was also the principal command station for all access control to the building. It was equipped with the latest in security technology including closed circuit television, radio communications, intrusion detection and fire alarm controls.

Up until two weeks earlier, Mark and his teammates had rotated through their assignments and spent their off-hours training in reaction drills, known as *Reacts*, for emergencies such as fires, bomb threats, intruders, riots and demonstrations. If they were off the compound when notified, they would drop everything and assemble in the React Room to receive orders and direction from the detachment commander. This room provided not only a storage area for weapons, ammunition, and personal protective equipment, but also as a safe and secure position to suit-up for any arising React event. Each potential React scenario was practiced and had its own standardized drill from which the MSGs could modify to fit the actual situation.

The team had grown closer in these final days of the US presence there. They were brothers. He joked that he was the only Texan on a team of New Englanders, and they made fun of his accent. He reminded them frequently that if they ever came to Dallas, then they would be the ones with the funny accents. They were impressed with his ability to understand what was going on around them as the North Vietnamese continued to advance south.

For a mere Lance Corporal, he seemed to have the mind of a senior strategist. He also had an uncanny ability to pick specific cards out of a deck, a trait that had occasionally earned him some additional spending money during the off-hours with his team. Some of his team mates jokingly called him Kreskin after the television mentalist.

He didn't mind the nickname because everyone in his unit had one. However, Mark had not told anyone about the dreams. He was a US Marine, and Marines didn't dream about combat; they assessed intelligence and responded appropriately and effectively. But from his arrival in country near the end of September, he had been plagued by recurring dreams of slaughter.

During the night of March 12, he had awakened in a cold sweat after seeing a mob of humanity slaughtered on a jungle highway, with a rotating "7" spinning over the top of the imagery. At first, he didn't understand it, but within days he would learn of the evacuation of the Central Highlands and the massacre of refugees in what would come to be known as the *Convoy of Tears.*

On March 10, 1975, three well-equipped North Vietnamese army divisions, laid siege to the city of Ban Me Thuot, which was defended by two reinforced regiments of the South Vietnamese Army. Despite a barrage of artillery fire, the South Vietnamese army fought well. However, they were worn down and, by March 12, the People's Army had essentially captured the city.

Unfortunately, it was at Ban Me Thuot that South Vietnamese Army officers began diverting helicopters from their military missions to pick up their families and flee to the south. This put a serious dent in the morale of their troops, and also gave US intelligence a foreshadowing of what was to come. Thousands of South Vietnamese families then began to flee the countryside, crowding the main roads and the pathways in a panicked flight for the coast. The exodus ultimately jammed highways and seaports unlike anything the region had ever witnessed. The refugees included not only those civilians who had helped the South's army or the Americans, but also a civilian population who had no reason to expect bad treatment from North Vietnam's army. They were just trying to get out.

The other disastrous effect this exhausting flight had on the South Vietnamese was that soldiers were leaving their posts to gather their families and escort them to safety. While this may have been a normal human response to the crisis, it accelerated the disintegration of the South's ability to command their units.

Leadership in the Army of the Republic of Viet Nam (ARVN) believed that the focus of the north's attack would be Pleiku, in the Central Highlands. But, upon the fall of Ban Me Thuot on March 14, they secretly ordered the withdrawal of the South's forces from the Central Highlands. In hindsight, this was a disastrous error. No one had developed any plans for the withdrawal, and the ill-timed directive to leave had the same effect as if the North Vietnamese Army had initiated it intentionally.

And as a result, Route 7B began to look like a miles-long parking lot, with every kind of motorized vehicle pressed into service, including buses, tanks, trucks, armored personnel carriers, private cars. Each vehicle was overloaded with civilians and military personnel of all ages from infants to geriatrics, often with people riding on the running boards or rooftops. Thousands of others took what they could carry and joined the convoy on foot, without food or water, for fifteen days. It was revoltingly hideous, as many of those persons not starved or dehydrated during their trip were victims of multiple rocket attacks and ambushes along the route. Of the estimated 400,000 civilians who initially took part in the march, only a handful actually reached their destinations in the Mekong region.

As the recurring dreams grew more realistic, Mark felt compelled to mention the context of them to Staff Sergeant Malcolm, his team leader, in a way that didn't make himself look crazy. He had approached the seasoned Marine near the React Room as he was typing a report on the morning of April 27.

"Hey Staff Sergeant, got a minute?"

"Yeah, Reynolds. What do you need?" the sergeant replied. His demeanor had softened towards the new addition to the MSG team, and with the pending chaos, he had lost that rigid, intense air about him that Mark had first seen upon his arrival several months earlier.

"I know I'm the new guy and all, but does the Major have a plan to get us out of here if Tan Son Nhut gets taken out?" Mark stared at his boots.

Malcom looked up from his typewriter, "What do you mean?"

Reynolds dragged the toe of his boot on the tile. "They're all around us." He began referring to the North Vietnamese troops. "It seems like they're letting us know that they are coming and if we want to leave, we've gotta leave now."

Malcolm regarded the young Lance Corporal with a degree of

respect that he wouldn't have accorded other subordinates on his team. After losing nearly a hundred US dollars on bets about whether or not he could find the three of clubs or the Jack of diamonds in a brand new deck of cards, he decided to cut his losses and start betting with LCPL Reynolds. "Scuttlebutt? What are you hearing?"

Malcolm knew that young Reynolds was freakishly accurate at these card games. But, having been raised in Boston, Malcolm had usually been one step ahead of the juvenile justice system through much of high school. He thought everything was a scam. He didn't have to know how the scam worked, just which way to bet.

"Nothing in particular." He stared at the tile under his boot. "They've taken everything else around us. They're sending a message to us to get out while we can. I'm just wondering how we get out of here if the airport is shut down?"

Malcolm was concerned, but direct. He didn't have all the answers, but he couldn't allow gossip and speculation to distract his team. "The Major has a pretty tight plan. In the event that our access to Ton Son Nhut is cut off, we evac from the roof with choppers. The Ambassador just has to give the word."

"Choppers?" Mark thought, then replied out loud, "There are thousands of people standing out there who expect us to get them out of here when the balloon goes up. The CH46 holds about twenty-five Marines, and the 53 can hold about fifty, maybe fifty-five. Between our teams and the 9th Marine Amphibious Brigade (MAB) guys, there are about a hundred of us." He looked up with his eyebrows raised. "That's a lot of choppers!"

The Staff Sergeant considered the numbers, recognizing the additional load created by the members of the MAB that had been sent to augment their security force on April 25. "Trust me Reynolds, the Major has a plan." Malcolm dismissed the Lance Corporal but told him to stay in contact and stay positive. He trusted the young Marine's intuition.

On April 28, a little past 6:00 p.m., three A-37 Dragonflies piloted by former South Vietnamese pilots, who had defected to the

Vietnamese People's Air Force during the fall of Da Nang, dropped six 250 pound bombs on the base, damaging aircraft and several buildings. South Vietnamese F-5s took off in pursuit, but they were unable to intercept the A-37s.

After the attack, C-130s leaving Tan Son Nhut reported receiving communist .51 caliber and 37 mm anti-aircraft fire, while sporadic PAVN rocket and artillery attacks also started to hit the airport and base. Because of this, C-130 flights were stopped temporarily after the air attack and wouldn't resume until the next day.

At about 4:00 a.m. on April 29, a C-130E, flown by a crew from the 776th Tactical Airlift Squadron, was destroyed by a 122 mm rocket while taxiing to pick up refugees after offloading cargo at the base. The crew evacuated the burning aircraft on the taxiway and departed the airfield on another C-130 that had previously landed. This was to be the last United States Air Force fixed-wing aircraft to leave Tan Son Nhut.

At 7:00 that morning, Major General Homer D. Smith, the Defense Attaché, advised Ambassador Martin that fixed wing evacuations would cease, and that Operation Frequent Wind, the helicopter evacuation of U.S. personnel and at-risk Vietnamese should commence. It appeared that Mark's prediction had come true.

Ambassador Martin, however, refused to accept General Smith's recommendation and instead insisted on visiting Tan Son Nhut to survey the situation for himself. Martin, who saw the departure from the region as a diplomatic failure, was not persuaded that the airfield was in fact disabled. Wishful thinking perhaps.

Finally though, after seeing firsthand the level of destruction caused by the airstrike and subsequent rocket attacks, Martin became convinced that Tan Son Nhut was no longer suitable for use by fixed wing aircraft. Thus, he reluctantly initiated Operation Frequent Wind just before eleven that morning.

To the end, Ambassador Martin had remained optimistic that a negotiated settlement could be reached whereby the United States would not have to pull out of South Vietnam and, in an effort to avert defeatism and panic he specifically instructed Major James

Kean, Commanding Officer of the Marine Security Guard Battalion, that he could not begin to remove the trees and shrubbery which were preventing the use of the Embassy parking lot as a helicopter landing zone.

Upon learning of these events, Staff Sergeant Malcom sent for Reynolds right away. "Okay, Reynolds, I have a meeting with the Non Commissioned Officer in Charge (NCOIC) and the Major in about fifteen minutes. What the fuck do you know, and how the fuck do you know it?"

"I know I'm glad we moved our shit out of Marine House!" Mark replied. The Marine House located at 204 Hong Thap Tu, during Mark's brief 6-month tour in Saigon prior to the evacuation, quartered the MSG Detachment, and was named Marshall Hall in memory of CPL James C. Marshall killed during the Tet Offensive. "We're not going back there."

"We're airlifting asses out of here as fast as we can," Malcolm said, "Care to place a bet on how we're going to get out of this?"

Mark thought for a moment before answering. "We're going to make it - the Marines and the staff - but..." his voice trailed off.

"So, if the Major gives me a chance to say something, what do I say?"

Mark stared at the floor, "We need to move food, water and ammo to the roof, right now. But, we gotta do it quietly. If people see us setting up for a final stand up there, they'll rush the gates."

All of the Marines knew that South Vietnamese leadership was out of options, and they had abandoned any unrealistic notion that the Communists might negotiate some sort of deal with Minh, who had just assumed power as the newest President. The reality was that North Vietnamese regular army troops and tanks had now surrounded Saigon, which had become a city in panic. Most western politicians, other than some of the French, realized that Minh had held communist leanings for too long and would just give South Viet Nam to the north as soon as they took power.

Mark continued, "There won't be a peace. We have to get out today."

Malcolm collected his paperwork, and stood up behind his desk. "Get some Marines and clear the trees out of the compound. I'll get the okay from the Major. We need an LZ pronto."

From 10:00 a.m. to 12:00 p.m., Mark and his fellow Marines worked quickly to cut down trees and move vehicles to create a Landing Zone in the embassy parking lot behind the Chancery building. Two LZs were now available in the embassy compound. The rooftop would be used for UH-1s and CH-46 Sea Knights, and the new parking lot LZ for the heavier CH-53 Sea Stallions.

As the Marines cleared the rubble from the parking lot, Mark reflected on recent political events that seemed doomed to failure. Ambassador Martin had done his best to shore up President Thieu, lobbying for additional US military and financial aid. His efforts were sincere, but they delayed the implementation of plans to evacuate American and South Vietnamese supporters of the administration from Saigon until it was far too late. Now they were in the shit.

Fortunately, two evacuation operations were already in action, and the execution of the third was in the hands of professional troops. The first of these, Operation Babylift, had been conducted between April 4 and 14, and some 2,600 Vietnamese children were taken safely to the United States to be adopted. But, Babylift was marred by a tragic accident on the first flight of the operation, April 4, 1975.

A C-5A transport had taken off and climbed to 23,000 feet when an explosive decompression blew out a huge section of the aft cargo door, cutting the control cables to the elevator and rudder. The pilot did a masterful job of flying the airplane, using power for pitch and ailerons for directional control. He managed to bring the aircraft back to within five miles of Tan Son Nhut, where he made a semi-controlled crash. However, of the 382 people aboard, 206 were killed, most of them children.

Nevertheless, all subsequent flights were made safely. The Babylift operation later came under criticism for its overt attempt to create good public relations, and for some of the criteria used in selecting the children. In the end, Babylift could be evaluated as yet another good-hearted attempt by the United States to do the right thing under difficult circumstances.

The second evacuation had been going on quietly for many days, relying on standard civilian and military airlift and virtually anything that would float. More than 50,000 people had been flown out by fixed wing aircraft, while another 73,000 left by sea. About 5,000 Americans were evacuated as well as everyone who wished to leave, including many foreigners. South Vietnamese who were airlifted out were for the most part people whose service to their government or to the United States made them candidates for execution by the Communists.

By the morning of April 29, there were approximately 10,000 people gathered around the Embassy, while some 2,500 evacuees were already in the embassy and consular compounds. The two major evacuation points chosen for Operation Frequent Wind were the DAO Compound adjacent to Tan Son Nhut Airport for American civilian and Vietnamese evacuees and the Embassy for Embassy staff. But, with Tan Son Nhut out of action, that left only the embassy grounds for the extraction.

The commanding officer of the Marine forces gathered Malcolm and the rest of his staff together to update them regarding his communications with his chain of command. The Major gazed out the window of the abandoned Secretary's office on the second floor of the U.S. embassy. The darkening sky took on the color of a dull metal, like aluminum, and the first of the intimidating clouds coming in from the sea had settled overhead.

The Officer scanned the Marine Security Guard duty roster. He had 46 U.S. Marine security guards here in the embassy compound, 15 across town at the U.S. Defense Attaché's Office, and the remains of two men killed in an earlier rocket attack at the Seventh Day Adventist Hospital somewhere in between. He shook his head.

"Well, as you know, they're playing our song," he said, referring to Bing Crosby's *White Christmas*. The supposedly covert signal for the evacuation of Saigon had been worked out some weeks earlier. An announcer for the Armed Forces Radio Network would read the words, "The temperature in Saigon is 105 degrees and rising." The code phrase was to be followed by a Bing Crosby recording of *I'm Dreaming of a White Christmas* playing continuously. The signal was known to all Americans, civilian and military, and therefore, to just about everyone else in the city.

He tried to smile. "As should be expected when dealing with civilians, we have a clusterfuck here. General Carey and Admiral Steele had been under the impression that everyone had already been extracted from here by bus, and convoyed to the DAO. That being the presumption, General Carey had scheduled only two air-lifts for the embassy, to accommodate ambassador Martin and a smaller remaining Marine contingent."

He looked around the room and noted the quizzical looks. "Obviously, I told them that we need choppers here, lots of them. In addition to the embassy staff, our Marines, and the 1,000-plus refugees already inside the walls, we're getting estimates that there could be as many as 10,000 Vietnamese surrounding the compound right now."

Seeing no questions thus far, he continued, "Apparently, the ambassador was reluctant to report specific numbers, but managed to relay that the embassy evacuation had not proceeded according to plan. When he told General Carey that there were hundreds of people camped on the grounds awaiting retrieval, well, you could say that Carey was...uh...miffed. He was under the impression that the embassy, if not now emptied by buses, soon would be. Carey has radioed Admiral Steele and informed him that an immediate adjustment in helicopter priorities is now needed."

The Major presented the withdrawal plan and got confirmation from the men on his staff that they knew what their jobs were, and they were prepared and equipped to carry them out. Satisfied that there were no other questions, he simply said, "Dismissed." Then, everyone left the room to get started on their respective tasks.

It was well after noon when the Marines in the compound heard the roar and then saw the first U.S. Navy A-7 Corsairs and Air Force F-4 Phantom jet fighters, inbound to provide cover for the first wave of *Marine Sea Stallions, Sea Knights*, and *Air Force Jolly Green Giants*. These squadrons, that would include 36 rescue helicopters, would also deposit an additional battalion of Fleet Marines as a show of force to secure the grounds.

By now, the leading edge of the rain squalls had formed a curtain falling across the eastern edge of Saigon, and Marine pilots were reporting almost zero visibility. Seventh Fleet air traffic controllers tracked the rain clouds on radar while simultaneously remaining alert for American aircraft straying out of the two predetermined corridors in and out of the city.

The Michigan corridor, at 6,500 feet, was reserved for inbound aircraft, and the Ohio corridor, at 5,500 feet, for outbound. Soon enough, both pilots and air traffic controllers knew, the monsoon clouds would force their aircraft below the flight corridors and down into range of small-arms fire and rocket-propelled grenades.

A light drizzle began to fall on the embassy compound. From the edge of the parking lot, the Major watched the helicopters overfly the embassy. It looked like they were headed toward the DAO near Tan Son Nhut. He went back inside and picked up the telephone, and was patched through to the DAO's Commanding Officer to let him know that aircraft were enroute to his location.

He then took an elevator to the roof where he located the NCOIC and said, "Choppers are on their way!" Both men peered over the edge at the parking lot. "I want the *fifty-threes* down there and the *forty-sixes* up here."

"Aye, sir!" the Top Sergeant replied.

And so it had begun. What would become the largest aerial evacuation in history was officially underway. But, it was almost 6 p.m. before the Marines in the compound and on the embassy roof, heard the washboard thumping of the helicopter rotors in the distance. A moment later a flight of four Sea Knights could be seen banking hard and lining up in formation for successive descents. The Marines had already cordoned off four groups of refugees, each consisting of 20 to 25 people, and were herding them up the stairs to the roof for boarding on the empty CH-46s. Not long after, the CH-53s could be seen approaching the parking lot.

The helicopters descended at 10-minute intervals. They found the top of the vertical funnel, slowed their forward progress, hovered for an instant, then one at a time made the dizzying 70-foot drop, as if hurtling down an amusement park water slide. It was tricky. If a helicopter crashed in the parking lot, there was nothing with which to move it, and thus no more choppers would be able to land.

The process ran continuously until the sun started going down and pilots grew concerned about visibility - especially the pilots who had to land in the parking lot. The pilot of one of the last choppers to make it in to the parking lot landing zone told the Major that Task Force 76 commander had ordered all CH-53 evacuations to cease at complete darkness. They might be able to get on and off the roof, but there was no way they could chance a blind vertical descent to the parking lot.

The Major told the pilot to relay a message to the Admiral that he would light the parking lot up like Broadway. He then ordered his Marines to round up and fuel every vehicle remaining in the compound, get them cranked up and get their headlights pointed at the landing zone. Within minutes, headlights illuminated the LZ.

Sometime around midnight, a corporal tapped Mark on his shoulder and said, "Top says to relieve you. You need to fall out and get some chow and rest...one hour." The corporal indicated the door to the embassy raising his fist and thumb over his shoulder.

Mark was dazed with fatigue, but knew that he wouldn't be able to sleep. He found the room where they'd laid out some C-rations and water, and he grabbed an olive-drab can of something off the table. He found a chair near the corner of the able and used his P-38 field can opener to chip away at the lid. It wasn't until he opened it that he realized he selected spaghetti and meatballs. It didn't matter. To him, all C-Rat entrees tasted the same. They looked pretty much the same too, having been compressed in a can for five to ten years.

He made sure that he drank plenty of water, as well as some of the Kool-Aid that someone had mixed, and when he finished his dinner, made sure his canteens were filled. It might be a while before any of them ate or drank again. He visited the head, and then returned to the line out near the gates.

"That was a fast hour," the corporal said with a sly grin.

"Can't sleep, and I don't want to wake up in a prison camp!" Mark replied trying to force a smile.

By 1:00 a.m., the vectoring helicopter pilots were having difficulty making out the headlights that had begun to dim as their vehicles ran out of fuel. It took Mark and his buddies a while to realize that the deafening rotor noise of the choppers had ceased. And, as he looked upwards towards the roof and the sky, he wondered if the evacuation had stopped.

It would be a while before word reached the compound that someone in Washington had ordered the flights temporarily suspended out of a concern for safety. Out in the Fleet, there was a heated discussion going on, with General Carey reminding the Admiral that mandatory rest time for the pilots notwithstanding, if they didn't pick up the pace of the evacuation then the only troops that would be greeting them upon their return to the Embassy would be North Vietnamese.

With that realization, every pilot that could be found on every ship, whether they were eating, sleeping or taking a dump, were summoned and ordered back into the air, and the first Marine squadrons began to ascend from the decks. Dawn was four hours away, and this was their last chance to get everyone they could out of Saigon.

It was about 2:15 in the morning when hope returned with two Marine H-46s vectoring in towards the Embassy. When the first one touched down on the roof, the pilot told the Major, "Nineteen more flights behind me, sir. That's it."

There were more than 800 more evacuees scattered around the compound, not counting approximately 200 Marines, and a handful of American civilians and other service members. The math indicated that some hard decisions had to be made.

Ambassador Martin had stoically chosen to remain behind in defiance of President Ford's director order to evacuate. But at 0330 hours, General Carey received a flash message from the White House that Ford wanted Martin out of there immediately. The message also said that no more Vietnamese were to be evacuated.

As the CH46, call sign Lady-Ace 09, touched down on the embassy roof, the pilot grabbed a grease pencil from his pocket and began to write on the laminated card on the clipboard strapped to his leg. The simple note he showed the Major read, "Ambassador Will Depart With Me. Now."

The Major told the pilot that he needed confirmation, so the Crew Chief handed him a headset. General Carey was on the other end, and told him that the order had come directly from the president. "The Ambassador is leaving now; if he refuses, arrest him. But get him on that chopper!" There was a pause and then he added, "All remaining lifts, will be limited to U.S. and amphibious personnel."

The Major respectfully reminded the General, "General, my Marines are on the wall, and then there's the front door of the embassy. Between my Marines and that front door are some 400 refugees still awaiting evacuation. I want you to understand clearly that when I pull my Marines back to the embassy, those people will be left behind."

Carey's voice crackled over the air. "And I want you, Major, to understand that the president of the United States directs you to do just that."

"Aye aye, Sir!" The Major handed the headset back to the crew chief.

Minutes later, a demoralized and hunched Ambassador Martin shuffled toward the helicopter. One of his bodyguards handed him the folded embassy flag, and the ambassador stepped into the waiting *Sea Knight*. As the 46 lifted off of the roof, the pilot keyed his microphone and relayed "Tiger is out." And, thus ended the diplomatic mission in Saigon on April 30, 1975 at 0458 hours.

The Major sprinted back over to the Master Gunnery Sergeant

who had been watching from the corner of the roof below the heli-pad, "No more CH-53s, Just Americans now. Get them to the roof."

Within minutes, the squad leaders were briefed, and they in turn passed the orders to each of their Marines on the wall. "On the Major's signal, we will withdraw calmly in a semicircle toward the embassy front door. No running. No shouting."

Staff Sergeant Malcolm repeated the command to Mark, who had not taken his eyes off the wall. "Got it? On my signal, withdraw calmly backwards until we get into a semicircle. We're backing into the building, and no one is going to follow us in."

Mark nodded, his attention focused on the crowd pushing against the gates. "Aye, Staff Sergeant!"

Moments later, the Major signaled and they began to form three concentric half-moons of about fifteen men each. As the entire mass of Marines edged slowly backward, the 400 Vietnamese in the compound began to sense that something was happening.

For a moment it seemed as if events were surreally transpiring in slow motion. The Vietnamese stared blankly at the American troops as the outermost perimeter, its flanks collapsing in on itself, backed into the lobby. Perhaps half of the Marines in the second perimeter had made it inside before a giant roar drowned out even the sounds of artillery falling on the city's outskirts.

On the command, Mark fell back to the position he'd been instructed, taking his spot in the semi-circle around the door. At each signal to move, he checked to his left and right to make sure he was still providing the necessary security coverage, and back-stepped until it was his time to go through the door.

"Here they come!" someone shouted, and the front gates immediately gave way.

Once inside the embassy, the Marines slammed the double doors and bolted them. They rode the elevators to the sixth floor, and once the squad leaders had done a headcount to make sure they had everyone, locked the power off, threw the keys down the elevator shafts, and made for the stairwells. With the outside perimeter abandoned, it was now a race against time; a race against whoever would be next to storm up the embassy stairs. A couple of the Marines tossed tear gas canisters down the stairwell to slow the crowd.

There were about 60 Marines and a few men from other services scattered about the rooftop. "I figure it will take three, maybe four runs at most," the Major said to the men. It did not take long for hundreds of angry South Vietnamese to flood up the embassy stairwell, breaking the chain link barriers as they came. The Marines heard the gates crash, one by one, until the mob was directly outside the barricaded steel door leading to the roof.

In the distance, the Marines heard the beating rotors of a helicopter approaching. The poor souls in the stairwell heard it too. There was a brief pause in the pandemonium, and then the door's hinges creaked and began to buckle.

As the first *Sea Knight's* rear wheels bounced onto the helipad, the sky was a graduated dark blue, somewhere between night and dawn. The chopper's engine reduced power, and the pilot leaned out and grinned.

Up above, the last pilot in line to land looked off in the distance towards the southeast. For a brief moment, he was certain that the sun had risen pocked with black dots, like a swarm of angry bees. He realized that the "bees" darkening the skies above the South China Sea were hundreds of South Vietnamese helicopters fleeing the coast and heading towards the fleet. The chopper in front of him lifted off and he maneuvered in to set his down.

After doing a brief headcount, the Top looked at the Major. "They'll never get us all in, sir."

The Major agreed, "Top," he said. "Give me nine guys I can bet my life on. We'll hold."

When the CH46 was loaded and ready to lift off, the pilot signaled a thumbs-up. But as he was checking his control panel, the major walked to the cockpit. The pilot, seeing him approach, pulled the headset from his ear and leaned out the window.

"Make sure you get back for us," the Major yelled over the noise of the engines. "Don't leave us here!"

The pilot nodded and the chopper lifted off and headed towards the sea. The remaining Marines were momentarily silent. They had all heard the stories about North Vietnamese prison camps and the insane treatment of Americans. It wasn't supposed to end like this.

"Everybody bring it in," one of the sergeants yelled.

One by one the Marines gathered about him. Each man's thoughts were polluted by fatigue, worry and general fear of the unknown. There was only one way out of Saigon and that was on a chopper. One asked, "You think the fleet's even still out there?"

"Of course it is," another replied.

"I ain't ending up in no camp," said yet another, who motioned toward one of the machine guns. "I got my spot picked out."

As each Marine spoke, Mark's head darted back and forth as if at a tennis match, absorbing what they were saying and trying not to let his anxiety make a bad situation worse.

"We better take a vote." one of the sergeants said. He had no doubt how it would come out. But he wanted to make it officia so that each man who remained had a chance to speak his mind.

One by one, they each voted to fight.

The Major looked over the rampart and checked his watch. It had been just over an hour.

Then suddenly, two of the guys spotted it simultaneously; a white contrail standing out against the blue sky far to the southeast.

"Major!"

As the Major raised his binoculars, he couldn't believe his eyes. There was a single inbound CH-46 being escorted by four Marine AH-Cobra gunships that were flying cover formations on the compass points, crisscrossing in attack formation every half mile. "Here comes rescue with a can of ass-whipping on the side!"

The sniping turned into a barrage as the chopper banked for its final approach and the CH-46 set its large black tires down on the rooftop helipad. Its crew chief dropped the tailgate. The glass in the side windows had been shot out.

The Major ran to the cockpit and shouted above the beating blades, "Waitin' for you. Didn't think you were coming."

The pilot grinned and gave the thumbs up. The Cobra gunships, nosed down for optimal firing, swooped in like hawks above the embassy. High above them, a Navy A-7 Corsair attack jet flew a pattern of interlacing circles, leaving a vapor trail as a sign of its presence.

The Major led the Marines up the ramp. "Pop the gas!" someone yelled, and a Gunnery Sergeant pulled the pins on two canisters of tear gas. He rolled them out the gunner's door. They hissed, tumbled off the helipad, and came to a stop.

However, the deployment of tear gas at that precise time might have been a mistake, as the rotors were sucking the gas vapors into the cockpit and the cabin of the helicopter. The pilots were momentarily blinded. The helicopter hopped and lurched, its tires bouncing once, twice, three times off the landing zone.

Through the fog, the Top could just make out the door to the roof. It buckled, and then broke, and the mob began to surge through.

Both pilots' eyes were red with fatigue and the effects of the tear gas, but in a moment most of it had blown off. They could see if they squinted hard enough. They had to get out of there now. Just as the mob surged up the outside staircase and onto the hot roof, the pilot coaxed all the power he could out of the engines.

The crew chief flipped his cigarette out of the ramp as the tear gas began to swirl around the helicopter, and the pilot applied the throttle, the tandem engines roaring to full life. It was something to dampen the screams of the people below. The CH46 began to lift off of the roof of the embassy, and the Marines on board strained to look out the windows to catch one last look at their mission. They had done their job. They were going home, mission accomplished. It was now 0753 hours.

Being one of the last to board, Mark looked out of the open ramp at the rear of the helicopter and for just a brief moment, saw her standing there. She was standing on the roof for Christ sakes, smiling. How had no one else seen her? She was beautiful: a raven-haired brown-eyed goddess, in her gray slacks and white blouse, and grey suede high heels. Why the hell would anyone be in high heels in Saigon today? He thought he remembered her from somewhere, but couldn't think right now. He was exhausted. As the aircraft banked to starboard, he could see her, just as plain as day. Smiling, and telling him, "See, I told you, you'd be okay!"

9

MONDAY, APRIL 25, 1977

Mark Reynolds strode proudly up the sidewalk towards the white doors on the two story red brick building. It was a beautiful day, and the sharp crease in his khaki shirt cut through the brand new sergeant stripes on his sleeve. He had been told to report to the first floor conference room in Edson Hall at 0800 hours and he was eight minutes early. He hated being late for anything.

Built in 1955, Edson Hall had been named for Medal of Honor recipient, Major General Merritt Austin Edson, and housed the Marine Corps Officer Communications School. The famed leader of Edson's Raiders, General Edson had been a Marine hero throughout WWII and a vocal proponent of the criticality of efficient communications in combat.

Mark was still a bit confused by his orders, since he was neither an officer, nor a communications specialist. However, a week earlier, his Company Commander had convinced him that this might be a unique career opportunity for him to work on a classified project. During the brief conversation, Captain McElroy was supportive of the assignment, but did not seem to know many details about the job.

"Communications, sir?" Reynolds asked. "But sir, I'm an infantry guy."

Captain McElroy flipped the pages in Mark's personnel file,

two-hole punched at the top and held in place by brown metal fasteners. "Every Marine is an infantry guy!" He flipped a couple of pages back and folded them behind the file so that he could lay it flat on his desk. "According to the request that filtered down from the Commandant, Intel is looking for people who have demonstrated superior intuitive skills on the battlefield. According to Gunny Malcolm, and your subsequent commanders since returning to the States, you are the most intuitive person they could think of."

Mark smiled. He knew Staff Sergeant Malcolm would be promoted after the chaos in Saigon. Mark owed him a congratulatory phone call when he was finished with the captain. "Thank you sir…I think. I'm not sure what my, uh, intuition has to do with commo or Intel."

"Apparently someone in the Pentagon thinks that it's an important attribute. And, you see these?" he asked, pointing at the captain's bars on his collar. "These mean I'm middle management. My boss tells me that they want Sergeant Reynolds to report to Edson Hall at Marine Corps Base Quantico Virginia next Monday at 0800 hours to learn about Communications as a secondary Military Occupational Specialty. Sergeant Reynolds, do you know what my answer to them is?"

"Yes, sir," Mark replied, appreciating the subtle sarcasm.

"That is precisely right young man." The captain smiled. "Look Sergeant, I really don't know what this is about, but what they told me is that this is a classified op, you're suited for it, and you might actually enjoy it. It's thirteen weeks out of your life, and if you decide you hate it, let me know, and the Fleet will welcome you back."

Mark shrugged, "Well sir, Staff Sergeant, uh, I mean Gunny. Malcolm said he would take care of me after 'Nam. Maybe this is his idea of taking care of me."

"Great!" Captain McElroy said, closing the file. "Give this to the First Sergeant on the way out and have him get your ass to Quantico."

Mark snapped to attention. "Aye, aye sir!" He executed a perfect about-face turn and marched out of the captain's office.

"Ooh rah!" the Captain responded as he reached for his telephone.

He dialed the number that his Brigade Commander had directed him to call immediately after the meeting. A female answered on the third ring. "Seven one two one."

The Captain's comments were succinct. "This is McElroy in Norfolk, please let him know that Reynolds is on his way." He frowned as he replaced the handset in the cradle of the black desk phone. Frustrated and slightly resentful of having to give up his men on a whim from the Pentagon, he had complied with the request. His duty was done.

Now, Mark's high gloss Corfam shoes beat out a soft thump on the tile floor that echoed off the concrete walls. He paused inside the door to see if there was a directory of sorts, but then moved on. The building wasn't that big, and he could hear voices near the end of the hall to his right, coming from an open door.

When he got to the doorway he was surprised to find a short, slightly stocky dark-haired woman in her early forties standing behind a podium at the front of the room. Inside, seated at some of the tables were two other Marines, both enlisted: an Army Warrant officer, and a Navy Chief, all at separate tables, and a man and a woman in civilian clothes, who sat together.

"Sergeant Reynolds reporting, Ma'am." he said as he entered the room.

"Hi Mark! Please come in, we've been expecting you. And there's no need for formalities here." She had a pleasant way about her. And a slight accent. "Please find a seat anywhere, and we'll get started."

There were ten tables, each with two chairs, and only seven attendees present. Since the only woman in the class was seated with the other civilian, Mark found a table along the right side of the room near the front. So much for opportunity. He opened his Samsonite briefcase, and pulled a notebook and pen out before he slid it under the table.

She smiled, "I guess some introductions are in order since most, if not all of you are wondering what the hell you're doing in a Communications class, and who the hell is the Middle-Eastern broad up front." She smiled as everyone laughed politely.

"To begin with, my name is Yasmina Sheppard. I was born in Beirut forty-some, oh hell, let's say thirty-some years ago. I moved to the United States in 1955 with my husband, who was a Marine. I have no military experience. Well, no uniformed military service, anyway, other than being married to one. He was killed in Da Nang in 1968, while I was pregnant with our second daughter. By education and occupation, I am, well, a scientific journalist now, living and working in California."

"We're going to be covering some really novel concepts of communications this week. It might make some of you uncomfortable." She paused, "So, if you thought you were here to learn about the PRC 10 radio or how to assemble a two-niner-something antenna, you'll be disappointed. Also, as far as intelligence work, I have never owned a decoder ring, I don't know how to shoot a gun, and I've never even seen a Minox spy camera."

She took a sip of coffee from a mug emblazoned with the Eagle, Globe and Anchor insignia. "And, if any of you must know, I prefer Sean Connery to Roger Moore and that…who was that Australian guy?"

"George Lazenby!" Army shouted with a smile.

"Yeah, him." She grinned. "Nevertheless, a couple of years ago the Department of Defense became interested in a particular mode of espionage communications that had not yet made the papers. It was quite controversial, and they would have thumbed their nose at it, if it weren't for the fact that our traditional intelligence channels were reporting that the Russians were already using it against us."

She took another sip of coffee, and then picked up a stack of papers from the table in front of her. "I am passing around the standard US Government Non-Disclosure agreement, which you will need to sign and give back. This will probably be the first of several that you will sign as you continue on with the program and are briefed on a variety of classified subjects."

One by one, she slid the documents in front of each attendee, "Each of you already has a Top Secret clearance. The material in this program will be classified at a higher level. And to complicate things, our clients, different agencies within the federal government, will often have you sign one for each project with which you're affiliated."

By the time she got to the back of the room, the people in front had signed their agreements and passed them to the center. She collected them and as she checked the names on each one, she continued, "I am not a US Government employee. I am a US Government contractor employed by an academic institution on the west coast. After your initial assessment period, if you continue to be affiliated with this project, you will retain your current military rank, pay and benefits, but you will be working for us full time."

Satisfied that she had agreements from everyone, she returned to the podium, and slid the stack into her briefcase. "I hope everyone here has an open mind."

She grabbed a piece of chalk from the tray. "Let's start with some general discussion. What are some different ways in which people communicate?"

As was typical during the first few minutes of any lecture, there was silence. "Oh, come on. If I told you that you could win cash and valuable prizes by playing along with us today, would you be willing to speak up? We're doing it right now."

Army raised his hand. "You mean, like talking?"

"Talking!" she said as she wrote it on the green board. "So let's break that out. We have face to face talking. What are some other variations on this?"

One of the Marines spoke up, "Well, you mentioned radio earlier."

"Yeah, radio." She wrote *RF* on the board.

And then the Marine added, "Telephone."

"Telephone, of course! My daughter's favorite appliance. How about some other ways?"

"Morse code, semaphore," Navy chimed in.

"Excellent," she wrote both on the board. "Morse code can be transmitted via RF or by line of sight by use of light pulses representing dots and dashes. And, semaphore; only the Navy would have thought of that!" She grinned.

The man in civilian clothes finally spoke, "How about letter-writing? You know, Pony Express?"

"Or non-verbal cues?" His female partner glared at him for a moment and then grinned.

Yasmina wrote non-verbal on the board. "Very good. About eighty five percent of all human communications is non-verbal: hand movements, facial expressions, body language."

"Any parents in here?" she asked the class. "What about feelings? Sometimes parents just know that something is wrong with their child. Usually we hear about this type of communications more often with mothers, rather than fathers."

She drew a woman stick figure on the board, holding hands with a child. "Some of you have heard stories about twins that are separated from great distances who can tell when the other experiences pain or great emotion." She drew a large question mark on the board. "How do we explain that particular type of communication?"

The class was quiet, so Yasmina went on. "How about synaptic transfer? In the central nervous system, a synapse is a small gap at the end of a neuron that allows a signal to pass from one neuron to the next. Synapses are found where nerve cells connect with other nerve cells. Synapses are key to the brain's function, especially when it comes to memory. But, information has to cross a gap to get from point A to point B. Have you ever wondered how it gets there?"

She tilted her head to the side, "Any physicists in the room? No? Then you've likely never heard of something called Quantum Entanglement. The term refers to the physical phenomenon that occurs when a pair or group of particles interact in a way such that the quantum state of each particle of the pair or group behaves in sync with the others, so to speak. This occurs even when the particles are separated by a large distance. This theory has caused a significant rift between classical and quantum physicists since 1938. In short, the particles seem to communicate even though they're not connected."

When she saw the glazed looks on everyone's faces, she switched gears. "Let's try a quick experiment. Everybody take a couple of deep breaths, and just relax." She flipped on the overhead projector and an image of a sailboat resting on a calm sea at sunrise appeared on the white screen. "I want you to take a moment to study this photograph. Look at the hues of the horizon meeting the sky, look at the colors of the water. Capture in your mind's eye every detail of this sailboat: its two masts, the deck, the portholes."

She paused. "Now I want you to close your eyes and relax. Everyone, close your eyes. Keep the image I just showed you in your mind. Now what I want you to do, is to imagine a large dolphin coming out of the water, leaping over the boat and re-entering the water on the opposite side."

She continued, "Keeping your eyes shut, by a show of hands, how many of you were able to imagine that?" She surveyed the room and noted that all hands were raised. "Good. How many of you, when you added the imaginary dolphin to the photo, saw the animal's movement? How many of you actually detected movement of the water? And how many of you added a splash in the water where the dolphin re-enters?" She smiled. All hands were still in the air.

She switched the light off and replaced the photo on the projector surface with another. "Great! You can open your eyes now. One last question; how many of you saw the dolphin come out of the water on the far side of the boat, and land in front of it, near the bow?"

Spontaneously, everyone in the room raised their hands at the same time. She turned the projector back on, displaying the same scene, but taken a few seconds later, with the descending dolphin entering the water in front of the boat with a splash. "Hmmm, would you look at that?"

Mark glanced around the room at the attendees looking at each other with grins of success. Everyone in the room had admitted to having seen the dolphin in their imagination leap over the bow of the boat and land, in just about the precise spot as the photo depicted.

Yasmina shrugged. "Some of you may say that we all saw it this way because we've seen something like that in the past, maybe in another photo, either for real, or in a TV show. Some of you might think that we had supplied a couple of photos that I selected based on your answers, which could statistically result in a similar perception in any population. Or, in everyday terms, that's logically how a good photographer would have captured such an event."

She took the photo off of the projector and replaced it with the photo of a physically attractive female, facing away from the camera, standing in a field of flowers. The sky was cobalt blue with a scattering of cumulous clouds high above. Her hands were at her sides. Her narrow waist and youthful looking hands suggested a younger woman, perhaps just out of her teens. "How about this shot? Study this photograph for a few seconds. Take in everything you can about the image."

She paused, and switched the overhead projector off again. "Got it? Now, close your eyes and think about the picture for a couple of seconds. This woman is now turning around to face you. Tell me what you can about her face."

After a few moments, a voice to Mark's left answered, "She's young, beautiful angular jaw, pretty smile. Large blue eyes, eyes with, uh, innocence."

"Good." Yasmina said. "Keeping your eyes closed, by a show of hands, is that what everyone got, or did someone get something different?"

The woman answered. "Yes. She's young; her eyes are blue, but she's, hmmm, not happy. She has something on her mind. She's in the field to think about something that's been bothering her."

"What's been bothering her?" Yasmina asked.

"She, uh, she's young. She's maybe in love with a guy that her parents don't approve of because he's older. They've maybe forbidden her to see him, and she's torn between her respect for her parents and her feelings for this guy."

Mark could hear Yasmina writing on the board before she spoke, "Interesting. Anyone else?"

Mark spoke up. "She's torn about her feelings, but she's waiting for someone, or something."

"Like what?" Yasmina queried.

"I don't know." Mark continued. "Maybe for the guy, maybe for something to come to her to tell her which way to go, what to decide."

"Fantastic everyone! How many people think she's turning to her left to look at you?" Yasmina noted that everyone except one of the Marines had their hands raised.

"Open your eyes." Yasmina pulled the photo off the machine and replaced it with the photo of the young girl, turning to look over her left shoulder at the camera. She was trying to smile, but a tear had formed in the corner of her eye.

"Is this what many of you saw?" She wrote the word 'Feelings' on the board. "Some of you not only saw the woman, but also perceived how she was feeling."

She turned the projector off again, and placed another photograph on the surface. She quickly looked around the room. "Okay. It looks like most of you brought something to write with. Anyone need a pen? No? Okay. Here's the last exercise of this group. Does everyone want to take another deep breath?"

She flipped the projector back on. It was something of a surreal animation, like some of the black-light posters Mark had seen for rock bands in the incense-laden head shops years before. It was basically an illustration of three concrete Islamic arches, connected but angled to form a three-sided patio. They were constructed with the rounded shape and a pointed arch at the top. A concrete floor, but no glass in the windows. The viewer was looking through the arches at a starry night, with a lighter hue along the horizon. Maybe just after dusk. It seemed that it was an elevated position, indicating great height above the landscape.

"Now what I want you to do, is, yeah, you guessed it; study this illustration, and then close your eyes."

When she was sure that they all had studied the image and closed their eyes, she continued, "Okay everyone, take a deep breath. In your mind, I want you to walk out on the surface and approach the windows. Tell me what you see when you look around. When you look up or down. What do you smell or hear? Tell me about what you see in the distance...off to the left or to the right."

"Take as long as you like. But, this time, when you open your eyes, I'd like you to take out a piece of paper and write down what you see. Be descriptive. Draw pictures if you like. Be as detailed as you can. Don't cheat off of anyone else because there is no right or wrong answer and what you come up with will ultimately be better than anything you copy from someone else."

"Okay? Use as much paper as you like. You might fill up one page and then get a feeling, a perception that you missed something. If that happens, just set the one page aside and start a new page. You have thirty minutes. Get started!" And with that, she walked out of the room.

Mark started right in. He closed his eyes again and felt himself move out on to the patio. The stone tiles were cool to his feet. It was high. It seemed like it was a parapet of sorts...a patio of some sort on top of a castle keep, but it overlooked a large expanse of land. He looked out into the evening at the stars in the sky and then looked down. There was a stream or small river cutting across a valley, with gentle rolling hills on either side. On his side of the valley, off to his left, there was a village. It was old. No electricity, but he saw flickering lights in the windows. Candles? There was smoke rising from the chimneys of the homes. No industry. Somewhere closer in the fields, cattle grazed.

His focus was distracted by one of the Marines in the back of the classroom, "What the fuck is this? What are we supposed to be doing here?"

He didn't open his eyes, but by now recognized some of the voices and heard the other Marine tell him, "Who cares... just write it up. This is better than marching twenty miles in ALICE gear all day."

Mark tried to focus again. He cleared his mind like he did when he was trying to guess at the playing cards in his parlor games. There was no money on the table for this, so he had nothing to lose by letting his mind go and just playing around with the task. What was the matter with the villagers? There was a certain solemnity to the illustration, a peace, but also a concern. War? Huh uh. Illness? Maybe.

There was something going on in the village that caused them to stay in their homes. What was it? He looked over his shoulder at the Army Warrant Officer. The guy was writing and sketching as if he were in a contest to fill up the most paper the fastest. The Navy Chief had a quizzical look in his eye, but was making feverish notes and drawings as fast as he could.

The two Marines seemed to be passing each other notes, responding and then passing them back. The two civilians looked at each other and shook their heads as if they shouldn't be doing this exercise. The woman glared at the man again and motioned to the paper, suggesting, "Get this done!"

Mark sat his pen down and focused. A second later, he picked it up and began to doodle. He drew a sideways "8" on the paper; the symbol for infinity. He over-drew the figure three or four times and then tapped the symbol a couple of times absentmindedly. All of a sudden, more details seemed to pop into his head. They weren't cows, they were sheep. There was a horse in a pen near one of the homes. In the adjacent field, there was a plow, dug into the dirt, but with the harness motionless on the ground.

He began drawing what he was seeing. Off to his right, there were higher mountain tops. Above the tree line there were rocks. Rocks, but no snow. He inhaled. There was a strong, sweet, heady scent that was almost sickening to him. Lilacs. Eastern Europe or western Asia? The architecture looked Islamic.

Where were they? In his mind, his hand touched the stone

and he felt its coolness and its sleekness: its consistency. Whoever owned this house, owned the village. Were the villagers afraid of the owner of this house?

The half hour passed faster than he had expected. Yasmina returned to the room and passed out 8X10" dark manila envelopes to each attendee. "I hope you had plenty of time to get your thoughts down. Please stick your notes, your doodles...or any other observations in the envelope I'm giving you. Seal it up and then write your name, legibly on the outside of the envelope."

Having retrieved all of the envelopes, she returned to the front and placed them in her briefcase. "Wasn't that fun everyone?"

There were some slight murmurs from the group, but no committals. With a smile, she went on. "Okay then, you all know me. We've had a chance to stretch our minds and have a little fun, so why don't we each introduce ourselves to each other?" When she noted the universal trepidation, she added, "Yes, public speaking. It sucks, but you have to do it if you want paid for today. You're not running for political office, so give us a sixty second summary of who you are, where you're from and what you do. Mark, you're up front...let's start with you...stand up."

Mark stood in place, turned and said, "Good morning. I'm Mark Reynolds. I'm from Dallas Texas and..." With a small shrug, he gestured at his uniform, "United States Marine Corps, almost three years. I'm currently assigned to..."

Yasmina interrupted, "We don't need current assignments. We don't want to violate any government secrets in here. And, by the way, you all can laugh in here when I say something funny!"

"Yes, Ma'am." Mark smiled and sat down.

"Thanks, Mark." Yasmina smiled. "How about you chief?"

The Navy Chief stood, "Hi. I'm Dan Wheeler, Chief Boatswain's Mate, US Navy. I'm originally from Nantucket; been in the Navy for fifteen years."

She moved her focus to the next row, "How about you, Army?"

He stood, his chair sliding backwards when it came into contact with the backs of his knees, "Hi all. I'm Joe Conner, Chief Warrant

Officer Two, US Army, uh, eleven years in service. I'm from Wichita Falls."

"Thanks Joe!" She smiled. "How about the rest of the Marine contingent here?"

The two sergeants looked at each other and then the first reluctantly rose. "Timothy Andrews. Sergeant. Pasadena, California. Six years USMC."

Before Andrews could be seated, the other Marine stood, "Brian Yates, Sergeant. Olympia, Washington ...uh...six years in."

"Thank you Marines." Yasmina looked at the couple in civilian attire. "Well, that just leaves you two!"

The man rose first, "Norman Webster. Buffalo, New York. United States Air Force, four years enlisted and two years, uh, civilian, GS-9"

As Norman sat down, his table partner stood. "Katie McBride, Pittsburgh, Pennsylvania. US Air Force Officer for four years, and civilian for almost four, uhmmm, GS-11."

"Thanks everyone. Now that you all know each other, I'm going to talk to you about someone we'll call 'Clair'." She wiped the board clean and then wrote as she spoke. "The one you're probably most familiar with depending on which kinds of movies you see or books you read, is, and this is where I usually lose people out of the class..." She looked over her shoulder. "You know, you can laugh at this; you have to have a sense of humor to make it in here!"

The chalk tapped as she wrote, "Clairvoyance. The psychic ability of clear seeing, images, pictures, a color, a face...even if it only flashes up from your sub-conscious for a split second."

"Clairaudience. Clear hearing of something remote to us: a voice telling you to do something. Not to be confused with schizophrenia or other delusional behavior, which we'll get into later in the week."

"Clairsentience: a feeling of emotion or and actual physical sensation transmitted from one person to another without any type of physical contact."

"Claircognizance: literally, clear knowing. Sometimes despite all evidence to the contrary, we just know something. And, we can't be talked out of it."

"And finally, Clairempathy: a type of communication - telepathy where a person tunes into the vibrations of another human being, or a place, or animal."

She turned back to the class, "So, before I freak you all out and send you running into the hallway, let me suggest that these are all attributes, or skills, that we are born with, to one degree or another. Some of these skills can be taught, or rather refined. They are also ways in which the Soviet Union has been gathering, stealing, classified information from us, since the sixties, maybe since World War Two."

"So, as you are continuing to breathe deeply and osmose this all in, in an objective and open-minded fashion, let me add that the 'Clairs' are all a part of what we call *Channeling*. That is, the ability to allow one's own mind to be used as a mechanism for the transfer of psychic information or energy."

Sergeant Yates looked dumbfounded, "Ma'am, with all due respect, are you telling me that the Marine Corps has sent me here to learn to be some sort of psychic?"

Yasmina replaced the piece of chalk in the tray. "Not exactly. The Marine Corps sent you here to brief you on one of the weapons being used by the Soviets, and possibly the Chinese, against our country. Whether or not you believe in it, is inconsequential. It is real. It is being used against us. And, we need to fight it. Your aptitude and intuition got you this far in the program. But, like leading the horse to water, I can't make you any more psychic than you were when you walked into the room. I can only teach you to better use and understand the skills, the gifts, you already have."

There was a brief silence before she spoke again. "And, since there seems to be a negative connotation within the scientific and government communities about any kind of psychic functioning, this program isn't about being psychic, per se. It's about teaching what they have chosen to call Remote Viewing. That is, under strict laboratory protocols, teaching someone to perceive and interpret non-local information. Specifically, information that can be learned while the viewer and target are separated over vast distances, and in some cases, time."

The two Marines looked at each other and then shrugged. "Okay. You say the Russians are doing this? Successfully?"

Yasmina nodded. "Indeed they are. If you stay with the program, you'll hear more about that down the road."

She paused. "Any other questions for now? I know this is all a little bit much to spring on someone, especially military personnel, but we have a limited amount of time to work with you and we need to give you as much as we can in the period that we have."

She placed another document on the projector surface and flipped on the lamp. "I doubt that any of you have seen this before, but this is something called the Zener test." Projected on the screen were five shapes; a square, a circle, a five-pointed star, a plus sign and three wavy but parallel lines.

"The targets used for these tests are the standard ESP Cards, sometimes called Zener Cards that have been used by thousands of parapsychologists like J.B. Rhine, in his classic studies of Extrasensory Perception. These show five different symbols. In this test, a card is individually selected from the stack, by a proctor in the next room. Each time a card is selected, the proctor will set it aside for one minute and then return it to the deck. The deck will be shuffled, face down, each time before another card is shown. Therefore, there should be no discernible pattern to the sequence of cards."

"You have to guess at 25 cards. This is not a contest. Your performance feedback will be given to you in a one-on-one meeting with our staffers later today or tomorrow. "

Yasmina looked around the room at the raised eyebrows. "Oh come on. This will be fun! None of you have had any training on this, which is good. We want you to focus on clearing your mind of all the crap that's running through it right now. Focus on the card, but don't take the whole minute. Use the first shape that pops into your mind, and write it down."

"There's twenty five of them?" Webster asked.

"Yep, twenty five. As a matter of fact, Katie, could I ask you to move to this desk up front? I want everyone to space out a bit for comfort, and to avoid getting test anxiety if they see their neighbor writing stuff faster than they are."

Yasmina pointed at two lights on top of the podium. "Everyone relax. When the green light comes on, I'll tell you to focus. When the red light comes on a minute later, I'll tell you to clear your mind and wait for the next green light to focus on your next target. Any questions?"

Hearing none, she stepped out of the classroom but was back in a moment. "Okay. Clear your heads, take a deep breath, and stand by for target number one!"

The light turned green and Yasmina started them off. "Here we go. Clear your minds and think only about the person in the other room. That person is staring at a card. Write down the shape you see."

Mark focused, but the first image that popped into his mind was a club. Dammit, this isn't cards! That image was followed in rapid succession by the square, then the circle, the plus sign, the wavy lines. Shit! It can't be all of them! It's only one card...

"Remember," Yasmina guided. "Take the first image that pops into your mind.

The star. It looked like a club, and it was the first thing to enter his mind. And so, next to the number 1 on his paper, he wrote, "Star".

The next three or four attempts were miserable. There was just too much garbage floating around in his brain. There were too many people in the room. He didn't like working under the clock so to speak. He was simply guessing. What was he going to have for dinner tonight? Was the Air Force officer single?

But, by the time he got to the last dozen, his mind and body started to work together to wipe the garbage out, and he began to see fleeting images. For some reason, he felt like he was going to be more successful with the last attempts than he was on the first.

As she called for the last five, he was almost certain that he'd nailed each one.

She made her trek around the room to collect everyone's responses. "Now see, wasn't that fun?"

There were some muffled groans from different tables and the Army Warrant rubbed his eyes.

"Seriously, guys?" She placed the responses into another manila envelope and stuffed it into a now-overflowing briefcase. "Well, I'm about to cheer you up."

"One of the things you're going to enjoy about this program is that we almost never put in a full day. We've learned that in order for people to perform well at this stuff they need to be well-fed and well rested. Therefore, you should spend the rest of the day walking around town, seeing the sites, getting something to eat and then getting to bed early."

"I have some administrative chores to do, so I'll be here for the next hour or so if anyone has any questions or concerns. If not, enjoy your day and I will see you tomorrow at eight; I mean, zero eight hundred!"

Mark stood and stretched, and tossed his notebook back into his briefcase. He loitered in class just long enough to give Katie and her associate a chance to walk out first. Call it silly, but before his transfer to Norfolk last month, he'd spent the last year by himself in Okinawa, and was anxious to start dating again. He was curious to see how Katie and her partner interacted outside of class.

He took his time walking to the parking lot, but was close enough to see that they had ridden together; a dark blue Chevrolet with US Government plates. Norm went straight to the driver's door, letting Katie open her own.

He smiled, "Company car. They just work together."

<hr />

On the other side of Marine Corps Base Quantico was the

expanded and modernized FBI Academy. Opened in 1972, it had been Hoover's dream to host the premier training program for law enforcement officers worldwide. Hoover died on May 2 that year, and never got to see the full reality of the project come to fruition.

The 550 acre complex included more than two dozen classrooms, eight conference rooms, two seven-story dormitories, a 1,000-seat auditorium, a dining hall, a full-sized gym with a swimming pool, a fully equipped library, and a new firing range. Other enhancements included specialized classrooms for forensic science training, four unique identification labs, more than a dozen darkrooms, and a mock-city classroom and crime scene room for practical exercises.

The superlative facilities enabled National Academy classes to expand to more than 200 students per session, including law enforcement leaders from around the world. In 1976, the National Executive Institute for the heads of the nation's largest law enforcement agencies was officially created.

Clarence Kelley was sworn in as the Director of the FBI on July 9, 1972. He was the first Director of the FBI to be appointed through the nomination and confirmation process. Among his contributions, Kelley was known for eliminating some of the practices that had been prevalent in the administrative division under J. Edgar Hoover's directorship, and also reopened relations with other intelligence agencies, such as the Central Intelligence Agency. In his last years as director, Hoover had all but broken off communications with the Agency.

Director Kelley looked across the desk at the tall and lanky senior agent. "You've certainly paid your dues, Fred. Your record of successes with the Bureau is unparalleled, and thanks to your leadership last week, barring any appeals, you put Leonard Peltier where he belongs. We'll get Jimmy Eagle one day too."

Fred Balmain looked down at the edge of the Director's desk and recalled the shooting. On June 26, 1975, Special Agents Jack R. Coler and Ronald A. Williams were on the Pine Ridge Indian Reservation searching for a young man named Jimmy Eagle, who was wanted for questioning in connection with the assault and robbery of two local ranch hands. A major shootout ensued, and both agents were killed before their back-up arrived.

The first trial for the suspects in the case took place in the summer of 1976 in Cedar Rapids, Iowa, after a motion for a change of venue was granted. However, Peltier had been in custody in Canada, fighting extradition, and so was not available for this trial. Charges against Jimmy Eagle, one of the individuals charged in the murders of the agents, were dismissed voluntarily by the government for lack of evidence.

"Thank you, sir." He looked back up. "I've always tried to do the right thing for the Bureau and for my country."

Now, at 55, Balmain didn't know if this was truly a promotion, or just a way for the Director to sideline him until mandatory retirement at 57. His promotion to Deputy Assistant Director for the Training Division meant that he was done in the Field, and that he would finish out his time at Quantico. It wasn't what he wanted, but it was better than early retirement.

Director Kelley smiled, "You've always been a tremendous asset. You were one of Director Hoover's most respected agents, and he wanted you looked after."

10

TUESDAY, APRIL 26, 1977

The morning was beautiful. The sun was out and the humidity was low, a light breeze coming in from the west. Mark was practically humming to himself as he found the classroom. Today, he felt rested, well-fed, and he was fifteen minutes early. As he entered the room, he saw Warrant Officer Conner and Yasmina talking about something humorous up front.

"Good morning!" he said to both of them.

They both smiled and nodded at him. He sat his briefcase on the floor beneath the same table he'd been at the day before and joined them up front. They were making small talk about restaurants in Frankfurt, and since Mark had never been there, he just listened.

As everyone filed in and took the same seats they had occupied the day before, Mark was excited to see that the Air Force duo sat apart, the way Yasmina had spaced them for the last exercise the day before. If there had been anything romantic between them before, then the ride home last night or the ride in this morning must have been chilly.

Yasmina opened her lecture. "Hopefully, you enjoyed our exercises yesterday. We're going to do more of the same today. First thing this morning, I'm going to give you an exercise that will take you a couple of hours to do. During this period, one-by-one, I'll ask you to step next door and spend a couple of minutes getting to know Dr. Kravitz." When she saw the concerned looks on several faces, she explained, "Don't worry, he's not a psychiatrist; he's a physicist, a scientist. He's my boss at the institute."

She grinned. "And, he's not here to get inside your head. He wants to help you get inside someone else's."

She moved back to the chalk board and began to outline their first project. "I wanted to give you something to work on independently since only one of you can meet with Dr. Kravitz at a time. So..."

She began writing, "What I'd like to see is, in as much detail as possible, your recollection of the two lowest periods in your life; the two times when you were at absolutely rock-bottom sad. Describe the situation, whether it was a job loss, death of a loved one, your girlfriend puked on your shoes; I don't care. Tell me what the situation was, and then describe, if you remember, exactly how you felt the day before and the day after. What did you do on those particular days that was different from any other day? Tell me how the event impacted your life. Tell me how you got through it"

"Then, I want you to work through the exact same process detailing the two happiest days of your life: marriage, birth of a child, big promotion, sex for the first time, whatever. Please be as detailed as possible about your feelings and perceptions before and after each event. How did these events make you feel, and why were they important?"

She put the chalk down. "These are not one-paragraph summaries. I want these to be thoughtful recollections as clear and as expressive as you can be. I want you to make me feel what you were feeling at those times. These will be private. You and I will be the only ones to read them."

"Any questions?" She looked around the room, "Okay then. Mark, you're up front so why don't you go first. Dr. Kravitz is in room 106 down the hall. When you get back we'll send the next victim."

Mark rose from his seat, "Do I need to take paper and pen?"

Yasmina waved him off, "No, it's just a friendly chat. Enjoy."

Mark headed down the hall to room 106 and knocked on the door frame.

"Come in," came the reply.

He entered the classroom and was momentarily stunned by the absence of all furniture, except for two chairs in the center of the room, facing each other, about five feet apart. The physics professor stood with a smile and warmly extended his hand. "Good morning Mark! I'm Leonard Kravitz. So nice to meet you!"

Mark felt as if he was meeting the twin brother of Art Garfunkel, who was wearing coke-bottle glasses that seemed to be a half-inch thick. "Good morning, sir," he said, accepting the slender hand and hoping his grip didn't crack the man's knuckles. His rug of tightly curled salt and pepper hair seemed like a part of a wig that had been pulled back too far, creating an extraordinarily large forehead.

"Please sit...be comfortable."

Mark sat in the seat indicated, and after the physicist sat down across from him he was aware that the man had nothing with which to take notes: no pen, no paper, and no briefcase. He was there to just chat. But he certainly looked the part of the physics professor; his jeans were faded and his jacket, while of good quality, appeared several years old and well-worn.

"So tell me Mark, what do you think so far about what you've heard?"

Mark tightened his bottom lip a bit, but tried not to frown. "Well, sir, on one hand this is all a little surprising for me. It's not really what I expected."

Dr. Kravitz smiled, "And, on the other hand?"

"Huh? Well, uh, " Mark cleared his throat. "On the other hand, confidentially, I believe that some of this is real. I mean, I think there are a lot of fakers making claims about being psychic, but I think that some people out there might really have some of these powers."

Kravitz nodded. "What would you say if I told you that everyone has these so-called powers, as you say, but that some people are just better at it than others?"

"Sir?"

"Some people are better at music and they'll make better musicians, but everyone can learn music. Some people are better at picking up golf than others, but everyone can learn the game. It comes down to their natural aptitudes, their interests, and of course, their training. So, in terms of psychic functioning, some people will be better at it than others."

"Sure." Mark shrugged. "That makes sense. But, Mrs. Sheppard made it seem so, uh, so normal. So matter-of fact. In our house, growing up, we just didn't talk about stuff like that."

"Ah. I take it that you had a pretty conventional Christian up-bringing?"

"Yes. I don't remember ever missing a Sunday of church - up until my senior year in High School. With dad's work schedule, it was usually mom that got me up and ready every Sunday morning. Up until I left for Boot Camp."

"You lost her a couple of years ago, isn't that right?"

Mark was surprised that the physicist knew something that personal about him. "Yes, sir. Some kind of respiratory infection that turned into pneumonia."

"I supposed you'll be writing about that in your exercise this morning?"

"Yes, sir."

"Mark, you don't have to call me 'sir'. Please call me Leonard. And, since you're going to write about her, we won't talk about your mom now." He adjusted his glasses. "Do you mind talking about Viet Nam, Saigon on that last day?"

"It's a blur, now. But, I don't mind."

"It's okay. I'm not looking for specifics here, but I'm fascinated by a couple of things. First, obviously, your card tricks. Marked deck?"

"No sir! I mean, Leonard." Mark shifted uncomfortably in his seat.

"Your sergeant at the time said you demonstrated freaky accuracy at picking cards out of any deck that was always shuffled by someone else. Fifty-two cards in a deck, and one gets pulled out face down and set apart from the others. So, you have one chance in fifty-two of guessing the right card. But he said that you were correct more than half the time. Is that right?"

Mark nodded a couple of times.

Kravitz prodded, "So? Give! Tell me how you did it? What do you see when you close your eyes and concentrate on the card?"

A grin started to form on the corner of Mark's mouth. For the first time in his life, he felt at ease talking about his special abilities. Kravitz made it all seem okay. "I guess I've never tried to describe it before. I think the color is what comes to my mind first. Sometimes I see, or think about something red or black. If I see a mix of colors, then I think it's a face card. Sometimes, I'll actually see a number or, like a photograph of the corner of a card pops into my mind. But, more often, I feel a certain intensity. Or power, like, the stronger the intensity, the higher the card."

Kravitz nodded slowly. "So, the two of clubs would feel dark and weak, whereas the King of diamonds would be colorful and powerful?"

"Yeah. Something like that. Sometimes, I'll see the shape of the suit and can actually count the diamonds or hearts or whatever."

"Amazing!" Kravitz sat forward in his seat. "Tell me more about Saigon - those last couple of days."

"It was a busy time." Mark thought as his gaze dropped to the floor.

"People described you as highly intuitive during that part of your life. Wasn't it you who suggested to sergeant Malcom to get supplies to the roof, even before a decision had been reached to evacuate the embassy from there?"

"Well, yeah. But, there was a mess all around us. It just seemed like the thing to do, and I wasn't the only one who was thinking about it."

Kravitz pondered the remark. "But, you were the only one who felt strongly enough about it to say something to your superiors."

"I suppose." Mark answered even though Kravitz' comment sounded more like a statement than a question.

Kravitz went on, "And didn't you later tell Sergeant Malcolm about the dream you had about the carnage surrounding the Convoy of Tears?"

"Wow," Mark replied, shocked at how much information Kravitz and his group had learned about him. "Yeah, but that was afterwards: a couple weeks after the evacuation, in a bar outside of Pearl. We were drinking and the conversation got a little crazy as the night went on."

"Have you always been this...intuitive?" Kravitz leaned forward more and brought his hands up in front of his mouth, making a steeple with his fingers, and touched his chin. "Was there a point in your life when you thought you might be, you know, different?"

Mark had never discussed this with anyone before in this much detail. "Well, I had scarlet fever when I was really young. I don't remember a lot of it. Except I remember being at the hospital and I was surrounded by doctors and nurses who all seemed pretty concerned. But, it wasn't like I saw them around me. It was more like I was in the room, watching them. Like a bystander. It was the same feeling I had when I got my tonsils taken out. They were putting me out, and I seemed to, this sounds stupid. I felt like I was floating out of my body and watching everything from, uh, from the ceiling."

"So, you don't recall those events themselves, but you recall the feeling, experiences, you had during those events?"

"Yeah, yeah, now that you mention it, that's a good way to say it."

Kravitz' pensive smile turned into a grin. "Mark, you're among friends here, and I think you will like working with us." He stood to shake hands again. "I don't want to keep you...and I have several other meetings to get to in the next couple of hours. When you get back to the classroom, can you send in the next person?"

"That's it?" Mark stood.

"That's it."

"But, I still have a couple of questions."

Kravitz ushered him towards the door. "Great! Hopefully that will never change. Enjoy your day."

Being Deputy Assistant Director for the Training Division, meant that Balmain would have a small office in Washington Headquarters, but that he would spend the majority of his time at the academy in Quantico. He enjoyed the Virginia countryside, and since his wife and he had found a nice country home outside of Lorton, Virginia, the commute between the two locations was about equidistant.

When he entered the lobby of the Academy, the receptionist recognized him right away. "Good morning Assistant Director!"

Balmain shook hands with the attractive twenty-something blonde. "Please call me Fred. Everyone does these days." She reminded him of someone. Some singer.

"Okay, Fred." She giggled, "I will when no one is around. Whenever real people are nearby, I'm supposed to call you Assistant Director. My name is Jill. Did you get your ID badge set up yet?"

"Hi, Jill. Nice to meet you." Balmain produced his site access control badge from his shirt pocket. "This one? Yes, I think we're set to go!"

She lowered her voice to just above a conspiratorial level. "Your badge gets you in everywhere, so if you lose it, please let me know right away!"

Balmain glanced down at the log book on the counter. "Sure thing. Do I need to sign in?"

Jill shook her head, "No sir. You're considered permanent staff."

"Permanent," he repeated with a sigh. "Does that mean they have a place to bury me out back somewhere?"

"Probably." She laughed. "We're on 550 acres surrounded by a Marine Corps base. They've probably buried a lot of bodies out there over the years!"

He nodded. "Is Garcia's office still down this way?"

"It sure is." Jill replied. "Third door on your left"

Paul Garcia was basically the site manager, responsible for everything other than academic content. If it broke, you called Paul. If you needed a new one, you called Paul. If you needed to lobby for additional budget money for something, you called Paul.

Having reached his mandatory retirement age, Garcia took the administrative position as a way of keeping close to the only family he had ever known. After graduation from West Point, he received a direct commission in the United States Army, and was quickly assigned to the 8th Army in Korea. There he volunteered for a special Ranger unit, and served with distinction until the unit was disbanded in March of 1951.

He returned to the United States after the war, and pursued a degree in Finance. One of his college roommates had been talking to recruiters for the FBI, and his enthusiasm over-flowed to Garcia. And so, after receiving his Master's Degree, he contacted the recruiters and was admitted to the FBI Academy. He had been an agent ever since, serving in eleven domestic offices and for almost two years in Brussels.

When Balmain stuck his head in Garcia looked up with elation. "Oh my God, Fred! How the hell are you?"

Balmain closed the office door and after vigorously shaking hands, sat down in one of the side chairs. What followed was more than an hour of story-telling, mostly true, occasionally embellished, but all satisfying.

When they had finished their coffee, Garcia said, "Well, I guess it's time for your official tour of the place. I know you've been here a dozen times, but you might as well see what you're inheriting!"

Balmain stood and opened the door for his longtime associate and friend to lead the way.

As Garcia led him down the hallway, he said, "I think you were one of the agents who was here for the commissioning of this place in 1972. It was totally state-of-the-art then, and we've done our best to keep up with technology."

Balmain nodded.

Garcia continued, "So, you've seen most of this before during your in-service training."

They took their time, looking in on some of the classrooms and observing the various teaching styles of the professional instructors. The classrooms were quite advanced for their day, with integrated electronics that could be controlled from the lecterns. With a push of a button, the instructor could dim the lights or call up closed circuit television, movies or film strip presentations. Student tables were all connected to the system with push-button controllers so that the instructor could ask a question, the students could select an answer, and the responses were automatically tabulated by a computer. The system kept track of performance statistics so that responses could be analyzed from class to class.

Through assigned seating, the instructor could immediately see who was absorbing the information and who wasn't. This would also allow them to amend their teaching style to make sure that each student had a firm grasp of the material before they moved on to another topic.

Further down the hall, an auditorium had been set up to look like a theater with realistic sets on stage. There was a living room and a separate bedroom. Forensics experts were detailing the proper way to collect, document and preserve evidence. Mannequins simulated corpses, and agents with acting interests served as interviewees.

The tour continued to a fingerprint lab where students were being taught the correct way to roll suspect fingerprints onto cards. From that point, they were given the opportunity to use modern lab equipment to develop latent prints using a fuming process. They would then photograph the print and then compare it to a list of suspect prints provided by the staff. The goal was to successfully match the latent to one of the samples.

They did a quick lap around the exterior of the campus before ending up back at the entrance to the main building. They wandered back down the hall to where they had begun. Garcia stopped and used his Master key to unlock a door. "This is your office. John Sebastian, your predecessor, took all of his personal effects, but there's a lot of stuff he left behind. We thought you might want to go through it and decide if it's worth keeping, or just trash it."

Garcia handed Balmain an office key. "I've got some things to take care of. Why don't you make yourself comfortable and I'll stop back by later and we'll go to lunch?"

Balmain looked around the office. "You bet. Great seeing you again!"

Garcia added, "You know, this is the original furniture from when we moved in here in seventy-two. If you like, I can put in a requisition to get you some more modern digs."

Balmain sighed, "Thanks, but there's no sense in further burdening the already over-burdened taxpayer. This will work for me. Actually, I think it's Headquarters' idea that I serve out my time here without causing any more trouble for them."

"Ain't that the way it always is!" Garcia chuckled as he walked away.

After Balmain closed the door, he sat down and adjusted the swivel chair to his liking. Sebastian had obviously been a much shorter man. Once he was comfortable, he looked at the laminated card that someone had left on his desk. It listed important names and numbers, instructions on how to get out if there was a fire, and some other basic building information.

In the center drawer of the desk, he found a key ring that had an extra key to the office and individual keys to the file cabinets. Like any good FBI agent, he tried each key to determine which key fit which lock. There were two lockable drawers in the desk and then four in the credenza behind the desk. They were all empty. But when he got to the taller four-drawer metal file cabinet, he found it crammed full of files and three-ring binders.

He shook his head slowly and began going through everything, starting with the top drawer. Much of the material was outdated information regarding personnel and budgeting that Balmain knew had to have been maintained elsewhere, and he questioned why he'd need a copy of reports that were as much as ten years old. He started a trash pile near the door.

After an hour and a half, the piles had grown and he was in the process of unlocking the last drawer, when there was a gentle knock on the door. "Yeah?"

Jill stuck her head in, "Sorry to interrupt. Mr. Garcia wants to know if you'd like to eat in the cafeteria today or if you'd rather go offsite?"

Balmain looked at her. That's it! She reminded him of that blonde singer from Abba. What was her name? Frida, something Swedish. "Oh, I don't care. Tell him it's his choice since he's buying!"

"Will do. He said he'd be ready in half an hour." She laughed. "Do you need anything?"

"Yeah." He stood up and maneuvered around the obstacle course being created by his piles of folders. "Can you find a couple of boxes for me to throw this stuff into? Also, do we have someone here that serves as the records retention custodian?"

"A what?"

"Uh, someone that knows how long we're required to keep different types of documents."

She raised an eyebrow. "I'll have to check on that. As for the boxes, I can get you those right now."

"Thanks," he said. But just as she was about to close the door on her way out, he asked, "Hey, not to be personal or anything, but what kind of perfume are you wearing?"

She giggled again. "Perfume? Mr. Sebastian didn't want us to wear perfume. He said it was too distracting for the young guys in the academy."

Balmain frowned. "Oh. Sorry. Don't worry about it."

Jill closed the door and he started sniffing around the office for the source. It was a pleasant scent. A stimulating and alluring scent, barely noticeable in the room. A scent that was vaguely familiar, but he'd not smelled in many years. He looked around the office and sniffed near the chairs. If anyone had seen him, they would have thought he'd lost his mind. Maybe he had.

Frustrated, he tossed the key ring onto the credenza, but with one bounce the keys slid off the back and fell to the floor behind the bulky piece of furniture. "Oh, fucking lovely!" he said aloud.

The wooden credenza was too close to the wall for him to reach his hand down behind it, and probably weighed more than a hundred pounds. He grunted as he slid it out a couple of inches across the commercial carpeting that seemed to come standard in government offices. When he got it out about three inches, he blindly reached over and down for the keys. His fingertips found the top of an errant file folder, so he pulled it up and tossed it on his desk. Now free of obstructions, he found the key ring on the floor and retrieved them before rocking the credenza back into place.

He laid the keyring on the desk near the phone, and deep in thought picked up the dusty file folder. He was a bit perturbed when he opened it and saw that the cover sheet indicated that it was a classified document. Across the front page was stamped "TOP SECRET ETERNA".

He exhaled slowly through his mouth. There were strict procedures governing the handling of classified information, and under no circumstances would it ever be stored in someone's office. It should have been locked up somewhere. Worse yet, Code Word classifications meant that a program was classified even higher than top-secret.

This was sensitive compartmentalized information that was intended for a very small audience. By adding a code word, only those who had been cleared, or read-in, for that specific code word could ever see it. And usually, it was the CIA that administered code word clearances. "Someone's going to get their tit in a ringer," he said softly as he flipped the cover page over.

As he began to read, his breathing slowed. It was a draft of a memo dated November 12, 1963 from President John F. Kennedy to the Director of the Central Intelligence Agency, and was entitled in the subject line: Classification of all UFO intelligence files affecting National Security.

Someone had redacted some of the information by using a black magic marker to cross out several names, as well as the official letterhead, but the gist of the document was still discernible.

Top Secret

*Memorandum for: The Director, (three or four words redacted),
Central Intelligence agency*

*As I had discussed with you previously, I have initiated (two or
three words redacted) and instructed James Webb to develop a
program with the Soviet Union in joint space and lunar exploration. It would be very helpful if you would have the high threat
cases reviewed with the purpose of identification of bona fide
as opposed to classified CIA and USAF sources. It is important
that we make a clear distinction between the knowns and unknowns in the event the Soviets try to mistake our extended cooperation as a cover for intelligence gathering of their defense
and space programs.*

*When this data has been sorted out, I would like you to arrange
a program of data sharing with NASA, where Unknowns are a
factor. This will help NASA mission directors in their defensive
responsibilities.*

*I would like an interim report on the data review no later than
February 1, 1964.*

/S/ John F. Kennedy

In the upper right hand corner of the document, someone had
handwritten the word *Draft*. The lower half of the page had been
redacted. However, in marginally decipherable handwriting, at the
bottom right, someone had written a name followed by *...has MJ
Directive...11/20/63.*

The next page caused him even greater concern. It appeared
to be a copy of an older document that had been snatched from a
fire, with charring and scorching through parts of it. It looked like a
government document, two-hole punched at the top. It was some
sort of memo from the Director of Central Intelligence (MJ-1) to

individuals or groups identified as: MJ-2, MJ-I, MJ-4, MJ-5, MJ-6 and MJ-7.

He read through the top portion of the memo that dealt with some sort of administrative issue concerning a duplication of activities. But the line that caught his attention was:

"As you must know, LANCER has made some inquiries regarding our activities, which we cannot allow. Please submit your views no later than October. Your action to this matter is critical to the continuance of this group."

At the top and bottom of the document were red ink stamps: TOP SECRET/MAJESTIC

LANCER had been President Kennedy's Secret Service code name. Balmain re-read the entire document. No date. No signature. It referenced four projects with which he was totally unfamiliar; Project MAJESTIC/JEHOVAH, Project EVINO, Project PARASITE and Project PAWNELION.

Balmain quickly flipped through the pages in the file, and realizing there was more to consume than he had time for, laid the folder open on his desk. Scratching his head, he looked at the date on the first document. November 12, 1963, just ten days before Kennedy had been assassinated. A thought that had been running through the back of his mind, creeped its way forward. It couldn't be!

Balmain's unit had been charged with investigating parts of the JFK assassination. Certainly, if the Director had known about some group in Washington that wanted the President muzzled, then he would have been told about it. From the swift, superficial review of the file, it would seem that someone high up in government wanted to stop the President from working with the Russians to explore space.

"Knowns, and unknowns?" What did that mean? Most people at the time believed the Soviets had been ahead of us in the space race. The prevailing thought was that they would get to the moon before the United States. But, the West didn't find out until later about a string of catastrophic failures that resulted in a loss of life as well as a scientific setback for them. So, what was Kennedy referring to? If we launched something, then it was known. If we didn't launch it, we pretty much knew that the Soviets did, so why would those birds be considered unknown?

He flipped once more through the file folder, and on several pages, he noted references to BLUEBOOK and to UFOs. "Wait a minute," he whispered slowly. BLUEBOOK was the Air Force's investigation into flying saucers. The FBI had maintained a strictly hands-off attitude towards reports and witnesses through the years, and as a protocol, simply referred witnesses to Air Force Headquarters. He suddenly remembered Hoover's mention of it years earlier.

Did Kennedy believe that they were something more than experimental Soviet craft? Was that why he was trying to get away from a policy of isolationism, and for us to join with the Soviets to explore space together? Did Kennedy think these sightings were actually something from some other planet? The idea was preposterous. But what if the phenomenon was real? Would that be a motive for...murder? He closed the file and turned it face down on his desk.

He sat in silence trying to resolve what he had just read, and at first, he didn't notice it. Then as he tilted his head to the side, and tried to clear his brain, he began to interpret the black-ink scrawl across the back of the folder, near the top. Naturally, he recognized the handwriting of the late founder of the FBI, but the message took him back in time.

"Shut it down and clean it up! 1/7/64." The phrase and the date were circled. Hoover had been looking at this file as he was closing down Balmain's investigation into the assassination of JFK.

He suddenly remembered where he had smelled that haunting perfume fragrance before. It was in a makeshift office suite in Dallas Texas, thirteen years ago, on a crisp day in January.

11

WEDNESDAY, APRIL 27, 1977

As Mark Reynolds pushed his briefcase under his desk, he noticed a smudge on one of his Corfam shoes. He wet a corner of his handkerchief with his tongue and diligently wiped the smudge away. It simply wouldn't do to have dirty shoes at Quantico.

Yasmina was energized and spirited as she kicked off the lecture on that sunny Wednesday morning. It was as if she had been drinking coffee since four in the morning. And, she seemed to have a way of bringing everyone in the room up to her level of excitement.

"This is going to be a great day. This is where, what do you say, the rubber meets the road. This morning I'd like to give you a basic orientation into remote viewing, and in the afternoon, we'll be moving down the hall to one of the other training rooms that has been set up with individual carrels, for some additional exercises."

She paused and scanned the room. "So, let's get into it!" She walked down the center of the room and passed out stapled packets about a quarter inch thick to each attendee. "This is yours to keep. It is unclassified material without any headers, and is for your reference so that you don't feel like you have to write at a hundred words per minute."

She recited from memory, like she had performed this act a hundred times. "Remote viewing is defined as *the ability to acquire accurate information about a distant or non-local person, place or event without using your physical senses or any other obvious means.* It's often associated with the idea of clairvoyance and sometimes called *anomalous cognition* or *second sight.* The difference between natural psychic receptivity and remote viewing is that our version of remote viewing, or RV, is a trained skill that the average person can learn to do. Let me say that again; the average person can be trained to remote view."

She returned to the lectern at the front of the room. "No one really knows for certain how remote viewing actually works, only that it does. One theory is that trained remote viewers are able to tap into the *Universal Mind,* or what has been known in some circles as the Akashic record, a kind of comprehensive storehouse of information about everything, where time and space are irrelevant. The remote viewer can enter what we call a hyperconscious state in which they can tune in to specific targets within the universal consciousness, of which all people and all things are a part."

She noticed some glazed-over looks, particularly among Marine sergeants Andrews and Yates. "It sounds like a lot of mystic-babble, but it's as good a guess as any as to what's really taking place. In short, we don't have a clue how it works. We just accept that it does."

She took a sip of her coffee. "There is a man that some of you will eventually meet. His name is Ingo Swann. Ingo is probably the best psychic on the planet, and he calls remote viewing a *form of virtual reality traveling that is brought under conscious control.* Ingo taught some physicists how to remote view, and they taught some military personnel...who are now teaching the rest of you. You are going to be the travelers, and your monitors, or taskers, will be your travel agents, so to speak."

She smiled. "If you think this practice is controversial, then you'd be right. Skeptics say that it doesn't work at all and some of the program's proponents believe it works 100 percent of the time. The fact is, it does really work, but not all of the time for all remote viewers. A highly skilled remote viewer may have a success rate that approaches 90 percent; meaning that they can correctly access a target nearly all of the time. However, the data obtained during the session may not be completely accurate."

"There are many factors involved, and some targets may be more complicated to reach and describe than others. And some remote viewers will key in on different aspects of a particular target that another viewer might not. Thus, the skeptics will always have reason to doubt, when in effect, an objective judge would say that there was something there."

"This practice of viewing information from a distance, that you will learn, can be traced back as far as the times of Ancient Greece, although it has transformed quite a bit over the years. The modern uses of this practice date back to around the 1930s when there were experiments being done on clairvoyance, out-of-body experiences, and telepathy in a series of Duke University's parapsychology experiments, conducted by J. B. Rhine."

"But in the wake of World War II, the US government began looking for ways to influence and control human behavior and, in addition to traditional psychological tactics, attention increasingly turned to parapsychology as well. Obviously, this research was not making the evening news."

"In the early 1950s, the Defense Department approached a medical doctor named Henry Andrija Puharich with a project to determine if certain mushrooms might unlock an individual's psychic powers. In typical government fashion, the CIA was also working on the same thing, at the same time, under the codename Project MKULTRA. Naturally, they hadn't told anyone about their work, so there was an understandable duplication among the different studies."

"During this time, Puharich was also researching other paranormal phenomenon like faith healing. Much of his early research is still considered classified by the former Atomic Energy Commission. Eventually, Puharich began exploring ESP and psychokinesis; the ability to move objects with one's mind, and began researching test subjects who appeared to have psychic potential. He's the guy that brought Uri Geller over here from Israel. Have you ever heard of him or seen him on television?" A couple of the attendees nodded.

"Remote viewing means different things to different people. For some, it means closing your eyes and imagining. For others, it might mean gazing into a crystal ball or reading tea leaves. How you get to where you need to be will be up to you. Remote Viewing can be all of these things. So it can get confusing."

She tried to simplify the concept. "Think about it like the general subject of martial arts. How do you learn martial arts? Well, first you have to do a little research. When you do, you find that there are many different types or styles martial arts; Kung Fu, Tae Kwon Do, Jujitsu, Karate...you know. You might be inept at one style and quite adept at others. So, the same is true of Remote Viewing."

"Thus, the goal today is to learn what you can about it, and then most importantly, let go of being right. You have to ditch your ego right now!"

"Some of you will do better today than others. This is not a contest!" She placed her hands on her hips. "The toughest part of your process will be to quiet your mind. You have to get rid of all the crap that bounces around the inside of your cranium every minute of your waking day so that you can allow sensory input a chance to work its way in there. And since this is a Communications class, we'll say that you need to be able to reduce the noise and amplify the signal. Our training is intended to help you improve the signal to noise ratio."

"Before you begin, you should try to place yourself in the proper physical and mental state. You should be open to receiving any and all information relative to whatever you decide to focus on, because you never know what pieces of information are vital until you are finished with the viewing. You will get sensory data all at once, in no logical order. Experienced psychics and beginners alike need this skill. So, when we break for lunch, get something good to eat, and start to relax."

She paused as if she was waiting for some sort of discussion or argument, but hearing none, she went on. "All right. In your notes somewhere, you'll see this. But even if you don't, your monitors will be bombarding you with this every time you sit down for a task."

"There are a ton of rules with this, but three fundamental ones that you need to know as you start your journey." She grabbed the chalk to write on the board. "Remote Viewing is not a religious experience. Christians, Jews, Muslims, and even atheists can remote view, but we'll introduce Buddha first."

"So, the first rule is to quiet your mind. Buddha described the human mind as being filled with drunken monkeys, jumping around, screeching, chattering, and carrying on endlessly. We all have monkey minds, Buddha taught us, with dozens of monkeys all clamoring for attention. Fear is an especially loud monkey, sounding the alarm incessantly, pointing out all the things we should be wary of and everything that could go wrong. Kick that shit out of there!"

"Second," she wrote, "Perceive the Target. When beginning to practice your remote viewing, you should note that it is not uncommon to view cloudy information that you receive that holds some type of attachment to your own personal memories or interactions. Sorting through what is real and what isn't a part of the viewing shouldn't be too troublesome if you know your own psychology well enough."

"You can prepare yourself for this by going into your remote viewing session with as clear and clean a state of mind and body as possible. Relaxation, or meditation of sorts, can help you here, as well as closing your eyes in order to better focus on viewing the target in your mind through some sort of portal, such as an imaginary window or even a magnifying glass. Hence the crystal ball." She looked over her shoulder, "No, the Defense Department doesn't issue those."

"After you establish the portal connection that you'd like to use, you should begin to draw or write out whatever initial impressions you receive, even if your eyes are closed. These initial impressions can be quite odd, and that's completely fine. Just do not halt the flow of information as you view or perceive whatever comes to you. It may seem quite nonsensical."

"And third. Describe." She wrote, with the clicking chalk echoing off the back wall. "Don't try to identify. We as humans try to label everything we see. Don't do that! Tell us what you see or perceive, but don't try to guess what it is."

"The subconscious mind does not communicate in any language. Viewers often get quick bits of information, much like the aperture of a camera that opens and closes so quickly, you almost don't notice it."

"So, it is those subtle flashes of color; a smell, a taste, an idea or even a quick picture in your mind that you should notice. You need to set aside all those naming words, words that identify something. Write them down off to the side of your page somewhere."

She put the chalk back in the tray and faced the audience. "I guess now is a good time to mention something called Analytic Overlay, or AOL. This is what happens when we start to get a flow of information in and try to solve the puzzle too fast. You need to avoid that as well. Questions?"

Katie McBride, the Air Force officer raised her hand. "I'm not trying to jump the gun on your lecture, but is all this part of clairvoyance or telepathy, or what? Are these terms all synonymous?"

"Great question." Yasmina turned to the board and picked up the chalk to write the key words. "Let's say that your target is a friend or colleague, sitting in a boat, on a large peaceful lake with an island in the center of it. This is a great target that has idertifiable features. If you mentally hovered over this scene from some sort of aerial perspective, then you'd be using clairvoyance."

"If, on the other hand, you read your friend's mind to see what he or she is seeing right at that moment, then that would be a form of telepathy. If you look ahead into the future and see the picture that your tasker will show you of this event or scene, after your viewing for feedback, and you are tuning in to what you might be seeing, then, that would be precognition. Meaning, you'd be seeing something that hasn't happened yet."

Katie nodded and scribbled some notes off to the side of her deck of handouts. "Got it. Thanks!"

"Like I said, at this stage of the game, you'll be bombarded by sensory input. Some of it may be relevant, but much of it may not be. The purpose of the training is to help the viewer separate true psychic perceptions from imagination. Think of it as a drawer organizer for your mind. Thoughts pour in, and controlled RV allows you to organize them on the page. This technique also introduces and utilizes a tool in the form of ideograms, which are symbols that the viewer develops to connect him or her to various aspects of the target site. They help to get the mind and the hand working together. But, I'll explain more about that tomorrow."

Yasmina smiled as she absorbed the facial expressions and body postures of the class. She was just about where she thought she needed to be at this stage of the game. Some were dubious, but all were curious. "Before the Department of the Army would agree to participate in this program, they sent a highly skeptical officer out to Palo Alto to check it out for himself. His plan was to see remote viewing in action. Two hours later, he was able to do it himself."

Norm Webster, the Air Force investigator raised his hand. Yasmina nodded at him and he asked, "So, what kinds of things is your organization being asked to, uh, view?"

"Another excellent question." She grimaced, "I'd like to be able to give you specifics, and I absolutely hate it when I have to tell someone that something is classified. But, for the most part, everything we do is classified. To try to answer your question, as it pertains to your particular interests, I can tell you that we have located missing military aircraft. I can tell you that we've been able to determine how a particular weapon works."

Webster twirled his pen around his fingers, "Then why aren't the armed services giving this more attention? Why aren't we hearing more about it?"

Yasmina replied thoughtfully, "There are a couple of answers to that question. First, we live in a very structured scientific environment where most scientists, and therefore politicians and military leaders, see this as hocus-pocus. No one is willing to stake their reputations or careers on something that is this far out there, if you know what I mean."

She took another sip of her coffee. "There's also the secrecy of it all. The Russians undoubtedly know that we're competing against them now in the ethereal space and the more we advertise our successes, the more paranoid they'll become."

She was quiet for a moment, "Then, of course, there's the business side of intelligence work. If you're a senator or congressman lobbying for money, what do you think creates more financial interest; a billion dollar spy satellite program, or a room full of psychics that cost less than a hundred grand a year?"

She raised her eyebrows. "It's really tough to finance a re-election campaign when there's no money on the table for people and equipment, earmarked for defense spending."

"Let's face it folks," she sighed "this is not a career builder on your resume. No colonel who's on the list for general, is going to want it known around Washington that his previous command was a bunch of psychics."

"Any other questions?" She waited for a response. "No? Okay then, who's ready for another Zener test? Now that you've had an opportunity to run through it once, let's try it again today and try to beat our performance from Monday."

⸻ ((◦)) ⸻

Balmain shook his head as he read through the strange file. Until he had a better understanding of what he had in his possession, he had decided against taking the file out of the office. At the end of the day, he put it back behind his credenza where he'd found it. As a consequence, he hadn't slept more than a couple of hours the night before. Too many thoughts bombarded his brain and left him with a myriad questions about the source and authenticity of the documents.

Chronologically, the file began with documents from the 1940s, including one from President Harry Truman, dated September 24, 1947, entitled *Memorandum for Secretary of Defense*. It was addressed to Secretary James Forrestal, recalling an earlier conversation between them, and authorizing the establishment of a project called MJ-12. It concentrated power and leadership for the project between the office of the President, the Director of the CIA, and Dr. Vannevar Bush, an electrical engineer who had headed the Office of Scientific Research during WWII and had been heavily involved in the Manhattan Project.

There were reports from the 1940s and 1950s of downed spacecraft that were recovered by the US Army, with one July 10, 1947 document that featured Hoover's identifiable handwritten comments off in the margin, "…demanding full access to the discs recovered".

Then there was a report from Maury Island, Washington dated June 21, 1947, which caught his attention due to the reference to the FBI and an agent of whom he'd heard.

It was about some boaters who were volunteer patrolmen, snagging logs that had slipped away from a nearby mill, into the channel where they could become a danger to watercraft in Puget Sound. The principal complainant, Harold Dahl reported that about two in the afternoon, he was on his patrol boat with two men, his son, and their dog.

As his boat approached the east shore of Maury Island, he looked in the sky and saw six objects floating about two thousand feet above them. The objects seemed to be made of some sort of reflective metal, doughnut shaped, and about one hundred feet in diameter. The center holes were about twenty-five feet in diameter. Dahl said he also saw round portholes and what he thought could have been observation windows. Five of the craft circled over the sixth, which dropped slowly, seemingly having mechanical difficulties. It stopped and hovered about five hundred feet above the water. Dahl put to shore because he was afraid the center aircraft was going to crash into his boat. Once ashore, Dahl took several pictures with his camera. The lower ship stayed in position for about five minutes, with the others still circling above. One of the ships left the formation and moved down, touching the lower ships. The two kept contact for several minutes, until Dahl said he heard a thud. Suddenly, thousands of pieces of what he thought were newspapers dropped from the inside of the center ship. Most of the debris landed in the bay, though some hit the beach. Dahl recovered a few pieces, finding it was a white, lightweight metal. Along with the white metal, the ship dropped about twenty tons of a dark metal, which he said looked like lava rock. When the lava rock hit the water, it was so hot that steam erupted. They took cover after several pieces landed on his boat. Some debris hit his son on the arm, burning him, and another piece struck his dog, killing him.

After the rain of metal, the craft rose into the air and headed west out to sea together with the others. Dahl tried to radio for help, but the radio did not work. They sailed back toward their dock, dropping the dog over the side as a burial at sea. Dahl took his son to the hospital for treatment and then told his boss, Fred Crisman, what had happened. Dahl gave Crisman the camera, and when the film was developed, the prints showed the strange air ships. However, the negatives had spots on them, which he suspected could have been damaged by exposure to light or radiation. Crisman said he initially did not believe Dahl's story, but nevertheless, he went back to Maury Island, where he gathered some rock samples. He said that while he was gathering the rocks, one of the airships appeared overhead, as if it was watching him. Dahl told investigators that the next morning, a man wearing a dark suit visited him, and suggested they go to breakfast together. Dahl drove his own car, following the stranger's new black Buick to a restaurant. While they ate, the stranger asked no specific questions, but rather recited the information that had been reported the day before. The man warned Dahl that if he went public with his claim, that the media would hound him and his family, and that he could be portrayed as a lunatic.

On the afternoon of July 31, Captain Lee Davidson and First

Lieutenant Frank Brown of the U.S. Army Air Force flew up to Tacoma from Hamilton Field, California. In addition to being pilots, the two men were intelligence specialists. They met with Ken Arnold, who had himself reported an encounter with strange objects during an earlier flight. Dahl and Crisman were also present for the meeting, which lasted for several hours.

One of the military officers told the group that he thought there might have been some credibility with the story, but that they had to return around midnight. They explained that they needed to be at Hamilton Field on August 1, which was the day the Air Force was to organizationally split from the Army.

The two officers took some of the slag samples and flew out of McChord Air Field around two o'clock in the morning on a B-25 bomber, with a crew of two other men. About twenty minutes later, the airplane crashed near Centralia, Washington. The two enlisted men managed to parachute to safety, but Davidson and Brown were killed.

The Air Force investigators determined that the crash had been nothing more than a terrible accident. One of the engines caught fire and the men began bailing out. But before Brown and Davidson could exit the aircraft, a wing broke and struck the tail section, severing it. The plane went into a spin, trapping the men inside. Another Air Force investigator later spoke with Dahl and Crisman, and visited their boat. He stated in his official report that the damage he saw did not match the damage the two sailors described. He could find no piles of metal on Maury Island, and the existing samples he saw looked like slag from a metal smelter. His conclusion matched that of an FBI investigator; that Dahl and Crisman had faked the incident to gain publicity for a magazine article. The FBI warned Dahl and Crisman that they believed their story to be a hoax and unless they dropped the matter, the government would likely prosecute the two men for a fraud, which had resulted in the deaths of the two Army officers. The admonition had the desired effect, as neither man wanted any trouble with the United States government. They were coerced into saying, according to the report dated August 14, 1947, "Dahl did not admit that his story was a hoax but only stated that if questioned by the authorities he was going to say it was a hoax because he did not want any further trouble over the matter."

What caught Balmain's attention, was the notation in the margin of the report. Someone had written "Forward to Banister."

Guy Banister. Now there was a name that jogged Balmain's memory, especially following Jim Garrison's ill-fated prosecution of Clay Shaw in New Orleans in 1969. After joining the Bureau in 1934, Banister was actually present at the killing of John Dillinger. His initial assignment with the Bureau had been Indianapolis, but he later moved to New York City where he was involved in the investigation of the American Communist Party.

Director Hoover was impressed by Banister's work and, in 1938, he was promoted to run the FBI office in Butte, Montana. During his tenure, he also served in Oklahoma City, Minneapolis and finally Chicago, where he was the Special Agent in Charge of the office before retiring from the FBI in 1954.

Banister moved home to Louisiana and, in January 1955, became Assistant Superintendent of the New Orleans Police Department, where he was given the task of investigating organized crime and corruption within the police force. It was later revealed that he was also involved in looking at the role that left-wing political activists were playing in the struggle for civil rights in New Orleans. In his spare time, he ran a network of informants that collected information on alleged communist and other subversive activities on the campuses of Tulane University and Louisiana State University. He regularly submitted reports on his findings to the FBI through quasi-official contacts.

After leaving the New Orleans Police Department over an embarrassing incident, Banister established his own private detective agency, and in June 1960, moved his office to 531 Lafayette Street on the ground floor of the Newman Building. Also located in the same building, with a different entrance around the corner, was the address of 544 Camp Street. This address would later be found stamped on Fair Play for Cuba Committee leaflets distributed by Lee Harvey Oswald, the suspected assassin of President John F. Kennedy.

The Newman Building also housed militant anti-Castro groups, including the Cuban Revolutionary Council, and Sergio Arcacha Smith's Crusade to Free Cuba Committee. As Garrison pointed out in his prosecution, Banister's office was within walking distance of the New Orleans offices of the FBI, CIA, Office of Naval Intelligence and the Reily Coffee Company, which had been Lee Harvey Oswald's employer at the time. Reily Coffee was also a strong supporter of anti-Castro causes.

Banister was implicated in a 1961 raid on a munitions depot in Houma, Louisiana, in which various weapons such as hand grenades and ammunition were stolen. Witnesses reported seeing such equipment stacked in Banister's back room. The New Orleans States-Item newspaper even reported an allegation that Banister served as a munitions supplier for the 1961 Bay of Pigs Invasion and continued to deal weapons from his office until 1963.

In 1962, Banister allegedly dispatched an associate, Maurice Brooks Gatlin; legal counsel of Banister's Anti-Communist League of the Caribbean, to Paris to deliver a suitcase containing $200,000 for the French OAS, a right-wing dissident paramilitary group. And, in 1963, Banister and anti-Castro activist David Ferrie began working for a lawyer named G. Wray Gill and his client, New Orleans Mafia boss Carlos Marcello. Court records indicated that this may have involved attempts to block Marcello's deportation to Guatemala.

In early 1962, Banister assisted David Ferrie in a dispute with Eastern Airlines regarding charges brought against Ferrie by the airline and New Orleans police for supposed crimes against nature and extortion. During this period, Ferrie was frequently seen at Banister's office, and Banister served as a character witness for Ferrie at his airline pilot's grievance board hearing in the summer of 1963.

Banister died of coronary thrombosis on June 6, 1964, and his private files disappeared among various people after his death.

Some witnesses alleged that the FBI and other agencies had sent agents in to seize them; filing cabinets and all.

Balmain let out a low whistle before commenting out loud. "So, Guy Bannister, a potential associate of Lee Harvey Oswald, was n-vestigating UFOs in the fifties?"

━━━◉━━━

Mark selected a carrel near the door, and one by one, the other students followed him into the room and located an empty work station. He stowed his briefcase under the desk, and looked at the dark manila envelope face down on the surface. Remembering their instructions from Yasmina, he didn't attempt to flip it over or hold it up to the light to get a hint as to what might be inside.

He inspected the headset hanging on the hook and noticed that the coiled cord ran into a volume control. He was only vaguely aware of the person walking behind him and taking the station next to his.

"I always wanted a private office," Katie McBride joked as she sat down. "This may be the closest I've gotten yet!"

Mark smiled. He was mildly excited, in both an emotional and physical way that she had opted to sit next to him. He looked down the row and saw that her partner was nowhere to be seen. He'd obviously taken a seat in the second or third row. "Hey, we have electricity and running water here! This is a step up from some of the places I've had to work. I'm Mark," he said reaching his hand around.

"I remember from Monday," she said with a smile. "Katie McBride."

After shaking hands he asked, "So what is a GS-11?"

She winked. "General Schedule. It's just another pay scale like E-something or O-something for enlisted and officer personnel in the services. Same philosophy. If you stay around long enough and don't get yourself in trouble, you get promoted."

"Uh huh. And what is it that you do when you're not learning to read minds?"

"Norm and I are civilian agents with the Air Force Office of Special Investigations. It's roughly the same thing as your Naval Investigative Service."

"You're a cop?" Mark chided jokingly.

She laughed, "I guess I am now. I started my career in the Air Force in science and technology. I was an Electrical Engineering grad from Brown. You?"

"Grunt, from Dallas." Mark grinned, using the slang term for an infantry Marine. "I went into the Corps right out of high school. Every once in a while, I think about going back to school on the GI Bill, but I just haven't had time yet. But if I ever do, I'll probably get into something like political science or history. The math and technical stuff really isn't my thing."

As Yasmina entered the classroom, Katie whispered, "Is there a place called the Anchored Eagle around here?"

Mark nodded, "Yeah, pretty good food! But, it gets kind of noisy at night if you know what I mean."

She had the most perfect set of teeth Mark had ever seen, and he seemed to focus on them as she spoke, "Do you feel like going there for lunch today? I'm in the mood to get out and try something different and it sounds like a good place."

Mark couldn't believe that she had just asked him out. A lunch date between colleagues, maybe. But it was still a date. "That sounds like fun!"

She smiled and slid her chair up into the carrel as Yasmina explained their first assignment.

"Okay on your desks, you will find a sealed envelope. As I mentioned in class, please leave it sealed. However, if you flip it over, you will see a number written on it. Write that number on each page of paper you use for this exercise."

She moved to the side of the classroom so that people could see her without having to stand up to look over the tops of the carrels. "This exercise will be easy. I want you to relax and quiet your mind. I want you to focus on the contents of your particular envelope...only yours. There are a lot of envelopes in the room right now. Just focus on the one in front of you."

"Write down the first impression that comes to your mind. Then, I want you to think about structure or shape. Draw what you see, not what you think it is. Don't try to name it. If you pick up other sensory input, or feelings, write that down as well. I'll give you about twenty minutes for this, so use all the time you need, but don't fall asleep. Begin."

Mark told himself that this was no different than trying to pick a card out of a deck. There were just more than fifty-two possibilities. He tried to clear his mind and concentrate but the monkeys were wreaking havoc on his brain. In addition to everything else that normally occupied his thoughts, he was now thinking about the attractive blond next to him, who had just invited him to lunch.

She was gorgeous. A little over five foot six, blond hair and piercing blue eyes, and the nicest smile he'd ever seen. Considering her height, he estimated her to be no more than a hundred thirty pounds, and she looked amazingly fit. She had a way of moving when she walked that suggested that even though she was a federal agent, she knew how to be a woman. As a matter of fact, she was a woman first, and a gun-toting agent second. There was something alluring and provocative about that.

The envelope. Concentrate on the envelope. Yasmina said to write down the first image that came to mind. A triangle. A really elongated triangle coming to a sharp point. It was outside somewhere. There were people around it, looking at it.

Katie had told the class that she was from Pittsburgh. But, she had chosen Brown for her degree. That was a well-known Ivy League school that had to have been expensive. It was in New Hampshire...no...Rhode Island. Scholarship...she must be pretty intelligent...she must've had a scholarship. Unless...maybe her parents were well-off? She'd never be happy, married to someone who drew sergeant's pay.

The envelope. Focus on the damn envelope. Mark tried to

re-position himself in his seat to be more comfortable, but was too distracted by all of the other attendees shifting in their seats, trying to do the same thing. He opened his eyes for a moment and put the earphones on. That should make things a little quieter.

There was a low frequency hum coming from the headset. He adjusted the volume all the way down and got rid of most of it. But in his brain, he could still hear it. Nevertheless, it was better than the room noise. After a while, he grew used to the hum and found it to be almost pleasant. It sounded like the beginning of an orchestration, just after the instruments have tuned, but before they played the first note. It was like the echo of, maybe a low "C".

The triangle had depth and dimension. At the base, It was square on the sides, climbing to a point. It was buried in the ground. It had meaning. It was tall; taller than anything around it. There was water nearby …natural water…but, also man-made…like a swimming pool. Maybe near a house on the beach. Someone important looks at it frequently.

Geez, she must be close to thirty! What did she say? Air Force officer for four years and a civilian for almost four…that's eight years since college. If she'd been twenty one when she graduated, she'd be twenty nine or thirty now. But, she was so sharp. She looked like she could pass for someone in their early twenties. She was in such good shape!

Mark had never dated a woman that was older than him. Hell, for the past four years, he hadn't dated any woman. He'd had a casual relationship with one of the female Marines in Okinawa, but that hadn't gotten him laid. What was Katie looking for? Just a lunch partner? Maybe she'd just broken up with someone or was going through a divorce and was ready to start something new? Maybe she just liked hitting on younger guys? Maybe guys in uniform? He was doing his sit-ups every morning; his stomach was flat and rock hard.

The envelope! What else was there about the triangle? What had Yasmina said? Pay attention to the sensory and dimensional information in your mental images. It means something. Maybe a large tombstone? Near a swimming pool? That didn't make any sense. Write it down.

Mark was in the middle of trying to draw what he was imagining when Dr. Kravitz entered the room. "Okay everyone, that's time! Everyone stand up and stretch."

Mark stood and stretched his arms out and then above his head, inhaling and exhaling purposefully. As he did, his gaze moved around the room and he noted that everyone else seemed as emotionally taxed as he. As his gaze moved to the woman next to him, he caught her smiling at him. "How'd you do?"

She shook her head. "No frickin' idea!"

Yasmina and Dr. Kravitz conferred briefly before she related, "As they say in show business, that's lunch! Please leave all of your notes underneath the envelopes on your desks and Dr. Kravitz and I will take a look at them while you guys are relaxing. Take an hour and a half, and when you return, we'll give you some feedback.

Katie reached below her desk and grabbed her purse. "I'm glad that's over. Let's get out of here!"

They got into her government-issued Chevy and headed down the road. She seemed to know where she was going, and ten minutes later, they pulled into the parking lot for the Anchored Eagle. Aside from her general perceptions about the class, during the brief drive Mark learned that her dad owned some sort of shopping mall in McKeesport, just southeast of Pittsburgh, and that Katie had become an engineer because she liked building things. She had a younger sister named Karen, who was a sophomore at Penn State and yearned to be an FBI agent, but because of the difference in their ages, they had not been as close growing up as she would have liked. She also had an on-again – off-again relationship with a TWA pilot named Terry. Luckily for Mark, it was currently in the off-again mode.

As they walked towards the entrance, Mark instinctively reached to open the door for her. This caused the patron in the grey suit coming out the door to stumble and drop the file folder he'd been carrying.

"Excuse me, sir," Mark said as he respectfully bent to retrieve the folder.

The tall lanky man in his fifties bent so fast to collect the file that Mark was afraid they would comically butt heads like in a cheap movie. "My mistake sergeant." He grabbed the file with both hands as if he was worried something would blow out of it, and as he dashed off towards the parking lot, gave Katie a quick glance. Mark took note, but couldn't tell; was it admiration or recognition?

Mark held the door open to allow his date inside. "Wow, he certainly looks like he's got a lot on his mind today!"

"FBI," she said.

Mark looked at her with a sly smile, "Using your psychic powers already?"

"Badge clipped to his belt," she said with a slight giggle. "Let's eat."

12

THURSDAY, APRIL 28, 1977

Mark Reynolds rolled over and looked at the luminous dial of the stainless Omega Seamaster on his wrist. It was just after two in the morning. The watch had been his high school graduation present from his mom and dad, and had been with him ever since, even in Saigon, when he worried that if he was taken prisoner, the watch would have ended up on some North Vietnamese colonel's wrist.

It took him a moment to remember where he was and how he got there.

After an enjoyable lunch, they had returned to class and sat through the feedback session provided by Yasmina and Dr. Kravitz. Katie's and Mark's scores were among the highest in the room and both were euphoric at their progress. As a means of celebration, they mutually recognized that a drink was in order and so after class, they agreed to meet at a place in Alexandria.

It was about a forty minute drive up Interstate 95, but rather than follow her, Mark wanted to go back to his room in Transient Billeting to change into civilian clothes. The rooms were clean and comfortable, but really not suitable for entertaining. At least not his. He had a queen size bed and a private bathroom, but that was about it.

Katie was stationed at Andrews Air Force Base and kept an apartment in the Landmark section of Alexandria. It was a relatively new high rise building near Interstate 395 and Van Dorn, with ample parking, and very close to a number of restaurants. So when they met for that drink, one led to two, which led to dinner, which led to another drink, which led to an invitation to see her apartment.

An uncontrollable smile came to his face. He knew he had to get back to Quantico and get some sleep before getting cleaned up and properly dressed for class. He gently slid out of bed and softly pulled the sheet up over her bare shoulder. He looked at her silently and was grateful that despite the alcohol-induced energy in the room, they'd had the presence of mind to talk for a bit first.

The apartment had a small kitchen, small bedroom, and small bathroom, so the tour only took a minute. When she turned to him to announce that he'd seen everything, they were too close. They touched and a second later they were in a passionate embrace, with his tongue trying to explore her neck, her ears and every erogenous zone above her shoulders. She was perky and beautiful, and he was heterosexual. That was really all it took.

She put her hands on his chest and whispered, "Hold on a sec."

"Too fast?" Mark replied, his heart beating through his shirt.

"No." She shook her head. "Not at all. But we need to face some facts, first."

She swallowed. "Your job and my job are going to take us different directions. With any luck, you'll be in Palo Alto in a week or so, and I'll be either here or somewhere else in the world."

Mark's excitation momentarily waned. "And?"

"And, if I tell you something now, it has to be our secret. You can't tell anyone else - especially anyone in the program."

By this point, Mark was ready to commit to anything she proposed. "Sure. What's the problem?"

"I'll lose my job if anyone finds out I told you this, but Norm and I are only guests in this program. We were given permission to sit in the class in order to see how they teach this stuff, the...uh... remote viewing. The OSI is considering using the lab's services, but they wanted to know more about the training methodologies before they would agree to spend any money, or consider evaluating the intelligence that can be produced. So, it's likely that I, we, might be a client in the near future."

Mark contemplated the impact of what she'd said. "So, where does that leave us?"

She smiled at him and he saw that perfect mouth. "It means that we should keep things friendly, and not read too much into tonight. What I mean is that it wouldn't be appropriate for us to start holding hands in class, or you carrying my books, or asking me to the prom. Know what I mean?"

"I do," he said before taking her in his arms and gently dancing her towards the bed.

Now, as he tried to find his socks in near darkness, he studied the curves that shaped the linen sheet covering her.

She rolled over and sat up. "Hey Marine! Are you trying to sneak out without paying?" A smile formed in the corner of her mouth as she brushed the blonde hair out of her sleepy eyes.

Mark smiled back, "Are you kidding? It was the best night of my life! If my car was paid for, I'd give it to you."

He went around to her side of the bed and sat down. He took her hand in his and she squeezed tightly as he whispered, "You're something else! I'll try to keep my hands and my eyes off of you today." He leaned forward and kissed her on the forehead. "See you in a few hours!"

——◆◆◆——

Balmain parked and hastened his pace to get to his office. He owed his wife an apology and needed to call her. What he had read and digested from the file over the last twenty four hours had made him particularly irritable that morning, and as a result, he took it out on her during breakfast. He stormed out of the house, leaving her with the feeling that she had done something to cause his foul disposition.

Obviously, he couldn't tell her the truth. She had been an FBI wife for thirty years and she was used to getting partial or vague explanations. "I'm so sorry, honey...it's the job." She was a good woman. She would understand.

"Is it the Peltier thing?" she'd asked patiently.

Balmain exhaled, "No. It's something going on in Washington. It's not your fault. It's not my fault. I love you."

Balmain stared at the file on his desk, now with a fresh scratch on the vintage manila folder from being dropped in the parking lot after yesterday's lunch. He'd never been so torn about a decision in his life.

He couldn't believe it. In front of him was evidence, of dubious origin no doubt, that elements of the US government may have had contact with spacecraft from somewhere other than earth. President Truman had attempted to reign in all of the relevant information to a special committee so they could study the phenomenon, and perhaps benefit militarily from what they had found.

There were numerous reports, from seemingly credible sources, but the FBI had simply pushed these investigations off on the Air Force, which in turn, coerced or cajoled witnesses into keeping quiet or revising their stories. Project BLUEBOOK was not an objective investigation into unexplained aerial phenomenon, but rather a means for the Air Force to explain the bulk of the reports coming in as nothing more than natural events or misidentified conventional aircraft. Also, their demonstrated intent was to discredit anyone who refused to change their story to meet the government narrative.

Neither was Project BLUEBOOK the comprehensive investigation that the public thought. Military and many civilian pilots had been told not to report sightings through BLUEBOOK, but rather through a separate government process under JANAP 146, instituted in 1966 with the NSA sitting in oversight. Thus, their reports could be labeled as classified and therefore made unavailable to the public. This caused some of the most credible sightings and evidence to be excluded from BLUEBOOK's published study.

It now appeared that the Joint Chiefs, the CIA and the FBI, at least at the highest levels, were knowledgeable of this and they all worked together to keep the secret. That is, until John F. Kennedy told the CIA he wanted to share this information with the Soviet Union. Ten days before his death, he let it be known that he wanted to open UFO files. Was it possible that all of the conspiracy theories about the Mafia, the Cubans, and even LBJ, were actually welcomed and promoted by the select group of world leaders who wanted to keep the true motive for his death a secret? The traditional conspiracy-chasers provided the perfect smokescreen.

But, why hadn't the media reacted? Normally, those vultures couldn't wait to expose something that would get them a Pulitzer. Since they seemed to mistrust everything that came out of government, why or how could they be so easily duped into thinking there was no story here? Why were they buying what the government was selling? Or was government control of the press higher up their respective organizational ladders than the public realized? Maybe higher up than the journalists themselves realized?

He bent the brown metal prongs straight up and slipped the pages off them. He quickly flipped through the individual sheets to make sure none of them had been stapled, and then walked down the hall.

"Jill?" he asked the receptionist. "Can you show me how to work that monstrous copier in there?"

She grinned, "Oh, no need. Just give it to me and I'll take care of it."

"No, that's okay." Balmain kept his grip on the documents. "Can you just show me how to make it work?"

"Sure, but you need this doo-hickey thing." She handed him a gray plastic box about the size of a pack of cigarettes that had what looked like an odometer on the end. "You just plug this in the slot on the side of the machine, and then make your copies. There's a guy that comes out once a month to look at the count and that's how they know how much to charge us for that month."

Balmain shrugged and took the counter with him to the copy room. When he was certain he was alone, he copied the entire file, feeling a little guiltier with each scan. When he was finished, he dropped the doo-hickey off on the reception counter and thanked her. He had just violated federal law by making copies of classified documents.

He wanted more information. But, who could he trust? How could he verify some of the claims made in these reports without letting anyone know of his interest? His contacts at CIA were cordial, but by no means safe to work through. His personal history of dodging and demeaning the media, did little to build any confidence with them either. There was the FBI library right there in Quantico, but it was a certainty that there would be nothing in there that hadn't been sanitized by every agency in the government.

He wiped his fingerprints off of the outer folder and on the individual pages where he might have touched them while reading or making copies. There was an old saying in the business, "Just because you're paranoid doesn't mean that they're not really out to get you." There was no sense giving some documents examiner more ammunition to torpedo his career if someone managed to get their hands on the file. He dropped the original back over the credenza where it had been for heaven-only-knows how long.

He stuck his fresh copies in the back of a mundane budget report for camouflage, and slid it into his briefcase. He spun the combination lock on his briefcase and pushed it under his desk before getting up and wandering down to Garcia's office.

"Got a minute?" Balmain said as Garcia looked up from the report he'd been reading.

"Sure, what's up?"

"Just curious." Balmain pursed his lips and frowned. "How long was Sebastian in this job before I got here?"

"I think about three years," he replied. "Why?"

"Just curious. I don't want to rock any boats organizationally and before I make any changes around here, I just wanted to know something about the academy's history. Who was here before him?"

Garcia thought for a moment. "MacArthur, Willis MacArthur. Everyone called him Mac."

Balmain nodded. "That's right. I kind of remember him. He wasn't here that long though, was he?"

Garcia shook his head and smiled, "Huh uh. A couple of years. He, uh, retired suddenly when a few of the women cadets made some claims of, you know, unprofessional conduct."

"Yeah, tall guy. Told everyone he thought he looked like Cary Grant. What ever happened to him?"

"Matter of fact, I think someone actually walked him out, if you know what I mean." Garcia winced, "He didn't last long after retirement. His wife heard about the allegations and left him. She got half of his pension in a speedy divorce and moved back home to someplace out west...Colorado or Wyoming maybe. He bought a boat somewhere down in the Keys, and invested his half of the settlement in a variety of distilleries, one bottle at a time. One night, he tried to go SCUBA diving after one too many cocktails."

"Dead?" Balmain asked, his eyebrows lifted so high he felt the skin tug at his ears.

"Oh yeah. Coast Guard got a call of a boat adrift and they found him about a quarter mile away, still in his gear, but his tank was empty."

Balmain pondered Garcia's recollection, "Was he the first Director out here when the place opened?"

"He was the first permanent one. Jack Cramer was an interim Director for a couple months, but as soon as MacArthur came in, he went back to Headquarters. He ran part of the Legal section there."

"Thanks!" Balmain turned to leave.

"Your turn to buy lunch Mr. Assistant Director!" Garcia shouted.

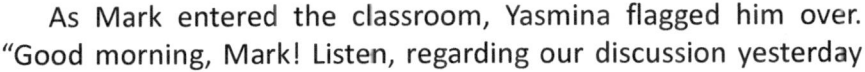

As Mark entered the classroom, Yasmina flagged him over. "Good morning, Mark! Listen, regarding our discussion yesterday afternoon, we're going to use the feedback from a couple of the viewings to help everyone understand what to look for and to better focus on their skills. Yours was one of the ones we selected. We won't be using any names, just the task reference numbers, so, no one will know it was yours. Are you okay with that?"

Mark nodded with a smile." Sure thing! I was kind of surprised that I got that close to the target."

Yasmina agreed, "Very close indeed! Your results and one other student's really exceeded our expectations!"

Mark, mildly sluggish from a lack of sleep, suddenly perked up. "Thanks!"

As the rest of the class had made their way in to their seats, Mark felt Katie brush past him a little closer than necessary on her way to her seat. "Good morning sergeant!" She said with a smile.

"Good morning," Mark said back, unable to keep from grinning.

Yasmina turned on the overhead projector and Mark immediately recognized one of the drawings he'd made of his triangle in yesterday's exercise, projected on the screen. "This is task number 77-234Q, viewed yesterday by one of your colleagues. As you can see, some of the most identifiable points that come out are the elongated triangular shape. But viewed three-dimensionally, we can see that it has depth, with the four sides coming to a sharp point. Originally seen as an elongated triangle, on successive pages..." she replaced the page on the screen with another from the same series. "...we see that this perception of a sharp triangle morphed into a pyramid, to like a toothpick buried in the ground, as the viewer indicates." She used her pencil to point to key features of the drawings. "But, something respected or revered as the viewer also notes."

"Off on the sides of the page, we see references to water, which include a perception of a natural body of water as well as something man-made, like a swimming pool. The viewer perceives this target to be of importance, that people are looking at it, and that important people look at it every day. It's made of a concrete-like material."

She summarized her findings, "So, a tall, elongated triangle with four sides that rises to a point, near the water, with people looking at it." She switched the projector off as she replaced the page on the screen with a photograph. "Any guesses?"

"A tombstone, or monument of some kind?" Warrant Officer Conner said.

"Maybe the Washington monument?" Katie asked.

"Bingo!" Yasmina declared, switching on the projector. There on the screen was Mark's target: a photograph depicting an aerial view of the Washington Monument, which included a portion of the adjacent Potomac and the reflecting pool that stretched out towards the Lincoln Memorial.

"In our business, we would call this a hit! We would score this as an eighty to ninety percent effort, because the viewer recognized the significant physical features and social importance. If he'd included the feature of the natural water as moving, and located it on the correct side of the monument, then this would have been a hundred percent. Well-done number 234!"

"The next work I'd like to display is number 77-517Q." She moved a drawing onto the projector surface. Even if Mark hadn't recognized the handwriting as Katie's, he still would have felt like this was her drawing. The technical detail and description, the careful, draftsman-like printing. Something an engineer would have produced.

Yasmina read the description as she pointed out features in the drawing. "Big structures in a circle, buried, old, might mean something spiritual and technical. In a field." On the next page the viewer notes, "Ancient...maybe associated with worship. Tall...wide... heavy...dense material, maybe rock."

"Stonehenge?" Chief Wheeler asked.

"Yeah...Stonehenge," Conner agreed.

"Bingo!" Yasmina cheered. She placed the accompanying photograph on the projector and the image of Stonehenge appeared on the screen. "Stonehenge is a prehistoric monument in Wiltshire, England, two miles west of Amesbury. It consists of a ring of standing stones, each around thirteen feet high, seven feet wide, and weighing around 25 tons."

She continued, "Archaeologists believe it was constructed around 3000 BC, and served as a gathering place for worship and for viewing celestial objects in the night sky. Like the description said, big rocks buried in a circle."

Yasmina clapped her hands. "Great work number 517! This is another ninety percent hit. Great description and sketch!" All of you had some valuable data. Remember, the goal isn't necessarily to be totally accurate with each exercise, but rather to learn something new about yourself each time."

She flipped the projector off. "When images come to mind, just write down what you see, and then try taking just the colors, textures, smells, sounds, tastes, shapes, patterns, positions, and sizes, whatever from the image that came to mind. Write this stuff down, even if it doesn't make any sense. Even if something is distracting you, write that down to get rid of it."

"You have to sift through the many thoughts that come to mind and get yourself to simply focus on describing what comes to you relative to the target site. So, write down the first thing that comes to your mind. Begin the session by describing the most basic impressions you have of the first target. What do you feel is the predominant thing in the target? Is it natural or artificial? Surrounded by land or water? Write several descriptors down."

"Information will be coming from the depths of your mind and autonomic nervous system. The idea is that your unconscious already knows everything there is to know about the target, it just has to communicate that information to your conscious mind. It does that through your body with very subtle sensations and feelings."

"You may start perceiving sizes, shapes and patterns. These are known as dimensionals. You may even start to feel an emotional reaction to the target. If it helps, imagine yourself floating several hundred feet over the target area. Is there anything surprising about the target that you didn't pick up on before, when viewed from a different angle?"

"If you didn't connect with anything in the photo, don't get frustrated. Like I said, at this stage, the main point of RV is to learn about yourself, not just to be accurate. Remember that remote viewing is an ability you have to cultivate. So, to the best of your abilities, just have fun!" She paused. "Questions?"

"So now, we'll work on one other exercise and then we'll take a break." She broke open a ream of paper and started distributing a dozen blank sheets to each attendee. "If you need to take a break, now's the time to go. Because, at exactly 10:00 o'clock today, that would be ten hundred for you military types, Dr. Kravitz will be standing at a remote location. In RV, we call this an outbounder experiment. Dr. Kravitz is the outbounder and no one, including me, knows where he is."

"Your job will be to see what he sees. Hear what he hears. Smell what he smells."

Mark stood and stretched as several of his colleagues left the room. As he rotated his torso he caught Katie smiling at him again, and he felt relieved. The smile meant that she didn't hate herself or him for the previous night. Everything was going to be fine.

At about two minutes until ten, Yasmina stuck her head out in the hallway and asked everyone to take their seats. Mark was excited, but a little anxious. He was already forgetting one of the cardinal rules; that the exercise was not about accuracy so much as it was to learn about himself. It wasn't a competition.

Yasmina checked her watch. "All right, class, the Outbounder has reached his target by now. Your target that is. For the next forty five minutes, I want you to relax and tell us everything you can about the target as it exists in current time. Use as much paper as you need. Begin!"

Mark took a couple of deep breaths, inhaling through his nose, and exhaling through his mouth. He cleared his mind of everything. Everything except Katie. Was she concentrating on the target, or was she thinking about him?

Focus, focus, focus! The first image. What's the first image? Gradually, the monkeys quieted down and were replaced with a darkened palette of subdued colors. There was kaleidoscopic movement. The colors morphed into a nebulous form that evolved into a large eye. Brown undulating iris, and expanding pupil. In his mind, he was drawn into it. Room noises faded into the distance.

Water. Was he looking at water? He was surrounded by water. Mark started sketching. Trees near water. Something jagged near water. Old. Useless. Worse than useless...never used.

He fell further into the pupil until he was immersed in darkness. Something intended for violence, or war. Never used. Poorly built. Graves without people. Something moving. Was it the target, or Kravitz?

Her body was so firm, her skin so very soft. They moved well together, as if they had known each other for years, and knew what the other enjoyed. When his tongue explored her neck and ears, it sent her into convulsive tremors. He couldn't remember the last time that he had felt so...

Focus! Concentrate on the Outbounder! Somewhere out there, Kravitz was trying to send him information, and Mark was certain that it had nothing to do with a thirty year old Air Force investigator.

A faint odor of salt water, and, fresh water? Brackish? Occasional odor of...sewage? He made notes and began to sketch. He drew a line across the center of the page and tried to draw something jagged above it. "No!" That wasn't it. He moved the paper to the side and started a fresh drawing. He drew another line across the page, sky above, something along the line...trees?

Old metal...rust. Fake trees with rust? No. She had a small mole on the back of her right calf...just inches below the crease of her knee.

Concentrate. It's like a shoreline. Trees overlooking water? Don't try to name it, just draw it! Something artificial, rusty sticking up. A lot of structure...jagged...doesn't make sense.

He tried to find the imaginary eye that he had slipped into earlier, but it was gone. He had hardly used any of his forty five minutes, and he was done. There was nothing inside him to see. All he could think about was how good Katie made him feel. He kept the pen in his right hand but put his forehead in his left. At the very least, he could look busy. He could look like he was trying.

Algae...scummy...smelly...He wrote it down. It was something.

He took another deep breath and let it out as slowly as he could. The target was outdoors. It was occasionally visited by curious people. But, not in cars...no road. He felt an emotional jolt, like slipping on virtual ice. What was her sister's name? Karen. She's a sophomore at Penn State. Wants to be an FBI agent. Mixed feelings...but she is important. Why? Katie only mentioned her in passing. Karen is...Karen will be important.

Focus! Concentrate on Kravitz. The target wasn't always there... it was brought there. Others like it were brought there. Many like it were brought there. No use for them. Obsolete before their time. Mark made the quick notations off on the side of the paper and then literally fell asleep, his forehead in his palm. He was exhausted from lack of sleep the night before.

Dr. Kravitz returned about 11:15 a.m., and after making small talk with the class, told them about his venture. He placed a photograph on the overhead projector, depicting his morning jaunt; an aerial view of a muddy bay with the shapes of dozens of ships barely visible beneath the surface.

He had taken a boat across to Mallows Bay, MD, which by water, was just a few miles southeast of Quantico. By boat, it was a ten minute trip. However, if he had driven, he would have had to have taken the interstate back to the beltway; and cross into Maryland on I-495, before turning back south. This would have taken more than an hour and a half.

His target had been the Ghost Fleet that was scuttled there. Built in April 1917, too late to see action in World War I, the U.S. constructed 1,000 wooden steamships, all of which were built in just 18 months. It was one of President Woodrow Wilson's first acts, after declaring war on Imperial Germany. After the war, there was nothing else to do with them. So, they were towed to their final resting place and sank.

At the time, German submarines were sinking more than 200

of the Allies' merchant ships each month. Meaning that one out of every four ships leaving England would end up on the ocean floor. Along with those ships, millions of tons of weapons, food and other supplies were lost at sea. This was a blockade by submarine, slowly starving the Allies. The United States, waking from its isolationist slumber, would need to crank out new merchant ships to break that blockade and come to the rescue of the Allies in Europe. One official bragged that the U.S. would turn out ships faster than Germany could build torpedoes to sink them. With a rapidly approaching due date, and a supply of steel that was reserved for ships that would see battle, the rush job was just that. It resulted in poorly constructed wooden ships that, despite the time saving methods used, didn't come anywhere close to being ready on schedule. By the time the Germans had surrendered, not a single ship from the order had crossed the ocean.

With the war over and steel once again in abundance, the unused ships became obsolete and were discarded, left to rot in the Potomac. Salvage attempts were made but were unsuccessful due to cost and sheer magnitude. The site was turned into a park and wildlife refuge, accessible only by shallow-draft boats or canoes.

Now, depending on the tides, the decayed remains of approximately 230 shipwrecks could be found littering the bay in what is believed to be the largest shipwreck fleet in the Western Hemisphere. Dozens can still be seen in the shallow waters, remnants of the priciest and most unnecessary shipbuilding project in history.

"Show of hands," he asked after concluding his briefing. "How many people here think they hit on parts of this target?"

Kravitz looked around the room and noticed all of the hands were up. "We'll meet one on one later today to look at your notes, but I'd like to point out some of the key elements that a judge would use to determine if you had a hit or not."

"First, if you got some kind of water gestalt, you get points for that. In order to tour this site, you have to go by shallow-draft boat or canoe. There's really no way to see it from shore."

"Second, if you had something about boats, especially boats

or military equipment that were no longer in use, that would be a point as well. This includes shapes or structures that seem to look like what's in the photograph."

"If you picked up something about smells, in the water, in the wood, oxidation of the iron fasteners: all would be appropriate."

"First, though, let's take a look at the variations that we all came up with. Dan, since this exercise had to do with ships, why don't you come up first, and show us what the Navy came up with? Remember everyone, there's no right or wrong answer on this. The goal is for us to understand the variety of images that can seem to be important."

Chief Boatswain's Mate Dan Wheeler shrugged and collected his notes, and begrudgingly accepted the challenge to be the first one of the group to present his work.

Balmain still had a few friends left in the Bureau, in positions where work could get done behind the scenes. One of them happened to be Josh Stanton, who was another career agent who took a civilian job with the Bureau so that he could stay close to the game. They had worked together in Miami years before when they were just out of the academy and on their first office assignment. Stanton was now a civilian data manager for the Personnel Department and had access to about everything in the Personnel Department, since it was his data.

He dialed the number, "Personnel, Stanton."

"Josh? It's Fred Balmain, how've you been?"

Josh sounded excited to hear from someone from the old days. "Good Lord, man! How are you? I'd heard you were back in town."

"Well, sort of. I'm in DC a couple days a week, but my office is in Quantico now. How's…"He had to think for a second. "…Nancy, isn't it?"

"Yeah, good memory. She's fine. She's back up at our place in

Maryland now, bitching about having to put up with me for the rest of the summer. We got that condo down in St. Augustine when I retired a few years ago, and she spends most of the winter down there with her sister."

"Is it a blessing or a curse?" Balmain joked.

"Hah!" He replied. "For her or for me?"

Fred tried to sound as nonchalant as he could, "Listen, I was talking to Garcia and just found out about Mac MacArthur. I'd heard some rumors at the time, but I didn't know until this morning that he'd...uh...drowned."

"Tch..." Stanton acknowledged. "Yeah. Silly shit. He had the world by the ass and decided to throw it away on tail. His wife left him and he became a world-class alcoholic. Absolute waste!"

Balmain considered his words carefully so as not to arouse suspicion. "Well, I think I met his ex while they were in Houston. I feel bad that I never got a chance to offer my condolences. Do you know where she's living now?"

"Yeah, hold on a minute." Balmain could hear Stanton clicking away on his keyboard. "What was his real first name?"

"I think it was Willis. Like I said, I remembered meeting him a few times, but it's been a while."

"Here it is." Josh read, "Got a pen?"

"Yeah." Balmain grabbed a pen and jotted down the information.

Josh read and clicked, "She gets his pension checks. Her name is Barbara, by the way, at 9031 Ahrens Avenue, Cheyenne, Wyoming 82006." Josh gave Balmain the phone number.

Balmain copied the number and read it back to him, "Got it! Thanks!" The FBI was a brotherhood, so Josh would not think it strange that a senior agent would want to pay his respects to a widow upon learning of the death of her husband, or rather, ex-husband.

After thanking his friend and expressing a need to get together, he grabbed his AT&T calling card out of his wallet so that he could make the call without the toll charges showing up on the Academy's monthly bill. After entering the string of digits, he could hear the phone ring on the other end.

"Hello?"

"Hello. Is this Barbara?"

"Yes, who's calling?" Her voice was a little weak, but it had been a long time.

"Barbara, this is Fred Balmain with the Bureau down in Quantico. I was in the Dallas office when you were in Houston and Mac and I worked on several cases together. I wanted to apologize for not calling you sooner, but I only learned of his passing this morning. I just wanted to offer my condolences to you and your family and to see if there was anything you needed?"

"That's very sweet of you. You said your name was Fred?"

"Yes, Fred Balmain, from Dallas."

"Oh Fred, we're doing okay now. The kids are out of school and have great jobs. I still have my health, so I consider myself blessed. I'm alone, but I keep busy. So, I guess I'm not at all lonely."

"Was he, uh, did he…"

"Was he seeing someone in Florida? No, I don't think so. He had his boat and a small apartment. I'm not sure he even had any furniture."

Balmain soothingly got her to talk about her marriage and the subsequent divorce before asking, "Did they ship his personal effects to you?"

"Yes, I received some boxes, but most of it was just that trash he'd been reading. Like I said, he didn't have much, and his half of his pension and the proceeds from the sale of the boat went to our kids."

"What trash?" Balmain asked innocently.

"Oh…you know. Fred, I was an FBI wife for thirty years and so naturally, I'd heard the stories about the parties and the golf junkets, and I learned to live with it. The stories those women at the academy told about him might have had some truth to them, but he really wasn't like that. What really did it for me was that he went so crazy towards the end of his career. He got obsessed with the whole flying saucer thing. He started collecting magazine and newspaper clippings and it got so that was all he could talk about."

Balmain was pensive. "Flying saucers?"

"Yes. That became his obsession. It got so we couldn't go out with friends, especially other agents, because that's all he ever wanted to talk about. Last time I spoke to him...Christmas just before he died, he had some truly lame-brain idea that someone from the government killed President Kennedy to keep him quiet about it all."

"He thought someone killed JFK because of flying saucers?" Balmain's breathing quickened.

"Yes. That was where his head was at the end. A few of the guys from the Bureau came by from time to time just to see if I was okay, but they never took it too seriously. They thought it was some sort of self-discovery phase he'd been going through, or early dementia. Then a couple weeks after he died, the Air Force sent two guys out to talk about it. I showed them his collection of magazine and newspaper articles. They asked what I was going to do with it, and when I said I was going to throw it out, they asked if they could have it."

Balmain frowned at the telephone. "You said Air Force? Were they in uniform? Did you get their names?"

"No. They were nice enough fellows though. They were in suits, but had some kind of Air Force ID card that said they were investigators."

"Did he ever mention anyone else's names during his, uh, references to the UFO thing?"

"Nope. It was strictly his obsession. His alone."

"Well, I'm so sorry things happened like this. I just want to wish you the very best and let you know that if you ever need anything, please give me a call. We're all family here."

She thanked him for the call and they hung up. He sat in silence for a moment. The Air Force sent people to her house, to collect old clippings that were worthless? They were looking for something, and hadn't found it yet.

13

FRIDAY, APRIL 29, 1977

J ust before being dismissed on Thursday afternoon, Yasmina
had thanked everyone for their participation, and scheduled
each attendee for a one-hour program review with her and Dr.
Kravitz. Mark wasn't sure what criteria, if any, had been used to decide who had what time slot, but the two other Marine sergeants,
Andrews and Yates, had been assigned 0900 and 1000 respectively.

Chief Wheeler was scheduled for 1100 and Mark for 1300, or in
civilian parlance, one o'clock in the afternoon. Joe Conner had been
given the two o'clock and Norm and Katie had been scheduled in
the 3:00 p.m. slot, which Mark already knew, was so that they could
have dinner and drinks with Yasmina and Dr. Kravitz to discuss their
observations and if, or how they felt that the RV program might
benefit the Department of the Air Force. Katie had confidentially
mentioned that they would be joined by her boss and maybe one
other agent from their office. But Mark was excited, because the
weekend belonged to him.

Thursday had been a great evening for Katie and Mark. Because
she was on an expense account, she was able to persuade Mark
that she should pick up the tab for the evening. It was the first t me
in his life that a woman he'd been out with on a date had ever paid
for dinner and drinks. Considering his southern upbringing, it was
quite a change for him socially, and he was more than a bit appre-
hensive at first. But, women's lib was working.

They agreed to spend the weekend together and take in the touristy sites like the Smithsonian, Arlington Cemetery, and the White House, before he had to return to Norfolk to clear quarters and drive out to Palo Alto. He was looking forward to it.

Mark had to bring his head back into the present. He anxiously entered the office two minutes early, and noted that even though there was no name on the door, it obviously belonged to a senior officer. There was quality wood paneling on the walls, as well as carpet and furniture that looked impressive. There was a small round conference table between the door and the desk and when he entered, he saw Dr. Kravitz and Yasmina seated there.

"Hi Mark! Come on in and have a seat!" Dr. Kravitz rose, and affectionately shook hands with him. He opened a file folder that had Mark's name on the tab.

"We were really impressed with your natural aptitude for remote viewing and we wanted to run through some of your exercises, and then talk about where you'd like to be this time next week."

Mark smiled, "Next week? Serving my country sir, wherever that is."

Yasmina spoke, "That's a great answer, Mark. So, let me ask you. Where do you think you could do the most good? Standing a security post in an embassy in Timbuktu, or facing down the Soviets or a band of terrorists without ever leaving the United States?"

"Ma'am?" Mark asked.

"You're a pretty intuitive guy, and we think you have the natural ability to be highly effective as a remote viewer for your country. As I mentioned on the first day of your orientation, we think we might actually be falling behind some of our enemies in using psychic warfare to our advantage. The Nazis started experimenting with psychic functioning and the occult back in the thirties, and after World War II, we knew that the Russians had grabbed ahold of their psychic talent, while we were trying to hire all of their rocket scientists."

"We might have started the space race together", Kravitz added, "but in the psychic space, we're behind. We need to even that race up and we need people like you who aren't afraid to take your gift to the next level."

Mark didn't know what to say. He was a Marine. His job was to defeat the enemy. But, in his mind, that had always required a helmet and a rifle. "What are you asking me to do?"

"You have about a year left on your enlistment." Kravitz flipped through the pages in his file. "How would you like to spend t in California? All, well, let's say most expenses paid."

"Doing what?" Mark asked cautiously.

Yasmina replied. "Our program right now consists of two major disciplines. We have a research component that attempts to study remote viewing and other psychic functioning under controlled laboratory protocols, and we also have an applications side."

Kravitz took over, "On the applications side, we receive targets from a variety of clients, usually intelligence or investigative agencies, that we assign for tasking. We set up the controls, the double-blind, direct the viewing and then provide the results back to the client. They review what we've sent them and make the decision as to whether or not our information is actionable."

Yasmina continued, "Much of the time, the clients don't share all of their relevant information regarding their request with us. So, we often send them a packet, that may not mean anything to us, but it fills in some important blanks for them. So, much of the time, we can't tell if our product has been valuable or not."

Kravitz added, "But, they continue to use us, so we figure that they must find some value in the information. Keep in mind that they come to us as a last resort. This means that if we get an accurate hit on a target, we did something that none of the other agencies could do. So, even if we only hit sixty to seventy five percent of the time, that's a hundred percent better than any of the other agencies."

He adjusted his eyeglasses. "I mentioned in class some of the things our team has been responsible for; discovery of the Russian Typhoon submarine, their work with particle beam weapons…finding kidnapped or missing individuals as a result of terrorism. These are all major contributions to our national security."

Mark thought for a moment. "I can't believe that more people aren't talking about this."

Kravitz shook his head, "We really don't want them to. Like we said earlier, if the Soviets were aware of how accurate we've already become, then it could cause them to panic. Intelligence in the cold war is managed to an appropriate balance. If one side has something the other side doesn't, it tips the scales. We're stable because we have a primal understanding of each other's strengths and weaknesses."

"So, while our enemies know that we are studying this field, they think they have the lead, and that's fine with us." Yasmina shifted in her seat as she crossed her legs under the table. "We're doing some things now that will seem to most people like total science fiction. Science fantasy! If specific details of this program were made public on the six o'clock news tonight, we'd panic our own citizens."

"And, no doubt, rock some religious institutions." It was Kravitz' turn. "In the few short days we were together, you learned how to quiet your mind and accurately identify certain shapes on the Zener cards. You were able to accurately perceive signals being sent from the next room, and from a remote site five miles from here. That's quite an accomplishment. And, we got all of you to a certain level of competency in this short time. But, like some people are better at certain things than others, you and another student excelled."

"You hit it out of the park." Yasmina interjected. "You have some natural abilities that we think we can work on and improve. We'd like you on our team in Palo Alto."

Mark was speechless. In only a week, he'd gone from a lean, mean infantry Marine, to a...a what? "Uhmm...and if I do this, what's my new MOS? What do I tell people I do?"

Kravitz replied slyly, "Your Military Occupational Specialty will be re-designated as an Intelligence Specialist; in your case it will be 02-31. You'll retain your E-5 paygrade and all of the benefits, plus you'll receive an additional housing allowance because of the cost of living out in California."

"And," Yasmina leaned slightly forward and smiled, "This will be a plainclothes assignment, so if you want to let your hair grow out a little, this will be the time."

"That was the spoonful of sugar." She lowered her voice. "Now for the medicine. This is a highly sensitive intelligence program. You can't tell anyone what you do. Not your family. Not your friends. Not even any of the people you met this week except for Dr. Kravitz and me, naturally. Your successes and failures will never be known outside of our department, and even if you are awarded a medal for something, the accompanying citation will be deliberately vague."

Kravitz remarked, "And you'll have to learn how to be paranoid. You'll need to be able to watch for surveillance, to be highly suspicious of people who try too hard to get to know you. Well, at least under unusual circumstances. But even the most casual meeting by chance, say, at a grocery store, could be a foreign power attempting to set you up for exploitation."

He closed the file and folded his hands on top of it. "In short, you'll be a highly classified instrument of the United States government, and therefore, potentially a target of anyone who seeks to do us harm."

—((•))—

Fred Balmain spent the morning at his office in the Headquarters Building located at 935 Pennsylvania Avenue Northwest, just up the street from the White House. The building had been a classic example of government bureaucracy in action, having originally been proposed thirty eight years earlier by Director Hoover. Once submitted, the project took fifteen years to put together from the time that Congress initially approved the plan.

It wasn't until June 28, 1974, the first FBI employees began arriving from nine different locations in the area, and by May 30, 1975, the Director, the Associate Director, and several other key divisions had moved in. President Gerald Ford officially dedicated the building on September 30, 1975, but the last wave of employees didn't move into the building until June 1977. By the time it was fully occupied, the building cost $106 million more than the original proposal in 1939.

After sorting through his mail that morning, Balmain had wandered the halls looking up friends that he hadn't seen in years. His relocation was as much social to him as it was professional. By 9:30 a.m., he had made his way to the conference room and found a seat at the table for what promised to be a very dull budget planning meeting.

Doug Wells, an old acquaintance of more than twenty years, took the seat next to him and the men spoke of some of the funnier incidents they'd been a part of through their assignments. Doug, himself now a Deputy Assistant Director, was there to lobby for the creation of a federally supported Hostage Rescue Team. He and others within the Bureau believed that there was a need for a special operations team to handle complex hostage situations, large-scale counter-terrorist operations, situations involving nuclear or biological agents, or operations that local law enforcement or regional FBI field offices were not trained or equipped to handle.

There was an Army Colonel named Beckwith who was in the final stages of creating such a team for military purposes. However, handcuffs were not a part of their uniform. In short, the Army team's job would be to neutralize assailants by force and safely leave with the rescued hostage. Doug Wells saw a need to build a similar team at the federal level with more of a law enforcement mission, making arrests rather than casualty counts.

Everyone grew silent as Director Kelley entered the room. After taking his seat, his first order of business was to introduce Fred Balmain to the rest of the group, since it was his first meeting in the new role.

"Gentlemen, many of you know Fred. He's been around for a long time and has graciously accepted the leadership position over our training academy. He'll be up here one or two days a week, and down at Quantico most of the time. Fred, did you want to say hello?"

Fred stood and waved, "Good morning everyone. I think I know most of you, and as time permits, I will schedule some time for us to visit. I'm in the book, so if you need anything immediately, please give me a call." Short and sweet, Fred sat back down as everyone nodded or waved a quiet welcome.

Director Kelley made some brief notes as the different department heads made their report of activities over the preceding month. Balmain had a hard time concentrating on the conversations, and found that he was probably not cut out to be a senior administrator. He grew bored quickly and lost interest in the topic. His mind drifted to the conversation he'd had with Mac's widow, and he was considering his next steps. He was sitting on a powder keg.

After the meeting, Doug Wells and he had walked the two blocks to the Congress Bar and Grille for a quick lunch. They continued their discussion about some of the lighter times the Bureau had faced before drifting into some of the sadder recollections surrounding the Peltier case and the loss of two agents.

Balmain looked at his watch and realized that it was already after 1:00 p.m. The two men returned to the Headquarters building and Balmain grabbed his briefcase and headed towards the parking garage. With the Washington traffic, he knew that it would be at least an hour and a half to get back to Quantico.

In fact, it was closer to an hour and forty-five minutes. As he walked through the main lobby, Jill grinned. "Wow, talk about perfect timing! You just missed them!"

"Missed who?" He asked.

"The furniture guys." She reached down to answer an incoming call. "They finished up about a half hour ago."

"The what?" Balmain looked at her quizzically and quickened his pace. Something was wrong. When he got to his office he could see Garcia standing in the doorway looking perplexed. "I thought you said you didn't want new furniture?"

"I didn't." Balmain brushed past him and began to open the file cabinet drawers. It looked like all of his files had been moved from the old cabinets to the new ones, with meticulous care. "Did you have something to do with this?"

"No way. The work order came through this morning along with a requisition that came from the Director's office. I thought you and he had worked something out."

"No." He was thinking quickly and he could feel his pulse pounding in his neck. "I just saw him a couple hours ago and he didn't mention anything." Balmain opened his file cabinet and credenza drawers one by one. It seemed like everything was where it belonged. Because of his current position, he had no classified information stored there, with the exception of something he wasn't supposed to have, which would have been exposed when they moved the credenza out.

Garcia smacked the door frame with the palm of his hand. "Well buddy, you must have friends in high places!" He laughed and turned to head back to his office.

As soon as his associate was gone, Balmain closed the door and moved the new credenza away from the wall. As he'd suspected, the file was gone. He pushed it back against the wall and systematically went through each drawer to make sure that the movers hadn't tried to re-file it somewhere else. Nothing. Whoever had brought the new furniture in had taken the file out.

He sat down and dialed the Director's Office.

The friendly, but efficient female voice answered. "Director Kelley's office."

"Hi Melinda, it's Fred Balmain. I wanted to personally thank the Director for the new office furniture. Did you handle that request for him?"

"Oh, hello Director Balmain. New furniture? No, I wasn't aware that he'd done that. He might have called the Supply office on his own. Do you want me to get him on the line?"

Balmain thought for a moment. "No. That's okay. I don't want to disturb him. I just wanted to say thanks!"

Balmain replaced the handset in the cradle. What had just happened? Was his line bugged? Did the widow MacArthur say something to someone? Did Josh in Personnel see something no-tated in the file, or was there some kind of electronic trigger in the network that detected the file access and alerted someone else in the system of his interest in Mac?

He couldn't report the missing file to anyone if he was never supposed to have seen it. Especially now that so much time had elapsed. If he tried to file an official report through proper chan-nels, someone upstairs would want to know why he put the file back behind the credenza instead of securing it in a more appropri-ate manner.

He picked up the telephone handset, paused, and placed it soft-ly back in the cradle. He couldn't call Barbara MacArthur. What was he supposed to say this time? Calling with condolences for a long dead ex-husband is one thing, but what would be his reason for calling her today?

"Hey Barb, just checking to see who you talked to about our call?" That would be so lame that it would arouse suspicion in a fifth grader. Or, "Hey Barb. Are your phones bugged?" Even lamer.

The furniture change could not have been a coincidence. Garcia was responsible for everything that was bought, sold or traded at the Academy. He believed his friend when he said that he had no knowledge of it. But, if the new furniture was truly a coincidence, then where was the file? Certainly, the FBI wouldn't contract with any furniture company that wasn't one hundred percent trustwor-thy. And, since when did movers relocate your files?

The usual process for moves was to empty your drawers and throw everything in boxes before they got there. The movers would take the old furniture out and put the new furniture in, and then you'd have to unpack your own boxes. Movers didn't want to ex-pend the extra time. Movers didn't want the liability if something got lost or damaged. Movers didn't take things out of an office. Especially an FBI office.

He needed to think. He needed to get out of there. He called his wife and told her he'd be late for dinner.

"How late?" she asked.

"I don't know. 6:30 or 7:00. Don't wait dinner for me."

"No problem, honey. I was just going to warm something up." She was so perfect for him.

He'd never been a big aficionado of guns, but this afternoon, he double checked that his Smith and Wesson Model 19 was loaded, and that he had an extra speed loader containing six rounds in his jacket pocket. He'd been issued a Smith and Wesson Model 13 several years earlier, but preferred to carry and qualify with his personally owned .357 magnum because it felt better in his hand, and it seemed like he could actually hit what he aimed at. And, with the two and a half inch barrel it seemed more comfortable on his belt, even though it was a little heavier. At least, if he ran out of ammunition he could always throw the damn thing at them.

He needed to walk. After locking his office and bidding good afternoon to Jill, he jumped in his car and headed up I-95 to Alexandria. The solitude of the drive and the fresh air of a walk through Old Town would give him a chance to clear his head.

An hour later, he was walking the brick sidewalks amid the well-preserved 18th and 19th century buildings of King Street. Lined with boutiques, restaurants and specialty shops, and steeped in history. Supposedly, the founding fathers dined at nearby Gadsby's Tavern, which was now a museum with period objects and photographs. The Carlyle House Historic Park was a restored Georgian mansion with a garden. And the Potomac River, just south of Washington, DC, served as a picturesque backdrop. He felt at home.

He sauntered and people-watched up the street with his hands in his pockets, experiencing the sounds and smells, with no particular destination in mind. How did they know? Who were they? At first he had questioned the authenticity of the file that he'd found. But now after a few days of reflection and increasingly questionable circumstances, he was starting to give more credence to it.

Balmain hadn't been aware of the young man with the light brown hair, until he'd stopped suddenly to look in a store window and noticed him out of the corner of his eye. He was wearing tight jeans and some sort of shirt that might have been more appropriate on the disco floor; something shiny with dark colors and some sort of floral print that seemed incongruous with the blue zipper jacket. The jacket looked like Air Force issue, as did the kid's haircut. As Balmain stopped, the kid also stopped abruptly and began to look in a storefront a couple of doors down.

Was he being paranoid? There was only one way to tell. Balmain maintained his meandering pace and continued on down the street for a couple of blocks until he spotted an alley across the street that he felt would meet his needs. He walked another block and crossed at the light. Using his peripheral vision, he could see the kid crossing as well. That was it. It was a tail. Not a good one, but the kid was definitely following him.

When Balmain got to the other side of the street he charged direction and started back the way from which he'd come. When he got to the alley he'd spotted, he stopped, looked at his watch and then furtively glanced left and right before turning right into the alley. As soon as he made the turn, he stopped and backed up into the brick wall and tried to steady his breathing.

He hadn't made an apprehension in more than ten years, and hadn't wrestled anyone, outside of annual defensive tactics training, in longer than that. He waited. And waited. Soon, he could hear the kid's approach, and when he turned the corner, Balmain let out a front snap kick to the young man's common peroneal nerve just above the knee.

Taking advantage of his pursuer's disorientation, he grabbed the guy's right arm and spun him into the brick wall. Before he could recover, he used his right leg to kick his quarry's shins so hard that the fellow's legs moved involuntarily backwards. He then slammed his head and chest into the wall.

Controlling his breathing, he whispered. "Federal agent, you're under arrest!"

"Wait!" the kid protested.

As the kid spoke, Balmain drew his Model 19 and drove the muzzle into his neck so hard he thought the young man would have a permanent bruise in the soft tissue under his chin or even a couple of broken teeth. "Wait my ass! Put the backs of your hands up against the wall. Do it now! Do it fucking now!"

The man in the blue jacket rotated his hands thumbs down so that the backs were against the brick and his palms were facing outward. In this position, he struggled to breathe as his legs pushed his head and neck at an unnatural angle into the wall. He gasped, "Wait dammit! I'm a federal agent too! My ID is in my pants pocket."

For no reason, and against everything he'd ever been taught, Balmain's thumb went to the hammer and cocked it. Fear, anger and adrenaline were now in control. By cocking the gun, Balmain had just changed the amount of pressure on the trigger necessary to make it shoot, go from thirteen pounds to less than four. If the kid flinched there'd be blood, brains and a hell of a report to write later on. He took his finger off the trigger.

"Yeah? And my Aunt Bessie is a stripper in the Bronx. Who are you working for?"

"Same as you, man!" The young man tried to grab a breath. "US Government... seriously...my ID is in my back pocket!"

Balmain moved his hand from between the man's shoulder blades down to his left pants pocket. Feeling a wallet, he said, "Don't you fucking move! I've had way too much coffee today and if you move, my finger may move on its own. And you won't like that."

Balmain's fingers pushed the wallet up and out of his pocket and then he opened the leather case. In the dimming light, he could still read the credentials. "United States Air Force, Office of Special Investigations? What the fuck is this?"

"I can't say," he replied.

Keeping the revolver under his chin, Balmain used his left elbow to slam the agent's neck up against the wall again. "Don't you fuck with me. I'll give you one chance to tell me why you're following an FBI agent, and then I'm going to start thinking about what I'm going to tell the Alexandria cops while you're bleeding out in this filthy alley."

"Wait!" The anxious agent pleaded, considering his alternatives. "We had a tip. It was about the file."

"What file?" Balmain demanded.

"You know, the file in your office."

A chill ran down Balmain's back but he had to ignore it. He was busy. "What fucking file?"

"They told us that you had possession of a classified file and we needed to see if," He sniffled. "Or, who, you might try to pass it off to."

"You're full of shit! You're making this up!" Balmain pushed the muzzle of the Model 19 deeper into the frightened agent's neck. "The movers...did you send the movers?" Balmain was scared.

"Yes." He admitted.

It was Balmain's turn to consider his options. He was emotionally prepared for something like this but hadn't expected it to unfold quite this way. "I don't know anything about any file. And, your people better have a really good explanation for breaking into an FBI office and going through my stuff."

"Sir, I don't make the rules. They told me to follow you and see if you met anyone. That's it."

"How'd you know where I was? I didn't see you behind me on ninety five."

"Bird Dog transmitter -under your bumper." The kid was having trouble breathing. "I have a receiver in the car."

"How many people? You and who else?" Balmain quickly looked around to see if he'd had a partner.

"Just me and another agent. He's with the car."

Balmain manipulated the agent's ID card out from behind the clear plastic window with one hand. "I'm keeping your ID. I'll mail it back to OSI at Andrews tomorrow. If you're not who you say you are, I'll have this all over the evening news tomorrow. Got me?"

"Yes, sir," he whimpered.

Balmain quickly patted the man down, but could not find a weapon. "When I let you go, I want you to start walking down this alley, and don't stop. If I think any of your people are watching me...

if I hear strange clicks on my telephone...or if it looks like my mail has been opened and re-sealed, I will fuck you up in ways that you or the Air Force can't even imagine. Hear me?"

"Yes, sir"

Balmain released the pressure on the agent, tossed his wallet on the ground and quickly left the alley. As soon as he de-cocked his gun and holstered it, he gave himself permission to shake uncontrollably.

⸺ ‹‹◉›› ⸺

Dr. Kravitz and Yasmina Sheppard entered La Planque at a little after six. Their reservation was for 6:15 p.m., so they glanced around to see if their guests had arrived before taking a seat at the bar. It was the finest French restaurant in Old Town, located on North Washington, across from Christ Church. Opened the previous year by Jean Chardon and his wife Marie, who had come to the United States from Beaugency, France in 1976, it boasted the finest cuisine in the area and a superlative wine selection. It drew an eclectic clientele from congressmen in tuxedos to artists in blue jeans.

Dr. Kravitz looked up when he saw the Air Force General arrive. They had met a week earlier, so they quickly recognized each other and exchanged a quiet greeting. Katie and Norm were with him.

"So nice to see you again General. How have you been?" Dr. Kravitz asked.

The General smiled and shook hands with Kravitz and then Yasmina. "We are well. It's nice to see you again."

Yasmina looked towards the door, "Did you have someone else joining us tonight?"

"Yes, Paul Scheller, one of our up and coming young agents." The General looked around annoyed. "But I don't seem him. He must have been detained." The General glanced at his watch. "Why don't we grab our table and he can join us when he arrives?"

The waiter led them to their table, and after the group had ordered a round of drinks, the General lowered his voice and leaned in close. "We were quite impressed with the results of the task we assigned you last week. I have to admit that I was rather skeptical about this process, but it looks like it paid off."

Kravitz smiled, "So, you were able to recover your missing item?"

The General nodded. "Yes. But the accuracy, and the means by which you steered us towards it leaves me wondering something."

"Yes?" Yasmina asked.

"From a security perspective, if your team is actually able to perform this efficiently, how do you turn them off at the end of the day?"

"I'm not sure what you mean." Yasmina said, curious.

Norm and Katie were silent. The General frowned. "Well, what I mean is, if your people can so very accurately see things, that can't be seen by anyone else, what keeps them from...well moonlighting? How do you know what they're viewing on their own time?"

"You mean, if they find something interesting, can they view it from home or anywhere else? Nothing." Kravitz acknowledged. "Psychic functioning doesn't diminish when you go home for the day. The difference between our group and any other gifted psychics in the world is that ours are professional intelligence officers, with active clearances and non-disclosure agreements in place."

Yasmina added, "So, you really can't turn them on or off. We're very selective in our program and only recruit people who are not only gifted, but trustworthy as well. But, if they're lying in bed or mowing the grass, you can't get them to disconnect from the universe."

The waiter returned with their drinks so they changed their conversation to the banality of the traffic around the Beltway during rush hour. After the waiter had carefully placed their drinks on the table and departed, the General started to speak again, but stopped when he saw his agent enter. "There he is."

Paul Scheller approached the table with apologies. "Good

evening everyone. I'm so sorry for my tardiness, but work took longer than I thought this evening."

The General introduced him to Kravitz and Yasmina, and then casually joked, "What's the other guy look like?"

The agent had an abrasion on his left cheek and the knuckles of his right hand had fresh Band-Aids applied. "Sorry, sir. I was carrying some file boxes out to the car and stumbled on the last stair step."

He'd tucked in the shirt tail of his disco shirt and replaced his blue zipper jacket with a sport coat in a superficial attempt to clean up. The General replied, "I see. Well, since everyone is here, I guess we can get started and I can tell you that Paul is one of the agents assigned to the case that we tasked you with last week."

14

TUESDAY, APRIL 22, 1980

S taff Sergeant Mark Reynolds sat at a table in the plain office, wearing blue jeans and his lucky Penn State T-shirt. There were no pictures anywhere, the colors of the walls and carpet were neutral, and the sound-insulated room guaranteed there was no noise coming in from the outside. His table was in the center of the room and angled to face a corner. The microphone and camera were positioned behind him, along with a single chair for the monitor to use during the session. On the corner of the table was a stack of blank paper, and a box with pens and pencils. On the other corner was a glass of water.

He was alone for the time being. He sat relaxed, with his shoes off and his feet up on the table, listening to soft music that had an underlying sub-audible binaural beat, facilitating relaxation and enabling him to quiet his mind. In the business of remote viewing, this period was known as the cool-down; that space of time allotted by the viewer to relax and sweep all of his physical problems, concerns, and issues into a mental dustpan and dump it in a box for safe-keeping.

The investigation into the potential use and effects of binaural tones had originally begun by German physicist Heinrich Wilhelm Dove in 1839, who published his findings in the scientific journal Repertorium der Physik. While research about the practice grew rapidly after that, the subject remained something of a scientific curiosity until 1973, with the publication of bio-physicist Gerald Oster's article, Auditory Beats in the Brain.

Dr. Oster's article collated the scattered pieces of relevant research on this controversial subject, offering fresh insight and supportive laboratory findings to the topic. Oster saw binaural beats as a powerful tool for cognitive and neurological research. Kravitz, with university backing was taking it to the next level.

A binaural beat was in fact, an auditory illusion perceived when two different pure-tone sine waves were presented to a listener, with one tone going to each ear. For example, if a 530 Hz pure tone was presented to a subject's right ear, while a 520 Hz pure tone was presented to the subject's left ear, the listener would perceive the illusion of a third tone. This third sound was called a binaural beat. In this example, the listener would have a perceived pitch correlating to a frequency of 10 Hz, which was the difference between the 530 Hz and 520 Hz pure tones presented to each ear.

Research indicated that different patterns of waves could bring about different physiological changes in the body. The Delta pattern could bring about a deeper, dreamless sleep in patients. The Theta pattern could improve meditation, creativity and rapid-eye-movement, or REM sleep. Alpha patterns could improve relaxation, and Betas could promote concentration and alertness. The research even indicated that a Gamma pattern could stimulate arousal during wakefulness.

Through the years, many people reported other sensations including a reduction of pain, or as an aid to help them sleep, meditate or have psychic experiences, including out of body experiences. For Mark, the process brought about accelerated relaxation and concentration at the same time.

He'd received the brief call from Dr. Kravitz about 7:00 the previous evening. "Don't watch the news. Get a good night's sleep and be in the office at 8:00 tomorrow morning."

To Mark, that meant he had a real-world tasking. Something big had come in and they wanted him to be free of any preconceived ideas as to the nature of his assignment. He was excited.

Even though he had enjoyed the research side of his exploration into remote viewing over the past three years, he very much relished the occasional opportunity to contribute to something real. And, the fact that Dr. Kravitz had told him not to watch the news, meant it was big indeed. They wanted him fresh. They did not want him front-loading his mind.

He was gratified by his role at the Institute. And, in light of his demonstrable successes, the Marine Corps offered him an early promotion to Staff Sergeant as an inducement to re-enlist for four more years. He certainly welcomed the pay increase, as living in the Palo Alto area was significantly more expensive than at most of the Marine bases. The Institute also kicked in a huge stipend to ensure that his apartment and surroundings were comfortable. Now, he finally felt like he belonged there.

When he was ready, he pushed the green button on the edge of the table. Moments later, Dr. Kravitz entered smiling and placed a manila envelope face down on the table. The two men had greeted each other earlier upon his arrival, so there was no need for conversation now. Mark placed the headphones on the floor under the table and reached for a piece of paper from the stack. He flipped over the envelope and noted the typed coordinate number: J23R47

Dr. Kravitz began the session. "Okay Mark, quiet your mind. You want as little mental noise as possible so that you can begin receiving sensory input. I need you to let go now. Write down the date, time and any ideas you want to let go of that may distract you while we're doing this viewing."

Mark wrote his name, the date and time on the upper right corner of the page, and then in the center of the page, he added the reference number, J23R47. He took a deep breath, loosened his arm and doodled a nonsensical ideogram in the upper left had corner of the page.

As one of the senior viewers taught, ideograms were the written physical language between the physical and subconscious mind. Each ideogram was a symbol for an idea, a concept, or a thing, that the viewer allowed to free-flow from his or her subconscious mind to their hand, to the paper. These ideas, concepts and things that ideograms represented were known as gestalts.

A simple gestalt could be the idea of land, or water, or life, or an event. The ideogram could help the viewer better identify and define the type of land; rocky, mountainous, or sandy? What type of water; still, moving, frozen?

Kravitz continued. "I need you to call the first target to your mind. Describe the most basic impressions you have of the target. What do you feel is the predominant thing in the target? Write your descriptors down."

It was a full minute before Mark recognized the first sensory input. As he relaxed, the familiar image of the large eye came into his mind and he drifted towards the huge iris and awaiting pupil. "It's a place, not here in the US. It's overseas...desert...a city in the desert."

Mark made some notes on the page and continued. "I see some sort of movement...military activity. Jets...aircraft, in a hurry. They're being sent to ...hmmm... to intercept an enemy of some kind."

Mark pushed the paper aside and started a new one with the same process of adding his name and the ideogram. He tapped the ideogram a few times in different places. "It's night time...like right around midnight or a little later...clear night...starry...pilots excited...they're not our pilots...foreign."

He drew a line through the center of the page, indicating ground, and he made some dots in the sky to portray stars. He shook his head, "Desert...Middle east...hmmm...some mountains... some water on borders...large country...cold in the north, warm in the south...Mediterranean?"

He tapped the ideogram again. "Pilots...military...chasing target..."

Dr. Kravitz spoke softly from behind him. "Focus on the target."

Mark, drew a small square up in the sky and then sketched in some lines radiating outwards from it. "Strange...bright...square... uhmmm...WHOA!" He sat upright.

Kravitz spoke again, "What do you see, Mark?"

"That thing can really move! I mean, it...like two or three thousand miles an hour." He drew zig zag lines emanating from the brilliant square he had just sketched. "It turns on a dime!"

"Tell me more about that." Kravitz said in a controlled voice.

"The pilots...uh...they try to shoot at it, but can't...uhmmm... one plane turns back...the other tries to chase it...but can't catch it. Fuck, this thing is fast! Pilot tries to eject, but can't."

"Describe it, Mark. What are they chasing?"

"It's...uh...it's square, with lights flashing around the outside... but they flash so fast, it might look like a steady...or pulsating light. It's...uh...about fifty feet long...and uh...not ours."

Kravitz tried not to allow his confusion to come through in his instructions. It was important for the monitor to be as neutral as possible to avoid cuing the viewer. "Whose is it?"

Mark concentrated, "It's not from here...it's...wow...uh...not from here."

Kravitz moved on, "Okay Mark...what happens next?"

"The pilots head back to the base...excited...frightened...they make a report to...they're embarrassed..."

"Who do they make their report to, Mark?"

"Uhmmm...to ...to us. One of our senior officers."

Kravitz stopped in the middle of the note he was writing. "I'm sorry, could you repeat what you just said?"

"Yeah...these pilots are still shaking...very tense, very nervous... aircraft systems were shut down remotely by something...our people are at the base...uh...Air Force...blue uniforms."

Kravitz saw the red light on the wall next to him blink on. "Mark, I want you to relax and stay focused on this location and time...this activity. I'll be right back."

As Kravitz left the room, Mark began to sketch out some of the things that he had perceived. He seemed to recognize the wing shape and dual exhaust of the jets as being Phantom, F-4's. But he couldn't discern any specific shape to their aerial target. It seemed boxy and non-aerodynamic. But, it was bright, and it really moved. Faster than anything he'd ever been aware of.

A few minutes passed and Kravitz returned, taking his seat behind Mark. "Okay Mark...you might have been seeing something in the past. We need you to move to present day. Same geographic area, but present day. Can you do that for me?"

Mark focused his mind as instructed. "Oh...yeah, big change...violent political change. Government has changed...no longer friendly. Violent revolution...religious zealots now in charge...students."

Mark made notes on the side of the paper, "Unrest...mobs in the street...burning things...flags...cars...chanting."

"Focus on the demonstration. Where are the demonstrations taking place?"

Mark tapped the ideogram again. "In the streets...government building...fence...large fence and wall...structure, like iron or steel...surrounds...like a compound."

Kravitz made some notes. "Tell me more about the compound."

Mark took a couple of deep breaths in through his nose and slowly, out his mouth. "Compound...in a city...was...like a sanctuary...uhmmm...several buildings, but main building looks like...a school." He tapped the ideogram. "Some of the people who work there actually call it a school... a nickname...uh...something High."

"People are trapped there...by other people. Can't leave...being held against their will...like prisoners."

"Tell me more about that, Mark."

"Surprised...fear...people inside tried to destroy...uh...not enough time. Taken by force...but...no shots were fired. They were... overwhelmed by ...uh...number of people coming in." Mark wrote AOL on the side of the paper and said, "I'm getting analytic overlay here...I'm thinking this is the US Embassy in Iran."

Kravitz was writing quickly. "Thanks, Mark...keep focusing on the building. How many people are in the building?"

Mark pushed his head into his hands. "Uh...wow...they come and go...uh...prisoners...uh...all or most of the people who worked there. Taken by surprise."

Kravitz pushed him. "You said most, did some of the people get away or are they injured?"

Mark ran his hands through his short hair, "Uh...some got away...went to someplace friendly to hide. But I get the feeling that they're home now."

"Mark, I want you to move forward in time by forty-eight hours and tell me what you see. Pull back higher if you have to. Move in time to forty-eight hours from now."

Mark saw the undulating iris, and dove further into the pupil of the large eye in his mind. "Uhmmm...tension in the school... anxiety...uhmmm..."

Kravitz spoke softly, "Can you pull back for me? Can you look around this place where the building and people are and tell me what's going on a few miles away?"

Mark reached for a new piece of paper. "Confusion."

"Okay Mark...relax just a moment. Information is coming from your mind and autonomic nervous system. Your unconscious already knows everything there is to know about the target, it just has to communicate that to your conscious mind. So just let go. Imagine yourself floating several thousand feet over the target area. Is there anything surprising about the target that you can perceive?"

"Uhmmm...night time...bad visibility...difficulty seeing, sand or something in the air. A military team...friendly military team there on a mission...but...they don't have enough equipment for the job and they've been told to pull out." Mark paused and took a sip of water. "They're worried that they've been discovered."

Mark pushed the paper aside with the other used sheets and grabbed a fresh piece off the pile. "Aircraft...some large with supplies and people...some helicopters. Need to move one of the choppers but can't taxi...sand." Mark did his best to sketch an overhead view of four cargo aircraft parked in a diamond formation, with smaller helicopters behind each one.

"I'm getting motion...circular...like the rotor on the chopper is moving. Oh, shit! There's some sort of crash...chaos...confusion... explosion... uhmmm desert, sand...fire ...someone in authority gives the order to abandon."

Mark was sweating. "Loss of life. People in a hurry...bodies left behind."

Kravitz noted the stress building up. "Okay, Mark. That should do it for now. Let's end this session and you can take a break."

Mark downed the remainder of the water in the glass. "You sure? I can keep going."

Kravitz flipped his notebook shut. "No. That was fine. Let's take a break. When you've finished writing up your summary, go out and take a walk."

—————◦«◉»◦◦————

Fred Balmain stood at the large window in his luxurious Chantilly office and looked out over Route 50 at the aircraft landing at Dulles. His office was large and well-appointed, consistent with his impressive title of Vice President Security Operations. The truth be known, Balmain felt as though any of a hundred other candidates would have been better qualified for his current position. But, being a retired FBI executive carried clout in the private sector.

Especially in the technology, finance, and aviation industries. Just about every federal contractor wanted to splash a retired FBI agent's name across their Annual Report. The credential brought something with it, even though he recognized that the average FBI agent knew absolutely nothing about running a private security department. Nevertheless, the office was twice the size of what he was used to and the work load was half as much.

He enjoyed watching the airport operations. Secretly, he wondered what it would have been like if he'd been a pilot instead of an FBI agent. Now, at fifty-eight, he was a little too old to make a career change. He glanced at the shadow-box frame on the wall with his badge and credentials, now perforated with the word RETIRED. It had been almost a year since he left the job and he realized that he had to adjust to the monotony of civilian life.

He would get used to it. His wife loved Virginia and accepting this job meant they wouldn't have to move. His thirty minute commute to Chantilly wasn't any further than he'd been driving when he worked at Quantico. The salary and bonus for his new job, combined with his FBI pension meant that they could now buy the retirement home on a golf course somewhere in the south.

His office door had been ajar, so he was mildly startled when he heard the voice. "Morning, Fred! Got a minute?"

Jim Amundson, the Vice President of Operations for the airline came in and closed the door. "How's things going for you? Are you starting to get the feel of the job?"

Balmain and Amundson shook hands. "Yes, indeed! They're keeping me busy with security assessments of the various airports and operations, and I'm up to my eyes in policy review. I love the job though, well, except the first time I heard that Concorde fly over. That thing is so loud I thought it was going to hit the building!"

Amundson chuckled appropriately, but it was obvious something was on his mind.

Balmain gestured to one of the leather seats in front of his desk. "Please have a seat. What can I do for you?"

He looked down and seemed to pick at his thumbnail. "Normally I wouldn't come to a security guy with an issue like this, but I've got a couple of pilots that I'd like to have interviewed by a guy who knows how to do interviews."

He looked up across the desk at Balmain. "There are some taboos in the commercial aviation business that you might or might not be aware of. They're not listed in our operations manual, but occasionally we get wind of something and have to check it out."

"Yes?" Balmain asked.

With his mouth closed, Amundson ran his tongue over his teeth and then took a deep breath. "They said they saw something last night on a flight from St. Louis to San Francisco and I need to know if they're telling the truth. And, if they are, I need to know what to do about it."

"Sure thing Jim. What's the problem? What did they see?"

Amundson smirked and raised his eyebrows. "They think they saw a flying saucer last night...well, a couple of them."

Balmain stared at him blankly for a moment. He hadn't thought about the file in months, and Amundson's statement took him right back to the anxiety he knew in his last days at the Bureau.

"They what?" he asked.

Amundson nodded. "Yeah, I know. We don't get these kinds of reports often and the airline is reluctant to make anything out of them because it hurts business. Also, merely reporting something like this has been known to sideline a pilot's career."

Amundson pulled a piece of paper from his jacket pocket and unfolded it. "Both of these guys are pretty solid. Square shooters, if you know what I mean. And, most of their flight plan has been verified, so I believe most of what they're telling me." He slid the page across the desk to Balmain.

"What do they say they saw?" Balmain looked at the paper. The pilot, Jack Krieger was forty-four years old, ex-Air Force and had been flying for almost twenty years, racking up more than 15,500 hours of flight time. His first officer was thirty five-year old Terrance Stubblefield who had logged 8,100 hours over the past eleven years. Both men had current FAA Flight Physicals in their files, and no disciplinary actions or complaints against them.

Amundson recalled, "They were at 34,000 feet and Salt Lake had just handed them off to Oakland Center for a routing update. They were somewhere over Nevada when a controller, supposedly from Nellis told them to immediately divert north. Oakland Center confirmed the instructions and routed them accordingly into SFO. But, as they were making their turn, they said they saw two brilliantly lit aircraft behaving in a non-aerodynamic fashion. Basically that they skipped their way south and it looked like they landed in, or near...uh..."

"Near where?"

Amundson sighed, "Look, I don't know if you've ever heard the rumors, but there is a base out there, a couple hours northwest of Las Vegas, and supposedly the military is testing some really weird things. Some people believe that there's a recovered flying saucer out there."

Balmain wasn't sure how to respond. Was Amundson on the level, or was he baiting him for some reason? "Recovered? From where?"

Amundson pointed towards the ceiling. "Out there somewhere. There've been stories going around since World War II, but I never put much stock in them. I've no reason to doubt these guys, but I'd sure like to learn more about the incident before I decide what to do about it."

"Sure." Balmain nodded. "When are they back?" He was going to play along until he determined if this was a legitimate contact or if he was being set up. And also, the subject was certainly stimulating and was the most interesting thing he'd encountered since working there.

"They landed at Dulles about an hour ago. I told them to stop by here before they go home. Do you want them one at a time or both together?"

"This isn't a criminal interview, and they've been together for the past 24 hours, so if they wanted to fabricate a story, they've had plenty of time. Let's keep it casual."

"Thanks!" Amundson got up. "I'll send them down as soon as they get here."

Balmain decided to make his office more conducive to a quiet and sensitive discussion among co-workers, rather than an employee-management meeting that might put them more on edge than they already were. He moved his chair around to the front of the desk so the three could face each other on equal turf. Next, he turned the blinds down a bit to reduce outside light coming in, making the room seem more shut off from the outside world. Finally, he called down to Vanessa, the receptionist and asked for a pitcher of water and three glasses.

About thirty minutes later, an exhausted and anxious Captain Jack Krieger and First Officer Terry Stubblefield arrived at his door.

When he heard the knock, Balmain turned from his spot at the window, sporting his biggest smile that he reserved for disarming the most agitated and uneasy visitors. "Hi guys! Come on in and have a seat."

He noted with amusement that Krieger took the seat on the left and Stubblefield took the seat on the right, as if their cockpit positions were ingrained wherever they went. "This is not a big deal, so you can relax. Amundson told me you had an interesting flight out to San Francisco, and I just wanted to hear more about it. But first, when did you guys eat and sleep last?"

Krieger answered, "We got a couple of hours on our layover in SFO, and grabbed a snack on the flight back a little while ago."

Balmain sat across from them, crossed his legs and rested his folded hands on his knee. He wanted to play the part of a curious administrator rather than some sort of corporate inquisitor. "Well, I won't keep you. I'm sure you want to get home."

Both men nodded and Stubblefield replied. "Yes, thank you!"

"So?" He began with an understanding glint. "Give me the five-W's. The details. What happened out there?"

The men looked at each other for a moment before Krieger opened up. "Well, we've been flying for a lot of years. And, between things we've heard in the military, and over drinks with other pilots, we thought we needed to talk to someone about this, but we weren't really sure who."

"It's okay." Balmain assured them. "What we say here is confidential, between the three of us. At some point we'll decide what we want to tell Jim Amundson. Does that work for you?"

The men nodded again. Captain Krieger waited a moment before speaking. "We were on our regular route to San Francisco, departing St. Louis a little after nine last night. It had been a pretty routine flight. A couple hours in, we got a radio call from someone at Nellis Air Force Base, telling us to divert to a heading of three five zero immediately for crossing traffic that was declaring an emergency." He scratched the stubble on his cheek. "A few seconds later, Oakland Center came on and confirmed the same heading, so we made our turn, staying on the same flight level: 34,000 feet."

"Listen guys, I'm not a pilot." Balmain said casually. "Is that some sort of oddity for the FAA to re-route you for something?"

Krieger responded, "No, not really. But, it was a really clear night, unlimited visibility."

"And?" Balmain probed.

Stubblefield jumped in. "Like he said, it was a clear night, and we were curious as to what kind of emergency would divert a commercial carrier with a hundred people on board at eleven at night... so we started watching for the cross traffic. You have to understand, that there was practically unlimited visibility. We could see for miles."

"Unlimited visibility, got it!" Balmain was interested. "And what did you see?"

"The weirdest fucking light show we've ever seen." Krieger continued. "There were two..."

"Sometimes three," Stubblefield interjected.

"Yeah, sometimes we could see three of these things...just brilliant lights...we couldn't really tell you what... they looked like. They were bobbing and weaving, bouncing across the sky and then they lined up and it looked like they went into...uh..."

Stubblefield spoke up again. "It looked like they went into that place called Area 51."

Balmain stared at them blankly for a moment. "Area 51? What's that?"

Krieger replied, "It's that secret base the Air Force uses out in the desert to test experimental aircraft, and..." He reached over and poured a glass of water. His hands were shaking. "There are rumors that an alien spacecraft crashed years ago and was taken there for inspection."

Balmain recalled a reference in the documents he'd seen to a place called Groom Lake. "So, you guys saw some experimental aircraft flying around, that landed at a military base. What's the big deal?"

Both men looked at each other before Stubblefield spoke. "Go ahead Jack, tell him the rest of it."

Jack took a large sip of water. "The targets lined up like they were going to land in formation." He paused and took a breath. "And then one of them broke off, and...I swear it covered ten...fifteen miles in the blink of an eye. The next thing we knew, it was pacing us off to starboard, maybe a half mile off our wing. The damn thing had to be three or four hundred feet long. It was long and cylindrical, like a cigar, and had a band of lights that ran its length, alternating colors; red, green, blue."

Krieger took another sip of water and looked at the floor. "There were windows above the band of lights. And as it gradually edged closer to us, maybe a couple hundred yards, we could see people inside."

Stubblefield cut in, "But they weren't, you know, people. Unless they were dressed for Halloween, these...uh, things...were definitely not human."

Balmain studied the men, their body language, mannerisms, and the uncontrolled tremor in their voices. They were telling the truth. "What are you saying?"

Krieger answered. "We weren't close enough to tell you what they were wearing, but I can tell you that they weren't human. They had large heads, spindly bodies. They were watching us...more than curiosity...they wanted to know if we were a threat."

Balmain squinted. "How did you determine that?"

"Just a feeling," Krieger answered.

"Okay, I hear you. What happened next?"

"I was watching from the right seat." Stubblefield raised his hands to simulate a maneuver. "After a minute or so, the thing dropped a few hundred feet and then shot under us, broke left and the next thing we saw, it had zipped back towards where the other two objects had been. It had to be moving more than two thousand miles an hour." It was quiet in the room.

"I'm going to ask a stupid question." Balmain broke the silence. "I don't suppose there were any markings on it like...Air Force... Made in America...anything like that?"

Krieger shook his head. "The thing was clean and smooth. No

markings, no seams, no rivets. It's as if the thing was made out of one piece of aluminum or something."

"Neither of you have ever seen anything like this before?"

"Never," they agreed.

"Any of the passengers see it?"

Both men shook their heads as Krieger speculated. "Doubtful. Most had their shades pulled and were dozing."

Balmain got up and stretched as he moved to his window. He believed them. He wanted to give them some kind of assurance that what they saw was real, and not a shared hallucination. But he couldn't. The file he'd seen didn't exist. "So. What do you want to do?"

"I don't know." Krieger remarked. "On one hand, I'd want our pilots to know that this stuff is out there and they need to be watching for it. On the other hand..."

Stubblefield added, "We don't want to be the ones that start the discussion. Bad things happen to pilots who report seeing flying saucers. Sometimes, they end up driving trucks and bagging groceries for a living."

Balmain's narrowing eyebrows automatically brought a frown to his mouth. "How much have you told Amundson? Anyone else?"

Krieger replied, "No one. Not a soul. We only told Amundson the same thing we told you."

Balmain looked back out the window, his hands in his pockets. "Well, you could call the Air Force, for whatever good that would do. If it was their aircraft, they'd already know about it. But, if it was something classified, they wouldn't want you talking about it either. On the other hand, you could call Life Magazine or National Geographic and give them a story. But, without any evidence, and an almost certain denial from the Air Force, they wouldn't print anything."

Balmain considered the repercussions of any guidance he could offer them. "Look, why don't you guys go home, get some sleep and think about it. Let me know what you want to do tomorrow."

"You believe us?" Krieger asked.

"I do." Balmain nodded slowly. "I wish I had something better to tell you, but this just isn't my area of expertise." He shook hands with both men as they rose to leave.

About ten minutes later Jim Amundson returned. "Well?"

Balmain glanced out the window again and then looked back at him. "My honest opinion? I think the men are telling the truth, and that the Air Force will lie if we ask them. So, it's probably in everyone's best interest, especially theirs, to forget about this and chalk it up to weird stuff that just happens."

Amundson joined Balmain at the window. "You believe them?"

Remembering Hamlet, Balmain quoted, "There are more things in Heaven and Earth, Horatio..." He exhaled through tight lips. "I believe them."

———«(O)»———

At 11:30 a.m., Dr. Kravitz entered the conference room and closed the door. He was old friends with the Air Force General and his OSI Agent, Paul Scheller, who waited patiently. But, it was the Army two-star general in the dark gray suit who could barely wait until the senior physicist had been seated. "What have you got for us?"

It was a classified briefing, being conducted for cleared personnel, in a facility that the Department of Defense had approved for such conversations. Kravitz adjusted his thick eyeglasses. "Well, General, the quick summary is that it looks like you have a rescue planned for the embassy personnel in Tehran. It will fail."

"What?" he asked, almost angrily.

"Sorry General." Kravitz flipped through his notes. "We put this task to four different viewers in the last eight hours and even though their perceptions differed slightly among them, they all have picked up on the sensation that your rescue team is fragmented; ships and helicopters from the Navy, large aircraft from the Air Force, and rescue troops from the Army. This is the first time they've worked together. This is the first time that they've ever tried to run an operation like this at night, in a desert environment.

The pilots aren't adequately trained, and the equipment hasn't been fully tested in the environment. And, you may not want to write this part down, the President has micro-managed the operation and has not allowed field commanders to have the back-up equipment they need, or the time to practice the mission under similar conditions."

The General made some notes on his pad. "How certain are you? How good are these guys of yours?"

"They're good General." Kravitz toyed with his glasses again. "There's more. You're going to lose people. It will be embarrassing for the United States. There will be an accident."

"Crap. You're sure?" The General muttered. "We've got to stop it."

Kravitz nodded sympathetically. "You'll try. But ultimately, there will be a delay in issuing the abort order. It'll be stalled in the White House."

15

FRIDAY, APRIL 25, 1980

Mark was filled with energy as he rumbled into the parking lot at the institute in his brown Chevy Nova. It was the Rally edition with the V-8; 350 cubic inch engine and four speed manual transmission. He'd been looking at more sensible and economically-priced cars at a local dealer's lot the previous week, but the sales manager showed him the car that he'd been using as a demonstrator for the past six months and Mark fell in love.

Financing had been quickly arranged, and even with 3,500 miles on the odometer, Mark felt like it was brand new. It was his. It still had a factory warranty, and provided Mark with the empowerment and recognition of adulthood and manliness he needed now that he was fighting a different kind of war. He couldn't wait to show Karen, even though he knew she'd roll her eyes at this perspicuous display of male extravagance.

She had called him the night before to let him know that she'd been hired at the Chicago offices of Arthur Andersen, one of the top accounting companies in the nation. In celebration, Katie and her husband were coming into Chicago Friday afternoon to spend the weekend, and Karen had invited Mark. He was booked on a flight departing San Francisco at 5:45 this afternoon, arriving in Chicago close to midnight.

Mark hadn't seen Karen since New Year's Day, but they had begun speaking on the phone at least weekly and realized that they had something more than just a dry sense of humor and mild physical attraction between them. They had grown as close as two people, two thousand miles apart, could grow.

Katie, now four months pregnant with their second child, had given up her position with the OSI a couple of years earlier, following Terry's long-overdue proposal of marriage. Wanting to get to work on starting a family, she found a more lucrative job that was much more in line with her education and interests, with an engineering company near the Beltway. There, she was excited to be working on some component for the new Space Shuttle. She was back to her first love - building things.

Katie and Mark had kept in touch after Quantico, and built a solid friendship through letters and phone calls. But when the sisters visited San Francisco a few months after he arrived there, his growing attraction to Karen seemed obvious and quite natural. Katie, by then officially engaged to her long time beau, had dutifully told her sister about the brief fling that she and Mark had while in a class together, but that didn't seem to bother her younger sibling. Mark's and Karen's personalities, and ages, were much more aligned, and it seemed like a logical match. On the other hand, the three of them were in agreement that Karen's fiancé Terry never needed to hear about it.

Mark took the elevator to the lower level, and when the doors opened, took the hallway to the right, entered his five-digit code on the keypad, and pulled the door open.

"Good morning Mark!" Beverly Owens, the receptionist and occasional office manager, greeted him without looking up from the VAX 11 terminal that connected her with the Digital Equipment Corporation's local network. She was busy getting client reports out and didn't want to break her pace. "Dr. Kravitz said to stop by his office when you got here."

"Thanks Bev!" Mark said as he punched his ID sequence into the keypad on the inner door. All of the doors in the institute were made of steel, set into a concrete block system, designed to withstand quite a pounding. Unfortunately, as everyone knew, all it took was for someone to pull a fire alarm and all of the doors in the building would automatically unlock until the fire alarm had been reset.

Mark headed down the hall to Dr. Kravitz' office, passing the closed door to the conference room on his right. He didn't linger but could hear voices coming through the door. It was rare to have a meeting before eight in the morning, but not totally suspicious in light of the work they had been doing for the military this past week. All of the RV team had been doing two or three tasks a day, all week.

He walked in to the secretarial alcove outside Dr. Kravitz' and Yasmina Sheppard's offices. "Are they both in the meeting down the hall?"

"Kravitz is." Stella Francis looked up from her terminal with a smile. "Yasmina had to take her daughter to the doctor. She'll be back around lunch time."

Mark poured himself a cup of coffee and then waited in Kravitz' office. He sorted through some of the magazines on his coffee table, but found nothing of interest. All of the magazines were about science and technology. None of which really appealed to Mark, except Popular Mechanics. It seemed that they always had the inside scoop on things that were of value to the average consumer, not just scientists. He had opened the most recent copy when Stella stuck her head in.

"Dr. Kravitz says he has something for you. You're in the cage!" She smiled.

The cage was their slang for the custom built room at the other end of the hall that had been specially constructed to filter out all ambient noise and any electrical or magnetic effects on the occupants. Once inside the door, there was a monitoring station set up with a microphone and speaker, but the viewer had to enter a second door to get inside. The walls of the room were constructed of another layer of concrete block, but between those two walls was a blanket of foam attached to a surface of chicken wire, that had been pressed into a metal that looked like aluminum foil. It wrapped the entire room, above the ceiling and below the floor.

Inside the room, where no radio waves could penetrate, was a single military cot with a pillow and blankets, a La-Z-Boy recliner, and a small portable table with some writing materials. It was totally soundproofed, so once inside, the viewers could hear nothing but their own breathing. They had learned over the past few years that in addition to providing scientific skeptics with a degree of comfort when evaluating psychic functioning, Faraday cages and other types of shielding facilitated the entire RV process.

Some physicists, including James Spottiswoode, believed that electromagnetic radiation from The Milky Way galaxy and the electromagnetic effects of solar flares both degraded psychic functioning in laboratory experiments. Electrical shielding seemed to help performance, and so did carrying out experiments when ambient radiation of any kind was at a minimum at the viewing location. A couple of years earlier, two of the institute's top performers successfully received messages sent from Palo Alto, while they were inside of a submarine submerged in 500 feet of sea water, 500 miles away. Thus, it seemed that while electronic waves could be shielded, thoughts couldn't.

Mark stopped at his desk, grabbed his Sony Walkman and a Hemi-sync tape, and then walked briskly to the cage. Inside the outer door, he flipped the session light on to let people know the room was occupied, and then he went through the second door. The cage door felt like it belonged on an armored refrigerator, and always made a poof sound when closed. Air was supplied through a special duct so that the occupant was comfortable and not otherwise subjected to bouts of claustrophobia. But other than that, the room was sealed off from the outside world.

He slipped off his Sperry Top-Siders and sat back in the recliner. He placed the earphone cups over his ears, and pushed the button on the Walkman. The binaural music was a bit loud for the isolation of the cage, so he adjusted the volume down. He regulated and deepened his breathing, trying to clear his mind. His upcoming weekend in Chicago was the toughest to clear out of there. He wondered if his Nova would be okay in the airport parking garage.

Would he be able to find a parking place? He wondered if his neighbor would collect his mail as they'd arranged. He wondered about the feedback session Dr. Kravitz had promised him before he had to leave early for his flight.

In his mind, as his breathing deepened and slowed, he swept all of these thoughts into the dustpan, and dumped them into the lock box. The screen inside his mind was now dark, with nothing but occasional shades of color floating to the surface, like an enveloping lava lamp. He was right where he needed to be, and with his eyes closed, found the switch on the table next to his chair and flipped it forward. Out in the monitoring station, the light went from red to green.

He drifted off to a light sleep for a few minutes, before Dr. Kravitz' voice could be heard over his music. "Good morning, Mark."

Mark stopped his tape and removed his earphones. "Good morning Doc. Busy day?"

"Yes, indeed. I hope you got some rest last night!"

Mark gave a thumbs-up sign to the camera in the corner of the room near the ceiling.

"That's great." Kravitz cleared his throat. "Mark, I have an envelope on the desk in front of me. Inside the envelope, there is a card with a question on it. Please focus on the question and provide me as much detail as you can."

Mark relaxed his breathing and the giant eye appeared. It was comfortable and welcoming. The large brown iris had just a tinge of green hue to it. It massaged the dark pupil causing it to slowly expand and contract ever so slightly as he moved towards it. He drifted inside to the darkened cavern that seemed safe and warm, where he floated and waited for images to appear.

"It's an event...night time...sky...stars..." He made some notes on his pad. "I'm getting movement...movement up in the air."

"There is structure...faster movement. Life." He began to draw an airplane in the sky. "Military...they are chasing something. Two jets...chasing something...in the sky."

Kravitz' voice came over the speaker in the cage "What are they chasing, Mark. Can you focus on that?"

Mark tucked his head and squeezed his eyes shut. "Aircraft.... uh...not well defined...very bright. Lights around the outside seem to pulsate very quickly. Not...not sleek like ours...very...uh...boxy. Lights run around the outside of the structure." He tried to sketch a rectangle within a rectangle, making dots where the lights would be in the narrow space between the two. "Moves quickly...motion... not straight though...it zigs and zags...like a hummingbird."

After drawing zig-zag lines across the page, he pushed it aside and reached for a new piece of paper. "Focusing on the box thing... there is life in it...not human...but lives...but the thing can work with or without people in it. It's like...it can fly by itself if it had to." He drew another rectangle and then a simplified tornado in the center. "Strange energy source. They can use energy...elements from our own atmosphere...they can communicate with us."

Mark made notes off to the side of his drawing. "They have communicated with us. They're here to watch us...to make sure we...uh...hmmm...don't abuse something."

"How do they communicate?" Kravitz asked.

"Telepathically...thought..." Mark made some notes. "Actual y... uhmmm..."

"Where are they from, Mark?"

"Yeow...not from here...they're...uh... from another star system...somewhere a few light years away by our measurements. But...they aren't the only ones who have visited. There are others from other galaxies that can...hmmm...bend space to make us closer...so they don't have to travel such distances...they uh...it's like going from one side of the paper to the other..." He drew a line across his page, and then folded the two sides together. "They don't travel...uhmmm...in a straight line...they fold space and just jump from one edge to the other. Time and space are not obstacles for them."

"Can you tell me more about the propulsion system?"

Mark reached for another piece of paper. He drew what looked like an upside down cup on a saucer. "It's actually small...not more than a foot or so in diameter. But...they don't all work like this. This one uses an element that's available here...well...eventually will be available...we'll make a few atoms of it, but we haven't discovered it yet...it takes a nuclear reaction."

"You mentioned they have communication with us. Who have they communicated with?"

Mark rubbed his forehead. "Government...military...only some senior people...not everyone. They're willing to share things... help us...but we're...uh...fragmented...too many governments...too many nationalities...some are okay, but others are violent."

Mark took a sip of water, and then tapped the strange ideogram he'd drawn in the upper left corner. "There's a danger in telling the world about them before we're ready. Jealousy...power... government and religion and science won't work together...they compete. They...uh...these...uh...entities actually work with us...not in the present, but the future us...some of these craft that we see are basically ours, a thousand years from now coming back to make sure we are advancing properly. Some are from far away, and some are us from the future."

"Focus on the communications piece, Mark. Tell me more about those with whom they've communicated."

Mark started to write and then paused to take a couple of large gulps of water. "Air Force...Army...General...uhmmm...bald man who was a general and is now the President."

Kravitz thought for a moment. Jimmy Carter had been in the Navy, and he certainly wasn't bald. "What time are you in now, Mark?"

"It's right after the war..."

"Viet Nam?"

"No," Mark replied. "World War II."

"Tell me more about that. Focus on the communications the President had with them."

Mark finished the water in his glass. "We developed a friendly relationship with them...as did some other countries. We exchanged technical information...and...hmmm...gold. We gave them gold."

Kravitz raised his eyebrows as he made note of the comment. "Why gold?"

"They need it for their atmosphere. They've been coming here for years...centuries...millennia to collect it...mine it...trade."

"Go on. Please continue."

"They understand that our politics here differs from country to country and even in this country, it changes every few years. The exchange program was set up because they think that we are peaceful here. We agreed to stop using nuclear weapons. But, they warn us not to let anyone know about them before we're all ready to know about them as one people...one planet. Or else...conflict... disbelief...uhmmm...or else..."

"Or else, what Mark?"

"Uhmmm...or else..." Mark lost the image of the bald-headed President and it was replaced by the image of a dapper, polished New Englander. "Uh...I'm getting some analytical overlay here...I'm starting to see Eisenhower and Kennedy...at some point before the inauguration...maybe in the oval office." He wrote AOL on the side of the sheet in large letters and circled it.

"I...uh..." Mark was suddenly aware of another presence in his mind. She was beautiful. Maybe about five foot five...black hair and beautiful penetrating brown eyes. A white blouse with a subtle print, gray slacks and gray heels. She was immaculate. Not a hair out of place, as she had pulled it tight behind her head. It accentuated her facial features and Mark couldn't take his eyes off of her.

"That's okay, Mark." Ignore the overlay and tell me more about their communications.

What was she doing here, in the Oval Office? She didn't work for Kennedy. She wasn't from his time. She certainly wasn't an alien, for if she was, Mark would have begged to be allowed on the ship. She was telling him something. She was pointing to something that Kennedy was writing.

Mark wasn't able to read the document the President seemed to be editing, but she was letting him know that Kennedy wants to share information...to open the files. He wants to work together with the Russians and Chinese to explore space together. Eisenhower told him not to do it, but he wants to do it anyway.

Her skin was soft, smooth and tanned. Was she Greek? Her dark skin made her teeth gleam even brighter. Her eyes sparkled. She took him by the hand and they drifted through the windows of the Oval Office and were suddenly projected two weeks into the future, where they hovered over Dealey Plaza. As the motorcade advanced, she pointed at it and shook her head solemnly from side to side. Together, they watched as the events unfolded, and then together experienced the grief of the nation.

"Mark?" Kravitz leaned closer to the microphone.

She smiled at him, and took him back to the Oval Office. Kennedy was having a heated discussion with a room full of powerful men. He couldn't understand what they were saying, but the President was firmly convinced of his decision. Mark turned to look for his guide, but she was gone.

"Mark? Are you still with us?"

Mark snapped out of his psychic detour. "I'm sorry. Uhmmm… some communicate telepathically…but not just with us. There are others from around the world that know about them and how easy it is to contact them."

Mark sat up in his chair and rubbed his face. "I'm sorry Doc, that's all I've got."

Kravitz opened the door to the cage and joined his protégé. "That's okay you did great. Are you all right? You seem a little stressed."

Mark rubbed his head. "I've got a big weekend coming up. It's hard to stay focused."

"Ah, yes. The young lady from Chicago? Not to worry. We'll follow up with everyone on this next week." Kravitz handed him the day's newspaper. "Here."

Mark took the San Francisco Chronicle from him and opened it to the front page and saw the headline. "Hostage Rescue Fails – US Planes Crash." The lead story, "8 Americans Die in Iran Operation."

"Your feedback from Tuesday." Kravitz said reverently.

⸻ ◉ ⸻

It was a cloudy day at Dulles, about seventy degrees. Fred Balmain looked out his window at the flights coming and going and tried to get the meeting with the two pilots, earlier that week, out of his head. He was ready to approach retirement both physically and mentally healthy, and looked forward to the impending and inevitable phase of his life with a stoic acceptance. He still felt young, but his doctors and insurance actuaries told him that he was quickly converging on that time in his life when he needed to focus on golf or fishing and leave stress to the next generation.

He had been reluctant to follow up the pilots' stories in any capacity; either as an ex-FBI agent or astute security director, for fear of opening a can of worms that he wanted to seal. But now as he stood, hands in his pockets, staring at life on the other side of the window, he wondered if he needed to do something. Something for them. Something for him. Maybe something for the rest of the world.

Why now? It was as if he'd done his best to bury the memories only to have an unseen force rip them open again. He'd been a good Christian all of his life. But now, he felt as if something dark was driving circumstances, driving him to get back into the game. Driving him to finish something that started long ago. It should have been a surprise when Vanessa buzzed him and told him there was a reporter on the line, but people talk. Maybe the pilots went public with their claim. But, why today?

He exhaled loudly through tight lips, and then returned to his desk to pick up the line. "Fred Balmain, can I help you?"

The male voice on the other end sounded respectful, but lacked confidence. "Mr. Balmain, thank you for taking my call. My name is Steve Albrecht. I'm a journalist. Well, sometimes I make movies and write books, but my background, I guess...well, you could just classify me as a reporter of sorts. I'm putting together some background information for a friend...and, well, I took a chance that you'd be in your office today."

Balmain's interest was only slightly piqued, although this didn't seem like other calls he'd taken from reporters over the past thirty years. Somehow, this sounded different. Why was a reporter calling him now? "What can I do for you, Mr. Albrecht?"

"Well, sir…" Albrecht paused. "I'd really like to buy you a drink. I…uh…first, let me say that I've read some things about you and was really impressed by your career. I appreciate your service to our country, and I certainly don't want you to think that I'm trying to get you to give away any of our country's secrets."

Balmain was curious. He should have put the man off, but he wanted to stay in the game for a while and learn more. "Then, what is it you want?"

Albrecht took a breath. "I'd like to talk to you about Dallas, 1963."

"If you're talking about the Kennedy assassination, then you know I wasn't actually in Dallas that day."

"Yes, I know." He paused. "But I know that you were one of the agents that ran a special task force to pursue different aspects of the case, before the Warren Commission took the investigation over."

"There were a lot of task forces…Miami, New Orleans…Mexico City…"

"I know, but I was told that you were pursuing leads relating to photographs or film of the assassination, that might not have been accounted for."

Balmain had to think. Albrecht's comments were technically dead on. But, since his role in that investigation was supposed to be confidential, how would a journalist have found out about it? "Where did you get your information, Mr. Albrecht?"

The journalist responded immediately, as if he had anticipated the question and rehearsed his response. "Sir, with all due respect, I want to assure you that I would no more tell you that, than I would tell anyone else about any conversations that you and I have had, or will have."

"Okay. So, what specifically do you want to know?" Balmain was now intrigued. If, for no other reason than to find out what the reporter knew and how he had come by the information.

"Well Mr. Balmain, you probably hate talking on the phone as much as I do. Can we meet this afternoon for a drink?"

Balmain frowned at the phone. "I don't know about that. I'm not sure that's a good...uh..."

Albrecht interrupted, "Sir, please let me assure you that I am on the level. I'm a firm believer that Oswald fired those shots. I'm not trying to create a new conspiracy theory. I'm actually trying to show that he did it."

He paused and then continued. "Look, I'm not trying to trap you into giving something away. Oswald pulled that trigger, starting the events in motion. I have circled back with some of the witnesses that were there that day, and several of them gave me your name. I just want to hear, first hand, about your recollections of those interviews. And, I don't want you to violate any privacy oaths. One drink? Off the record?"

The fellow sounded legitimate, but Balmain questioned the timing of the contact. One drink, off the record? He grunted to himself, "There's no such thing as off the record when you're talking to a reporter." He turned in his seat so that he could look out his window. "All right. One drink. Where would you like to meet?"

I'm staying at the Crystal City Marriot. I took the Metro over from National. I could meet you anywhere, but if you don't mind coming back towards the city, I could meet you in the hotel bar. It's at 1999 Richmond Hwy, Arlington..."

"I know where it is," Balmain cut him off. "I'll be there at four. How will I know you?"

"Well," he laughed. "Receding hairline and goatee beard. I look like a college professor or...well...J. Allen Hynek, without the glasses or the pipe."

Balmain's heart skipped a beat. Why in the world would this guy have compared himself to the guy that the Air Force had assigned to debunk flying saucer reports throughout BLUEBOOK? He asked innocently, "Who?"

"Oh, uh, a guy that's been on TV. Anyway, I'm fifty and look like a college professor. I'll have on a brown tweed jacket, and I have a salt and pepper goatee." He laughed. "There can't be that many guys in the bar this afternoon that look like that."

Balmain packed up his things and locked up the files he'd been working on. Expense fraud, internal theft, and a falsified employment application. Hardly the kind of subterfuge he'd been used to. And missed. On his way out, he stopped at Amundson's door. "Hey Jim, I'm knocking off early today. I've got to meet someone in the city."

"Yeah," he looked up. "I'm getting out of here early today too. Enjoy!"

Balmain knew that this time of day on a Friday, the Beltway would be at best, constipated and at worst, a parking lot. So, he drove down the street to the Dulles Metro Station, and bought a ticket. He would have to change trains at the Rosslyn station to get to Crystal City, but he'd ridden the route so many times, he knew he could make the twenty-two mile trip in about fifty minutes. And, there was actually a Metro station on the ground floor of the hotel.

He could only imagine what the Beltway traffic would be like on a Friday afternoon, but was soon certain he'd made the right choice. He arrived ten minutes early, and found the bar was empty of customers. He took a seat on one of the corners as the bartender looked over. "Afternoon! What can I get you?"

"Dewar's and water?"

"Coming right up."

The bartender generously mixed the drink, over-pouring the shot glass before tilting it over the ice. As he brought the drink over, he offered Balmain a copy the day's Washington Post. Balmain laid a twenty dollar bill on the counter and opened the paper, "8 Americans Die in Iran Operation." He shook his head.

A few minutes later, a couple in their thirties came in and took a booth in the far corner. Friday afternoon? Booth in the corner? Hotel bar? Balmain grinned as he speculated about the depth of the affair they were having. He wondered if they had hotel reservations yet, or if they were just going to wing it. Five minutes later, a college-professor in a brown tweed jacket entered.

Balmain nodded at him, and the slightly overweight gent pulled out a stool and extended his hand. "You must be Mr. Balmain?"

"Fred." Balmain replied.

"Steve." They shook hands, and the journalist adjusted the stool so that the two men could face each other. "Thank you for meeting me on a Friday afternoon. I'm sure you have many things you'd rather be doing this evening."

"It's okay." Balmain hoisted his glass in a toast. "Tell me about your book."

Albrecht started to answer, but the bartender, anxious to add to his tip jar, suddenly materialized to take the new guest's drink order.

"Gimlet." Albrecht replied.

The bartender nodded and departed in search of gin and lime juice.

"Fighting scurvy?" Balmain asked.

"Excuse me?"

"The Gimlet was created by British sailors as a means of getting toasted while preventing scurvy. You've no-doubt heard the derogatory expression, Limeys?"

"I always wondered where that came from." He moved a zippered leather folio around on the counter and rested his arm on it. "So, how do you like civilian life?"

Balmain was restless but figured that this guy was nervous and he wouldn't be able to get to the point without some degree of small-talk. "The money is good, and so far, no one has tried to kill me. How do you like writing?"

He tapped the folio nervously. The bartender returned with the drink and moved a basket of mixed nuts closer to them. When he left to take care of the couple in the corner, Albrecht continued.

"I enjoy it. Sometimes it's lucrative and sometimes it isn't. Feast or famine as they say." He took a sip of his drink. His dark tan had just a slight hue of red meaning that he spent time in the sun but had recently been over-exposed. His accent was a neutral Midwest. He didn't have the southern drawl of Virginia or the

Mid-Atlantic-Baltimore patois. He was probably transplanted from somewhere in the Midwest to somewhere south, or west.

"And besides me, what brings you to the District?" Balmain asked, hoping to prod the conversation along.

Albrecht took a healthy swig of his Gimlet. "Well, there have been a tremendous number of books and articles written about the Kennedy assassination. There are books that focus on the evidence, like David Lifton's recent book, and those that use a couple of factual points to support some wide-eyed conspiracy theory or another, which really only serves to get the author some air time on the evening news."

He stared down at his folio. "I've even heard that there's a guy writing one now that says the Secret Service accidentally fired a rifle from the car behind the limo, while the agent was attempting to respond to the sounds of gunfire." He paused briefly to see if Balmain would offer a reaction or response. When none came, he continued, "I guess they'll be writing about this for some time to come."

"Yes." Balmain sampled his scotch. "I'm familiar with several of these theories."

Albrecht drummed his fingers on his folio. "Yes. Many say the Mafia...or the Cubans...or even LBJ or Jackie...the CIA...Lord knows, many people had a motive."

Balmain regarded the fidgety writer for a moment. "Mr. Albrecht, if you have interviewed the same people I interviewed, then you know that most of these conspiracy theories are simply not true. They make great copy, but there's just no substance to them. How could I help you? What could you possibly expect me to add?"

Albrecht downed his drink and signaled the bartender for another. "Not to sound trite, but I'd like to fulfill a dying man's last wish."

"Huh?"

"A few months ago, I got a call from a retired Air Force officer. He was in a nursing home and was darting in and out of consciousness due to the pain medication he was receiving for a terminal brain tumor. He had gotten my name from someone who had read an article of mine, and he asked me to visit him in Tempe."

"Arizona?" Balmain asked reaching for his scotch.

"Correct. He had been assigned to the Chief of Staff's office during the Kennedy administration, the Air Force Chief of Staff. And in this role, he occasionally came into possession of classified briefing documents intended for the President of the United States. He said that he had a story to tell and as long as I waited until after he was gone to publish anything, he would give me all the information he had."

"And?" Balmain tried not to appear impatient.

"Well, what he told me was that earlier in his career, he was a Squadron Commander at Edwards Air Force Base in 1954 when Dwight Eisenhower visited out there. This fellow was a Major then. Evidently Ike was there to inspect some relatively advanced aircraft." He paused. "Have you ever heard this story?"

"Huh uh." Balmain was waiting for something that tied to JFK. "Eisenhower was a five-star general before being elected to be our Commander-in-Chief. I assume he visited a lot of military bases."

The bartender delivered Albrecht's gimlet. He took a sip. "It turns out my source's nephew was an Air Force photographer, who was sent along to cover the Ike visit. He was on temporary duty, just visiting Edwards for a day or two, so they planned to get together after the event at the Base for dinner. He was just there to take some pictures for public relations...you know..."

Balmain shook his head. "No, I don't know. What's this got to do with Kennedy?"

"I'm getting to that. Something pretty exciting took place during that visit, and the nephew got pictures of it. However, afterwards he was forced to surrender his film, and they put him on the first transport back to his base in Texas. He and his uncle, my source, were told to keep their silence or face military criminal charges."

"No dinner?" Balmain quipped sarcastically.

"No dinner." He sipped his drink. "This same nephew, in November

1963 happened to be on a rooftop across from Dealey Plaza during the assassination and had 8MM footage of the JFK assassination that he took from a totally unique angle. It captured the event clearly, but from an angle that the Warren Commission wouldn't have wanted to see, since it might have invalidated their findings."

If Balmain had been hooked up to a polygraph right then, the galvanic skin response sensor would have gone off the chart. He felt an electrical charge shoot through his body as he tried to analyze what he was hearing. Something wasn't adding up. It couldn't be! Keeping his voice even, he asked, "If he had footage of the assassination, why didn't he turn it in? Lord knows we were looking for everything that was snapped that day."

"Because there was something else on that roll." Albrecht unzipped the folio and slid out a black and white enlargement; a photo of a silver disk about thirty feet in diameter, hovering in front of a group of military officers. Seamless, bright aluminum, it didn't have any doors or windows. Neither did it have any visible landing gear. "This is a still shot taken by my source's nephew at Edwards Air Force Base in 1954." He slid the picture to Balmain.

"And this," Albrecht pulled another enlargement out. "...is a blow-up of some of the 8MM frames that were on the tail end of the film that the nephew shot at Dealey Plaza."

Balmain looked at the enlargement of the roll and compared the images of the silver disk in November, 1963 to the one allegedly shot in 1954. They were virtually identical. A chill ran down his spine as he remembered the case. It couldn't be the same guy. They'd seen that film at Headquarters, and it was underexposed garbage. Worthless!

Albrecht took another sip of his drink. "The Colonel told me that on the afternoon of the 22nd his nephew had raced back to his base to get the film of the assassination developed. But when he got to the lab, there were several senior officers there screaming at him to get to the flight line. So, he grabbed some extra film out of the refrigerator, but in his haste, never had time to switch it out, uh, before filming the, uh, visitor to the base."

Balmain stared at him without comment. He was trying to decide if this guy was sincere or setting him up for a very elaborate sting.

"Afterwards, he returned to the base photo lab to process the film, but by the time it was ready, it was after nine in the evening. He was alone in the lab, and the NCO in charge of the lab, who by the way was the only guy that had the combination to the classified materials safe, had already left for the day. Because of the film's importance, the nephew thought it would be safer with him, so he took it home with him."

Balmain continued his silence. It was a good interview technique to get the other person to talk, but in actuality, he just didn't know what to say.

"When the nephew returned to work the next day, the base security police were there, taking a report. Someone had broken in and stolen every piece of film in the place, and even hacked their way into the records safe."

Albrecht traced his index finger around the rim of the martini glass. "The nephew called his uncle, and after telling him about the film's contents, panicked and took off."

"The Air Force listed him as Absent Without Leave, AWOL, and he totally disappeared for a couple of weeks. But then, he called the Colonel and told him that he'd been staying at a family cabin in Jamaica Beach, down near Galveston, and he wanted to come home."

"The Colonel contacted the Air Force OSI and set up the meeting." Albrecht took another swig of the Gimlet. "But the OSI Agents claimed that when they got to the cabin, he wasn't there. The next thing the Colonel heard was a couple weeks later, his nephew had died in a warehouse fire in Dallas."

Balmain already knew the answer before he asked. "And the nephew's name?"

"Harold M. Ramey. He was a staff sergeant, assigned to the photo lab at..."

"Sheppard Air Force Base," Balmain finished the sentence for him.

16

The weather in Chicago had been crazy, rising to a record high of 91 degrees on April 22, before plummeting to highs in the mid-forties over the weekend. After a gratifying reunion with the sisters and Captain Terry, as he was known in the family, Karen had darted between lanes, cursing at slower drivers and pushing the Cutlass Supreme to the limits of its performance. Or so it felt to Mark. But after the harrowing experience, she successfully dropped him at the departures area by 6:22, allowing him ample time to check in and get to his gate for the 7:05 a.m. departure back to San Francisco.

After a brief kiss curbside, he grabbed his bag, and leapt out of the car. They'd said their passionate good-byes earlier and agreed to try to maintain a long-distance relationship, at least until she was able to accumulate some vacation time. They had calculated all of the holidays throughout the remainder of the year, and made tentative plans for each one. Mark was excited. He was now part of a couple.

He dashed to the ticket counter to check in, and found that he had been given a Captain's Upgrade to first class. He was surprised, and asked the ticket agent what that was.

She winked and lowered her voice, "Well, it's usually reserved for family members of employees or for really special guests that one of our captains wants to reward."

"Oh, thank you," he replied to her. Captain Terry must have made a phone call to someone and Mark realized that he would have to call him after he arrived in San Francisco to offer his thanks.

The First Class service started at the boarding area as the gate agent recognized the code on his ticket and told him that he could board the aircraft any time he'd like. Once aboard, the cabin attendant took his jacket and asked him if he'd like anything to drink before take-off.

His seat, 1-C, was in the first row on the aisle, across from the galley, and seemed more like the La-Z-Boy recliner at the institute than the coach airline seats he was used to. It was certainly more comfortable than the orange webbing he'd sat in on a couple of the Marine Corps' C-130s. He remembered his first flight on one several years earlier. About an hour into the flight, he needed to use the restroom and wandered aft in search. When he got to the ramp and the pallets of cargo strapped down, he turned and found a Navy Chief reading a newspaper.

"Where's the head, Chief?" he'd asked.

"Starboard bulkhead, aft." The chief nodded to the rear of the aircraft.

Mark carefully walked back, balancing his steps amid the turbulence and looked down. There, attached to the inside frame of the aircraft was a plastic funnel with a drainage hose descending through the floor. He looked back at the Chief, who nodded with a sly smile.

Now, just a few years later, he was relaxing in his airborne recliner with an attractive flight attendant bringing him drinks. He smiled and shook his head.

His thoughts drifted from the relaxing and fulfilling weekend back to his disturbing RV session the Friday before. It had taken him a while to get those thoughts out of his mind on his way into O'Hare. His session had affected him. The psychic revelation he'd experienced came as a complete shock to him. It was one thing to think that the country had been lied to about the JFK assassination, but it was even stranger to find that woman who was pointing the way for him. She was showing him things. But, who was she?

He'd finally remembered her on Friday night as the aircraft had lifted its wheels off the runway at San Francisco International Airport. As he drifted in and out of a light sleep, he knew that he'd last seen her on the roof of the Embassy in Saigon five years earlier. Who was she?

She was a psychic interloper of sorts, as was he. She didn't belong in Kennedy's time any more than she had belonged in Saigon. But, he was certain he didn't know her. They had never met. Why did she seem so familiar to him? Why did she care about him?

The taxi seemed long, but they were second in line for take-off, and when their turn came, the G-forces pushed him back in his seat, and he relaxed. Thrust was good. Thrust meant speed, and speed meant lift, and lift meant that everything was working the way it was supposed to. He heard the wheels retract into the belly of the aircraft, and it was only seconds before the captain turned off the No Smoking light.

He looked around the first class cabin of the 727 Stretch model and saw a couple of guys in suits, a guy with long hair wearing jeans, and his bubbly traveling companion. In his mind, he decided that the guy was in the entertainment profession and the young lady was, well, not a wife. Maybe a friend. Maybe a groupie or something. The rest of the First Class section was empty.

After breakfast of eggs and sausage, the cabin attendant came by and asked if he'd like anything else. A cocktail perhaps. He declined and depressed the button in the armrest to push his seat back.

He relaxed and drifted off into light sleep. The JFK assassination had been a significant event in his life when he was growing up. It was important to everyone in that era, but even more so for the kids of Dallas. It was something they'd never forget. He took his Walkman out of the seat pocket, and depressed the Play button as he put the earphones over his head.

He cleared his mind of the events of the weekend and the noise of the cabin, and it wasn't long before he unintentionally fell into the pupil of his mental eye. As the cares of the physical world receded in the distance, he was vividly transported back to his home in Dallas as a child. He smelled the turkey at Christmas dinner and experienced the happiness that had come with family. His Uncle Dirk and Aunt Jeanine in the kitchen, and his cousins in the back yard.

The fruity smells of Mom's Primrose and Winter Jasmine in her garden, the trip to the theater to watch James Garner. In his head, he heard the theme song from the movie; a catchy tune that he always enjoyed when watching reruns of the Doris Day movie on television. The song brought him comfort. Her voice soothed and energized him at the same time.

The difference in the binaural sine tones entering each ear made the song emerge and then recede in his mind, fading into the hollow distance. He mentally pulled away from the theater on Christmas evening, and pushed further back in time by a month, no, a little more: November 22 at 12:25 p.m. Central time.

The exuberant young president feels the wind on his face in the open Lincoln. Amid the roar of the crowds and exhaust of the motorcycles alongside the car, he feels like he is at the right place and time in history. He is excited about how this visit will help him in the polls. Despite having the socially inept and sometimes worrisome Johnson in tow, he has made some difficult choices that will work out well for his campaign and ultimately, for the country.

He waves to the adoring crowd and is charged by their energy. He knows they are closer than the Secret Service would like, and frowns at Jackie's bodyguard as he runs forward to crouch on the platform behind the rear bumper. Agent Hill glances at him, but returns his focus to the encroaching lines of people along the left side of the limousine. After a couple blocks, Hill reluctantly decides to jump off the platform and return to the running board of the follow-up vehicle.

His son's birthday is three days away. They'll need to do something special. Maybe another ride in the Marine helicopter. John loves airplanes. Ahead, the crowds seem to open up a little. He can see the daylight of Dealey Plaza ahead. Just a few more minutes to the Trade Mart luncheon.

There's got to be a way to get the Russians, and maybe the Chinese to join him in the exploration of space. He knows that we can't go into the universe in competition with each other. We have to venture out as one people. The magicians have told him that people are watching. Not our people...their people. The magicians? Faceless entities that run the country. The MAJIC group. What a silly name. Less than a dozen people knew what the letters stood for.

The motorcade turns right onto Houston Street. Kennedy can smell fresh air. Women call to him to look their way so that they can take his picture. Women are a weakness for him. His wife understands. She doesn't condone, but she understands. He's got to stabilize his desires if he's going to run the country. His trysts, if they become known publicly, could undermine everything he's worked for, and ruin any chances that Bobby might have to take the reins of the nation as the next president.

Huge elements of emotion surround him. He's enveloped by positive energy...lots of complex emotions...happy, cheerful thoughts are flooding through his mind. Then, something happens. He's surprised and concerned for just a moment. There's an adrenaline rush, his heart rate increases. But, it's only a momentary concern. Time is slowing down for him. He's very confused. He feels like Caesar, realizing too late that the Senators have conspired to kill him. Then total calmness, more like a mixture of elation and calm, a spiritual awakening. Celestial awareness, a feeling of not caring about the past. The past no longer matters.

Mark was suddenly laden with guilt. It was as if he was intruding on someone's private moment. The transition from physical to spiritual life was not something he should have been a part of. He moved ahead to the hospital. Jackie is weeping, her pink outfit soaked in blood. The doctors are working to get his heart started, but they know there is no chance. The President is clinically dead. A priest who has been summoned is reluctant to administer last rites, but eventually acquiesces. The head injury is too severe and all the doctors can do is to perform a medical drama to assure the widow that everything that could be done would be done.

Mark felt a chill. A closeness of someone. It was vivid. From his left, he could perceive a man with a dark complexion, bald or shaved head. His sharp nose made Mark think of someone with an African, no, an Egyptian lineage. He was wearing a college sweat-shirt, but the arms had been cut off at the shoulders. He was wiry and muscular, maybe in his early forties. He was leaning in towards Mark, but not to talk to him. It felt more like the man was studying him. Inspecting him.

Then from his right, he could feel someone pulling him. It was her. It was the woman in the gray slacks that seemed to appear whenever he was in trouble. She pulled him away from Dallas, and for a moment they hung in darkness, weightless in the cavern of the giant pupil that took him from reality to other places. She seemed to know something. She put her finger to her lips and shook her head slowly from side to side as if she was telling him he can't talk about this anymore. This has to stay a secret for a while longer. It's not his job to reveal what he knows.

Mark felt the intense pressure in his head at the same time the cabin attendant's soft touch on his shoulder brought him back to the present. "Sir?"

He'd slept through the descent and he needed to clear his ears. He popped his jaw a couple of times as she leaned over to help him return his seatback to its upright position. "We'll be landing in San Francisco in a couple of minutes. Can I get you anything else?"

"No, thank you," he replied hazily. He looked at his watch. He'd been out for over three hours.

⸺»《◉》«⸺

Fred Balmain glanced at his watch. It was almost 11:15 a.m., and he needed to meet Arguelles at 11:45, so he picked up the dark expandable folder to make sure that the two envelopes were appropriately sealed. One contained his Last Will and Testament, which he and his wife Sarah had reviewed and updated over the weekend. And, the fatter one was a complete set of the copies of the documents he'd found behind his credenza at his office at Quantico years earlier.

The meeting with the reporter had caused him some concerns and excited a part of him that he thought he'd lost. There was a mystery that needed to be solved, and he was a part of it. He replaced the two envelopes in the folder and slipped the elastic band around the top, snapping it into place.

Madison's was about half way between Dulles and Balmain's office and was supposedly established by some distant relative of President James Madison. It featured great steaks and tall booths that facilitated intimate conversations, and so it was an acceptable meeting place for lunch. Political leaders and power brokers from the public and private sectors often dined there because of its proximity to the airport, and because it was usually void of reporters who stalked the D.C. area restaurants looking for stories.

Mondays were usually light, and because the restaurant seemed to cater to more of a late-lunch crowd anyway, Balmain wasn't surprised to find very few cars in the parking lot. Once inside, it took his eyes a moment to adjust to the low light provided by the flickering gas lanterns, reminiscent of the early 1800s, matching the rest of the restaurant's theme. Waiters and waitresses were attired in period costume and did their best to create the atmosphere of a bygone era. Until you got the bill of course; major credit cards accepted. Balmain hadn't seen Mike's dark red Fleetwood Brougham in the parking lot, so he decided to grab a seat.

Mike Arguelles, born Miguel, had been in the CIA, only a couple of years. Long enough to know that he didn't want to work for the CIA. An absolute champion of ethics and capitalism, he and his family had made it out of Cuba before the Bay of Pigs, and still fostered some resentment about the Agency's handling of the operation. He and Balmain had crossed paths a couple of times when he was lecturing on legal matters at both The Farm in Williamsburg, and at Quantico. The Farm, of course was the nickname for Camp Peary, the CIA's supposedly secret training site off Interstate 64, with an exit sign that was clearly marked.

The hostess, attired and adorned like Martha Washington, led Balmain to a booth in the corner, and in keeping with his FBI training, he took the seat that faced the door. He ordered an iced tea and then sat, elbows on the table, with his chin resting on his steepled hands.

The meeting with Albrecht had left him with more questions than answers. He'd spent Saturday at the library trying to find references to the supposed filmmaker. There were very few. Checking crisscross directories, he was able to tie the name on the business card to an actual person, with an actual business, but that didn't mean anything. No spook ever took on a cover that wouldn't at least withstand some cursory investigation.

Albrecht had been involved in books about the Roswell incident and some other fringe subjects, but there was nothing Balmain found that could substantiate whether he was really interested in the topic, or if he was just a well-place covert operative of…of someone. He was alarmed that Albrecht had produced images from an 8MM roll of film that Washington had said was underexposed and of no value. It had to be from the same source that he'd investigated in 1963. That is, unless there had been two people filming from the roof of the Post Office building. Just not possible.

And, why would he have come to Balmain? This fellow obviously had a resource inside the Justice Department that knew what the purpose of Balmain's team had been. Albrecht had been cagey about his sources, but extraordinarily accurate. His business card showed a Post Office box in Albuquerque, but that didn't mean anything either. He could have been from anywhere.

By the end of the interview, Balmain was left confused as to the exact nature of Albrecht's request. Was he confirming whether or not the FBI knew that flying saucers were visiting US Air Force Bases? Or was he trying to tie the JFK assassination to the President's desire to open up the records? Either premise would be shocking to the general public. If it was true that an alien presence had been interacting with us for years, or centuries, what would that do to religious institutions...the Vatican? To Judaism? To Islam? To global strategic policy?

He'd inspected the photographs as good as he could in the dimly lit bar, and without a magnifying glass, he couldn't be certain as to their authenticity. He was no expert, but he'd seen thousands of photos through the years and they looked as genuine as anything he'd ever seen. He'd flipped each of them over and noted that the reverse sides were clean. There were no lab stamps indicating a processing date or location, meaning that they weren't commercially enlarged. No surprise there. Anyone who had this kind of material wouldn't have taken it down the street to their neighborhood photo shop.

Balmain had tried to press him for more information about his background, but all he learned was that the journalist had started his career as a high school teacher of foreign languages and political science. No schools were mentioned. By the end of the evening, he had been forced into the position of either accepting the journalist at his word or not.

The turning point of the afternoon came not with the meeting itself, but afterwards, on their way out. At the end of their meeting, Albrecht had offered him a phone number to call, with certain instructions. "If you have any questions or would like to talk again, please call this number and leave a message, or tell whoever answers that you'd like to bet the spread on the next ball game; it doesn't matter which one."

Balmain looked at the business card for Steven Albrecht, Author, Producer. "Albuquerque?"

"Yes." He finished his Gimlet. "That's where I live now. If no one answers and you have to leave a message, I will get back to you as soon as I can."

As they left the bar, Balmain noticed that the couple in the corner must have reached a decision as to their evening's activities, because they both rose as the man left cash on the table. From that distance, it didn't look like they'd touched their drinks.

The male half of their team seemed to loiter in the lobby as Albrecht moved towards the elevators. The female followed Balmain down the escalator to the Metro terminal. She looked like any of Washington's other young impressionable college graduates who came from a good family, good school, with good credentials, determined to make a name for themselves in the center of government. Maybe a lawyer, maybe a would-be politician.

She didn't seem to have any interest in him whatsoever. She didn't even ride in the same car. But, Balmain's concerns grew just a bit when she changed trains in Rosslyn and boarded the same westbound train he was taking. However, she disembarked at the Wiehle-Reston East Station, one station before Balmain himself got off.

On one hand, it was exhilarating to be back in a situation that accelerated his heart and sharpened his senses. On the other hand, he had no idea what he had gotten into. Were they following Albrecht and, therefore, naturally anyone he met with? Albrecht didn't seem to have the skills or tradecraft to make it in the undercover world. So, if he'd been followed from Albuquerque he probably wouldn't have known it. Then again, maybe thirty-some years of field work had made Balmain just a little paranoid.

Nevertheless, the full impact of what he was doing prompted him to sit down with Sarah Friday night and take a look at their wills. She didn't seem concerned about the timing. They'd been talking about it for a while and she was happy today. She had some new wicker baskets to display for her friends when they visited. Expensive wicker baskets, made in Ohio, of all places.

After they'd reviewed the paperwork, she'd gone upstairs to get ready for bed. Balmain had gone into his study, and tediously removed the books and memorabilia from the bookshelf. Once empty, he was able to slide it out and pull back the carpeting from the floor to expose the envelope and the documents that had given him many sleepless nights. And during the most recent sleepless night, he made his decision.

Mike Arguelles entered at precisely 11:45 a.m., and after

seeing Balmain in the corner, waved off Martha Washington and started that way. He moved well for a large man. At about six feet tall, his weight was probably close to 260 pounds, and the bald head and gray moustache made him look a bit older than he was. He was still fit, though. He moved between the tables with the pep and precision of an all-star running back, a smile on his face.

Mike's brief tenure with The Company, or The Outfit as some agents referred to it, led Balmain to believe that he could be trusted. Like many Cubans looking for a better life, Mike was prepared to support his new country, but expected them to deliver on their promises. That was why we paid taxes. He'd done extensive pro-bono work in the fields of human rights, specifically for people and groups who had fled dictatorships in the southern Americas.

He could afford to donate some of his time for charitable causes. He had been a successful engineer for a major arms manufacturer before having a change of vision and studying law at Georgetown. His legal education had been paid by the US Government. In a few brief years, he had managed to start a family of four sons, build a house, and amass a collection of Mont Blanc pens and pencils, some of which he proudly touted in his shirt pocket each day. His collection of firearms was even more impressive and was valued at many thousands of dollars.

Balmain rose and the two men shook hands. "Hi Mike. Thank you for coming."

Arguelles grinned and slid his briefcase into the booth. "Are you kidding? A free lunch at Madison's? I wouldn't miss it."

Another ersatz Martha Washington took their orders and disappeared as the two men caught up and eventually got down to business. Balmain passed the expandable file folder to him.

"Sarah and I wanted to update our wills, so we made a few minor changes." Balmain sipped his iced tea and stared at the folder. "But, there's something else I need you to do...attorney-client confidentiality. No questions."

As soon as they opened the cabin door, Mark was up and headed down the jet-way. Since he had carried his only luggage onboard with him, he bypassed the baggage claim area and almost sprinted to the parking garage to check on his Nova. He was excited to see that his pride and joy, while a bit dusty, appeared unscathed.

Kravitz had given him the time off without marking it down as vacation time, so he felt obligated to go straight to the institute from the airport and at least try to put in as much of a full day as he could. "Hi Mark!" Kravitz beamed as he adjusted his glasses. "How's that girl of yours...Karen is it?"

"She's great, Doc. We had a great weekend," Mark answered, a bit embarrassed.

Yasmina and Dr. Kravitz exchange a mischievous grin. "Well, in light of your busy weekend, we thought we'd take it easy on you today." Yasmina smiled conspiratorially as she handed him a sheet of paper with several locations listed. "We've got a new viewer in the cage today and we're going to let you be the outbounder."

"Yeah!" Mark exclaimed.

Being the outbounder was the gravy job. All one had to do was to drive somewhere and find some structure or event of significance, and look at it; experience everything about it for an hour and then come back to the Institute. It would be the viewer's task to try to interpret any psychic feelings or perceptions and determine as much about the outbounder's target as they could. In short, it was a free day of sightseeing for Mark.

Mark looked at the list. Some of the locations he was familiar with, and others, he'd never heard of. He needed something that was visually inspiring, something with impact that would offer the viewer some vivid gestalts to identify.

"Thanks!" Mark said as he grabbed a map off of the table and started for the door. He would have one hour to find the site he selected and get into position.

St. Mary of the Assumption Cathedral was located at 1111 Gough Street in San Francisco, about three miles east of the Golden Gate Bridge. Striking in appearance and visible from the air for miles, the bright modernistic cathedral was a distinct landmark in the cityscape of San Francisco, which any trained remote viewer would have no trouble keying in on. Designed by architects Pietro Belluschi and Pier Luigi Nervi using what was considered the most superlative engineering, the form of the chapel attracted visitors from all parts of the world.

Groundbreaking occurred in August of 1965, and two years later Apostolic Delegate Luigi Raimondi blessed the cornerstone. Construction was completed in 1970, with architecture emphasizing both the vertical and the horizontal elements. The intent was that the eyes were drawn upward with the sweeping of the white cupola, as human hearts were meant to uplift towards the heavens and God.

The brilliant white hyperbolic paraboloid created a graceful flow upwards 190 feet where the four corners met in a cross. The cathedral was crowned with a 55 foot golden cross at its apex. Stained glass ran up all four sides of the building. At the top plane of the structure, the four lines of glass changed direction, running horizontal and creating a cross with the mosaic glass patterns.

The organ, built by Fratelli Ruffatti was one of the most acclaimed in the world. The soaring concrete pedestal platform was a magnificent art form in its own right and held an impressive 4,842 pipes.

Mark parked on Gough just south of Geary Boulevard, checked his watch for the correct time, and then walked the circumference of the building taking note of the impressive and expressive modern architecture. After his tour, he sat on a concrete bench gazing up at the tower. It truly was a spectacular piece of engineering.

During his hour, he watched people come and go, and experienced the sights, sounds and smells of the area. A bit cool and windy, the air seemed fresh and brisk, and he tried to focus on where he was and what he was doing. He did not want to drift back to thoughts about JFK or his weekend in Chicago. He was being viewed and he didn't want the viewer getting the wrong signals.

He checked his watch. It was 12:45 p.m., and time to return to the Institute. He got up from his bench and started back to his car. As he turned around he felt a momentary spear of confusion poke him in the back. He didn't know why, but for a brief second he felt fear and pain. He shook it off and walked towards the street.

Johnny T. Ribbs sat behind the wheel of the tan Chrysler Cordoba. The padded half-landau roof was torn in places and the entire car showed general signs of neglect. It was four years old but only four hours stolen from a parking lot near the bus station.

At twenty six, Johnny T had spent most of his adult life in jails of one kind or another. A ne'er-do-well with two brothers who had never met their fathers, he fled Baton Rouge, and traveled west, believing that he could be an actor or stuntman in the movie business. However, show business was not in his future as he was stuck in menial jobs for a year before realizing it was a lot easier to make a living thrusting a gun into someone's face, and simply taking what you wanted.

His luck over the years had been miserable until he had recently met a Hollywood casting agent in the drunk tank the week before in the County jail. His cellmate explained how some guy had been nailing his wife, and that if Johnny wanted to pick up five thousand dollars in a hurry, all he'd have to do is wait for this guy to go to his car at a certain place and time, and take care of him. Reliable transportation and the necessary tools would be provided.

Johnny T needed the money. He didn't really trust the offer or the man making it, but if there was a chance he could get five grand for an hour's work, he couldn't pass it up. He'd do it and be out of San Francisco within minutes. Five thousand dollars would give him an opportunity to start fresh somewhere. "Half before, and half after." Johnny had told his new client.

The client agreed and told him where he would find the car the following Monday. There would be $2,500 in the glove box. The man gave Johnny a slip of paper with an address on it and told him when the job was over to drop the car at that residence and check the mail box. The rest of his cash would be waiting for him there.

And sure enough, in the glovebox, as his client had promised, was an envelope containing an assortment of used bills adding up to $2,500. There was also a loaded .38 revolver. Johnny wasn't book-smart, but he was genuinely fearful of shooting someone with a gun that might eventually link him to other crimes that he'd had nothing to do with. So, he didn't touch it.

The type-written note that accompanied the payment gave him a description of his target, as well as the car to look for and where to find it. Johnny had followed the brown Nova from the Institute to the church and now was just waiting. He just waited and chain-smoked his Winstons until he saw the guy coming back to his car.

He was nervous. In the hour he'd been parked there, he'd seen several young white men that could have been his mark. However, they had walked past the Chevy Nova without as much as a glance. But at 12:45 p.m., his patience was rewarded. He started the massive V-8 engine and checked his mirrors to ensure that he was clear of oncoming traffic. After backing a few feet from the car in front of him, he dropped the transmission into drive and put his left foot on the brake.

It was him! His target came around the front of the Nova and reached into his pocket for his keys. Johnny slammed his right foot down on the gas pedal and the engine roared to life, the tires squealing as they fought to find traction. He lifted off the gas a bit for fear that he'd fish-tail and hit another car, but he made it into the lane, straightened his wheel and applied pressure again. He fought the normal impulse to swerve at the last minute. It was unnatural to intentionally drive into another human being. He'd never even run over an animal before.

As his speed increased, he guided the steering wheel to the right and kept his foot down. The right front fender of the Cordoba caught the left rear side of the Nova right behind the driver's door, just as Mark tried to insert his key into the lock. At the sound of the crash, Mark jumped instinctively, which is probably what dissipated the energy.

With less weight on his frame, the impact spun his legs out from under him and he slid across the hood of the car before his back smashed into the windshield with such force that as the car sped off, his body never touched the trunk before slamming into the asphalt.

He felt pain. But, pain was good. You have to be alive to feel pain. He was aware of people rushing to his aid and yelling for someone else to call an ambulance. As silly as it sounded, he felt bad for his Nova. It had taken some of the impact and might have saved his life. His poor Nova.

Someone yelled to him, "Hang in there!"

As another onlooker tried to get some padding under his head, someone else yelled, "No! Don't touch his head. He might have a neck injury."

Then, just before he lost consciousness, he saw her. His raven-haired brown-eyed goddess. Didn't she have any other clothes? She always had the same blouse and gray slacks on. But, it was so comforting to see her. To feel her near him.

She leaned close and whispered, "I'm sorry about this. You're going to be okay."

17

WEDNESDAY, APRIL 30, 1980

The doctors were impressed. Despite the trauma that the hit and run victim had suffered, they felt that he would eventually make a full recovery. Physically anyway. As with all head injuries, it would take a while before they could fully understand the long term effects of the skull fracture. His right tibia had been fractured, and his spine had taken quite a shock, but the only thing that concerned them was the head injury.

He was responding to verbal commands, but his memory was still a bit sketchy. It was not uncommon for trauma victims to have some level of amnesia after a significant event. But only time would tell. His vital signs were stable, but he had difficulty recalling anything that had happened in the past twenty four hours. They felt it best to get him up and moving as soon as he could and to have him talk to people he knew to gradually regain those missing puzzle pieces that make up reality.

When he was aware of someone in his room, Mark opened his eyes to see a nurse doing something with the corner of his bedsheet.

"Just making you comfortable. How are you feeling today?"

Mark inhaled through his nose. The nasal cannula supplied fresh oxygen, but it was dry. He wanted to cough, but was afraid if he did, something inside would break. "Honestly? I feel like shit."

"That's fair." She smiled at him. "My name is Lynda. I'm one of your day nurses."

He tried to laugh. "Lynda...the Day nurse...like Lynda Day, the actress on *Mission Impossible*?"

"Don't I wish," she replied, tugging at his sheets. "You've had some visitors. It seems like you've got a lot of friends."

Mark knew that he was in a hospital, but felt detached from himself due to the narcotics they had put him on. He knew he had pain throughout his body, but it was as if the drugs were helping him just ignore it. "I thought so. I've heard people coming and going, but I can't remember who or when. Who's been here?"

"Yeah, that's the drugs," she acknowledged. "One of them is downstairs right now. I think she said her name was Jasmine or something."

"Yasmina?"

"Yeah, that's probably right." She finished tucking and stood up. "Friend of yours?"

Mark searched his memory. "I think so."

Lynda collected some trays and left, and an indeterminate period of time later, a short, squat Mediterranean-looking woman entered. "Hey, you're awake! How you feeling?"

Mark looked at her for a moment, through the narcotic haze. "Yasmina?"

She walked up to the side of his bed and took his hand carefully, so as not to disturb the IV. "Yeah. They say you took quite a spill. How much do you remember?"

Mark pushed himself to recall the incident, "I was looking at something...a church, I think. I don't remember anything after that."

"You were on assignment...for the Institute."

Mark frowned, "The Marine Corps Institute?"

Yasmina studied him for a moment. "No, Mark. For us. What do you remember about your job?"

"I'm a Marine," he responded.

"Yes, but do you remember what you were doing for us?"

"No. I'm sorry."

"What's the last thing you remember before the accident?" she asked, with a moderate amount of concern in her voice.

"I don't know. I don't remember the accident."

"Do you remember Viet Nam?"

"Yes. I was on the wall at the Embassy when we withdrew."

"Do you remember how we met?"

"It was at Quantico, wasn't it? I was in a class..."

She squeezed his hand. "Hey, listen. There's a nice young lady named Karen who's been calling us every couple of hours to check on you. Girlfriend?"

"Yes, uh, from Chicago. Is that where I'm from?"

"No, sweetie. You're from Dallas. Does that mean anything to you?"

"Mom...Dad...family and friends." Tears formed in the corners of his eyes. "Mom died a few years ago. Dad's still with the fire department."

"You remember Karen, though?"

"Yes."

"Do you remember her sister, Katie?"

"Yes...blond...cute...pregnant. We saw them last weekend. I think it was last weekend. Shit, what is today?"

"It's okay, Mark. They've got you on some pain killers. Do you remember anyone coming to visit you since you've been here?"

"Uhmmm, doctors... I think you and Dr. Kravitz were here yesterday. Some others." He tried hard to focus. "Two guys from the government. I couldn't open my eyes, but I could hear them."

"Were they Marines? The Marine Corps sent a young officer by yesterday to check on you."

"No, I don't think so. They asked about...uhmmm...Eterna or something. I didn't know what they meant."

After a long silence, Yasmina's tone changed. "What did they ask you about Eterna?"

"They weren't really asking me. It's like they were talking to each other, by the window...almost a whisper. I don't think they knew I heard them."

"What did they want to know about Eterna?"

Mark felt a wave of emotion sweep over him as he realized he wasn't as okay as he thought. "I couldn't hear the entire conversation; just bits and pieces. They spoke to each other. They wanted to know how much had leaked out about something called Eterna." Mark tried to hold back tears. "I don't know. I'm sorry."

Yasmina looked at him as a mother would look at her son in the same predicament, and squeezed his hand again. "I have to get back to work, and you need to get some rest. The nurse has my number, so if you need anything, please ask her to call me."

Mark closed his eyes and drifted off to narcotic-induced sleep. It was sometime later when the two guys in suits entered his room.

"Mr. Reynolds?" the taller of the two asked.

"Yes."

"I'm Inspector Phillips with the San Francisco Police, and this is Special Agent Reynaldo with the US Secret Service. We'd like to talk to you about your accident, if you feel up to it?"

Mark tried to push himself up in bed a bit, and as he struggled against the pain and the drugs, became aware that sometime during his nap, someone had removed the nasal cannula. "Yes. But I have to warn you, I don't remember much about the accident."

"No problem sir. We'll be in and out as fast as we can." Phillips opened a vinyl-covered notebook and produced five color Polaroid pictures of Black men in their mid-twenties. Mark determined that they were booking shots, each with San Francisco Police Department and a date across the bottom. "Do you know any of these men?"

Mark stared at the photos and tried to search his memory. "No. None of them look familiar at all."

Phillips asked again, "You're sure? You've never seen any of them anywhere?"

"Nope, don't know them. Who are they?"

"Does the name Johnny T. Ribbs mean anything to you?" He tucked the photos back into a pocket in his notebook.

Mark tried to shake his head, but he could feel pain breaking through the fog of analgesics. "No...huh uh. I don't think I've ever met anyone named Ribbs."

"What's the last thing you do remember?"

He tried to put the pieces of the puzzle together, but the colors and shapes just weren't fitting. "I'm so sorry. I was doing something...on the job...I remember looking at a church" His breathing deepened. "Geezus! I don't know. I can't remember anything before that except my weekend."

"What did you do over the weekend?"

"I went to see, uh, my girlfriend and her family in Chicago. I got back to town, and I went to church. No. I was sent to the church."

"Who told you to go to the church, Mark?"

"I don't know; it must've been Yasmina. She said that I work with her."

"Yasmina sent you to the church. Is that Mrs. Sheppard?"

"Yeah...Sheppard."

"What do you do for Mrs. Sheppard?" the Inspector probed.

"I don't know."

"Is Mrs. Sheppard in the Marines?"

"No...she's a...uh...civilian contractor. Her group works for the government." Mark cleared his throat. He needed to cough.

"What's the name of the group, Mark?"

"I don't know. She called it the Institute. It must be something academic; she's not a Marine." He paused. "But, her husband was."

The Inspector looked across the bed at the man he'd introduced as Reynaldo. After some sort of non-verbal signal was exchanged, he continued. "Mark, you were hit by a stolen car driven by a small time, habitual offender by the name of Johnny Ribbs. The car was found a few miles from where you were hit. It had been burned out, with Ribbs inside it. Are you sure you've never heard of him?"

"No...I'm sure. You said a habitual offender...what does that mean?"

"He was a small-time hoodlum with a lengthy conviction history. We're just following our evidence, and trying to piece this all together. The thing is, he was found with about twenty five hundred dollars in counterfeit US currency on him."

"Counterfeit?" Mark frowned. "I guess that explains what Raymondo, uh, the Secret Service guy is doing here."

The shorter gentleman finally spoke. "Reynaldo...Gil Reynaldo. And yes. We're trying to determine what Ribbs was doing over on that side of town with counterfeit currency, before he got roasted. Obviously, it doesn't look like he got a chance to pass any of it."

Reynaldo moved towards the end of the bed so that Mark didn't have to turn his head to see them. "We think he might have met his counterfeiter around the church, and thought that you might have seen something while you were there."

Mark closed his eyes and tried to remember details about the church. He could see the tall white structure in his mind, but that was it. It was like a dream that one recalls when they wake up, but soon forgets as the morning moves on. With every second, he remembered less and less of his afternoon. "Huh uh...sorry."

"No problem, man," Phillips said. "We're going to leave our cards on the table. If you think of something else, please give us a call."

Mark nodded carefully, and was asleep before they were out of the room.

⊰⊱⊰⊱

Yasmina grabbed her purse off the front seat and dashed up the steps to the Institute without bothering to lock her car door. She didn't care. On the elevator to her floor, she tapped her foot anxiously and when the car stopped, she pushed the doors open. She was so angry, she entered her code incorrectly on the access control keypad and had to re-enter it a second time before the door unlocked.

She opened the door to the conference room so quickly that if anyone had been standing on the other side, they would have been rewarded with a concussion as bad as Mark Reynolds had received in the accident. She tossed her purse unceremoniously into the corner before squaring off, hands on her hips, addressing the men gathered around the table.

"Doctor Kravitz, my apologies, but I'm about to cost the Institute a client." Her face was flushed and rage was in her brown eyes. "First, I want the truth. I won't tolerate any bullshit answers from any of you, and I won't allow any of you to quote some ridiculous national security protocol as a basis for not answering my questions. Are we fucking clear, gentlemen?"

Kravitz offered a surprised look, but was silent. If Yasmina was upset, there was a good reason. He looked at the three men across the table, wearing civilian clothes.

"Which of you visited the hospital in the past twenty-four hours?"

"The hospital?" The oldest of the three asked carefully.

"Yes, the hospital. Mark Reynolds is in the hospital recovering from injuries he sustained in a hit and run crash on Monday. He received a couple of visitors that he did not recognize, and while they thought he was unconscious, they began to discuss ETERNA. I want to know which of you it was."

The three men looked at each other questioningly. The fifty-something gentleman was the most organizationally powerful, of the group. He was a three star general in the United States Air Force, and in addition to overseeing the Office of Special Investigations, he was also the appointed representative for the Air Force's controversial foray into Remote Viewing. "I just flew in from Washington this morning, and came straight here from the airport."

The red-headed man in his forties, looked like he had played football at one time or another. His clothes were a bit tight on him, accentuating his bulky frame, and indicating to others that he had recently added some weight or didn't like to shop for clothes. He represented the Directorate of Operations at CIA in Langley. "I came in this morning as well - commercial flight out of National."

As everyone's gaze drifted towards the distinguished white-haired chap at the end of the table who was clad in the expensive blue suit and crisp white shirt, he winced slightly. Joseph Barnes didn't like being the center of attention. After all, he'd spent more than thirty years protecting people who enjoyed the spotlight. He had retired from the US Secret Service three years earlier, but they had kept him on the payroll in a civilian capacity to oversee the projects with which no other career-track agent wanted to be associated. The Service's use of Remote Viewing was one of those. And so was ETERNA. He now took on the projects for which the Secret Service, or any of its sister agencies would have needed a level of deniability, cloaking their involvement.

He didn't seem to be the least bit rattled as he spoke. "Well then. I guess it's my turn to issue an official denial." He laid his pen on his notepad. "As you know, my work on your project is highly sensitive. When our San Francisco office learned that the police department had picked up a homicide case involving counterfeit currency, we knew they would assign an agent. But when I saw that the suspect was linked to a hit and run of a Mark Reynolds who was employed here, I wanted to ascertain what Mr. Reynolds remembered about the accident, and about ETERNA, before our field office agent got to him."

Yasmina's eyes were cold. "Reynolds wasn't on ETERNA. He simply stumbled on a fast-mover while viewing another target last week. It was an attractor." She explained, using the team's slang for an event that a viewer attaches to inadvertently, because it's more interesting to him or her than the actual target. "As soon as he did, we stopped the session and directed him back towards the appropriate target."

"He was on ETERNA." Barnes insisted. "One of our viewers has seen him. Whether it was a sanctioned session or not, Reynolds found his way into it."

Kravitz interrupted, "You're running your own viewers at Secret Service?"

Barnes shrugged. "Not officially. We have a couple of agents who've been dabbling in it, and are getting better. One of them has seen Reynolds and an unidentified female bi-locating to JFK's Oval Office in the weeks leading up to the assassination."

"A woman?" Yasmina asked, somewhat calmer now that she had exposed the source of the leak. "We don't have any female viewers here, besides me."

"We know. We're not sure who she is or how she fits in. All our agent was able to perceive was that she's American and not malevolent."

The Air Force General chimed in, "If you'll recall, Dr. Kravitz, this...this moonlighting is something that concerned me three years ago when we first met."

Kravitz defended himself and his group. "And General, as you'll recall, I said that all of our people are vetted and have signed non-disclosure agreements. The fact that Mark might have seen something psychically, that thousands of other psychics from around the world have probably already seen, is not significant. Half the world's population doesn't believe in psychic functioning. And your control of the media and government continues to support that. Without any type of confirmation or validation, these reports are nothing more than someone's dreams or fantasies."

"Precisely." Yasmina pulled a chair away from the table and sat down. "The US Government's practice of ridiculing anyone who stumbles onto national secrets, or in this case, a correct theory, or makes reports of any unidentified phenomenon has been publicly castrated. It has shifted public perception of reports, and the people who make them, as being looney."

She continued, "So, Mr. Barnes, I want to know more about the guy that supposedly hit our viewer. I believe his name is Ribbs?"

Barnes shrugged. "There's not much to tell. He's a derelict from Louisiana - moved west in search of fame and fortune and decided crime was a better career choice. My guess is he was probably a bit sociopathic. Most of them are."

Kravitz pushed his glasses higher on his nose. "You think the accident with Mark was just that? Nothing more sinister?"

"Our agent is working with SFPD on the assumption that Ribbs was in the area to meet his counterfeiter. They only found about fifteen dollars and change on him in genuine currency. We believe he had made his purchase and was in a hurry to get away."

"How's he doing, by the way? Your guy, Reynolds." Barnes asked, masterfully changing the subject.

Yasmina took a deep breath and then exhaled. "He'll survive, but he has significant memory loss. No memory of the accident, and no memory of his work here. Other than a romantic weekend with his girlfriend, he doesn't remember much of the last two or three years. His memory of Viet Nam and his childhood before that seems fine."

Kravitz reached over and grasped her hand, "Much of the time these head injuries self-resolve. You wait, he'll be as good as new."

She smiled at Kravitz and then returned her gaze to the other three men. "That still leaves the matter of ETERNA."

She crossed her legs and placed her hands in her lap. "I think we need to re-group and decide how much of ETERNA might have leaked out. Not from us, but from your agencies."

There were looks of concern passed around the table. No one wanted to be the first person to speak.

The CIA official that they knew as George Mason kicked it off. "Well, since our agency was created in 1947, right after Roswell, maybe I should start." His lecture sounded practiced.

"The concept of ETERNA began with President Harry Truman under a couple of earlier code names; MAJIC and JEHOVAH...which were later brought together as MJ. We'd had visual contact with unknown spacecraft for years. Some would even say centuries. But it wasn't until after the war that Truman decided we needed to further explore the phenomenon. So, after the Roswell incident in New Mexico, he decided to transition elements of the wartime Office of Strategic Services into the new Central Intelligence Agency."

"During this transition, knowledge of the program was limited to a handful of senior defense and scientific leaders. Some of these people sat on a committee that became known as MJ-12. Information that came in regarding extra-terrestrial or extra-dimensional sightings was passed to this group for further investigation, after the initial investigators explained the reports away publicly as nonsense, or hallucinations or something earthly that the Air Force might be testing."

"This practice had worked at Roswell, even after they'd already issued a press release about a downed saucer. We came back with a story that it was really a weather balloon and had the airfield's Intelligence officer pose with that kite. It was a test to see if we could control the story. Even a fifth grader could have identified the material as a weather balloon, but we were able to convince the public that intelligence personnel assigned to a nuclear bombardment wing wouldn't know the difference."

"After Roswell, there were some other interactions which most of you know about. There was principal consensus among the group members that we had to keep this bottled up tight. And for the first couple of years, everyone played by those rules. Then in early 1949, it began to look like James Forrestal was having a change of opinion. He'd gotten too close to the investigations and became adamant that we needed to be forthcoming with the public."

"He'd begun to differ with Truman on a number of topics and had met with Dewey a couple times to discuss staying on if Dewey won the upcoming election. He'd become a liability. Truman asked for his resignation, and even though he'd previously expressed a desire to resign, he seemed shocked. He withdrew psychologically and fell into a state of depression."

"The rest of the MJ committee was nervous over what he might say or do, so they got him a room at the Medical Center at Bethesda. On the sixteenth floor. I think you know the rest. After two months of near isolation from his family, his brother called to let the staff know that he was going to take him out of Bethesda the next day. So, the Secretary fell out of the window while trying to hang himself. The short answer to the question is that under Truman, less than twenty people were read into ETERNA."

"I guess you could say that Truman started the informational clamp-down. He commissioned the Robertson Panel, which initiated project BLUEBOOK, replacing projects SIGN in 1948 and later project GRUDGE in 1949. Under the name BLUEBOOK, it ran from 1952 to 1969, to determine if UFOs were a threat to national security, and to scientifically analyze UFO-related data."

"But it was LBJ who pushed the Condon Committee to close it

down. Before they'd had their first meeting, the committee leader, a physics professor named Edward Condon, said that most UFO's could be explained and that the unidentified ones simply didn't warrant further interest. That was a strange thing for him to say since he was a vocal proponent of quantum mechanics. He'd gotten pulled off the Manhattan Project for being troublesome about information security; something the House Un-American Activities Committee found interesting."

"Dwight Eisenhower had been dialed in early on, primarily due to his military service prior to being elected president. It has been unfortunately leaked that he made several visits to air bases, which included personal inspections of alien equipment as well as a meet-and-greet on two separate installations. He saw their technology and wanted it for us. He clamped down on the information even further and pressed BLUEBOOK to take more of a debunking position rather than one of objective investigation. His intent was to discredit reports and reporters and get the flying saucer story off the front pages."

"Ike was worried that too much information about our extra-terrestrial visitors had already leaked out, so he re-classified the program and gave it the new name, ETERNA."

He paused. "In short, the total number of people who had knowledge of ETERNA was still less than twenty-five. Others were pulled in for investigative or technical purposes, but their work was done in a compartmentalized fashion, and they never knew the extent or impact of what they were working on."

"Since we're here to talk about JFK, let's come back to him after we finish talking about the other presidents."

"So, moving on to Johnson; he was a self-serving narcissistic dufus. He literally didn't give a damn about UFOs as long as he was gaining power and could reward his cronies who worshipped him like a king. He was so heavily invested in the industrial complex, that the idea of global peace was just counter-intuitive to him. As for JFK's death, his feelings ranged from ambivalence to ecstasy, as the two never liked each other anyway. Total people in Johnson's administration that were read in to ETERNA? None. The members who had been on the Program during Kennedy, and those that remained from Eisenhower, were still less than two dozen."

Mason sighed. "Nixon pretty much screwed it up for future presidents by taking Jackie Gleason to Homestead Air Force Base to look at some...well...foreign artifacts. He arrived at the south gate, without an appointment, without official Secret Service protection, or anything else except a good buzz on."

"He was able to persuade security personnel to let him and Gleason into a secure...a highly secure area that he'd obviously been to before. Gleason kept his end of the bargain and remained mum on the visit for several years. At some point he told his wife about it. She recalled the meeting with Nixon and said that when her husband had returned home, he drank more heavily than usual, and lapsed into a depression for the next two weeks. Gleason was a big student of Ufology, and built a home in Westchester County New York shaped like a flying saucer on eight acres."

"Under Nixon, the program added Richard Helms, who was head of CIA, and of course, a guy that you know of more from Watergate than from his work with Allen Dulles, E. Howard Hunt. Although, Hunt was more of an action figure than a voting member of the group."

"Ford's administration was interesting from the standpoint that when he was a US Representative from Michigan, he was one of the first key political figures to push back on BLUEBOOK after an entire town, including cops, lawyers and other stable individuals saw a variety of unidentifiable lights in the sky, for an entire week back in 1966."

"The same lights were spotted by officers in Ohio, just across the Michigan border, and by observers at Selfridge Air Force Base. This is when J. Allen Hynek came up with the now laughable swamp gas explanation, and Ford decided that his constituents were entitled to a better explanation. As some people indicated at the time, the toothpaste was out of the tube, and the government just couldn't put it back."

"However, even though he'd pushed back while a rep in MI, he was told flat-out that since he'd publicly agreed with the Warren Commission report, he was basically done in politics if he said anything. He knew, but of course there was nothing he could do about it."

"So if we now look to the current administration, let me start by saying that Jimmy Carter, while Governor of Georgia, was one of the first key political figures to make his own UFO report.

"During his campaign for president, he said he was in Leary, Georgia, waiting outside for a Lion's Club Meeting to begin, at about 7:30 p.m., when he spotted what he publicly called the darndest thing he'd ever seen in the sky. Carter, and another dozen people witnessed the same event. He told a reporter that, after the experience, he vowed never again to ridicule anyone who claimed to have seen a UFO. And, he promised that, if elected president, he would encourage the government to release every piece of information they had about UFOs to the public and to scientists."

"After winning the presidency, though, he received a briefing from then CIA head George H. W. Bush, and afterwards people in his office said that he broke down and wept. Rumor has it that Bush told Carter that most of it was need-to-know, and that Carter, even as president, didn't have a need to know the full details."

He continued, "We don't know what Stansfield Turner shared when Carter appointed him to head CIA, or rather what George Bush left for him to share. But he was another agency director who tried to quash reports in the media."

"Carter later backed away from his campaign pledge, saying that the release of some information might have defense implications and pose a threat to national security."

Yasmina interrupted him. "But, ETERNA was only partially about the alien issue. It was also about the motive for the assassination. Kennedy had many enemies from outside and within. Who really pulled Oswald's strings, and in the end, who killed him?"

"So now we go back to John F. Kennedy. JFK realized what was going on and wanted to share it with the world. He wanted to see us explore space together; all countries contributing to the quest."

"Perhaps Eisenhower had shared the entire program with him, much as he had with his Vice President, who was at the time, Richard Nixon. Regardless, Kennedy's family had wealth and influence and they were now cemented in Washington D.C. politics, whether the rest of Washington liked it or not. So, much as the Senators met to decide Caesar's fate, so too met the influential members of the group that had been charged with protecting the secrecy of the program. In the end, they realized that there was only one course of action."

Yasmina thought for a moment. "Did Hoover know this in 1963?"

The Air Force general spoke softly. "Hoover was involved on the fringes. So, one might assume that he was aware, perhaps after the fact. Our office officially briefed him on it in 1964."

She looked at the dapper gent at the end of the table. "And, the Secret Service?"

Barnes replied, exasperated. "We didn't know...not then. Why would we do something to jeopardize the safety of a sitting president, when we would be held out to be the laughing stocks of the security profession?"

Yasmina placed her palms face down on the table. "My first role as a government psychic was in 1963, providing Hoover and the FBI with information that would lead them to the sources of evidence that had been undiscovered. Was the Secret Service aware of that?"

"No, but..." Barnes replied, "We will continue to hold the position that we will not confirm nor deny any reports that persons other than Lee Harvey Oswald were involved in the murder of our President. This would include any suggestion that one of our agents, accidentally fired the fatal shot. Of course, if you have photographic evidence that supports your claim, we would be eager to look at it."

"I see," she said. "Do you think such evidence still exists?"

Barnes remembered that day in Dealey Plaza when FBI Special Agent Fred Balmain handed him the photos of the dead airman. "Unofficially, we can tell you that the US Secret Service and FBI believe there is evidence of the assassination which is yet to be discovered."

———⊳«◉»⊲———

A Colonel and a Command Sergeant Major, neither of whom Mark recognized, walked into his room. After a few soft words about his health, continued recovery and commitment to duty, the Colonel presented Mark with a Navy and Marine Corps Commendation Medal; which, as they read from the citation, were presented to him for sustained acts of heroism or meritorious service, not in combat.

"I won't go through the cheesy motion of trying to pin this on you while you're still defecating in a bedpan. Here's the presentation case with the medal and a ribbon, and a copy of the citaton that will go into your DD-214. Hang onto it and when you put your dress uniform on again, I expect to see it in its proper place on your ribbon bar!" Then he smiled.

"I believe you've got a girlfriend in Chicago, isn't that right?"

"Thank you sir!" Mark took the case. "Yes, sir. Her name's Karen"

"Well, son, the Commandant of the Marine Corps says that you are to be reunited with her at your earliest opportunity."

The gruff CSM added with a smile "So what the fuck are you goldbrickin' in this civilian hospital for? Son, you have orders for the Naval Hospital Great Lakes. Get out of that fucking rack and get your shit together. You're going to Chicago tonight! "

"What about Yasmina?" Mark was trying to wake himself from the drugs.

The Colonel looked at him knowingly. "Your friend, Mrs. Sheppard is a Gold Star wife. She's the one who called the Commandant about your situation and he said to get you home right the fuck now!"

"Grab your shit and get your sorry ass in this wheelchair, Marine!" The CSM winked.

———•《◎》•———

The discussion with her clients had run well past five and by the time it was over, she just needed to get out of there. After racing home, Yasmina closed her door and locked it behind her. She tossed her keys into the dish by the door and felt alone. It seemed like events had come full circle for her today.

"Hi Mom! How was your day?"

"Hi sweetie!" She hugged her daughter and changed the subject to school. She didn't want the embrace to end. "How did you do on the Geometry test today?"

She smiled. "I got an A, of course! " After studying her mom for a moment, she continued. "Oh my gosh Mom. Are you okay?"

"I'm fine, sweetie! Mom's just had a really long day!"

Nerissa smiled the innocence of any twelve year old happy to see her mom at the end of a busy day. "Oh, I'm so sorry, mom. Would you like to bake some brownies? That always makes me feel better.

18

SATURDAY, OCTOBER 22, 1983

F orty eight hours earlier, SSGT Mark Reynolds had been working on guard schedules from his office in the Marine Barracks in Beirut. He had been deployed as a part of the Multi-National Peacekeeping Force after the April 18 bombing of the US Embassy in West Beirut. A suicide terrorist driving a van packed with 2,000 pounds of highly explosive pentaerythritol tetranitrate, known to the Marines as PETN, crashed into the embassy lobby detonating the payload. This attack was a clear sign of opposition to MNF presence.

Mark had physically recovered from the injuries sustained in the hit and run accident three years earlier. He had made a rapid recovery and was able to resume his duties with the Marine Corps Embassy Security Group. Unfortunately, there was a three year gap in his memory, prior to the accident, which the Navy doctors said was most likely permanent. Nevertheless, he had passed all of the physical and academic requirements to return to his former duties, once he'd been discharged from the Naval Hospital Great Lakes. And now, he was back in it.

Tensions were high in the region. Various Islamic factions were at war with the western world, and there was no better representative for western interests, in their minds, that the United States. Following the April bombing, the Marines provided a reinforced rifle company to take over security of the embassy compound to enable rescue and recovery operations. Once recovery operations were concluded, a heavily reinforced rifle platoon was stationed at the embassy through the end of May 1983, when 2nd Battalion, 6th Marines was relieved by 1st Battalion, 8th Marines.

The Multinational Force in Lebanon was an international peace-keeping force created in August 1982 following the US-led ceasefire between the PLO and Israel, to end their involvement in the conflict between Lebanon's pro-government and pro-Syrian factions.

The ceasefire, begun in 1981, held until June 3, 1982, when the Abu Nidal Organization attempted to assassinate Shlomo Argov, Israel's ambassador to the United Kingdom. Israel blamed the PLO for the attack, and three days later invaded Lebanon. West Beirut was under siege for seven weeks before the PLO finally acceded to a new agreement for their withdrawal.

It was this agreement that provided for the deployment of a Multinational Force to assist the Lebanese Armed Forces in evacuating the PLO, Syrian forces, and other foreign combatants involved in Lebanon's civil war. One US Marine Amphibious Unit was assigned to Beirut International Airport as a 1,400-man force, which also provided external security troops at U.S. diplomatic facilities in the greater Beirut area.

Additional combat support elements of the MAU were stationed aboard amphibious ships offshore, but with Mark's experience in Saigon, the Headquarters group decided he needed to be on the ground in support of their mission.

Mark was heavily engrossed in his paperwork when Master Sergeant Fielding came in and sat down.

"Got a minute?"

Mark looked up from his paperwork and immediately detected that something was wrong. "Sure, Top. What's up?"

He hesitated for a moment. "I'm afraid I've got some bad news for you. The Red Cross just notified the Executive Officer that your father, uh, he had a stroke last night, and didn't make it."

Mark looked at him for a second as if he hadn't heard what had just been said. "Dad? You're sure?"

"Yeah, man. I'm sorry. The XO has you on a flight out of here and back to Dallas in a couple of hours. You have thirty days leave, starting now." He stood and extended his hand. "I am so very sorry to have to be the one to tell you. Let me know what you need, and we'll see that it gets done."

Mark stared at the papers on his desk. He was torn between his love of family and an overwhelming feeling that he was needed there. "Thanks Top. I...uh..."

"I know. It's time to take care of your family. I'll get the sched-ules posted. Like I said, the XO has you on a contract flight back to Andrews leaving at 1400 hours today. When you touch down, check with the agent and they'll get you through to Dallas on commercial. We'll take care of all this stuff until you get back."

═══◄◉►═══

Karen's green eyes were bright, but sympathetic. She had ar-rived a day earlier and had been staying at the family home with Susan, Dan's companion for the past three years. The two women had gotten along well from the first time they'd met at Mark and Karen's wedding a year earlier. Their personalities and interests were a natural fit, and they both welcomed each other into the Reynolds family.

Like Dan, Susan had lost her spouse some years back, and still grieving, did not think it appropriate to wed another man. At least, not yet. Dan understood and shared the same fears, so the two had agreed to a committed companionship instead of a traditional marriage. It had worked well for them and enabled them to get on with their lives with mutual support. They had fun together. They healed together.

Like Karen, Susan was perky, opinionated, and active. Although she was twenty years older, the two had become close and could have easily been sisters. They were both quite physically fit; Susan because of her vanity, and Karen because she was getting ready to take the test to become an FBI agent, and driven to be in tip-top shape.

Karen was excited to see him. His deployment was originally planned to run until December 15, but with the loss of his father they would now have thirty days together before he had to return to the chaos and noise of Beirut. And, if things quieted down over there, maybe he wouldn't have to go back.

She had been good for Mark. After his release from the hospital, she had been patient, then encouraging and then demanding. She knew that he would not feel like himself again until he was physically able to do everything he'd been able to do prior to the accident. She could help him with everything, except his memory.

Mark's loss of memory bothered him significantly for a while and then he gradually grew to accept it. He had no idea what he did in the Marine Corps for almost three years. Some kind of intelligence work. And Katie, while she had a good idea of his role, since they had attended class together, never tried to help him fill in the blanks. She couldn't. Katie knew her sister would have found that sort of occupation weird, and so she never told Karen the specifics of that week in Quantico. Just that she and Mark had met during an intelligence seminar. Karen was far too practical and dogmatic to believe in something as spurious as psychic functioning. To Karen, if you couldn't prove it, it didn't exist.

It was almost one in the afternoon when he landed, and between time zone differences and aircraft changes, he was tired, hungry, and needed a shower. Nevertheless, as soon as he saw her, he perked right up.

"Hi baby!" He dropped his carry-on bag and took her in his arms. As he kissed her hard on the mouth he wished he'd had a chance to gargle first. He hugged her so tight he was afraid he'd crack one of her ribs.

"You look good!" she said, her head up against his chest. "I am so very sorry about your dad. I don't know what to say. It was so sudden and he seemed like he was in perfect health."

Mark had many hours on several airplanes to sort through his emotions. He would have wanted to be there for his dad at the end, but knew that his father understood his drive to be a Marine. "You look great! I have missed you so much!"

She took his arm and they went to baggage claim to pick up his over-stuffed sea bag. While they waited, she grinned at him. "How's schoolwork going?"

He shrugged, "It's been crazy over there. I was only able to sign up for one class this semester, but this puts me over the requirements for an Associate's Degree. Once I get stateside again, I can start doubling up and get my Bachelor's in another twelve months."

She hadn't expected to see him for another month when his deployment officially ended, and although she was saddened by the event that brought him back, she was excited to be next to him now. "Oh, that's fantastic! This is going to open up so many opportunities for you!"

The conveyor belt started to whir and clank and she took his hand. "Katie's at the house. She left the kids with Terry since she thought they might be more of a handful than a help."

"Yeah, probably better that way," Mark concurred. "How's she getting along with Susan?"

"Katie gets along with everyone, and she realizes that this week is about your dad. She would be able to get along with anyone for that long."

Karen tightened her grip on Mark's hand. "You're going to think I'm childish, but...uhmm, there was a period when I was afraid that I'd never see you again. I was so afraid something would happen to you over there."

Mark nodded. "I know, sweetie, but it's what I do. They really take good care of us and the officers over there are great at their jobs."

They watched as Mark's olive-drab sea bag emerged from the depths of the baggage area and slid silently down to the conveyor assembly. Karen giggled, "Geez...you pack like a girl! How much stuff did you bring back with you?"

Mark shrugged with a smile, "Yeah, I brought everything. You just never know if they're going to redeploy you somewhere else, and I decided to pack it all."

When they got to the house, there was kissing and hugging and a few tears. Mark and the three ladies talked about their memories of Dan, and finally Mark decided to walk around the house. Since turning eighteen, he had lived with the Corps. The house brought back memories of his childhood. He wandered from room to room, finding a different memory in each. He felt sad that one couldn't bring back those times, but knew inside that he'd made the right decision about his pathway in life. He returned to the kitchen, and took a seat at the table.

Susan opened a bottle of Cabernet and then found four wine glasses in the cupboard. "He'd been fine up until a week ago. He got dizzy and the left side of his face went numb. I took him into the doctor and they ran some tests. They said that he'd had something called a TIA, a transient ischemic attack. A mini-stroke I guess."

She evenly filled the glasses until the bottle was empty, and then continued. "He was so embarrassed about it. I told him that he needed to take it easy for a while, but you know your dad. He was insistent about not telling anyone, and getting back to work as soon as he could." She sat the empty bottle aside.

She distributed the glasses to everyone around the kitchen table and then sat down with a sigh. "He was so organized. Even though he wanted to get back to work, he wanted to make sure that his affairs were in order, so he showed me where his will was, and he told me that if anything happened to him, he'd like to be cremated. It was such fatalistic talk for a man who was trying so hard to get back to his job and his friends."

Katie found some chips in the cupboard, and some lunch meat in the fridge that they used to make a nice assortment of snacks. A quickly sliced cucumber finished out the presentation.

Susan sipped her Cabernet pensively. "Not bad. This is one of the bottles Dan and I brought back from Mondavi this summer. Napa was such a great trip. He knew almost nothing about wine until that trip. But, it was as if he had some sort of, you know, an awakening. He really got interested in it and we had so much fun going to wine tastings around here."

A tear started to form in her eye. "He was so alive during those last few months. He was looking forward to retirement and we were going to move into my place up in North Dallas. We'd talked about going somewhere else, but my kids would never have forgiven me if I gave up their childhood home." She took another sip of her wine. "He was just so, I don't know, in touch with things."

"Last Tuesday he insisted on sitting out under the stars all night. We put the patio recliners back and just watched the stars and talked about life. Then, a shooting star went across the sky and he looked at me and said that I should let you know," she turned to Mark. "...that if anything happened to him, he was leaving you a bottle of Four Roses."

"Four Roses? Whiskey?" Mark chuckled politely. "I wonder how old it is. Mom used to hate it so he usually kept a bottle hidden from her."

Karen smiled. "Your mom didn't know he drank?"

"Oh, she knew," Mark confessed. "They drank beer together, and an occasional glass of wine. But, he kept a bottle hidden from her so that when they got on each other's nerves, he'd sneak away and have a quiet shot."

"Well, it's here somewhere," Susan inserted. "I've started going through some of the stuff that he wanted to donate: Salvation Army or Volunteers of America. Something like that. So far, though, I haven't found any old bottles of Four Roses."

Katie felt that Susan was experiencing a tremendous amount of grief and tried to get her to talk more. "So, what else did you two like to talk about?"

Mark listened to the conversation for a while and then began to detach mentally as the sights and smells of his childhood came back to him. He began thinking about the experiences he'd had, growing up in this house, which now seemed smaller to him. Playing with his friends and cousins, learning how to mow the grass, helping his dad change the oil on the family cars. Another bottle of wine was sacrificed as the group reminisced.

It was getting close to dinner time and the mood was sober even if the occupants weren't. Karen changed the subject. "We need to get out of here for a while. We're in Dallas. There must be a steak place close by."

Susan nodded. "You know it! Do you feel like dressing up, or something more casual?"

Katie jumped in, "I'm game either way, but I think we need to take a cab. After all that wine, I'm not sure any of us should be driving."

The ladies laughed, and Susan found a copy of the Yellow Pages in one of the kitchen drawers. She chose the cab company with the biggest ad. She provided their address and the name of the restaurant that she thought everyone would like. "Twenty minutes? Great!"

She hung up. "Well, you heard it. We have about twenty minutes to get cleaned up, and only one and a half bathrooms to do it."

Mark shrugged. "Would you guys mind bringing me back something? The snacks filled me up, so to be honest, I'm not that hungry now. If y'all don't mind, I'd kind of like to just hang out here for a while."

The three ladies understood, and moved to the bedrooms and bathrooms to make themselves presentable for dinner. About twenty minutes later, the cab rolled up in front of the house and they departed, with the promise that they would bring Mark back a steak sandwich.

When they were gone, he wandered the house again, his fingertips touching the walls and furniture in each room. The tactile contact helped his memory leap back to happier times. His mom and dad chasing each other through the house in games that he wouldn't understand until he was older. Laughter and fun on the holidays. The occasional parties Dad would throw for his firemen friends and their families.

He went to his old room and opened the dresser drawers.

There, he found things that he hadn't thought about in years: old underwear, GI Joe accessories and equipment, an old Boy Scout pocket knife. Then there was an old fruitcake tin in which he kept his most prized possessions of childhood: his high school ring, an assortment of keys that went to locks that he couldn't remember. Some of his dad's firefighting uniform buttons, awards, collar insignia with various numbers of bugles to indicate the different ranks, and an old invitation to his high school graduation. Even a picture of him and his prom date from his senior year.

He briefly checked all of the closets and his dad's desk drawers. He found his dad's cache of 8MM home movies that were taken over several years of family vacations. The most memorable ones were the trips to the beaches in Florida, and Six Flags, the amusement park that opened in nearby Arlington in 1961, which was supposed to rival Disneyland in size and scope.

The park got its name because there were six themed areas within the park. Each was themed after one of the six countries whose flag had flown over Texas during the state's history. It was Mark's first test of Geography when his mom made him identify the flags and name the countries: Spain, Mexico, France, Texas, the Old South and the United States of America. He pulled the box out of the drawer and carried it with him. He would want to save those memories.

But, as Susan had earlier mentioned, there was no bottle of Four Roses to be found. He paused in the hallway momentarily. Dad had been an engineer before becoming a fireman. Where would an engineer hide a bottle of booze? A bottle of booze that he didn't want his wife or young son to find?

He grabbed a flashlight out of the kitchen and headed to the basement. It smelled musty. There were cobwebs in many places, but the basement didn't seem nearly as cluttered as he would have expected after all these years.

He stood in the center of the basement. It made perfect sense. This was the place that his dad liked to hide out in, whenever he and mom argued about something. He looked slowly around the room, side to side, up and down. He pulled one of the old folding chairs out of the corner, and stood on it to look up at the rafters. There in one corner, he found some old newspapers, folded to fit into the cross-braces.

He carefully opened them and saw that they were copies of the Baltimore Sun. One was from May 1, 1977, and the other was from May 8, the following Sunday. He hopped down off the chair, and unfolded the legs of the old card table that had served as a second table for many family gatherings through the years. During parties, it had been the kid's table. Every family had one, and it seemed like a rite of passage to be old enough to eventually sit with the adults.

He carefully laid the newspapers on the table and then resumed his search. There were some cardboard boxes in the corner that he looked through. More newspapers and magazines. But, no sign of a bottle of Four Roses. As he flipped through the various magazines in the first box, he noted that they were from a variety of publications, but they all seemed to be focused on the Kennedy assassination.

Among most Dallas residents of the time, there had been a keen engrossment in the topic, but Mark couldn't recall his dad ever expressing that much of an interest in it. He opened the other boxes and realized that the first two were full of magazines or news articles about the assassination. The third was about flying saucers. It was odd. His dad hadn't seemed curious about UFOs, either.

They had discussed some of the absurd theories about the assassination over the years as Mark was growing up, but once the Warren Commission had issued its ruling, the subject just didn't make good dinner conversation. And, he couldn't recall a time when the subject of UFOs or aliens had surfaced either.

His gaze wandered around the unadorned basement. He'd looked about everywhere. Flipping through one of the magazines relating to the assassination, he said out loud, "Where would someone hide a bottle of booze? A fireman? An engineer? He flipped the magazine upside down and got up again. Slowly, he wandered the circumference of the musty basement and when he got to one corner, he noticed that the two by four frame of that section wasn't quite as dusty as the rest of them. He jiggled it and saw that it was loose, and then smiled to himself.

The scratch marks on the wood indicated that someone had moved this piece of wood out from under the other studs at some point in the past. As it began to swivel out, he realized that someone had been in here several times over the past few years. As it rotated, out it exposed a hole in the concrete block below. When he shined his flashlight down through the hole, he could see that there was something in there, and reached in to retrieve it.

There was a small cloth bag that had bulk. Success! He gently pulled the bag up out of the hole and took his new treasure over to the card table for further investigation. Inside, was the illusive bottle of Four Roses whiskey, promised him as a part of his estate. There was also a canister with 8MM film, and a small envelope with a note. He lined up each of the coveted contents on the table and then went upstairs to find a glass and some ice.

When he returned, he poured a healthy dose of the whiskey into the glass and swirled the ice around before lifting it into the air. "Here's to you Dad. Sorry I wasn't with you. I miss you already!"

The libation felt cool to the tongue, but warm to the throat. Within seconds, he felt the sedative effects wind their way around his blood stream. He sat the glass down and retrieved the envelope. It was addressed to him, in his dad's handwriting. He carefully tore it open and read the one-page letter, which had been typed on his mom's old Royal typewriter. He'd used it to write essays and papers in school, and immediately recognized both the cloth ribbon print and strike of the "L" key that was out of alignment.

Dear Mark,

If you're reading this, it means you'll be drinking by yourself, much as I did the first night I looked at the enclosed film. Years ago, I promised your mother that I'd never discuss it with you or anyone else for as long as we both lived. I have honored my promise. Once you watch the film <u>all the way through</u>, I would ask that you not discuss it with anyone until you give some serious *thought as to whether the damage outweighs the contribution to history and our way of life. I know you'll figure it out.*

Love always,
Dad

Mark took another sip of his drink and re-read the note. Although his dad had been a practical joker at times, his tone in the note seemed quite serious. He ran back upstairs and found the Bell and Howell projector in the living room closet and returned to the basement to set it up.

Yasmina Sheppard stuck her head in Nerissa's room. The girl had been sitting at her desk most of the day, looking out her window at the orange tree in the back yard. "Hey sweetie! You haven't eaten anything all day. What's the matter?"

The fifteen year old was blossoming from a skinny tomboy into a striking teen, with promise for rare beauty as an adult. "I'm sorry, Mom. I just don't feel well."

Yasmina sat on the end of the girl's bed. "I told you that you can talk to me about anything. I can tell when something's bugging you, so why don't you tell me what it is and then we can go make some Dawood Basha for dinner. You know you love those meatballs and rice!"

She turned sideways in her chair. "I had another one of those dreams last night."

Yasmina tightened her lips into a forced smile. "The one where you saw grandma Khoury?"

She nodded. "She's trying to tell me something. Something bad is going to happen to our people."

"Honey, Teta loved you very much. Maybe she just wants you to know that she's still looking out for you." Yasmina knew that these types of psychic experiences could be a blessing or a curse, especially for a high schooler. She had decided long ago not to push her daughter towards it, or discourage her from it, but to discuss it with her openly whenever she had the opportunity. "So, what did Teta tell you...exactly?"

She looked back through the window at the orange tree outside, and tried to hold back a tear. "She showed me a man will drive a truck into a building and he's going to blow it up. It will be soon, and people we know will be hurt by it. She said it's too late to stop it."

Mike Arguelles sat quietly in his office, not far from Dulles Airport. After circling the obituary, he laid the newspaper aside. He knew this day would eventually come.

Interment Ceremony;
Arlington National Cemetery
9:00 October 25, 1983
Frederick John Balmain
11/12/23 – 6/12/83

On June 1, 1983 Fred Balmain of Lorton, Virginia passed away suddenly while on vacation in Northern Michigan. Raised in Silver Spring MD, Balmain entered the US Army in 1941 and served in the European Theater of Operations during WWII, where he was awarded the Silver Star and Purple Heart and received several other commendations. After completing his Bachelor's Degree in Economics, Fred joined the FBI in 1949 and served in a variety of positions until retiring in in 1979. Fred loved the outdoors, friends, fishing, and above all, his family. He is survived by best friend and devoted wife of 23 years, Sarah and their son Jeff.

Arguelles retrieved the envelope from the back of his safe. It was time to exercise his responsibilities and fulfill a promise to a friend.

———◦((◦))◦———

It was getting late, and the ladies would be returning home soon. The first time through the film, Mark watched the events of November 22, 1963 unfold from an angle that he had never before seen. That no one, except maybe his dad, had seen. As the motorcade accelerated through the triple-underpass and out of view, he had been tempted to stop the film and rewind it. But his dad had instructed him to watch it all the way through.

As the next scene opened, he was confused as to what he was looking at. He couldn't tell if it was some sort of trick photography, or perhaps a demonstration of a new type of military aircraft. But, there it was. There they were. A stainless steel flying saucer landing at a US Air Force base, while another made sharp, hummingbird movements overhead. He watched the reaction of the military officers in the frame. They exuded amusement and satisfaction as opposed to fear. Some shook their heads in wonderment, but it seemed as if they had gathered specifically to watch this demonstration of aerial adroitness and were applauding the results.

Mark was stunned. The JFK assassination and flying saucers on the same film? It didn't make sense. He rewound the film and played it through one more time. He refocused the lens to make it as sharp as he could, and stepped closer to the wall. The motorcade entered Dealey Plaza. Having a lifelong familiarity of the assassination details, he quickly looked at the top of the frame and saw that Oswald was at his perch. Mark squinted and backed up to the table and stopped the projector. He reversed it a few frames and paused.

There was someone moving behind Oswald. Someone was stacking boxes behind Oswald. Oswald was supposed to have been on the sixth floor by himself. Nevertheless, from this angle, a viewer could see that there was a stocky male wearing a white short-sleeve shirt, moving boxes into place behind Oswald just seconds before he opened fire. From this angle, the man's face wasn't visible; just his beefy forearms. By the time the rifle barrel was seen protruding out the window, the second man was gone.

Mark rewound the film and played it through from the start again. The motorcade enters Dealey Plaza, turning north on Houston from Main. The camera begins to pan up. Oswald is visible and the man in the white shirt is a few feet behind him for just a split-second. The limousine turns west on Elm. The rifle protrudes from the window by a couple of inches, and there is a muzzle flash.

Below, agents in the follow up car react. One agent jumps off the running board of the follow-up vehicle and races to the limousine as a second agent reaches for a rifle and chambers a round. The responding agent is still several feet behind the limousine when the President's head explodes. He is too late.

There is too much to comprehend. A second person present behind Oswald would have totally changed the Warren Commission's ruling and been solid evidence of some sort of conspiracy to murder the President. But, even the assassination event itself could have been overshadowed by what Mark saw at the end of the film. Flying saucers landing at a US Air Force base? Was this real?

No wonder his dad had kept this film hidden all these years. Mark wondered how he'd ever come into possession of it. Certainly, no one else had ever seen it. Maybe that explained his dad's secret obsession with the JFK assassination and the whole UFO thing. Not wanting to reveal that he knew any more about either subject would have been sufficient reason for them never to have discussed it all these years.

While he rewound the film again to get it back on its original reel, he reached for the Baltimore Sun newspaper and found the article that must have piqued his dad's interest. Dated May 1, 1977, the article had been written by Ralph Reppert and detailed the investigative work conducted by a Howard Donahue on the ballistics of a 6.5MM Mannlicher Carcano rifle, similar to what Oswald used.

Donahue had been one of eleven qualified marksmen asked by CBS television to participate in a re-creation of the assassination, and the only one to demonstrate that it would have been possible for Lee Harvey Oswald to have fired three shots in the time specified by the Warren Commission investigation. However, Donahue's experience illustrated other concerns regarding the Warren report. In particular, the fact that the testimony of ballistics experts seemed to have been largely omitted from the Commission's review and presentation of evidence.

Donahue further investigated on his own, and eventually came to the conclusion that the bullet that struck Kennedy in the head had in fact been accidentally fired by a Secret Service agent riding in the follow-up car. The Reppert article postulated that after Oswald's first shot, many of the agents turned completely around and visually acquired someone in a sixth floor corner window of the School Book Depository building.

Donahue speculated that during this rapidly unfolding sequence of events, an agent who had been seated on the convertible's rear deck with his feet on the seat, reached down for an AR-15 rifle, released the safety and lifted it briefly to chamber a round.

As Oswald's second shot was fired, the President's car and the follow-up car containing Secret Service agents suddenly sped up, creating an unstable platform. In the microsecond that the agent had the muzzle of the rifle pointed forward to chamber the round, he fell backwards, and the rifle discharged. In a tragic denouement, the rifle is pointed toward Kennedy at that instant, and the bullet struck him in the back of the head, on the right side.

If the article was accurate, it couldn't have been intentional. At the time he chambered the round, the agent is looking to his right and rear. The rifle is only even visible for a fraction of a second before he lowers it back towards the seat. With the dozens of photographs and movie footage shot that day, certainly there had to have been a photograph that had captured that instant.

Mark had seen dozens of photographs of the assassination over the years. There had been hundreds of people who had written articles and books on various conspiracy theories. With so many people digging into the case, how could it be possible that such a photograph wouldn't have surfaced by now? Certainly, someone would have turned such evidence in to the proper authorities? The FBI? Certainly, the Bureau would have scoured the area looking for such evidence.

It was just after eleven in the evening when the ladies returned home. Excited and alarmed they called his name.

"Mark!" It was Karen's voice he heard above the others as he climbed the steps. "Have you heard?"

"Heard what?"

She broke into tears as she ran to give him a hug. "Oh, I am so glad you're here. It's just awful!"

"What's awful? What's the matter?"

Karen couldn't talk, so Katie explained, "We just heard on the radio, that the Marine Barracks in Beirut was bombed. Your barracks. They're saying that there have been hundreds killed or injured.'

Mark hugged his wife tightly. He was emotionally drained already, and just didn't know what to say.

19

Yasmina Sheppard doodled on her notepad in her comfortable office in Reston, Virginia. As she prepared for her next meeting, she looked at the small gold picture frame on the corner of her desk that contained pictures of her two daughters, Aleyna and Nerissa, and reflected on the conversation she'd had two years earlier in Palo Alto with their government sponsor.

"The Russians know what we're doing. Hell, everyone knows what we're doing," the senior CIA official said bluntly. "We need to reign this in and keep it off the front page. We're going to go private with it so that we don't have to deal with FOIA requests. We're going to publicly state that Remote Viewing was only marginally successful. We're going to tell the world that the US Government didn't get anything out of it and we're getting out of the business. We can't have our enemies knowing that we can see what they are doing anywhere, anytime. Imagine the impact on open society when it leaks that we have people who can see everything they do, everywhere, all the time?"

The official rubbed his forehead. "Half of Americans don't trust their government now. Open acknowledgement of psychic spying would cost us the other half as well. I can't allow anyone to tip our hand as to how successful we've...you've really been."

Yasmina looked at him quietly. It didn't take a psychic to know what was coming.

He continued, "Your people will keep their positions, but we have to modify the relationship. Companies like…you know… are going to pick it up and run with it. The government can contract with them through the black operations budget, but we won't have to answer any questions. Similarly, unless they get into some unforeseeable court battle, contractors don't have to produce a single document on it."

"How secure is this funding?" Yasmina asked.

"Very," was the flat answer. "The Black Ops budget gets approved every year, by both sides of the Aisle. Everyone wants covert work done, but to protect their political careers, none of them want to know specifically where the money goes or how it gets used. It runs around forty to fifty billion dollars a year, so your department's draw on it isn't even a rounding error."

"And, you'll take care of all my people?" She looked at him across the desk.

"Absolutely." He opened his briefcase and withdrew several documents. "Here are the employment contracts for anyone who wants to come over. And, while they have to maintain their secrecy oaths about any specifics of cases they worked on, they are free to write their memoirs, consult on their own with industry, and continue working independently or jointly in any capacity they feel practical."

"Just like that?" Yasmina had worked for the government for too long, and was understandably skeptical.

"Just like that," he replied. "We can't keep the program secret forever, but we truly need your services."

"And Dr. Kravitz?" she inquired. It was a deal-breaker.

"Per our agreement, Dr. Kravitz will receive the pension you set forth in the earlier discussion, and receive retirement pay and benefits equal to a Brigadier General, for life. He is also free to publish and speak on his area of expertise as he chooses. Again though, provided he honors the tenets of his various clearances with the United States Government."

Yasmina nodded and quickly looked through the employment

agreements. They looked fairly standard, and quite banal. They were generically worded for positions of Technical Consultant, and so general in nature, they could have pertained to accountants, lawyers or encyclopedia salesmen. "I'll meet with the team and explain your offer. I am in support of this, but they need to make up their own minds."

"I understand," he said, zipping his briefcase shut. "Everything is going private in the next ten years. Look, in time, we will be moving the entire UFO problem into the private sector as well, for the very same reason. The Air Force told the world they were out of the UFO business in 1969, but pretty soon, the new program is going to leak. We have to get this out of government hands, and into the private sector for insulation."

"What about Lieutenant Colonel Corso?" She looked over the top of her reading glasses.

The CIA man grimaced. "Corso isn't your problem. He didn't work for you, and there's nothing I can do for him now. He's going to publish that book on Roswell, and let the world know about the technology we reaped, and how we got it to the scientific community without them even realizing where their ideas came from. He went outside the circle, and he'll have to be, uh, discredited to some degree."

Yasmina moved the stack of employment agreements to the side of her desk. "And ETERNA?"

He sighed almost painfully. "ETERNA never happened. And, Ms. Sheppard, the term should never be used again. You know the rules. Bad things can happen to people who, uh, you know."

And now, two years later, she doodled and wondered if she'd made the right decision; for her team, for herself, and now for her daughter Nerissa, who at thirty had become one of the most talented and brilliant psychics ever to come through the program.

Nerissa was her only family now. Her other daughter Aleyna, born before they had emigrated from Lebanon in 1955, never had a chance to see first grade. Taken to the hospital for a case of scarlet fever in 1960, she failed to respond to the antibiotics and died after her fever suddenly rose to over 107 degrees.

It had been a devastating loss for Yasmina and her husband. But it was this loss that propelled Yasmina to begin exploring her psychic inner self, in attempts to reach out to her daughter on the other side. Her own mother, Nerissa's Teta, had been known for having the so-called second sight: highly accurate knowledge about people, places and things for no explainable reason. The idea of non-local communication had been ingrained in her since birth. It was perfectly natural.

And when mother and daughter had connected, somewhere in the astral dimension, it had driven Yasmina to find out how body and mind worked. She needed to know how was she able to transcend the physical realm and experience her daughter, who was at total peace on the other side. It seemed so real to her that she concentrated all of her energies on an undergraduate degree in Biophysiology, which only whetted her appetite for knowledge. By the end of 1968, she had buried a husband, given birth to a beautiful new daughter, and received her Doctorate of Medicine from the George Washington University.

On one hand, she was satisfied with her success in understanding the human body. But, it did little to satisfy her quest to understand those things that could not be seen or proven in the laboratory. So, much to the disdain of her professors, although she had completed the degree, she declined the internship and residency. She had never had any intention of practicing medicine. She just wanted as much knowledge as she could get. And, for this reason, she shied from using the initials after her name, or ever alluding to her impressive credentials until she met a curly-headed guy from California.

One day, as she approached graduation day, she'd attended a lecture given by a physicist named Kravitz, and she knew she had found that link she had been looking for. Dr. Kravitz had offered her the bridge between science and the unknown that she had been driven to find. She collaborated on projects and helped research his papers, but she did not want to be listed as a co-author or researcher. When working with people, she wanted them to accept her as just an ordinary person, rather than a formally schooled scientist.

She had found a home. And now, so had Nerissa, who had blessed Yasmina with a grandson whom she adored. Maybe it was genetic, or maybe it was something else. Nerissa had shattered performance metrics in every conceivable area of psychic functioning. By the time she had entered college at eighteen, her remote viewing skills were more accurate than anything the Institute had witnessed. Her precognitive and retro-cognitive sessions were amazingly hyper-accurate in controlled laboratory experiments, which the usual receptacle of skeptics could not explain away. And, lab monitors were shocked at her reports made while bi-locating on the most difficult of targets. She had been a rare find for the Institute, and had early on captured the attention of the government.

Nerissa had, in effect, paid her way through college as a part time Remote Viewer, working under the mentorship of her mother and Dr. Kravitz. Having grown up in the business, it seemed like a logical career progression. However, she remained guarded when talking to her friends about her hidden talents.

When she wasn't remote viewing for the government or attending classes at San Jose State's Lucas College of Business, she picked up extra money by singing in a couple of oldies bands in the Bay area. Her perfect pitch and narrow vibrato were often compared to Doris Day, and she performed renditions of the film and music legend's hit songs so flawlessly, that people could close their eyes and imagine the famed singer was in the room with them.

Nerissa often sang at home or in her car because she felt that it relaxed her and took her to a different dimension. It gave her the opportunity to shed her student persona, full of numbers and analyses, and quiet her mind as she moved to a different side of her brain.

Being raised in a Lebanese-American household had also prepared Nerissa to rapidly learn Lebanese Arabic and French, with native proficiency. Her language skills, her natural beauty and her unparalleled psychic functioning caused the CIA to salivate. They called upon her often to help them wade through the unique political discord in the Middle East.

However, she was far too valuable to send abroad. Her skills had to be exploited in a room in Langley. The US government couldn't risk sending her anywhere in the Middle East, even with the level of protection afforded a sitting President. She was a precious commodity, and there were too many people watching.

It was almost two in the afternoon when Yasmina looked up at the soft knock on the door. "Hey sweetie!"

"Hi mom! I stopped home to check on Hunter."

"How's my little prince?" Yasmina asked.

Nerissa smiled. "Eating, sleeping and crapping on schedule "

Yasmina looked down at her notes and whispered, "Close the door, would ya?"

Nerissa glanced at her mom for a second and then slowly pushed the door shut until she heard the latch click into place. Once she seated herself, she crossed her legs and placed her hands in her lap. It was her way of forcing herself to look comfortable. "Okay. What's up?"

Yasmina considered her various clearances and obligations and decided that blood was thicker than water. Nerissa needed to know the full story. Well, as much of the story as she herself knew. "The Canadian job you did last week."

Nerissa shrugged. "What about it?"

Yasmina opened the folder on her desk. "The results of the session were fairly detailed and the client would like to know more. You were asked to RV a coordinate target and you provided the following data." She flipped the page and read from her daughter's report:

"There are at least four types of alien species, possibly as many as eight, and they have been visiting earth for thousands of years."

"The different species probably have different agendas and

should not be considered as one entity. Most are friendly, but at least one species is not."

"There are live ETs on earth at this present time, and one of the species may be called the Tall Whites by some governments. It's possible that two of them are currently working in some capacity within some department of the United States government on some sort of technology exchange program."

"A cabal formed by the Council on Foreign Relations and the Trilateral Commission, which includes Bilderberg members, members of the international banking and oil cartels, and select members of the military are planning to create one world government. And, they are suppressing information about alien existence and visitation from the public."

Nerissa listened, and when her mother paused, she commented. "Yeah. That's what I saw. What's the issue?"

Yasmina closed the file and looked across the desk. "The target you were given, was to report on what a former Canadian Defence Minister learned about UFOs while in office. It turns out that he has broken away from the Liberal Party and has formed a new political party. The, uh, Canadian Action Party. The current government is strongly aligned with our own Defense Department and wanted to know what he knows, and could possibly take public."

"This guy is well-respected up there. He's not some kook they can easily humiliate in the news. This guy oversaw the unification of their Army, Navy and Air Force into one organization. They're concerned."

Yasmina continued. "He's extremely well-connected globally, especially in the area of monetary reform, and has highly placed friends on every continent. He favors economic neo-liberalism; that is, deregulation, free trade and above all, the privatization of many of the government's programs. In short, he wants to take Canada the same way the US government wants to take us. He's an educated engineer and author who served a long career in Canadian politics."

Nerissa looked at her mom quietly for a moment. "I wrote what I saw. Is the client not happy with the product?"

"Our product, yes. The situation, no." Yasmina opened another file folder on her desk. "The Agency wants you back at Langley for another project tomorrow. My problem is that the CIA, the Air Force OSI and now the Canadians are all trying to RV the same things. They're not talking to each other and I'm afraid that innocent people are going to get hurt. That is, if they haven't been already."

"Connors RV'd a target last week and saw the Internet exploding exponentially over the next few years. This means that information will travel around the global network almost as fast as it travels around the astral space now."

"More and more people are entering and leaving black operations programs every year, and many are trying to talk about what they know. The government is going to privatize much of what they've been doing, simply to dodge FOIA requests and enhance deniability. People are learning more and more about who we are as a planet and how we fit into the overall cosmos. There's talk that even the Vatican may yield their position on life in the cosmos. But yet, a group of self-appointed governors have chosen to keep everything a secret."

"So, why this hush-hush meeting, Mom?"

She unconsciously reached for her coffee mug and took a sip of cold, stale coffee left over from earlier in the morning. Wincing, she said, "It's a matter of time before this group, this cabal, begins to ask us to do things that we've agreed were unethical. Even though we can do things, doesn't make them right. I think that eventually, some agency, maybe not ours, but some agency somewhere, will be asked to control behavior remotely. Or maybe, they'll be asked to disrupt someone's physiological functioning - give them a stroke or something."

Nerissa looked down. She knew that these types of experiments had been conducted under controlled conditions, sometimes successfully. "What are you suggesting?"

Yasmina got up from her desk and walked around to her

daughter's side. Stroking her hair lightly, she whispered. "I think we need an insurance policy."

———◦《◉》◦———

Karen Reynolds kicked her shoes off the second she was inside the door. It was scorching hot outside, she was tired and her feet hurt. She sat the bag of groceries on the kitchen counter and thought to herself that she would rather do anything this evening besides cook dinner.

When she got to the bedroom, she quickly shed her jacket and began to pull her belt through the pant loops and out of the pancake holster that held her duty weapon; one of the newly issued Glock .40 caliber semi-automatics. She dropped the magazine out of it and quickly racked the slide to eject the round in the chamber, before sliding the components under a towel on the top shelf of the closet.

It was almost 5:30 p.m., and she had half-expected Mark to beat her home. However, she had the place to herself and decided not to waste the moment. She started running the shower and while the hot water found its way to the second floor, she checked the phone's voicemail for messages. Nothing.

A half hour later, she felt like a new person. But not a person who wanted to fix dinner. So, after drying off and donning her gym clothes, she checked the newspaper for movies. She was in the mood for something light and funny. The week had been stressful, and she needed a break.

The embezzlement case she had been working on with fellow agent Brad Tinsler was nearing a conclusion, and would be a huge public relations coup for the Bureau, as well as providing a boost to their respective careers. While the work had required long tedious hours, the unfortunate byproduct had been the change in her personal relationship with her coworker.

The extended hours had required meals together. At first, it was take-out at the conference table in the office. Then, the occasional walk down the street to one of Washington's finer restaurants. The dinners became more frequent and ultimately included drinks. Drinks led to more intimate conversations, until one night, they stopped at one of the nicer hotels in Crystal City to have a drink on the way home.

She didn't know why she allowed it to happen. Perhaps it was because Mark, now a Major, was working longer hours himself, and she so hated the loneliness caused by his deployments. She felt somewhat responsible though for the predicament, since she was the one who had pushed him to get his degree. She'd pushed him to go through the Marine Corps Officer Candidate School to obtain a commission, and she'd been enormously supportive of him as his career path progressed from second lieutenant to first lieutenant in just eighteen months.

It was another thirty months and two deployments before he made captain. Now, after twenty - three years of service, he was a major, and looking at retirement in less than a year. Probably due to their shared interests in law enforcement, his goal was to take his pension, and at age forty one, join a small police department outside of Dallas as a second career. With Karen's seniority, she was guaranteed a transfer to the Dallas Field Office in about the same period of time. Things could really work out for them, despite the relationship's drift in separate directions over the past few years.

She loved her husband. They had been good together. She felt immense guilt at the thought that she could stray from her vows and have an affair with a coworker, especially a coworker with a wife and kids at home. So many times she had debated with herself the pros and cons of telling Mark. She knew that if she did, he would be devastated. She didn't want a divorce any more than she wanted to keep something like this from him. Even though she had been with Tinsler several times over the preceding months, she wished it had never happened and that it would just go away.

Tinsler wasn't a bad looking guy. But, she hadn't done it strictly because of the physical attraction. They had much in common.

Their personalities were similar. Their beliefs were similar. And, due to their work on the case, she seemed to be spending more time with him than she was with her husband. Or, for that matter, their eight year old son, Carter.

Carter, named after a grandfather he never got the chance to meet, Daniel Carter Reynolds, was an energetic third grader who was smart and likeable. It bothered Mark and Karen that he spent so much time with sitters, friends and relatives during these years when his parents were focused on their careers. Still, he seemed to adapt well and was exceedingly proud to tell his friends that dad was a major in the Marines and mom was an FBI agent.

She couldn't risk the fallout. No one had ever been divorced in her strict Catholic family, and she couldn't be the first. She would do whatever it took to keep her marriage going, and if that meant lying and accepting the guilt it brought, then so be it. She had to end the affair, put it behind her and make sure that Mark never knew about it. She declared to herself that she would break it off with Tinsler next Monday.

She tried to analyze what had caused her and Mark to grow apart, besides their busy schedules. Tinsler was a down to earth kind of guy. If he couldn't prove it, it didn't exist. His agnostic beliefs had been something of a wake-up call for a woman who'd grown up in the church, never questioning the teachings or philosophies of the Vatican.

Mark, on the other hand, had seemed to grow more spiritual over the years, and his interests had perturbed her. For some reason he'd grown to accept that life on other planets was real. Whenever there was a television program about UFOs or the like, he would monopolize the TV. Weekend trips to the mall always included a trip to the book store, and off he would head to the section that contained books on UFOs and psychic drivel.

He'd grown more intrigued about conspiracy theories of varying natures, whether it was flying saucers, the Loch Ness monster, or who might have killed President Kennedy. It was all hogwash to Karen. She shared Tinsler's beliefs that if you couldn't prove it, then it didn't exist. She chalked Mark's interests off to a simple change of life. He was approaching retirement and she was certain that he was searching for a new interest to occupy his active brain, or some sort of validation that his life had been worthwhile.

Mark finally arrived home a few minutes after six and found his wife wiping down the counter in the kitchen. He dropped his briefcase on the floor and lovingly threw his arms around her from the rear quietly, as if he'd been slipping up on an enemy sentry. "Hey babe! How was your day?" He kissed her lightly on the neck.

She turned and smiled. "Long and hectic." She gave him a quick kiss on the mouth. "I was thinking about a movie tonight."

She reached for the newspaper that was folded and opened to the movie section. "Here's one with Bette Midler and Dennis Farina...That Old Feeling. It's rated PG-13, but I think Carter would be okay with it and would enjoy getting out with us. We can get hotdogs there, and neither of us would have to cook."

Mark glanced at the advertisement and nodded. "Yeah, that looks good. Give me a few minutes for a shower and I'll be ready. Is he upstairs?"

"Huh uh, Carol's, next door. I was just getting ready to call her to send him home. Go take your shower and I'll get him cleaned up."

Forty minutes later, Mark was in civilian clothes and he and his family climbed into his year-old Chevy Tahoe. It was roomy and comfortable and was their only personal vehicle since Karen had sold her Audi when the FBI issued her a Chevy Lumina. She was allowed to make personal stops or run the occasional errand on the way home in her Official Government Vehicle, but taking the family to the movies was expressly forbidden. Often referred to by agents as their G-Ride, some pushed the limits of the policy more than others, but since the government was self-insured, an agent could get in serious trouble by abusing the privilege.

Dan dropped Karen and Carter at the main entrance and went on to park the Tahoe while Karen bought the tickets. Upon entering the theater, he inhaled the invigorating smell of popcorn. There was something about the smell of popcorn that made him feel alive and relaxed at the same time. It brought back so many pleasant childhood memories.

Because the film had been out for a while, the tickets were cheap, attendance was light, and they had their pick of seats. They found three together on an aisle in the center section and settled in to watch the trailers from upcoming films. Carter had his own popcorn and Raisinettes, while Mark and Karen tried to get mustard on their hotdogs and not on their clothes. The lights eventually dimmed all the way as they settled in to relax and watch.

The movie was entertaining and cute. A young woman invites her divorced parents to her wedding. And even though they haven't seen each other in fourteen years, a heated argument ensues, indicating some unresolved friction between them still lingers. Surprisingly though, the two reconnect and decide to run away from their respective spouses for a few days to rekindle an old spark. While at a swank hotel, they spy another reception and decide to crash it, since there is music and dancing and they're both in the mood to have fun.

The two main characters begin to dance to a soft Latin song, One Shining Moment. As the gentle bongos drove the piano and soulful guitar, the claves offered a pleasant syncopation. Marc Anthony sang expressively of wandering through a sea of loneliness until finally meeting the woman of his dreams.

The speakers in the theater pumped the music into Mark's ears in amplified stereo; with different frequencies entering each ear. With this binaural effect, Mark suddenly felt as if an electrical charge had permeated his body. As his senses sharpened, the characters' dialogue began to fade into the background and the song's lyrics and accompaniment seemed to crescendo, overpowering his subconscious. It was something about the frequencies of the musical notes. They were stimulating parts of his brain that he hadn't used in years.

He felt light headed; like he was present, but watching himself from outside his body. There was suddenly a fragrance. A woman's perfume. Nothing he had ever smelled before. Nothing that he noticed when he and his family had taken their seats. It was pleasant, exotic, and so clean. It excited him.

Then for just a brief moment, he saw her as if in a fleeting dream. She was the most stunning woman he'd ever seen. She was dark, not Latin…but maybe Mediterranean. She looked familiar. He should know her, but he didn't. And, in an instant, she was gone and his memory transported him back to Dallas in 1983.

He was in his dad's basement, watching the movie and reading the note his father had left him. He re-experienced the inner turmoil about what to do with this startling evidence. Evidence of so many different things. It had overwhelmed him then. If released publicly, it could be traced back to him and could ruin his career in the Marines. It could ruin Karen's chances of becoming an FBI agent.

The images of those days flashed past his mind at an amazing speed: the funeral, the fire department's touching tribute, his final private moment with his dad before they closed the casket.

Time slowed in Mark's mind as the Latin music seemed to echo from inside his head. He was alone with his dad, the mourner's collecting in the lobby of the funeral home. The quick glance over his shoulder, the tactile sensation of lifting his dad's lifeless elbow as he slipped the film canister under the body. It would be safe there. No one would ever find it. If he needed it again, it could be recovered with a court's order of exhumation. But in the meantime, no person, no government would ever think of looking for it there. The film had been safe with his dad all these years, and now it would remain safe for many more.

Her scent filled his nostrils again and she appeared for a second in the corner of his mind. She smiled and nodded, and was gone. Marc Anthony's ballad erupted in crescendo in the theater and in his mind.

As his memory jumped back and forth from Saigon to his accident, he shivered. What was he missing? He should know more about the assassination. Why couldn't he remember? He was certain he knew more about the reason for JFK's assassination, but the cobwebs in his head won't allow him access to that hard drive in his hippocampus.

And, who was this woman? Why did he think he should know her? In all of his reading about the assassination, he'd never come across a woman like her. She was beautiful. He felt she knew him. But how?

The song ended, and Mark was drawn back to the present. He was shivering and sweating. He had to control his breathing so that Karen did not notice. He sat confused, staring at the screen, but not watching the movie. Who was he? What memories had he lost in those three years before the accident?

After the movie was over and the lights came back up, they collected their trash and got up to leave. "What happened to you? Did you zone out or something?" Karen asked.

"What do you mean?"

She frowned at him in a playful way. "It seemed like you were really enjoying the first part of the movie, and then, you zoned out. You didn't laugh, you didn't move in your seat. I thought you fell asleep, but your eyes were open."

Mark was embarrassed. "Oh, sorry. I've just got a lot on my mind. I started thinking about work stuff and couldn't concentrate on the movie."

She took his arm. "No worries. I'm kinda tired myself."

When they returned home, Carter took his bath and got ready for bed, but was still too energized to fall asleep. The sugar in the candy and soft drinks at the theater were having the same effect on him as a handful of amphetamine.

Mark picked the boy up and spun him around over his head before carefully simulating a body slam onto his bed. "Here you are champ – bedtime!"

"Dad, I can't sleep."

"You've gotta. We're going to mow the grass and trim the shrubs tomorrow."

"Sing something to me," he requested.

"Sing to you?" Mark chuckled. "What do you want me to sing, I'll Be Missing You? The Marines' Hymn?"

"You know, that song you sang to me when I was a kid and I was sick."

"You're still a kid, and with all that candy I'm surprised you're not sick now." Mark said sarcastically.

"Come on, dad. You know!"

"You mean the one from that movie?" Mark remembered the lullaby from his favorite movie, Move Over Darling.

Mark was the same age then as Carter was now, when they went to see it play on Christmas Day in the Texas Theater. He had enjoyed listening to Doris Day's character sing it to her kids, and when Carter had a particularly nasty dose of the flu a couple years earlier, he sang it to him as a means of cheering him up. Mark didn't consider himself a singer, but Carter seemed to enjoy it.

After clearing his throat, he sang softly and could imagine Doris' soft vocals taking him to a place in the distant reaches of space. He sang as he traveled past the moon and on through the Milky Way.

And at that very same instant, forty-four miles away, in a two-story condo in Reston, Virginia, Nerissa was singing the same song, an octave higher, to her one year old son Hunter, with such precision that it was if Doris Day was in the room. As Hunter drifted off to sleep, she thought about the conversation with her mother, and how careful they'd have to be.

20

FRIDAY, OCTOBER 16, 2015

With mixed emotions and a nostalgic ceremony that included the best wishes of the Commandant, Major Mark Reynolds had retired from the USMC in March 1998. As much as he loved the Corps, he knew it was time to move on. And, thanks to the FBI Human Resources office, Karen was granted a transfer to the Dallas Field office a month later.

Together they found a 2,800 square foot ranch home in Plano, and after the couple dug in to their new surroundings, Mark completed the 728 hours of required training through a local police academy and passed the TCOLE Peace Officer licensing examination. He was commissioned as a police officer by the Plano Police Department, and excitedly embarked on his second career.

Nationally accredited since 1992, the department consisted of more than 400 sworn Officers, 178 full-time civilian employees, and 79 civilian part-time employees who had completed various training programs and served in a support capacity. Located in Collin County, Plano was a thriving and comfortable city with a population of nearly 285,000, and was voted one of the best places to live in Texas. Life in Plano offered residents highly rated schools, and a quiet suburban retreat; surrounded by restaurants, coffee shops, and parks. Families got along because residents tended to have moderate political views.

After paying his dues on the street for a couple of years, he'd been assigned to the Criminal Investigative Services Division, and following the attacks of September 11, 2001, was reassigned to the new Homeland Security Unit. The new role provided exciting opportunities that allowed Mark to serve on task forces with various federal agencies investigating a wide range of national security issues. But one particular case in 2008 had brought with it initially some confusion and eventually, a new awakening.

While working with ATF and Customs agents, Mark and some of his team members had been dispatched to Crawford, Texas for a briefing by US Secret Service agents assigned to the George W. Bush detail at the Crawford Ranch. Leaving Dallas on Tuesday, January 8th, they made the two-hour drive to the command post, and after formal introductions, proceeded to a nearby watering hole for more informal ones.

The team was to spend three days with regional law enforcement agencies, providing joint training on the interdiction efforts surrounding illegal immigration. But, that evening, Stephenville gained national media attention when dozens of residents, including police officers and fire fighters reported sightings of unidentified flying objects.

Descriptions varied, but several residents described one craft as the size of a football field, while others said it was as much as a mile long. Several observers reported military aircraft pursuing objects in the sky that were much smaller but flew in such controlled formations that it appeared they were showing off for spectators.

It was there that Mark met Stan Marchand, a hearty physical specimen of six feet, with a forty-four inch chest and thirty-two inch waist, who pumped iron consistently, and other men's wives occasionally. His aquiline nose and perennially tanned skin were a product of his Egyptian lineage and combined with his natural charm and perfect smile, made the ladies immediately attracted to him. His hair had begun to thin in his thirties, and now that he was in his fifties, the current style permitted him to shave his head, adding to his masculine persona.

Stan was one of the most outgoing and congenial agents the

Secret Service had ever had on their rolls. But, it was this pattern of affable behavior, particularly with married women, that had gotten him kicked off the White House detail. However, by the time the Service's internal investigation into his off-duty avocation was over, W, as TRAILBLAZER had been informally known to his agents, had taken a liking to Stan and had him assigned to the Western White House as the Detail Leader for the residential security team.

Located on 1,600 acres near the tiny town of Crawford, about 25 miles west of Waco, the 4,000 square foot environmentally friendly home appeared relatively modest, designed by David Heymann, a professor at the University of Texas at Austin's School of Architecture. With an eye for sustainable design, Heymann incorporated more green features than any of the so-called environmental politicians of the time had heretofore attempted with any of their dwellings.

A central closet in the four-bedroom home held geothermal heat pumps drawing ground water through pipes sunk 300 feet into the ground. The water averaged about 67 degrees year-round, heating the house in winter and cooling it in the summer. The system used no fossil fuels such as oil or natural gas, and it consumed 25 percent of the electricity required for a conventional heating/cooling systems of similar size. Wastewater from showers, sinks and toilets drained into underground purifying tanks and then into the 40,000 gallon cistern. The collected water then was used to irrigate the land surrounding the house.

In contrast, Al Gore's 20-room mansion boasted eight bathrooms and was heated by natural gas. His property also featured a pool with a pool house, and a separate guest house, all heated by gas. In one month alone, his Tennessee homestead consumed more energy than the average American household in an entire year. His average bill for electricity and natural gas was estimated at $2,400.00 per month. In natural gas alone, the property consumed more than 20 times the national average for an American home. But, he got a Nobel Prize in 2007 for his work in the area of climate change.

The Bush Prairie Chapel Ranch in McLennan County, had been dubbed the Western White House and welcomed numerous heads of state over the years, including Russian president Vladimir Putin and Saudi King Abdullah bin Abdulaziz. However, when TRAILBLAZER wasn't in residence, the pace of activity for the small security detail was obviously not what they had been used to in Washington.

Stan and the President got along well and after a personal understanding between them that all of the Bush women were off-limits to him, he'd be allowed to finish out his career in charge of the soon-to-be former president's protection detail when he returned to private life in the next year. Knowing it wasn't a bad gig, Stan accepted the offer.

Following the official briefing and tour, Stan had loaded the group into the black Suburban, and drove them to the cigar bar in Crawford, where they spent the evening smoking a variety of Latin American stogies, drinking single malt scotch, and embellishing the details of their storied careers. All humorous, naturally. Agents never discussed the realities of their jobs with outsiders. Only the funny parables.

Halfway through their third or fourth drinks, no one was keeping score, Stan's cell phone had gone off. The change in his demeanor was stark as he switched immediately to his most sober of voices,

Mark and the other task force agents recognized the seriousness of the call as they watched Stan move to the outside patio to talk in a more quiet setting. The group watched through the window as Stan listened, nodded, and pocketed his cell phone and then pensively returned inside.

He was deep in thought, but after a moment he polled his group. "Okay, I've got two questions. First, who has breath mints, and second, who wants overtime tonight?"

Mark looked quickly at his ATF and Customs counterparts and then at Brad Forbes, another Secret Service Agent assigned to the Ranch, who'd earlier given them a tour of the property.

"What's up?" Forbes asked, pushing his drink away.

Marchand thought for a moment. "That was the Boss. He just

got a call from the congressman up in Erath County, who just got a call from the Governor." He paused, frowning. "We need to interview a couple dozen people."

"About what?" Forbes asked again, dumping Tic-Tacs into his palm and passing the plastic container around.

"You guys are all T-S, right?" Marchand asked quietly.

Everyone nodded, including Mark who'd had to undergo a security clearance investigation in order to handle Top Secret information.

"Well..." He signaled the bartender for the check. "It would seem that several people have reported seeing unidentified flying objects that were being chased by F-16s tonight. They were seen heading from Stephenville, southeast, this direction."

Forbes raised his eyebrows. "Are you fucking with us?"

Stan shook his head. "I wish. The reports have been coming in all night from all around there. The Air Guard scrambled some F-16s out of Ft. Worth and Ellington. But whatever it, they were, they couldn't catch them."

The bartender slid a check across the bar that he had marked no charge/SS on. Stan nodded and smiled and then left a one hundred dollar bill on the bar as the group headed to the parking lot.

"It's an hour drive. Does anyone have to take a leak?"

Everyone shook their heads and jumped into the huge Suburban.

The Suburban turned north on Route 6 and Stan reached under the dash to grab the mic on his radio. "Twenty One Alpha is northbound on Route 6. Advise Texas DPS and counties that we may be running hot."

The control room back at the Western White House acknowledged the communication, and Stan flipped a switch that activated the emergency lights concealed behind the grill and within the headlight and taillight assemblies. In the darkness, the massive Suburban was now visible for almost a mile in any direction.

Mark was suddenly alive again. He was excited and anxious. It was a feeling he hadn't had since that day in Viet Nam as they tried in vain to hold the wall. The feelings of anxiety as they waited for that chopper, wondering if they'd been left behind. But it was something else. Ever since that night in his father's basement, he'd developed that intense curiosity about strange objects in the sky. He knew that they were real, and the government did as well. And now, he was being assigned to interview people who had seem them first hand.

His pulse raced with the knowledge that he would be meeting people with a story to tell. Adding to his consternation was the realization that the Chevrolet Suburban, despite all of its positive attributes, was never intended to continuously run and swerve at speeds in excess of ninety miles an hour. He also knew that nearly twice as many police officers, and Secret Service agents for that matter, died in traffic crashes than gunfire. Nevertheless, he was on an adrenaline high.

Less than an hour later, they were pulling in to the Stephenville Police station on Belknap. As Stan backed the Suburban into a space marked Police Parking Only, he reached down into the pocket on the door and pulled out a bottle of Scope mouthwash. After taking a healthy swig, he passed the bottle to Forbes, who did the same and passed it to the back seat. "No business cards. First names only guys. I don't want anyone trying to follow up with us on this later on."

Stan moved to the back of the Suburban and popped the rear hatch. Inside was a Pelican case with an assortment of gear. He grabbed four of the dark blue raid jackets, as they were known: windbreakers that had large white letters on the back; FEDERAL AGENT. "Here. Put these on. If anyone asks you where you work, just tell them Homeland Security and leave it at that."

The sheriff and the police chief had done their best to corral as many witnesses as they could. Some appeared quiet and stunned. Others were almost festive. It was nearly four in the morning by the time they had interviewed everyone who had seen the strange lights in the sky. When they had talked to as many people as were willing to speak, they met with the Sheriff and the police chief to summarize the results of the interviews.

One trucking entrepreneur was sitting around a fire outside the home of a friend in Selden, Texas. Then he saw the lights: orbs that glowed at first, then began to flash. "There was no regular pattern to the flashing," he said. "They lined up horizontally, seven of them, then changed into an arch. They lined up vertically, and I saw two rectangles of bright flame. That's when I knew it was a life-changing experience."

He said he watched the lights drift north toward Stephenville, the seat of Erath County. "They came back a few minutes later, this time followed by two jets, F-16s, I think." The witness, who owned and flew a Cessna, had seen plenty of military planes over the years. "The jets looked like they were chasing the lights, and the lights seemed to be toying with them. It was like a 100 horse-power car trying to keep up with a 1000 horsepower one."

Others, including several police officers reported that a UFO hovered over the farming community for about five minutes streaking away into the night sky at an immeasurable speed.

One fellow saw the object when he was out clearing brush off a hilltop near the town of Selden. He described the unidentified object as being an enormous aircraft with flashing strobe lights, but it was totally silent. He estimated that it sped away at more than 3,000 mph, followed by two fighter jets that were hopelessly outmaneuvered. He said it took the unusual aircraft just a few seconds to cross a section of sky that it takes twenty minutes to fly in a conventional propeller aircraft. And, it was enormous. He estimated that what he saw was almost a half-mile wide and a mile long, adding that it was "bigger than a Wal-Mart."

The reporter from the *Stephenville Empire-Tribune*, who was covering the story, said that about forty people saw the objects, but that many were too uncomfortable to admit their sightings until they could be sure they wouldn't be ridiculed.

One of the police officers interviewed said he was walking to his car when he saw a red glow that reminded him of pictures he'd seen of an erupting volcano at night. He said the object was suspended 3,000 feet in the air, and that he was so awestruck that he called his son to come and see. He was reluctant to be quoted on the record for fear that his career would be in jeopardy.

When they had finished their summary of the interviews, Stan talked quietly with the police chief and the sheriff, shook hands and then slid into the driver's seat. As the Suburban roared to life, Stan turned to Forbes. "Well, luckily, no one got any pictures."

"Luckily?" Mark asked.

He shifted into drive and pulled the Suburban out onto the street. He looked at Forbes. "Read 'em in."

Forbes turned in his seat to look at Mark and the agents from Customs and ATF. "Boys, it's like this. We went to a cigar bar, got blind stinking drunk, and then we went our separate ways. We were never here. This never happened. Tomorrow morning, the Adjutant General from the State of Texas will have gotten word from the Air Force Chief of Staff in Washington that this was nothing but a mis-identified training exercise of a squadron of F-16s."

"What?" Mark asked, knowing that what these people had seen was truly significant.

Forbes turned back to look out the passenger window. "Your wife, she's with the Bureau. Right?"

"Yeah, but..."

"And you- you get a pension from the Marine Corps, right?"

Mark began to process what was going on. "So?"

"So, bad shit happens to people who find themselves crossing into black projects, who try to talk too much about stuff they know. Nothing personal, I'm just trying to help you understand."

"Black projects?" Mark carefully evaluated what he was hearing. "Wait a minute. You know these people saw something real."

Forbes shook his head and frowned. "Doesn't matter."

The ATF agent spoke up, "But this came from the President. He's going to want some explanation, isn't he?"

Forbes offered a deferential look towards his supervisor. Stan was silent for a few moments before answering. "Look, his dad was the only President of the United States to also serve as the Director of the CIA. He already knows. He's just not in a position to ever do anything about it. None of us are."

After another moment of silence, Stan continued, "TIMBERWOLF,

George-forty-one, when he headed CIA, was the guy that told Carter that he didn't have a need to know about this stuff, after Carter had specifically asked for a briefing. And, Carter was the first modern politician ever to report seeing a UFO first hand. He had a definite interest in the subject. Think about it; the President of the United States asked for a briefing on extra-terrestrial activity, and the head of the C-I fucking A told him he didn't have a need to know."

They drove in silence for what seemed longer than it was, each man pondering what they had learned from the interviews and trying to understand it all in their own way. It wasn't group hallucinations. It wasn't secret aircraft being tested by the government. It wasn't swamp gas. There would be paid skeptics to flaunt their credentials and suggest it was some sort of flying spiders that glowed in the dark, or some equally stupid explanation.

Mark looked out the window at the passing landscape and the sun beginning to brighten the eastern sky. He was exhausted and needed rest. He didn't think his eyes closed but for a moment, he was in a dream-like state. He remembered the film in the basement years before and replayed it in his mind. The subtle smell of an alluring perfume filled his nostrils and he felt a comforting presence telling him that he wasn't alone. It would be okay.

Somewhere south of Stephenville, they stopped for breakfast. They had to run a class for a dozen cops in two hours, and pretend like they'd had a good night's rest.

—————»((•))«—————

Now, seven years later, Mark rubbed his temples as he tried to move data around the Excel spreadsheet. He hated paperwork. He rejoiced in the fact that after lunch he would be playing golf with Marchand. It would be a peaceful break from the drama that had been going on at home.

After thirty three years of marriage, Mark's relationship with his wife often vacillated between being platonic roommates, to a toxic atmosphere of mutual mistrust. Karen was convinced that Mark had a girlfriend, and Mark was suspicious that she had someone as well. They kept up an amicable air in public, but behind closed doors, the relationship was rocky.

They had managed to keep up a stable front for Carter and his wife who had stayed with them for a few months as they transitioned to new assignments and a new home, but after they left, Karen had moved back into one of the guest rooms down the hall. They had drifted as far as two people could. They were cordial, but Mark felt that there should be more. Over the past ten years, they had talked about separating several times, but Karen vehemently opposed any talk of divorce.

She was only three months short of mandatory retirement with the Bureau and whenever the subject came up, she always argued to postpone any decisions about their future until after her retirement.

Carter had his own family now and was doing well. He had followed his mom educationally, but his dad occupationally. After receiving his bachelor's degree in accounting, he joined the Marine Corps, completed OCS and was now a captain, stationed at the Marine Corps Combat Service Support School for Financial Management in Camp Johnson, North Carolina. In another three months, he and Rebecca would be having their first child. Rebecca was a Marine Corps brat, whose father had served in Viet Nam, a few years before Mark's tour.

It was after the Stephenville event that Mark had been increasingly bothered by inexplicable headaches, vivid dreams and feelings about incidents that eventually came true. He had been seeing things that hadn't occurred yet. He was seeing things that had occurred elsewhere that he should have had no way of knowing. Sometimes, he would have a flash of imagery while he was awake and there were times he was worried that this spontaneous daydreaming could cause him to have an accident. He didn't want to admit these events to himself, and tried to forget about them. But they kept happening with increasing regularity.

Mark had discussed these experiences with Karen, who rather than feign sympathy, simply told him to go see a doctor. And while that could have been sage medical advice, if ever discovered by an outsider, could have ended his career in law enforcement. There was a stigma attached to visiting a psychologist. Even though the department had an Employee Assistance Program, there was always a fear that a visit would somehow become common knowledge, and then whispers around the briefing room would spread.

They struggled to find common ground. When her mom had passed away a couple years earlier, she had left Karen a modest inheritance that she split with her sister Katie. With Carter grown, college paid off, and no bills to speak of, Mark and Karen decided to join Gleneagles Country Club. They used some of the inheritance for the $30,000 initiation fee, and decided that they'd use the club to do things together. She took golf lessons, but after a couple of rounds on the challenging course with narrow fairways, she gave it up. She spent the majority of her time there on the tennis courts or in the fitness center.

As it turned out, the membership just gave them another outlet in which to do things separately. Mark didn't play tennis and Karen didn't play golf. So, they developed a different group of friends who used the club at different times on different days of the week.

Mark tried to loosen his back and swung the club as easily as he could. He focused on bringing the club head back slower, and then following through at roughly the same speed. After the third practice swing, Marchand joined him to watch the couple in front of them tee-off.

Stan Marchand had finally retired from the Secret Service, and having been a Marine before, he and Mark hit it off from the first time they met in Crawford in 2008. Stan went out of his way to be the opposite of ostentatious, going so far on numerous occasions to wear workout shirts with the sleeves cut off, often challenging the dress code of the upscale club. He wanted to make it clear that he didn't have to pretend to be something he wasn't.

As they stretched, they both focused on the woman. "Wow. There she is again!" Mark commented, shaking his head.

She was the special type of stunning that you'd expect to have seen on TV or in the movies. The tanned, firm body of a college cheerleader, her swing and form were impeccable. Her drive went at least two hundred yards right down the center of the fairway.

He remembered the first time he'd seen her, a couple weeks earlier. Marchand seemed less interested in her than was Mark, but had mentioned at the time, "They were in front of me in the club-house when I checked in. She said her name was Mary something. I think the guy she's with is a guest. I've seen them in the fitness center a couple of times."

"Son of a bitch!" Mark looked at her figure and flawless skin that contrasted against the white golf skirt and sleeveless top she wore. "Geeezus. She's fucking amazing!"

"Yeah!" He shook his head. "The guy she's with must be loaded. He's got to be twenty years older than her," Marchand replied with an underlying hint of a suitable target being covertly acquired. He was reluctant to openly admit interest in any woman that hadn't already been captivated by his charm.

But now, as his marriage continued to erode, Mark saw Mary more frequently on the golf course and watched sometimes as she crushed an opponent on the tennis courts. Several times he'd seen her in the fitness center lifting weights and running the treadmill like a woman possessed. Her escort was obviously just there to talk to her. He never broke a sweat. But, the circumstances had never been right for Mark to approach her and find out more about her. It was more than physical attraction. Mark felt like he knew her, or, needed to.

Karen had friends in the club. So Mark figured that it was common knowledge that he was married, and he couldn't take the chance that a simple act of saying hello could be reported back to an angry spouse and blown out of proportion.

Stan and Mark followed Mary and her escort around the course all day, occasionally catching up to them on the next tee box following a par three, as they waited for the foursome in front of them to move on towards the next green. At one point, Mary's golf partner looked at Stan and nodded almost imperceptibly. It seemed like more than a casual greeting between two strangers. Mark had seen that nod before when tactical operators from different agencies recognized a counterpart, even when they'd never met.

By the fourteenth hole, Marchand finally looked at Mark and said, "Your game sucks already. Why don't you just hit in to her so you can run up and apologize and introduce yourself?"

"Are you kidding me?" Mark replied slamming his putter into the bag on the back of the cart. "The way I'm hitting today, I'd probably hit that asshole she's with, and he'd turn out to be a personal injury attorney."

Marchand, whose handicap hovered around a five, chuckled. "I'll hit her and toss you the club."

"No!" Mark said with a grin. "I'm in enough trouble at home already. I don't need any more shit in my life." Still, there was something about her. Mark felt like he knew her from somewhere and he couldn't get her out of his mind.

"Do you know that guy?" Mark asked.

Stan shrugged, wiping one of his club faces with the towel attached to his bag. "No, huh uh."

When the round was over, they headed to the bar to add up their scorecard. Mark caught a quick glimpse of Mary and her companion heading into the parking lot, loading their clubs into a BMW convertible.

"Yeah." He thought. "That guy must have money!" For the first time in many years, despite all of the conflict and drama at home, Mark desperately wished he was single. But, he had no idea of what he was getting into.

—————)(◉)(—————

Nerissa had been in Toronto on April 11, 2015, a special gift for Hunter's 18th birthday. He would be entering the Air Force Academy in Colorado Springs in the fall and with her upcoming temporary assignment away from home, she thought it would be a good opportunity to spend some time with him before he began to focus on getting himself physically and intellectually in shape for four years of hard work. He would be spending a couple of months with grandma, his Teta, before leaving for Colorado, and Nerissa would only be able to see him a couple weekends a month.

The Agency had continued to frown on her leaving the country for any reason, but her clients determined that a trip to Toronto would be safe enough. Seeing the sites and taking in some of the finer restaurants, she'd let Hunter sleep in that Saturday morning, while she slipped away to the conference. She felt guilty, but was certain that the guys in *the tank*, as the pool of viewers had become known, wouldn't detect anything.

On Saturday morning, former Defence Minister Paul Hellyer was the keynote speaker at a Toronto symposium on UFO secrecy. The event saw more than 150 people gather at a University of Toronto auditorium for the elder politician's fascinating review of the world's problems. Nerissa looked around the room at the guests and thought that they were a diverse representation of society. Some were academics or scientists, some were politicians or interested military personnel, and of course, some looked like they slept with tin foil on their heads at night to keep the government from reading their minds.

Hellyer had been a vocal critic of government secrecy around UFOs for several decades and was working with several private individuals promoting *Disclosure*. And, for a while, years earlier, had been one of the Institute's remote viewing targets of considerable interest. He knew things. He also knew important people, and therefore, was not easy for the government, any government, to discredit.

"In short," Hellyer explained, "There is a secret cabal's stranglehold on the international banking system, inhibiting humankind's ability to adopt the technology available from extraterrestrial visitors, and to apply it to the climate crisis of global warming."

"Most of us do not know what is going on," Hellyer said. "And the problem, is that what you don't see is what you get."

Hellyer's words had resonated with her and solidified her resolve that she and her mother had been on the right track years earlier. While he had stopped short at naming names, he strongly intimated the organizations that were in control of the truth, but were concealing it for their own power-hungry reasons.

While many believed that Hellyer's comments were based partly on fact and largely on some easily believed speculation, Nerissa knew better. His comments were dead on. His beliefs had helped drive her towards targets that would help her achieve her objectives. Without knowing it, he gave her targets to psychically investigate.

In her spare time, she had begun seeing, feeling the structure and vision of many of the world's most powerful organizations and people. She knew their secrets. She had seen things that the paparazzi weren't able to see. She knew where the bodies were buried.

It had begun with a session on some of the groups that Hellyer had mentioned in his lectures and books, as being part of a loosely knit cabal. To her surprise, some of the top members of the groups had certain proclivities for perverted sexual liaisons, often with children. She began to sense a connection between the rich and famous and a billionaire hedge-fund manager based in New York, Jeff Tabachnik.

Her psychic wanderings had taken her inside such controversial networks as The Bilderberg Meeting: an annual conference established in 1954 to open dialogue between the powerful elites in Europe and North America. The group's agenda, publicly espoused, was to prevent another world war, and focus on bolstering a group vision around free market Western capitalism and its interests around the globe.

On its rolls were political leaders, magnates from industry, finance, academia, and of course, the media. At any given time throughout its history, membership averaged between 120 and 150 people who were free to use the information gained at meetings, without having to cite a source. This practice was said to encourage candid debate, while maintaining privacy.

Then, there was the Trilateral Commission, formed in 1973 by private citizens of Japan, North American nations and Western European nations to foster substantive political and economic dialogue across the world. The idea of the Commission was developed during a time of considerable discord among the United States and its allies in Western Europe, Japan, and Canada. In Nerissa's subsequent research of their membership, a name stood out. Jeffrey Tabachnik. Based in New York, with lavish homes around the world, and his own private island in the Caribbean, Tabachnik knew people. Important people.

Essentially, liberal internationalists from Europe, Japan, and the United States, they were the intellectual elite. Some claimed that Jimmy Carter's entire government had been recruited from there. The Trilateral Commission was concerned with trying to induce what they called more moderation in democracy. In other words, turning people back to passivity and obedience so they wouldn't put so many constraints on their government. Ironically, Jimmy Carter had been the first President to openly press for information about extraterrestrials.

In particular, the Trilateral Commission seemed worried about young people. They were concerned about the institutions responsible for the indoctrination of the young, including schools, universities, churches and so on, pushing the message that the established institutions weren't doing their jobs. The media would help.

Critics accused the Commission of promoting a global consensus among the international ruling classes in order to manage international affairs in the interest of the financial and industrial elites under the Trilateral umbrella. You were with them or you weren't.

And ultimately, there was the Council on Foreign Relations, founded in 1921, a United States nonprofit think tank specializing in U.S. foreign policy and international affairs. It was headquartered in New York City, with an additional office in Washington, D.C. Its membership numbered nearly 5,000 and included senior politicians, more than a dozen former Cabinet officials, CIA directors, bankers, lawyers, professors, and senior media figures.

The CFR meetings convened government officials, global business leaders and prominent members of the intelligence and foreign-policy community to discuss international issues. They had published the bi-monthly journal Foreign Affairs since 1922, and ran the David Rockefeller Studies Program, which influenced foreign policy by making recommendations to the presidential administrations and diplomatic community, testifying before Congress, interacting with the media, and publishing opinions on foreign policy issues. The media. Of course they had their hooks in the media. Who owned the major media outlets, anyway?

Some of the people whose hearts and minds she'd invaded over the years met at least annually at The Bohemian Club, a private retreat north of San Francisco in Sonoma County. It was where the Manhattan Project blossomed, resulting in the production of an atomic bomb that killed thousands, and sent a message around the cosmos that the blue planet on the edges of the Milky Way had learned how to split the atom. Somewhere, light years away, an intelligent entity must have thought, "Uh oh, looks like the kids found the matches."

Founded in 1872 from a regular meeting of journalists, artists, and musicians, it soon began to accept businessmen and entrepreneurs as permanent members, as well as offering temporary membership to university presidents and military commanders who were serving in the San Francisco Bay Area. Now, the club concealed a membership of many local and global leaders, ranging from artists to businessmen and former or potential Presidents of the United States.

Like the cellular amoeba, barely noticeable on its own, when it becomes amoebic dysentery, the destruction of any one particular amoeboid will not stop the disease. Control over the world's political and financial systems was not placed with elected officials, but as Hellyer had suspected, an anonymous cabal. There was no one single person at the top.

Eisenhower, the President who at one time threatened to send the Army into Area 51 if they didn't permit his inspection team access to the site, tried his best to warn the world of this amoebic process in his farewell speech.

Delivered in a television broadcast on January 17, 1961, he warned that the nation must guard against the potential influence of what he termed the military–industrial complex. He pub icly expressed concerns about plans for the future, the dangers of massive spending in this military-industrial arena and of the domination of science through federal funding. Conversely, he foresaw the domination of science-based public policy by what he called the scientific-technological elite.

Nerissa switched on the small TV in the kitchen as she searched the refrigerator for something to make for dinner. Set to one of the cable news channels, she stopped and turned to catch the tail end of a feature story. A reporter was interviewing a member of the Vatican's astronomy program about the recent change in the church's position on extraterrestrial life.

"...there's no conflict between the possibility of alien life, even intelligent life, and the teachings of the Catholic Church. Just as there is a multiplicity of creatures on Earth, there can be other beings, even intelligent, created by God," The Jesuit astronomer paused for a moment and then continued. "This is not in contrast with our faith because we can't put limits on God's creative freedom."

Most in the world would believe the Vatican saw this as a logical idea whose time had simply come. Nerissa knew better. It was confirmation that her plan was working.

21

Mark rolled his F-150 pickup into the club's parking lot a little after noon. He and Stan had a 1:30 p.m. tee time, and they planned to grab a sandwich first in the club house. As he pulled in, he saw the empty parking space next to his, and thought about the day before.

Stunning as always, she was in the process of tossing her tennis bag into the trunk of the BMW convertible. He couldn't believe his luck. He smiled at Mary as he retrieved his golf bag from the bed of the truck and closed the top.

They made eye contact, and she smiled back at him.

"I've seen you around here a few times, but I don't think we've ever met," he said with a bit less confidence than he'd intended.

She moved a few inches closer and he got a whiff of her scent, an alluring perfume combined with perspiration. It was exotic and seductive.

He reached to shake her hand. "My name is Mark. Mark Reynolds."

As she introduced herself, she took his hand and he felt an immediate warmth, an undeniable comfort. He was certain they'd met somewhere in his past. He already knew her name was Mary and he was so enraptured by the chance meeting, he missed it the first time she said it.

"Hi Mary. How do you do?"

She grinned widely, "No…Neri…N-E-R-I…short for Nerissa. Nerissa Cavendish."

"Oh…" He returned the grin. "I've never met a Nerissa before. Charming name!"

"It's actually from the Merchant of Venice. Mom is a big Shakespeare fan."

He held her hand a second or two longer than was necessary. He felt something pass between them - perhaps in her touch, perhaps in the knowing look in her eyes. "Are you a Dallas native?"

"No." She offered a light grin as if she knew he was firting, but that she would never let it go anywhere. "I'm in Process Management for a company and I'm only here for a few months on a project."

Mark was momentarily disheartened that as suddenly as he'd discovered her, she would one day soon be gone.

"Where's home?" he asked pocketing his keys.

She looked briefly down and then back into his eyes. "I'm not sure." She smiled again. "I was born in California, but have been living in Virginia for most of my adult life."

Mark took a chance. "And, is Mr. Cavendish with you?"

Still smiling, she shook her head. "Not any more. We've been divorced for several years."

"Hmmm…beautiful woman away from home. Maybe I could give you a call later and we could get a drink?"

"Can't today." She beamed as she moved towards the driver side of the car and opened her door. "Maybe some other time."

Mark moved with her and when she was seated and reaching for her seatbelt, he gently closed the door. "Well, how can I get ahold of you later to see if you've changed your mind?"

She raised her eyebrows and winked. "We're both here four or five days a week. I'm sure I'll run into you again." The BMW sprang to life, and she waved briefly as she backed out of the parking space and drove away. She affected him. And, there was something in that brief exchange that told him he needed to move forward with his life.

He knew he needed to get off his butt and push for a divorce. Their lives were no longer the storybook romance from thirty years earlier. Neither of them were growing anymore, either as individuals or as a couple. Their façade wasn't fooling their friends or family.

And so, it was later that night around the pool, after Karen and he had each had three drinks and an hour of sobbing, that Karen broke down. "Please just tell me her name. Tell me her name and I'll give you the divorce. I just need to know."

Their differences gradually eroded the marriage to the point of no return. Mark Reynolds likened it to swimming against the current at every bend, and with Carter gainfully employed in the United States Marine Corps, he decided that it was time to move on. He hadn't expected Karen to be so shocked. They had, after all, been sleeping in separate bedrooms for the past five years. He truly expected her to say, "What took you so long?"

Instead, what followed was a roller coaster of emotion ranging from anger to sadness to bargaining, and finally focusing on anger. In thirty years, he had never seen her like this. She was convinced that he'd had a girlfriend for the past ten years, and she would not believe anything Mark told her.

"Tell me! Just tell me her name!" she repeated.

The truth was, that there was no name to give her. But her sobs turned to screams and she broke down and began to beg, and for some reason Mark believed that he had to give her something to satisfy her need. She fell to her knees in front of him and began pulling on his shirt in hysterics. "Tell me...please tell me..."

And in an instant of insanity, he heard himself mutter the word, "Neri." It was the only name that came to mind. It was the only name that had been on his mind. And the truth was that she had absolutely nothing to do with their marital problems. She was just in the right time and place to make Mark realize that it was time for him to move on and find someone new. "She's just someone I met at the club. I hardly know her. We're certainly not sleeping together like you and Tinsler."

At the mention of her former partner's name, Karen froze, an icy stare penetrating Mark's eyes.

"It's a small world," Mark added quietly. "News travels."

Without another word, Karen simply picked up her glass, returned inside and went upstairs to bed.

This morning, she was back to being the cold and sarcastic roommate he'd had known for the past few months, and barely said a word to him before leaving for work.

Now, he looked again at the empty parking space and then around the lot to see if he could see Neri's BMW anywhere. He suddenly felt empty and lonely, but picked up his clubs and made for the clubhouse.

Marchand was waiting for him. "Golf on a Monday? You okay?"

Mark was ready to start talking about retirement from the police department. His seniority and overtime had given him substantial time off, and he looked forward to things that got him out of the toxic atmosphere at home. "Yeah. Thanks for meeting me. Karen is off today and since I finished up early at the PD, I felt like I needed to stay away for a few hours."

"Hey, brother, I'm retired and I've got nothin' else to do!"

It was a good day for golf. The temperature topped out at seventy five with the humidity around fifty percent. The broken clouds and light breeze made it perfect. Just enough wind to blame a bad shot on the gust and not the golfer. At the turn, they grabbed more drinks before tackling the back nine with a sense of humor and a good buzz.

The course was practically empty on this Monday, and the duo found themselves back in the clubhouse by five thirty, feasting on hot dogs and Single Malt Scotch. They ran into a couple of Customs guys that they knew, and when the second round of drinks came, they all realized it was going to be a long evening.

The General and his wife sat down for a light evening meal at the kitchen island as the six o'clock news came on in the background. When the anchor led the story, he immediately froze and shifted his attention to the television. He'd been expecting it. Just not so soon.

He suddenly remembered how his hand had trembled as he re-read the note that had come in the inter-office mail pouch a week earlier. The outer envelope was fresh, with no previous delivery stations listed on the cover. It could have come from his own assistant's desk. Inside the pouch was a simple greeting card envelope like one would expect for a birthday. But the message was far from cordial. On a plain white 5" by 7" piece of paper was typed:

Someone in your organization will leak the existence of the AATIP program to the media. You will not impede its release and will not attempt to investigate the source. You will allow unofficial sources within your ranks to merely acknowledge that the program exists, but not comment as to the authenticity of the subject matter released. At some point in the next 24 months you'll be told to publicly verify the authenticity of the videos. Tabachnik recorded your meeting at the Bohemian Lodge last June.

ETERNA
TS//SAR-E

Whoever had sent the note, not only had access to the Pentagon's internal mail system, but also knew the portion marking for a special access program. A program he had heard of years earlier, but never been read into.

He'd been in the Oval Office assisting the then Air Force Chief of Staff with briefing documents relating to Soviet activity in Afghanistan. As he bent to recover a file the Chief of Staff had dropped on the President's desk, his eyes darted to a file folder peeking out from underneath another stack of documents. As the President noticed his wandering eyes, he quickly pushed the papers together and dumped them into a desk drawer, an angry look on his face.

He had only seen it for an instant: TOP SECRET//SPECIAL ACCESS REQUIRED-ETERNA.

When they had returned to the Pentagon later that day, the Chief of Staff had brought him in to his office, closing the door swiftly behind them. He still remembered vividly the admonition and scolding, "Need I remind you Colonel, that what you see in the White House is never to be discussed anywhere, anytime."

"No, sir!" He was hoping for a promotion to flag grade soon, and there was no way he would ever do anything to jeopardize it. "I totally understand, sir."

He had not heard the term in the years since. And the simple fact that he hadn't, meant that ETERNA was something that was highly classified, and that it had probably been re-classified and re-named several times throughout the years to prevent disclosure under the Freedom of Information Act.

The general's initial shock and curiosity turned rapidly to anger when he read the last line of the note again. How would anyone know about his relationship with Jeff Tabachnik? He reached into his briefcase and found the secure cell phone in the hidden compartment. He typed in the five-digit sequence that would automatically delete the number at the end of the call. There would be no record that this call was ever made.

His hand was now shaking more, and his fingers misdialed the first digit after the area code. He hit the end button and redialed.

"Yes, General?" The male voice on the other end was as clear as if the two men were standing next to each other.

"We need to meet. Quickly."

The voice on the other end was calm, controlled. "Why General?"

"I need to know who you spoke to about our June meeting, or any of the other meetings."

The stable voice on the other end was without emotion, almost automated. Instead of expressing any urgency or interest, it was almost as if the call didn't matter. "We have an agreement, General. I speak to no one about the arrangements I make with any of my clients. They depend on that."

"Well, someone knows. We need to meet," the General said, somewhat exasperated.

"I'll be at my home in Manhattan. Come by around seven," Tabachnik replied with no more urgency than if he'd ordered a pizza. He could feign interest and charm for brief periods of time, but in reality, he was void of any feelings for others. He was a sociopath.

The General had finished early, and hopped the shuttle to New York, but the meeting had done little to re-assure him. Despite Tabachnik's assertive guarantees, he had much to be paranoid about. The financial investments he had made with the back-door money from defense contractors had more than doubled in the last year, and thanks to Tabachnik, was well hidden from prying eyes in several offshore accounts.

If that information leaked, he would be exposed to criminal charges and embarrassment, but he would still have his family. If his other interests in what Tabachnik offered his special clients came to light, his family would be disgraced; he'd be alone, and branded as a sex criminal.

The network anchor resumed, with a tinge of amusement in his voice as if he wasn't sure if the story was real or not.

The Pentagon is not commenting on a newly released video which shows U.S. Navy pilots encountering an unidentified flying object earlier this year, but has garnered calls for more research into what these mysterious objects could be.

The footage was released today by a privately funded scientific research and media group, led by a team of former intelligence and scientific advisors to the US Government. The clip is said to be an 'authentic DoD video that captures the high-speed flight of an unidentified aircraft at low altitude,' and 'reveals a previously undisclosed Navy encounter that occurred off the East Coast this year.

Supposedly, there are additional videos to be released soon. The Department of Defense declined to comment on this particular video, but confirmed to our network that the U.S. government ran a program for investigating reports of unidentified flying objects until 2012.

The Advanced Aviation Threat Identification Program ended in the 2012 time frame. It was determined that there were other, higher priority issues that merited funding and it was in the best interest of the DoD to make a change. The DoD takes seriously all threats and potential threats to our people, our assets, and our mission and takes action whenever credible information is developed.

"Oh my God, George. Isn't that…"
The General nodded. "Yeah. Nothing will come of it. Let's eat."

⸻ ⸺《◉》⸺ ⸻

By the time Mark returred home it was after seven, and he was moderately drunk. But, he knew something was wrong. All it took was an index finger to push the door open enough to step through and smell the death. Mark recognized the familiar smell and sensation. When someone walks into a room occupied by the recently deceased, they are greeted by the usual caustic smells of traumatic violence like burnt gun powder, feces, urine and the *copper-esque* smell of blood. But there was something else. The feeling.

And, on this crisp October evening in Plano, he was greeted by a grizzly site. Neri Cavendish was lying face-up in a pool of her own blood; her surprise still visible on a beautiful face that had turred ashen and cold. One eye was closed, but the other half-open, as sometimes happens following the physical death. It took him a moment to accept what he was seeing. She hadn't deserved this.

He fought back the shock to take in the scene. He stood

motionless in the doorway, looking at both of them on the floor of his living room. In the darkness, they looked in peaceful repose. Karen's Sig P229 had left her grip, but rested on the floor under the fingertips of her right hand. The single gunshot wound with the star pattern in the right rear side of Neri's head indicated that Karen had fired up close when Neri's head was turned. Then, apparently, knelt down beside her and shot herself in the chest.

Mark couldn't add the pieces up. How...why would Neri be in his house with Karen?

Forty - seven years old, she was just someone he passed at Gleneagles a few times, exchanging a smile or a greeting. She had been so beautiful. With the unforgettable body of a college cheer-leader, she turned every heterosexual male head. And because of his situation at home, he had begun to look forward to the smiles when they passed.

She just happened to have been in his space that day. Why had he been so attracted to Nerissa Cavendish? And why, oh why, could he have been so reckless to give Karen her name. Karen was a sea-soned investigator. She was also a vindictive and frightened spouse. How could he have been so foolish?

And that was it. With a couple of shots, Karen had managed to punish him for his desires, his thoughts and of course, his actions. She'd not sworn any kind of revenge, and Mark had not believed her capable of something like this. Statistically, everyone swears revenge for something at one time or another, but they rarely act out. Who knows, maybe she was punishing the FBI for something as well.

As Reynolds looked at the two of them on the floor, now forever joined by one act, his mind became blank. He wanted to cry, but he couldn't breathe. The images indelibly etched in his mind, he would always look back on that conversation by the pool and think, "Why did I give her that name?"

Reynolds fell to his knees, a pain in his stomach radiating to his chest. A scream emerged from within, and he rolled to the floor. He grabbed for Neri's hand, and then lost consciousness. There was suddenly a feeling of peace. There was an almost deafening absence of sound. He knew he was unconscious, but he felt dizzy, as if the floor of the house was turning upside down.

There was a brilliant flash of light in his mind that quickly faded to black. As he felt his breathing slow, the black void filled with the impression of an eye. A close up of an eye. Very close, as if the eye was by itself in a universe of darkness. The brown iris seemed to expand and contract, drawing him towards an enlarging pupil. As he drew nearer, the pupil seemed to invite him in closer and he found himself entering the hollow space. Peaceful. Drifting.

There was no reason for alarm. He felt safe. Confused, but safe. He was following his emotions, and was curious to see where he was being led. But, it was like he had been through this eye before. Somewhere.

As he floated down this tunnel, a collage of color and imagery appeared along the sides, which made no sense to him. Then, as he moved further, faces seemed to appear. Distinct faces. He didn't know any of them, but it seemed as though he should have.

And then he saw her. Neri was there. Her face was vibrant and alive and her eyes were seducing him just like he remembered. They were looking at just him. He took her hand and tried to talk. There was so much he needed to tell her.

She smiled back at him. A warm and welcoming smile that he had seen before, both in reality and in his dreams. They embraced, and he felt her complete forgiveness. Together, their minds synced and they were taken back on a psychic journey to when he was a young child. In only seconds, they saw their lives fast-forward as if watching a video. They were at the movie the night he told Karen that he wanted to retire.

But, Neri had been there that night as well. They floated together like two divers emerging from the darker depths of a calm azure sea, towards the light of the surface. Their embrace became stronger and emotion overwhelmed them. It was as if their molecular structure was fusing them together. They were becoming one entity, slowly floating towards the surface of the sea.

The soft beat of the Latin song he remembered from that night at the theater in Quantico filled his head - the strike of the claves echoing off non-existent walls, on beats three, six and eight.

Together, they broke the surface of the water and ascended into a darkening sky. High above the clouds, they entered the isolation of space, and were surrounded by stars. In moments, they lived a complete lifetime together. He was at her high school and college graduations. She sat nearby as he was sworn in as a US Marine. They were present at each other's weddings.

Never having met her father, she was walked down the aisle by Dr. Kravitz, the only father figure she'd ever known. But she was happy. She knew her dad was watching. It was as if he was in the church, wearing his finest dress blue uniform, medals dangling on his chest as he moved. His officer's Mameluke sword glinted in the sunlight breaking through the panes of the church windows. The Ivory-colored plastic grip, fixed with the star screws, the flash of the gold-plated guard. He was proud of his baby girl.

As the music grew in intensity, he saw Neri's work at the Institute, all of her contributions, and her relationships with her coworkers and clients. She was so very gifted. She had helped so many people. She had so much left to give. But now in this space, Neri and he were two souls lost in space and time.

He saw the birth of her son, Hunter. And then, as they hung weightless somewhere in the cosmos, he saw Hunter growing up without a mother. He saw the pain and neglect of the relationship that Neri had gone through with her ex-husband, and was witness to the damage that would happen now with Hunter having to live with his dad full time.

The music faded abruptly. He pushed Neri away from him, and looked into her brilliant brown eyes. "I did this to you. I have to make this right"

"You can't...you can't change what's happened," she concedes. "But, you can come with me."

"I have to fix this," he cries.

There was an explosion of energy that blinded and deafened

him. He felt sickened as G-forces unlike anything he'd ever experienced yanked him in several directions at once.

⸺⟨◉⟩⸺

Karen screamed, "Please just tell me her name. Tell me her name and I'll give you the divorce. I just need to know."

Reynolds was stunned, disoriented, "What?"

Karen's sobs turned to screams and she broke down and began to beg, and Mark believed that he was hallucinating. She fell to her knees and began pulling on his shirt in hysterics. "Tell me. Please tell me."

Mark shook his head as if trying to clear his ears after coming out of the pool. The room was still spinning. Wait, the ground was spinning. Where was he?

Karen grabbed his shirt so hard, the fabric ripped. "Just give me her name, and I'll do whatever you ask!"

Mark could feel his mouth start to form the words, "N...N..." and then a sharp pain seemed to come up from his jaw, through the back of his eye and into the top of his head. "N...N...aaaghh!" he screamed, and fell out of the lawn chair on to the concrete patio near the edge of the pool, as the searing pain in his head made him reach for his temples. He was out.

Karen kicked at him. "Stop it! Don't pull this shit on me! Give me her name!"

⸺⟨◉⟩⸺

Reynolds was only vaguely aware that some time had passed, and that there were people talking, "I'm going to slip this over your head. It's just to hold the mask in place so you can breathe easier."

He opened his eyes and saw the two medics kneeling next to him. He blinked. "What's going on? Where am I?"

"You're at home. You lost consciousness, and your wife called us," he replied.

"My wife?" He was trying to figure out how his wife could have called when he'd seen her dead just moments earlier. "She's dead."

"Oh, you fucking wish, you son of a bitch!" Karen retorted from somewhere off to his left.

They were on the deck by the pool, not inside the bloodstained living room of his home. "What is today?" Reynolds asked, trying to add the pieces up. He was sober, and it wasn't dark anymore. Or maybe it wasn't dark…yet? He had never felt so disoriented.

"How long was I out?" he asked the medic with difficulty. Half his face wasn't working.

The medic glanced at Karen and then replied, "Just a couple of minutes. It looked like you banged your head when you fell out of your chair. You might have had a TIA…a mini-stroke. So, I think you ought to come with us and get checked out at the ER."

⸺⸺◦《◦》◦⸺⸺

Knowing he was fully insured, the doctors wanted to keep him in the hospital for as long as possible. As he opened his eyes, he saw the blurry presence of Stan Marchand leaning over him, as if for an inspection of sorts. Stan was wearing his favorite University of Cincinnati sweatshirt with the arms cut off.

Mark looked at his friend for a couple of minutes before the images started to flood back into his mind, and he suddenly realized where he had really met Stan the first time. Not in Crawford in 2008, but in a psychic session with Neri. They were in the Kennedy Oval Office and she was showing him some documents on Kennedy's desk. The dark skin, the shaved head, the sleeveless sweatshirt. It was Stan all right, but nothing made sense.

His memory, excised years earlier in the hit and run accident, was flooding back. He remembered the assignment to Quantico and his posting to the Institute in California, and his work for the government as a remote viewer. It was coming back, and he felt like he'd been given the keys to his own mental attic as he was rummaging through old things to see what was up there.

It took him a moment to assemble the broken pieces of his past. When Mark could finally speak, he said, "You know, don't you? You were there."

"I know," he replied nonchalantly.

"So, the Secret Service has known about me since the seventies?"

"Not really. They don't know about you at all. I've known about you since about 1990. But, they didn't know what I was viewing or when I was viewing. The Service doesn't sanction such things officially. Occasionally, I would let them know about a feeling, or a vision if you want to call it that, if I thought it would prevent something from endangering one of our Protectees. But..."

"But, when I met you in Crawford, you knew who I was?"

"Not at first. It wasn't until the drive to Stephenville than I somehow pieced together that you were the one I'd seen remote viewing the Oval Office with the woman. I had that brief, fleeting sensation that we'd met before. Some people call it a shining moment: when things come together in your subconscious and break through to the conscious mind."

Mark thought about Stan's word choice. "That woman? You didn't know about Neri?"

Stan tilted his head and furrowed his brow. "Who the fuck is Neri?"

"Neri - the smoking hot woman at the club. You thought her name was Mary. The one that always hangs out with the tall guy you thought was creepy."

Stan Marchand straightened his back, a look of amazement coming over his face. "The woman I perceived you with in JFK's Oval Office was... her?" He put his hands on his hips and grunted. "Wow. I didn't see that one coming!"

He pursed his lips. "Usually when I view, you know, bi-locate, I sense energies. Sometimes they're male; sometimes they're female. Sometimes I can perceive faces, and sometimes just a presence. In that session, I was able to see you in the room, but I could only sense her presence. I couldn't see her physically."

"But, that was in 1980. You weren't with the Secret Service yet."

He shrugged. "You might have RV'd it in 1980, but I didn't have my session until sometime in 1993. Remember, there is no such thing as time and space in the psychic realm. We were all coming together from different places and different times. Who knows when Neri would have RV'd the same dimension? She'd have been a kid in 1980, and I was still in college."

He scratched his three-day growth of beard. "But in that one psychic event, we all came together for basically the same purpose. To find out what happened to JFK."

Mark exhaled slowly. He was trying to bring his tortured mind and body together. "So, what did happen?"

He shook his head. "A fucking comedy of errors. Yeah, the mob wanted him out. Yes, Castro was pissed. And yes, he had no friends in the CIA. But it was the magicians, slang for what used to be called MAJIC for a while. As Clinton once said, there's a government within the government that the President can't see. It's made up of a consortium of business and government leaders from around the world. Presidents come and presidents go, but the cabal is timeless. It's self-perpetuating."

Marchand slid one of the chairs over to the edge of the bed and sat down. Mark propped himself up a bit so that he could still see him. He continued in a voice just above a whisper, "Before your accident, you were on to it. Kennedy had gotten into a significant beef with the real government, the government represented by the representatives of the people. When word leaked that he wanted to work with the Soviets to identify these extraterrestrial visitors and share technology globally, they warned him. When the warning didn't change his mind, they assembled a team of, well, basically mercenaries that came from military and intelligence ranks, to stage an assassination and make it look like someone else did it."

"Oswald really was a patsy?"

"No," he grunted. "Oswald was a murdering bastard. He pulled the trigger. He just didn't know the real reason he was being moved into play. In intelligence parlance, you might say it was a false-flag exercise that was carried out using our own flag."

"But, the film," Mark interrupted softly. "I...uh..."

Stan nodded. "Yeah...the fucking film. And so, the punch line to the comedy of errors. Castro really was going to kill Kennedy on that trip. He had two shooters in place along the route. The first team just lost their nerve at the last minute, and backed away. They didn't know Oswald was around the corner in the Schoolbook Depository. There was a second team behind the fence on the grassy knoll area that were waiting for him, but when they saw the fatal shot, they packed up and left without firing a shot."

He sighed, "And no one could have known that an overly excited agent could have had an unintentional discharge of his weapon, at the split second it was aimed at Kennedy's head. No one could have foreseen that."

Marchand rubbed his eyes wearily. "It wasn't until the autopsy that the doctors realized they'd have a hard time explaining how Oswald's round-nosed bullet could have exploded in Kennedy's head like that. That's how Barnes got involved."

"Barnes?"

"Joseph Barnes, US Secret Service, retired in 1979 after years of distinguished service to his country. They brought him back as a consultant. He was the guy they sent to Dallas to clean up the crime scene. To make sure there was no evidence that could be recovered, that pointed to anyone but Oswald. He was also the guy that orchestrated your accident. Not as a consultant to the Secret Service, but representing some other interested parties in Langley."

Knowing that Mark had figured most of it out already, he went on. "He had some other clean-up to do through the years. It started with an Air Force photographic specialist named Ramey who was to surrender the film to Barnes in a Dallas Warehouse in December 1963. They found Ramey dead in a fire, but no film. The FBI later produced a film that they purported to be the one recovered at the scene, but that film was worthless; under-exposed all the way through. But with Ramey dead, then there'd be no way to conclusively say what was, or should have been on it." He paused. "But of course you'd eventually find the real one. Well, one of the real ones. During the month that he was missing, Ramey was making a duplicate of his film. When he was finished, he spliced undeveloped film around the spool so that if anyone ever found it, like a firefighter, it would look like unprocessed stuff. He sent the other copy to his uncle."

"Then there was an FBI agent named MacArthur, who ran the training academy in Quantico. He was supposedly given documentation by a CIA contact; internal correspondence from CIA to the MJ group discussing Kennedy's interest in opening UFO files to the Soviets as a gesture of good will, and suggesting an appropriate response. Some of those documents were sent just two weeks before the assassination."

"MacArthur's death was made to look like a SCUBA accident, but the documents were never recovered. They finally showed up in some guy's book a few years later and the government, especially the FBI, went to great lengths to call them out as forgeries and discredit the author. In the end, the author was told to publicly state that he'd somehow hoaxed it, or his family would suffer. He acquiesced, temporarily, and later came back and said the docs were real, but he'd been pressured to say they weren't."

Marchand tugged at his ear, still deep in thought. "There were others through the years, even a reporter from the Baltimore Sun. Everyone even loosely associated with ETERNA is gone now. Hell, Barnes himself has been gone for ten years now. And, as far as the film goes, I know where it is, and as long as it stays there, no one else will ever need to know of its existence."

Mark lay quietly for a moment, trying to understand what he was learning. "Did you know me before the accident?"

Stan looked down at the floor and then turned and glanced towards the window. After a few long seconds, he answered his friend as best as he could. "I didn't know about your accident or Barnes, for that matter until well into the nineties."

"I was remote viewing some missing files and sort of happened upon Joseph Barnes. He joined the Service in fifty-one, and after serving in the DC Field Office, got White House duty when Eisenhower took over in fifty-three. He crossed into intelligence work and represented the Service with CIA and DIA. He made a lot of friends over there."

"Barnes was given some eight-by-ten photos of the Ramey crime scene, by an FBI agent named Balmain. That would have been in sixty-three when Barnes was cleaning up Dealey Plaza. They kept in touch through the years and Barnes always wondered how much Balmain might really have known."

"An Air Force OSI team searched Balmain's home and office covertly, but never found anything. It's been a long trail, and you were a part of it. At some points, a victim. That's a long-winded way of saying that I didn't meet the real Mark Reynolds until that afternoon at W's ranch."

Mark looked at the IV port going into his arm. "So, where does that leave us?"

Marchand laughed. "Retired and playing golf three days a week. All this stuff will come out in time. As public opinion shifts, the government within the government will become more visible and it'll have to be more honest about its purposes, or face global insurrection."

Marchand stood, and returned the chair to its original spot on the other side of the room. "Despite his lack of experience in politics, Harry Truman proved to be one hell of a surprising leader. He managed the Roswell incident, developed the MJ group, and made it so that information about the extraterrestrial presence would be classified above what POTUS could see. Remember, the only way Eisenhower got to see Area 51 was after he threatened to send the Army in to take it by force." He shook his head slowly. "Kennedy should have seen the writing on the wall."

"In a way, Truman created the cabal, or at least created the environment in which it could propagate. Nowadays, the power lies not with elected officials, because they are here today and gone tomorrow. The power lies with senior career leaders who will stay in their position for twenty-five to thirty years. Someday though, that's exactly how they'll be found and eliminated. Some of us know what to look for."

Mark raised his right hand off the bed and Stan grasped it. "Thanks. You probably went out on a limb to tell me this."

"No biggie, brother. They're letting you out of here tomorrow morning. I'll be back to pick you up."

"Thanks," Mark said as he closed his eyes.

Sometime later, he was aware of her alluring perfume, and he opened his eyes just enough to see Neri standing next to his bed. She looked great. She had on blue gym shorts and a white tee shirt. She touched his hand and smiled. "You're going to be okay."

She felt soft and warm. "Will I see you again?" he asked.

Neri smiled at him knowingly. "You never know. My project is finished, so I have to go now. Please don't try to find me for a while. When the time is right, I'll find you." She kissed him on the forehead, and he closed his eyes.

"Hi Mr. Reynolds. Time for your medication!" The stout nurse smiled.

Mark sat up in bed confused and looked around. "Where's Neri?"

The nurse looked at him. "Neri?"

"The, uh, woman that was just here."

She handed him a small paper cup containing a pill. "Sorry, sir. I haven't seen anyone in here since your friend left, the dark one. Say, he's not single by any chance, is he?"

Mark smiled and swallowed the pill with a mouthful of water. He knew they'd always be able to find each other, no matter where they were.

Epilogue

Nerissa Khoury Cavendish walked purposefully up the side street that paralleled Richmond Highway, towards the office building in Crystal City Virginia. She was wearing gray slacks, gray open-toed pumps, and a white blouse with a light floral pattern. The elastic around the mid-section allowed an occasional glimpse of exquisite flat abdominal muscles. Her thick dark hair was up today.

She entered the revolving door, and nodded at the security guard behind the desk, before waving her American Express card over a small sensor near the turnstiles. Her soft, sensuous hands replaced the card in her wallet, allowing others nearby to get a glimpse of the brilliant oval opal on her left ring finger.

She took the elevator to the eighth floor and when the doors opened, walked to the second door on the right.

The woman behind the desk looked up briefly, and nodded without expression. Neri passed the opal ring in front of a concea ed reader near the door, and when she heard a click, she entered the small office and said hello to the man in the blue slacks and white shirt behind the desk.

He nodded casually. "Good work. Do you want to tell me how you did it?

"Did what? She asked innocently.

"The dominoes. The Pentagon, the Vatican?"

She smiled innocently. "Why Paul, whatever do you mean?"

He frowned. "Oh, come on! The Catholic Church has been around for two thousand years, and suddenly it's okay to believe in life on other planets?" He reached on the corner of the desk for the newspaper folded open to the news report about the Pentagon's secret UFO program. He flipped it across the desk towards her. "And, I suppose you had nothing to do with this?"

"I was on vacation, Paul. Do I ask you what you do when you're on vacation?"

He sighed heavily. "So, he got to you, huh?"

"You mean Reynolds? Yeah, I suppose. A little."

He grimaced. "What about Tabachnik? What happens when the dominoes lead back to him, and his clients get a little too nervous? You know how that's going to end for him, right?"

"Who cares?" she shrugged.

They both looked towards the office door as Denny Caldwell came in. The former AFOSI Agent was approaching sixty and was considered too old for regular agent duties, which required mandatory retirement at age fifty-seven. However, the six foot four inch bean pole did enjoy undercover work. For the last month, he'd been playing the part of Neri's love interest, on location in Dallas. The role suited him well, growing up on a ranch in Wyoming. He could pass for a Texan.

"Hi Denny. Have a seat." Paul nodded at him, and then retrieved the manila packet from his center desk drawer. He opened the envelope, and pulled out a single sheet of paper. It was a standard Property Acknowledgement form to indicate receipt of the enclosed documents.

Paul slid the receipt across the desk to Neri, and placed a ballpoint pen on top of it. "The Agency needs a favor. It shouldn't take you more than a week. Sign this."

Neri quickly read the short paragraph, signed in the designated space, and passed it back across the desk. She'd signed enough of them in the past few years to recite the text from memory.

Paul glanced at her signature. She was still signing her name as Cavendish, even though her ex-husband had already remarried. Satisfied, he dumped the contents of the envelope on the desk, and sorted through them, "One Lebanese passport issued to Nerissa Fayad, one Canadian driver's license in the same name. One MasterCard, and one American Express card, both issued to Nerissa Fayad. Miscellaneous pictures of non-existent family members." He passed the documents across the table like a poker player folding his hand. "Don't forget to lock your other ID in the safe before you leave today."

Paul watched her carefully load each item into the empty wallet she'd brought with her for just this purpose. "Why do you always like to use your real first name on these jobs?"

"Nerissa, Merchant of Venice." She looked past him, out the window. "She was a loyal servant who successfully used disguises to accomplish her goals."

Paul rolled his eyes. "One more thing. We were worried about you. You were completely off grid for more than two hours last Monday."

She sat calmly in front of the desk, and placed her purse on the floor beside her. "What do you mean?"

"Look at this." He slid the report across the desk.

She reached down, opened her purse, and removed the red horn rimmed glasses, which with her hair up, made her look like a character from the 1960s, perhaps like a dark Senta Berger when she was at her peak.

Neri looked at the report, frowning, "So? This can't be right. What are you saying?"

The career spook she knew only as Paul had a deadpan expression, "You never should have kicked your surveillance team loose. That violated your safety protocol."

"I know," Neri replied. "I felt like I had to ditch Denny to get closer to the subject. I felt it." She looked at Caldwell. "I'm sorry."

He shrugged. "Don't worry about it."

"Neri, you're not getting it." Paul continued, "You weren't just off the electronic grid, you were off the psychic grid as well. When you didn't show for your debrief with Denny last Monday, he reported it. You switched your tracker off, and we tasked the tank to find you. None of the viewers could find you for more than two hours."

"I don't understand." She shrugged.

Paul looked at her without a smile. "Neri, for two hours, it's like you didn't exist. You were dead. Well, maybe not dead, but not alive either. You, and your energy, spirit, whatever you want to call it, were, well, nowhere. That is the only way we can describe it. But, he found out a way to get you back."

"Reynolds?" She slid the report back across the desk. "That's not possible. If I had crossed over I wouldn't be here. Dead is dead. You can't reverse it."

Paul Scheller pursed his lips, "Maybe it is. Consider that your death had not been discovered by anyone, and insufficient time had passed for anyone to be concerned about your whereabouts. Well, except us. Only minimal time parallax. I'm not sure we can explain it, but you had to have been physically dead at some point. Neither can we explain why the guys in the tank didn't see it."

Neri was silent for a long moment, looking out the window behind his desk. It was a beautiful day in the Beltway. Cobalt blue skies with just a few puffy white clouds. "What are you suggesting, that Mark Reynolds could do something that other psychics couldn't see?"

"He found a way to go back in time, make a structural alteration in reality, which resulted in the event that caused your death to never happen."

Over the years, her own psychic functioning had developed to the point that she could bi-locate throughout the cosmos. She could increase a person's body temperature by a few degrees without them knowing it. Her original forays into simple telekinesis experimentation were now considered elementary stuff to her.

Given the right circumstances, she could move things, bend things, and cause machines to malfunction. She thought back to her RV session of FBI Agent Balmain's first day running the Academy in

Quantico. Her psychic abilities caused the key ring that he'd tossed on the credenza, to slide an extra three inches off the back and onto the floor. If she hadn't taken that action, he would have never found the documents relating to ETERNA. She had read him as being a good man, who would do the right thing.

It was how she learned about the film. After realizing Balmain's lifelong interest in the Kennedy assassination, she traveled further back in time to his Dallas operation and listened to the conversation he'd had with Director Hoover. It was her psychic messaging to Mark's father that day in the car when he suddenly realized that he had to supplant a duplicate film in the warehouse for the FBI to find. Otherwise, Dan's future would have been bleak at best, and Mark might have grown up without a father.

It was Neri who had chatted briefly with a dead Lee Harvey Oswald in order to find out what he had been told to do and why. Their visit had taken place in the astral space, but had been witnessed by a young Mark Reynolds, who mentally perceived them in the theater, Christmas night 1963. She knew at that reading, that Mark would have tremendous psychic potential, but that he had to be protected.

She told her mother, Yasmina, about her psychic findings, and with a few connections in Naval Intelligence, Yasmina had gotten Mark transferred to the Remote Viewing program after Viet Nam. Nerissa and Yasmina had been protecting Mark for a long time, but felt guilty that they had failed him when Barnes' clandestine team went after him with the hit and run accident in San Francisco. Psychic espionage was getting better, but it still wasn't perfect. There were still mistakes. Barnes wanted to protect the Service's image, and saw Mark's silence as the only way to do it. By then, Barnes had lost his focus, and some would say, his mind.

"Neri? Still with us?" Paul asked.

She was silent. It would explain the loss of consciousness that she had on that evening. The haziness that clouded her thoughts for two hours. It would explain the dream about a phone call from an FBI agent, Mark's wife, who invited her to their home. She was curious, and felt compelled to go. She felt anxious, but not in danger. She'd seen her future, and it didn't end there.

She'd seen her son, Hunter marry a wonderful girl that he hadn't met yet, who would give him three children of his own, and that her mother, Yasmina would live to see them as well. She hadn't been worried about her physical safety. Now she wondered if the phone call from Karen Reynolds wasn't really a dream, after all.

"What?" she asked.

"We need him back," Paul replied calmly. "Whatever psychic talent he had, must have returned and we can't risk losing that. Neither can we risk someone else getting ahold of him."

"We have to let him go," she stated "He has paid his dues and we need to leave him alone"

"How can we?"

An hour later, Neri said goodbye to Paul, and started her long walk back to her room at the Crystal City Marriott. She fumbled in her purse for a moment and found the burn phone: the phone that she'd picked up the day before at the carry out. She looked briefly at the email and attachments that she had already staged in her untraceable outbound email, and hit the send button.

In a moment, the world's largest media outlets would have the files they needed to move forward with the story of the century. Disclosure was starting whether the government wanted it or not. It might take a couple of years, but it was coming. They would certainly deny everything, but it would do no good. The toothpaste would be out of the tube.

There wouldn't be as much resistance from the cabal now. They wouldn't be able to quiet the media this time with shallow denials or aspersions of lunacy upon witnesses. For the past three months, she had been psychically looking in on some of the most powerful families in the world. The families that owned or controlled the media. And government. And industry. One by one, she had invaded their private thoughts and saw where evidence of their filthy transgressions had been buried.

And, she had been able to collect the material to humiliate

them publicly if they tried to block or spin a story. Important people were about to be exposed and deposed. The government would eventually be forced to admit that they had been in contact with civilizations from other planets. We were now small in the universe. But, we were truly one people. When reality eventually filtered out, it would not be long before Kennedy's murder tied back to the surreptitious cowards who hid in the shadows. They hid while they prospered, but they couldn't hide forever.

Her test cases with the Vatican and the Pentagon had already proved successful. She could do it.

While Mark had begun to get his memory back, he was still in a daze regarding the incident that had gotten him hospitalized. The golf game with Stan was real. The murder-suicide scene at his house was real. Had he actually been able to go back in time and re-write history so to speak? Or had he simply had a hyper-realistic premonition the night before of what would happen if he had given Karen Neri's name?

In attempt to stabilize his head and find some answers, Mark found Neri's contact information in the online club directory. He fired up the venerable F-150 and then drove the route down Beeker Drive towards her place on Manchester Avenue.

He turned down her street and began looking at house numbers, then semi-consciously lifted his right foot off the accelerator pedal. As the Ford pickup slowed, he saw the For Sale sign in Neri's front yard. At the end of the drive were stacked some old mattresses and cardboard boxes that would be collected tomorrow by the garbage workers.

Neri was gone for now. But, when the time was right, he knew she'd find him.

www.ingramcontent.com/pod-product-compliance
Lightning Source LLC
Chambersburg PA
CBHW070303030726
47505CB00004B/892